Barbara H. Solomon is a professor of English and women's studies at Iona College in New Rochelle, New York. She is also Director of Writing for the Department of English. Among the anthologies she has edited are the Signet/Mentor editions of *Bernice Bobs Her Hair and Other Stories of F. Scott Fitzgerald*; *Rediscoveries: American Short Stories by Women, 1832–1916*; *Herland and Selected Stories of Charlotte Perkins Gilman*; *Other Voices, Other Vistas: 25 Non-Western Stories*; *American Families*; and *The Awakening and Selected Stories of Kate Chopin*. She is currently researching contemporary American stories about the lives of women.

THE HAVES AND HAVE-NOTS

30 STORIES ABOUT MONEY AND CLASS IN AMERICA

EDITED BY

Barbara H. Solomon

SIGNET CLASSICS

SIGNET CLASSICS
Published by New American Library, a division of
Penguin Group (USA) Inc., 375 Hudson Street,
New York, New York 10014, USA
Penguin Group (Canada), 10 Alcorn Avenue, Toronto,
Ontario M4V 3B2, Canada (a division of Pearson Penguin Canada Inc.)
Penguin Books Ltd., 80 Strand, London WC2R 0RL, England
Penguin Ireland, 25 St. Stephen's Green, Dublin 2,
Ireland (a division of Penguin Books Ltd.)
Penguin Group (Australia), 250 Camberwell Road, Camberwell, Victoria 3124,
Australia (a division of Pearson Australia Group Pty. Ltd.)
Penguin Books India Pvt. Ltd., 11 Community Centre, Panchsheel Park,
New Delhi - 110 017, India
Penguin Group (NZ), cnr Airborne and Rosedale Roads, Albany,
Auckland 1310, New Zealand (a division of Pearson New Zealand Ltd.)
Penguin Books (South Africa) (Pty.) Ltd., 24 Sturdee Avenue,
Rosebank, Johannesburg 2196, South Africa

Penguin Books Ltd., Registered Offices:
80 Strand, London WC2R 0RL, England

Published by Signet Classics, an imprint of New American Library,
a division of Penguin Group (USA) Inc.

First Signet Classics Printing, October 1999
10 9 8 7 6 5 4 3 2

Copyright © Barbara Solomon, 1999
All rights reserved

The following page constitutes a continuation of this copyright page.

This book is for my brother Mel Hochster,
his wife, Margie Morris, and their family,
Lani and Michael, Hallie, Louis,
Daniel, and Sophie.

CONTENTS

ACKNOWLEDGMENTS

I would like to thank Iona College Professors Stanley J. Solomon and Cedric R. Winslow for their perceptive reading of my text. At the Department of English, a great deal of assistance was provided by two graduate research assistants: Kimberly Hall-Kouril and Dorothy B. Brophy. At Ryan Library, Adrienne Franco and Robert Monteleone were helpful in securing some of the materials needed for this collection.

INTRODUCTION

On the most obvious level, the phrase "haves and have-nots" refers to those who are wealthy and those who are poor. But as many American writers have demonstrated, the consequences of having an ample income or living in poverty are far reaching, dramatic, and, sometimes, surprising.

Wealthy people, of course, have numerous advantages that can be readily catalogued. Their housing is spacious, comfortable, and safe, located in pleasant and desirable neighborhoods where their children attend good public or private schools. Their children can expect to attend school as long as they wish, going to college and earning graduate or professional degrees at their parents' expense. They have access to state-of-the-art computers both in school and at home.

On the other hand, the children of the poor and even the lower middle class often must live in dangerous neighborhoods, inhabited by, or in close proximity to, gangs and drug dealers. Their schools will likely be overcrowded, in need of basic repairs, staffed by teachers and administrators who are more focused on keeping order and offering remedial help and vocational courses than on providing advanced placement, honors, and a range of arts and science enrichment courses. These children will have fewer opportunities to learn up-to-date computer skills at school or to use computers at home.

During the summer, wealthy children may travel with their parents, broadening their perspectives of other cultures and, perhaps, acquiring the rudiments of foreign languages. Often, they will spend much of the summer at expensive camps where they swim, ride horses, canoe, play tennis, golf, and dance. Nature counselors may teach them interesting information about the environment while drama counselors may arrange talent shows or amateur musicals in which they can perform. In contrast, children of the urban poor generally spend the summer on the streets or in small parks where their activities are unsupervised by adults. Children of the rural poor are often needed during the summer to help with farming or household chores.

Now, one might well ask, Can there possibly be any advantage to being poor? Significantly, many successful individuals have attributed their positive character traits and zest for life to having come from a background of poverty or from a very modest, working-class family. Having experienced need, insecurity, and unfulfilled desires, they have focused on obtaining wealth for themselves and making certain that their children will never know deprivation. Their success often gives them an important satisfaction beyond the purchasing power of money. Writing in *The Gospel of Wealth,* Andrew Carnegie, who rose from bobbin boy in a cotton factory at the age of twelve to a millionaire steel magnate and philanthropist, asserts:

> As a rule, there is more genuine satisfaction, a truer life, and more obtained from life in the humble cottages of the poor than in the palaces of the rich. I always pity the sons and daughters of rich men, who are attended by servants, and have governesses at a later age, but am glad to remember that they do not know what they have missed.

Certainly, becoming successful and wealthy often helps to create a positive self-image and sense of well-being. These also result from accomplishments, from work well done and rewarded, from creative ideas and original plans, and from good organizational skills; in short, from recognition by the world that the individual has some skill or produces some product that is valuable to others.

For more than three centuries, the American colonies and, later, the United States have been a place for many "have-nots" to make the "American Dream" come true for themselves and to become "haves." And the spirit of optimism that people have, knowing that this transformation can occur, has grown out of some key elements in the history of the nation, a nation that has differed dramatically from every other country in the world. Four characteristics have contributed to the unparalleled success stories of America.

First, throughout the eighteenth and nineteenth centuries, the United States had a frontier that beckoned to millions of settlers, holding out natural resources undreamed of in other parts of the world. For farmers or ranchers there was land, often to be had cheaply or even, under some conditions, for free. Seemingly, there were endless forests to supply lumber and pristine lakes, rivers, and streams to supply potable water and a variety of fish. There were also rich deposits of coal, oil, silver, copper, and gold.

Critical to the development of these resources was a population of both native-born Americans and immigrants who were connected by a deeply held cluster of values—the work ethic. This ethic held that industry and thrift should be rewarded with—as Benjamin Franklin says—"a State of Affluence and some Degree of Reputation in the World." These Americans believed in self-improvement and progress as well as in the nobility of all kinds of work. They also, if somewhat vaguely, often linked material success with spiritual improvement.

Next, by and large, America was characterized by a flexible class structure. Indeed, many believed that America was a classless society. In contrast to England and other European countries with their history of aristocrats and landed gentry, this country was filled by numerous communities in which family connections or inherited money counted for little unless an individual was capable, smart, healthy, energetic, and adaptable. Although ordinary Americans might be fascinated by the lives of foreign aristocrats or American millionaires, class snobbery itself, at least since the Jacksonian era, has been highly suspect.

Finally, at the same time that much of the country was being settled and coming of age, astounding technological advances seemed to offer another kind of frontier and to bring the nation closer together. Steam engines and electric power changed the ways people worked and lived. Railroads at first connected towns and cities and shortly thereafter connected the East and West coasts. Toward the end of the nineteenth century, electric lights transformed cities. Then came the telegraph, the telephone, movie theaters, airplanes, and, most important, mass-produced and affordable automobiles. At home, radios, vacuum cleaners, refrigerators, washers, dryers, and, later, television sets, CD players, VCRs, and computers became commonplace.

At times, however, many Americans have feared that their nation, which had been knit together by history, ideology, and industrialization, might be becoming two nations, having less in common and becoming more antagonistic to one another. These two nations are populated by the "haves" and the "have-nots." In our age, the means by which great wealth is accumulated has changed in ways that are apparent to most Americans. An energetic couple may have three jobs between them and work long hours to try to save money. But each morning they may read in the papers about some stock being split, or about the merger of two giant banks, or about the successful takeover of one giant corporation by another so that those with investments have acquired additional millions. The simple notion of an individual or employee performing a service to earn income is coming to seem hopelessly outdated. And those without invested capital (sometimes estimated to be 60% of the population) often fall further behind in debt each day.

Fiction about the "haves" and "have-nots" has often been a source of valuable insights about our view of ourselves and the world, about our ideals, dreams, values, relationships and behavior. The stories in this volume vividly dramatize the changes in marriage, family life, and the workplace over a period of one hundred fifty years. Although all of the authors whose work appears in this volume have depicted the influence of poverty or wealth on the lives of their characters, for some this has been an occasional theme, but for others it has been a lifelong obsession.

A number of writers represented in this collection are generally grouped together because they share certain basic beliefs and literary aims. The Naturalists—Rebecca Harding Davis, Stephen Crane, Frank Norris, Jack London, and Theodore Dreiser—typically depict destitute or lower-class characters whose fate is not a matter of free will. Instead, the people they portray are overcome by forces beyond their control. Often in their works, children or young people are victimized by a degree and kind of poverty that prevents individuals from bettering themselves. Convinced that a person's destiny is the result of his or her heredity interacting with the environment, the Naturalists employ many disturbing details to explore the oppressive world in which their characters are trapped.

Another loosely connected group of writers whose work appears in this volume, which includes F. Scott Fitzgerald, John Cheever, J. F. Powers, Francine Prose, and Ethan Canin, might be described as psychological realists. They tend to emphasize the idea that character is fate. Generally, they depict middle-class men and women who are faced with problems and who need to make some kind of decision or change in their lives. Although economic situations may have some impact on these characters, unlike the driven characters of Naturalistic fiction, they frequently make choices that are significantly influenced by their preferences, goals, and ideals.

Other connections exist between the stories in this volume, but a useful one concerns the kinds of problems or situations experienced by the central characters. Thus, clusters of stories can be formed because they illuminate a particular topic. Of course, some stories dramatize two or three issues and could be placed in more than one group. (For example, John Cheever's "The Sorrows of Gin" is about "Disappointment" as well as "Interactions.") Within a group, each story is discussed chronologically by date of its publication in a book. While these stories serve to make us conscious of the implications of being a "have" or a "have-not," as with all good literature, they do much more than that. They provide a glimpse into lives that we might never encounter elsewhere. They are often informed by the sympathy the author has for the characters and by the wisdom the author has about their situations. They are a window on the spectrum of the American experience.

Four American Dreams

Four of the stories in this collection depict a young person who has a vivid ideal of achieving success in America. Alice Dunbar-Nelson's "Hope Deferred" (1914) chronicles the attempt of Louis Edwards to secure a job as a civil engineer, the work he has been educated to do. F. Scott Fitzgerald's "Winter Dreams" (1922) traces the experience of Dexter Green during four dramatic episodes of his life, beginning at age fourteen and ending when he is thirty-two years old. James T. Farrell's "A Jazz-Age Clerk" (1932) dramatizes the events during the one-hour lunch break that Jack Stratton spends in Chicago's business district. The selections from Sandra Cisneros's *The House on Mango Street* (1987) are a narrative from the viewpoint of Esperanza, a child of Mexican-American heritage. She lives with her parents, sister, and brothers on a street where many women lead bitter and restricted lives.

"Hope Deferred" opens with Louis Edwards's job interview at a firm that represents his last hope of securing the civil engineer's work that he knows he can do. His rejection is obviously the result of the color of his skin. As an African-American, he has spent almost a year looking for a position. Because he is poor, with "a sheaf of unpaid bills," his wife, Margaret, worries that she will prove to be a burden to her husband. She tells him that if he did not have to support her, Louis would "have a better chance to hold out" until some employer could discover his value.

Louis puts aside his professional aspirations to become the head waiter at a restaurant where the regular employees are on strike. One consolation he has is that there are now three or four black waiters working with him at a restaurant that formerly had no African-American employees. But this educated, optimistic, and idealistic young man is about to gauge just how far he is from fulfilling the American Dream.

Early in "Winter Dreams," Fitzgerald indicates that Dexter Green is a middle-class adolescent who caddies for the very affluent members of the Sherry Island Golf Club for pocket money rather than out of real need. The club inspires his dreams of dramatic triumphs:

> He became a golf champion and defeated Mr. T. A. Hedrick in a marvellous match played a hundred times over the fairways of his imagination, a match each detail of which he changed about untiringly—sometimes he won with almost laughable ease, sometimes he came up magnificently from behind. Again, stepping from a Pierce-Arrow automobile, like Mr. Mortimer Jones, he strolled frigidly into the lounge of the Sherry Island Golf Club—or perhaps, surrounded by an admiring crowd, he gave an exhibition of fancy diving from the spring-board of the club raft. . . .

For Dexter, realizing the American Dream consists of three elements: first, making a great deal of money; second, becoming an insider—an accepted member of upper-class society; third—and possibly most important—winning the golden girl, the wealthy, beautiful, exciting, and scornful Judy Jones to be his wife.

Many of Dexter's decisions revolve around preparing himself for the upper-class identity of his dreams. He chooses a prestigious Eastern university over the state university his father could more easily afford. After he has established himself as an affluent and successful businessman, he is ready to complete his new identity:

> When the time had come for him to wear good clothes, he had known who were the best tailors in America, and the best tailors in America had made him the suit he wore this evening. He had acquired that particular reserve peculiar to his university, that set it off from other universities. He recognized the value to him of such a mannerism and he had adopted it; he knew that to be careless in dress and manner required more confidence than to be careful. But carelessness was for his children. His mother's name had been Krimslich. She was a Bohemian of the peasant

class and she had talked broken English to the end of
her days. Her son must keep to the set patterns.

The element of Dexter's dream that will prove most
challenging and destructive for him is his quest to marry
self-assured and fickle Judy Jones. As do so many other
Fitzgerald heroes, Dexter dreams of becoming worthy of
the most desirable girl, a girl who may well prove to be
beyond his attainment.

In "A Jazz-Age Clerk," James T. Farrell depicts a
young man who suffers considerably from a lack of
money and who thinks of his unfulfilled desires almost
constantly. But Jack Stratton, in a shabby and faded blue
suit and wearing a hat stained with hair dressing, evokes
surprisingly little sympathy. He is a have-not in significant ways other than his financial situation.

Jack, who works as a clerk in Chicago, prefers his
lunch hour from one o'clock to two rather than the usual
time of twelve to one. Because he desires above all to
impress others, even strangers, he has convinced himself
that "people seeing him on the streets between one and
two might figure that he was a lad with a pretty good
job, because one o'clock was the time when many businessmen took their lunch in order to avoid the noonday
jams in the Loop."

Although Jack thinks all the time of having wealth,
he has no plans for succeeding. The processes through
which people set goals for themselves, get additional education, acquire and practice valuable skills, or prove
themselves to employers have no place in his thoughts.
Instead, Jack catalogues all the reasons he is poor and
sees himself as a victim of bad luck and circumstances
beyond his control:

He hadn't had anything to start on. Father and mother
with no dough. One year in high school, and that without clothes, no athletic ability, no money, nothing that
could get him into fraternities and make the girls go
for him. But, gee, in high school there'd been all kinds
of hot and classy girls! Only why should they have
looked at an unimportant freshman like himself? And
anyway, that was all over. Now he was working at a

job with no future. Maybe he ought to be glad for
what he had, but, gee, he couldn't help feeling that
some guys got all the breaks, while he got almost
none.

Throughout the story, Jack consoles himself with fanta-
sies about the beautiful women he sees on the street.
Even his daydreams about them are based on threadbare
clichés. He thinks of women as sex objects who are acquired by males who spend great sums of money on
them. With Jack's inability to relate to others and his
emphasis on the most superficial aspects of life, his lack
of wealth seems to be only one of his major problems.

In Sandra Cisneros's *The House on Mango Street*,
Esperanza lives with her parents, her sister Nenny, and
two brothers in a crowded house she doesn't like. As a
Mexican-American child, Esperanza is keenly aware of
her family's poverty and minority background. She observes the girls and women around her and determines
that, unlike many of them, she won't depend on a male
to "rescue her" from poverty and to take her away from
Mango Street. Instead, she is inspired by her own version of the American Dream. Although her culture's
ideal for a woman is a life devoted to a husband and
children, her ideal is to become a writer and to achieve
her own success. She wants her own identity, not one
passed over to her as someone's wife or mother.

Because she understands the qualities a writer needs
in order to work, because she has begun to write, and
because she is an independent person, Esperanza is
clearly a "have" among many "have-nots." Her compas-
sion for others, her good self-image, and her focused
goals are her most important assets. Among the joys of
the American Dream that she imagines is that she will
return to Mango Street to help those who can't get away.
Her dream is both personal and communal.

Disappointment

"The Untold Lie" (1919) by Sherwood Anderson and
"Where We Are Now" (1988) by Ethan Canin depict

central characters as they face the limitations of their lives. Both are married men who have realized that the American Dream will not come true for them.

In "The Untold Lie," Ray Pearson is a farm laborer in Ohio. About fifty years old and married with six children, his shoulders are stooped from hard work and his hands are chapped. Two catalysts cause him to consider the way his life has turned out. First, he is stirred by the loveliness of the October countryside with "low hills [that] are all splashed with yellows and reds." The promise and beauty of the bushes, fields, and hills cause him to want to protest against his round of endless toil as the provider for his family.

The second catalyst comes in the form of a question that Hal Winters, a fellow farm hand, asks him. Hal tells Ray that he has made a young woman pregnant and asks Ray whether he ought to marry her. Both men share the same view that marrying is like putting oneself "into the harness to be worn out like an old horse." Hal's question and the beauty of the autumn landscape serve to remind Ray of the dreams he has not thought about for years. He remembers that

> at the time he married, he had planned to go west to his uncle in Portland, Oregon—how he hadn't wanted to be a farm hand, but had thought when he got out West he would go to sea and be a sailor or get a job on a ranch and ride a horse into Western towns, shouting and laughing and waking the people in the houses with his wild cries.

As he races to catch up with Hal, it seems as though he wants to empower the young man to fulfill the dreams that he has had to put aside. But, of course, each must choose his own dreams.

Charlie, the first-person narrator in "Where We Are Now," describes himself and Jodi, his wife of eleven years. He is a physical education teacher and assistant baseball and basketball coach in the Hollywood school system. Jodi works at the circulation desk of the public library. When Charlie was in his early twenties, he hoped to have a career as a minor league pitcher. He had "struck out nine men in a row and pitched to half a dozen hitters who are in the majors now," but nothing came of his dream of being discovered by an agent. After getting his undergraduate degree, he took stock of his abilities, read biographies of inspiring men, and decided that "to turn your life around you had to start from the inside." He remembers having "a coach in college who said he wasn't trying to teach us to be pro-ballplayers; he was trying to teach us to be decent people." Charlie seems to be a very decent person, a thoughtful and caring husband who seems pretty well satisfied with his life.

Jodi, on the other hand, is not satisfied with their way of life. As a student, she wanted to be an actress. Later, she attempted to become a playwright and then considered opening a bookstore. She wants to move out of their apartment, which "is in a building with no grass or bushes, only a social room, the plastic chairs and a carpet made of Astroturf." When the couple argue about the apartment, she points out that "the elevator stops a foot below the floors, so you have to step up to get out; the cold water comes out rusty in the mornings; three weeks ago a man was robbed in the hallway by a kid with a bread knife." Although Charlie is well aware of these unpleasant aspects of their apartment, it seems that he is not particularly disturbed by them. He is at ease with his disappointments, with his circumstances, with where he is now.

Interactions

Several stories in this collection depict the conflicts or problems that arise when affluent characters interact with those who are poor or lower-middle class. One element that such stories often share is the attitude of the wealthy that they must protect what belongs to them from the poor whom they imagine to be jealous and hostile. When there is a significant disparity between the lifestyles and financial circumstances of people, one rarely finds close relationships or friendship.

In John Cheever's story "The Sorrows of Gin" (1953), the Lawtons are a comfortable, suburban family. Their most pressing problem seems to be finding and keeping an acceptable live-in cook. Rosemary, who has been with them for a few days, seems to be a competent cook and is also kind to their daughter, Amy, who is about nine years old. She is very honest as she tells Amy how discouraging it is to be a servant in someone else's house: " 'You're always surrounded by a family, and yet you're never part of it. Your pride is often hurt. The Madams seem condescending and inconsiderate. I'm not blaming the ladies I've worked for. It's just the nature of the relationship.' " Amy feels grown-up when Rosemary confides in her and is on her way to developing an affection for the cook.

On one evening when the Lawtons are out, Amy must put up with Mrs. Henlein, a babysitter she dislikes. Mistakenly believing that Mrs. Henlein has spent the evening drinking his gin, Mr. Lawton accuses this older woman of being drunk. Outraged by his unfounded accusation, Mrs. Henlein voices her contempt for a man who has wealth, but one whom she considers her inferior, a nouveau riche upstart in terms of heritage and background. She tells him:

> "Oh, you disgust me—you disgust me in your ignorance of all the trouble I've had. . . . I lived in this neighborhood my whole life. I can remember when it was full of good farming people and there was fish in the rivers. My father had four acres of sweet meadowland and a name that was known far and wide."

Mrs. Henlein is among those who have been displaced when developers subdivide rural property in order to build bedroom communities for affluent commuters.

While Mr. Lawton is concerned about the theft of his personal supply of alcohol, and Mrs. Henlein's behavior is only a passing irritation, the wealthy couple depicted in T. Coraghessan Boyle's "Peace of Mind" (1989), Hilary and Ellis Hunsicker, are concerned about protecting their family and property from violent and sadistic criminals. Giselle Nyerges, a very effective saleswoman for an elaborate household alarm system, has regaled the couple with stories of masked intruders who torture, rob, and rape their victims. The lurid details of various burglaries that are part of her sales pitch have the desired effect: the couple purchases the "Armed Response" alarm system she is selling.

Ellis thinks about his wife and daughters' vulnerability:

> He'd been a fool, he saw that now. How could he have thought, even for a minute, that they'd be safe out here in the suburbs? The world was violent, rotten, corrupt, seething with hatred and perversion, and there was no escaping it. Everything you worked for, everything you loved, had to be locked up as if you were in a castle under siege.

When the couple entertains guests, Ellis defends buying the newly installed and expensive alarm system. He tells his friend Sid that "it's a society of haves and have-nots, and like it or not, we're the haves." An obvious perspective frequently developed by the "haves" is fairly evident. Those who possess money often become fearful of outsiders. Their reasonable need to be cautious can spill over into distrust, anxiety, or dislike of those who are not of their social and financial class and background or who do not share their values. Interestingly, in this story, the "have-not," Everett Coles, is not the victim of extreme poverty. He is, in fact, a homeowner who has some valuable possessions. In depicting Coles, Boyle touches on the varied elements of modern life that can lead to frustration and rage.

In a very different story, "Why I Am a Danger to the Public" (1989), Barbara Kingsolver depicts a woman who lacks wealth but who by any other standard is a "have." Vicki Morales, the narrator, is a Mexican-American copper mine worker. A single mother raising two children, she has worked for eight years for Ellington, a mining company that owns the local stores, the miners' houses, and, in a certain sense, even the town police force. In spite of the company and other workers' prejudice, she began working at the mine first "on the track gang, laying down rails for the cars that go into the pit." After her husband left her, in spite of much opposition at the company, she earned a promotion to become a crane operator. She recalls the way she demanded employment: "I went up the hill and made such a ruckus they had to hire me up there, hire me or shoot me . . ." Vicki thinks of her job with pride, describing the sort of work many women in her situation would have to settle for: "I was not going to support my kids in no little short skirt down at the Frosty King."

When Vonda Fangham unexpectedly visits Vicki's company house during a bitter strike against the mine, Vicki remembers that they were little girls about the same age growing up in the town. But the gulf between them has always been vast. Vonda's father owns a drug store that had a popular soda fountain. When Vonda admits she doesn't remember Vicki as one of the children who came into the store, Vicki can easily explain the reason to her: " 'People my color was not allowed to go in there and set at the soda fountain. We had to get paper cups and take our drinks outside. Remember that? I used to think and *think* about why that was. I thought our germs must be so nasty they wouldn't wash off the glasses.' " Although Vicki is a "have-not" in terms of wealth, she is clearly superior to Vonda in every other respect.

Charity and Welfare

Two stories, "The Free Vacation House" (1920) by Anzia Yezierska and "Jack in the Pot" by Dorothy West (1995), dramatize the failure of private charities and governmental assistance programs to address the needs of the poor in an appropriate way. Many wealthy Americans resent that a portion of their taxes is spent on providing welfare for people they consider to be lazy, immoral, or even criminal. And because the urban poor are much more visible than the rural poor, they sometimes become the scapegoats of taxpayers who have no idea of the actual amount of money expended on welfare payments and who tend to stereotype all welfare recipients.

In Yezierska's "The Free Vacation House," the narrator, who is a mother of six children, describes the two-week vacation in the country from which she and her children have just returned. A Jewish immigrant, she was dismayed to learn that the trip—for which her name was submitted—was funded by charities. She tells the interviewer sent to screen her: "Ain't the charities those who help beggars out? I ain't no beggar. I'm not asking for no charity. My husband, he works." But, overwhelmed by endless housework and caring for her children, she decides that she will take the country vacation after all.

Almost immediately, this mother has cause to resent the insensitivity and disdain with which she and other charity recipients are treated. At the charity office, she must answer the same questions she has previously been asked, but this time without privacy. Next, she and the other mothers must have a superficial medical examination:

> I wish I could ease out my heart a little, and tell in words how that doctor looked on us, just because we were poor and had no money to pay. He only used the ends from his finger-tips to examine us with. From the way he was afraid to touch us or come near us, he made us feel like we had some catching sickness that he was trying not to get on him.

Her treatment at the country house reflects a similar contempt for the impoverished mothers and children. Rigid rules and the sounding of bells for various activities are employed to control the "guests'" behavior from morning until night. The organizers of the two-week vacations clearly have a philosophy of keeping the poor in their place, and that place is not among the flowers.

In West's "Jack in the Pot," Mr. and Mrs. Edmunds have been on relief for two years. During that time, Mr. Edmunds has "doggedly" tried to find work, trudging through the city each day. West sketches the economic history of the couple:

> Once he had had a little stationery store. After losing it, he had spent his small savings and sold or pawned every decent article of clothing before applying for relief. Even so, there had been a long investigation

while he and his wife slowly starved. . . . He never
got over being ashamed.

Every aspect of the Edmunds's lives reflects the stigma
of being on relief. For example, Mr. Spiro, the owner of
the store where Mrs. Edmunds shops regularly, has "put
in inferior stock because most of his customers were
poor-paying reliefers." He extends credit to her, but in-
timidates her with a reference to his conversation with
her relief investigator. Similarly, the couple has been
waiting for weeks for the janitor of their tenement to
supply window strips for their apartment. The janitor
knows that the building is not kept warm, and often the
tenants pound on their radiators to try to get some heat.
But he tells Mrs. Edmunds, "It's that ol' furnace. I done
tol' the agent time and again, but they ain' fixin' to fix
up this house 'long as you all is relief folks."

Mr. Edmunds summarizes the couple's quality of life
on welfare: " 'We don't live human. I never see a paper
'cept when I pick one up on the subway. I ain't had a
cigarette in three years. We ain't got a radio. We don't
have no company. All the pleasure you get is a ten-cent
movie one day a week. I don't even get that.' "

Living in fear that the investigator will cut off their
relief money if they seem to have unexplained luxuries,
they are embarrassed and frightened to be having
chicken for dinner on the day of her visit. The govern-
ment's principle in allocating relief money seems to be
to spend enough to keep the recipients alive—but just
barely.

Generosity

The stories "Miss Esther's Guest" (1893) by Sarah
Orne Jewett, "The Gift of the Magi" (1906) by O.
Henry, and "Elephant" (1988) by Raymond Carver illus-
trate the idea that the lack of money that causes some
hardship or strain may also bring out the best in people.
Acts of kindness, generosity, or love can lead to enriched
and deeply satisfying experiences. In "Miss Esther's
Guest," Esther Porley, who is sixty-four years old, over-

comes her timidity and decides to offer hospitality to a
charity guest. This individual is to be sent from Boston
for a vacation in Daleham, her village, through the arrangements of the Committee for the Country Week, a
charitable, church-related organization. Esther explains
her reasons for hosting a guest to the minister's wife:

> "I've thought and flustered a sight over taking this
> step," said good old Esther abruptly. "I had to con-
> quer a sight o' reluctance, I must say. I've got so used
> to livin' by myself that I sha'n't know how to consider
> another. But I see I ain't got common feelin' for oth-
> ers unless I can set my own comfort aside once in a
> while. I've brought you my name as one of those that
> will take one o' them city folks that needs a spell o'
> change. It come straight home to me how I should be
> feeling it by this time, if my lot had been cast in one
> o' them city garrets that the minister described so
> affecting."

With her frayed silk shawl and well-darned gloves, she
is clearly a woman who lives frugally, but she believes
that she should share part of the small income she inherited upon her mother's death:

> "I ain't rich, but we was able to save a little some-
> thing, and now I'm eatin' of it all up alone. It come
> to me I should like to have somebody take a taste out
> o' mother's part. Now, don't you let 'em send me no
> rampin' boys like them Barnard's folks had come last
> year, that vexed dumb creatur's so; and I don't know
> how to cope with no kind o' men-folks or strange girls,
> but I should know how to do for a woman that's get-
> ting well along in years, an' has come to feel kind
> o' spent."

The delightful turn of events that occurs when the recipient of her charitable offer arrives reassures us that un-
selfish behavior and goodness are sometimes fittingly
rewarded.

   In O. Henry's "The Gift of the Magi," Della and Jim
Young are struggling to make ends meet on an income

that has been reduced from $30 a week to $20 a week. After one subtracts the $8.00 weekly rent they pay for a furnished apartment, it is easy to see why neither spouse has the money to purchase a suitable gift as Christmas approaches. Each spouse has a high standard for the appropriate gift for the other. It must be a meaningful object of good quality. It must convey how well each understands the other and must be an unexpected and luxurious gift that will long give pleasure. The Christmas gifts they finally exchange reflect their joy and pride in one another, their willingness to make sacrifices for love, and a generosity of spirit that is not often conveyed by the objects that people present to one another during the holiday season.

In "Elephant" (1988) by Raymond Carver, the narrator has been helping to support his former wife, seventy-five-year-old mother, daughter and her two children as well as his son who is in college, when his brother, Billy, telephones to say that he has lost his job. He needs a loan from his brother or he and his family will lose their house. The narrator has a modest job and a simple lifestyle, but he must make changes to raise the monthly sums he sends to his family:

> So I started cutting back. I had to quit eating out, for instance. Since I lived alone, eating out was something I liked to do, but it became a thing of the past. And I had to watch myself when it came to thinking about movies. I couldn't buy clothes or get my teeth fixed. The car was falling apart. I needed new shoes, but forgot it.

Perhaps one of the insights Carver dramatizes best in this story is that a caring family member is only as wealthy as the poorest relative needing support.

The Tenement and the Factory

Three early stories seem to be calculated critiques of the American Dream, the ideal that hard work, persistence, and frugality will enable poor individuals to overcome the circumstances of lower-class life, to rise above the situation of their parents, and to succeed in making more comfortable lives for themselves. "Life in the Iron Mills" (1861) by Rebecca Harding Davis, "Maggie: A Girl of the Streets" (1893) by Stephen Crane, and "The Apostate" (1911) by Jack London depict characters who are born into a world in which they and their families are mired in a never-ending round of toil in which they earn subsistence wages. Their earnings are insufficient to purchase any but the unwholesome, cheap food and minimal shelter that make it possible for them to return to work day after day. Another important element these stories have in common is that the young people live in households in which the family provides little, if any, solace, support, or wisdom. In the case of Crane's story, familial indifference, alcoholism, and the double standard for sexual behavior combine to trap Maggie in a downward spiral.

Rebecca Harding Davis, the earliest Naturalist writer in America, identifies her central character in "Life in the Iron Mills," Hugh Wolfe, as a victim of both his heredity as a descendent of a Cornish tin miner and his environment as a furnace tender—known as a puddler—who lives in the slums among other impoverished mill workers. Davis, reflecting the prejudices of her era, believes that the reader would be able to identify the Welsh emigrants who work at the iron foundry as inferior human beings: "They are a trifle more filthy; their muscles are not so brawny; they stoop more." Hugh and his father lead lives like those of the others "of their class: incessant labor, sleeping in kennel-like rooms, eating rank pork and molasses." Nineteen-year-old Hugh may very likely have begun working at the iron mill when he was nine or ten. The figure he has sculpted from waste iron proclaims his vision and talent as an artist. But his lack of education and a brutalizing round of toil have resulted in "a sickly mill-boy" whose mind has become "greedy, dwarfed, full of thwarted energy and unused powers."

As Davis does in "Life in the Iron Mills," Jack London in "The Apostate" indicts industrial America's factories and businesses. The story is virtually the work history of a poor young boy and of the toll exacted from him as a child laborer. London prefaces "The Apostate" with a satiric version of the Lord's Prayer, one that communicates the tyranny of the workplace and mocks the Puritan work ethic.

Johnny, the fatherless central character, had gone to work winding bobbins at the age of seven. Although his wages, combined with those of his mother, have kept him and his younger siblings from starving, they eat the poorest quality food and never get enough of it to feel full. London uses the term "chronic underfeeding" to explain the boy's physical condition. Johnny suffers from a lint cough from working at the cloth mills, but when at the age of nine he gets piecework in a glass factory, his physical condition deteriorates further:

> It was simple work, the tying of glass stoppers into small bottles. . . . He held the bottles between his knees so that he might work with both hands. Thus, in a sitting position and bending over his own knees, his narrow shoulders grew humped and his chest was contracted for ten hours each day. This was not good for the lungs, but he tied three hundred dozen bottles a day.

London also emphasizes the other effect of the boy's repetitious labor: he loses the ability to think and to dream. The mind-numbing work reduces him to a "human machine."

In "Maggie: A Girl of the Streets," Stephen Crane chronicles the life of Maggie Johnson, first as a child in a poor tenement family in New York City and later as a pretty, but unsophisticated, young woman who struggles to rise above her dismal circumstances. Unlike Davis and London, Crane does not dwell on the details of his character's harsh work environment. He quickly mentions Maggie's introduction to toil at a collars and cuffs factory: "She received a stool and a machine in a room where sat twenty girls of various shades of yellow discontent. She perched on the stool and treaded at her machine all day, turning out collars."

The most destructive forces in Maggie's life, however,

are her own family members, especially her alcoholic mother and combative brother, Jimmie. With a narrow perspective informed by her drunk and abusive mother, tenement life, and the sweatshop, Maggie is totally unable to evaluate the character of her brother's friend, Pete, who becomes her suitor. While Jimmie and Pete feel free to satisfy their sexual appetites and try to seduce any young woman who crosses their path, Maggie is the victim of her romantic idealism, innocent illusions, and familial hypocrisy. Crane's story, like those of Davis and London, pits overwhelming forces against an individual.

The Farm and the System

Some people mired in poverty are bitter about a system that impedes those who lack money from rising in the world and enables those who have wealth to gain more wealth with relative ease. "Under the Lion's Paw" (1889) by Hamlin Garland and "A Deal in Wheat" (1903) by Frank Norris depict farm families victimized by the system. With even a modest "cushion of funds" these families may have been able to hold out or succeed during difficult times, but people who lack money are generally not in a position to bargain or to wait for the best opportunity. American farmers are always at risk in two ways: first, nature is unpredictable, and crops can be ruined overnight. Second, the prices that farmers get for their crops can vary greatly, being subject to both market conditions and artificial manipulation.

In "Under the Lion's Paw," Tim and Nettie Haskins and their three children have been driven off their Kansas farm by four years of grasshopper plagues. As Haskins explains to his generous new friend and mentor Steve Council:

> [The grasshoppers] wiped us out. They chawed everything that was green. They jest set around waitin' f'r us to die t' eat us, too. My God! I ust t' dream of 'em sittin' round on the bedpost, six feet long, workin' their jaws. They eet the fork-handles. They got worse

'n' worse till they jest rolled on one another, piled up
like snow in winter.

Fortunately, Haskins has Council to negotiate the
rental of a farm far from the old one. Council gets very
fair terms from Jim Butler, a land speculator who has
acquired twenty farms, many now worked by the tenant
farmers who once owned them. Butler has become a
landlord who no longer needs to work, but his wealth
seems to have been accumulated through the disasters
and failures of others.

Even after Haskins has been able to rent a property
on fair terms, he fears that his lack of money to stock
and seed the farm will prevent him from making "a good
farm of it." The labor of husband, wife, and their oldest
child goes into harvesting their first crop:

> Clothing dripping with sweat, arms aching, filled with
> briers, fingers raw and bleeding, backs broken with
> the weight of heavy bundles, Haskins and his man
> toiled on. Tommy [his son] drove the harvester, while
> his father and a hired man bound on the machine. . . .
> almost every night after supper, when the hand went
> to bed, Haskins returned to the field shocking the
> bound grain in the light of the moon.

But as Garland seems determined to demonstrate, those
who work hard, manage resources carefully, and make
sacrifices must also take into account the system and the
greed of those who know how to use it.

Frank Norris's "A Deal in Wheat" (1903) begins in
late summer with a Kansas wheat grower and his wife
trying to sell their harvested crop. Sam and Emma Lewiston have been informed that wheat dealers will pay
them 66 cents a bushel for wheat that cost almost $1.00
a bushel to produce. Even as they deliberate about what
to do, the price of wheat falls to 62 cents. They must
sell the wheat.

Norris's story is structured around a series of scenes
depicting the system by which farm products are bought
and sold by investors who stand to gain or lose a fortune.
Two opposite factions, the bears—or sellers—headed by

Mr. Truslow, and the bulls—or buyers—headed by Mr. Hornung, have been trying to manipulate prices in their favor. By the beginning of the following April, "Hornung had disclosed his hand, and in place of mere rumors, the definite and authoritative news that May wheat had been cornered in the Chicago Pit went flashing around the world from Liverpool to Odessa and from Duluth to Buenos Aires."

The same wheat that the Lewistons had to sell at a price that ruined them and drove them off their farm has been "steadily shouldered" by Hornung and his associates so that it has reached $1.50 a bushel and the investor has cleared more than $100,000 through these wheat dealings. The moves and countermoves of Truslow and Hornung are strategies in an elaborate battle that sometimes seems more like a challenging game that some men enjoy playing. But this game determines the cost of the wheat that is reflected in the price of bread. Norris's subject is clearly the system by which farmers and working men can be ruined while "the great operators, who never saw the wheat they traded in, bought and sold the world's food, gambled in the nourishment of entire nations, [and] practiced their tricks, chicanery, and oblique shifty 'deal.' "

The Single Young Woman

Several stories depict a single young woman in a range of economic and social circumstances. In two of them, "Louisa" (1891) by Mary Wilkins Freeman and "The Second Choice" (1918) by Theodore Dreiser, the central character is courted by a suitor she does not love. In a third story, "Everyone Had a Lobster" (1988) by Francine Prose, a woman and man, vacationing among a group of affluent young professionals at a summer rental house, are attracted to each other.

In Freeman's "Louisa," Louisa Britton has lost the position as the local school-teacher that she had held for eight years. Since she is the sole support of her widowed mother and grandfather, she is desperately trying to earn enough money to feed her family:

The Brittons had been and were in sore straits. All they had in the world was this little house with the acre of land. Louisa's meager school money had bought their food and clothing since her father died. Now it was almost starvation for them. Louisa was struggling to wrest a little sustenance from their stony acre of land, toiling like a European peasant woman, sacrificing her New England dignity.

Mrs. Britton is horrified that her daughter has worked at cleaning a neighbor's house and raking hay in that neighbor's field.

From her mother's point of view, all Louisa needs to do to rescue the family is to encourage the town's only eligible and wealthy bachelor, Jonathan Nye, who has begun to call on Louisa. Mrs. Britton tells her daughter that the Nyes can afford to have meat every day. On the other hand, at the Britton household, "There was nothing for dinner but the hot biscuits and tea. . . . Their chief dependence for food through the summer was their garden, but that had failed them in some respects." Louisa's mother puts enormous pressure on her to marry for money. Since Louisa does not love Jonathan and does not wish to marry without love, the conflict between mother and daughter is intense.

In Dreiser's "The Second Choice," the pressure on Shirley to marry is largely self-generated. A middle-class young woman, Shirley was generally contented with her home and situation while she was being courted by Barton, a reliable young man who works at a train terminal. When she falls in love with Arthur, a handsome, adventurous, and ambitious young man, she becomes discontented, critical of her job at a drug company as well as of her parents and the modest house they own:

Some girls were so much more fortunate. They had fine clothes, fine homes, a world of pleasure and opportunity in which to move. They did not always have to scrimp and save and work to pay their own way. And yet she had always been compelled to do it, but had never complained until now—or until he came, and after. Bethune Street, with its commonplace front yards and houses nearly all alike, and this house, so like the others, room for room and porch for porch, and her parents, too, really like all the others, had seemed good enough, quite satisfactory, indeed, until then. But now, now!

Shirley blames herself and her circumstances as being too dull for Arthur. Dreiser, however, intends the reader to recognize the serious problems of Arthur's character that are far more important to the relationship than any finery Shirley could purchase to please him. Arthur has a destructive effect on her self-image and self-confidence, since their relationship is far more important to her than it is to him.

The young woman in Francine Prose's "Everyone Had a Lobster" seems the most vulnerable of the three women depicted in these stories. She has been living for six weeks in a Long Island beach house rented by a group of affluent singles. Valerie is the only one who pays no rent, but the others don't seem to care because she amuses them. They find her "entertaining" and "brave" and think of her as someone "right out there, right on the edge by which they meant she had no income and was a bit manic, lean, a fearless swimmer." In short, these successful, young professionals enjoy having a Bohemian in their midst, someone who perhaps reminds them of their freer, more idealistic earlier selves or their friends in the past.

But the reader quickly learns that Valerie is expected to be "constantly cheery and up" as her contribution to the group. Increasingly, she needs a stimulant to keep herself upbeat. She has "found an African bark called kavakava that she can get at health food stores and that she chews to get a noticeable buzz." The poorest person and most peripheral in the group, Valerie feels further alienated from those around her one evening when she sees a video they had made earlier that day while she was away. The tape of their morning at the beach shows that while Gary, one of their party, is floundering in the water, the others are too preoccupied with their own interests to find out whether he needs help. The video then records the image of Gary being pulled out of the ocean by the Coast Guard. Valerie is astounded that he can "sit there and joke with these assholes who had almost let him drown, who were too selfish and lazy to even find out if he had been drowning." The use of kavakava won't provide Valerie with an antidote to the casual sexuality, lack of intimacy, and inability to feel any commitment to another person that characterizes the lives of these people.

Three Wives

Three very different stories, "Mrs. Beazley's Deeds" (1916) by Charlotte Perkins Gilman, "Blue Island" (1953) by J. F. Powers, and "Over the Hill" (1990) by Kate Braverman, depict the economic element of marriage as a major force experienced differently by wives and husbands. Many Americans overemphasize the impact of love and romance on a marriage and underestimate the significance of financial issues. Often, people acknowledge the importance of economic decisions in marriage only in the case of extreme wealth or poverty. But the wide disparity between a husband's and wife's earning power and control over financial matters, though not readily apparent, may become a serious problem.

In an early story, "Mrs. Beazley's Deeds," Charlotte Perkins Gilman dramatizes the conscious economic tyranny that William Beazley exerts over his wife, Maria. In spite of her objections, he has sold most of the property that his wife had inherited from her father. He has compelled her to sign the deeds for these sales, keeping a stern "hand on his wife" and punishing their children as a way of controlling her. When Mrs. Beazley pleads with her husband not to sell the last remaining lot in Rockwell, the place where she was born, "Mr. Beazley minded her outcry no more than he minded the squawking of a to-be beheaded hen." He resents the law that requires Maria to sign the documents for the sale of the land, telling her " 'this fool law is a mere formality—you know the real law—"Wives submit yourselves to your husbands!" ' "

As yet another demonstration of his power over—and

contempt for—his wife, Mr. Beazley has arranged to take a paying boarder into his small house without consulting her. The presence of an extra person will create additional work for his exhausted wife and displace the children from their beds. Although William feels smugly pleased with his action, it will have unexpected consequences for the entire family.

In "Blue Island" by J. F. Powers, Ethel Davicci is an insecure wife, very conscious of the difference between her husband Ralph's economic status and her own background. She had worked as a waitress in the Mohawk Inn, one of several businesses he owns. When she became pregnant with their child, Ralph married Ethel, and she is very much aware that he need not have done so. Ethel owes all of her comforts to Ralph's generosity: namely, a house on Blue Island, complete with two new large oil paintings and sterling silver for eighteen. Ethel's feeling of indebtedness, along with Ralph's wealth and goal of becoming an all-American suburbanite, are destructive forces. Theirs is by no means a marriage of equals. Ethel remains very much Ralph's employee, taking orders from him about where to shop and arranging a social event that is important to him. As his "employee/wife," Ethel fears Ralph's displeasure and lies to him when anything occurs that he might not consider appropriate. For example, he "had told her to open a charge account [at a nearby store], and she hadn't, and she never knew when he'd stop there and try to use it. There was a sign up in the store that said: In God We Trust—All Others Pay Cash."

Ralph's problems of identity as a newly rich Italian-American have a considerable impact on the couple's lives. While Ralph is now a "have," he feels out of place and uncomfortable in the affluent suburb of Blue Island. In an effort to become assimilated, he has grown apart from his family and becomes furious if any of his relatives call him by his real name—Rock or Rocky. He doesn't know how to relate to his neighbors. Part of Ethel's marital responsibility is to invite and entertain their new neighbors and to help Ralph, who has minimal social skill or poise, to become acquainted and accepted in a middle- or upper-middle-class community. His warped version of the American Dream is making him anxious and unhappy. Ethel, who has more insight about their problems than Ralph, is paying a high price as his submissive wife.

In "Over the Hill" by Kate Braverman, Jessica, her husband Frank, and their two children live in an expensive home in Beverly Hills. Frank continually reminds Jessica that his money pays for their luxurious circumstances. He knows that Jessica is unhappy and wants to leave him, but he also realizes that she is a fearful and dependent woman. Thus, Frank can intimidate and manipulate her by dramatizing how poor Jessica and the children will be if she leaves him. As a successful divorce lawyer, Frank knows how to use the judicial system to his advantage. His goal is to frighten Jessica with a vision of the poverty she will endure without him:

> He gives her a computer printout that his accountant has devised. Lists of numbers for services, car insurance, health insurance, homeowners' insurance, gas and water and electricity, food, liquor, chauffeur, car payments, house repairs, school tuition, psychiatrist, swimming pool maintenance, tennis lessons, violin lessons, restaurants, airline and theater tickets, hairdresser, clothing, pediatrician, dentist, orthodontist. There are more numbers, three full pages of them, but Jessica has seen enough.

Frank has told Jessica that he will not pay for the children's private school or for her psychiatrist, and he seems to enjoy visiting vacant urban apartments to show his wife where she would have to live without him. Jessica can't help but contrast these cramped and depressing places with the area where she lives, an acre on a hillside that displays the kind of world Frank and his wealthy neighbors can create:

> This is the climate that only money can buy. There is no vegetation too exotic or difficult. Here the Japanese and Mexican gardeners arrive at sunrise with bulbs from Australia, China, India, Madagascar, Kauai, and Peru. There should be lilies in the pools, she thinks,

and peacocks and jaguars in the tall night grass. Or perhaps they already have this, closer to Sunset Boulevard, in the gated villas she drives past.

A divorce, like marriage itself, is an economic process as well as an emotional one. Jessica, like many other wives, has discovered that women and children are often the losers in such a process.

Motherhood

Motherhood can prove to be difficult even under the best of circumstances. In few, if any, other endeavors are the stakes so high and the formal training so lacking. Several stories in this volume explore the guilt or unhappiness when a mother, sometimes a single parent, must rear her child without adequate resources. Other stories depict relationships between mothers and children in which external circumstances such as wealth or poverty are only part of a complex tangle of emotions, needs, and bonds.

In "A Pair of Silk Stockings" (1897), Kate Chopin—a turn-of-the-century writer with a surprisingly contemporary perspective—portrays Mrs. Sommers as a dedicated and self-sacrificing mother. Chopin explains the reason why Mrs. Sommers does not dwell on the "better days" she had known before her marriage. "She had no time—no second of time to devote to the past. The needs of the present absorbed her every faculty. A vision of the future like some dim, gaunt monster sometimes appalled her, but luckily to-morrow never comes."

Finding herself "the unexpected possessor of fifteen dollars," she makes plans to spend the entire sum very judiciously on clothing and shoes for her sons and daughters. Her excitement at having the opportunity to make so many purchases at one time is such that "between getting the children fed and the place righted, and preparing herself for the shopping bout, she had actually forgotten to eat any luncheon at all!" The poor quality of her own clothing, especially her shoes, stockings, and gloves, reflects the sacrifices that she typically makes because of a lack of money.

But as Mrs. Sommers tries on well-made and satisfying apparel, the restraint she has been imposing on herself unexpectedly begins to give way: "She was not thinking at all. She seemed for the time to be taking a rest from that laborious and fatiguing function and to have abandoned herself to some mechanical impulse that directed her actions and freed her of responsibility." Unlike some stereotypical mothers in sentimental fiction, this realistically depicted mother has cultivated tastes, deeply felt needs, and a strong sense of identity that she has put aside—at great cost—for the benefit of her children.

In "He" (1930) by Katherine Anne Porter, Mrs. Whipple's ten-year-old son's being retarded complicates her relationships with all three of her children. Her pride and defensiveness about her son's disability and the family's poverty frequently cause her to use poor judgment. Since she can not bear the thought of being pitied, she continually admonishes her husband: "Don't ever let a soul hear us complain," and "nobody's going to get a chance to look down on us." Lacking self-knowledge and rationalizing her behavior, Mrs. Whipple gives her daughter, Emly, the extra blanket that was on her son's cot and reassures herself that "He never seemed to mind the cold."

When her brother announces that he and his family plan to visit the Whipples on a particular Sunday, Mrs. Whipple insists that they butcher and serve a suckling pig to impress her relatives. Mr. Whipple strongly objects to her plan because he knows that if the pig is allowed to mature, it could supply three hundred pounds of pork instead of one meal for nine people. Intensifying the Whipples' difficult situation on the farm is "a hard winter" with a loss of about half of their crop and the death of one of their plow horses. No matter what Mrs. Whipple says about her love for "Him," she believes that caring for her retarded son will result in denying her other two children the meager resources that they deserve and need.

Tillie Olsen's "I Stand Here Ironing" (1961) is an interior monologue or meditation of a mother of five children about her oldest daughter, nineteen-year-old Emily. Abandoned by her husband when Emily was eight months old, this mother in the 1930s must support herself and her infant in a pre-relief, pre-WPA world of the Great Depression.

She is brutally honest about the choices she has made and admits that with her first-born she lacked not only money but the wisdom that she would gain later that would benefit her other children. But almost all of her actions reflected her poverty and need to earn a living for herself and Emily. As she catalogs her hurtful decision to send Emily to a nursery school and, later, to a charity convalescent home where the child was supposed to get good food and extra care, it is apparent that her financial status made her powerless to protect her young child. Of the unpleasant nursery school the mother comments:

> [Emily] was two. Old enough for nursery school they said, and I did not know then what I know now—the fatigue of the long days, and the lacerations of group life in nurseries that are only parking places for children.
>
> Except that it would have made no difference if I had known. It was the only way we could be together, the only way I could hold a job.

Emily's mother acknowledges making mistakes in her treatment of her daughter that would never be made by an affluent mother. She and her second husband convince themselves that Emily is old enough to be left alone when they go out for what they think of as only a short time. Upon their return, they find that "the front door is open, the clock on the floor in the hall." A desperate Emily tells them: "It wasn't just a little while. I didn't cry. Three times I called you, just three times, and then I ran downstairs to open the door so you could come faster."

This mother realizes all too well that a lack of money led to compromises about her child's comfort and happiness. Rushed earlier because she was working, impatient and tired later because her other children needed her attention, she regrets the fact that Emily did not receive the kind of nurturing she would have wished for the daughter she loves so dearly.

In "Everyday Use" (1973) by Alice Walker, Mrs. Johnson is awaiting the arrival of Dee, one of her two daughters, for a visit. As the story's first-person narrator, Mrs. Johnson describes herself, communicating. that she is a farm worker, a strong woman with a very positive self-image:

> I am a large, big-boned woman with rough, man-working hands. In the winter I wear flannel nightgowns to bed and overalls during the day. I can kill and clean a hog as mercilessly as a man. My fat keeps me hot in zero weather. I can work outside all day, breaking ice to get water for washing; I can eat pork liver cooked over the open fire after it comes steaming from the hog.

Dee and Maggie, her daughters, are almost total opposites. Dee is attractive, articulate, fashionable, affluent, self-assured, selfish, and insensitive to the feelings of others. She seems to have been away from and out of touch with her family for some time. One of the first things Dee does is to correct her mother about how to address her. Named after both an aunt and a grandmother, this daughter has rejected her name in favor of a new African name: Wangero Leewanika Kemanjo. Among other changes, Wangero demands some of Mrs. Johnson's household items that she once scorned but now wants to take home with her. She has discovered that sophisticated people value hand-crafted, one-of-a-kind furnishings, and she has plans to use them as decorations.

Mrs. Johnson is very conscious of the contemptuous way that Wangero treats her sister. A timid, good-natured, and "homely" young woman, Maggie is "ashamed of the burn scars down her arms and legs" and she eyes "her sister with a mixture of envy and awe." Clearly, Mrs. Johnson's sympathies lie with Maggie, her "have-not" daughter with whom she shares many day-to-day activities as well as family values. She is surprisingly tolerant of the daughter who looks down on her and criticizes her way of life. But without rejecting Wangero, Mrs. Johnson knows that she must acknowledge the superiority of the simple goodness and generosity of her modest and unassuming daughter.

Coincidentally, in "Kiswana Browne" (1980) by Gloria Naylor, the central character, like Dee Johnson, has changed her name, choosing one of African derivation. In this story, the mother, Mrs. Browne, who lives in the affluent African-American neighborhood of Linden Hills, calls on her daughter, who has recently moved into an apartment on Brewster Place, a run-down street. Mrs. Browne continues to call her daughter Melanie although she is well aware that the name she prefers is Kiswana. Clearly an idealist and a dreamer, Kiswana has no telephone because she can not afford the $75.00 deposit that is required for installation.

This mother and her daughter are divided by differing political and social agendas as well as by the wealth of the mother and the poverty of the daughter, who does not want to accept financial help from her parents. The central conflicts between them revolve around the activist choices Kiswana made when she was a college student during the civil rights movement and the working-class lifestyle she now has. Kiswana dropped out of school because she believed that her "place was in the streets with my people, fighting for equality and a better community." Mrs. Browne, who is an articulate, upper-middle-class woman, believes that it would have been far better for her daughter to have stayed in school so that she could have qualified for an influential job in which she could have been helpful to African-Americans from within the system. Mrs. Browne describes her vision of the way that Kiswana could succeed:

> "You don't have to sell out, as you say, and work for some corporation, but you could become an assemblywoman or a civil liberties lawyer or open a freedom school in this very neighborhood. That way you could really help the community. But what help are you going to be to these people on Brewster while you're living hand-to-mouth on file-clerk jobs waiting for a revolution? You're wasting your talents, child."

Although Kiswana distrusts her mother's middle-class values and thinks that Mrs. Browne has too little commitment to effect change, she does really want her mother's approval. She has begun to notice how similar they are in certain subtle respects, and she is beginning to develop a new perspective about her mother as a woman.

Conclusion

The insights dramatized in these stories about success and failure anticipate the findings of psychological and sociological studies conducted decades after the publication of the literature. Many authors seem capable of distilling important truths of human nature and goals as they explore the behavior of individuals in complex or troubled situations. In a *New York Times* article about people who have materialistic goals, Alfie Kohn observes that in recent years,

> psychological researchers have been amassing an impressive body of data suggesting that satisfaction simply is not for sale. Not only does having more things prove to be unfulfilling, but people for whom affluence is a priority in life tend to experience an unusual degree of anxiety and depression as well as a lower overall level of well-being. Likewise, those who would like nothing more than to be famous or attractive do not fare as well, psychologically speaking, as those who primarily want to develop close relationships, become more self-aware, or contribute to the community.

The pursuit of the "American Dream" of material success increasingly appears to have major, unhappy side-effects. First, of course, is the disappointment when the consumer discovers that the joys of new car technology or new cosmetic items are limited and fleeting. Next comes the tension and strain for those who have paid for such items by long-term loans or by charging them on credit cards. For many families, increased debt means increased working hours for already overburdened parents.

On the other hand, as several stories in this collection demonstrate, the quality of life in very poor households is often marked by friction, competition for resources, or a sense of bitterness and demoralization. The belief that those who succeeded did so through virtues such as being industrious, thrifty, honest, and responsible frequently seems to have been replaced by the conviction that having good connections to wealthy and successful people (it's who you know) or being at the right place at the right time (it's a matter of luck) or knowing how to use the system are key elements in becoming a "have." Literature that examines the American Dream, dramatizes the character traits of our heroes and anti-heroes, depicts successful or failed relationships, and challenges us to analyze our assumptions and values continues to illuminate the American experience and to grow increasingly relevant at the beginning of a new century.

—Barbara H. Solomon

Iona College
New Rochelle, New York

ALICE DUNBAR-NELSON
(1875–1935)

Born Alice Ruth Moore in New Orleans, Louisiana, Alice Dunbar-Nelson was one of two daughters of Patricia and Joseph Moore. Her mother, a former Louisiana slave, was a seamstress, and her father, who was possibly of white Creole heritage, was a seaman. Alice was graduated from Straight College in New Orleans in 1892, and during the next four years she taught elementary school in New Orleans and began to publish her poetry and fiction. In 1898, she married Paul Lawrence Dunbar, a gifted and well-known black poet, and became a teacher in New York City's school system. Divorced from Dunbar, she began to teach at Howard High School in Wilmington, Delaware, and in 1916 she married Robert J. Nelson, a journalist. A political activist, she founded two institutions to aid young African-American women: the White Rose Home for Girls in Harlem and the Industrial School for Colored Girls in Marshalltown, Delaware. She published two collections, *Violets and Other Tales* (1895), a volume of stories and poems, and *The Goodness of St. Rocque and Other Stories* (1899). These books, along with numerous other stories that appeared in magazines or that remained as unpublished manuscripts, the novella *A Modern Undine*, and a selection of her plays, poems, and newspaper columns are reprinted in the three volumes of *The Works of Alice Dunbar-Nelson*, edited by Gloria T. Hull (1988). *Give Us Each Day: The Diary of Alice Dunbar-Nelson* was published in 1984.

Hope Deferred

THE direct rays of the August sun smote on the pavements of the city and made the soda-water signs in front of the drug stores alluringly suggestive of relief. Women in scant garments, displaying a maximum of form and a minimum of taste, crept along the pavements, their mussy light frocks suggesting a futile disposition on the part of the wearers to keep cool. Traditional looking fat men mopped their faces, and dived frantically into screened doors to emerge redder and more perspiring. The presence of small boys, scantily clad and of dusky hue and languid steps, marked the city, if not distinctively southern, at least one on the borderland between the North and the South.

Edwards joined the perspiring mob on the hot streets and mopped his face with the rest. His shoes were dusty, his collar wilted. As he caught a glimpse of himself in a mirror of a shop window, he smiled grimly. "Hardly a man to present himself before one of the Lords of Creation to ask a favor," he muttered to himself.

Edwards was young; so young that he had not outgrown his ideals. Rather than allow that to happen, he had chosen one to share them with him, and the man who can find a woman willing to face poverty for her husband's ideals has a treasure far above rubies, and more precious than one with a thorough understanding of domestic science. But ideals do not always supply the immediate wants of the body, and it was the need of the wholly material that drove Edwards wilted, warm and discouraged into the August sunshine.

The man in the office to which the elevator boy directed him looked up impatiently from his desk. The windows of the room were open on a courtyard where green tree tops waved in a humid breeze; an electric fan whirred, and sent forth flashes of coolness; cool looking leather chairs invited the dusty traveler to sink into their depths.

Edwards was not invited to rest, however. Cold gray eyes in an impassive pallid face fixed him with a sneering stare, and a thin icy voice cut in on his half spoken words with a curt dismissal in its tone.

"Sorry, Mr.—Er—, but I shan't be able to grant your request."

His "Good Morning" in response to Edwards' reply as he turned out of the room was of the curtest, and left the impression of decided relief at an unpleasant duty discharged.

"Now where?" He had exhausted every avenue, and this last closed the door of hope with a finality that left no doubt in his mind. He dragged himself down the little side street, which led home, instinctively, as a child draws near to its mother in its trouble.

Margaret met him at the door, and their faces lighted up with the glow that always irradiated them in each other's presence. She drew him into the green shade of the little room, and her eyes asked, though her lips did not frame the question.

"No hope," he made reply to her unspoken words.

She sat down suddenly as one grown weak.

"If I could only just stick it out, little girl," he said, "but we need food, clothes, and only money buys them, you know."

"Perhaps it would have been better if we hadn't married—" she suggested timidly. That thought had been uppermost in her mind for some days lately.

"Because you are tired of poverty?" he queried, the smile on his lips belying his words.

She rose and put her arms about his neck. "You know better than that; but because if you did not have me, you could live on less, and thus have a better chance to hold out until they see your worth."

"I'm afraid they never will." He tried to keep his tones even, but in spite of himself a tremor shook his words. "The man I saw to-day is my last hope; he is the chief clerk, and what he says controls the opinions of others. If I could have gotten past his decision, I might have influenced the senior member of the firm, but he is a man who leaves details to subordinates, and Mr. Hanan was suspicious of me from the first. He isn't sure," he continued with a little laugh, which he tried to make sound spontaneous, "whether I am a stupendous fraud, or an escaped lunatic."

"We can wait; your chance will come," she soothed him with a rare smile.

"But in the meanwhile—" he finished for her and paused himself.

A sheaf of unpaid bills in the afternoon mail, with the curt and wholly unnecessary "Please Remit" in boldly impertinent characters across the bottom of every one drove Edwards out into the wilting sun. He knew the main street from end to end; he could tell how many trolley poles were on its corners; he felt that he almost knew the stones in the buildings, and that the pavements were worn with the constant passing of his feet, so often in the past four months had he walked, at first buoyantly, then hopefully, at last wearily up and down its length.

The usual idle crowd jostled around the baseball bulletins. Edwards joined them mechanically. "I can be a sidewalk fan, even if I am impecunious." He smiled to himself as he said the words, and then listened idly to a voice at his side. "We are getting metropolitan, see that!"

The "that" was an item above the baseball score. Edwards looked and the letters burned themselves like white fire into his consciousness.

STRIKE SPREADS TO OUR CITY.
WAITERS AT ADAMS' WALK OUT
AFTER BREAKFAST THIS MORNING.

"Good!" he said aloud. The man at his side smiled appreciatively at him; the home team had scored another run, but unheeding that Edwards walked down the street with a lighter step than he had known for days.

The proprietor of Adams' restaurant belied both his name and his vocation. He should have been rubicund, corpulent, American; instead he was wiry, lank, foreign in appearance. His teeth projected over a full lower lip, his eyes set far back in his head and were concealed by wrinkles that seemed to have been acquired by years of squinting into men's motives.

"Of course I want waiters," he replied to Edwards' question, "any fool knows that." He paused, drew in his lower lip within the safe confines of his long teeth, squinted his eyes intently on Edwards. "But do I want colored waiters? Now, do I?"

"It seems to me there's no choice for you in the matter," said Edwards good-humoredly.

The reply seemed to amuse the restaurant keeper immensely; he slapped the younger man on the back with a familiarity that made him wince both physically and spiritually.

"I guess I'll take you for head waiter." He was inclined to be jocular, even in the face of the disaster which the morning's strike had brought him. "Peel off and go to work. Say, stop!" as Edwards looked around to take his bearings, "What's your name?"

"Louis Edwards."

"Uh huh, had any experience?"

"Yes, some years ago, when I was in school."

"Uh huh, then waiting ain't your general work."

"No."

"Uh huh, what do you do for a living?"

"I'm a civil engineer."

One eyebrow of the saturnine Adams shot up, and he withdrew his lower lip entirely under his teeth.

"Well, say man, if you're an engineer, what you want to be strike-breaking here in a waiter's coat for, eh?"

Edwards' face darkened, and he shrugged his shoulders. "They don't need me, I guess," he replied briefly. It was an effort, and the restaurant keeper saw it, but his wonder overcame his sympathy.

"Don't need you with all that going on at the Monarch works? Why, man, I'd a thought every engineer this side o' hell would be needed out there."

"So did I; that's why I came here, but—"

"Say, kid, I'm sorry for you, I surely am; you go on to work."

"And so," narrated Edwards to Margaret, after midnight, when he had gotten in from his first day's work, "I became at once head waiter, first assistant, all the other waiters, chief boss, steward, and high-muck-a-muck, with all the emoluments and perquisites thereof."

Margaret was silent; with her ready sympathy she knew that no words of hers were needed then, they would only add to the burdens he had to bear. Nothing could be more bitter than this apparent blasting of his lifelong hopes, this seeming lowering of his standard. She said nothing, but the pressure of her slim brown hand in his meant more than words to them both.

"It's hard to keep the vision true," he groaned.

If it was hard that night, it grew doubly so within the next few weeks. Not lightly were the deposed waiters to take their own self-dismissal and supplanting. Daily they menaced the restaurant with their surly attentions, ugly and ominous. Adams shot out his lower lip from the confines of his long teeth and swore in a various language that he'd run his own place if he had to get every nigger in Africa to help him. The three or four men whom he was able to induce to stay with him in the face of missiles of every nature, threatened every day to give up the battle. Edwards was the force that held them together. He used every argument from the purely material one of holding on to the job now that they had it, through the negative one of loyalty to the man in his hour of need, to the altruistic one of keeping the place open for colored men for all time. There were none of them of such value as his own personality, and the fact that he stuck through all the turmoil. He wiped the mud from his face, picked up the putrid vegetables that often strewed the floor, barricaded the doors at night, replaced orders that were destroyed by well-aimed stones, and stood by Adams' side when the fight threatened to grow serious.

Adams was appreciative. "Say, kid, I don't know what I'd a done without you, now that's honest. Take it from me, when you need a friend anywhere on earth, and you can send me a wireless, I'm right there with the goods in answer to your S. O. S."

This was on the afternoon when the patrol, lined up in front of the restaurant, gathered in a few of the most disturbing ones, none of whom, by the way, had ever been employed in the place. "Sympathy" had pervaded the town.

The humid August days melted into the sultry ones of September. The self-dismissed waiters had quieted down, and save for an occasional missile, annoyed Adams and his corps of dark-skinned helpers no longer. Edwards had resigned himself to his temporary discomforts. He felt, with the optimism of the idealist, that it was only for a little while; the fact that he had sought work at his profession for nearly a year had not yet discouraged him. He would explain carefully to Margaret when the day's work was over, that it was only for a little while; he would earn enough at this to enable them to get away, and then in some other place he would be

able to stand up with the proud consciousness that all
his training had not been in vain.

He was revolving all these plans in his mind one Saturday night. It was at the hour when business was dull,
and he leaned against the window and sought entertainment from the crowd on the street. Saturday night, with
all the blare and glare and garishness dear to the heart
of the middle-class provincial of the smaller cities, was
holding court on the city streets. The hot September sun
had left humidity and closeness in its wake, and the evening mists had scarce had time to cast coolness over the
town. Shop windows glared wares through colored lights,
and phonographs shrilled popular tunes from open store
doors to attract unwary passersby. Half-grown boys and
girls, happy in the license of Saturday night on the
crowded streets, jostled one another and pushed in long
lines, shouted familiar epithets at other pedestrians with
all the abandon of the ill-breeding common to the class.
One crowd, in particular, attracted Edwards' attention.
The girls were brave in semi-decollete waists, scant short
skirts and exaggerated heads, built up in fanciful designs;
the boys with flamboyant red neckties, striking hat-
bands, and white trousers. They made a snake line, boys
and girls, hands on each others' shoulders, and rushed
shouting through the press of shoppers, scattering the
inattentive right and left. Edwards' lip curled, "Now, if
those were colored boys and girls—"

His reflections were never finished, for a patron
moved towards his table, and the critic of human life
became once more the deferential waiter.

He did not move a muscle of his face as he placed
the glass of water on the table, handed the menu card,
and stood at attention waiting for the order, although
he had recognized at first glance the half-sneering face
of his old hope—Hanan, of the great concern which had
no need of him. To Hanan, the man who brought his
order was but one of the horde of menials who satisfied
his daily wants and soothed his vanity when the cares of
the day had ceased pressing on his shoulders. He had
not even looked at the man's face, and for this Edwards
was grateful.

A new note had crept into the noise on the streets;

there was in it now, not so much mirth and ribaldry as menace and anger. Edwards looked outside in slight alarm; he had grown used to that note in the clamor of the streets, particularly on Saturday nights; it meant that the whole restaurant must be prepared to quell a disturbance. The snake line had changed; there were only flamboyant hat-bands in it now, the decollete shirt waists and scant skirts had taken refuge on another corner. Something in the shouting attracted Hanan's attention, and he looked up wonderingly.

"What are they saying?" he inquired. Edwards did not answer; he was so familiar with the old cry that he thought it unnecessary.

"Yah! Yah! Old Adams hires niggers! Hires niggers!"

"Why, that is so." Hanan looked up at Edwards' dark face for the first time. "This is quite an innovation for Adams' place. How did it happen?"

"We are strikebreakers," replied the waiter quietly, then he grew hot, for a gleam of recognition came into Hanan's eyes.

"Oh, yes, I see. Aren't you the young man who asked me for employment as an engineer at the Monarch works?"

Edwards bowed, he could not answer; hurt pride surged up within him and made his eyes hot and his hands clammy.

"Well, er—I'm glad you've found a place to work; very sensible of you, I'm sure. I should think, too, that it is work for which you would be more fitted than engineering."

Edwards started to reply, but the hot words were checked on his lips. The shouting had reached a shrillness which boded immediate results, and with the precision of a missile from a warship's gun, a stone hurtled through the glass of the long window. It struck Edwards' hand, glanced through the dishes on the tray which he was in the act of setting on the table, and tipped half its contents over Hanan's knee. He sprang to his feet angrily, striving to brush the debris of his dinner from his immaculate clothing, and turned angrily upon Edwards.

"That is criminally careless of you!" he flared, his eyes blazing in his pallid face. "You could have prevented that; you're not even a good waiter, much less an engineer."

And then something snapped in the darker man's head. The long strain of the fruitless summer; the struggle of keeping together the men who worked under him in the restaurant; the heat, and the task of enduring what was to him the humiliation of serving, and this last injustice, all culminated in a blinding flash in his brain. Reason, intelligence, all was obscured, save a man hatred, and a desire to wreak his wrongs on the man, who, for the time being, represented the author of them. He sprang at the white man's throat and bore him to the floor. They wrestled and fought together, struggling, biting, snarling, like brutes in the debris of food and the clutter of overturned chairs and tables.

The telephone rang insistently. Adams wiped his hands on a towel, and carefully moved a paint brush out of the way, as he picked up the receiver.

"Hello!" he called. "Yes, this is Adams, the restaurant keeper. Who? Uh huh. Wants to know if I'll go his bail? Say, that nigger's got softening of the brain. Course not, let him serve his time, making all that row in my place; never had no row here before. No, I don't never want to see him again."

He hung up the receiver with a bang, and went back to his painting. He had almost finished his sign, and he smiled as he ended it with a flourish:

WAITERS WANTED. NONE BUT
WHITE MEN NEED APPLY

Out in the county workhouse, Edwards sat on his cot, his head buried in his hands. He wondered what Margaret was doing all this long hot Sunday, if the tears were blinding her sight as they did his; then he started to his feet, as the warden called his name. Margaret stood before him, her arms outstretched, her mouth quivering with tenderness and sympathy, her whole form yearning toward him with a passion of maternal love.

"Margaret! You here, in this place?"

"Aren't you here?" She smiled bravely, and drew his

head towards the refuge of her bosom. "Did you think I wouldn't come to see you?"

"To think I should have brought you to this," he moaned.

She stilled his reproaches and heard the story from his lips. Then she murmured with bloodless mouth, "How long will it be?"

"A long time, dearest—and you?"

"I can go home, and work," she answered briefly, "and wait for you, be it ten months or ten years—and then—?"

"And then—" they stared into each other's eyes like frightened children. Suddenly his form straightened up, and the vision of his ideal irradiated his face with hope and happiness.

"And then, Beloved," he cried, "then we will start all over again. Somewhere, I am needed; somewhere in this world there are wanted dark-skinned men like me to dig and blast and build bridges and make straight the roads of the world, and I am going to find that place—with you."

She smiled back trustfully at him. "Only keep true to your ideal, dearest," she whispered, "and you will find the place. Your window faces the south, Louis. Look up and out of it all the while you are here, for it is there, in our own southland, that you will find the realization of your dream."

—1914

F. SCOTT FITZGERALD
(1896–1940)

Born in St. Paul, Minnesota, F. Scott Fitzgerald attended St. Paul Academy, the Newman School in Hackensack, New Jersey, and Princeton University. He left Princeton without earning a degree, partly because he spent so much time writing for the college's *Nassau Literary Magazine*, the Triangle Club, and *The Tiger* that his grades suffered. In 1917, he enlisted in the army and, while stationed at Camp Sheridan in Montgomery, Alabama, he met Zelda Sayre, a beautiful and lively debutante. During the time that they were engaged to be married, Fitzgerald feared he would lose Zelda because he was not wealthy enough to provide the kind of lifestyle she demanded. Upon publication of his first novel, *This Side of Paradise*, in the spring of 1920, Zelda traveled to New York, where she and Scott were married in the rectory of St. Patrick's Cathedral. During the next decade, the era Fitzgerald named "The Jazz Age," the couple lived at various times in New York, Paris, and on the Riviera. He published *The Beautiful and Damned* (1922), *The Great Gatsby* (1925), *Tender Is the Night* (1934), and left the unfinished manuscript of *The Last Tycoon*, which was edited by Edmund Wilson and published in 1941. Among Fitzgerald's story collections are *Flappers and Philosophers* (1921), *Tales of the Jazz Age* (1922), *All the Sad Young Men* (1926), and *Taps at Reveille* (1935).

Winter Dreams

SOME of the caddies were poor as sin and lived in one-room houses with a neurasthenic cow in the front yard, but Dexter Green's father owned the second best grocery-store in Black Bear—the best one was "The Hub," patronized by the wealthy people from Sherry Island—and Dexter caddied only for pocket-money.

In the fall when the days became crisp and gray, and the long Minnesota winter shut down like the white lid of a box, Dexter's skis moved over the snow that hid the fairways of the golf course. At these times the country gave him a feeling of profound melancholy—it offended him that the links should lie in enforced fallowness, haunted by ragged sparrows for the long season. It was dreary, too, that on the tees where the gay colors fluttered in summer there were now only the desolate sand-boxes knee-deep in crusted ice. When he crossed the hills the wind blew cold as misery, and if the sun was out he tramped with his eyes squinted up against the hard dimensionless glare.

In April the winter ceased abruptly. The snow ran down into Black Bear Lake scarcely tarrying for the early golfers to brave the season with red and black balls. Without elation, without an interval of moist glory, the cold was gone.

Dexter knew that there was something dismal about this Northern spring, just as he knew there was something gorgeous about the fall. Fall made him clinch his hands and tremble and repeat idiotic sentences to himself, and make brisk abrupt gestures of command to imaginary audiences and armies. October filled him with hope which November raised to a sort of ecstatic triumph, and in this mood the fleeting brilliant impressions of the summer at Sherry Island were ready grist to his mill. He became a golf champion and defeated Mr. T. A. Hedrick in a marvellous match played a hundred times over the fairways of his imagination, a match each detail of which he changed about untiringly—sometimes he won with almost laughable ease, sometimes he came up magnificently from behind. Again, stepping from a Pierce-Arrow automobile, like Mr. Mortimer Jones, he strolled frigidly into the lounge of the Sherry Island Golf Club—or perhaps, surrounded by an admiring crowd, he gave an exhibition of fancy diving from the spring-board of the club raft. . . . Among those who watched him in open-mouthed wonder was Mr. Mortimer Jones.

And one day it came to pass that Mr. Jones—himself and not his ghost—came up to Dexter with tears in his eyes and said that Dexter was the——best caddy in the club, and wouldn't he decide not to quit if Mr. Jones made it worth his while, because every other——caddy in the club lost one ball a hole for him—regularly——.

"No, sir," said Dexter decisively, "I don't want to caddy any more." Then, after a pause: "I'm too old."

"You're not more than fourteen. Why the devil did you decide just this morning that you wanted to quit? You promised that next week you'd go over to the State tournament with me."

"I decided I was too old."

Dexter handed in his "A Class" badge, collected what money was due him from the caddy master, and walked home to Black Bear Village.

"The best——caddy I ever saw," shouted Mr. Mortimer Jones over a drink that afternoon. "Never lost a ball! Willing! Intelligent! Quiet! Honest! Grateful!"

The little girl who had done this was eleven—beautifully ugly as little girls are apt to be who are destined after a few years to be inexpressibly lovely and bring no end of misery to a great number of men. The spark, however, was perceptible. There was a general ungodliness in the way her lips twisted down at the corners when she smiled, and in the—Heaven help us!—in the almost passionate quality of her eyes. Vitality is born early in such women. It was utterly in evidence now, shining through her thin frame in a sort of glow.

She had come eagerly out on to the course at nine o'clock with a white linen nurse and five small new golf-clubs in a white canvas bag which the nurse was carrying. When Dexter first saw her she was standing by the caddy house, rather ill at ease and trying to conceal the fact by engaging her nurse in an obviously unnatural conversation graced by startling and irrelevant grimaces from herself.

"Well, it's certainly a nice day, Hilda," Dexter heard her say. She drew down the corners of her mouth, smiled, and glanced furtively around, her eyes in transit falling for an instant on Dexter.

Then to the nurse:

"Well, I guess there aren't very many people out here this morning, are there?"

The smile again—radiant, blatantly artificial—convincing.

"I don't know what we're supposed to do now," said the nurse looking nowhere in particular.

"Oh, that's all right. I'll fix it up."

Dexter stood perfectly still, his mouth slightly ajar. He knew that if he moved forward a step his stare would be in her line of vision—if he moved backward he would lose his full view of her face. For a moment he had not realized how young she was. Now he remembered having seen her several times the year before—in bloomers.

Suddenly, involuntarily, he laughed, a short abrupt laugh—then, startled by himself, he turned and began to walk quickly away.

"Boy!"

Dexter stopped.

"Boy——"

Beyond question he was addressed. Not only that, but he was treated to that absurd smile, that preposterous smile—the memory of which at least a dozen men were to carry into middle age.

"Boy, do you know where the golf teacher is?"

"He's giving a lesson."

"Well, do you know where the caddy-master is?"

"He isn't here yet this morning."

"Oh." For a moment this baffled her. She stood alternately on her right and left foot.

"We'd like to get a caddy," said the nurse. "Mrs. Mortimer Jones sent us out to play golf, and we don't know how without we get a caddy."

Here she was stopped by an ominous glance from Miss Jones, followed immediately by the smile.

"There aren't any caddies here except me," said Dexter to the nurse, "and I got to stay here in charge until the caddy-master gets here."

"Oh."

Miss Jones and her retinue now withdrew, and at a proper distance from Dexter became involved in a heated conversation, which was concluded by Miss Jones taking one of the clubs and hitting it on the ground with violence. For further emphasis she raised it again and was about to bring it down smartly upon the nurse's bosom, when the nurse seized the club and twisted it from her hands.

"You damn little mean old *thing!*" cried Miss Jones wildly.

Another argument ensued. Realizing that the elements of comedy were implied in the scene, Dexter several times began to laugh, but each time restrained the laugh before it reached audibility. He could not resist the monstrous conviction that the little girl was justified in beating the nurse.

The situation was resolved by the fortuitous appearance of the caddy-master, who was appealed to immediately by the nurse.

"Miss Jones is to have a little caddy, and this one says he can't go."

"Mr. McKenna said I was to wait here till you came," said Dexter quickly.

"Well, he's here now." Miss Jones smiled cheerfully at the caddy-master. Then she dropped her bag and set off at a haughty mince toward the first tee.

"Well?" The caddy-master turned to Dexter. "What you standing there like a dummy for? Go pick up the young lady's clubs."

"I don't think I'll go out to-day," said Dexter.

"You don't——"

"I think I'll quit."

The enormity of his decision frightened him. He was a favorite caddy, and the thirty dollars a month he earned through the summer were not to be made elsewhere around the lake. But he had received a strong emotional shock, and his perturbation required a violent and immediate outlet.

It is not so simple as that, either. As so frequently would be the case in the future, Dexter was unconsciously dictated to by his winter dreams.

II

Now, of course, the quality and the seasonability of these winter dreams varied, but the stuff of them remained. They persuaded Dexter several years later to pass up a business course at the State university—his father, prospering now, would have paid his way—for the precarious advantage of attending an older and more

famous university in the East, where he was bothered
by his scanty funds. But do not get the impression, because his winter dreams happened to be concerned at
first with musings on the rich, that there was anything
merely snobbish in the boy. He wanted not association
with glittering things and glittering people—he wanted
the glittering things themselves. Often he reached out
for the best without knowing why he wanted it—and
sometimes he ran up against the mysterious denials and
prohibitions in which life indulges. It is with one of those
denials and not with his career as a whole that this
story deals.

He made money. It was rather amazing. After college
he went to the city from which Black Bear Lake draws
its wealthy patrons. When he was only twenty-three and
had been there not quite two years, there were already
people who liked to say: "Now *there's* a boy—" All
about him rich men's sons were peddling bonds precariously, or investing patrimonies precariously, or plodding
through the two dozen volumes of the "George Washington Commercial Course," but Dexter borrowed a
thousand dollars on his college degree and his confident
mouth, and bought a partnership in a laundry.

It was a small laundry when he went into it, but Dexter made a specialty of learning how the English washed
fine woolen golf-stockings without shrinking them, and
within a year he was catering to the trade that wore
knickerbockers. Men were insisting that their Shetland
hose and sweaters go to his laundry, just as they had
insisted on a caddy who could find golf-balls. A little
later he was doing their wives' lingerie as well—and running five branches in different parts of the city. Before
he was twenty-seven he owned the largest string of laundries in his section of the country. It was then that he
sold out and went to New York. But the part of his
story that concerns us goes back to the days when he
was making his first big success.

When he was twenty-three Mr. Hart—one of the gray-
haired men who liked to say "Now there's a boy"—gave
him a guest card to the Sherry Island Golf Club for a
week-end. So he signed his name one day on the register, and that afternoon played golf in a foursome with

Mr. Hart and Mr. Sandwood and Mr. T. A. Hedrick. He did not consider it necessary to remark that he had once carried Mr. Hart's bag over these same links, and that he knew every trap and gully with his eyes shut—but he found himself glancing at the four caddies who trailed them, trying to catch a gleam or gesture that would remind him of himself, that would lessen the gap which lay between his present and his past.

It was a curious day, slashed abruptly with fleeting, familiar impressions. One minute he had the sense of being a trespasser—in the next he was impressed by the tremendous superiority he felt toward Mr. T. A. Hedrick, who was a bore and not even a good golfer any more.

Then, because of a ball Mr. Hart lost near the fifteenth green, an enormous thing happened. While they were searching the stiff grasses of the rough there was a clear call of "Fore!" from behind a hill in their rear. And as they all turned abruptly from their search a bright new ball sliced abruptly over the hill and caught Mr. T. A. Hedrick in the abdomen.

"By Gad!" cried Mr. T. A. Hedrick, "they ought to put some of these crazy women off the course. It's getting to be outrageous."

A head and a voice came up together over the hill:

"Do you mind if we go through?"

"You hit me in the stomach!" declared Mr. Hedrick wildly.

"Did I?" The girl approached the group of men. "I'm sorry. I yelled 'Fore!' "

Her glance fell casually on each of the men—then scanned the fairway for her ball.

"Did I bounce into the rough?"

It was impossible to determine whether this question was ingenuous or malicious. In a moment, however, she left no doubt, for as her partner came up over the hill she called cheerfully:

"Here I am! I'd have gone on the green except that I hit something."

As she took her stance for a short mashie shot, Dexter looked at her closely. She wore a blue gingham dress, rimmed at throat and shoulders with a white edging that accentuated her tan. The quality of exaggeration, of thinness, which had made her passionate eyes and downturning mouth absurd at eleven, was gone now. She was arrestingly beautiful. The color in her cheeks was centered like the color in a picture—it was not a "high" color, but a sort of fluctuating and feverish warmth, so shaded that it seemed at any moment it would recede and disappear. This color and the mobility of her mouth gave a continual impression of flux, of intense life, of passionate vitality—balanced only partially by the sad luxury of her eyes.

She swung her mashie impatiently and without interest, pitching the ball into a sand-pit on the other side of the green. With a quick, insincere smile and a careless "Thank you!" she went on after it.

"That Judy Jones!" remarked Mr. Hedrick on the next tee, as they waited—some moments—for her to play on ahead. "All she needs is to be turned up and spanked for six months and then to be married off to an old-fashioned cavalry captain."

"My God, she's good-looking!" said Mr. Sandwood, who was just over thirty.

"Good-looking!" cried Mr. Hedrick contemptuously, "she always looks as if she wanted to be kissed! Turning those big cow-eyes on every calf in town!"

It was doubtful if Mr. Hedrick intended a reference to the maternal instinct.

"She'd play pretty good golf if she'd try," said Mr. Sandwood.

"She has no form," said Mr. Hedrick solemnly.

"She has a nice figure," said Mr. Sandwood.

"Better thank the Lord she doesn't drive a swifter ball," said Mr. Hart, winking at Dexter.

Later in the afternoon the sun went down with a riotous swirl of gold and varying blues and scarlets, and left the dry, rustling night of Western summer. Dexter watched from the veranda of the Golf Club, watched the even overlap of the waters in the little wind, silver molasses under the harvest-moon. Then the moon held a finger to her lips and the lake became a clear pool, pale and quiet. Dexter put on his bathing-suit and swam out to the farthest raft, where he stretched dripping on the wet canvas of the spring-board.

There was a fish jumping and a star shining and the lights around the lake were gleaming. Over on a dark peninsula a piano was playing the songs of last summer and of summers before that—songs from "Chin-Chin" and "The Count of Luxemburg" and "The Chocolate Soldier"—and because the sound of a piano over a stretch of water had always seemed beautiful to Dexter he lay perfectly quiet and listened.

The tune the piano was playing at that moment had been gay and new five years before when Dexter was a sophomore at college. They had played it at a prom once when he could not afford the luxury of proms, and he had stood outside the gymnasium and listened. The sound of the tune precipitated in him a sort of ecstasy and it was with that ecstasy he viewed what happened to him now. It was a mood of intense appreciation, a sense that, for once, he was magnificently attuned to life and that everything about him was radiating a brightness and a glamour he might never know again.

A low, pale oblong detached itself suddenly from the darkness of the Island, spitting forth the reverberated sound of a racing motorboat. Two white streamers of cleft water rolled themselves out behind it and almost immediately the boat was beside him, drowning out the hot tinkle of the piano in the drone of its spray. Dexter raising himself on his arms was aware of a figure standing at the wheel, of two dark eyes regarding him over the lengthening space of water—then the boat had gone by and was sweeping in an immense and purposeless circle of spray round and round in the middle of the lake. With equal eccentricity one of the circles flattened out and headed back toward the raft.

"Who's that?" she called, shutting off her motor. She was so near now that Dexter could see her bathing-suit, which consisted apparently of pink rompers.

The nose of the boat bumped the raft, and as the latter tilted rakishly he was precipitated toward her. With different degrees of interest they recognized each other.

"Aren't you one of those men we played through this afternoon?" she demanded.

He was.

"Well, do you know how to drive a motor-boat? Because if you do I wish you'd drive this one so I can ride on the surf-board behind. My name is Judy Jones"—she favored him with an absurd smirk—rather, what tried to be a smirk, for, twist her mouth as she might, it was not grotesque, it was merely beautiful—"and I live in a house over there on the Island, and in that house there is a man waiting for me. When he drove up at the door I drove out of the dock because he says I'm his ideal."

There was a fish jumping and a star shining and the lights around the lake were gleaming. Dexter sat beside Judy Jones and she explained how her boat was driven. Then she was in the water, swimming to the floating surf-board with a sinuous crawl. Watching her was without effort to the eye, watching a branch waving or a sea-gull flying. Her arms, burned to butternut, moved sinuously among the dull platinum ripples, elbow appearing first, casting the forearm back with a cadence of falling water, then reaching out and down, stabbing a path ahead.

They moved out into the lake; turning, Dexter saw that she was kneeling on the low rear of the now uptilted surf-board.

"Go faster," she called, "fast as it'll go."

Obediently he jammed the lever forward and the white spray mounted at the bow. When he looked around again the girl was standing up on the rushing board, her arms spread wide, her eyes lifted toward the moon.

"It's awful cold," she shouted. "What's your name?"

He told her.

"Well, why don't you come to dinner to-morrow night?"

His heart turned over like the fly-wheel of the boat, and, for the second time, her casual whim gave a new direction to his life.

III

Next evening while he waited for her to come downstairs, Dexter peopled the soft deep summer room and the sun-porch that opened from it with the men who had already loved Judy Jones. He knew the sort of men they were—the men who when he first went to college had entered from the great prep schools with graceful clothes and the deep tan of healthy summers. He had seen that, in one sense, he was better than these men. He was newer and stronger. Yet in acknowledging to himself that he wished his children to be like them he was admitting that he was but the rough, strong stuff from which they eternally sprang.

When the time had come for him to wear good clothes, he had known who were the best tailors in America, and the best tailors in America had made him the suit he wore this evening. He had acquired that particular reserve peculiar to his university, that set it off from other universities. He recognized the value to him of such a mannerism and he had adopted it; he knew that to be careless in dress and manner required more confidence than to be careful. But carelessness was for his children. His mother's name had been Krimslich. She was a Bohemian of the peasant class and she had talked broken English to the end of her days. Her son must keep to the set patterns.

At a little after seven Judy Jones came down-stairs. She wore a blue silk afternoon dress, and he was disappointed at first that she had not put on something more elaborate. This feeling was accentuated when, after a brief greeting, she went to the door of a butler's pantry and pushing it open called: "You can serve dinner, Martha." He had rather expected that a butler would announce dinner, that there would be a cocktail. Then he put these thoughts behind him as they sat down side by side on a lounge and looked at each other.

"Father and mother won't be here," she said thoughtfully.

He remembered the last time he had seen her father, and he was glad the parents were not to be here tonight—they might wonder who he was. He had been born in Keeble, a Minnesota village fifty miles farther north, and he always gave Keeble as his home instead of Black Bear Village. Country towns were well enough to come from if they weren't inconveniently in sight and used as footstools by fashionable lakes.

They talked of his university, which she had visited frequently during the past two years, and of the near-by city which supplied Sherry Island with its patrons, and whither Dexter would return next day to his prospering laundries.

During dinner she slipped into a moody depression which gave Dexter a feeling of uneasiness. Whatever petulance she uttered in her throaty voice worried him. Whatever she smiled at—at him, at a chicken liver, at nothing—it disturbed him that her smile could have no root in mirth, or even in amusement. When the scarlet corners of her lips curved down, it was less a smile than an invitation to a kiss.

Then, after dinner, she led him out on the dark sun-porch and deliberately changed the atmosphere.

"Do you mind if I weep a little?" she said.

"I'm afraid I'm boring you," he responded quickly.

"You're not. I like you. But I've just had a terrible afternoon. There was a man I cared about, and this afternoon he told me out of a clear sky that he was poor as a church-mouse. He'd never even hinted it before. Does this sound horribly mundane?"

"Perhaps he was afraid to tell you."

"Suppose he was," she answered. "He didn't start right. You see, if I'd thought of him as poor—well, I've been mad about loads of poor men, and fully intended to marry them all. But in this case, I hadn't thought of him that way, and my interest in him wasn't strong enough to survive the shock. As if a girl calmly informed her fiancé, that she was a widow. He might not object to widows, but——

"Let's start right," she interrupted herself suddenly. "Who are you, anyhow?"

For a moment Dexter hesitated. Then:

"I'm nobody," he announced. "My career is largely a matter of futures."

"Are you poor?"

"No," he said frankly, "I'm probably making more money than any man my age in the Northwest. I know that's an obnoxious remark, but you advised me to start right."

There was a pause. Then she smiled and the corners of her mouth drooped and an almost imperceptible sway brought her closer to him, looking up into his eyes. A lump rose in Dexter's throat, and he waited breathless for the experiment, facing the unpredictable compound that would form mysteriously from the elements of their lips. Then he saw—she communicated her excitement to him, lavishly, deeply, with kisses that were not a promise but a fulfillment. They aroused in him not hunger demanding renewal but surfeit that would demand more surfeit . . . kisses that were like charity, creating want by holding back nothing at all.

It did not take him many hours to decide that he had wanted Judy Jones ever since he was a proud, desirous little boy.

IV

It began like that—and continued, with varying shades of intensity, on such a note right up to the dénouement. Dexter surrendered a part of himself to the most direct and unprincipled personality with which he had ever come in contact. Whatever Judy wanted, she went after with the full pressure of her charm. There was no divergence of method, no jockeying for position or premeditation of effects—there was a very little mental side to any of her affairs. She simply made men conscious to the highest degree of her physical loveliness. Dexter had no desire to change her. Her deficiencies were knit up with a passionate energy that transcended and justified them.

When, as Judy's head lay against his shoulder that first night, she whispered, "I don't know what's the matter with me. Last night I thought I was in love with a man and to-night I think I'm in love with you—"—it seemed to him a beautiful and romantic thing to say. It was the exquisite excitability that for the moment he controlled and owned. But a week later he was compelled to view this same quality in a different light. She took him in her roadster to a picnic supper, and after supper she disappeared, likewise in her roadster, with another man.

Dexter became enormously upset and was scarcely able to be decently civil to the other people present. When she assured him that she had not kissed the other man, he knew she was lying—yet he was glad that she had taken the trouble to lie to him.

He was, as he found before the summer ended, one of a varying dozen who circulated about her. Each of them had at one time been favored above all others—about half of them still basked in the solace of occasional sentimental revivals. Whenever one showed signs of dropping out through long neglect, she granted him a brief honeyed hour, which encouraged him to tag along for a year or so longer. Judy made these forays upon the helpless and defeated without malice, indeed half unconscious that there was anything mischievous in what she did.

When a new man came to town every one dropped out—dates were automatically cancelled.

The helpless part of trying to do anything about it was that she did it all herself. She was not a girl who could be "won" in the kinetic sense—she was proof against cleverness, she was proof against charm; if any of these assailed her too strongly she would immediately resolve the affair to a physical basis, and under the magic of her physical splendor the strong as well as the brilliant played her game and not their own. She was entertained only by the gratification of her desires and by the direct exercise of her own charm. Perhaps from so much youthful love, so many youthful lovers, she had come, in self-defense, to nourish herself wholly from within.

Succeeding Dexter's first exhilaration came restlessness and dissatisfaction. The helpless ecstasy of losing himself in her was opiate rather than tonic. It was fortunate for his work during the winter that those moments of ecstasy came infrequently. Early in their acquaintance it had seemed for a while that there was a deep and spontaneous mutual attraction—that first August, for example—three days of long evenings on her dusky veranda, of strange wan kisses through the late afternoon, in shadowy alcoves or behind the protecting trellises of the garden arbors, of mornings when she was fresh as a dream and almost shy at meeting him in the clarity of the rising day. There was all the ecstasy of an engagement about it, sharpened by his realization that there was no engagement. It was during those three days that, for the first time, he had asked her to marry him. She said "maybe some day," she said "kiss me," she said "I'd like to marry you," she said "I love you"—she said—nothing.

The three days were interrupted by the arrival of a New York man who visited at her house for half September. To Dexter's agony, rumor engaged them. The man was the son of the president of a great trust company. But at the end of a month it was reported that Judy was yawning. At a dance one night she sat all evening in a motor-boat with a local beau, while the New Yorker searched the club for her frantically. She told the local beau that she was bored with her visitor, and two days later he left. She was seen with him at the station, and it was reported that he looked very mournful indeed.

On this note the summer ended. Dexter was twenty-four, and he found himself increasingly in a position to do as he wished. He joined two clubs in the city and lived at one of them. Though he was by no means an integral part of the stag-lines at these clubs, he managed to be on hand at dances where Judy Jones was likely to appear. He could have gone out socially as much as he liked—he was an eligible young man, now, and popular with down-town fathers. His confessed devotion to Judy Jones had rather solidified his position. But he had no social aspirations and rather despised the dancing men who were always on tap for the Thursday or Saturday parties and who filled in at dinners with the younger married set. Already he was playing with the idea of going East to New York. He wanted to take Judy Jones with him. No disillusion as to the world in which she had grown up could cure his illusion as to her desirability.

Remember that—for only in the light of it can what he did for her be understood.

Eighteen months after he first met Judy Jones he became engaged to another girl. Her name was Irene Scheerer, and her father was one of the men who had always believed in Dexter. Irene was light-haired and sweet and honorable, and a little stout, and she had two suitors whom she pleasantly relinquished when Dexter formally asked her to marry him.

Summer, fall, winter, spring, another summer, another fall—so much he had given of his active life to the incorrigible lips of Judy Jones. She had treated him with interest, with encouragement, with malice, with indifference, with contempt. She had inflicted on him the innumerable little slights and indignities possible in such a case—as if in revenge for having ever cared for him at all. She had beckoned him and yawned at him and beckoned him again and he had responded often with bitterness and narrowed eyes. She had brought him ecstatic happiness and intolerable agony of spirit. She had caused him untold inconvenience and not a little trouble. She had insulted him, and she had ridden over him, and she had played his interest in her against his interest in his work—for fun. She had done everything to him except to criticise him—this she had not done—it seemed to him only because it might have sullied the utter indifference she manifested and sincerely felt toward him.

When autumn had come and gone again it occurred to him that he could not have Judy Jones. He had to beat this into his mind but he convinced himself at last. He lay awake at night for a while and argued it over. He told himself the trouble and the pain she had caused him, he enumerated her glaring deficiencies as a wife. Then he said to himself that he loved her, and after a while he fell asleep. For a week, lest he imagined her husky voice over the telephone or her eyes opposite him at lunch, he worked hard and late, and at night he went to his office and plotted out his years.

At the end of a week he went to a dance and cut in on her once. For almost the first time since they had met he did not ask her to sit out with him or tell her that she was lovely. It hurt him that she did not miss these things—that was all. He was not jealous when he saw that there was a new man to-night. He had been hardened against jealousy long before.

He stayed late at the dance. He sat for an hour with Irene Scheerer and talked about books and about music. He knew very little about either. But he was beginning to be master of his own time now, and he had a rather priggish notion that he—the young and already fabulously successful Dexter Green—should know more about such things.

That was in October, when he was twenty-five. In January, Dexter and Irene became engaged. It was to be announced in June, and they were to be married three months later.

The Minnesota winter prolonged itself interminably, and it was almost May when the winds came soft and the snow ran down into Black Bear Lake at last. For the first time in over a year Dexter was enjoying a certain tranquillity of spirit. Judy Jones had been in Florida, and afterward in Hot Springs, and somewhere she had been engaged, and somewhere she had broken it off. At first, when Dexter had definitely given her up, it had made him sad that people still linked them together and asked for news of her, but when he began to be placed at dinner next to Irene Scheerer people didn't ask him about her any more—they told him about her. He ceased to be an authority on her.

May at last. Dexter walked the streets at night when the darkness was damp as rain, wondering that so soon, with so little done, so much of ecstasy had gone from him. May one year back had been marked by Judy's poignant, unforgivable, yet forgiven turbulence—it had been one of those rare times when he fancied she had grown to care for him. That old penny's worth of happiness he had spent for this bushel of content. He knew that Irene would be no more than a curtain spread behind him, a hand moving among gleaming teacups, a voice calling to children . . . fire and loveliness were gone, the magic of nights and the wonder of the varying hours and seasons . . . slender lips, down-turning, dropping to his lips and bearing him up into a heaven of eyes. . . . The thing was deep in him. He was too strong and alive for it to die lightly.

In the middle of May when the weather balanced for a few days on the thin bridge that led to deep summer he turned in one night at Irene's house. Their engagement was to be announced in a week now—no one would be surprised at it. And to-night they would sit together on the lounge at the University Club and look on for an hour at the dancers. It gave him a sense of solidity to go with her—she was so sturdily popular, so intensely "great."

He mounted the steps of the brownstone house and stepped inside.

"Irene," he called.

Mrs. Scheerer came out of the living-room to meet him.

"Dexter," she said, "Irene's gone up-stairs with a splitting headache. She wanted to go with you but I made her go to bed."

"Nothing serious, I—"

"Oh, no. She's going to play golf with you in the morning. You can spare her for just one night, can't you, Dexter?"

Her smile was kind. She and Dexter liked each other. In the living-room he talked for a moment before he said good-night.

Returning to the University Club, where he had rooms, he stood in the doorway for a moment and watched the dancers. He leaned against the door-post, nodded at a man or two—yawned.

"Hello, darling."

The familiar voice at his elbow startled him. Judy Jones had left a man and crossed the room to him—Judy Jones, a slender enamelled doll in cloth of gold: gold in a band at her head, gold in two slipper points at her dress's hem. The fragile glow of her face seemed to blossom as she smiled at him. A breeze of warmth and light blew through the room. His hands in the pockets of his dinner-jacket tightened spasmodically. He was filled with a sudden excitement.

"When did you get back?" he asked casually.

"Come here and I'll tell you about it."

She turned and he followed her. She had been away—he could have wept at the wonder of her return. She had passed through enchanted streets, doing things that were like provocative music. All mysterious happenings, all fresh and quickening hopes, had gone away with her, come back with her now.

She turned in the doorway.

"Have you a car here? If you haven't, I have."

"I have a coupé."

In then, with a rustle of golden cloth. He slammed the door. Into so many cars she had stepped—like this—like that—her back against the leather, so—her elbow resting on the door—waiting. She would have been soiled long since had there been anything to soil her—except herself—but this was her own self outpouring.

With an effort he forced himself to start the car and back into the street. This was nothing, he must remember. She had done this before, and he had put her behind him, as he would have crossed a bad account from his books.

He drove slowly down-town and, affecting abstraction, traversed the deserted streets of the business section, peopled here and there where a movie was giving out its crowd or where consumptive or pugilistic youth lounged in front of pool halls. The clink of glasses and the slap of hands on the bars issued from saloons, cloisters of glazed glass and dirty yellow light.

She was watching him closely and the silence was embarrassing, yet in this crisis he could find no casual word with which to profane the hour. At a convenient turning he began to zigzag back toward the University Club.

"Have you missed me?" she asked suddenly.

"Everybody missed you."

He wondered if she knew of Irene Scheerer. She had been back only a day—her absence had been almost contemporaneous with his engagement.

"What a remark!" Judy laughed sadly—without sadness. She looked at him searchingly. He became absorbed in the dashboard.

"You're handsomer than you used to be," she said thoughtfully. "Dexter, you have the most rememberable eyes."

He could have laughed at this, but he did not laugh. It was the sort of thing that was said to sophomores. Yet it stabbed at him.

"I'm awfully tired of everything, darling." She called every one darling, endowing the endearment with careless, individual comraderie. "I wish you'd marry me."

The directness of this confused him. He should have told her now that he was going to marry another girl, but he could not tell her. He could as easily have sworn that he had never loved her.

"I think we'd get along," she continued, on the same note, "unless probably you've forgotten me and fallen in love with another girl."

Her confidence was obviously enormous. She had said, in effect, that she found such a thing impossible to believe, that if it were true he had merely committed a childish indiscretion—and probably to show off. She would forgive him, because it was not a matter of any moment but rather something to be brushed aside lightly.

"Of course you could never love anybody but me," she continued, "I like the way you love me. Oh, Dexter, have you forgotten last year?"

"No, I haven't forgotten."

"Neither have I!"

Was she sincerely moved—or was she carried along by the wave of her own acting?

"I wish we could be like that again," she said, and he forced himself to answer:

"I don't think we can."

"I suppose not. . . . I hear you're giving Irene Scheerer a violent rush."

There was not the faintest emphasis on the name, yet Dexter was suddenly ashamed.

"Oh, take me home," cried Judy suddenly; "I don't want to go back to that idiotic dance—with those children."

Then, as he turned up the street that led to the residence district, Judy began to cry quietly to herself. He had never seen her cry before.

The dark street lightened, the dwellings of the rich loomed up around them, he stopped his coupé in front of the great white bulk of the Mortimer Joneses' house, somnolent, gorgeous, drenched with the splendor of the damp moonlight. Its solidity startled him. The strong walls, the steel of the girders, the breadth and beam and pomp of it were there only to bring out the contrast with the young beauty beside him. It was sturdy to accentuate her slightness—as if to show what a breeze could be generated by a butterfly's wing.

He sat perfectly quiet, his nerves in wild clamor, afraid that if he moved he would find her irresistibly in his arms. Two tears had rolled down her wet face and trembled on her upper lip.

"I'm more beautiful than anybody else," she said brokenly, "why can't I be happy?" Her moist eyes tore at his stability—her mouth turned slowly downward with an exquisite sadness: "I'd like to marry you if you'll have me, Dexter. I suppose you think I'm not worth having, but I'll be so beautiful for you, Dexter."

A million phrases of anger, pride, passion, hatred, tenderness fought on his lips. Then a perfect wave of emotion washed over him, carrying off with it a sediment of wisdom, of convention, of doubt, of honor. This was his girl who was speaking, his own, his beautiful, his pride.

"Won't you come in?" He heard her draw in her breath sharply.

Waiting.

"All right," his voice was trembling, "I'll come in."

V

It was strange that neither when it was over nor a long time afterward did he regret that night. Looking at it from the perspective of ten years, the fact that Judy's flare for him endured just one month seemed of little importance. Nor did it matter that by his yielding he subjected himself to a deeper agony in the end and gave serious hurt to Irene Scheerer and to Irene's parents, who had befriended him. There was nothing sufficiently pictorial about Irene's grief to stamp itself on his mind.

Dexter was at bottom hard-minded. The attitude of the city on his action was of no importance to him, not because he was going to leave the city, but because any outside attitude on the situation seemed superficial. He was completely indifferent to popular opinion. Nor, when he had seen that it was no use, that he did not possess in himself the power to move fundamentally or to hold Judy Jones, did he bear any malice toward her. He loved her, and he would love her until the day he was too old for loving—but he could not have her. So he tasted the deep pain that is reserved only for the strong, just as he had tasted for a little while the deep happiness.

Even the ultimate falsity of the grounds upon which Judy terminated the engagement that she did not want to "take him away" from Irene—Judy, who had wanted nothing else—did not revolt him. He was beyond any revulsion or any amusement.

He went East in February with the intention of selling out his laundries and settling in New York—but the war came to America in March and changed his plans. He returned to the West, handed over the management of the business to his partner, and went into the first officers' training-camp in late April. He was one of those young thousands who greeted the war with a certain amount of relief, welcoming the liberation from webs of tangled emotion.

VI

This story is not his biography, remember, although things creep into it which have nothing to do with those dreams he had when he was young. We are almost done with them and with him now. There is only one more incident to be related here, and it happens seven years farther on.

It took place in New York, where he had done well—so well that there were no barriers too high for him. He was thirty-two years old, and, except for one flying trip immediately after the war, he had not been West in seven years. A man named Devlin from Detroit came into his office to see him in a business way, and then and there this incident occurred, and closed out, so to speak, this particular side of his life.

"So you're from the Middle West," said the man Devlin with careless curiosity. "That's funny—I thought men like you were probably born and raised on Wall Street. You know—wife of one of my best friends in Detroit came from your city. I was an usher at the wedding."

Dexter waited with no apprehension of what was coming.

"Judy Simms," said Devlin with no particular interest; "Judy Jones she was once."

"Yes, I knew her." A dull impatience spread over him. He had heard, of course, that she was married— perhaps deliberately he had heard no more.

"Awfully nice girl," brooded Devlin meaninglessly, "I'm sort of sorry for her."

"Why?" Something in Dexter was alert, receptive, at once.

"Oh, Lud Simms has gone to pieces in a way. I don't mean he ill-uses her, but he drinks and runs around——"

"Doesn't she run around?"

"No. Stays at home with her kids."

"Oh."

"She's a little too old for him," said Devlin.

"Too old!" cried Dexter. "Why, man, she's only twenty-seven."

He was possessed with a wild notion of rushing out into the streets and taking a train to Detroit. He rose to his feet spasmodically.

"I guess you're busy," Devlin apologized quickly. "I didn't realize——"

"No, I'm not busy," said Dexter, steadying his voice. "I'm not busy at all. Not busy at all. Did you say she was—twenty-seven? No, I said she was twenty-seven."

"Yes, you did," agreed Devlin dryly.

"Go on, then. Go on."

"What do you mean?"

"About Judy Jones."

Devlin looked at him helplessly.

"Well, that's—I told you all there is to it. He treats her like the devil. Oh, they're not going to get divorced or anything. When he's particularly outrageous she forgives him. In fact, I'm inclined to think she loves him. She was a pretty girl when she first came to Detroit."

A pretty girl! The phrase struck Dexter as ludicrous.

"Isn't she—a pretty girl, any more?"

"Oh, she's all right."

"Look here," said Dexter, sitting down suddenly. "I don't understand. You say she was a 'pretty girl' and now you say she's 'all right.' I don't understand what you mean—Judy Jones wasn't a pretty girl, at all. She

was a great beauty. Why, I knew her, I knew her. She
was——"

Devlin laughed pleasantly.

"I'm not trying to start a row," he said. "I think Judy's
a nice girl and I like her. I can't understand how a man
like Lud Simms could fall madly in love with her, but
he did." Then he added: "Most of the women like her."

Dexter looked closely at Devlin, thinking wildly that
there must be a reason for this, some insensitivity in the
man or some private malice.

"Lots of women fade just like *that*." Devlin snapped
his fingers. "You must have seen it happen. Perhaps I've
forgotten how pretty she was at her wedding. I've seen
her so much since then, you see. She has nice eyes."

A sort of dullness settled down upon Dexter. For the
first time in his life he felt like getting very drunk. He
knew that he was laughing loudly at something Devlin
had said, but he did not know what it was or why it was
funny. When, in a few minutes, Devlin went he lay down
on his lounge and looked out the window at the New
York sky-line into which the sun was sinking in dull
lovely shades of pink and gold.

He had thought that having nothing else to lose he
was invulnerable at last—but he knew that he had just
lost something more, as surely as if he had married Judy
Jones and seen her fade away before his eyes.

The dream was gone. Something had been taken from
him. In a sort of panic he pushed the palms of his hands
into his eyes and tried to bring up a picture of the waters
lapping on Sherry Island and the moonlit veranda, and
gingham on the golf-links and the dry sun and the gold
color of her neck's soft down. And her mouth damp to
his kisses and her eyes plaintive with melancholy and
her freshness like new fine linen in the morning. Why,
these things were no longer in the world! They had existed and they existed no longer.

For the first time in years the tears were streaming
down his face. But they were for himself now. He did
not care about mouth and eyes and moving hands. He
wanted to care, and he could not care. For he had gone
away and he could never go back any more. The gates
were closed, the sun was gone down, and there was no

beauty but the gray beauty of steel that withstands all time. Even the grief he could have borne was left behind in the country of illusion, of youth, of the richness of life, where his winter dreams had flourished.

"Long ago," he said, "long ago, there was something in me, but now that thing is gone. Now that thing is gone, that thing is gone. I cannot cry. I cannot care. That thing will come back no more."

—1922

JAMES T. FARRELL
(1904—1979)

Born and raised on Chicago's South Side, James Thomas Farrell attended parochial elementary and high schools followed by three years of study at the University of Chicago and evening classes at De Paul University. He worked at a range of jobs, including at a shoe store, gas station, advertising company, funeral parlor, and newspaper. His fiction typically depicts poor Chicago characters of Irish descent, and he published more than twenty-five novels. His first three novels form a trilogy about the same character: *Young Lonigan* (1932), *The Young Manhood of Studs Lonigan* (1934), and *Judgment Day* (1935). These works chronicle the degeneration of William (Studs) Lonigan, an adolescent who is corrupted by his Chicago slum environment, becomes a brutal hoodlum, and dies by the age of twenty-nine. In 1937, the trilogy won a $2,500 Book-of-the-Month Club prize. Farrell's second novel cycle, a history of the life of Danny O'Neill, includes *A World I Never Made* (1936), which was the subject of an obscenity court case in 1937; *No Star Is Lost* (1939); *Father and Son* (1940); *My Days of Anger* (1943); and *The Face of Time* (1953). Among his story collections are *$1000 a Week and Other Stories* (1942), *An American Dream Girl* (1950), and *A Dangerous Woman and Other Short Stories* (1957).

A Jazz-Age Clerk

I

JACK Stratton worked from ten to eight answering telephone calls in the Wagon Department of the Continental Express Company. What he liked best about his job was his lunch hour from one to two. Ordinarily, clerks went to lunch at twelve o'clock, and he believed that people seeing him on the streets between one and two might figure that he was a lad with a pretty good job, because one o'clock was the time when many businessmen took their lunch in order to avoid the noonday jams in the Loop.

One sunny day in early spring Jack went out to lunch. He felt good. He would have felt even better if only his faded powder-blue suit were not so old, and if only it were already the next pay day, because then he hoped to be able to make a down payment and get a new suit on the installment plan. When he had got this powder-blue suit, he'd thought that it was the real thing. All the cake-eaters were wearing them. But it was a cheap suit that had faded quickly. And his brown hat, fixed square-shaped the way the cakes were wearing them, was old and greasy from the stacomb that he smeared on his hair every day. Yes, he would have been feeling much better if he were dogged out in a new outfit. Well, he would some day, he decided. He walked toward Van Buren Street.

It was a narrow, dusty street, with garages, a continental filling station and terminal, and the rear ends of old office buildings and restaurants. On the other side he spotted a girl, and told himself that she was so hot she could start a new Chicago fire all by herself. He snapped his fingers and watched her pass. Daddy! He burst into song:

> Teasing eyes, teasing eyes,
> You're the little girl that sets my heart afire . . .

Teasing! He expressed his feelings with a low whistle. He guessed that working in the Loop had its advantages. At least there were plenty of shebas to look at. He shifted his gait into a hopping two-step. Self-conscious, he checked himself. People might laugh at him in the street, just as Gas-House McGinty, Heinie Mueller, and some of the others in the office laughed at him. Some day he would like to show them, clean up on a few of the wise-aleck clerks. And he would, too! They were dumb, that was all, and they didn't know what was the real thing in the world today. They didn't have enough sense to be cake-eaters. And nicknaming him Jenny, like they had. Some day he would Jenny them! He began walking in a kind of waltzing dance step, his body quivering as he moved. Another song burst into his thoughts, "Tiger Rose."

Sadness and self-pity drove the half-sung chorus out of his mind. He wanted girls, a girl, and he wanted money to spend on clothes so that he could impress the broads, and to spend on dances, dates, going places. But he was only making eighty-five dollars a month. That was more than he had expected when he started looking for a job, and he couldn't kick. He knew fellows who only made their fifteen a week. But his pay wasn't any too much. And since his old man was out of work, most of his jack had to go to his mother toward keeping up the home. Gee, he wished that the old man would find another job, and then he could have a little more to spend.

He saw an athletically built blonde, who was just bow-wows, the kind to look at and weep. He jerked his shoulders in rhythm and sang:

> I'm runnin' wild, I'm runnin' wild,
> I lost control . . .

Now, if there would only be some mama like that in the restaurant, and if he could only get next to her.

The restaurant where he usually ate was owned by a Greek, and was a small establishment with a tile floor and an imitation marble counter. He took a counter seat in the front, several stools removed from the nearest customer. Kitty, the slatternly peroxide-blonde waitress, greeted him with a yellow-toothed yawn, and at the same time she rubbed a fat hand over her low forehead. He looked up at her face; it was crusted with powder.

"Hello," he said.

A customer got up and went to the glass case to pay his check. Kitty left Jack, collected, rang the cash register, deposited the silver in the drawer, and returned. The expression on her face was stupid, bored. Jack snapped his fingers, rolled his eyes, and sang a jazz song.

"What yuh want today, Dapper Dan?" she asked.

"Ham and coffee."

Swinging her head sidewise, she shouted the sandwich order to the chef. Other customers left and she collected.

He was the only one remaining in the restaurant. Suddenly he was conscious of his shabbiness. He reached down to touch the raggedy cuffs of his bell-bottom trousers. He felt the thinness at the right elbow of his coat. Kitty slid a ham sandwich at him, and then she slopped a cup of coffee across the counter.

"Big times tonight!" he said while applying mustard to his sandwich.

"Huh?" she mumbled lifelessly.

"Dance at the South Hall out in Englewood where I live," he said, biting into his sandwich.

"Takin' yours along?" she asked lackadaisically.

"I told her to keep the home fires burning tonight. I like a little variety and change, sister."

His shoulders swung to the singing of a few lines from "The Darktown Strutters' Ball."

"Cancha sing something that's new," Kitty said petulantly.

"I just learned this one this week at the Song Shop on Quincy Street. Listen!"

> *No, no, Nora, nobody but you, dear,*
> *You know, Nora, yours truly is true, dear . . .*

"Aha!" he interrupted with a leer.

> *And when you accuse me of flirting*

"Like that?" he interpolated with a lascivious wink.

> *I wouldn't, I couldn't, I love you so,*
> *I've had chances, too many to mention . . .*

"Always get chances," he interposed.

> *Never give them a bit of attention.*
> *No, no, Nora. No? No?*

"Nice tune," Kitty said dopily as Jack bent down to drink coffee.

"Fast! And tonight I'm grabbing myself a keen number and stepping myself right up over those blue clouds into heaven."

"You're conceited."

He finished his sandwich. His coffee cup was half full. He looked at the cuts of pie in the dessert case before him. He dug his hand into his right trouser pocket. He swallowed his coffee in one gulp and slid off the stool. He paid Kitty fifteen cents, which she rang up.

"Toodle-oo!"

" 'Bye, sheik," she said patronizingly.

II

Overhead, the elevated trains thundered, drowning out the racket of street traffic. He stood on the sidewalk, hands in pockets, hat tilted, watching the crowd. He decided that today he'd sit in the lobby of a good hotel instead of going to the Song Shop and listening to the new tunes being sung. It would be restful.

If he only had on decent clothes, he could sit in a lobby and seem like a young fellow, maybe, with a rich old man or a good job that paid a big salary. A man in a hurry bumped into him and, hastening on, snottily suggested that he quit taking up the whole sidewalk. Jack looked after him, shrugged his shoulders, laughed. He bent his eyes on the moving legs of a girl ahead of him. He realized that if he got his shoes shined, he would improve his appearance. He hated to spend the dime, though, because when he got home tonight he could shine his own shoes. But his appearance would be improved, and he wouldn't look quite so poor. It was all in accordance with the principles of clever dressing. Always have on something new, outstanding or shiny, a loud tie, a clean shirt, a new hat, shined shoes, and then something else you were wearing that was shabby wouldn't be so noticed. He applied his principle by dropping into a shoe-shine parlor.

A young Negro energetically shined his shoes, and Jack day-dreamed about how he would stroll nonchalantly into the lobby of the Potter Hotel and find himself a chair that he could slump into, just so natural. He could spread his legs out so that the first thing anyone

noticed about him would be his shined shoes. His
thoughts leaped. Wouldn't it be luck if some ritzy queen
fell for him! It would just be . . . delicious. Daddy! His
mood lifted.

Adventure-bound, hopeful and gay, he hustled toward
the new Potter Hotel. His courage deserted him as he
passed the uniformed doorman who stood with a set and
frowning face, seeming to tell Jack that he wasn't
wanted. He paused at the entrance to the enormous
lobby, with its gold decorations, its hanging diamond-
like chandeliers, its lavish display of comfortable furniture. He told himself in awe that it was like a palace.
He noticed men and women, sitting, standing, moving
around, talking, reading newspapers, and for a moment
he felt as if he were in a moving picture world, the hero
in a picture walking into this hotel lobby like a palace
fit for the richest of kings or businessmen. He skirted
several bellboys and found a chair in a corner, but it
was not obscure, because there was a passageway all
round the lobby and many people would pass him while
he sat. A feeling of awe, as if he were in a church where
talking was not permitted, filled his consciousness. He
wished that he hadn't come here where he didn't belong,
and at the same time he was glad that he'd come.

Several yards away from him he noticed a gray-haired
man in a gray suit, whose pleasingly wrinkled face
seemed calm, contented, mellowed. He tried to make
himself seem as calm and as at ease as this man. For
want of something to do, he ran the palm of his hand
through his greasy hair; it was meticulously parted in the
center. He sedulously drew out his dirty handkerchief to
wipe the grease off his hand. To his right, he heard a
well-dressed fellow discussing the stock market with a
friend. A bellboy wended in and out, intoning:

"Call for Mr. Wagner . . . Call for Mr. Wagner . . .
Call for Mr. Wagner . . . Call for Mr. Wagner . . . Mr.
Wagner please . . ."

He was unable to chase out his confusion of feelings
in this alien atmosphere of the well-dressed, the well-
fed, the prosperous. He wished he could live a life that
had as much glitter as there must be in the lives of these
people. He thought how some day he wanted to be able

to sit in a swanky hotel lobby like this one, well-dressed, and have a bell hop pass along calling out his name. He tried to visualize himself, a little older, a successful rich businessman in the lobby with the bellboy droning for him.

"Call for Mr. Stratton . . . Call for Mr. John Stratton . . . Call for Mr. John Stratton . . . Mr. John Stratton . . ."

And it would be some millionaire on the wire waiting to close an important deal that would net him a handsome piece of change. He'd close the deal and come back to wait for a mama. Maybe she'd be some hot movie actress like Gloria Swanson who would be like the sweetheart of the world in her pictures. And he would be waiting for this movie actress more beautiful than even Gloria Swanson, thinking how when he had been nothing but a punk clerk at the express company he'd come to sit in the same lobby, wearing shabby clothes, dreaming of the day when things would happen to him.

He watched a tall and handsome young fellow stroll by. Must be collegiate! Must have had his gray suit made to order and have paid fifty, seventy-five bucks for it, maybe even more. The threads of his daydream suddenly snapped. All the confidence went out of him, so that he felt shaky, trembly. He wished again that he hadn't come here. He felt as if everyone in the lobby were looking at him, knowing he didn't belong and wanting to see him tossed out on his can. He looked unobtrusively at two snappily dressed young fellows on his left. They were out of earshot, but he wondered what they were saying. They probably had everything they wanted and did anything they cared to do, had automobiles, money on which to date up queens . . . everything. The one wearing a Scotch tweed suit drew out a fat cigar, removed the band, smelled the cigar, bit off the end, lit it like a businessman in a movie. If only his life were that of a hero in the movies! Ah! That was class, the way that fellow in the tweeds had pulled out his cigar and lit it. Yes, when his own dream ship came in and he could afford to smoke four-bit cigars, he would have to remember to light them the way that fellow did.

"Call for Mr. O'Flaherty . . . Call for Mr. Al O'Flaherty . . . Call for Mr. Al O'Flaherty . . . Call for Mr. Al O'Flaherty . . ."

Wouldn't it be the dogs to be paged like that on important business calls! But he had no right even to think of such things. It wouldn't ever be for him. His lot in life deepened his wretchedness. He hadn't had anything to start on. Father and mother with no dough. One year in high school, and that without clothes, no athletic ability, no money, nothing that could get him into fraternities and make the girls go for him. But, gee, in high school there'd been all kinds of hot and classy girls! Only why should they have looked at an unimportant freshman like himself? And anyway, that was all over. Now he was working at a job with no future. Maybe he ought to be glad for what he had, but, gee, he couldn't help feeling that some guys got all the breaks, while he got almost none. All these people, they belonged to a world he would never enter.

A bellboy coming toward him. Gee! He sat stricken in a paralyzing fright. He pushed back the dirty cuffs of his shirt so that they were invisible. He tried to think up a reason he could give for being in the lobby when the bell hop came and questioned him. He'd say he was waiting for somebody who was staying at the hotel. But they could check up on the name. He'd say he was waiting for a friend coming in from New York who was going to stay here. The bellboy coming! He wanted to get up and leave. He had no will. He was so afraid that he began to sweat under the armpits, and his forehead perspired. Coming!

The bellboy passed by his chair as if no one were sitting in it, and bent down to speak with the calm-faced man. The man rose and followed the bellboy across the lobby. Jack again pulled out his soiled handkerchief, crushed it into a ball so that it couldn't be noticed, and wiped his forehead.

He watched a slim, voluptuous blonde woman cross the lobby. She was the dogs, the snake's hips, and the stars all rolled into something in a black dress. Those lips of hers. She had lip-appeal, sister, lip-appeal, sex-appeal, and she had it, and she was like a shower of stars. Looked like a woman some rich bird had put in the velvet. He followed her tantalizing, sensuous movements with thirsting eyes. She was a trifle taller than he, he guessed . . . but . . . hot . . . She sat down beside a middleaged man in a conservative blue suit, crossed her legs. . . . Legs! Wouldn't he like to have the bucks to buy the most expensive stockings money could buy for those legs! She lit a cigarette and he bet himself that it was an expensive Turkish cigarette. Oh, sister!

Tantalizing, he told himself, not removing his eyes from her legs.

Yes, all he wanted was the money to have a mama like that. There wasn't a movie queen in Hollywood that had a nickel on that one. He imagined that she was his woman, seated beside him, talking to him, saying that she would rather have lunch at the Fraternity Row today. She was saying she was crazy, just crazy, about him and didn't care two cents for anyone else in the world. She was wild for him. . . .

"Call for Mr. Jones . . . Mr. Jones please! . . . Mr. Jones!"

The voice of the bellboy was like a jolt, awakening him. He looked at his Ingersoll watch. Two minutes to two. He'd be late, and Collins, his boss, might bawl the hell out of him, and then all the fellows in the office would razz him, call him Jenny, the drugstore cowboy. He placed his hat on carefully and moved swiftly out of the lobby. Hurrying along the street, he fell into a dance step. Then he ran until he pulled up, winded. Four minutes after two. What excuse could he give Collins? He paused to look at a girl in pink. Nice! He unwittingly broke into song.

I'm Al-a-ba-ma bound . . .

He again worried about himself, thought of the things he wanted and couldn't have. He started running, hoping that Collins wouldn't bawl him out. Two seven!

—1932

SANDRA CISNEROS
(B. 1954)

Born in Chicago to a Mexican father and a Mexican-American mother, Sandra Cisneros was the only daughter in a family with seven children. During her childhood, her family often lived in Mexico City as well as Chicago. She received a B.A. from Loyola University and an M.F.A. from the University of Iowa Writers' Workshop. She has worked as a high school teacher for drop-out students and a Loyola University recruiter and counselor for minority students as well as having visiting professorships at California State University at Chico, the University of California at Berkeley, the University of California at Irvine, the University of Michigan, and the University of New Mexico. She has been awarded two National Endowment for the Arts Fellowships (1982, 1988), a Paisano Dobie Fellowship (1986), a Lannan Foundation Literary Award (1991), an H.D.L. from the State University of New York at Purchase (1993), and a MacArthur Foundation Fellowship (1995). According to Cisneros, in a course at the University of Iowa she discovered the unique voice in which she writes, a narrative voice influenced by the two different speech patterns of her parents. She has published three collections of poetry: *Bad Boys* (1980), *My Wicked, Wicked Ways* (1987) and *Loose Woman* (1994). She published *The House on Mango Street*, a collection of connected vignettes written from the point of view of a first-person Latina girl, in 1984 and *Woman Hollering Creek and Other Stories* in 1991.

Three Sketches from
The House on Mango Street

WE didn't always live on Mango Street. Before that we lived on Loomis on the third floor, and before that we lived on Keeler. Before Keeler it was Paulina, and before that I can't remember. But what I remember most

is moving a lot. Each time it seemed there'd be one more
of us. By the time we got to Mango Street we were six—
Mama, Papa, Carlos, Kiki, my sister Nenny and me.

The house on Mango Street is ours and we don't have
to pay rent to anybody or share the yard with the people
downstairs or be careful not to make too much noise and
there isn't a landlord banging on the ceiling with a broom.
But even so, it's not the house we'd thought we'd get.

We had to leave the flat on Loomis quick. The water
pipes broke and the landlord wouldn't fix them because
the house was too old. We had to leave fast. We were
using the washroom next door and carrying water over in
empty milk gallons. That's why Mama and Papa looked
for a house, and that's why we moved into the house on
Mango Street, far away, on the other side of town.

They always told us that one day we would move into
a house, a real house that would be ours for always so
we wouldn't have to move each year. And our house
would have running water and pipes that worked. And
inside it would have real stairs, not hallway stairs, but
stairs inside like the houses on T.V. And we'd have a
basement and at least three washrooms so when we took
a bath we didn't have to tell everybody. Our house
would be white with trees around it, a great big yard
and grass growing without a fence. This was the house
Papa talked about when he held a lottery ticket and this
was the house Mama dreamed up in the stories she told
us before we went to bed.

But the house on Mango Street is not the way they
told it at all. It's small and red with tight little steps in
front and windows so small you'd think they were holding their breath. Bricks are crumbling in places, and the
front door is so swollen you have to push hard to get
in. There is no front yard, only four little elms the city
planted by the curb. Out back is a small garage for the
car we don't own yet and a small yard that looks smaller
between the two buildings on either side. There are
stairs in our house, but they're ordinary hallway stairs,
and the house has only one washroom, very small.
Everybody has to share a bedroom—Mama and Papa,
Carlos and Kiki, me and Nenny.

Once when we were living on Loomis, a nun from my

school passed by and saw me playing out front. The laundromat downstairs had been boarded up because it had been robbed two days before and the owner had painted on the wood YES WE'RE OPEN so as not to lose business.

Where do you live? she asked.

There, I said pointing up to the third floor.

You live *there*?

There. I had to look to where she pointed—the third floor, the paint peeling, wooden bars Papa had nailed on the windows so we wouldn't fall out. You live *there*? The way she said it made me feel like nothing. *There.* I lived *there.* I nodded.

I knew then I had to have a house. A real house. One I could point to. But this isn't it. The house on Mango Street isn't it. For the time being, Mama said. Temporary, said Papa. But I know how those things go.

A Rice Sandwich

The special kids, the ones who wear keys around their necks, get to eat in the canteen. The canteen! Even the name sounds important. And these kids at lunch time go there because their mothers aren't home or home is too far away to get to.

My home isn't far but it's not close either, and somehow I got it in my head one day to ask my mother to make me a sandwich and write a note to the principal so I could eat in the canteen too.

Oh no, she says pointing the butter knife at me as if I'm starting trouble, no sir. Next thing you know everybody will be wanting a bag lunch—I'll be up all night cutting bread into little triangles, this one with mayonnaise, this one with mustard, no pickles on mine, but mustard on one side please. You kids just like to invent more work for me.

But Nenny says she doesn't want to eat at school—ever—because she likes to go home with her best friend Gloria who lives across the schoolyard. Gloria's mama has a big color T.V. and all they do is watch cartoons. Kiki and Carlos, on the other hand, are patrol boys.

They don't want to eat at school either. They like to stand out in the cold especially if it's raining. They think suffering is good for you ever since they saw that movie "300 Spartans."

I'm no Spartan and hold up an anemic wrist to prove it. I can't even blow up a balloon without getting dizzy. And besides, I know how to make my own lunch. If I ate at school there'd be less dishes to wash. You would see me less and less and like me better. Everyday at noon my chair would be empty. Where is my favorite daughter you would cry, and when I came home finally at 3 p.m. you would appreciate me.

Okay, okay, my mother says after three days of this. And the following morning I get to go to school with my mother's letter and a rice sandwich because we don't have lunch meat.

Mondays or Fridays, it doesn't matter, mornings always go by slow and this day especially. But lunch time came finally and I got to get in line with the stay-at-school kids. Everything is fine until the nun who knows all the canteen kids by heart looks at me and says: you, who sent you here? And since I am shy, I don't say anything, just hold out my hand with the letter. This is no good, she says, till Sister Superior gives the okay. Go upstairs and see her. And so I went.

I had to wait for two kids in front of me to get hollered at, one because he did something in class, the other because he didn't. My turn came and I stood in front of the big desk with holy pictures under the glass while the Sister Superior read my letter. It went like this:

Dear Sister Superior, Please let Esperanza eat in the lunch room because she lives too far away and she gets tired. As you can see she is very skinny. I hope to God she does not faint. Thanking you, Mrs. E. Cordero.

You don't live far, she says. You live across the boulevard. That's only four blocks. Not even. Three maybe. Three long blocks away from here. I bet I can see your house from my window. Which one? Come here. Which one is your house?

And then she made me stand up on a box of books and point. That one? she said pointing to a row of ugly 3-flats, the ones even the raggedy men are ashamed to go into. Yes, I nodded even though I knew that wasn't my house and started to cry. I always cry when nuns yell at me, even if they're not yelling.

Then she was sorry and said I could stay—just for today, not tomorrow or the day after—you go home. And I said yes and could I please have a Kleenex—I had to blow my nose.

In the canteen, which was nothing special, lots of boys and girls watched while I cried and ate my sandwich, the bread already greasy and the rice cold.

Bums in the Attic

I want a house on a hill like the ones with the gardens where Papa works. We go on Sundays, Papa's day off. I used to go. I don't anymore. You don't like to go out with us, Papa says. Getting too old? Getting too stuck-up, says Nenny. I don't tell them I am ashamed—all of us staring out the window like the hungry. I am tired of looking at what we can't have. When we win the lottery . . . Mama begins, and then I stop listening.

People who live on hills sleep so close to the stars they forget those of us who live too much on earth. They don't look down at all except to be content to live on hills. They have nothing to do with last week's garbage or fear of rats. Night comes. Nothing wakes them but the wind.

One day I'll own my own house, but I won't forget who I am or where I came from. Passing bums will ask, Can I come in? I'll offer them the attic, ask them to stay, because I know how it is to be without a house.

Some days after dinner, guests and I will sit in front of a fire. Floorboards will squeak upstairs. The attic grumble.

Rats? they'll ask.

Bums, I'll say, and I'll be happy.

—1989

SHERWOOD ANDERSON
(1876–1941)

Anderson, early in his life, feared that he might turn out like his father, Irwin, a jovial, theatrical raconteur who failed miserably to provide for his wife and family. To make up for his father's lack of ambition and money, the young Anderson worked energetically at a series of menial jobs which included delivery boy, farmhand, newsboy, factory employee, stablehand, and warehouse workman. At the age of thirty he had settled down to a conventional existence as a middle-class businessman, but during the next few years the writing that he had been doing in his spare time became increasingly important to him. The tension between the demands of his job and the need to devote himself to writing, which more and more preoccupied him, contributed to a nervous breakdown at the age of thirty-six. He left Ohio for Chicago to take a job there as an advertising copywriter, hoping it would provide financial support while allowing the time he needed for his literary career. His first novel, *Windy McPherson's Son*, appeared in 1916, and his first collection of tales, *Winesburg, Ohio*, followed three years later. Best known as a short story writer, he published three other collections: *The Triumph of the Egg* (1921), *Horses and Men* (1923), and *Death in the Woods and Other Stories* (1933).

The Untold Lie

RAY Pearson and Hal Winters were farm hands employed on a farm three miles north of Winesburg. On Saturday afternoons they came into town and wandered about through the streets with other fellows from the country.

Ray was a quiet, rather nervous man of perhaps fifty with a brown beard and shoulders rounded by too much and too hard labor. In his nature he was as unlike Hal Winters as two men can be unlike.

Ray was an altogether serious man and had a little

sharp-featured wife who had also a sharp voice. The two, with half a dozen thin-legged children, lived in a tumble-down frame house beside a creek at the back end of the Wills farm where Ray was employed.

Hal Winters, his fellow employee, was a young fellow. He was not of the Ned Winters family, who were very respectable people in Winesburg, but was one of the three sons of the old man called Windpeter Winters who had a sawmill near Unionville, six miles away, and who was looked upon by everyone in Winesburg as a confirmed old reprobate.

People from the part of Northern Ohio in which Winesburg lies will remember old Windpeter by his unusual and tragic death. He got drunk one evening in town and started to drive home to Unionville along the railroad tracks. Henry Brattenburg, the butcher, who lived out that way, stopped him at the edge of the town and told him he was sure to meet the down train but Windpeter slashed at him with his whip and drove on. When the train struck and killed him and his two horses a farmer and his wife who were driving home along a nearby road saw the accident. They said that old Windpeter stood up on the seat of his wagon, raving and swearing at the onrushing locomotive, and that he fairly screamed with delight when the team, maddened by his incessant slashing at them, rushed straight ahead to certain death. Boys like young George Willard and Seth Richmond will remember the incident quite vividly because, although everyone in our town said that the old man would go straight to hell and that the community was better off without him, they had a secret conviction that he knew what he was doing and admired his foolish courage. Most boys have seasons of wishing they could die gloriously instead of just being grocery clerks and going on with their humdrum lives.

But this is not the story of Windpeter Winters nor yet of his son Hal who worked on the Wills farm with Ray Pearson. It is Ray's story. It will, however, be necessary to talk a little of young Hal so that you will get into the spirit of it.

Hal was a bad one. Everyone said that. There were three of the Winters boys in that family, John, Hal, and

Edward, all broad shouldered big fellows like old Wind-peter himself and all fighters and woman-chasers and generally all-around bad ones.

Hal was the worst of the lot and always up to some devilment. He once stole a load of boards from his fa-ther's mill and sold them in Winesburg. With the money he bought himself a suit of cheap, flashy clothes. Then he got drunk and when his father came raving into town to find him, they met and fought with their fists on Main Street and were arrested and put into jail together.

Hal went to work on the Wills farm because there was a country school teacher out that way who had taken his fancy. He was only twenty-two then but had already been in two or three of what were spoken of in Wines-burg as "women scrapes." Everyone who heard of his infatuation for the school teacher was sure it would turn out badly. "He'll only get her into trouble, you'll see," was the word that went around.

And so these two men, Ray and Hal, were at work in a field on a day in the late October. They were husking corn and occasionally something was said and they laughed. Then came silence. Ray, who was the more sen-sitive and always minded things more, had chapped hands and they hurt. He put them into his coat pockets and looked away across the fields. He was in a sad dis-tracted mood and was affected by the beauty of the country. If you knew the Winesburg country in the fall and how the low hills are all splashed with yellows and reds you would understand his feeling. He began to think of the time, long ago when he was a young fellow living with his father, then a baker in Winesburg, and how on such days he had wandered away to the woods to gather nuts, hunt rabbits, or just to loaf about and smoke his pipe. His marriage had come about through one of his days of wandering. He had induced a girl who waited on trade in his father's shop to go with him and something had happened. He was thinking of that after-noon and how it had affected his whole life when a spirit of protest awoke in him. He had forgotten about Hal and muttered words. "Tricked by Gad, that's what I was, tricked by life and made a fool of," he said in a low voice.

As though understanding his thoughts, Hal Winters spoke up. "Well, has it been worth while? What about it, eh? What about marriage and all that?" he asked and then laughed. Hal tried to keep on laughing but he too was in an earnest mood. He began to talk earnestly. "Has a fellow got to do it?" he asked. "Has he got to be harnessed up and driven through life like a horse?"

Hal didn't wait for an answer but sprang to his feet and began to walk back and forth between the corn shocks. He was getting more and more excited. Bending down suddenly he picked up an ear of the yellow corn and threw it at the fence. "I've got Nell Gunther in trouble," he said. "I'm telling you, but you keep your mouth shut."

Ray Pearson arose and stood staring. He was almost a foot shorter than Hal, and when the younger man came and put his two hands on the older man's shoulders they made a picture. There they stood in the big empty field with the quiet corn shocks standing in rows behind them and the red and yellow hills in the distance, and from being just two indifferent workmen they had become all alive to each other. Hal sensed it and because that was his way he laughed. "Well, old daddy," he said awkwardly, "come on, advise me. I've got Nell in trouble. Perhaps you've been in the same fix yourself. I know what every one would say is the right thing to do, but what do you say? Shall I marry and settle down? Shall I put myself into the harness to be worn out like an old horse? You know me, Ray. There can't any one break me but I can break myself. Shall I do it or shall I tell Nell to go to the devil? Come on, you tell me. Whatever you say, Ray, I'll do."

Ray couldn't answer. He shook Hal's hands loose and turning walked straight away toward the barn. He was a sensitive man and there were tears in his eyes. He knew there was only one thing to say to Hal Winters, son of old Windpeter Winters, only one thing that all his own training and all the beliefs of the people he knew would approve, but for his life he couldn't say what he knew he should say.

At half-past four that afternoon Ray was puttering about the barnyard when his wife came up the lane along the creek and called him. After the talk with Hal he hadn't returned to the corn field but worked about the barn. He had already done the evening chores and had seen Hal, dressed and ready for a roistering night in town, come out of the farmhouse and go into the road. Along the path to his own house he trudged behind his wife, looking at the ground and thinking. He couldn't make out what was wrong. Every time he raised his eyes and saw the beauty of the country in the failing light he wanted to do something he had never done before, shout or scream or hit his wife with his fists or something equally unexpected and terrifying. Along the path he went scratching his head and trying to make it out. He looked hard at his wife's back but she seemed all right.

She only wanted him to go into town for groceries and as soon as she had told him what she wanted began to scold. "You're always puttering," she said. "Now I want you to hustle. There isn't anything in the house for supper and you've got to get to town and back in a hurry."

Ray went into his own house and took an overcoat from a hook back of the door. It was torn about the pockets and the collar was shiny. His wife went into the bedroom and presently came out with a soiled cloth in one hand and three silver dollars in the other. Somewhere in the house a child wept bitterly and a dog that had been sleeping by the stove arose and yawned. Again the wife scolded. "The children will cry and cry. Why are you always puttering?" she asked.

Ray went out of the house and climbed the fence into a field. It was just growing dark and the scene that lay before him was lovely. All the low hills were washed with color and even the little clusters of bushes in the corners by the fences were alive with beauty. The whole world seemed to Ray Pearson to have become alive with something just as he and Hal had suddenly become alive when they stood in the corn field staring into each other's eyes.

The beauty of the country about Winesburg was too much for Ray on that fall evening. That is all there was to it. He could not stand it. Of a sudden he forgot all about being a quiet old farm hand and throwing off the torn overcoat began to run across the field. As he ran he shouted a protest against his life, against all life, against everything that makes life ugly. "There was no promise made," he cried into the empty spaces that lay about him. "I didn't promise my Minnie anything and Hal hasn't made any promise to Nell. I know he hasn't. She went into the woods with him because she wanted to go. What he wanted she wanted. Why should I pay? Why should Hal pay? Why should any one pay? I don't want Hal to become old and worn out. I'll tell him. I won't let it go on. I'll catch Hal before he gets to town and I'll tell him."

Ray ran clumsily and once he stumbled and fell down. "I must catch Hal and tell him," he kept thinking and although his breath came in gasps he kept running harder and harder. As he ran he thought of things that hadn't come into his mind for years—how at the time he married he had planned to go west to his uncle in Portland, Oregon—how he hadn't wanted to be a farm hand, but had thought when he got out west he would go to sea and be a sailor or get a job on a ranch and ride a horse into western towns, shouting and laughing and waking the people in the houses with his wild cries. Then as he ran he remembered his children and in fancy felt their hands clutching at him. All of his thoughts of himself were involved with the thoughts of Hal and he thought the children were clutching at the younger man also. "They are the accidents of life, Hal," he cried. "They are not mine or yours. I had nothing to do with them."

Darkness began to spread over the fields as Ray Pearson ran on and on. His breath came in little sobs. When he came to the fence at the edge of the road and confronted Hal Winters, all dressed up and smoking a pipe as he walked jauntily along, he could not have told what he thought or what he wanted.

Ray Pearson lost his nerve and this is really the end of the story of what happened to him. It was almost dark when he got to the fence and he put his hands on the top bar and stood staring. Hal Winters jumped a ditch and coming up close to Ray put his hands into his pockets and laughed. He seemed to have lost his own sense of what had happened in the corn field and when he put up a strong hand and took hold of the lapel of Ray's coat he shook the old man as he might have shaken a dog that had misbehaved.

"You came to tell me, eh?" he said. "Well, never mind telling me anything. I'm not a coward and I've already made up my mind." He laughed again and jumped back across the ditch. "Nell ain't no fool," he said. "She didn't ask me to marry her. I want to marry her. I want to settle down and have kids."

Ray Pearson also laughed. He felt like laughing at himself and all the world.

As the form of Hal Winters disappeared in the dusk that lay over the road that led to Winesburg, he turned and walked slowly back across the fields to where he had left his torn overcoat. As he went some memory of pleasant evenings spent with the thin-legged children in the tumble-down house by the creek must have come into his mind, for he muttered words. "It's just as well. Whatever I told him would have been a lie," he said softly, and then his form also disappeared into the darkness of the fields.

—1919

ETHAN CANIN

(B. 1960)

The son of a violinist and painter, Ethan Canin grew up in Ann Arbor, Michigan; Oberlin, Ohio; Philadelphia, Pennsylvania and San Francisco, California. At Stanford, he studied engineering and English; at the University of Iowa he earned an M.F.A.; at Harvard Medical School he earned an M.D. While a resident at the University of California at San Francisco, he gave up medicine in order to become a fulltime writer. He has been awarded a Houghton Mifflin Literary Fellowship (1988), a Henfield Transatlantic Review Award (1989), and a grant from the National Endowment for the Arts (1989). At the age of nineteen he published his first short story, and at the age of twenty-seven he published his first story collection, *Emperor of the Air* (1988). He is the author of two novels, *Blue River* (1991) and *For Kings and Planets* (1998), as well as a second volume of stories, *The Palace Thief* (1994). Presently, he teaches at the University of Iowa Writers' Workshop.

Where We Are Now

WHEN I met Jodi, she was an English major at Simmons College, in Boston, and for a while after that she tried to be a stage actress. Then she tried writing a play, and when that didn't work out she thought about opening a bookstore. We've been married eleven years now, and these days she checks out books at the public library. I don't mean she reads them; I mean she works at the circulation desk.

We've been arguing lately about where we live. Our apartment is in a building with no grass or bushes, only a social room, with plastic chairs and a carpet made of Astroturf. Not many people want to throw a party on Astroturf, Jodi says. She points out other things, too: the elevator stops a foot below the floors, so you have to step up to get out; the cold water comes out rusty in the mornings; three weeks ago a man was robbed in the hallway by a kid with a bread knife. The next Sunday night Jodi rolled over in bed, turned on the light, and said, "Charlie, let's look at houses."

It was one in the morning. From the fourth floor, through the night haze, I could see part of West Hollywood, a sliver of the observatory, lights from the mansions in the canyon.

"There," I said, pointing through the window. "Houses."

"No, let's look at houses to buy."

I covered my eyes with my arm. "Lovebird," I said, "where will we find a house we can afford?"

"We can start this weekend," she said.

That night after dinner she read aloud from the real estate section. "Santa Monica," she read. "Two bedrooms, yard, half-mile to beach."

"How much?"

She looked closer at the paper. "We can look other places."

She read to herself for a while. Then she said that prices seemed lower in some areas near the Los Angeles airport.

"How much?"

"A two-bedroom for $160,000."

I glanced at her.

"Just because we look doesn't mean we have to buy it," she said.

"There's a real estate agent involved."

"She won't mind."

"It's not honest," I said.

She closed the paper and went to the window. I watched a muscle in her neck move from side to side. "You know what it's like?" she said, looking into the street.

"I just don't want to waste the woman's time," I answered.

"It's like being married to a priest."

I knew why she said that. I'm nothing like a priest. I'm a physical education teacher in the Hollywood schools and an assistant coach—basketball and baseball. The other night I'd had a couple of other coaches over to the house. We aren't all that much alike—I'll read a biography on the weekend, listen to classical music maybe a third of the time—but I still like to have them over. We were sitting in the living room, drinking beer and talking about the future. One of the coaches has a two-year-old son at home. He didn't have a lot of money, he said, so he thought it was important to teach his kid morality. I wasn't sure he was serious, but when he finished I told a story anyway about an incident that had happened a few weeks before at school. I'd found out that a kid in a gym class I was teaching, a quiet boy and a decent student, had stolen a hat from a men's store. So I made him return it and write a letter of apology to the owner. When I told the part about how the man was so impressed with the letter that he offered the boy a job, Jodi remarked that I was lucky it hadn't turned out the other way.

"What do you mean?" I asked.

"He could have called the police," she said. "He could have thanked you for bringing the boy in and then called the police."

"I just don't think so."

"Why not? The boy could have ended up in jail."

"I just don't think so," I said. "I think most people will respond to honesty. I think that's where people like us have to lead the way."

It's an important point, I said, and took a drink of beer to take the edge off what I was saying. Too much money makes you lose sight of things, I told them. I stopped talking then, but I could have said more. All you have to do is look around: in Beverly Hills there's a restaurant where a piece of veal costs thirty dollars. I don't mind being an assistant coach at a high school, even though you hear now about the fellow who earns a hundred thousand dollars with the fitness truck that comes right to people's homes. The truck has Nautilus, and a sound system you wouldn't expect. He keeps the stars in shape that way—Kirk Douglas, the movie executives. The man with the truck doesn't live in Hollywood. He probably lives out at the beach, in Santa Monica or Malibu.

But Hollywood's fine if people don't compare it with the ideas they have. Once in a while, at a party, someone

from out of town will ask me whether any children of
movie stars are in my classes. Sometimes Jodi says the
answer is yes but that it would violate confidentiality to
reveal their names. Other times I explain that movie
stars don't live in Hollywood these days, that most of
them don't even work here, that Hollywood is just car
washes and food joints, and that the theater with the
stars' footprints out front isn't much of a theater anymore. The kids race hot rods by it on Thursday nights.

Hollywood is all right, though, I say. It's got sun and
wide streets and is close to everything.

But Jodi wants to look anyway.

Next Sunday I drive, and Jodi gives directions from the
map. The house is in El Segundo. While I'm parking I
hear a loud noise, and a 747 flies right over our heads.
I watch it come down over the freeway.

"Didn't one of them land on the road once?" I ask.

"I don't remember it," Jodi says. She looks at the
map. "The house should be on this block."

"I think it was in Dallas. I think it came right down
on top of a car."

I think about that for a minute. It shakes me up to
see a huge plane so low. I think of the people inside the
one that landed on the road—descending, watching the
flaps and the ailerons, the houses and automobiles coming into view.

"The ad says there are nice trees in back," says Jodi.

She leads us to the house. It's two stories, yellow
stucco walls, with a cement yard and a low wire fence
along the sidewalk. The roof is tar paper. Down the
front under the drainpipes are two long green stains.

"Don't worry," she says. "Just because we look
doesn't mean anything." She knocks on the door and
slips her arm into mine. "Maybe you can see the ocean
from the bedroom windows."

She knocks again. Then she pushes the door a little,
and we walk into the living room. There are quick footsteps, and a woman comes out of the hallway. "Good
afternoon," she says. "Would you sign in, please?"

She points to a vinyl-covered book on the coffee table,
and Jodi crosses the room and writes something in it.

Then the agent hands me a sheet of paper with small type on it and a badly copied picture. I've never shopped for a house before. I see two columns of abbreviations, some numbers. It's hard to tell what the picture is of, but then I recognize the long stains under the drainpipes. I fold the sheet and put it into my pants pocket. Then I sit down on the couch and look around. The walls are light yellow, and one of them is covered with a mirror that has gold marbling in it. On the floor is a cream-colored shag rug, with a matted area near the front door where a couch or maybe a trunk once stood. Above the mantel is a painting of a blue whale.

"Do the appliances and plumbing work?" Jodi asks.

"Everything works," says the agent.

Jodi turns the ceiling light on and off. She opens and closes the door to a closet in the corner, and I glimpse a tricycle and a bag full of empty bottles. I wonder what the family does on a Sunday afternoon when buyers look at their house.

"The rooms have a nice feel," the agent says. "You know what I mean?"

"I'm not sure I do," I say.

"It's hard to explain," she says, "but you'll see."

"We understand," says Jodi.

In the marbled mirror I watch Jodi's reflection. Three windows look onto the front yard, and she unlatches and lifts each one.

"I like a careful buyer," says the agent.

"You can never be too thorough," Jodi answers. Then she adds, "We're just looking."

The agent smiles, drumming her fingers against her wrist. I know she's trying to develop a strategy. In college I learned about strategies. I worked for a while selling magazines over the phone: talk to the man if you think they want it; talk to the woman if you think they don't. I was thinking of playing ball then, semi-pro, and the magazine work was evenings. I was twenty-three years old. I thought I was just doing work until I was discovered.

"Why don't you two look around," I say now to the agent. "I'll stay here."

"Perfect," she says.

She leads Jodi into the next room. I hear a door open and shut, and then they begin talking about the floors, the walls, the ceiling. We aren't going to buy the house, and I don't like being here. When I hear the two of them walk out through the back door into the yard, I get up from the couch and go over to look at the painting above the mantel. It's an underwater view, looking below the whale as it swims toward the surface. Above, the sunny sky is broken by ripples. On the mantel is a little pile of plaster powder, and as I stand there, I realize that the painting has just recently been hung. I go back to the couch. Once on a trip up the coast I saw a whale that the tide had trapped in a lagoon. It was north of Los Angeles, along the coastal highway, in a cove sheltered by two piers of man-moved boulders. Cars were parked along the shoulder. People were setting up their cameras while the whale moved around in the lagoon, stirring up the bottom. I don't like to think about trapped animals, though, so instead I sit down and try to plan what to do tomorrow at practice. The season hasn't started yet, and we're still working on base-running—the double steal, leading from the inside of the bag. Baseball isn't a thing you think about, though; baseball *comes*. I'm an assistant coach and maybe could have been a minor league pitcher, but when I think of it I realize I know only seven or eight things about the whole game. We learn so slowly, I think.

I get up and go over to the painting again. I glance behind me. I put my head next to the wall, lift the frame a little bit, and when I look I see that behind it the plaster is stained brown from an interior leak. I take a deep breath and then put the frame back. From outside in the yard I hear the women speaking about basement storage space, and rather than listen I cross the room and enter a hallway. It smells of grease. On the wall, at waist level, are children's hand marks that go all the way to the far end. I walk down there and enter the kitchen. In it are a Formica table and four plastic chairs, everything made large by the low ceiling. I see a door in the corner, and when I cross the room and open it I'm surprised to find a stairway with brooms and mops hung above the banister. The incline is steep, and when I go up I find myself in the rear of an upstairs closet. Below me Jodi and the agent are still talking. I push through the clothes hanging in front of me and open the door.

I'm in the master bedroom now. A king-size bed stands in front of me, but something's funny about it, and when I look closer I think that it might be two single beds pushed together. It's covered by a spread. I stop for a moment to think. I don't think I'm doing anything wrong. We came here to see the house, and when people show their homes they take out everything of value so that they won't have to worry. I go to the window. Framing it is a new-looking lace curtain, pinched up in a tie-back. I look out at a crab apple tree and some telephone wires and try to calculate where the ocean might be. The shadows point west, but the coastline is irregular in this area and juts in different directions. The view of the crab apple is pretty, spotted with shade and light—but then I see that in the corner behind the curtain the glass is splintered and has been taped. I lift the curtain and look at the pane. The crack spreads like a spider web. Then I walk back to the bed. I flatten my hands and slip them into the crevice between the two mattresses, and when I extend my arms the two halves come apart. I push the beds back together and sit down. Then I look into the corner, and my heart skips because I see that against the far wall, half-hidden by the open door, is an old woman in a chair.

"Excuse me," I say.

"That's all right," she says. She folds her hands. "The window cracked ten years ago."

"My wife and I are looking at the house."

"I know."

I walk to the window. "A nice view," I say, pretending to look at something in the yard. The woman doesn't say anything. I can hear water running in the pipes, some children outside. Tiny, pale apples hang among the leaves of the tree.

"You know," I say, "we're not really looking at the house to buy it."

I walk back to the bed. The skin on the woman's arms is mottled and hangs in folds. "We can't afford to buy it," I say. "I don't make enough money to buy a house and—I don't know why, but my wife wants to look at them anyway. She wants people to think we have enough money to buy a house."

The woman looks at me.

"It's crazy," I say, "but what are you going to do in that kind of situation?"

She clears her throat. "My son-in-law," she begins, "wants to sell the house so he can throw the money away." Her voice is slow, and I think she has no saliva in her mouth. "He has a friend who goes to South America and swallows everything, then comes back through customs with a plastic bag in his bowel."

She stops. I look at her. "He's selling the house to invest the money in drugs?"

"I'm glad you don't want to buy," she says.

I might have had a small career in baseball, but I've learned in the past eleven years to talk about other things. I was twenty-three the last pitch I threw. The season was over and Jodi was in the stands in a wool coat. I was about to get a college degree in physical education. I knew how to splint a broken bone and how to cut the grass on a golf green, and then I decided that to turn your life around you had to start from the inside. I had a coach in college who said he wasn't trying to teach us to be pro ballplayers; he was trying to teach us to be decent people.

When we got married, I told Jodi that no matter what happened, no matter where things went, she could always trust me. We'd been seeing each other for a year, and in that time I'd been reading books. Not baseball books. Biographies: Martin Luther King, Gandhi. To play baseball right you have to forget that you're a person; you're muscles, bone, the need for sleep and food. So when you stop, you're saved by someone else's ideas. This isn't true just for baseball players. It's true for anyone who's failed at what he loves.

A friend got me the coaching job in California, and as soon as we were married we came west. Jodi still wanted to be an actress. We rented a room in a house with six other people, and she took classes in dance in the mornings and speech in the afternoons. Los Angeles is full of actors. Sometimes at parties we counted them. After a couple of years she started writing a play, and until we moved into where we are now we used to read pieces of it out loud to our six housemates.

By then I was already a little friendly with the people at school, but when I was out of the house, even after two years in Los Angeles, I was alone. People were worried about their own lives. In college I'd spent almost all my time with another ballplayer, Mitchell Lighty, and I wasn't used to new people. A couple of years after we graduated, Mitchell left to play pro ball in Panama City, and he came out to Los Angeles on his way there. The night before his plane left, he and I went downtown to a bar on the top floor of a big hotel. We sat by a window, and after a few drinks we went out onto the balcony. The air was cool. Plants grew along the edge, ivy was woven into the railing, and birds perched among the leaves. I was amazed to see the birds resting there thirty stories up on the side of the building. When I brushed the plants the birds took off into the air, and when I leaned over to watch them, I became dizzy with the distance to the sidewalk and with the small, rectangular shapes of the cars. The birds sailed in wide circles over the street and came back to the balcony. Then Mitchell put his drink on a chair, took both my hands, and stepped up onto the railing. He stood there on the metal crossbar, his wrists locked in my hands, leaning into the air.

"For God's sake," I whispered. He leaned farther out, pulling me toward the railing. A waiter appeared at the sliding door next to us. "Take it easy," I said. "Come on down." Mitchell let go of one of my hands, kicked up one leg, and swung out over the street. His black wingtip shoe swiveled on the railing. The birds had scattered, and now they were circling, chattering angrily as he rocked. I was holding on with my pitching arm. My legs were pressed against the iron bars, and just when I began to feel the lead, just when the muscles began to shake, Mitchell jumped back onto the balcony. The waiter came through the sliding door and grabbed him, but in the years after that—the years after Mitchell got married and decided to stay in Panama City—I thought of that incident as the important moment of my life.

I don't know why. I've struck out nine men in a row and pitched to half a dozen hitters who are in the majors now, but when I think back over my life, about what I've done, not much more than that stands out.

As we lie in bed that night, Jodi reads aloud from the real estate listings. She uses abbreviations: BR, AC, D/D. As she goes down the page—San Marino, Santa Ana, Santa Monica—I nod occasionally or make a comment.

When I wake up later, early in the morning, the newspaper is still next to her on the bed. I can see its pale edge in the moonlight. Sometimes I wake up like this, maybe from some sound in the night, and when I do, I like to lie with my eyes closed and feel the difference between the bed and the night air. I like to take stock of things. These are the moments when I'm most in love with my wife. She's next to me, and her face when she sleeps is untroubled. Women say now that they don't want to be protected, but when I watch her slow breathing, her parted lips, I think what a delicate thing a life is. I lean over and touch her mouth.

When I was in school I saw different girls, but since I've been married to Jodi I've been faithful. Except for once, a few years ago, I've almost never thought about someone else. I have a friend at school, Ed Ryan, a history teacher, who told me about the time he had an affair, and about how his marriage broke up right afterward. It wasn't a happy thing to see. She was a cocktail waitress at a bar a few blocks from school, he said. Ed told me the whole long story, about how he and the waitress had fallen in love so suddenly that he had no choice about leaving his wife. After the marriage was over, though, Ed gained fifteen or twenty pounds. One night, coming home from school, he hit a tree and wrecked his car. A few days later he came in early to work and found that all the windows in his classroom had been broken. At first I believed him when he said he thought his wife had done it, but that afternoon we were talking and I realized what had really happened.

We were in a lunch place. "You know," Ed said, "sometimes you think you know a person." He was looking into his glass. "You can sleep next to a woman, you can know the way she smiles when she's turned on, you can see in her hands when she wants to talk about something. Then you wake up one day and some signal's been exchanged—and you don't know what it is, but you think for the first time, *Maybe I don't know her.* Just something. You never know what the signal is." I looked at him then and realized that there was no cocktail waitress and that Ed had broken the windows.

I turn in bed now and look at Jodi. Then I slide the newspaper off the blanket. We know each other, I think. The time I came close to adultery was a few years ago, with a secretary at school, a temporary who worked afternoons. She was a dark girl, didn't say much, and she wore turquoise bracelets on both wrists. She kept finding reasons to come into my office, which I share with the two other coaches. It's three desks, a window, a chalkboard. One night I was there late, after everyone else had gone, and she came by to do something. It was already dark. We talked for a while, and then she took off one of her bracelets to show me. She said she wanted me to see how beautiful it was, how the turquoise changed color in dim light. She put it into my hand, and then I knew for sure what was going on. I looked at it for a long time, listening to the little sounds in the building, before I looked up.

"Charlie?" Jodi says now in the dark.

"Yes?"

"Would you do whatever I asked you to do?"

"What do you mean?"

"I mean, would you do anything in the world that I asked you to do?"

"That depends," I say.

"On what?"

"On what you asked. If you asked me to rob someone, then maybe I wouldn't."

I hear her roll over, and I know she's looking at me. "But don't you think I would have a good reason to ask you if I did?"

"Probably."

"And wouldn't you do it just because I asked?"

She turns away again and I try to think of an answer. We've already argued once today, while she was making dinner, but I don't want to lie to her. That's what we argued about earlier. She asked me what I thought of the house we looked at, and I told her the truth, that a house just wasn't important to me.

"Then what is important to you?"

I was putting the forks and knives on the table. "Leveling with other people is important to me," I answered. "And you're important to me." Then I said, "And whales."

"What?"

"Whales are important to me."

That was when it started. We didn't say much after that, so it wasn't an argument exactly. I don't know why I mentioned the whales. They're great animals, the biggest things on earth, but they're not important to me.

"What if it was something not so bad," she says now, "but still something you didn't want to do?"

"What?"

The moonlight is shining in her hair. "What if I asked you to do something that ordinarily you wouldn't do yourself—would you do it if I asked?"

"And it wasn't something so bad?"

"Right."

"Yes," I say. "Then I would do it."

"What I want you to do," she says on Wednesday, "is look at another house." We're eating dinner. "But I want them to take us seriously," she says. "I want to act as if we're really thinking of buying it, right on the verge. You know—maybe we will, maybe we won't."

I take a sip of water, look out the window. "That's ridiculous," I say. "Nobody walks in off the street and decides in an afternoon whether to buy a house."

"Maybe we've been looking at it from a distance for a long time," she says, "assessing things." She isn't eating her dinner. I cooked it, chicken, and it's steaming on her plate. "Maybe we've been waiting for the market to change."

"Why is it so important to you?"

"It just is. And you said you'd do it if it was important to me. Didn't you say that?"

"I had a conversation with the old woman in the yellow house."

"What?"

"When we looked at the other house," I say, "I went off by myself for a while. I talked with the old woman who was sitting upstairs."

"What did you say?"

"Do you remember her?"

"Yes."

"She told me that the owner was selling the house so he could use the money to smuggle drugs."

"So?"

"So," I say, "you have to be careful."

This Sunday Jodi drives. The day is bright and blue, with a breeze from the ocean, and along Santa Monica Boulevard the palm fronds are rustling. I'm in my suit. If Jodi talks to the agent about offers, I've decided I'll stay to the back, nod or shrug at questions. She parks the car on a side street and we walk around the corner and go into the lobby of one of the hotels. We sit down in cloth chairs near the entrance. A bellman carries over an ashtray on a stand and sets it between us; Jodi hands him a bill from her purse. I look at her. The bellman is the age of my father. He moves away fast, and I lean forward to get my shoulder loose in my suit. I'm not sure if the lobby chairs are only for guests, and I'm ready to get up if someone asks. Then a woman comes in and Jodi stands and introduces herself. "Charlie Gordon," I say when the woman puts her hand out. She's in a gray pinstripe skirt and a jacket with a white flower in the lapel. After she says something to Jodi, she leads us outside to the parking circle, where a car is brought around by the valet, a French car, and Jodi and I get in back. The seats are leather.

"Is the weather always this nice?" Jodi asks. We pull out onto Wilshire Boulevard.

"Almost always," the woman says. "That's another thing I love about Los Angeles—the weather. Los Angeles has the most perfect weather on earth."

We drive out toward the ocean, and as the woman moves in and out of the lines of traffic, I look around the car. It's well kept, maybe leased. No gum wrappers or old coffee cups under the seat.

"Then you're looking for a second home?" the woman says.

"My husband's business makes it necessary for us to have a home in Los Angeles."

I look at Jodi. She's sitting back in the seat, her hand resting on the armrest.

"Most of the year, of course, we'll be in Dallas."

The street is curved and long with a grass island in the middle and eucalyptus along its length, and each time the car banks, I feel the nerves firing in my gut. I look at Jodi. I look at her forehead. I look at the way her hair falls on her neck, at her breasts, and I realize, the car shifting under us, that I don't trust her.

We turn and head up a hill. The street twists, and we go in and out of the shade from a bridge of elms. I can't see anything behind the hedges.

"The neighborhood is lovely," the woman says. "We have a twenty-four-hour security patrol, and the bushes hide everything from the street. We don't have sidewalks."

"No sidewalks?" I say.

"That discourages sightseeing," says Jodi.

We turn into a driveway. It heads down between two hedges to the far end, where a gravel half-circle has been cut around the trunk of a low, spreading fig tree. We stop, the agent opens Jodi's door, and we get out and stand there, looking at the house. It's a mansion.

The walls are white. There are clay tiles on the roof, sloped eaves, hanging vines. A narrow window runs straight up from the ground. Through it I can see a staircase and a chandelier. In college once, at the end of the season, the team had a party at a mansion like this one. It had windows everywhere, panes of glass as tall as flagpoles. The fellow who owned it had played ball for a while when he was young, and then gotten out and made big money. He was in something like hair care or combs then, and at the door each of us got a leather travel kit with our name embossed and some of his products inside. At the buffet table the oranges were cut so that the peels came off like the leather on a split baseball. He showed us through the house and then brought us into the yard. He told us that after all these years the game was still inside him. We stood on the lawn. It was landscaped with shrubs and willows, but he said he had bought the place because the yard was big enough for a four-hundred-foot straightaway center field.

Now the agent leads us up the porch stairs. She rings the bell and then opens the door; inside, the light is everywhere. It streams from the windows, shines on the wood, falls in slants from every height. There are oriental carpets on the floor, plants, a piano. The agent opens her portfolio and hands us each a beige piece of paper. It's textured like a wedding invitation, and at the top, above the figures, is an ink drawing of the house. The boughs of the fig tree frame the paper. I look down at it in my hand, the way I used to look down at a baseball.

The agent motions us into the living room. From there she leads us back through a glass-walled study, wisteria and bougainvillaea hanging from the ceiling, down a hallway into the kitchen. Through the windows spread the grounds of the estate. Now is the time, I think to myself, when I should explain everything.

"I think I'll go out back," Jodi says. "You two can look around in here."

"Certainly," the agent says.

After she leaves, I pretend to look through the kitchen. I open cabinets, run the water. The tap has a charcoal filter. The agent says things about the plumbing and the foundation; I nod and then walk back into the study. She follows me.

"I know you'll find the terms agreeable," she says.

"The terms."

"And one can't surpass the house, as one can see."

"You could fit a diamond in the yard."

She smiles a little bit.

"A baseball diamond," I say. I lean forward and examine the paned windows carefully. They are newly washed, clear as air. Among them hang the vines of bougainvillaea. "But some people look at houses for other reasons."

"Of course."

"I know of a fellow who's selling his house to buy drugs in South America."

She looks down, touches the flower in her jacket.

"People don't care about an honest living anymore," I say.

She smiles and looks up at me. "They don't," she says. "You're absolutely right. One sees that everywhere now. What line of work are you in, Mr. Gordon?"

I lean against the glassed wall. Outside, violet petals are spinning down beneath the jacarandas. "We're not really from Dallas," I say.

"Oh?"

Through the window I see Jodi come out onto the lawn around the corner of the house. The grass is beautiful. It's green and long like an outfield. Jodi steps up into the middle of it and raises her hands above her head, arches her back like a dancer. She was in a play the first time I ever saw her, stretching like that, onstage in a college auditorium. I was in the audience, wearing a baseball shirt. At intermission I went home and changed my clothes so that I could introduce myself. That was twelve years ago.

"No," I say to the agent. "We're not really from Dallas. We moved outside of Dallas a while back. We live in Highland Park now."

She nods.

"I'm an investor," I say.

—1988

JOHN CHEEVER

(1912–1982)

Born and raised in Quincy, Massachusetts, John Cheever published his first story, "Expelled," in *The New Republic* at the age of eighteen, using some details of his own expulsion from Thayer Academy in South Braintree, Massachusetts. Best known as a short fiction writer, his story collections include: *The Way Some People Live: A Book of Stories* (1943), *The Enormous Radio and Other Stories* (1953), *The Housebreaker of Shady Hill and Other Stories* (1958), *Some People, Places, and Things That Will Not Appear in My Next Novel* (1961), *The Brigadier and the Golf Widow* (1964), *The World of Apples* (1973), and *The Stories of John Cheever* (1978), a retrospective collection. The author of five novels, *The Wapshot Chronicle* (1957), *The Wapshot Scandal* (1964), *Bullet Park* (1969), *Falconer* (1977), and *Oh What a Paradise It Seems* (1982), Cheever won the National Book Award and the Pulitzer Prize, and received the Howells Medal for Fiction from the National Academy of Arts and Letters.

The Sorrows of Gin

IT was Sunday afternoon, and from her bedroom Amy could hear the Beardens coming in, followed a little while later by the Farquarsons and the Parminters. She went on reading *Black Beauty* until she felt in her bones that they might be eating something good. Then she closed her book and went down the stairs. The living-room door was shut, but through it she could hear the noise of loud talk and laughter. They must have been gossiping or worse, because they all stopped talking when she entered the room.

"Hi, Amy," Mr. Farquarson said.

"Mr. Farquarson spoke to you, Amy," her father said.

"Hello, Mr. Farquarson," she said. By standing outside the group for a minute, until they had resumed their conversation, and then by slipping past Mrs. Farquarson, she was able to swoop down on the nut dish and take a handful.

"Amy!" Mr. Lawton said.

"I'm sorry, Daddy," she said, retreating out of the circle, toward the piano.

"Put those nuts back," he said.

"I've handled them, Daddy," she said.

"Well, pass the nuts, dear," her mother said sweetly. "Perhaps someone else would like nuts."

Amy filled her mouth with the nuts she had taken, returned to the coffee table, and passed the nut dish.

"Thank you, Amy," they said, taking a peanut or two.

"How do you like your new school, Amy?" Mrs. Bearden asked.

"I like it," Amy said. "I like private schools better than public schools. It isn't so much like a factory."

"What grade are you in?" Mrs. Bearden asked.

"Fourth," she said.

Her father took Mr. Parminter's glass and his own, and got up to go into the dining room and refill them. She fell into the chair he had left vacant.

"Don't sit in your father's chair, Amy," her mother said, not realizing that Amy's legs were worn out from riding a bicycle, while her father had done nothing but sit down all day.

As she walked toward the French doors, she heard her mother beginning to talk about the new cook. It was a good example of the interesting things they found to talk about.

"You'd better put your bicycle in the garage," her father said, returning with the fresh drinks. "It looks like rain."

Amy went out onto the terrace and looked at the sky, but it was not very cloudy, it wouldn't rain, and his advice, like all the advice he gave her, was superfluous. They were always at her. "Put your bicycle away." "Open the door for Grandmother, Amy." "Feed the cat." "Do your homework." "Pass the nuts." "Help Mrs. Bearden with her parcels." "Amy, please try and take more pains with your appearance."

They all stood, and her father came to the door and

called her. "We're going over to the Parminters' for supper," he said. "Cook's here, so you won't be alone. Be sure and go to bed at eight like a good girl. And come and kiss me good night."

After their cars had driven off, Amy wandered through the kitchen to the cook's bedroom beyond it and knocked on the door. "Come in," a voice said, and when Amy entered, she found the cook, whose name was Rosemary, in her bathrobe, reading the Bible. Rosemary smiled at Amy. Her smile was sweet and her old eyes were blue. "Your parents have gone out again?" she asked. Amy said that they had, and the old woman invited her to sit down. "They do seem to enjoy themselves, don't they? During the four days I've been here, they've been out every night, or had people in." She put the Bible face down on her lap and smiled, but not at Amy. "Of course, the drinking that goes on here is all sociable, and what your parents do is none of my business, is it? I worry about drink more than most people, because of my poor sister. My poor sister drank too much. For ten years, I went to visit her on Sunday afternoons, and most of the time she was *non compos mentis*. Sometimes I'd find her huddled up on the floor with one or two sherry bottles empty beside her. Sometimes she'd seem sober enough to a stranger, but I could tell in a second by the way she spoke her words that she'd drunk enough not to be herself any more. Now my poor sister is gone, I don't have anyone to visit at all."

"What happened to your sister?" Amy asked.

"She was a lovely person, with a peaches-and-cream complexion and fair hair," Rosemary said. "Gin makes some people gay—it makes them laugh and cry—but with my sister it only made her sullen and withdrawn. When she was drinking, she would retreat into herself. Drink made her contrary. If I'd say the weather was fine, she'd tell me I was wrong. If I'd say it was raining, she'd say it was clearing. She'd correct me about everything I said, however small it was. She died in Bellevue Hospital one summer while I was working in Maine. She was the only family I had."

The directness with which Rosemary spoke had the effect on Amy of making her feel grown, and for once

politeness came to her easily. "You must miss your sister
a great deal," she said.

"I was just sitting here now thinking about her. She
was in service, like me, and it's lonely work. You're always surrounded by a family, and yet you're never a
part of it. Your pride is often hurt. The Madams seem
condescending and inconsiderate. I'm not blaming the
ladies I've worked for. It's just the nature of the relationship. They order chicken salad, and you get up before
dawn to get ahead of yourself, and just as you've finished
the chicken salad, they change their minds and want
crab-meat soup."

"My mother changes her mind all the time," Amy
said.

"Sometimes you're in a country place with nobody
else in help. You're tired, but not too tired to feel lonely.
You go out onto the servants' porch when the pots and
pans are done, planning to enjoy God's creation, and
although the front of the house may have a fine view of
the lake or the mountains, the view from the back is
never much. But there is the sky and the trees and the
stars and the birds singing and the pleasure of resting
your feet. But then you hear them in the front of the
house, laughing and talking with their guests and their
sons and daughters. If you're new and they whisper, you
can be sure they're talking about you. That takes all the
pleasure out of the evening."

"Oh," Amy said.

"I've worked all kinds of places—places where there
were eight or nine in help and places where I was expected to burn the rubbish myself, on winter nights, and
shovel the snow. In a house where there's a lot of help,
there's usually some devil among them—some old butler
or parlormaid—who tries to make your life miserable
from the beginning. 'The Madam doesn't like it this
way,' and 'The Madam doesn't like it that way,' and
'I've been with the Madam for twenty years,' they tell
you. It takes a diplomat to get along. Then there is the
rooms they give you, and every one of them I've ever
seen is cheerless. If you have a bottle in your suitcase,
it's a terrible temptation in the beginning not to take a
drink to raise your spirits. But I have a strong character.

It was different with my poor sister. She used to complain about nervousness, but, sitting here thinking about her tonight, I wonder if she suffered from nervousness at all. I wonder if she didn't make it all up. I wonder if she just wasn't meant to be in service. Toward the end, the only work she could get was out in the country, where nobody else would go, and she never lasted much more than a week or two. She'd take a little gin for her nervousness, then a little for her tiredness, and when she'd drunk her own bottle and everything she could steal, they'd hear about it in the front part of the house. There was usually a scene, and my poor sister always liked to have the last word. Oh, if I had had my way, they'd be a law against it! It's not my business to advise you to take anything from your father, but I'd be proud of you if you'd empty his gin bottle into the sink now and then—the filthy stuff! But it's made me feel better to talk with you, sweetheart. It's made me not miss my poor sister so much. Now I'll read a little more in my Bible, and then I'll get you some supper."

The Lawtons had had a bad year with cooks—there had been five of them. The arrival of Rosemary had made Marcia Lawton think back to a vague theory of dispensations; she had suffered, and now she was being rewarded. Rosemary was clean, industrious, and cheerful, and her table—as the Lawtons said—was just like the Chambord. On Wednesday night after dinner, she took the train to New York, promising to return on the evening train Thursday. Thursday morning, Marcia went into the cook's room. It was a distasteful but a habitual precaution. The absence of anything personal in the room—a package of cigarettes, a fountain pen, an alarm clock, a radio, or anything else that could tie the old woman to the place—gave her the uneasy feeling that she was being deceived, as she had so often been deceived by cooks in the past. She opened the closet door and saw a single uniform hanging there and, on the closet floor, Rosemary's old suitcase and the white shoes she wore in the kitchen. The suitcase was locked, but when Marcia lifted it, it seemed to be nearly empty.

Mr. Lawton and Amy drove to the station after dinner

on Thursday to meet the eight-sixteen train. The top of
the car was down, and the brisk air, the starlight, and
the company of her father made the little girl feel kindly
toward the world. The railroad station in Shady Hill re-
sembled the railroad stations in old movies she had seen
on television, where detectives and spies, bluebeards and
their trusting victims, were met to be driven off to remote country estates. Amy liked the station, particularly
toward dark. She imagined that the people who traveled
on the locals were engaged on errands that were more
urgent and sinister than commuting. Except when there
was a heavy fog or a snowstorm, the club car that her
father traveled on seemed to have the gloss and the monotony of the rest of his life. The locals that ran at odd
hours belonged to a world of deeper contrasts, where
she would like to live.

They were a few minutes early, and Amy got out of
the car and stood on the platform. She wondered what
the fringe of string that hung above the tracks at either
end of the station was for, but she knew enough not to
ask her father, because he wouldn't be able to tell her.
She could hear the train before it came into view, and
the noise excited her and made her happy. When the
train drew in to the station and stopped, she looked in
the lighted windows for Rosemary and didn't see her.
Mr. Lawton got out of the car and joined Amy on the
platform. They could see the conductor bending over
someone in a seat, and finally the cook arose. She clung
to the conductor as he led her out to the platform of
the car, and she was crying. "Like peaches and cream,"
Amy heard her sob. "A lovely, lovely person." The conductor spoke to her kindly, put his arm around her
shoulders, and eased her down the steps. Then the train
pulled out, and she stood there drying her tears. "Don't
say a word, Mr. Lawton," she said, "and I won't say
anything." She held out a small paper bag. "Here's a
present for you, little girl."

"Thank you, Rosemary," Amy said. She looked into
the paper bag and saw that it contained several packets
of Japanese water flowers.

Rosemary walked toward the car with the caution of
someone who can hardly find her way in the dim light.

A sour smell came from her. Her best coat was spotted with mud and ripped in the back. Mr. Lawton told Amy to get in the back seat of the car, and made the cook sit in front, beside him. He slammed the car door shut after her angrily, and then went around to the driver's seat and drove home. Rosemary reached into her handbag and took out a Coca-Cola bottle with a cork stopper and took a drink. Amy could tell by the smell that the Coca-Cola bottle was filled with gin.

"Rosemary!" Mr. Lawton said.

"I'm lonely," the cook said. "I'm lonely, and I'm afraid, and it's all I've got."

He said nothing more until he had turned into their drive and brought the car around to the back door. "Go and get your suitcase, Rosemary," he said. "I'll wait here in the car."

As soon as the cook had staggered into the house, he told Amy to go in by the front door. "Go upstairs to your room and get ready for bed."

Her mother called down the stairs when Amy came in, to ask if Rosemary had returned. Amy didn't answer. She went to the bar, took an open gin bottle, and emptied it into the pantry sink. She was nearly crying when she encountered her mother in the living room, and told her that her father was taking the cook back to the station.

When Amy came home from school the next day, she found a heavy, black-haired woman cleaning the living room. The car Mr. Lawton usually drove to the station was at the garage for a checkup, and Amy drove to the station with her mother to meet him. As he came across the station platform, she could tell by the lack of color in his face that he had had a hard day. He kissed her mother, touched Amy on the head, and got behind the wheel.

"You know," her mother said, "there's something terribly wrong with the guest-room shower."

"Damn it, Marcia," he said, "I wish you wouldn't always greet me with bad news!"

His grating voice oppressed Amy, and she began to fiddle with the button that raised and lowered the window.

"Stop that, Amy!" he said.

"Oh, well, the shower isn't important," her mother said. She laughed weakly.

"When I got back from San Francisco last week," he said, "you couldn't wait to tell me that we need a new oil burner."

"Well, I've got a part-time cook. That's good news."

"Is she a lush?" her father asked.

"Don't be disagreeable, dear. She'll get us some dinner and wash the dishes and take the bus home. We're going to the Farquarsons'."

"I'm really too tired to go anywhere," he said.

"Who's going to take care of me?" Amy asked.

"You always have a good time at the Farquarsons'," her mother said.

"Well, let's leave early," he said.

"Who's going to take care of me?" Amy asked.

"Mrs. Henlein," her mother said.

When they got home, Amy went over to the piano.

Her father washed his hands in the bathroom off the hall and then went to the bar. He came into the living room holding the empty gin bottle. "What's her name?" he asked.

"Ruby," her mother said.

"She's exceptional. She's drunk a quart of gin on her first day."

"Oh dear!" her mother said. "Well, let's not make any trouble now."

"Everybody is drinking my liquor," her father shouted, "and I am God-damned sick and tired of it!"

"There's plenty of gin in the closet," her mother said. "Open another bottle."

"We paid that gardener three dollars an hour and all he did was sneak in here and drink up my Scotch. The sitter we had before we got Mrs. Henlein used to water my bourbon, and I don't have to remind you about Rosemary. The cook before Rosemary not only drank everything in my liquor cabinet but she drank all the rum, kirsch, sherry, and wine that we had in the kitchen for cooking. Then, there's that Polish woman we had last summer. Even that old laundress. *And* the painters. I think they must have put some kind of a mark on my door. I think the agency must have checked me off as an easy touch."

"Well, let's get through dinner, and then you can speak to her."

"The hell with that!" he said. "I'm not going to encourage people to rob me. *Ruby!*" He shouted her name several times, but she didn't answer. Then she appeared in the dining-room doorway anyway, wearing her hat and coat.

"I'm sick," she said. Amy could see that she was frightened.

"I should think that you would be," her father said.

"I'm sick," the cook mumbled, "and I can't find anything around here, and I'm going home."

"Good," he said. "Good! I'm through with paying people to come in here and drink my liquor."

The cook started out the front way, and Marcia Lawton followed her into the front hall to pay her something. Amy had watched this scene from the piano bench, a position that was withdrawn but that still gave her a good view. She saw her father get a fresh bottle of gin and make a shaker of Martinis. He looked very unhappy.

"Well," her mother said when she came back into the room. "You know, she didn't look drunk."

"Please don't argue with me, Marcia," her father said. He poured two cocktails, said "Cheers," and drank a little. "We can get some dinner at Orpheo's," he said.

"I suppose so," her mother said. "I'll rustle up something for Amy." She went into the kitchen, and Amy opened her music to "Reflets d'Automne." "COUNT," her music teacher had written. "COUNT and lightly, lightly . . ." Amy began to play. Whenever she made a mistake, she said "Darn it!" and started at the beginning again. In the middle of "Reflets d'Automne" it struck her that *she* was the one who had emptied the gin bottle. Her perplexity was so intense that she stopped playing, but her feelings did not go beyond perplexity, although she did not have the strength to continue playing the piano. Her mother relieved her. "Your supper's in the kitchen, dear," she said. "And you can take a popsicle out of the deep freeze for dessert. Just one."

Marcia Lawton held her empty glass toward her hus-

band, who filled it from the shaker. Then she went upstairs. Mr. Lawton remained in the room, and, studying
her father closely, Amy saw that his tense look had
begun to soften. He did not seem so unhappy any more,
and as she passed him on her way to the kitchen, he
smiled at her tenderly and patted her on the top of
the head.

When Amy had finished her supper, eaten her popsicle, and exploded the bag it came in, she returned to
the piano and played "Chopsticks" for a while. Her father came downstairs in his evening clothes, put his
drink on the mantelpiece, and went to the French doors
to look at his terrace and his garden. Amy noticed that
the transformation that had begun with a softening of
his features was even more advanced. At last, he seemed
happy. Amy wondered if he was drunk, although his
walk was not unsteady. If anything, it was more steady.

Her parents never achieved the kind of rolling, swinging gait that she saw impersonated by a tightrope walker
in the circus each year while the band struck up "Show
Me the Way to Go Home" and that she liked to imitate
herself sometimes. She liked to turn round and round
and round on the lawn, until, staggering and a little sick,
she would whoop, "I'm drunk! I'm a drunken man!"
and reel over the grass, righting herself as she was about
to fall and finding herself not unhappy at having lost for
a second her ability to see the world. But she had never
seen her parents like that. She had never seen them
hanging on to a lamppost and singing and reeling, but
she had seen them fall down. They were never indeco-
rous—they seemed to get more decorous and formal the
more they drank—but sometimes her father would get
up to fill everybody's glass and he would walk straight
enough but his shoes would seem to stick to the carpet.
And sometimes, when he got to the dining-room door,
he would miss it by a foot or more. Once, she had seen
him walk into the wall with such force that he collapsed
onto the floor and broke most of the glasses he was
carrying. One or two people laughed, but the laughter
was not general or hearty, and most of them pretended
that he had not fallen down at all. When her father got
to his feet, he went right on to the bar as if nothing had

happened. Amy had once seen Mrs. Farquarson miss the chair she was about to sit in, by a foot, and thump down onto the floor, but nobody laughed then, and they pretended that Mrs. Farquarson hadn't fallen down at all. They seemed like actors in a play. In the school play, when you knocked over a paper tree you were supposed to pick it up without showing what you were doing, so that you would not spoil the illusion of being in a deep forest, and that was the way *they* were when somebody fell down.

Now her father had that stiff, funny walk that was so different from the way he tramped up and down the station platform in the morning, and she could see that he was looking for something. He was looking for his drink. It was right on the mantelpiece, but he didn't look there. He looked on all the tables in the living room. Then he went out onto the terrace and looked there, and then he came back into the living room and looked on all the tables again. Then he went back onto the terrace, and then back over the living-room tables, looking three times in the same place, although he was always telling her to look intelligently when she lost her sneakers or her raincoat. "Look for it, Amy," he was always saying. "Try and remember where you left it. I can't buy you a new raincoat every time it rains." Finally he gave up and poured himself a cocktail in another glass. "I'm going to get Mrs. Henlein," he told Amy, as if this were an important piece of information.

Amy's only feeling for Mrs. Henlein was indifference, and when her father returned with the sitter, Amy thought of the nights, stretching into weeks—the years, almost—when she had been cooped up with Mrs. Henlein. Mrs. Henlein was very polite and was always telling Amy what was ladylike and what was not. Mrs. Henlein also wanted to know where Amy's parents were going and what kind of party it was, although it was none of her business. She always sat down on the sofa as if she owned the place, and talked about people she had never even been introduced to, and asked Amy to bring her the newspaper, although she had no authority at all.

When Marcia Lawton came down, Mrs. Henlein wished her good evening. "Have a lovely party," she called after the Lawtons as they went out the door. Then she turned to Amy. "Where are your parents going, sweetheart?

"But you must know, sweetheart. Put on your thinking cap and try and remember. Are they going to the club?"

"No," Amy said.

"I wonder if they could be going to the Trenchers'," Mrs. Henlein said. "The Trenchers' house was lighted up when we came by."

"They're not going to the Trenchers'," Amy said. "They hate the Trenchers."

"Well, where are they going, sweetheart?" Mrs. Henlein asked.

"They're going to the Farquarsons'," Amy said.

"Well, that's all I wanted to know, sweetheart," Mrs. Henlein said. "Now get me the newspaper and hand it to me politely. *Politely,*" she said, as Amy approached her with the paper. "It doesn't mean anything when you do things for your elders unless you do them politely." She put on her glasses and began to read the paper.

Amy went upstairs to her room. In a glass on her table were the Japanese flowers that Rosemary had brought her, blooming stalely in water that was colored pink from the dyes. Amy went down the back stairs and through the kitchen into the dining room. Her father's cocktail things were spread over the bar. She emptied the gin bottle into the pantry sink and then put it back where she had found it. It was too late to ride her bicycle and too early to go to bed, and she knew that if she got anything interesting on the television, like a murder, Mrs. Henlein would make her turn it off. Then she remembered that her father had brought her home from his trip West a book about horses, and she ran cheerfully up the back stairs to read her new book.

It was after two when the Lawtons returned. Mrs. Henlein, asleep on the living-room sofa dreaming about a dusty attic, was awakened by their voices in the hall. Marcia Lawton paid her, and thanked her, and asked if anyone had called, and then went upstairs. Mr. Lawton was in the dining room, rattling the bottles around. Mrs. Henlein, anxious to get into her own bed and back to sleep, prayed that he wasn't going to pour himself another drink, as they so often did. She was driven home night after night by drunken gentlemen. He stood in the door of the dining room, holding an empty bottle in his hand. "You must be stinking, Mrs. Henlein," he said.

"Hmm," she said. She didn't understand.

"You drank a full quart of gin," he said.

The lackluster old woman—half between wakefulness and sleep—gathered together her bones and groped for her gray hair. It was in her nature to collect stray cats, pile the bathroom up to the ceiling with interesting and valuable newspapers, rouge, talk to herself, sleep in her underwear in case of fire, quarrel over the price of soup bones, and have it circulated around the neighborhood that when she finally died in her dusty junk heap, the mattress would be full of bankbooks and the pillow stuffed with hundred-dollar bills. She had resisted all these rich temptations in order to appear a lady, and she was repaid by being called a common thief. She began to scream at him.

"You take that back, Mr. Lawton! You take back every one of those words you just said! I never stole anything in my whole life, and nobody in my family ever stole anything, and I don't have to stand here and be insulted by a drunk man. Why, as for drinking, I haven't drunk enough to fill an eyeglass for twenty-five years. Mr. Henlein took me to a place of refreshment twenty-five years ago, and I drank two Manhattan cocktails that made me so sick and dizzy that I've never liked the stuff ever since. How dare you speak to me like this! Calling me a thief and a drunken woman! Oh, you disgust me— you disgust me in your ignorance of all the trouble I've had. Do you know what I had for Christmas dinner last year? I had a bacon sandwich. Son of a bitch!" She began to weep. "I'm glad I said it!" she screamed. "It's the first time I've used a dirty word in my whole life and I'm glad I said it. Son of a bitch!" A sense of liberation, as if she stood at the bow of a great ship, came over her. "I lived in this neighborhood my whole life. I can remember when it was full of good farming people and there was fish in the rivers. My father had four acres of sweet meadowland and a name that was known far and wide, and on my mother's side I'm descended from patroons, Dutch nobility. My mother was the spit and image of Queen Wilhelmina. You think you can get away with insulting me, but you're very, very, very much mistaken." She went to the telephone and, picking up the receiver, screamed, "Police! Police! Police! This is Mrs. Henlein, and I'm over at the Lawtons'. He's drunk, and he's calling me insulting names, and I want you to come over here and arrest him!"

The voices woke Amy, and, lying in her bed, she perceived vaguely the pitiful corruption of the adult world; how crude and frail it was, like a piece of worn burlap, patched with stupidities and mistakes, useless and ugly, and yet they never saw its worthlessness, and when you pointed it out to them, they were indignant. But as the voices went on and she heard the cry "Police! Police!" she was frightened. She did not see how they could arrest her, although they could find her fingerprints on the empty bottle, but it was not her own danger that frightened her but the collapse, in the middle of the night, of her father's house. It was all her fault, and when she heard her father speaking into the extension telephone in the library, she felt sunk in guilt. Her father tried to be good and kind—and, remembering the expensive illustrated book about horses that he had brought her from the West, she had to set her teeth to keep from crying. She covered her head with a pillow and realized miserably that she would have to go away. She had plenty of friends from the time when they used to live in New York, or she could spend the night in the Park or hide in a museum. She would have to go away.

"Good morning," her father said at breakfast. "Ready for a good day!" Cheered by the swelling light in the sky, by the recollection of the manner in which he had handled Mrs. Henlein and kept the police from coming, refreshed by his sleep, and pleased at the thought of playing golf, Mr. Lawton spoke with feeling, but the words seemed to Amy offensive and fatuous; they took away her appetite, and she slumped over her cereal bowl, stirring it with a spoon. "Don't slump, Amy," he said. Then she remembered the night, the screaming, the resolve to go. His cheerfulness refreshed her memory.

Her decision was settled. She had a ballet lesson at ten, and she was going to have lunch with Lillian Towele. Then she would leave.

Children prepare for a sea voyage with a toothbrush and a Teddy bear; they equip themselves for a trip around the world with a pair of odd socks, a conch shell, and a thermometer; books and stones and peacock feathers, candy bars, tennis balls, soiled handkerchiefs, and skeins of old string appear to them to be the necessities of travel, and Amy packed, that afternoon, with the impulsiveness of her kind. She was late coming home from lunch, and her getaway was delayed, but she didn't mind. She could catch one of the late-afternoon locals; one of the cooks' trains. Her father was playing golf and her mother was off somewhere. A part-time worker was cleaning the living room. When Amy had finished packing, she went into her parents' bedroom and flushed the toilet. While the water murmured, she took a twenty-dollar bill from her mother's desk. Then she went downstairs and left the house and walked around Blenhollow Circle and down Alewives Lane to the station. No regrets or goodbyes formed in her mind. She went over the names of the friends she had in the city. In case she decided not to spend the night in a museum. When she opened the door of the waiting room, Mr. Flanagan, the stationmaster, was poking his coal fire.

"I want to buy a ticket to New York," Amy said.

"One-way or round-trip?"

"One-way, please."

Mr. Flanagan went through the door into the ticket office and raised the glass window. "I'm afraid I haven't got a half-fare ticket for you, Amy," he said. "I'll have to write one."

"That's all right," she said. She put the twenty-dollar bill on the counter.

"And in order to change that," he said, "I'll have to go over to the other side. Here's the four-thirty-two coming in now, but you'll be able to get the five-ten." She didn't protest, and went and sat beside her cardboard suitcase, which was printed with European hotel and place names. When the local had come and gone, Mr. Flanagan shut his glass window and walked over the footbridge to the northbound platform and called the Lawtons'. Mr. Lawton had just come in from his game and was mixing himself a cocktail. "I think your daughter's planning to take some kind of a trip," Mr. Flanagan said.

It was dark by the time Mr. Lawton got down to the station. He saw his daughter through the station window. The girl sitting on the bench, the rich names on her paper suitcase, touched him as it was in her power to touch him only when she seemed helpless or when she was very sick. Someone had walked over his grave! He shivered with longing, he felt his skin coarsen as when, driving home late and alone, a shower of leaves on the wind crossed the beam of his headlights, liberating him for a second at the most from the literal symbols of his life—the buttonless shirts, the vouchers and bank statements, the order blanks, and the empty glasses. He seemed to listen—God knows for what. Commands, drums, the crackle of signal fires, the music of the glockenspiel—how sweet it sounds on the Alpine air—singing from a tavern in the pass, the honking of wild swans; he seemed to smell the salt air in the churches of Venice. Then, as it was with the leaves, the power of her figure to trouble him was ended: his gooseflesh vanished. He was himself. Oh, why should she want to run away? Travel—and who knew better than a man who spent three days of every fortnight on the road—was a world of overheated plane cabins and repetitious magazines, where even the coffee, even the champagne, tasted of plastics. How could he teach her that home sweet home was the best place of all?

—1953

T. CORAGHESSAN BOYLE
(B. 1948)

Born and raised in Peekskill, New York, Thomas Coraghessan Boyle earned a B.A. at the State University of New York at Potsdam, an M.F.A. at the University of Iowa Writers' Workshop, and a Ph.D. in nineteenth-century English literature at the University of Iowa. At the age of seventeen, he changed his name from Thomas John, replacing John with a maternal family name that is pronounced Cor-RAG-ah-sen. A professor of creative writing at the University of Southern California, he lives in a Frank Lloyd Wright house outside of Santa Barbara. An enthusiastic reader of his own fiction, Boyle has given numerous readings throughout the country and has appeared on television programs such as "Today," "Late Night with David Letterman," and "The Charlie Rose Show." He is the author of seven novels: *Water Music* (1982); *Budding Prospects* (1984); *World's End* (1987), which won the 1988 Pen/Faulkner Award for Best American Fiction; *East Is East* (1990); *The Road to Wellville* (1993), which was made into a film starring Anthony Hopkins and Bridget Fonda; *The Tortilla Curtain* (1995); and *Riven Rock* (1998). His stories are collected in *Descent of Man* (1979), which received the 1980 St. Lawrence Award for short fiction; *Greasy Lake* (1985); *If the River Was Whiskey* (1989); *Without a Hero* (1994); and *T. C. Boyle Stories* (1998), a collection of sixty-eight tales.

Peace of Mind

FIRST she told them the story of the family surprised over their corn muffins by the masked intruder. "He was a black man," she said, dropping her voice and at the same time allowing a hint of tremolo to creep into it, "and he was wearing a lifelike mask of President Reagan. He just jimmied the lock and waltzed in the front door with the morning paper as if he was delivering flowers or something. . . . They thought it was a joke at first." Giselle's voice became hushed now, confidential, as she described how he'd brutalized the children, humiliated the wife—"Sexually, if you know what I mean"—and bound them all to the kitchen chair with twists of sheer pantyhose. Worse, she said, he dug a scratchy old copy of Sam and Dave's "Soul Man" out of the record collection and made them listen to it over and over as he looted the house. They knew he was finished when Sam and Dave choked off, the stereo rudely torn from the socket and thrown in with the rest of their things"—she paused here to draw a calculated breath—"And at seven-thirty A.M., no less."

She had them, she could see it in the way the pretty little wife's eyes went dark with hate and the balding husband clutched fitfully at his pockets—she had them, but she poured it on anyway, flexing her verbal muscles, not yet noon and a sale, a big sale, already in the bag. So she gave them an abbreviated version of the story of the elderly lady and the overworked Mexican from the knife-sharpening service and wrung some hideous new truths from the tale of the housewife who came home to find a strange car in her garage. "A strange car?" the husband prompted, after she'd paused to level a doleful, frightened look on the wife. Giselle sighed. "Two white men met her at the door. They were in their early forties, nicely dressed, polite—she thought they were real-estate people or something. They escorted her into the house, bundled up the rugs, the paintings, the Camcorder and VCR and then took turns desecrating"—that was the term she used, it got them every time—"desecrating her naked body with the cigarette lighter from her very own car."

The husband and wife exchanged a glance, then signed on for the whole shmeer—five thousand and some-odd dollars for the alarm system—every window, door, keyhole, and crevice wired—and sixty bucks a month for a pair of "Armed Response" signs to stick in the lawn. Giselle slid into the front seat of the Mercedes and cranked up the salsa music that made her feel as if every day was a fiesta, and then let out a long slow breath. She checked her watch and drew a circle around the next name on her list. It was a few minutes past twelve, crime was rampant, and she was feeling lucky. She tapped her foot and whistled along with the sour, jostling trumpets—no doubt about it, she'd have another sale before lunch.

The balding husband stood at the window and watched the Mercedes back out of the driveway, drift into gear, and glide soundlessly up the street. It took him a moment to realize he was still clutching his checkbook. "God, Hil," he said (or, rather, croaked—something seemed to be wrong with his throat), "it's a lot of money."

The pretty little wife, Hilary, crouched frozen on the couch, legs drawn up to her chest, feet bare, toenails glistening. "They stuff your underwear in your mouth," she whispered, "that's the worst thing. Can you imagine that, I mean the taste of it—your own underwear?"

Ellis didn't answer. He was thinking of the masked intruder—that maniac disguised as the President—and of his own children, whose heedless squeals of joy came to him like hosannas from the swingset out back. He'd been a fool, he saw that now. How could he have thought, even for a minute, that they'd be safe out here in the suburbs? The world was violent, rotten, corrupt, seething with hatred and perversion, and there was no escaping it. Everything you worked for, everything you loved, had to be locked up as if you were in a castle under siege.

"I wonder what they did to her," Hilary said.

"Who?"

"That woman—the one with the cigarette lighter. I heard they burn their initials into you."

Yes, of course they did, he thought—why wouldn't they? They sold crack in the elementary schools, pissed in the alleys, battered old women for their Social Security checks. They'd cleaned out Denny Davidson while he was in the Bahamas and ripped the stereo out of Phyllis Steubig's Peugeot. And just last week they'd stolen two brand-new Ironcast aluminum garbage cans from the curb in front of the neighbor's house—just dumped the trash in the street and drove off with them. "What do you think, Hil?" he said. "We can still get out of it."

"I don't care what it costs," she murmured, her voice drained of emotion. "I won't be able to sleep till it's in."

Ellis crossed the room to gaze out on the sun-dappled backyard. Mifty and Corinne were on the swings, pumping hard, lifting up into the sky and falling back again with a pure rhythmic grace that was suddenly so poignant he could feel a sob rising in his throat. "I won't either," he said, turning to his wife and spreading his hands as if in supplication. "We've got to have it."

"Yes," she said.

"If only for our peace of mind."

Giselle was pretty good with directions—she had to be, in her business—but still she had to pull over three times to consult her Thomas' Guide before she found the next address on her list. The house was in a seedy, run-down neighborhood of blasted trees, gutted cars, and tacky little houses, the kind of neighborhood that just made her blood boil—how could people live like that? she wondered, flicking off the tape in disgust. Didn't they have any self-respect? She hit the accelerator, scattering a pack of snarling, hyenalike dogs, dodged a stained mattress and a pair of overturned trash cans and swung into the driveway of a house that looked as if it had been bombed, partially reconstructed, and then bombed again. There has to be some mistake, she thought. She glanced up and caught the eye of the man sitting on the porch next door. He was fat and shirtless, his chest and arms emblazoned with lurid tattoos, and he was in the act of lifting a beer can to his lips when he saw that she was peering at him from behind the frosted window of her car. Slowly, as if it cost him an enormous effort, he lowered the beer can and raised the middle finger of his free hand.

She rechecked her list. 7718 Picador Drive. There was no number on the house in front of her, but the house to the left was 7716 and the one to the right 7720. This was it, all right. She stepped out of the car with her briefcase, squared her shoulders, and slammed the door, all the while wondering what in god's name the owner of a place like this would want with an alarm system. These were the sort of people who broke into houses—

and here she turned to give the fat man an icy glare—
not the ones who had anything to protect. But then what
did she care?—a sale was a sale. She set the car alarm
with a fierce snap of her wrist, waited for the reassuring
bleat of response from the bowels of the car, and
marched up the walk.

The man who answered the door was tall and
stooped—mid-fifties, she guessed—and he looked like a
scholar in his wire-rims and the dingy cardigan with the
leather elbow patches. His hair was the color of freshly
turned dirt and his eyes, slightly distorted and swimming
behind the thick lenses, were as blue as the skies over
Oklahoma. "Mr. Coles?" she said.

He looked her up and down, taking his time. "And
what're you supposed to be," he breathed in a wheezy
humorless drawl, "the Avon Lady or something?" It was
then that she noticed the nervous little woman frozen in
the shadows of the hallway behind him. "Everett," the
woman said in a soft, pleading tone, but the man took
no notice of her. "Or don't tell me," he said, "you're
selling Girl Scout cookies, right?"

When it came to sales, Giselle was unshakable. She
saw her opening and thrust out her hand. "Giselle Nyerges," she said, "I'm from SecureCo. You contacted us
about a home security system?"

The woman vanished. The fat man next door blew
into his fist and produced a rude noise and Everett
Coles, with a grin that showed too much gum, took her
hand and led her into the house.

Inside, the place wasn't as bad as she'd expected. K-
Mart taste, of course, furniture made of particle board,
hopelessly tacky bric-a-brac, needlepoint homilies on the
walls, but at least it was spare. And clean. The man led
her through the living room to the open-beam kitchen
and threw himself down in a chair at the Formica table.
A sliding glass door gave onto the dusty expanse of the
backyard. "So," he said. "Let's hear it."

"First I want to tell you how happy I am that you're
considering a SecureCo home security system, Mr.
Coles," she said, sitting opposite him and throwing the
latches on her briefcase with a professional snap. "I
don't know if you heard about it," she said, the conspira-

torial whisper creeping into her voice, "but just last week they found a couple—both retirees, on a fixed income—bludgeoned to death in their home not three blocks from here. And they'd been security-conscious too—deadbolts on the doors and safety locks on the windows. The killer was this black man—a Negro—and he was wearing a lifelike mask of President Reagan. . . . Well, he found this croquet mallet . . ."

She faltered. The man was looking at her in the oddest way. Really, he was. He was grinning still—grinning as if she were telling a joke—and there was something wrong with his eyes. They seemed to be jerking back and forth in the sockets, jittering like the shiny little balls in a pinball machine. "I know it's not a pleasant story, Mr. Coles," she said, "but I like my customers to know that, that . . ." Those eyes were driving her crazy. She looked down, shuffling through the papers in her briefcase.

"They crowd you," he said.

"Pardon?" Looking up again.

"Sons of bitches," he growled, "they crowd you."

She found herself gazing over his shoulder at the neat little needlepoint display on the kitchen wall: SEMPER FIDELIS; HOME SWEET HOME; BURN, BABY, BURN.

"You like?" he said.

Burn, Baby, Burn?

"Did them myself." He dropped the grin and gazed out on nothing. "Got a lot of time on my hands."

She felt herself slipping. This wasn't the way it was supposed to go at all. She was wondering if she should hit him with another horror story or get down to inspecting the house and writing up an estimate, when he asked if she wanted a drink. "Thank you, no," she said. And then, with a smile, "It's a bit early in the day for me."

He said nothing, just looked at her with those jumpy blue eyes till she had to turn away. "Shit," he spat suddenly, "come down off your high horse, lady, let your hair down, loosen up."

She cleared her throat. "Yes, well, shouldn't we have a look around so I can assess your needs?"

"Gin," he said, and his voice was flat and calm again,

"it's the elixir of life." He made no move to get up from the table. "You're a good-looking woman, you know that?"

"Thank you," she said in her smallest voice. "Shouldn't we—?"

"Got them high heels and pretty little ankles, nice earrings, hair all done up, and that smart little tweed suit—of course you know you're a good-looking woman. Bet it don't hurt the sales a bit, huh?"

She couldn't help herself now. All she wanted was to get up from the table and away from those jittery eyes, sale or no sale. "Listen," she said, "listen to me. There was this woman and she came home and there was this strange car in her garage—"

"No," he said, "you listen to me."

" 'Panty Rapist Escapes,' " Hilary read aloud in a clear declamatory tone, setting down her coffee mug and spreading out the "Metro" section as if it were a sacred text. " 'Norbert Baptiste, twenty-seven, of Silverlake, dubbed the Panty Rapist because he gagged his victims with their own underthings . . .' " She broke off to give her husband a look of muted triumph. "You see," she said, lifting the coffee mug to her lips, "I told you. *With their own underthings.*"

Ellis Hunsicker was puzzling over the boxscores of the previous night's ballgames, secure as a snail in its shell. It was early Saturday morning, Mifty and Corinne were in the den watching cartoons, and the house alarm was still set from the previous night. In a while, after he'd finished his muesli and his second cup of coffee, he'd punch in the code and disarm the thing and then maybe do a little gardening and afterward take the girls to the park. He wasn't really listening, and he murmured a half-hearted reply.

"And can you imagine Tina Carfarct trying to tell me we were just wasting our money on the alarm system?" She pinched her voice in mockery: " 'I hate to tell you, Hil, but this is the safest neighborhood in L.A.' Jesus, she's like a Pollyanna or something, but you know what it is, don't you?"

Ellis looked up from the paper.

"They're too cheap, that's what—her and Sid both. They're going to take their chances, hope it happens to the next guy, and all to save a few thousand dollars. It's sick. It really is."

Night before last they'd had the Carfarcts and their twelve-year-old boy, Brewster, over for dinner—a nice sole amandine and scalloped potatoes Ellis had whipped up himself—and the chief object of conversation was, of course, the alarm system. "I don't know," Sid had said (Sid was forty, handsome as a prince, an investment counselor who'd once taught high-school social studies), "it's kind of like being a prisoner in your own home."

"All that money," Tina chimed in, sucking at the cherry of her second Manhattan, "I mean I don't think I could stand it. Like Sid says, I'd feel like I was a prisoner or something, afraid to step out into my own yard because some phantom mugger might be lurking in the marigolds."

"The guy in the Reagan mask was no phantom," Hilary said, leaning across the table to slash the air with the flat of her hand, bracelets ajangle. "Or those two men—*white* men—who accosted that woman in her own garage—" She was so wrought up she couldn't go on. She turned to her husband, tears welling in her eyes. "Go on," she'd said, "tell them."

It was then that Tina had made her "safest neighborhood in L.A." remark and Sid, draining his glass and setting it down carefully on the table, had said in a phlegmy, ruminative voice, "I don't know, it's like you've got no faith in your fellow man," to which Ellis had snapped, "Don't be naive, Sid."

Even Tina scored him for that one. "Oh, come off it, Sid," she said, giving him a sour look.

"Let's face it," Ellis said, "it's a society of haves and have-nots, and like it or not, we're the haves."

"I don't deny there's a lot of crazies out there and all," Tina went on, swiveling to face Ellis, "it's just that the whole idea of having an alarm on everything—I mean you can't park your car at the mall without it—is just, well, it's a sad thing. I mean next thing you know people'll be wearing these body alarms to work, rub up against them in a crowd and—bingo!—lights flash and sirens go off." She sat back, pleased with herself, a tiny, elegant blonde in a low-cut cocktail dress and a smug grin, untouched, unafraid, a woman without a care in the world.

But then Sid wanted to see the thing and all four of them were at the front door, gathered round the glowing black plastic panel as if it were some rare jewel, some treasure built into the wall. Ellis was opening the closet to show them the big metal box that contained the system's "brain," as the SecureCo woman had called it, when Sid, taken by the allure of the thing, lightly touched the tip of his index finger to the neat glowing red strip at the bottom that read EMERGENCY.

Instantly, the scene was transformed. Whereas a moment earlier they'd been calm, civilized people having a drink before a calm, civilized meal, they were suddenly transformed into hand-wringing zombies, helpless in the face of the technology that assaulted them. For Sid had activated the alarm and no one, least of all Ellis, knew what to do about it. The EMERGENCY strip was flashing wildly, the alarm beep-beep-beeping, the girls and the Carfarcts' boy fleeing the TV room in confusion, four pairs of hands fluttering helplessly over the box, and Ellis trying to dredge up the disarm code from the uncertain pocket of memory in which it was stored. "One-two-two-one!" Hilary shouted. Tina was holding her ears and making a face. Sid looked abashed.

When at last—after two false starts—Ellis had succeeded in disarming the thing and they'd settled back with their drinks and exclamations of "Jesus!" and "I thought I was going to die," there was a knock at the door. It was a man in a SecureCo uniform, with nightstick and gun. He was tall and he had a mustache. He invited himself in. "There a problem?" he asked.

"No, no," Ellis said, standing in the entranceway, heart pounding, acutely aware of his guests' eyes on him, "it's a new system and we, uh—it was a mistake."

"Name?" the man said.

"Hunsicker. Ellis."

"Code word?"

Here Ellis faltered. The code word, to be used for purposes of positive identification in just such a situation as this, was Hilary's inspiration. Pick something easy to remember, the SecureCo woman had said, and Hilary had chosen the name of the kids' pet rabbit, Honey Bunny. Ellis couldn't say the words. Not in front of this humorless man in the mustache, not with Sid and Tina watching him with those tight mocking smiles on their lips . . .

"Code word?" the man repeated.

Hilary was sunk into the couch at the far end of the coffee table. She leaned forward and raised her hand like a child in class, waving it to catch the guard's attention. "Honey Bunny," she said in a gasp that made the hair prickle at the back of Ellis' neck, "it's Honey Bunny."

That had been two nights ago.

But now, in the clear light of Saturday morning, after sleeping the sleep of the just—and prudent (Panty Rapist—all the Panty Rapists in the world could escape and it was nothing to him)—feeling self-satisfied and content right on down to the felt lining of his slippers, Ellis sat back, stretched, and gave his wife a rich little smile. "I guess it's a matter of priorities, honey," he said. "Sid and Tina can think what they want, but you know what I say—better safe than sorry."

When she talked about it afterward—with her husband at Gennaro's that night (she was too upset to cook), with her sister, with Betty Berger on the telephone—Giselle said she'd never been so scared in all her life. She meant it too. This was no horror story clipped from the newspaper, this was real. And it happened to her.

The guy was crazy. Creepy. Sick. He'd kept her there over four hours, and he had no intention of buying anything—she could see that in the first fifteen minutes. He just wanted an audience. Somebody to rant at, to threaten, to pin down with those jittery blue eyes. Richard had wanted her to go to the police, but she balked. What had he done, really? Scared her, yes. Bruised her arm. But what could the police do—she'd gone there of her own free will.

Her own free will. He'd said that. Those were his exact words.

Indignant, maybe a little shaken, she'd got up from the kitchen table to stuff her papers back into the briefcase. He was cursing under his breath, muttering darkly about the idiots on the freeway in their big-ass Mercedeses, crowding him, about spics and niggers and junior-high kids cutting through his yard—"Free country, my ass!" he'd shouted suddenly. "Free for every punk and weirdo and greaser to crap all over what little bit I got left, but let me get up from this table and put a couple holes in one of the little peckerheads and we'll see how it is. And I suppose you're going to protect me, huh, Miss Mercedes Benz with your heels and stockings and your big high-tech alarm system, huh?"

When she snapped the briefcase closed—no sale, nothing, just get me out of here, she was thinking—that was when he grabbed her arm. "Sit down," he snarled, and she tried to shake free but couldn't, he was strong with the rage of the psychopath, the lion in its den, the loony up against the wall.

"You're hurting me," she said as he forced her back down. "Mr. . . . Coles!" and she heard her own voice jump with anger, fright, pain.

"Yeah, that's right," he said, tightening his grip, "but you came here of your own free will, didn't you? Thought you were going to sucker me, huh? Run me a song and dance and lay your high-tech crap and your big bad SecureCo guards on me—oh, I've seen them, bunch of titsuckers and college wimps, who they going to stop? Huh?" He dropped her arm and challenged her with his jumpy mad tight-jawed glare.

She tried to get up but he roared, "Sit down! We got business here, goddamnit!" And then he was calling for his wife: "Glenys! Woman! Get your ass in here."

If she'd expected anything from the wife, any help or melioration, Giselle could see at a glance just how hopeless it was. The woman wouldn't look at her. She appeared in the doorway, pale as death, her hands trembling, staring at the carpet like a whipped dog. "Two G&T's," Coles said, sucking in his breath as if he were on the very edge of something, at the very beginning, "tall, with a wedge of lime."

"But—" Giselle began to protest, looking from Coles to the woman.

"You'll drink with me, all right." Coles' voice came at her like a blade of ice. "Get friendly, huh? Show me what you got." And then he turned away, his face violent with disgust. "SecureCo," he spat. He looked up, staring past her. "You going to keep the sons of bitches away from me, you going to keep them off my back, you going to give me any guarantees?" His voice rose. "I got a gun collection worth twelve thousand dollars in there—you going to answer for that? For my color TV? The goddamned trash can even?"

Giselle sat rigid, wondering if she could make a break for the back door and wondering if he was the type to keep it locked.

"Sell me," he demanded, looking at her now.

The woman set down the gin-and-tonics and then faded back into the shadows of the hallway. Giselle said nothing.

"Tell me about the man in the mask," he said, grinning again, grinning wide, too wide, "tell me about those poor old retired people. Come on," he said, his eyes taunting her, "sell me. I want it. I do. I mean I really need you people and your high-tech bullshit . . ."

He held her eyes, gulped half his drink, and set the glass down again. "I mean really," he said. "For my peace of mind."

It wasn't the fender-bender on the freeway the night before or the two hundred illegals lined up and looking for work on Canoga Avenue at dawn, and it wasn't the heart-clenching hate he still felt after being forced into early retirement two years ago or the fact that he'd sat up all night drinking gin while Glenys slept and the police and insurance companies filed their reports—it wasn't any of that that finally drove Everett Coles over the line. Not that he'd admit, anyway. It wasn't that little whore from SecureCo either (that's what she was, a whore, selling her tits and her lips and her ankles and all the rest of it too) or the veiny old hag from Westec or even the self-satisfied, smirking son of a bitch from Metropolitan Life, though he'd felt himself slipping on that one ("Death and dismemberment!" he'd hooted in the man's face, so thoroughly irritated, rubbed wrong, and just plain pissed he could think of nothing but the big glistening Mannlicher on the wall in the den). . . . No, it was Rance Ruby's stupid, fat-faced, shit-licking excuse of a kid.

Picture him sitting there in the first faint glow of early morning, the bottle mostly gone now and the fire in his guts over that moron with the barking face who'd run into him on the freeway just about put out, and then he looks up from the kitchen table and what does he see but this sorry lardassed spawn of a sorry tattooed beer-swilling lardass of a father cutting through the yard with his black death's-head T-shirt and his looseleaf and book jackets, and that's it. There's no more thinking, no more reason, no insurance or hope. He's up out of the chair like a shot and into the den, and then he's punching the barrel of the Mannlicher right through the glass of the den window. The fat little fuck, he's out there under the grape-fruit tree, shirttail hanging out, turning at the sound, and then *ka-boom,* there's about half of him left.

Next minute Everett Coles is in his car, fender rubbing against the tire in back where that sorry sack of shit ran into him, and slamming out of the driveway. He's got the Mannlicher on the seat beside him and a couple fistfuls of ammunition and he's peppering the side of Ruby's turd-colored house with a blast from his Weath-erby pump-action shotgun. He grazes a parked camper on his way up the block, slams over a couple of garbage cans, and leans out the window to take the head off somebody's yapping poodle as he careens out onto the boulevard, every wire gone loose in his head.

Ellis Hunsicker woke early. He'd dreamt he was a little cloud—the little cloud of the bedtime story he'd read Mifty and Corinne the night before—scudding along in the vast blue sky, free and untethered, the sun smiling on him as it does in picturebooks, when all at once he'd felt himself swept irresistibly forward, moving faster and faster, caught up in a huge, darkening, malevolent thun-derhead that rose up faceless from the far side of the day . . . and then he woke. It was just first light. Hilary

•

was breathing gently beside him. The alarm panel
glowed soothingly in the shadow of the half-open door.

It was funny how quickly he'd got used to the thing,
he reflected, yawning and scratching himself there in the
muted light. A week ago he'd made a fool of himself
over it in front of Sid and Tina, and now it was just
another appliance, no more threatening or unusual—and
no less vital—than the microwave, the Cuisinart, or the
clock radio. The last two mornings, in fact, he'd been
awakened not by the clock radio but by the insistent
beeping of the house alarm—Mifty had set it off going
out the back door to cuddle her rabbit. He thought now
of getting up to shut the thing off—it was an hour yet
before he'd have to be up for work—but he didn't. The
bed was warm, the birds had begun to whisper outside,
and he shut his eyes, drifting off like a little cloud.

When he woke again it was to the beep-beep-beep of
the house alarm and to the hazy apprehension of some
godawful crash—a jet breaking the sound barrier, the
first rumbling clap of the quake he lived in constant fear
of—an apprehension that something was amiss, that this
beep-beep-beeping, familiar though it seemed, was
somehow different, more high-pitched and admonitory
than the beep-beep-beeping occasioned by a child going
out to cuddle a bunny. He sat up. Hilary rose to her
elbows beside him, looking bewildered, and in that instant the alarm was silenced forever by the unmistakable
roar of a gunblast. Ellis' heart froze. Hilary cried out,
there was the heavy thump of footsteps below, a faint
choked whimper as of little girls startled in their sleep
and then a strange voice—high, hoarse, and raging—that
chewed up the morning like a set of jaws. "Armed response!" the voice howled. "Armed response, goddamnit! Armed response!"

The couple strained forward like mourners at a funeral.
Giselle had them, she knew that. They'd looked scared
when she came to the door, a pair of timid rabbity faces
peering out at her from behind the matching frames of
their prescription glasses, and they seated themselves on
the edge of the couch as if they were afraid of their own
furniture. She had them wringing their hands and darting

uneasy glances out the window as she described the per-
petrator—"A white man, dressed like a schoolteacher,
but with these wicked, jittery eyes that just sent a shiver
through you." She focused on the woman as she described the victims. There was a boy, just fourteen years
old, on his way to school, and a woman in a Mercedes
driving down to the corner store for coffee filters. And
then the family—they must have read about it—all of
them, and not three blocks from where they were now
sitting. "He was thirty-five years old," she said in a
husky voice, "an engineer at Rocketdyne, his whole life
ahead of him . . . and she, she was one of these supernice
people who . . . and the children . . ." She couldn't go
on. The man—Mr. Dunsinane, wasn't that the name?—
leaned forward and handed her a Kleenex. Oh, she had
them, all right. She could have sold them the super-de-
luxe laser alert system, stock in the company, mikes for
every flower in the garden, but the old charge just
wasn't there.

"I'm sorry," she whispered, fighting back a sob.

It was weird, she thought, pressing the Kleenex to her
face, but the masked intruder had never affected her like
this, or the knife-sharpening Mexican either. It was
Coles, of course, and those sick jumpy eyes of his, but
it was the signs too. She couldn't stop thinking about
those signs—if they hadn't been there, that is, stuck in
the lawn like a red flag in front of a bull . . . But there
was no future in that. No, she told the story anyway,
told it despite the chill that came over her and the thick-
ening in her throat.

She had to. If only for her peace of mind.

—1989

BARBARA KINGSOLVER

(B. 1955)

Born in Annapolis, Maryland, Barbara Kingsolver received a B.A. at De Pauw University and an M.S. at the University of Arizona, where she worked as a research assistant in the Physiology Department. She was a technical writer and freelance journalist before becoming a full-time writer in 1987. Among her honors are a feature-writing award from the Arizona Press Club (1986), American Library Association Awards for *The Bean Trees* (1988) and *Homeland* (1990), a PEN Fiction Prize for *Animal Dreams* (1991), a Woodrow Wilson Foundation/Lila Wallace Fellowship (1992–93), and a D. Litt from De Pauw University (1994). Kingsolver's first novel, *The Bean Trees* (1988), has been published in sixty-five countries, and a sequel, *Pigs in Heaven,* was published in 1993. She has published two other novels, *Animal Dreams* (1990) and *The Poisonwood Bible* (1998), as well as two nonfiction works, *Holding the Line: Women in the Great Arizona Mine Strike of 1983* (1989), which chronicles the role of women during the Phelps Dodge Copper Company strike, and *High Tide in Tucson: Essays from Now or Never* (1995). *Another America/Otra America* (1992) is a collection of her poetry that includes her Spanish translations of these poems. Twelve of her stories are collected in *Homeland and Other Stories* (1989).

Why I Am a Danger to the Public

BUENO, if I get backed into a corner I can just about raise up the dead. I'll fight, sure. But I am no lady wrestler. If you could see me you would know this thing is a *joke*—Tony, my oldest, is already taller than me, and he's only eleven. So why are they so scared of me I have to be in jail? I'll tell you.

Number one, this strike. There has never been one that turned so many old friends *chingándose*, not here in Bolton. And you can't get away from it because Ellington don't just run the mine, they own our houses, the water we drink and the dirt in our shoes and pretty much the state of New Mexico as I understand it. So if something is breathing, it's on one side or the other. And in a town like this that matters because everybody you know some way, you go to the same church or they used to babysit your kids, something. Nobody is a stranger.

My sister went down to Las Cruces New Mexico and got a job down there, but me, no. I stayed here and got married to Junior Morales. Junior was my one big mistake. But I like Bolton. From far away Bolton looks like some kind of all-colored junk that got swept up off the street after a big old party and stuffed down in the canyon. Our houses are all exactly alike, company houses, but people paint them yellow, purple, colors you wouldn't think a house could be. If you go down to the Big Dipper and come walking home *loca* you still know which one is yours. The copper mine is at the top of the canyon and the streets run straight uphill; some of them you can't drive up, you got to walk. There's steps. Oliver P. Snapp, that used to be the mailman for the west side, died of a heart attack one time right out there in his blue shorts. So the new mailman refuses to deliver to those houses; they have to pick up their mail at the P.O.

Now, this business with me and Vonda Fangham, I can't even tell you what got it started. I never had one thing in the world against her, no more than anybody else did. But this was around the fourth or fifth week so everybody knew by then who was striking and who was crossing. It don't take long to tell rats from cheese, and every night there was a big old fight in the Big Dipper. Somebody punching out his brother or his best friend. All that and no paycheck, can you imagine?

So it was a Saturday and there was just me and Corvallis Smith up at the picket line, setting in front of the picket shack passing the time of day. Corvallis is *un tipo,* he is real tall and lifts weights and wears his hair in those corn rows that hang down in the back with little pieces of aluminum foil on the ends. But good-looking in a certain way. I went out with Corvallis one time just so people would have something to talk about, and sure

enough, they had me getting ready to have brown and
black polka-dotted babies. All you got to do to get pregnant around here is have two beers with somebody in
the Dipper, so watch out.

"What do you hear from Junior," he says. That's a
joke; everybody says it including my friends. See, when
Manuela wasn't hardly even born one minute and Tony
still in diapers, Junior says, "Vicki, I can't find a corner
to piss in around this town." He said there was jobs in
Tucson and he would send a whole lot of money. Ha
ha. That's how I got started up at Ellington. I was not
going to support my kids in no little short skirt down at
the Frosty King. That was eight years ago. I got started
on the track gang, laying down rails for the cars that go
into the pit, and now I am a crane operator. See, when
Junior left I went up the hill and made such a rackus
they had to hire me up there, hire me or shoot me, one.

"Oh, I hear from him about the same as I hear from
Oliver P. Snapp," I say to Corvallis. That's the rest of
the joke.

It was a real slow morning. Cecil Smoot was supposed
to be on the picket shift with us but he wasn't there yet.
Cecil will show up late when the Angel Gabriel calls the
Judgment, saying he had to give his Datsun a lube job.

"Well, looka here," says Corvallis. "Here come the
ladies." There is this club called Wives of Working Men,
just started since the strike. Meaning Wives of Scabs.
About six of them was coming up the hill all cram-
packed into Vonda Fangham's daddy's air-condition Lincoln. She pulls the car right up next to where mine is
at. My car is a Buick older than both my two kids put
together. It gets me where I have to go.

They set and look at us for one or two minutes. Out
in that hot sun, sticking to our T-shirts, and me in my
work boots—I can't see no point in treating it like a
damn tea party—and Corvallis, he's an eyeful anyway.
All of a sudden the windows on the Lincoln all slide
down. It has those electric windows.

"Isn't this a ni-i-ice day," says one of them, Doreen
Carter. Doreen visited her sister in Laurel, Mississippi,
for three weeks one time and now she has an accent.
"Bein' payday an' all," she says. Her husband is the

minister of Saint's Grace, which is scab headquarters. I
quit going. I was raised up to believe in God and the
union, but listen, if it comes to pushing or shoving I
know which one of the two is going to keep tires on
the car.

"Well, yes, it is a real nice day," another one of them
says. They're all fanning theirselves with something
paper. I look, and Corvallis looks. They're fanning theirselves with their husbands' paychecks.

I haven't had a paycheck since July. My son couldn't
go to Morse with his baseball team Friday night because
they had to have three dollars for supper at McDonald's.
Three damn dollars.

The windows start to go back up and they're getting
ready to drive off, and I say, "Vonda Fangham, *vete
al infierno.*"

The windows whoosh back down.

"What did you say?" Vonda wants to know.

"I said, I'm surprised to see you in there with the scab
ladies. I didn't know you had went and got married to
a yellow-spine scab just so somebody would let you in
their club."

Well, Corvallis laughs at that. But Vonda just gives
me this look. She has a little sharp nose and yellow hair
and teeth too big to fit behind her lips. For some reason
she was a big deal in high school, and it's not her personality either. She was the queen of everything. Cheerlead-
ers, drama club, every school play they ever had, I think.

I stare at her right back, ready to make a day out of
it if I have to. The heat is rising up off that big blue
hood like it's a lake all set to boil over.

"What I said was, Vonda Fangham, you can go to
hell."

"I can't hear a word you're saying," she says. "Trash
can't talk."

"This trash can go to bed at night and know I haven't
cheated nobody out of a living. You want to see trash,
chica, you ought to come up here at the shift change
and see what kind of shit rolls over that picket line."

Well, that shit I was talking about was their husbands,
so up go the windows and off they fly. Vonda just about
goes in the ditch trying to get that big car turned around.

To tell you the truth I knew Vonda was engaged to get married to Tommy Jones, a scab. People said, Well, at least now Vonda will be just Vonda Jones. That name Fangham is *feo,* and the family has this whole certain way of showing off. Her dad's store, Fangham Drugs, has the biggest sign in town, as if he has to advertise. As if somebody would forget it was there and drive fifty-one miles over the mountains to Morse to go to another drugstore.

I couldn't care less about Tommy and Vonda getting engaged, I was just hurt when he crossed the line. Tommy was a real good man, I used to think. He was not ashamed like most good-looking guys are to act decent every once in a while. Me and him started out on the same track crew and he saved my butt one time covering the extra weight for me when I sprang my wrist. And he never acted like I owed him for it. Some guys, they would try to put the moves on me out by the slag pile. Shit, that was hell. And then I would be downtown in the drugstore and Carol Finch or somebody would go *huh-hmm,* clear her throat and roll her eyes, like, "Over here is what you want," looking at the condoms. Just because I'm up there with their husbands all day I am supposed to be screwing around. In all that mud, just think about it, in our steel toe boots that weigh around ten pounds, and our hard hats. And then the guys gave me shit too when I started training as a crane operator, saying a woman don't have no business taking up the good-paying jobs. You figure it out.

Tommy was different. He was a lone ranger. He didn't grow up here or have family, and in Bolton you can move in here and live for about fifty years and people still call you that fellow from El Paso, or wherever it was you come from. They say that's why he went in, that he was afraid if he lost his job he would lose Vonda too. But we all had something to lose.

That same day I come home and found Manuela and Tony in the closet. Like poor little kitties in there setting on the shoes. Tony was okay pretty much but Manuela was crying, screaming. I thought she would dig her eyes out.

Tony kept going, "They was up here looking for you!"

"Who was?" I asked him.

"Scab men," he said. "Clifford Owens and Mr. Alphonso and them police from out of town. The ones with the guns."

"The State Police?" I said. I couldn't believe it. "The State Police was up here? What did they want?"

"They wanted to know where you was at." Tony almost started to cry. "Mama, I didn't tell them."

"He didn't," Manuela said.

"Well, I was just up at the damn picket shack. Anybody could have found me if they wanted to." I could have swore I saw Owens's car go right by the picket shack, anyway.

"They kept on saying where was you at, and we didn't tell them. We said you hadn't done nothing."

"Well, you're right, I haven't done nothing. Why didn't you go over to Uncle Manny's? He's supposed to be watching you guys."

"We was scared to go outside!" Manuela screamed. She was jumping from one foot to the other and hugging herself. "They said they'd get us!"

"Tony, did they say that? Did they threaten you?"

"They said stay away from the picket rallies," Tony said. "The one with the gun said he seen us and took all our pitchers. He said, your mama's got too big a mouth for her own good."

At the last picket rally I was up on Lalo Ruiz's shoulders with a bull horn. I've had almost every office in my local, and sergeant-at-arms twice because the guys say I have no toleration for BS. They got one of those big old trophies down at the union hall that says on it "MEN OF COPPER," and one time Lalo says, "Vicki ain't no Man of Copper, she's a damn stick of *mesquite*. She might break but she sure as hell won't bend."

Well, I want my kids to know what this is about. When school starts, if some kid makes fun of their last-year's blue jeans and calls them trash I want them to hold their heads up. I take them to picket rallies so they'll know that. No law says you can't set up on nobody with a bull horn. They might have took my picture, though. I wouldn't be surprised.

"All I ever done was defend my union," I told the kids. "Even cops have to follow the laws, and it isn't no crime to defend your union. Your grandpapa done it and his papa and now me."

Well, my grandpapa one time got put on a railroad car like a cow, for being a Wobbly and a Mexican. My kids have heard that story a million times. He got dumped out in the desert someplace with no water or even a cloth for his head, and it took him two months to get back. All that time my granny and Tía Sonia thought he was dead.

I hugged Tony and Manuela and then we went and locked the door. I had to pull up on it while they jimmied the latch because that damn door had not been locked one time in seven years.

What we thought about when we wanted to feel better was: What a God-awful mess they got up there in the mine. Most of those scabs was out-of-towners and didn't have no idea what end of the gun to shoot. I heard it took them about one month to figure out how to start the equipment. Before the walkout there was some parts switched around between my crane and a locomotive, but we didn't have to do that because the scabs tied up the cat's back legs all by theirselves. Laying pieces of track backwards, running the conveyors too fast, I hate to think what else.

We even heard that one foreman, Willie Bunford, quit because of all the jackasses on the machinery, that he feared for his life. Willie Bunford used to be my foreman. He made fun of how I said his name, "Wee-lee!" so I called him Mr. Bunford. So I have an accent, so what. When I was first starting on the crane he said, "You aren't going to get PG now, are you, Miss Morales, after I wasted four weeks training you as an operator? I know how you Mexican gals love to have babies." I said, "Mr. Bunford, as far as this job goes you can consider me a man." So I had to stick to that. I couldn't call up and say I'm staying in bed today because of my monthly. Then what does he do but lay off two weeks with so-call whiplash from a car accident on Top Street when I saw the whole story: Winnie Hask backing into his car in front of the Big Dipper and him not in it. If a man can get whiplash from his car getting bashed in while he is drinking beer across the street, well, that's a new one.

So I didn't cry for no Willie Bunford. At least he had the sense to get out of there. None of those scabs knew how to run the oxygen machine, so we were waiting for the whole damn place to blow up. I said to the guys, Let's go sit on Bolt Mountain with some beer and watch the fireworks.

The first eviction I heard about was the Frank Mickliffs, up the street from me, and then Joe Gomez on Alameda. Ellington wanted to clear out some company houses for the new hires, but how they decided who to throw out we didn't know. Then Janie Marley found out from her friend that babysits for the sister-in-law of a scab that company men were driving scab wives around town letting them pick out whatever house they wanted. Like they're going shopping and we're the peaches getting squeezed.

Friday of that same week I was out on my front porch thinking about a cold beer, just thinking, though, because of no cash, and here come an Ellington car. They slowed way, way down when they went by, then on up Church Street going about fifteen and then they come back. It was Vonda in there. She nodded her head at my house and the guy put something down on paper. They made a damn picture show out of it.

Oh, I was furious. I have been living in that house almost the whole time I worked for Ellington and it's all the home my kids ever had. It's a real good house. It's yellow. I have a big front porch where you can see just about everything, all of Bolton, and a railing so the kids won't fall over in the gulch, and a big yard. I keep it up nice, and my brother Manny being right next door helps out. I have this mother duck with her babies all lined up that the kids bought me at Fangham's for Mother's Day, and I planted marigolds in a circle around them. No way on this earth was I turning my house over to a scab.

The first thing I did was march over to Manny's house

and knock on the door and walk in. "Manny," I say to him, "I don't want you mowing my yard anymore unless you feel like doing a favor for Miss Vonda." Manny is just pulling the pop top off a Coke and his mouth goes open at the same time; he just stares.

"Oh, no," he says.

"Oh, yes."

I went back over to my yard and Manny come hopping out putting on his shoes, to see what I'm going to do, I guess. He's my little brother but Mama always says "*Madre Santa*, Manuel, keep an eye on Vicki!" Well, what I was going to do was my own damn business. I pulled up the ducks, they have those metal things that poke in the ground, and then I pulled up the marigolds and threw them out on the sidewalk. If I had to get the neighbor kids to help make my house the ugliest one, I was ready to do it.

Well. The next morning I was standing in the kitchen drinking coffee, and Manny come through the door with this funny look on his face and says, "The tooth fairy has been to see you."

What in the world. I ran outside and there was *pink* petunias planted right in the circle where I already pulled up the marigolds. To think Vonda could sneak into my yard like a common thief and do a thing like that.

"Get the kids," I said. I went out and started pulling out petunias. I hate pink. And I hate how they smelled, they had these sticky roots. Manny woke up the kids and they come out and helped.

"This is fun, Mom," Tony said. He wiped his cheek and a line of dirt ran across like a scar. They were in their pajamas.

"Son, we're doing it for the union," I said. We threw them out on the sidewalk with the marigolds, to dry up and die.

After that I was scared to look out the window in the morning. God knows what Vonda might put in my yard, more flowers or one of those ugly pink flamingos they sell at Fangham's yard and garden department. I wouldn't put nothing past Vonda.

*   *   *

Whatever happened, we thought when the strike was over we would have our jobs. You could put up with high water and heck, thinking of that. It's like having a baby, you just grit your teeth and keep your eyes on the prize. But then Ellington started sending out termination notices saying, You will have no job to come back to whatsoever. They would fire you for any excuse, mainly strike-related misconduct, which means nothing, you looked cross-eyed at a policeman or whatever. People got scared.

The national office of the union was no help; they said, To hell with it, boys, take the pay cut and go on back. I had a fit at the union meeting. I told them it's not the pay cut, it's what all else they would take if we give in. "Ellington would not have hired me in two million years if it wasn't for the union raising a rackus about all people are created equal," I said. "Or half of you either because they don't like cunts or coloreds." I'm not that big of a person but I was standing up in front, and when I cussed, they shut up. "If my papa had been a chickenshit like you guys, I would be down at the Frosty King tonight in a little short skirt," I said. "You bunch of no-goods would be on welfare and your kids pushing drugs to pay the rent." Some of the guys laughed, but some didn't.

Men get pissed off in this certain way, though, where they have to tear something up. Lalo said, "Well, hell, let's drive a truck over the plant gate and shut the damn mine down." And there they go, off and running, making plans to do it. Corvallis had a baseball cap on backwards and was sitting back with his arms crossed like, Honey, don't look at me. I could have killed him.

"Great, you guys, you do something cute like that and we're dead ducks," I said. "We don't have to do but one thing, wait it out."

"Till when?" Lalo wanted to know. "Till hell freezes?" He is kind of a short guy with about twelve tattoos on each arm.

"Till they get fed up with the scabs pissing around and want to get the mine running. If it comes down to busting heads, no way. Do you hear me? They'll have the National Guards in here."

I knew I was right. The Boots in this town, the cops, they're on Ellington payroll. I've seen strikes before. When I was ten years old I saw a cop get a Mexican man down on the ground and kick his face till blood ran out of his ear. You would think I was the only one in that room that was born and raised in Bolton.

Ellington was trying to get back up to full production. They had them working twelve-hour shifts and seven-day weeks like Abraham Lincoln had never freed the slaves. We started hearing about people getting hurt, but just rumors; it wasn't going to run in the paper. Ellington owns the paper.

The first I knew about it really was when Vonda come right to my house. I was running the vacuum cleaner and had the radio turned up all the way so I didn't hear her drive up. I just heard a knock on the door, and when I opened it: Vonda. Her skin looked like a flour tortilla. "What in the world," I said.

Her bracelets were going clack-clack-clack, she was shaking so hard. "I never thought I'd be coming to you," she said, like I was Dear Abby. "But something's happened to Tommy."

"Oh," I said. I had heard some real awful things: that a guy was pulled into a smelter furnace, and another guy got his legs run over on the tracks. I could picture Tommy either way, no legs or burnt up. We stood there a long time. Vonda looked like she might pass out. "Okay, come in," I told her. "Set down there and I'll get you a drink of water. Water is all we got around here." I stepped over the vacuum cleaner on the way to the kitchen. I wasn't going to put it away.

When I come back she was looking around the room all nervous, breathing like a bird. I turned down the radio.

"How are the kids?" she wanted to know, of all things.

"The kids are fine. Tell me what happened to Tommy."

"Something serious to do with his foot, that's all I know. Either cut off or half cut off, they won't tell me." She pulled this little hanky out of her purse and blew her nose. "They sent him to Morse in the helicopter ambulance, but they won't say what hospital because I'm not next of kin. He doesn't have any next of kin here, I *told* them that. I informed them I was the fiancée." She blew her nose again. "All they'll tell me is they don't want him in the Bolton hospital. I can't understand why."

"Because they don't want nobody to know about it," I told her. "They're covering up all the accidents."

"Well, why would they want to do that?"

"Vonda, excuse me please, but don't be stupid. They want to do that so we won't know how close we are to winning the strike."

Vonda took a little sip of water. She had on a yellow sun dress and her arms looked so skinny, like just bones with freckles. "Well, I know what you think of me," she finally said, "but for Tommy's sake maybe you can get the union to do something. Have an investigation so he'll at least get his compensation pay. I know you have a lot of influence on the union."

"I don't know if I do or not," I told her. I puffed my breath out and leaned my head back on the sofa. I pulled the bandana off my head and rubbed my hair in a circle. It's so easy to know what's right and so hard to do it.

"Vonda," I said, "I thought a lot of Tommy before all this shit. He helped me one time when I needed it real bad." She looked at me. She probably hated thinking of me and him being friends. "I'm sure Tommy knows he done the wrong thing," I said. "But it gets me how you people treat us like kitchen trash and then come running to the union as soon as you need help."

She picked up her glass and brushed at the water on the coffee table. I forgot napkins. "Yes, I see that now, and I'll try to make up for my mistake," she said.

Give me a break, Vonda, was what I was thinking. "Well, we'll see," I said. "There is a meeting coming up and I'll see what I can do. If you show up on the picket line tomorrow."

Vonda looked like she swallowed one of her ice cubes. She went over to the TV and picked up the kids' pictures one at a time, Manuela then Tony. Put them back down. Went over to the *armario* built by my grandpapa.

"What a nice little statue," she said.

"That's St. Joseph. Saint of people that work with their hands."

She turned around and looked at me. "I'm sorry about the house. I won't take your house. It wouldn't be right."

"I'm glad you feel that way, because I wasn't moving."

"Oh," she said.

"Vonda, I can remember when me and you were little girls and your daddy was already running the drugstore. You used to set up on a stool behind the counter and run the soda-water machine. You had a charm bracelet with everything in the world on it, poodle dogs and hearts and a real little pill box that opened."

Vonda smiled. "I don't have the foggiest idea what ever happened to that bracelet. Would you like it for your girl?"

I stared at her. "But you don't remember me, do you?"

"Well, I remember a whole lot of people coming in the store. You in particular, I guess not."

"I guess not," I said. "People my color was not allowed to go in there and set at the soda fountain. We had to get paper cups and take our drinks outside. Remember that? I used to think and *think* about why that was. I thought our germs must be so nasty they wouldn't wash off the glasses."

"Well, things have changed, haven't they?" Vonda said.

"Yeah." I put my feet up on the coffee table. It's my damn table. "Things changed because the UTU and the Machinists and my papa's union the Boilermakers took this whole fucking company town to court in 1973, that's why. This house right here was for whites only. And if there wasn't no union forcing Ellington to abide by the law, it still would be."

She was kind of looking out the window. She probably was thinking about what she was going to cook for supper.

"You think it wouldn't? You think Ellington would

build a nice house for everybody if they could still put half of us in those falling-down shacks down by the river like I grew up in?"

"Well, you've been very kind to hear me out," she said. "I'll do what you want, tomorrow. Right now I'd better be on my way."

I went out on the porch and watched her go down the sidewalk—click click, on her little spike heels. Her ankles wobbled.

"Vonda," I yelled out after her, "don't wear high heels on the line tomorrow. For safety's sake."

She never turned around.

Next day the guys were making bets on Vonda showing up or not. The odds were not real good in her favor. I had to laugh, but myself I really thought she would. It was a huge picket line for the morning shift change. The Women's Auxiliary thought it would boost up the morale, which needed a kick in the butt or somebody would be busting down the plant gate. Corvallis told me that some guys had a meeting after the real meeting and planned it out. But I knew that if I kept showing up at the union meetings and standing on the table and jumping and hollering, they wouldn't do it. Sometimes guys will listen to a woman.

The sun was just coming up over the canyon and already it was a hot day. Cicada bugs buzzing in the *palo-verdes* like damn rattlesnakes. Me and Janie Marley were talking about our kids; she has a boy one size down from Tony and we trade clothes around. All of a sudden Janie grabs my elbow and says, "Look who's here." It was Vonda getting out of the Lincoln. Not in high heels either. She had on a tennis outfit and plastic sunglasses and a baseball bat slung over her shoulder. She stopped a little ways from the line and was looking around, waiting for the Virgin Mary to come down, I guess, and save her. Nobody was collecting any bets.

"Come on, Vonda," I said. I took her by the arm and stood her between me and Janie. "I'm glad you made it." But she wasn't talking, just looking around a lot.

After a while I said, "We're not supposed to have bats up here. I know a guy that got his termination papers for

carrying a crescent wrench in his back pocket. He had
forgot it was even in there." I looked at Vonda to see
if she was paying attention. "It was Rusty Cochran," I
said, "you know him. He's up at your dad's every other
day for a prescription. They had that baby with the hole
in his heart."

But Vonda held on to the bat like it was the last man
in the world and she got him. "I'm only doing this for
Tommy," she says.

"Well, so what," I said. "I'm doing it for my kids. So
they can eat."

She kept squinting her eyes down the highway.

A bunch of people started yelling, "Here come the
ladies!" Some of the women from the Auxiliary were
even saying it. And here come trouble. They were in
Doreen's car, waving signs out the windows: "We Support Our Working Men" and other shit not worth repeating. Doreen was driving. She jerked right dead to a
stop, right in front of us. She looked at Vonda and you
would think she had broke both her hinges the way her
mouth was hanging open, and Vonda looked back at
Doreen, and the rest of us couldn't wait to see what
was next.

Doreen took a U-turn and almost ran over Cecil
Smoot, and they beat it back to town like bats out of
hell. Ten minutes later here come her car back up the
hill again. Only this time her husband Milton was driving, and three other men from Saint's Grace was all in
there besides Doreen. Two of them are cops.

"I don't know what they're up to but we don't need
you getting in trouble," I told Vonda. I took the bat
away from her and put it over my shoulder. She looked
real white, and I patted her arm and said, "Don't
worry." I can't believe I did that, now. Looking back.

They pulled up in front of us again but they didn't get
out, just all five of them stared and then they drove off,
like whatever they come for they got.

That was yesterday. Last night I was washing the
dishes and somebody come to the house. The kids were
watching TV. I heard Tony slide the dead bolt over and
then he yelled, "Mom, it's the Boot."

Before I can even put down a plate and get into the living room Larry Trevizo has pushed right by him into the house. I come out wiping my hands and see him there holding up his badge.

"Chief of Police, ma'am," he says, just like that, like I don't know who the hell he is. Like we didn't go through every grade of school together and go see *Suddenly Last Summer* one time in high school.

He says, "Mrs. Morales, I'm serving you with injunction papers."

"Oh, is that a fact," I say. "And may I ask what for?"

Tony already turned off the TV and is standing by me with his arms crossed, the meanest-looking damn eleven-year-old you ever hope to see in your life. All I can think of is the guys in the meeting, how they get so they just want to bust something in.

"Yes you may ask what for," Larry says, and starts to read, not looking any of us in the eye: "For being a danger to the public. Inciting a riot. Strike-related misconduct." And then real low he says something about Vonda Fangham and a baseball bat.

"What was that last thing?"

He clears his throat. "And for kidnapping Vonda Fangham and threatening her with a baseball bat. We got the affidavits."

"*Pa'fuera!*" I tell Larry Trevizo. I ordered him out of my house right then, told him if he wanted to see somebody get hurt with a baseball bat he could hang around my living room and find out. I trusted myself but not Tony. Larry got out of there.

The injunction papers said I was not to be in any public gathering of more than five people or I would be arrested. And what do you know, a squad of Boots was already lined up by the picket shack at the crack of dawn this morning with their hands on their sticks, just waiting. They knew I would be up there, I see that. They knew I would do just exactly all the right things. Like the guys say, Vicki might break but she don't bend.

They cuffed me and took me up to the jailhouse, which is in back of the Ellington main office, and took off my belt and my earrings so I wouldn't kill myself or escape. "With an earring?" I said. I was laughing. I could see this old rotten building through the office window; it used to be something or other but now there's chickens living in it. You could dig out of there with an earring, for sure. I said, "What's that over there, the Mexican jail? You better put me in there!"

I thought they would just book me and let me go like they did some other ones, before this. But no, I have to stay put. Five hundred thousand bond. I don't think this whole town could come up with that, not if they signed over every pink, purple, and blue house in Bolton.

It didn't hit me till right then about the guys wanting to tear into the plant. What they might do.

"Look, I got to get out by tonight," I told the cops. I don't know their names, it was some State Police I have never seen, seem like they just come up out of nowhere. I was getting edgy. "I have a union meeting and it's real important. Believe me, you don't want me to miss it."

They smiled. And then I got that terrible feeling you get when you see somebody has been looking you in the eye and smiling and setting a trap, and there you are in it like a damn rat.

What is going to happen I don't know. I'm keeping my ears open. I found out my kids are driving Manny to distraction—Tony told his social-studies class he would rather have a jailbird than a scab mom, and they sent him home with a note that he was causing a dangerous disturbance in class.

I also learned that Tommy Jones was not in any accident. He got called off his shift one day and was took to Morse in a helicopter with no explanation. They put him up at Howard Johnson's over there for five days, his meals and everything, just told him not to call nobody, and today he's back at work. They say he is all in one piece.

Well, I am too.

—1989

ANZIA YEZIERSKA
(C. 1885–1970)

The youngest of nine children, Anzia Yezierska became an immigrant in America when her family left Poland and settled in the Jewish ghetto on the Lower East Side of Manhattan. By 1915, she had begun to write and publish stories that reflected her experience as a sweatshop worker who struggled to gain an education, attending English classes after long days at work. In 1919, her story "The Fat of the Land" was awarded the Edward J. O'Brien prize, and in 1920, *Hungry Hearts*, a collection of ten of her stories, was published. A surprisingly popular success, the book was the basis of a Hollywood silent film produced by Samuel Goldwyn. Paid $10,000 for the film rights, Yezierska seemed to be experiencing the American Dream. During a prolific period, she published another story collection, *Children of Loneliness* (1923) as well as the novels *Salome of the Tenements* (1922), *Bread Givers* (1925), *Arrogant Beggar* (1927), and *All I Could Never Be* (1932). Among the first Jewish-American women writers, she depicted the hardships of Jewish immigrant family members, particularly women, in a prose style that echoed the syntax and vocabulary of the Yiddish-speaking ghetto community. Her success, however, did not extend into the mid-1930s and -40s, and she found it difficult to publish her later works. Her autobiography, *Red Ribbon on a White Horse*, appeared in 1950; *The Open Cage: An Anzia Yezierska Collection*, edited by Alice Kessler-Harris, was published in 1979.

The Free Vacation House

HOW came it that I went to the free vacation house was like this:

One day the visiting teacher from the school comes to find out for why don't I get the children ready for school in time; for why are they so often late.

I let out on her my whole bitter heart. I told her my

head was on wheels from worrying. When I get up in the morning, I don't know on what to turn first: should I nurse the baby, or make Sam's breakfast, or attend on the older children. I only got two hands.

"My dear woman," she says, "you are about to have a nervous breakdown. You need to get away to the country for a rest and vacation."

"Gott im Himmel!" says I. "Don't I know I need a rest? But how? On what money can I go to the country?"

"I know of a nice country place for mothers and children that will not cost you anything. It is free."

"Free! I never heard from it."

"Some kind people have made arrangements so no one need pay," she explains.

Later, in a few days, I just finished up with Masha and Mendel and Frieda and Sonya to send them to school, and I was getting Aby ready for kindergarten, when I hear a knock on the door, and a lady comes in. She had a white starched dress like a nurse and carried a black satchel in her hand.

"I am from the Social Betterment Society," she tells me. "You want to go to the country?"

Before I could say something, she goes over to the baby and pulls out the rubber nipple from her mouth, and to me, she says, "You must not get the child used to sucking this; it is very unsanitary."

"Gott im Himmel!" I beg the lady. "Please don't begin with that child, or she'll holler my head off. She must have the nipple. I'm too nervous to hear her scream like that."

When I put the nipple back again in the baby's mouth, the lady takes herself a seat, and then takes out a big black book from her satchel. Then she begins to question me. What is my first name? How old I am? From where come I? How long I'm already in this country? Do I keep any boarders? What is my husband's first name? How old he is? How long he is in this country? By what trade he works? How much wages he gets for a week? How much money do I spend out for rent? How old are the children, and everything about them.

"My goodness!" I cry out. "For why is it necessary all

this to know? For why must I tell you all my business? What difference does it make already if I keep boarders, or I don't keep boarders? If Masha had the whooping-cough or Sonya had the measles? Or whether I spend out for my rent ten dollars or twenty? Or whether I come from Schnipishock or Kovner Gubernie?"

"We must make a record of all the applicants, and investigate each case," she tells me. "There are so many who apply to the charities, we can help only those who are most worthy."

"Charities!" I scream out. "Ain't the charities those who help the beggars out? I ain't no beggar. I'm not asking for no charity. My husband, he works."

"Miss Holcomb, the visiting teacher, said that you wanted to go to the country, and I had to make out this report before investigating your case."

"Oh! Oh!" I choke and bit my lips. "Is the free country from which Miss Holcomb told me, is it from the charities? She was telling me some kind people made arrangements for any mother what needs to go there."

"If your application is approved, you will be notified," she says to me, and out she goes.

When she is gone I think to myself, I'd better knock out from my head this idea about the country. For so long I lived, I did n't know nothing about the charities. For why should I come down among the beggars now?

Then I looked around me in the kitchen. On one side was the big wash-tub with clothes, waiting for me to wash. On the table was a pile of breakfast dishes yet. In the sink was the potatoes, waiting to be peeled. The baby was beginning to cry for the bottle. Aby was hollering and pulling me to take him to kindergarten. I felt if I didn't get away from here for a little while, I would land in a crazy house, or from the window jump down. Which was worser, to land in a crazy house, jump from the window down, or go to the country from the charities?

In about two weeks later around comes the same lady with the satchel again in my house.

"You can go to the country to-morrow," she tells me. "And you must come to the charity building to-morrow at nine o'clock sharp. Here is a card with the address.

Don't lose it, because you must hand it to the lady in the office."

I look on the card, and there I see my name wrote; and by it, in big printed letters, that word "CHARITY."

"Must I go to the charity office?" I ask, feeling my heart to sink. "For why must I come there?"

"It is the rule that everybody comes to the office first, and from there they are taken to the country."

I shivered to think how I would feel, suppose somebody from my friends should see me walking into the charity office with my children. They would n't know that it is only for the country I go there. They might think I go to beg. Have I come down so low as to be seen by the charities? But what's the use? Should I knock my head on the walls? I had to go.

When I come to the office, I already found a crowd of women and children sitting on long benches and waiting. I took myself a seat with them, and we were sitting and sitting and looking on one another, sideways and crosswise, and with lowered eyes, like guilty criminals. Each one felt like hiding herself from all the rest. Each one felt black with shame in the face.

We may have been sitting and waiting for an hour or more. But every second was seeming years to me. The children began to get restless. Mendel wanted water. The baby on my arms was falling asleep. Aby was crying for something to eat.

"For why are we sittin' here like fat cats?" says the woman next to me. "Ain't we going to the country to-day yet?"

At last a lady comes to the desk and begins calling us our names, one by one. I nearly dropped to the floor when over she begins to ask: Do you keep boarders? How much do you spend out for rent? How much wages does your man get for a week?

Did n't the nurse tell them all about us already? It was bitter enough to have to tell the nurse everything, but in my own house nobody was hearing my troubles, only the nurse. But in the office there was so many strangers all around me. For why should everybody have to know my business? At every question I wanted to holler out: "Stop! Stop! I don't want no vacations! I'll

better run home with my children." At every question I
felt like she was stabbing a knife into my heart. And she
kept on stabbing me more and more, but I could not
help it, and they were all looking at me. I could n't move
from her. I had to answer everything.

When she got through with me, my face was red like
fire. I was burning with hurts and wounds. I felt like
everything was bleeding in me.

When all the names was already called, a man doctor
with a nurse comes in, and tells us to form a line, to be
examined. I wish I could ease out my heart a little, and
tell in words how that doctor looked on us, just because
we were poor and had no money to pay. He only used
the ends from his finger-tips to examine us with. From
the way he was afraid to touch us or come near us, he
made us feel like we had some catching sickness that he
was trying not to get on him.

The doctor got finished with us in about five minutes,
so quick he worked. Then we was told to walk after the
nurse, who was leading the way for us through the street
to the car. Everybody what passed us in the street turned
around to look on us. I kept down my eyes and held
down my head and I felt like sinking into the sidewalk.
All the time I was trembling for fear somebody what
knows me might yet pass and see me. For why did they
make us walk through the street, after the nurse, like
stupid cows? Were n't all of us smart enough to find our
way without the nurse? Why should the whole world
have to see that we are from the charities?

When we got into the train, I opened my eyes, and
lifted up my head, and straightened out my chest, and
again began to breathe. It was a beautiful, sun-shiny day.
I knocked open the window from the train, and the
fresh-smelling country air rushed upon my face and
made me feel so fine! I looked out from the window and
instead of seeing the iron fire-escapes with garbage-cans
and bedclothes, that I always seen when from my flat I
looked—instead of seeing only walls and wash-lines between walls, I saw the blue sky, and green grass and
trees and flowers.

Ah, how grand I felt, just on the sky to look! Ah, how

grand I felt just to see the green grass—and the free space—and no houses!

"Get away from me, my troubles!" I said. "Leave me rest a minute. Leave me breathe and straighten out my bones. Forget the unpaid butcher's bill. Forget the rent. Forget the wash-tub and the cook-stove and the pots and pans. Forget the charities!"

"Tickets, please," calls the train conductor.

I felt knocked out from heaven all at once. I had to point to the nurse what held our tickets, and I was feeling the conductor looking on me as if to say, "Oh, you are only from the charities."

By the time we came to the vacation house I already forgot all about my knock-down. I was again filled with the beauty of the country. I never in all my life yet seen such a swell house like that vacation house. Like the grandest palace it looked. All round the front, flowers from all colors was smelling out the sweetest perfume. Here and there was shady trees with comfortable chairs under them to sit down on.

When I only came inside, my mouth opened wide and my breathing stopped still from wonder. I never yet seen such an order and such a cleanliness. From all the corners from the room, the cleanliness was shining like a looking-glass. The floor was so white scrubbed you could eat on it. You could n't find a speck of dust on nothing, if you was looking for it with eyeglasses on.

I was beginning to feel happy and glad that I come, when, Gott im Himmel! again a lady begins to ask us out the same questions what the nurse already asked me in my home and what was asked over again in the charity office. How much wages my husband makes out for a week? How much money I spend out for rent? Do I keep boarders?

We were hungry enough to faint. So worn out was I from excitement, and from the long ride, that my knees were bending under me ready to break from tiredness. The children were pulling me to pieces, nagging me for a drink, for something to eat and such like. But still we had to stand out the whole list of questionings. When she already got through asking us out everything, she gave to each of us a tag with our name written on it.

She told us to tie the tag on our hand. Then like tagged horses at a horse sale in the street, they marched us into the dining-room.

There was rows of long tables, covered with pure-white oil-cloth. A vase with bought flowers was standing on the middle from each table. Each person got a clean napkin for himself. Laid out by the side from each person's plate was a silver knife and fork and spoon and teaspoon. When we only sat ourselves down, girls with white starched aprons was passing around the eatings.

I soon forgot again all my troubles. For the first time in ten years I sat down to a meal what I did not have to cook or worry about. For the first time in ten years I sat down to the table like a somebody. Ah, how grand it feels, to have handed you over the eatings and everything you need. Just as I was beginning to like it and let myself feel good, in comes a fat lady all in white, with a teacher's look on her face. I could tell already, right away by the way she looked on us, that she was the boss from this place.

"I want to read you the rules from this house, before you leave this room," says she to us.

Then she began like this: We dassen't stand on the front grass where the flowers are. We dassen't stay on the front porch. We dassen't sit on the chairs under the shady trees. We must stay always in the back and sit on those long wooden benches there. We dassen't come in the front sitting-room or walk on the front steps what have carpet on it—we must walk on the back iron steps. Everything on the front from the house must be kept perfect for the show for visitors. We dassen't lay down on the beds in the daytime, the beds must always be made up perfect for the show for visitors.

"Gott im Himmel!" thinks I to myself; "ain't there going to be no end to the things we dassen't do in this place?"

But still she went on. The children over two years dassen't stay around by the mothers. They must stay by the nurse in the play-room. By the meal-times, they can see their mothers. The children dassen't run around the house or tear up flowers or do anything. They dassen't holler or play rough in the play-room. They must always behave and obey the nurse.

We must always listen to the bells. Bell one was for getting up. Bell two, for getting babies' bottles. Bell three, for coming to breakfast. Bell four, for bathing the babies. If we come later, after the ring from the bell, then we'll not get what we need. If the bottle bell rings and we don't come right away for the bottle, then the baby don't get no bottle. If the breakfast bell rings, and we don't come right away down to the breakfast, then there won't be no breakfast for us.

When she got through with reading the rules, I was wondering which side of the house I was to walk on. At every step was some rule what said don't move here, and don't go there, don't stand there, and don't sit there. If I tried to remember the endless rules, it would only make me dizzy in the head. I was thinking for why, with so many rules, didn't they also have already another rule, about how much air in our lungs to breathe.

On every few days there came to the house swell ladies in automobiles. It was for them that the front from the house had to be always perfect. For them was all the beautiful smelling flowers. For them the front porch, the front sitting-room, and the easy stairs with the carpet on it.

Always when the rich ladies came the fat lady, what was the boss from the vacation house, showed off to them the front. Then she took them over to the back to look on us, where we was sitting together, on long wooden benches, like prisoners. I was always feeling cheap like dirt, and mad that I had to be there, when they smiled down on us.

"How nice for these poor creatures to have a restful place like this," I heard one lady say.

The next day I already felt like going back. The children what had to stay by the nurse in the play-room did n't like it neither.

"Mamma," says Mendel to me, "I wisht I was home and out in the street. They don't let us do nothing here. It's worser than school."

"Ain't it a play-room?" asks I. "Don't they let you play?"

"Gee wiss! play-room, they call it! The nurse hollers on us all the time. She don't let us do nothing."

The reasons why I stayed out the whole two weeks is this: I think to myself, so much shame in the face I suffered to come here, let me at least make the best from it already. Let me at least save up for two weeks what I got to spend out for grocery and butcher for my back bills to pay out. And then also think I to myself, if I go back on Monday, I got to do the big washing; on Tuesday waits for me the ironing; on Wednesday, the scrubbing and cleaning, and so goes it on. How bad it is already in this place, it's a change from the very same sameness of what I'm having day in and day out at home. And so I stayed out this vacation to the bitter end.

But at last the day for going out from this prison came. On the way riding back, I kept thinking to myself: "This is such a beautiful vacation house. For why do they make it so hard for us? When a mother needs a vacation, why must they tear the insides out from her first, by making her come down to the charity office? Why drag us from the charity office through the streets? And when we live through the shame of the charities and when we come already to the vacation house, for why do they boss the life out of us with so many rules and bells? For why don't they let us lay down our heads on the bed when we are tired? For why must we always stick in the back, like dogs what have got to be chained in one spot? If they would let us walk around free, would we bite off something from the front part of the house?

"If the best part of the house what is comfortable is made up for a show for visitors, why ain't they keeping the whole business for a show for visitors? For why do they have to fool in worn-out mothers, to make them think they'll give them a rest? Do they need the worn-out mothers as part of the show? I guess that is it, already."

When I got back in my home, so happy and thankful I was I could cry from thankfulness. How good it was feeling for me to be able to move around my own house, like I pleased. I was always kicking that my rooms was small and narrow, but now my small rooms seemed to grow so big like the park. I looked out from my window on the fire-escapes, full with bedding and garbage-cans, and on the wash-lines full with the clothes. All these ugly things was grand in my eyes. Even the high brick walls all around made me feel like a bird what just jumped out from a cage. And I cried out, "Gott sei dank! Gott sei dank!"

—1920

DOROTHY WEST
(1907–1998)

The daughter of a former slave who became a successful businessman, Dorothy West was born and raised in Boston. She was tutored at home before she attended public schools and Girl's Latin School and, later, studied at Boston University and Columbia University School of Journalism. She was the youngest of the distinguished group of African-American writers and artists who were known for the Harlem Renaissance movement in the 1920s and became a close friend of Langston Hughes, Countee Cullen, and Zora Neale Hurston. During the 1930s, she founded two magazines, *Challenge* and *New Challenge*, in which she hoped to publish the work of young black writers to keep the spirit of the Harlem Renaissance alive. She also became a Harlem welfare investigator and worked for the Federal Writers Project. From 1947 to 1998, she lived at her family's former vacation home in Oak Bluffs on Martha's Vineyard and contributed regularly to *The Vineyard Gazette*. Although she began publishing her work as a teenager, her first novel, *The Living Is Easy*, was not published until 1948. In 1995, at the age of eighty-eight, she became a best-selling author when she published two books, the novel *The Wedding* and the story and essay collection *The Richer, The Poorer*. *The Wedding*, which depicts well-educated, upper-middle-class African-American families on Martha's Vineyard, was filmed as a two-part television movie by Oprah Winfrey in 1998.

Jack in the Pot

WHEN she walked down the aisle of the theater, clutching the money in her hand, hearing the applause and laughter, seeing, dimly, the grinning black faces, she was trembling so violently that she did not know how she could ever regain her seat.

It was unbelievable. Week after week she had come on Wednesday afternoon to this smelly, third-run neigh-

borhood movie house, paid her dime, received her beano
card, and gone inside to wait through an indifferent fea-
ture until the house lights came on, and a too jovial
white man wheeled a board onto the stage and busily
fished in a bowl for numbers.

Today it had happened. As the too jovial white man
called each number, she found a corresponding one on
her card. When he called the seventh number and explained dramatically that whoever had punched five
numbers in a row had won the jackpot of fifty-five dollars, she listened in smiling disbelief that there was that
much money in his pocket. It was then that the woman
beside her leaned toward her and said excitedly, "Look,
lady, you got it!"

She did not remember going down the aisle. Undoubt-
edly her neighbor had prodded her to her feet. When it
was over, she tottered dazedly to her seat, and sat in a
dreamy stupor, scarcely able to believe her good fortune.

The drawing continued, the last dollar was given away,
the theater darkened, and the afternoon crowd filed out.
The little gray woman, collecting her wits, followed
them.

She revived in the sharp air. Her head cleared and
happiness swelled in her throat. She had fifty-five dollars
in her purse. It was wonderful to think about.

She reached her own intersection and paused before
Mr. Spiro's general market. Here she regularly shopped,
settling part of her bill fortnightly out of her relief check.
When Mr. Spiro put in inferior stock because most of
his customers were poor-paying reliefers, she had wanted
to shop elsewhere. But she could never get paid up.

Excitement smote her. She would go in, settle her account, and say good-bye to Mr. Spiro forever. Resolutely
she turned into the market.

Mr. Spiro, broad and unkempt, began to boom heart-
ily, from behind the counter, "Hello, Mrs. Edmunds."

She lowered her eyes and asked diffidently, "How
much is my bill, Mr. Spiro?"

He recoiled in horror. "Do I worry about your bill,
Mrs. Edmunds? Don't you pay something when you get
your relief check? Ain't you one of my best customers?"

"I'd like to settle," said Mrs. Edmunds breathlessly.

Mr. Spiro eyed her shrewdly. His voice was soft and insinuating. "You got cash, Mrs. Edmunds? You hit the number? Every other week you give me something on account. This week you want to settle. Am I losing your trade? Ain't I always treated you right?"

"Sure, Mr. Spiro," she answered nervously. "I was telling my husband just last night, ain't another man treats me like Mr. Spiro. And I said I wished I could settle my bill."

"Gee," he said triumphantly, "it's like I said. You're one of my best customers. Worrying about your bill when I ain't even worrying. I was telling your investigator . . . ," he paused significantly, "when Mr. Edmunds gets a job, I know I'll get the balance. Mr. Edmunds got himself a job maybe?"

She was stiff with fright. "No, I'd have told you right off, and her, too. I ain't one to cheat on relief. I was only saying how I wished I could settle. I wasn't saying that I was."

"Well, then, what you want for supper?" Mr. Spiro asked soothingly.

"Loaf of bread," she answered gratefully, "two pork chops, one kinda thick, can of spaghetti, little can of milk."

The purchases were itemized. Mrs. Edmunds said good night and left the store. She felt sick and ashamed, for she had turned tail in the moment that was to have been her triumph over tyranny.

A little boy came toward her in the familiar rags of the neighborhood children. Suddenly Mrs. Edmunds could bear no longer the intolerable weight of her mean provisions.

"Little boy," she said.

"Ma'am?" He stopped and stared at her.

"Here." She held out the bag to him. "Take it home to your mama. It's food. It's clean."

He blinked, then snatched the bag from her hands, and turned and ran very fast in the direction from which he had come.

Mrs. Edmunds felt better at once. Now she could buy a really good supper. She walked ten blocks to a better neighborhood and the cold did not bother her. Her misshapen shoes were winged.

She pushed inside a resplendent store and marched to the meat counter. A porterhouse steak caught her eye. She could not look past it. It was big and thick and beautiful.

The clerk leaned toward her. "Steak, moddom?"

"That one."

It was glorious not to care about the cost of things. She bought mushrooms, fresh peas, cauliflower, tomatoes, a pound of good coffee, a pint of real cream, a dozen dinner rolls, and a maple walnut layer cake.

The winter stars were pricking the sky when she entered the dimly lit hallway of the old-law tenement in which she lived. The dank smell smote her instantly after the long walk in the brisk, clear air. The Smith boy's dog had dirtied the hall again. Mr. Johnson, the janitor, was mournfully mopping up.

"Evenin', Mis' Edmunds, ma'am," he said plaintively.

"Evening," Mrs. Edmunds said coldly. Suddenly she hated Mr. Johnson. He was so humble.

Five young children shared the uninhabitable basement with him. They were always half sick, and he was always neglecting his duties to tend to them. The tenants were continually deciding to report him to the agent, and then at the last moment deciding not to.

"I'll be up tomorrow to see 'bout them windows, Mis' Edmunds, ma'am. My baby kep' frettin' today, and I been so busy doctorin'."

"Those children need a mother," said Mrs. Edmunds severely. "You ought to get married again."

"My wife ain' daid," cried Mr. Johnson, shocked out of his servility. "She's in that T.B. home. Been there two years and 'bout on the road to health."

"Well," said Mrs. Edmunds inconclusively, and then added briskly, "I been waiting weeks and weeks for them window strips. Winter's half over. If the place was kept warm—"

"Yes'm, Mis' Edmunds," he said hastily, his bloodshot eyes imploring. "It's that ol' furnace. I done tol' the agent time and again, but they ain' fixin' to fix up this house 'long as you all is relief folks."

*   *   *

The steak was sizzling on the stove when Mr. Edmunds'
key turned in the lock of the tiny three-room flat. His
step dragged down the hall. Mrs. Edmunds knew what
that meant: "No man wanted." Two years ago Mr. Edmunds had begun, doggedly, to canvass the city for
work, leaving home soon after breakfast and rarely returning before supper.

Once he had had a little stationery store. After losing
it, he had spent his small savings and sold or pawned
every decent article of furniture and clothing before
applying for relief. Even so, there had been a long investigation while he and his wife slowly starved. Fear had
been implanted in Mrs. Edmunds. Thereafter she was
never wholly unafraid. Mr. Edmunds had had to stand
by and watch his wife starve. He never got over being
ashamed.

Mr. Edmunds stood in the kitchen doorway, holding
his rain-streaked hat in his knotted hand. He was forty-
nine, and he looked like an old man.

"I'm back," he said. "Cooking supper."

It was not a question. He seemed unaware of the in-
toxicating odors.

She smiled at him brightly. "Smell good?"

He shook suddenly with the cold that was still in him.
"Smells like always to me."

Her face fell in disappointment, but she said gently,
"You oughtn't to be walking 'round this kind of
weather."

"I was looking for work," he said fiercely. "Work's
not going to come knocking."

She did not want to quarrel with him. He was too
cold, and their supper was too fine.

"Things'll pick up in the spring," she said soothingly.

"Not for me," he answered gloomily. "Look how I
look. Like a bum. I wouldn't hire me, myself."

"What you want me to do about it?" she asked
furiously.

"Nothing," he said with wry humor, "unless you can
make money, and make me just about fifty dollars."

She caught her breath and stared at his shabbiness.

She had seen him look like this so long that she had forgotten that clothes would make a difference.

She nodded toward the stove. "That steak and all. Guess you think I got a fortune. Well, I won a little old measly dollar at the movies."

His face lightened, and his eyes grew soft with affection. "You shouldn't have bought a steak," he said. "Wish you'd bought yourself something you been wanting. Like gloves. Some good warm gloves. Hurts my heart when I see you with cold hands."

She was ashamed, and wished she knew how to cross the room to kiss him. "Go wash," she said gruffly. "Steak's 'most too done already."

It was a wonderful dinner. Both of them had been starved for fresh meat. Mrs. Edmunds' face was flushed, and there was color in her lips, as if the good blood of the meat had filtered through her skin. Mr. Edmunds ate a pound and a half of the two-pound steak, and his hands seemed steadier with each sharp thrust of the knife.

Over coffee and cake they talked contentedly. Mrs. Edmunds wanted to tell the truth about the money, and waited for an opening.

"We'll move out of this hole some day soon," said Mr. Edmunds. "Things won't be like this always." He was full and warm and confident.

"If I had fifty dollars," Mrs. Edmunds began cautiously, "I believe I'd move tomorrow. Pay up these people what I owe, and get me a fit place to live in."

"Fifty dollars would be a drop in the bucket. You got to have something coming in steady."

He had hurt her again. "Fifty dollars is more than you got," she said meanly.

"It's more than you got, too," he said mildly. "Look at it like this. If you had fifty dollars and made a change, them relief folks would worry you like a pack of wolves. But say, f' instance, you had fifty dollars, and I had a job, we could walk out of here without a howdy-do to anybody."

It would have been anticlimactic to tell him about the money. She got up. "I'll do the dishes. You sit still."

He noticed no change in her and went on earnestly, "Lord's bound to put something in my way soon. Things is got to break for us. We don't live human. I never see a paper 'cept when I pick one up on the subway. I ain't had a cigarette in three years. We ain't got a radio. We don't have no company. All the pleasure you get is a ten-cent movie one day a week. I don't even get that."

Presently Mrs. Edmunds ventured, "You think the investigator would notice if we got a little radio for the bedroom?"

"Somebody got one to give away?" His voice was eager.

"Maybe."

"Well, seeing how she could check with the party what give it to you, I think it would be all right."

"Well, ne' mind—" Her voice petered out.

It was his turn to try. "Want to play me a game of cards?"

He had not asked her for months. She cleared her throat. "I'll play a hand or two."

He stretched luxuriously. "I feel so good. Feeling like this, bet I'll land something tomorrow."

She said very gently, "The investigator comes tomorrow."

He smiled quickly to hide his disappointment. "Clean forgot. It don't matter. That meal was so good it'll carry me straight through Friday."

She opened her mouth to tell him about the jackpot, to promise him as many meals as there was money. Suddenly someone upstairs pounded on the radiator for heat. In a moment someone downstairs pounded. Presently their side of the house resounded. It was maddening. Mrs. Edmunds was bitterly aware that her hands and feet were like ice.

" 'Tisn't no use," she cried wildly to the walls. She burst into tears. " 'Tisn't nothing no use."

Her husband crossed quickly to her. He kissed her cheek. "I'm going to make all this up to you. You'll see."

By half past eight they were in bed. By quarter to nine Mrs. Edmunds was quietly sleeping. Mr. Edmunds lay staring at the ceiling. It kept coming closer.

Mrs. Edmunds waked first and decided to go again to the grand market. She dressed and went out into the street. An ambulance stood in front of the door. In a minute an intern emerged from the basement, carrying a bundled child. Mr. Johnson followed, his eyes more bleary and bloodshot than ever.

Mrs. Edmunds rushed up to him. "The baby?" she asked anxiously.

His face worked pitifully. "Yes, ma'am, Mis' Edmunds. Pneumonia. I heard you folks knockin' for heat last night but my hands was too full. I ain't forgot about them windows, though. I'll be up tomorrow bright and early."

Mr. Edmunds stood in the kitchen door. "I smell meat in the morning?" he asked incredulously. He sat down, and she spread the feast, kidneys, and omelet, hot buttered rolls, and strawberry jam. "You mind," he said happily, "explaining this mystery? Was that dollar of yours made out of elastic?"

"It wasn't a dollar like I said. It was five. I wanted to surprise you."

She did not look at him and her voice was breathless. She had decided to wait until after the investigator's visit to tell him the whole truth about the money. Otherwise they might both be nervous and betray themselves by their guilty knowledge.

"We got chicken for dinner," she added shyly.

"Lord, I don't know when I had a piece of chicken."

They ate, and the morning passed glowingly. With Mr. Edmunds' help, Mrs. Edmunds moved the furniture and gave the flat a thorough cleaning. She liked for the investigator to find her busy. She felt less embarrassed about being on relief when it could be seen that she occupied her time.

The afternoon waned. The Edmundses sat in the living room, and there was nothing to do. They were hungry but dared not start dinner. With activity suspended, they became aware of the penetrating cold and the rattling windows. Mr. Edmunds began to have that wild look of waiting for the investigator.

Mrs. Edmunds suddenly had an idea. She would go and get a newspaper and a package of cigarettes for him.

At the corner, she ran into Mr. Johnson. Rather he ran into her, for he turned the corner with his head down, and his gait as unsteady as if he had been drinking.

"That you, Mr. Johnson?" she said sharply.

He raised his head, and she saw that he was not drunk.

"Yes, ma'am, Mis' Edmunds."

"The baby—is she worse?"

Tears welled out of his eyes. "The Lord done took her."

Tears stood in her own eyes. "God knows I'm sorry to hear that. Let me know if there's anything I can do."

"Thank you, Mis' Edmunds, ma'am. But ain't nothin' nobody can do. I been pricin' funerals. I can get one for fifty dollars. But I been to my brother, and he ain't got it. I been everywhere. Couldn't raise no more than ten dollars." He was suddenly embarrassed. "I know all you tenants is on relief. I wasn't fixin' to ask you all."

"Fifty dollars," she said strainedly, "is a lot of money."

"God'd have to pass a miracle for me to raise it. Guess the city'll have to bury her. You reckon they'll let me take flowers?"

"You being the father, I guess they would," she said weakly.

When she returned home the flat was a little warmer. She entered the living room. Her husband's face brightened.

"You bought a paper!"

She held out the cigarettes. "You smoke this kind?" she asked lifelessly.

He jumped up and crossed to her. "I declare I don't know how to thank you! Wish that investigator'd come. I sure want to taste them."

"Go ahead and smoke," she cried fiercely. "It's none of her business. We got our rights same as working people."

She turned into the bedroom. She was utterly spent. Too much had happened in the last twenty-four hours.

"Guess I'll stretch out for a bit. I'm not going to sleep.

If I do drop off, listen out for the investigator. The bell needs fixing. She might have to knock."

At half past five Mr. Edmunds put down the newspaper and tiptoed to the bedroom door. His wife was still asleep. He stood for a moment in indecision, then decided it was long past the hour when the investigator usually called, and went down the hall to the kitchen. He wanted to prepare supper as a surprise. He opened the window, took the foodstuffs out of the crate that in winter served as icebox, and set them on the table.

The doorbell tinkled faintly.

He went to the door and opened it. The investigator stepped inside. She was small and young and white.

"Good evening, miss," he said.

"I'm sorry to call so late," she apologized. "I've been busy all day with an evicted family. But I knew you were expecting me, and I didn't want you to stay in tomorrow."

"You come on up front, miss," he said. "I'll wake up my wife. She wasn't feeling so well and went to lie down."

She saw the light from the kitchen, and the dark rooms beyond.

"Don't wake Mrs. Edmunds," she said kindly, "if she isn't well. I'll just sit in the kitchen for a minute with you."

He looked down at her, but her open, honest face did not disarm him. He braced himself for whatever was to follow.

"Go right on in, miss," he said.

He took the dish towel and dusted the clean chair. "Sit down, miss."

He stood facing her with a furrow between his brows, and his arms folded. There was an awkward pause. She cast about for something to say, and saw the table.

"I interrupted your dinner preparations."

His voice and his face hardened for the blow.

"I was getting dinner for my wife. It's chicken."

"It looks like a nice one," she said pleasantly.

He was baffled. "We ain't had chicken once in three years."

"I understand," she said sincerely. "Sometimes I spend my whole salary on something I want very much."

"You ain't much like an investigator," he said in surprise. "One we had before you woulda raised Ned." He sat down suddenly, his defenses down. "Miss, I been wanting to ask you this for a long time. You ever have any men's clothes?"

Her voice was distressed. "Every once in a while. But with so many people needing assistance, we can only give them to our employables. But I'll keep your request in mind."

He did not answer. He just sat staring at the floor, presenting an adjustment problem. There was nothing else to say to him.

She rose. "I'll be going now, Mr. Edmunds."

"I'll tell my wife you was here, miss."

A voice called from the bedroom. "Is that you talking?"

"It's the investigator lady," he said. "She's just going."

Mrs. Edmunds came hurrying down the hall, the sleep in her face and tousled hair.

"I was just lying down, ma'am. I didn't mean to go to sleep. My husband should've called me."

"I didn't want him to wake you."

"And he kept you sitting in the kitchen."

She glanced inside to assure herself that it was sufficiently spotless for the fine clothes of the investigator. She saw the laden table, and felt so ill that water welled into her mouth.

"The investigator lady knows about the chicken," Mr. Edmunds said quickly. "She—"

"It was only five dollars," his wife interrupted, wringing her hands.

"Five dollars for a chicken?" The investigator was shocked and incredulous.

"She didn't buy that chicken out of none of your relief money," Mr. Edmunds said defiantly. "It was money she won at a movie."

"It was only five dollars," Mrs. Edmunds repeated tearfully.

"We ain't trying to conceal nothing," Mr. Edmunds

snarled. He was cornered and fighting. "If you'd asked me how we come by the chicken, I'd have told you."

"For God's sake, ma'am, don't cut us off," Mrs. Edmunds moaned. "I'll never go to another movie. It was only ten cents. I didn't know I was doing wrong." She burst into tears.

The investigator stood tense. They had both been screaming at her. She was tired and so irritated that she wanted to scream back.

"Mrs. Edmunds," she said sharply, "get hold of yourself. I'm not going to cut you off. That's ridiculous. You won five dollars at a movie and you bought some food. That's fine. I wish my family could win five dollars for food."

She turned and tore out of the flat. They heard her stumbling and sobbing down the stairs.

"You feel like eating?" Mrs. Edmunds asked dully.

"I guess we're both hungry. That's why we got so upset."

"Maybe we'd better eat, then."

"Let me fix it."

"No." She entered the kitchen. "I kinda want to see you just sitting and smoking a cigarette."

He sat down and reached in his pocket with some eagerness. "I ain't had one yet." He lit a cigarette, inhaled, and felt better immediately.

"You think," she said bleakly, "she'll write that up in our case?"

"I don't know, dear."

"You think they'll close our case if she does?"

"I don't know that neither, dear."

She clutched the sink for support. "My God, what would we do?"

The smoke curled around him luxuriously. "Don't think about it till it happens."

"I got to think about it. The rent, the gas, the light, the food."

"They wouldn't hardly close our case for five dollars."

"Maybe they'd think it was more."

"You could prove it by the movie manager."

She went numb all over. Then suddenly she got mad about it.

It was nine o'clock when they sat down in the living room. The heat came up grudgingly. Mrs. Edmunds wrapped herself in her sweater and read the funnies. Mr. Edmunds was happily inhaling his second cigarette. They were both replete and in good humor.

The window rattled and Mr. Edmunds looked around at it lazily. "Been about two months since you asked Mr. Johnson for weather strips."

The paper shook in her hand. She did not look up. "He promised to fix it this morning, but his baby died."

"His baby! You don't say!"

She kept her eyes glued to the paper. "Pneumonia."

His voice filled with sympathy. He crushed out his cigarette. "Believe I'll go down and sit with him a while."

"He's not there," she said hastily. "I met him when I was going to the store. He said he'd be out all evening."

"I bet the poor man's trying to raise some money."

She let the paper fall in her lap, and clasped her hands to keep them from trembling. She lied again, as she had been lying steadily in the past twenty-four hours, as she had not lied before in all her life.

"He didn't say nothing to me about raising money."

"Wasn't no need to. Where would you get the first five cents to give him?"

"I guess," she cried jealously, "you want me to give him the rest of my money."

"No," he said. "I want you to spend what little's left on yourself. Me, I wish I had fifty dollars to give him."

"As poor as you are," she asked angrily, "you'd give him that much money? That's easy to say when you haven't got it."

"I look at it this way," he said simply. "I think how I'd feel in his shoes."

"You got your own troubles," she argued heatedly. "The Johnson baby is better off dead. You'd be a fool to put fifty dollars in the ground. I'd spend my fifty dollars on the living."

"Tain't no use to work yourself up," he said. "You ain't got fifty dollars, and neither have I. We'll be quar-

reling in a minute over make-believe money. Let's go
to bed."

Mrs. Edmunds waked at seven and tried to lie quietly
by her husband's side, but lying still was torture. She
dressed and went into the kitchen, and felt too listless
to make her coffee. She sat down at the table and
dropped her head on her folded arms. No tears came.
There was only the burning in her throat and behind
her eyes.

She sat in this manner for half an hour. Suddenly she
heard a man's slow tread outside her front door. Terror
gripped her. The steps moved on down the hall, but for
a moment her knees were water. When she could control
her trembling, she stood up and knew that she had to
get out of the house. It could not contain her and Mr.
Johnson.

She walked quickly away from her neighborhood. It
was a raw day, and her feet and hands were beginning
to grow numb. She felt sorry for herself. Other people
were hurrying past in overshoes and heavy gloves. There
were fifty-one dollars in her purse. It was her right to
do what she pleased with them. Determinedly she turned
into the subway.

In a downtown department store she rode the escalator to the dress department. She walked up and down
the rows of lovely garments, stopping to finger critically,
standing back to admire.

A salesgirl came toward her, looking straight at her
with soft, expectant eyes.

"Do you wish to be waited on, madam?"

Mrs. Edmunds opened her mouth to say "Yes," but
the word would not come. She stared at the girl stupidly.
"I was just looking," she said.

In the shoe department, she saw a pair of comfort
shoes and sat down timidly in a fine leather chair.

A salesman lounged toward her. "Something in shoes?"

"Yes, sir. That comfort shoe."

"Size?" His voice was bored.

"I don't know," she said.

"I'll have to measure you," he said reproachfully.

"Give me your foot." He sat down on a stool and held out his hand.

She dragged her eyes up to his face. "How much you say those shoes cost?"

"I didn't say. Eight dollars."

She rose with acute relief. "I ain't got that much with me."

She retreated unsteadily. Something was making her knees weak and her head light.

Her legs steadied. She went quickly to the down escalator. She reached the third floor and was briskly crossing to the next down escalator when she saw the little dresses. A banner screamed that they were selling at the sacrifice price of one dollar. She decided to examine them.

She pushed through the crowd of women, and emerged triumphantly within reach of the dresses. She searched carefully. There were pinks and blues and yellows. She was looking for white. She pushed back through the crowd. In her careful hands lay a little white dress. It was spun gold and gossamer.

Boldly she beckoned a salesgirl. "I'll take this, miss," she said.

All the way home she was excited and close to tears. She was in a fever to see Mr. Johnson. She would let the regret come later. A child lay dead and waiting burial.

She turned her corner at a run. Going down the rickety basement stairs, she prayed that Mr. Johnson was on the premises.

She pounded on his door and he opened it. The agony in his face told her instantly that he had been unable to borrow the money. She tried to speak, and her tongue tripped over her eagerness.

Fear took hold of her and rattled her teeth. "Mr. Johnson, what about the funeral?"

"I give the baby to the student doctors."

"Oh my God, Mr. Johnson! Oh my God!"

"I bought her some flowers."

She turned and went blindly up the stairs. Drooping in the front doorway was a frost-nipped bunch of white flowers. She dragged herself up to her flat. Once she stopped to hide the package under her coat. She would never look at that little white dress again. The ten five-dollar bills were ten five-pound stones in her purse. They almost hurled her backward.

She turned the key in her lock. Mr. Edmunds stood at the door. He looked rested and confident.

"I been waiting for you. I just started to go."

"You had any breakfast?" she asked tonelessly.

"I made some coffee. It was all I wanted."

"I shoulda made some oatmeal before I went out."

"You have on the big pot time I come home. Bet I'll land something good," he boasted. "You brought good luck in this house. We ain't seen the last of it." He pecked her cheek and went out, hurrying as if he were late for work.

She plodded into the bedroom. The steam was coming up fine. She sank down on the side of the bed and unbuttoned her coat. The package fell on her lap. She took the ten five-dollar bills and pushed them between a fold of the package. It was burial money. She could never use it for anything else. She hid the package under the mattress.

Wearily she buttoned up her coat and opened her purse again. It was empty, for the few cents remaining from her last relief check had been spent indiscriminately with her prize money.

She went into the kitchen to take stock of her needs. There was nothing left from their feasts. She felt the coffeepot. It was still hot, but her throat was too constricted for her to attempt to swallow.

She took her paper shopping bag and started out to Mr. Spiro's.

—1995

SARAH ORNE JEWETT

(1849–1909)

At nineteen, under a pseudonym, Sarah Orne Jewett published her first short story, "Jenny Garrow's Lovers," thus embarking on a long and successful career as an author. Although she was graduated from Berwick Academy, the strongest educational influence in her life was her father, Dr. Theodore Herman Jewett, a country physician. Traveling with her father about South Berwick, Maine, as he visited his patients, the young girl absorbed a great many impressions of human nature and became as well a perceptive observer of the New England seacoast and countryside. To a large extent, these experiences informed her vision as she began to write fresh and vivid short stories of rural American life. Among her works are *Deephaven* (1877), *Country By-Ways* (1881), *A Country Doctor* (1884), *A Marsh Island* (1885), *A White Heron and Other Stories* (1886), and *The Queen's Twin and Other Stories* (1899). Her most famous and most representative work is *The Country of the Pointed Firs* (1896).

Miss Esther's Guest

I

OLD Miss Porley put on her silk shawl, and arranged it carefully over her thin shoulders, and pinned it with a hand that shook a little as if she were much excited. She bent forward to examine the shawl in the mahogany-framed mirror, for there was a frayed and tender spot in the silk where she had pinned it so many years. The shawl was very old; it had been her mother's, and she disliked to wear it too often, but she never could make up her mind to go out into the street in summer, as some of her neighbors did, with nothing over her shoulders at all. Next she put on her bonnet and tried to set it straight, allowing for a wave in the looking-glass

that made one side of her face appear much longer than
the other; then she drew on a pair of well-darned silk
gloves; one had a wide crack all the way up the back of
the hand, but they were still neat and decent for everyday wear, if she were careful to keep her left hand under
the edge of the shawl. She had discussed the propriety
of drawing the raveled silk together, but a thick seam
would look very ugly, and there was something acciden-
tal about the crack.

Then, after hesitating a few moments, she took a small
piece of folded white letter-paper from the table and
went out of the house, locking the door and trying it,
and stepped away bravely down the village street. Everybody said, "How do you do, Miss Porley?" or "Good-
mornin', Esther." Every one in Daleham knew the good
woman; she was one of the unchanging persons, always
to be found in her place, and always pleased and friendly
and ready to take an interest in old and young. She and
her mother, who had early been left a widow, had been
for many years the village tailoresses and makers of little
boys' clothes. Mrs. Porley had been dead three years,
however, and her daughter "Easter," as old friends
called our heroine, had lived quite alone. She was made
very sorrowful by her loneliness, but she never could be
persuaded to take anybody to board: she could not bear
to think of any one's taking her mother's place.

It was a warm summer morning, and Miss Porley had
not very far to walk, but she was still more shaky and
excited by the time she reached the First Church parsonage. She stood at the gate undecidedly, and, after she
pushed it open a little way, she drew back again, and
felt a curious beating at her heart and general reluctance
of mind and body. At that moment the minister's wife,
a pleasant young woman with a smiling, eager face,
looked out of the window and asked the tremulous visitor to come in. Miss Esther straightened herself and
went briskly up the walk; she was very fond of the minister's wife, who had only been in Daleham a few months.

"Won't you take off your shawl?" asked Mrs. Wayton
affectionately; "I have just been making gingerbread,
and you shall have a piece as soon as it cools."

"I don't know's I ought to stop," answered Miss Esther, flushing quickly. "I came on business; I won't keep you long."

"Oh, please stay a little while," urged the hostess. "I'll take my sewing, if you don't mind; there are two or three things that I want to ask you about."

"I've thought and flustered a sight over taking this step," said good old Esther abruptly. "I had to conquer a sight o' reluctance, I must say. I've got so used to livin' by myself that I sha'n't know how to consider another. But I see I ain't got common feelin' for others unless I can set my own comfort aside once in a while. I've brought you my name as one of those that will take one o' them city folks that needs a spell o' change. It come straight home to me how I should be feeling it by this time, if my lot had been cast in one o' them city garrets that the minister described so affecting. If 't hadn't been for kind consideration somewheres, mother an' me might have sewed all them pleasant years away in the city that we enjoyed so in our own home, and our garden to step right out into when our sides set in to ache. And I ain't rich, but we was able to save a little something, and now I'm eatin' of it all up alone. It come to me I should like to have somebody take a taste out o' mother's part. Now, don't you let 'em send me no rampin' boys like them Barnard's folks had come last year, that vexed dumb creatur's so; and I don't know how to cope with no kind o' men-folks or strange girls, but I should know how to do for a woman that's getting well along in years, an' has come to feel kind o' spent. P'raps we ain't no right to pick an' choose, but I should know best how to make that sort comfortable on 'count of doin' for mother and studying what she preferred."

Miss Esther rose with quaint formality and put the folded paper, on which she had neatly written her name and address, into Mrs. Wayton's hand. Mrs. Wayton rose soberly to receive it, and then they both sat down again.

"I'm sure that you will feel more than repaid for your kindness, dear Miss Esther," said the minister's wife. "I know one of the ladies who have charge of the arrangements for the Country Week, and I will explain as well as I can the kind of guest you have in mind. I quite envy her: I have often thought, when I was busy and tired,

how much I should like to run along the street and make
you a visit in your dear old-fashioned little house."

"I should be more than pleased to have you, I'm
sure," said Miss Esther, startled into a bright smile and
forgetting her anxiety. "Come any day, and take me just
as I am. We used to have a good deal o' company years
ago, when there was a number o' mother's folks still
livin' over Ashfield way. Sure as we had a pile o' work
on hand and was hurrying for dear life an' limb, a
wagon-load would light down at the front gate to spend
the day an' have an early tea. Mother never was one to
get flustered same's I do 'bout everything. She was a
lovely cook, and she'd fill 'em up an' cheer 'em, and git
'em off early as she could, an' then we'd be kind o'
waked up an' spirited ourselves, and would set up late
sewin' and talkin' the company over, an' I 'd have things
saved to tell her that had been said while she was out
o' the room. I make such a towse over everything myself,
but mother was waked right up and felt pleased an'
smart, if anything unexpected happened. I miss her more
every year," and Miss Esther gave a great sigh. "I s'pose
't wa'n't reasonable to expect that I could have her to
help me through with old age, but I'm a poor tool,
alone."

"Oh, no, you mustn't say that!" exclaimed the minister's wife. "Why, nobody could get along without you.
I wish I had come to Daleham in time to know your
mother too."

Miss Esther shook her head sadly. "She would have
set everything by you and Mr. Wayton. Now I must be
getting back in case I'm wanted, but you let 'em send
me somebody right away, while my bush beans is so nice.
An' if any o' your little boy's clothes wants repairin', just
give 'em to me; 't will be a real pleasant thing to set a
few stitches. Or the minister's; ain't there something
needed for him?"

Mrs. Wayton was about to say no, when she became
conscious of the pleading old face before her. "I'm sure
you are most kind, dear friend," she answered, "and I
do have a great deal to do. I'll bring you two or three
things to-night that are beyond my art, as I go to evening
meeting. Mr. Wayton frayed out his best coat sleeve yes-

terday, and I was disheartened, for we had counted upon
his not having a new one before the fall."

" 'T would be mere play to me," said Miss Esther,
and presently she went smiling down the street.

II

The Committee for the Country Week in a certain
ward of Boston were considering the long list of children, and mothers with babies, and sewing-women, who
were looking forward, some of them for the first time in
many years, to a country holiday. Some were to go as
guests to hospitable, generous farmhouses that opened
their doors willingly now and then to tired city people;
for some persons board could be paid.

The immediate arrangements of that time were settled
at last, except that Mrs. Belton, the chairman, suddenly
took a letter from her pocket. "I had almost forgotten
this," she said; "it is another place offered in dear quiet
old Daleham. My friend, the minister's wife there, writes
me a word about it: 'The applicant desires especially an
old person, being used to the care of an aged parent and
sure of her power of making such a one comfortable,
and she would like to have her guest come as soon as
possible.' My friend asks me to choose a person of some
refinement—'one who would appreciate the delicate simplicity and quaint ways of the hostess.' "

Mrs. Belton glanced hurriedly down the page. "I believe that's all," she said. "How about that nice old sew-
ing-woman, Mrs. Connolly, in Bantry Street?"

"Oh, no!" someone entreated, looking up from her
writing. "Why isn't it just the place for my old Mr. Rill,
the dear old Englishman who lives alone up four flights
in Town Court and has the bullfinch? He used to en-
grave seals, and his eyes gave out, and he is so thrifty
with his own bit of savings and an atom of a pension.
Someone pays his expenses to the country, and this
sounds like a place he would be sure to like. I've been
watching for the right chance."

"Take it, then," said the busy chairman, and there was
a little more writing and talking, and then the committee

meeting was over which settled Miss Esther Porley's
fate.

III

The journey to Daleham was a great experience to
Mr. Rill. He was a sensible old person, who knew well
that he was getting stiffer and clumsier than need be in
his garret, and that, as certain friends had said, a short
time spent in the country would cheer and invigorate
him. There had been occasional propositions that he
should leave his garret altogether and go to the country
to live, or at least to the suburbs of the city. He could
not see things close at hand so well as he could take a
wide outlook, and as his outlook from the one garret
window was a still higher brick wall and many chimneys,
he was losing a great deal that he might have had. But
so long as he was expected to take an interest in the
unseen and unknown he failed to accede to any plans
about the country home, and declared that he was well
enough in his high abode. He had lost a sister a few
years before who had been his mainstay, but with his
hands so well used to delicate work he had been less
bungling in his simple household affairs than many another man might have been. But he was very lonely and
was growing anxious; as he was rattled along in the train
toward Daleham he held the chirping bullfinch's cage
fast with both hands, and said to himself now and then,
"This may lead to something: the country air smells very
good to me."

The Daleham station was not very far out of the village, so that Miss Esther Porley put on her silk shawl
and bonnet and everyday gloves just before four o'clock
that afternoon, and went to meet her Country Week
guest. Word had come the day before that the person
for Miss Porley's would start two days in advance of the
little company of children and helpless women, and since
this message had come from the parsonage Miss Esther
had worked diligently, late and early, to have her house
in proper order. Whatever her mother had liked was
thought of and provided. There were going to be rye
short-cakes for tea, and there were some sprigs of thyme

and sweet-balm in an old-fashioned wine-glass on the keeping-room table; mother always said they were so freshening. And Miss Esther had taken out a little shoulder-shawl and folded it over the arm of the rocking-chair by the window that looked out into the small garden where the London-pride was in full bloom, and the morning-glories had just begun to climb. Miss Esther was sixty-four herself, but still looked upon age as well in the distance.

She was always a prompt person, and had some minutes to wait at the station; then the time passed and the train was late. At last she saw the smoke far in the distance, and her heart began to sink. Perhaps she would not find it easy to get on with the old lady, and—well it was only for a week, and she had thought it right and best to take such a step, and now it would soon be over.

The train stopped, and there was no old lady at all.

Miss Esther had stood far back to get away from the smoke and roar—she was always as afraid of the cars as she could be—but as they moved away she took a few steps forward to scan the platform. There was no black bonnet with a worn lace veil, and no old lady with a burden of bundles; there were only the station master and two or three men, and an idle boy or two, and one clean-faced, bent old man with a bird-cage in one hand and an old carpet-bag in the other. She thought of the rye short-cakes for supper and all that she had done to make her small home pleasant, and her fire of excitement suddenly fell into ashes.

The old man with the bird-cage suddenly turned toward her. "Can you direct me to Miss Esther Porley's?" said he.

"I can," replied Miss Esther, looking at him with curiosity.

"I was directed to her house," said the pleasant old fellow, "by Mrs. Belton, of the Country Week Committee. My eyesight is poor. I should be glad if anybody would help me to find the place."

"You step this way with me, sir," said Miss Esther. She was afraid that the men on the platform heard every word they said, but nobody took particular notice, and off they walked down the road together. Miss Esther was enraged with the Country Week Committee.

"*You* were sent to—Miss Porley's?" she asked grimly, turning to look at him.

"I was, indeed," said Mr. Rill.

"I am Miss Porley, and I expected an old lady," she managed to say, and they both stopped and looked at each other with apprehension.

"I do declare!" faltered the old seal-cutter anxiously. "What had I better do, ma'am? They most certain give me your name. May be you could recommend me somewheres else, an' I can get home to-morrow if 't ain't convenient."

They were standing under a willow-tree in the shade; Mr. Rill took off his heavy hat—it was a silk hat of bygone shape; a golden robin began to sing, high in the willow, and the old bullfinch twittered and chirped in the cage. Miss Esther heard some footsteps coming behind them along the road. She changed color; she tried to remember that she was a woman of mature years and considerable experience.

" 'T ain't a mite o' matter, sir," she said cheerfully. "I guess you'll find everything comfortable for you;" and they turned, much relieved, and walked along together.

"That's Lawyer Barstow's house," she said calmly, a minute afterward, "the handsomest place in town, we think 't is," and Mr. Rill answered politely that Daleham was a pretty place; he had not been out of the city for so many years that everything looked beautiful as a picture.

IV

Miss Porley rapidly recovered her composure, and bent her energies to the preparing of an early tea. She showed her guest to the snug bedroom under the low gambrel roof, and when she apologized for his having to go upstairs, he begged her to remember that it was nothing but a step to a man who was used to four long flights. They were both excited at finding a proper nail for the birdcage outside the window, though Miss Esther said that she should love to have the pretty bird downstairs where they could see it and hear it sing. She said to herself over and over that if she could have her long-lost brother come home from sea, she should like to have him look and behave as gentle and kind as Mr. Rill. Somehow she found herself singing a cheerful hymn as she mixed and stirred the short-cakes. She could not help wishing that her mother were there to enjoy this surprise, but it did seem very odd, after so many years, to have a man in the house. It had not happened for fifteen years, at least, when they had entertained Deacon Sparks and wife, delegates from the neighboring town of East Wilby to the County Conference.

The neighbors did not laugh at Miss Esther openly or cause her to blush with self-consciousness, however much they may have discussed the situation and smiled behind her back. She took the presence of her guest with delighted simplicity, and the country week was extended to a fortnight, and then to a month. At last, one day Miss Esther and Mr. Rill were seen on their way to the railroad station, with a large bundle apiece beside the carpet-bag, though someone noticed that the bull-finch was left behind. Miss Esther came back alone, looking very woebegone and lonely, and if the truth must be known, she found her house too solitary. She looked into the woodhouse where there was a great store of kindlings, neatly piled, and her water-pail was filled to the brim, her garden-paths were clean of weeds and swept, and yet everywhere she looked it seemed more lonely than ever. She pinned on her shawl again and went along the street to the parsonage.

"My old lady's just gone," she said to the minister's wife. "I was so lonesome I could not stay in the house."

"You found him a very pleasant visitor, didn't you, Miss Esther?" asked Mrs. Wayton, laughing a little.

"I did so; he wa'n't like other men—kind and friendly and fatherly, and never stayed round when I was occupied, but entertained himself down street considerable, an' was as industrious as a bee, always asking me if there wa'n't something he could do about house. He and a sister some years older used to keep house together, and it was her long sickness used up what they'd saved, and yet he's got a little somethin', and there are friends he used to work for, jewelers, a big firm, that gives him somethin' regular. He's goin' to see"—and Miss Esther blushed crimson—"he's goin' to see if they'd be willin' to pay it just the same if he come to reside in Daleham. He thinks the air agrees with him here."

"Does he indeed?" inquired the minister's wife, with deep interest and a look of amusement.

"Yes 'm," said Miss Esther simply; "but don't you go an' say nothin' yet. I don't want folks to make a joke of it. Seems to me if he does feel to come back, and remains of the same mind he went away, we might be judicious to take the step—"

"Why, Miss Esther!" exclaimed the listener.

"Not till fall—not till fall," said Miss Esther hastily. "I ain't going to count on it too much anyway. I expect we could get along; there's considerable goodness left in me, and you can always work better when you've got somebody beside yourself to work for. There, now I've told you I feel as if I was blown away in a gale."

"Why, I don't know what to say at such a piece of news!" exclaimed Mrs. Wayton again.

"I don't know's there's anything *to* say," gravely answered Miss Esther. "But I did laugh just now coming in the gate to think what a twitter I got into the day I fetched you that piece of paper."

"Why, I must go right and tell Mr. Wayton!" said the minister's wife.

"Oh, don't you, Mis' Wayton; no, no!" begged Miss Esther, looking quite coy and girlish. "I really don't know's it's quite settled—it don't seem's if it could be. I'm going to hear from him in the course of a week. But I suppose *he* thinks it's settled; he's left the bird."

—1893

O. HENRY
(1862–1910)

Born William Sidney Porter in Greensboro, North Carolina, the man who would publish his well-loved stories under the pseudonym O. Henry was raised by an aunt and uncle. Married, with one daughter, he was working as a bank teller when he was accused of embezzling funds. Initially, he fled to Central America to avoid prosecution, but when he learned that his wife was dying, he returned to be with her and surrendered to the authorities. Convicted of the crime after a controversial trial, he was sentenced to five years in the federal prison at Columbus, Ohio. There he became the prison pharmacist and he began to write and publish his stories. Choosing the pen name O. Henry, he sold the first of these stories, "Whistling Dick's Christmas Stocking," to *McClure's Magazine* from jail in 1899. Released for good behavior after he had served three years and three months of his sentence, he settled in New York City, where he quickly achieved fame and success as a writer who celebrated the City in a popular series of stories that had surprise endings. Among the numerous collections of his stories are *Cabbages and Kings* (1904), *The Four Million* (1906), *The Trimmed Lamp* (1907), *Heart of the West* (1907), *The Voice of the City* (1908), *Options* (1909), *Strictly Business* (1910), and *Whirligigs* (1910). In his honor, in 1918, the first volume of *O. Henry Prize Stories* was published. For this continuing series, editors choose from among the best stories published each year, award prizes to the authors, and republish those stories, with others, in a memorial volume.

The Gift of the Magi

ONE dollar and eighty-seven cents. That was all. And sixty cents of it was in pennies. Pennies saved one and two at a time by bulldozing the grocer and the vegetable man and the butcher until one's cheeks burned with the silent imputation of parsimony that such close dealing implied. Three times Della counted it. One dollar and eighty-seven cents. And the next day would be Christmas.

There was clearly nothing to do but flop down on the shabby little couch and howl. So Della did it. Which instigates the moral reflection that life is made up of sobs, sniffles, and smiles, with sniffles predominating.

While the mistress of the home is gradually subsiding from the first stage to the second, take a look at the home. A furnished flat at $8 per week. It did not exactly beggar description, but it certainly had that word on the lookout for the mendicancy squad.

In the vestibule below was a letter-box into which no letter would go, and an electric button from which no mortal finger could coax a ring. Also appertaining thereunto was a card bearing the name "Mr. James Dillingham Young."

The "Dillingham" had been flung to the breeze during a former period of prosperity when its possessor was being paid $30 per week. Now, when the income was shrunk to $20, the letters of "Dillingham" looked blurred, as though they were thinking seriously of contracting to a modest and unassuming D. But whenever Mr. James Dillingham Young came home and reached his flat above he was called "Jim" and greatly hugged by Mrs. James Dillingham Young, already introduced to you as Della. Which is all very good.

Della finished her cry and attended to her cheeks with the powder rag. She stood by the window and looked out dully at a gray cat walking a gray fence in a gray backyard. Tomorrow would be Christmas Day, and she had only $1.87 with which to buy Jim a present. She had been saving every penny she could for months, with this result. Twenty dollars a week doesn't go far. Expenses had been greater than she had calculated. They always are. Only $1.87 to buy a present for Jim. Her Jim. Many a happy hour she had spent planning for something nice for him. Something fine and rare and sterling—something just a little bit near to being worthy of the honor of being owned by Jim.

There was a pier-glass between the windows of the

room. Perhaps you have seen a pier-glass in an $8 flat. A very thin and very agile person may, by observing his reflection in a rapid sequence of longitudinal strips, obtain a fairly accurate conception of his looks. Della, being slender, had mastered the art.

Suddenly she whirled from the window and stood before the glass. Her eyes were shining brilliantly, but her face had lost its color within twenty seconds. Rapidly she pulled down her hair and let it fall to its full length.

Now, there were two possessions of the James Dillingham Youngs in which they both took a mighty pride. One was Jim's gold watch that had been his father's and his grandfather's. The other was Della's hair. Had the Queen of Sheba lived in the flat across the airshaft, Della would have let her hair hang out the window some day to dry just to depreciate Her Majesty's jewels and gifts. Had King Solomon been the janitor, with all his treasures piled up in the basement, Jim would have pulled out his watch every time he passed, just to see him pluck at his beard from envy.

So now Della's beautiful hair fell about her rippling and shining like a cascade of brown waters. It reached below her knee and made itself almost a garment for her. And then she did it up again nervously and quickly. Once she faltered for a minute and stood still while a tear or two splashed on the worn red carpet.

On went her old brown jacket; on went her old brown hat. With a whirl of skirts and with the brilliant sparkle still in her eyes, she fluttered out the door and down the stairs to the street.

Where she stopped the sign read: "Mme. Sofronie. Hair Goods of All Kinds." One flight up Della ran, and collected herself, panting. Madame, large, too white, chilly, hardly looked the "Sofronie."

"Will you buy my hair?" asked Della.

"I buy hair," said Madame. "Take yer hat off and let's have a sight at the looks of it."

Down rippled the brown cascade.

"Twenty dollars," said Madame, lifting the mass with a practised hand.

"Give it to me quick," said Della.

Oh, and the next two hours tripped by on rosy wings.

Forget the hashed metaphor. She was ransacking the stores for Jim's present.

She found it at last. It surely had been made for Jim and no one else. There was no other like it in any of the stores, and she had turned all of them inside out. It was a platinum fob chain simple and chaste in design, properly proclaiming its value by substance alone and not by meretricious ornamentation—as all good things should do. It was even worthy of The Watch. As soon as she saw it she knew that it must be Jim's. It was like him. Quietness and value—the description applied to both. Twenty-one dollars they took from her for it, and she hurried home with the 87 cents. With that chain on his watch Jim might be properly anxious about the time in any company. Grand as the watch was, he sometimes looked at it on the sly on account of the old leather strap that he used in place of a chain.

When Della reached home her intoxication gave way a little to prudence and reason. She got out her curling irons and lighted the gas and went to work repairing the ravages made by generosity added to love. Which is always a tremendous task, dear friends—a mammoth task.

Within forty minutes her head was covered with tiny, close-lying curls that made her look wonderfully like a truant schoolboy. She looked at her reflection in the mirror long, carefully, and critically.

"If Jim doesn't kill me," she said to herself, "before he takes a second look at me, he'll say I look like a Coney Island chorus girl. But what could I do—oh! what could I do with a dollar and eighty-seven cents?"

At 7 o'clock the coffee was made and the frying-pan was on the back of the stove hot and ready to cook the chops.

Jim was never late. Della doubled the fob chain in her hand and sat on the corner of the table near the door that he always entered. Then she heard his step on the stair away down on the first flight, and she turned white for just a moment. She had a habit of saying little silent prayers about the simplest everyday things, and now she whispered: "Please God, make him think I am still pretty."

The door opened and Jim stepped in and closed it.

He looked thin and very serious. Poor fellow, he was only twenty-two—and to be burdened with a family! He needed a new overcoat and he was without gloves.

Jim stopped inside the door, as immovable as a setter at the scent of quail. His eyes were fixed upon Della, and there was an expression in them that she could not read, and it terrified her. It was not anger, nor surprise, nor disapproval, nor horror, nor any of the sentiments that she had been prepared for. He simply stared at her fixedly with that peculiar expression on his face.

Della wriggled off the table and went for him.

"Jim, darling," she cried, "don't look at me that way. I had my hair cut off and sold it because I couldn't have lived through Christmas without giving you a present. It'll grow out again—you won't mind, will you? I just had to do it. My hair grows awfully fast. Say 'Merry Christmas!' Jim, and let's be happy. You don't know what a nice—what a beautiful, nice gift I've got for you."

"You've cut off your hair?" asked Jim, laboriously, as if he had not arrived at that patent fact yet even after the hardest mental labor.

"Cut it off and sold it," said Della. "Don't you like me just as well, anyhow? I'm me without my hair, ain't I?"

Jim looked about the room curiously.

"You say your hair is gone?" he said, with an air almost of idiocy.

"You needn't look for it," said Della. "It's sold, I tell you—sold and gone, too. It's Christmas Eve, boy. Be good to me, for it went for you. Maybe the hairs of my head were numbered," she went on with a sudden serious sweetness, "but nobody could ever count my love for you. Shall I put the chops on, Jim?"

Out of his trance Jim seemed quickly to wake. He enfolded his Della. For ten seconds let us regard with discreet scrutiny some inconsequential object in the other direction. Eight dollars a week or a million a year—what is the difference? A mathematician or a wit would give you the wrong answer. The magi brought valuable gifts, but that was not among them. This dark assertion will be illuminated later on.

Jim drew a package from his overcoat pocket and threw it upon the table.

"Don't make any mistake, Dell," he said, "about me. I don't think there's anything in the way of a haircut or a shave or a shampoo that could make me like my girl any less. But if you'll unwrap that package you may see why you had me going a while at first."

White fingers and nimble tore at the string and paper. And then an ecstatic scream of joy; and then, alas! a quick feminine change to hysterical tears and wails, necessitating the immediate employment of all the comforting powers of the lord of the flat.

For there lay The Combs—the set of combs, side and back, that Della had worshipped for long in a Broadway window. Beautiful combs, pure tortoise shell, with jewelled rims—just the shade to wear in the beautiful vanished hair. They were expensive combs, she knew, and her heart had simply craved and yearned over them without the least hope of possession. And now, they were hers, but the tresses that should have adorned the coveted adornments were gone.

But she hugged them to her bosom, and at length she was able to look up with dim eyes and a smile and say: "My hair grows so fast, Jim!"

And then Della leaped up like a little singed cat and cried, "Oh, oh!"

Jim had not yet seen his beautiful present. She held it out to him eagerly upon her open palm. The dull precious metal seemed to flash with a reflection of her bright and ardent spirit.

"Isn't it a dandy, Jim? I hunted all over town to find it. You'll have to look at the time a hundred times a day now. Give me your watch. I want to see how it looks on it."

Instead of obeying, Jim tumbled down on the couch and put his hands under the back of his head and smiled.

"Dell," said he, "let's put our Christmas presents away and keep 'em a while. They're too nice to use just at present. I sold the watch to get the money to buy your combs. And now suppose you put the chops on."

The magi, as you know, were wise men—wonderfully wise men—who brought gifts to the Babe in the manger. They invented the art of giving Christmas presents. Being wise, their gifts were no doubt wise ones, possibly bearing the privilege of exchange in case of duplication. And here I have lamely related to you the uneventful chronicle of two foolish children in a flat who most unwisely sacrificed for each other the greatest treasures of their house. But in a last word to the wise of these days let it be said that of all who give gifts these two were the wisest. Of all who give and receive gifts, such as they are wisest. Everywhere they are wisest. They are the magi.

—1906

RAYMOND CARVER
(1939–1988)

Born in Clatskanie, Oregon, Raymond Carver grew up in Yakima, Washington, where his father worked as a logger. After graduating from Humboldt State College in California, he studied at the University of Iowa's Writers' Workshop. His collections of stories include *Put Yourself in My Shoes* (1974), *Will You Please Be Quiet, Please?* (1976), *Furious Seasons and Other Stories* (1977), *What We Talk About When We Talk About Love* (1981), *The Pheasant* (1982), *Cathedral* (1983), *If It Please You* (1984), *The Stories of Raymond Carver* (1985), and *Where I'm Calling From* (1988). In addition he published three collections of poems in small press editions: *Near Klamath* (1968), *Winter Insomnia* (1970), *At Night the Salmon Move* (1976), as well as *Where Water Comes Together with Other Water* (1985) and *Ultramarine* (1986). A recipient of a Guggenheim Fellowship in 1979, Carver received a National Endowment for the Arts Discovery Award for Poetry and was elected in 1988 to the American Academy and Institute of Arts and Letters.

Elephant

I knew it was a mistake to let my brother have the money. I didn't need anybody else owing me. But when he called and said he couldn't make the payment on his house, what could I do? I'd never been inside his house—he lived a thousand miles away, in California; I'd never even *seen* his house—but I didn't want him to lose it. He cried over the phone and said he was losing everything he'd worked for. He said he'd pay me back. February, he said. Maybe sooner. No later, anyway, than March. He said his income-tax refund was on the way. Plus, he said, he had a little investment that would mature in February. He acted secretive about the investment thing, so I didn't press for details.

"Trust me on this," he said. "I won't let you down."

He'd lost his job last July, when the company he worked for, a fiberglass-insulation plant, decided to lay off two hundred employees. He'd been living on his unemployment since then, but now the unemployment was gone, and his savings were gone, too. And he didn't have health insurance any longer. When his job went, the insurance went. His wife, who was ten years older, was diabetic and needed treatment. He'd had to sell the other car—her car, an old station wagon—and a week ago he'd pawned his TV. He told me he'd hurt his back carrying the TV up and down the street where the pawnshops did business. He went from place to place, he said, trying to get the best offer. Somebody finally gave him a hundred dollars for it, this big Sony TV. He told me about the TV, and then about throwing his back out, as if this ought to cinch it with me, unless I had a stone in place of a heart.

"I've gone belly up," he said. "But you can help me pull out of it."

"How much?" I said.

"Five hundred. I could use more, sure, who couldn't?" he said. "But I want to be realistic. I can pay back five hundred. More than that, I'll tell you the truth, I'm not so sure. Brother, I hate to ask. But you're my last resort. Irma Jean and I are going to be on the street before long. I won't let you down," he said. That's what he said. Those were his exact words.

We talked a little more—mostly about our mother and her problems—but, to make a long story short, I sent him the money. I had to. I felt I had to, at any rate—which amounts to the same thing. I wrote him a letter when I sent the check and said he should pay the money back to our mother, who lived in the same town he lived in and who was poor and greedy. I'd been mailing checks to her every month, rain or shine, for three years. But I was thinking that if he paid her the money he owed me it might take me off the hook there and let me breathe for a while. I wouldn't have to worry on that score for a couple of months, anyway. Also, and this is the truth, I thought maybe he'd be more likely to pay her, since they lived right there in the same town and he saw her from time to time. All I was doing was trying to cover myself some way. The thing is, he might have the best intentions of paying me back, but things happen sometimes. Things get in the way of best intentions. Out of sight, out of mind, as they say. But he wouldn't stiff his own mother. Nobody would do that.

I spent hours writing letters, trying to make sure everybody knew what could be expected and what was required. I even phoned out there to my mother several times, trying to explain it to her. But she was suspicious over the whole deal. I went through it with her on the phone step by step, but she was still suspicious. I told her the money that was supposed to come from me on the first of March and on the first of April would instead come from Billy, who owed the money to me. She'd get her money, and she didn't have to worry. The only difference was that Billy would pay it to her those two months instead of me. He'd pay her the money I'd normally be sending to her, but instead of him mailing it to me and then me having to turn around and send it to her he'd pay it to her directly. On any account, she didn't have to worry. She'd get her money, but for those two months it'd come from him—from the money he owed me. My God, I don't know how much I spent on phone calls. And I wish I had fifty cents for every letter I wrote, telling him what I'd told her and telling her what to expect from him—that sort of thing.

But my mother didn't trust Billy. "What if he can't come up with it?" she said to me over the phone. "What then? He's in bad shape, and I'm sorry for him," she said. "But, son, what I want to know is, what if he isn't about to pay me? What if he can't? Then what?"

"Then I'll pay you myself," I said. "Just like always. If he doesn't pay you, I'll pay you. But he'll pay you. Don't worry. He says he will, and he will."

"I don't want to worry," she said. "But I worry anyway. I worry about my boys, and after that I worry about myself. I never thought I'd see one of my boys in this shape. I'm just glad your dad isn't alive to see it."

In three months my brother gave her fifty dollars of what he owed me and was supposed to pay to her. Or maybe it was seventy-five dollars he gave her. There are conflicting stories—two conflicting stories, his and hers.

But that's all he paid her of the five hundred—fifty dollars or else seventy-five dollars, according to whose story you want to listen to. I had to make up the rest to her. I had to keep shelling out, same as always. My brother was finished. That's what he told me—that he was finished—when I called to see what was up, after my mother had phoned, looking for her money.

My mother said, "I made the mailman go back and check inside his truck, to see if your letter might have fallen down behind the seat. Then I went around and asked the neighbors did they get any of my mail by mistake. I'm going crazy with worry about this situation, honey." Then she said, "What's a mother supposed to think?" Who was looking out for her best interests in this business? She wanted to know that, and she wanted to know when she could expect her money.

So that's when I got on the phone to my brother to see if this was just a simple delay or a full-fledged collapse. But, according to Billy, he was a goner. He was absolutely done for. He was putting his house on the market immediately. He just hoped he hadn't waited too long to try and move it. And there wasn't anything left inside the house that he could sell. He'd sold off everything except the kitchen table and chairs. "I wish I could sell my blood," he said. "But who'd buy it? With my luck, I probably have an incurable disease." And, naturally, the investment thing hadn't worked out. When I asked him about it over the phone, all he said was that it hadn't materialized. His tax refund didn't make it, either—the I.R.S. had some kind of lien on his return. "When it rains it pours," he said. "I'm sorry, brother. I didn't mean for this to happen."

"I understand," I said. And I did. But it didn't make it any easier. Anyway, one thing and the other, I didn't get my money from him, and neither did my mother. I had to keep on sending her money every month.

I was sore, yes. Who wouldn't be? My heart went out to him, and I wished trouble hadn't knocked on his door. But my own back was against the wall now. At least, though, whatever happens to him from here on, he won't come back to me for more money—seeing as how he still owes me. Nobody would do that to you. That's how I figured, anyway. But that's how little I knew.

I kept my nose to the grindstone. I got up early every morning and went to work and worked hard all day. When I came home I plopped into the big chair and just sat there. I was so tired it took me a while to get around to unlacing my shoes. Then I just went on sitting there. I was too tired to even get up and turn on the TV.

I was sorry about my brother's troubles. But I had troubles of my own. In addition to my mother, I had several other people on my payroll. I had a former wife I was sending money to every month. I had to do that. I didn't want to, but the court said I had to. And I had a daughter with two kids in Bellingham, and I had to send her something every month. Her kids had to eat, didn't they? She was living with a swine who wouldn't even *look* for work, a guy who couldn't hold a job if they handed him one. The time or two he did find something, he overslept, or his car broke down on the way in to work, or else he'd just be let go, no explanation, and that was that.

Once, long ago, when I used to think like a man about these things, I threatened to kill that guy. But that's neither here nor there. Besides, I was drinking in those days. In any case, the bastard is still hanging around.

My daughter would write these letters and say how they were living on oatmeal, she and her kids. (I guess he was starving, too, but she knew better than to mention that guy's name in her letters to me.) She'd tell me that if I could just carry her until summer things would pick up for her. Things would turn around for her, she was sure, in the summer. If nothing else worked out— but she was sure it would; she had several irons in the fire—she could always get a job in the fish cannery that was not far from where she lived. She'd wear rubber boots and rubber clothes and gloves and pack salmon into cans. Or else she might sell root beer from a vending stand beside the road to people who lined up in their cars at the border, waiting to get into Canada. People sitting in their cars in the middle of summer were going to be thirsty, right? They were going to be crying out for cold drinks. Anyway, one thing or the other, whatever line of work she decided on, she'd do fine in the summer. She just had to make it until then, and that's where I came in.

My daughter said she knew she had to change her life. She wanted to stand on her own two feet like everyone else. She wanted to quit looking at herself as a victim. "I'm not a victim," she said to me over the phone one night. "I'm just a young woman with two kids and a son-of-a-bitch bum who lives with me. No different from lots of other women. I'm not afraid of hard work. Just give me a chance. That's all I ask of the world." She said she could do without for herself. But until her break came, until opportunity knocked, it was the kids she worried about. The kids were always asking her when Grandpop was going to visit, she said. Right this minute they were drawing pictures of the swing sets and swimming pool at the motel I'd stayed in when I'd visited a year ago. But summer was the thing, she said. If she could make it until summer, her troubles would be over. Things would change then—she knew they would. And with a little help from me she could make it. "I don't know what I'd do without you, Dad." That's what she said. It nearly broke my heart. Sure I had to help her. I was glad to be even halfway in a position to help her. I had a job, didn't I? Compared to her and everyone else in my family, I had it made. Compared to the rest, I lived on Easy Street.

I sent the money she asked for. I sent money every time she asked. And then I told her I thought it'd be simpler if I just sent a sum of money, not a whole lot, but money even so, on the first of each month. It would be money she could count on, and it would be *her* money, no one else's—hers and the kids'. That's what I hoped for, anyway. I wished there was some way I could be sure the bastard who lived with her couldn't get his hands on so much as an orange or a piece of bread that my money bought. But I couldn't. I just had to go ahead and send the money and stop worrying about whether he'd soon be tucking into a plate of my eggs and biscuits.

My mother and my daughter and my former wife. That's three people on the payroll right there, not counting my brother. But my son needed money, too. After he graduated from high school, he packed his things, left his mother's house, and went to a college back East. A college in New Hampshire, of all places. Who's ever heard of New Hampshire? But he was the first kid in the family, on either side of the family, to even *want* to go to college, so everybody thought it was a good idea. I thought so, too, at first. How'd I know it was going to wind up costing me an arm and a leg? He borrowed left and right from the banks to keep himself going. He didn't want to have to work a job and go to school at the same time. That's what he said. And, sure, I guess I can understand it. In a way, I can even sympathize. Who likes to work? I don't. But after he'd borrowed everything he could, everything in sight, including enough to finance a junior year in Germany, I had to begin sending him money, and a lot of it. When, finally, I said I couldn't send any more, he wrote back and said if that was the case, if that was really the way I felt, he was going to deal drugs or else rob a bank—whatever he had to do to get money to live on. I'd be lucky if he wasn't shot or sent to prison.

I wrote back and said I'd changed my mind and I could send him a little more after all. What else could I do? I didn't want his blood on my hands. I didn't want to think of my kid being packed off to prison, or something even worse. I had plenty on my conscience as it was.

That's four people, right? Not counting my brother, who wasn't a regular yet. I was going crazy with it. I worried night and day. I couldn't sleep over it. I was paying out nearly as much money every month as I was bringing in. You don't have to be a genius, or know anything about economics, to understand that this state of affairs couldn't keep on. I had to get a loan to keep up my end of things. That was another monthly payment.

So I started cutting back. I had to quit eating out, for instance. Since I lived alone, eating out was something I liked to do, but it became a thing of the past. And I had to watch myself when it came to thinking about movies. I couldn't buy clothes or get my teeth fixed. The car was falling apart. I needed new shoes, but forget it.

Once in a while I'd get fed up with it and write letters to all of them, threatening to change my name and telling them I was going to quit my job. I'd tell them I was planning a move to Australia. And the thing was, I was serious when I'd say that about Australia, even though I didn't know the first thing about Australia. I just knew it was on the other side of the world, and that's where I wanted to be.

But when it came right down to it, none of them really believed I'd go to Australia. They had me, and they knew it. They knew I was desperate, and they were sorry and they said so. But they counted on it all blowing over before the first of the month, when I had to sit down and make out the checks.

After one of my letters where I talked about moving to Australia, my mother wrote that she didn't want to be a burden any longer. Just as soon as the swelling went down in her legs, she said, she was going out to look for work. She was seventy-five years old, but maybe she could go back to waitressing, she said. I wrote her back and told her not to be silly. I said I was glad I could help her. And I was. I was glad I could help. I just needed to win the lottery.

My daughter knew Australia was just a way of saying to everybody that I'd had it. She knew I needed a break and something to cheer me up. So she wrote that she was going to leave her kids with somebody and take the cannery job when the season rolled around. She was young and strong, she said. She thought she could work the twelve-to-fourteen-hour-a-day shifts, seven days a week, no problem. She'd just have to tell herself she could do it, get herself psyched up for it, and her body would listen. She just had to line up the right kind of babysitter. That'd be the big thing. It was going to require a special kind of sitter, seeing as how the hours would be long and the kids were hyper to begin with, because of all the Popsicles and Tootsie Rolls, M&M's, and the like that they put away every day. It's the stuff kids like to eat, right? Anyway, she thought she could find the right person if she kept looking. But she had to buy the boots and clothes for the work, and that's where I could help.

My son wrote that he was sorry for his part in things and thought he and I would both be better off if he ended it once and for all. For one thing, he'd discovered he was allergic to cocaine. It made his eyes stream and affected his breathing, he said. This meant he couldn't test the drugs in the transactions he'd need to make. So, before it could even begin, his career as a drug dealer was over. No, he said, better a bullet in the temple and end it all right here. Or maybe hanging. That would save him the trouble of borrowing a gun. And save us the price of bullets. That's actually what he said in his letter, if you can believe it. He enclosed a picture of himself that somebody had taken last summer when he was in the study-abroad program in Germany. He was standing under a big tree with thick limbs hanging down a few feet over his head. In the picture, he wasn't smiling.

My former wife didn't have anything to say on the matter. She didn't have to. She knew she'd get her money the first of each month, even if it had to come all the way from Sydney. If she didn't get it, she just had to pick up the phone and call her lawyer.

This is where things stood when my brother called one Sunday afternoon in early May. I had the windows open, and a nice breeze moved through the house. The radio was playing. The hillside behind the house was in bloom. But I began to sweat when I heard his voice on the line. I hadn't heard from him since the dispute over the five hundred, so I couldn't believe he was going to try and touch me for more money now. But I began to sweat anyway. He asked how things stood with me, and I launched into the payroll thing and all. I talked about oatmeal, cocaine, fish canneries, suicide, bank jobs, and how I couldn't go to the movies or eat out. I said I had a hole in my shoe. I talked about the payments that went on and on to my former wife. He knew all about this, of course. He knew everything I was telling him. Still, he said he was sorry to hear it. I kept talking. It was his dime. But as he talked I started thinking, *How are you going to pay for this call, Billy?* Then it came to me that *I* was going to pay for it. It was only a matter of minutes, or seconds, until it was all decided.

I looked out the window. The sky was blue, with a

few white clouds in it. Some birds clung to a telephone wire. I wiped my face on my sleeve. I didn't know what else I could say. So I suddenly stopped talking and just stared out the window at the mountains, and waited. And that's when my brother said, "I hate to ask you this, but—" When he said that, my heart did this sinking thing. And then he went ahead and asked.

This time it was a thousand. A thousand! He was worse off than when he'd called that other time. He let me have some details. The bill collectors were at the door—the door! he said—and the windows rattled, the house shook, when they hammered with their fists. *Blam, blam, blam,* he said. There was no place to hide from them. His house was about to be pulled out from under him. "Help me, brother," he said.

Where was I going to raise a thousand dollars? I took a good grip on the receiver, turned away from the window, and said, "But you didn't pay me back the last time you borrowed money. What about that?"

"I didn't?" he said, acting surprised. "I guess I thought I had. I wanted to, anyway. I tried to, so help me God."

"You were supposed to pay that money to Mom," I said. "But you didn't. I had to keep giving her money every month, same as always. There's no end to it, Billy. Listen, I take one step forward and I go two steps back. I'm going under. You're all going under, and you're pulling me down with you."

"I paid her *some* of it," he said. "I did pay her a little. Just for the record," he said, "I paid her something."

"She said you gave her fifty dollars and that was all."

"No," he said. "I gave her seventy-five. She forgot about the other twenty-five. I was over there one afternoon, and I gave her two tens and a five. I gave her some cash, and she just forgot about it. Her memory's going. Look," he said, "I promise I'll be good for it this time, I swear to God. Add up what I still owe you and add it to this money here I'm trying to borrow, and I'll send you a check. We'll exchange checks. Hold on to my check for two months, that's all I'm asking. I'll be out of the woods in two months' time. Then you'll have your money. July 1st, I promise, no later, and this time

I *can* swear to it. We're in the process of selling this little piece of property that Irma Jean inherited a while back from her uncle. It's as good as sold. The deal has closed. It's just a question now of working out a couple of minor details and signing the papers. Plus, I've got this job lined up. It's definite. I'll have to drive fifty miles round trip every day, but that's no problem—hell, no. I'd drive a hundred and fifty if I had to, and be glad to do it. I'm saying I'll have money in the bank in two months' time. You'll get your money, all of it, by July 1st, and you can count on it."

"Billy, I love you," I said. "But I've got a load to carry. I'm carrying a very heavy load these days, in case you didn't know."

"That's why I won't let you down on this," he said. "You have my word of honor. You can trust me on this absolutely. I promise you my check will be good in two months, no later. Two months is all I'm asking for. Brother, I don't know where else to turn. You're my last hope."

I did it, sure. To my surprise, I still had some credit with the bank, so I borrowed the money, and I sent it to him. Our checks crossed in the mail. I stuck a thumbtack through his check and put it up on the kitchen wall next to the calendar and the picture of my son standing under that tree. And then I waited.

I kept waiting. My brother wrote and asked me not to cash the check on the day we'd agreed to. Please wait a while longer is what he said. Some things had come up. The job he'd been promised had fallen through at the last minute. That was one thing that came up. And that little piece of property belonging to his wife hadn't sold after all. At the last minute, she'd had a change of heart about selling it. It had been in her family for generations. What could he do? It was her land, and she wouldn't listen to reason, he said.

My daughter telephoned around this time to say that somebody had broken into her trailer and ripped her off. Everything in the trailer. Every stick of furniture was gone when she came home from work after her first night at the cannery. There wasn't even a chair left for her to sit down on. Her bed had been stolen, too. They were going to have to sleep on the floor like Gypsies, she said.

"Where was what's-his-name when this happened?" I said.

She said he'd been out looking for work earlier in the day. She guessed he was with friends. Actually, she didn't know his whereabouts at the time of the crime, or even right now, for that matter. "I hope he's at the bottom of the river," she said. The kids had been with the sitter when the ripoff happened. But, anyway, if she could just borrow enough from me to buy some second-hand furniture she'd pay me back, she said, when she got her first check. If she had some money from me before the end of the week—I could wire it, maybe—she could pick up some essentials. "Somebody's violated my space," she said. "I feel like I've been raped."

My son wrote from New Hampshire that it was essential he go back to Europe. His life hung in the balance, he said. He was graduating at the end of summer session, but he couldn't stand to live in America a day longer after that. This was a materialist society, and he simply couldn't take it anymore. People over here, in the U.S., couldn't hold a conversation unless *money* figured in it some way, and he was sick of it. He wasn't a Yuppie, and didn't want to become a Yuppie. That wasn't his thing. He'd get out of my hair, he said, if he could just borrow enough from me, this one last time, to buy a ticket to Germany.

I didn't hear anything from my former wife. I didn't have to. We both knew how things stood there.

My mother wrote that she was having to do without support hose and wasn't able to have her hair tinted. She'd thought this would be the year she could put some money back for the rainy days ahead, but it wasn't working out that way. She could see it wasn't in the cards. "How are you?" she wanted to know. "How's everybody else? I hope you're okay."

I put more checks in the mail. Then I held my breath and waited.

While I was waiting, I had this dream one night. Two dreams, really. I dreamt them on the same night. In the first dream, my dad was alive once more, and he was giving me a ride on his shoulders. I was this little kid, maybe five or six years old. *Get up here,* he said, and he took me by the hands and swung me onto his shoulders. I was high off the ground, but I wasn't afraid. He was holding on to me. We were holding on to each other. Then he began to move down the sidewalk. I brought my hands up from his shoulders and put them around his forehead. *Don't muss my hair,* he said. *You can let go,* he said, *I've got you. You won't fall.* When he said that, I became aware of the strong grip of his hands around my ankles. Then I did let go. I turned loose and held my arms out on either side of me. I kept them out there like that for balance. My dad went on walking while I rode on his shoulders. I pretended he was an elephant. I don't know where we were going. Maybe we were going to the store, or else to the park so he could push me in the swing.

I woke up then, got out of bed, and used the bathroom. It was starting to get light out, and it was only an hour or so until I had to get up. I thought about making coffee and getting dressed. But then I decided to go back to bed. I didn't plan to sleep, though. I thought I'd just lie there for a while with my hands behind my neck and watch it turn light out and maybe think about my dad a little, since I hadn't thought about him in a long time. He just wasn't part of my life any longer, waking or sleeping. Anyway, I got back in bed. But it couldn't have been more than a minute before I fell asleep once more, and when I did I got into this other dream. My former wife was in it, though she wasn't my former wife in the dream. She was still my wife. My kids were in it, too. They were little, and they were eating potato chips. In my dream, I thought I could smell the potato chips and hear them being eaten. We were on a blanket, and we were close to some water. There was a sense of satisfaction and well-being in the dream. Then, suddenly, I found myself in the company of some other people—people I didn't know—and the next thing that happened was that I was kicking the window out of my son's car and threatening his life, as I did once, a long time ago. He was inside the car as my shoe smashed through the glass. That's when my eyes flew open, and I woke up.

The alarm was going off. I reached over and pushed the switch and lay there for a few minutes more, my heart racing. In the second dream, somebody had offered me some whiskey, and I drank it. Drinking that whiskey was the thing that scared me. That was the worst thing that could have happened. That was rock bottom. Compared to that, everything else was a picnic. I lay there for a minute longer, trying to calm down. Then I got up.

I made coffee and sat at the kitchen table in front of the window. I pushed my cup back and forth in little circles on the table and began to think seriously about Australia again. And then, all of a sudden, I could imagine how it must have sounded to my family when I'd threatened them with a move to Australia. They would have been shocked at first, and even a little scared. Then, because they knew me, they'd probably started laughing. Now, thinking about their laughter, I had to laugh, too. *Ha, ha, ha.* That was exactly the sound I made there at the table—*ha, ha, ha*—as if I'd read somewhere how to laugh.

What was it I planned to do in Australia, anyway? The truth was, I wouldn't be going there any more than I'd be going to Timbuktu, the moon, or the North Pole. Hell, I didn't want to go to Australia. But once I understood this, once I understood I wouldn't be going there—or anywhere else, for that matter—I began to feel better. I lit another cigarette and poured some more coffee. There wasn't any milk for the coffee, but I didn't care. I could skip having milk in my coffee for a day and it wouldn't kill me. Pretty soon I packed the lunch and filled the thermos and put the thermos in the lunch pail. Then I went outside.

It was a fine morning. The sun lay over the mountains behind the town, and a flock of birds was moving from one part of the valley to another. I didn't bother to lock the door. I remembered what had happened to my daughter, but decided I didn't have anything worth stealing anyway. There was nothing in the house I couldn't live without. I had the TV, but I was sick of watching TV. They'd be doing me a favor if they broke in and took it off my hands.

I felt pretty good, all things considered, and I decided to walk to work. It wasn't all that far, and I had time to spare. I'd save a little gas, sure, but that wasn't the main consideration. It was summer, after all, and before long summer would be over. Summer, I couldn't help thinking, had been the time everybody's luck had been going to change.

I started walking alongside the road, and it was then, for some reason, I began to think about my son. I wished him well, wherever he was. If he'd made it back to Germany by now—and he should have—I hoped he was happy. He hadn't written yet to give me his address, but I was sure I'd hear something before long. And my daughter, God love her and keep her. I hoped she was doing okay. I decided to write her a letter that evening and tell her I was rooting for her. My mother was alive and more or less in good health, and I felt lucky there, too. If all went well, I'd have her for several more years. Birds were calling, and some cars passed me on the highway. Good luck to you, too, brother, I thought. I hope your ship comes in. Pay me back when you get it. And my former wife, the woman I used to love so much. She was alive, and she was well, too—so far as I knew, anyway. I wished her happiness. When all was said and done, I decided things could be a lot worse. Just now, of course, things were hard for everyone. People's luck had gone south on them was all. But things were bound to change soon. Things would pick up in the fall maybe. There was lots to hope for.

I kept on walking. Then I began to whistle. I felt I had the right to whistle if I wanted to. I let my arms swing as I walked. But the lunch pail kept throwing me off balance. I had sandwiches, an apple, and some cookies in there, not to mention the thermos. I stopped in front of Smitty's, an old café that had gravel in the parking area and boards over the windows. The place had been boarded up for as long as I could remember. I decided to put the lunch pail down for a minute. I did that, and then I raised my arms—raised them up level with my shoulders. I was standing there like that, like a goof, when somebody tooted a car horn and pulled off the highway into the parking area. I picked up my lunch

pail and went over to the car. It was a guy I knew from
work whose name was George. He reached over and
opened the door on the passenger's side. "Hey, get in,
buddy," he said.

"Hello, George," I said. I got in and shut the door,
and the car sped off, throwing gravel from under the
tires.

"I saw you," George said. "Yeah, I did, I saw you.
You're in training for something, but I don't know
what." He looked at me and then looked at the road
again. He was going fast. "You always walk down the
road with your arms out like that?" He laughed—*ha, ha,
ha*—and stepped on the gas.

"Sometimes," I said. "It depends, I guess. Actually, I
was standing," I said. I lit a cigarette and leaned back
in the seat.

"So what's new?" George said. He put a cigar in his
mouth, but he didn't light it.

"Nothing's new," I said. "What's new with you?"

George shrugged. Then he grinned. He was going very
fast now. Wind buffeted the car and whistled by outside
the windows. He was driving as if we were late for work.
But we weren't late. We had lots of time, and I told
him so.

Nevertheless, he cranked it up. We passed the turnoff
and kept going. We were moving by then, heading
straight toward the mountains. He took the cigar out of
his mouth and put it in his shirt pocket. "I borrowed
some money and had this baby overhauled," he said.
Then he said he wanted me to see something. He
punched it and gave it everything he could. I fastened
my seat belt and held on.

"*Go*," I said. "What are you waiting for, George?"
And that's when we really flew. Wind howled outside
the windows. He had it floored, and we were going flat
out. We streaked down that road in his big unpaid-for
car.

—1988

REBECCA HARDING DAVIS
(1831–1910)

Born Rebecca Blaine Harding in Washington, Pennsylvania, Rebecca Harding spent her childhood in Wheeling, Virginia (now West Virginia), a mill town on the Ohio River. From the age of fourteen to seventeen, Davis studied at the Washington Female Seminary in Washington, Pennsylvania, and was graduated as class valedictorian in 1848. For the next thirteen years, she lived with her financially comfortable family in Wheeling. In 1861, the *Atlantic Monthly* published "Life in the Iron Mills," paying Davis $50 and requesting additional submissions. She quickly supplied *Margret Howth: A Story of To-day*, "John Lamar," and *David Gaunt*, a Civil War novel, all published in the *Atlantic Monthly* between 1861 and 1862. In 1863, she married L. Clarke Davis, an attorney, and the couple settled in Philadelphia. Although Davis published some "potboilers," her serious fiction often dealt with major social issues such as governmental bribery and corruption and race relations after the Civil War. Among her novels are *Waiting for the Verdict* (1868), *Dallas Galbraith* (1868), *Put Out of the Way* (1870), *A Law Unto Herself* (1878), *Dr. Warrick's Daughters* (1896), and *Frances Waldeaux* (1896). Her stories and sketches are collected in *Silhouettes of American Life* (1892) and *Bits of Gossip* (1904).

Life in the Iron Mills

> "Is this the end?
> O Life, as futile, then, as frail!
> What hope of answer of redress?"

A cloudy day: do you know what that is in a town of iron-works? The sky sank down before dawn, muddy, flat, immovable. The air is thick, clammy with the breath of crowded human beings. It stifles me. I open the window, and, looking out, can scarcely see through

the rain the grocer's shop opposite, where a crowd of
drunken Irishmen are puffing Lynchburg tobacco in their
pipes. I can detect the scent through all the foul smells
ranging loose in the air.

The idiosyncrasy of this town is smoke. It rolls sullenly
in slow folds from the great chimneys of the iron-foundries,
and settles down in black, slimy pools on the muddy
streets. Smoke on the wharves, smoke on the dingy
boats, on the yellow river,—clinging in a coating of greasy
soot to the house-front, the two faded poplars, the faces
of the passers-by. The long train of mules, dragging
masses of pig-iron through the narrow street, have a foul
vapor hanging to their reeking sides. Here, inside, is a
little broken figure of an angel pointing upward from
the mantel-shelf; but even its wings are covered with
smoke, clotted and black. Smoke everywhere! A dirty
canary chirps desolately in a cage beside me. Its dream
of green fields and sunshine is a very old dream,—almost
worn out, I think.

From the back-window I can see a narrow brick-yard
sloping down to the river-side, strewed with rain-butts
and tubs. The river, dull and tawny-colored, (*la belle
rivière!*) drags itself sluggishly along, tired of the heavy
weight of boats and coal-barges. What wonder? When I
was a child, I used to fancy a look of weary, dumb appeal
upon the face of the negro-like river slavishly bearing its
burden day after day. Something of the same idle notion
comes to me to-day, when from the street-window I look
on the slow stream of human life creeping past, night
and morning, to the great mills. Masses of men, with
dull, besotted faces bent to the ground, sharpened here
and there by pain or cunning; skin and muscle and flesh
begrimed with smoke and ashes; stooping all night over
boiling caldrons of metal, laired by day in dens of drunkenness and infamy; breathing from infancy to death an
air saturated with fog and grease and soot, vileness for
soul and body. What do you make of a case like that,
amateur psychologist? You call it an altogether serious
thing to be alive: to these men it is a drunken jest, a
joke,—horrible to angels perhaps, to them commonplace
enough. My fancy about the river was an idle one: it is
no type of such a life. What if it be stagnant and slimy

here? It knows that beyond there waits for it odorous sunlight,—quaint old gardens, dusky with soft, green foliage of apple-trees, and flushing crimson with roses,—air, and fields, and mountains. The future of the Welsh puddler passing just now is not so pleasant. To be stowed away, after his grimy work is done, in a hole in the muddy graveyard, and after that,—*not* air, nor green fields, nor curious roses.

Can you see how foggy the day is? As I stand here, idly tapping the window-pane, and looking out through the rain at the dirty back-yard and the coal-boats below, fragments of an old story float up before me,—a story of this old house into which I happened to come to-day. You may think it a tiresome story enough, as foggy as the day, sharpened by no sudden flashes of pain or pleasure.—I know: only the outline of a dull life, that long since, with thousands of dull lives like its own, was vainly lived and lost: thousands of them,—massed, vile, slimy lives, like those of the torpid lizards in yonder stagnant water-butt.—Lost? There is a curious point for you to settle, my friend, who study psychology in a lazy, *dilettante* way. Stop a moment. I am going to be honest. This is what I want you to do. I want you to hide your disgust, take no heed to your clean clothes, and come right down with me,—here, into the thickest of the fog and mud and foul effluvia. I want you to hear this story. There is a secret down here, in this nightmare fog, that has lain dumb for centuries: I want to make it a real thing to you. You, Egoist, or Pantheist, or Arminian, busy in making straight paths for your feet on the hills, do not see it clearly,—this terrible question which men here have gone mad and died trying to answer. I dare not put this secret into words. I told you it was dumb. These men, going by with drunken faces and brains full of unawakened power, do not ask it of Society or of God. Their lives ask it; their deaths ask it. There is no reply. I will tell you plainly that I have a great hope; and I bring it to you to be tested. It is this: that this terrible dumb question is its own reply; that it is not the sentence of death we think it, but, from the very extremity of its darkness, the most solemn prophecy which the world has known of the Hope to come. I dare make my meaning no clearer, but will only tell my story. It will, perhaps, seem to you as foul and dark as this thick vapor about us, and as pregnant with death; but if your eyes are free as mine are to look deeper, no perfume-tinted dawn will be so fair with promise of the day that shall surely come.

My story is very simple,—only what I remember of the life of one of these men,—a furnace-tender in one of Kirby & John's rolling-mills,—Hugh Wolfe. You know the mills? They took the great order for the Lower Virginia railroads there last winter; run usually with about a thousand men. I cannot tell why I choose the half-forgotten story of this Wolfe more than that of myriads of these furnace-hands. Perhaps because there is a secret underlying sympathy between that story and this day with its impure fog and thwarted sunshine,—or perhaps simply for the reason that this house is the one where the Wolfes lived. There were the father and son,—both hands, as I said, in one of Kirby & John's mills for making railroad-iron,—and Deborah, their cousin, a picker in some of the cotton-mills. The house was rented then to half a dozen families. The Wolfes had two of the cellar-rooms. The old man, like many of the puddlers and feeders of the mills, was Welsh,—had spent half of his life in the Cornish tin-mines. You may pick the Welsh emigrants, Cornish miners, out of the throng passing the windows, any day. They are a trifle more filthy; their muscles are not so brawny; they stoop more. When they are drunk, they neither yell, nor shout, nor stagger, but skulk along like beaten hounds. A pure, unmixed blood, I fancy: shows itself in the slight angular bodies and sharply-cut facial lines. It is nearly thirty years since the Wolfes lived here. Their lives were like those of their class: incessant labor, sleeping in kennel-like rooms, eating rank pork and molasses, drinking—God and the distillers only know what; with an occasional night in jail, to atone for some drunken excess. Is that all of their lives?—of the portion given to them and these their duplicates swarming the streets to-day?—nothing beneath?—all? So many a political reformer will tell you,— and many a private reformer, too, who has gone among them with a heart tender with Christ's charity, and come out outraged, hardened.

One rainy night, about eleven o'clock, a crowd of half-clothed women stopped outside of the cellar-door. They were going home from the cotton-mill.

"Good-night, Deb," said one, a mulatto, steadying herself against the gas-post. She needed the post to steady her. So did more than one of them.

"Dah's a ball to Miss Potts' to-night. Ye'd best come."

"Inteet, Deb, if hur'll come, hur'll hef fun," said a shrill Welsh voice in the crowd.

Two or three dirty hands were thrust out to catch the gown of the woman, who was groping for the latch of the door.

"No."

"No? Where's Kit Small, then?"

"Begorra! on the spools. Alleys behint, though we helped her, we dud. An wid ye! Let Deb alone! It's ondacent frettin' a quite body. Be the powers, an' we'll have a night of it! there'll be lashin's o' drink,—the Vargent be blessed and praised for 't!"

They went on, the mulatto inclining for a moment to show fight, and drag the woman Wolfe off with them; but, being pacified, she staggered away.

Deborah groped her way into the cellar, and, after considerable stumbling, kindled a match, and lighted a tallow dip, that sent a yellow glimmer over the room. It was low, damp,—the earthen floor covered with a green, slimy moss,—a fetid air smothering the breath. Old Wolfe lay asleep on a heap of straw, wrapped in a torn horse-blanket. He was a pale, meek little man, with a white face and red rabbit-eyes. The woman Deborah was like him; only her face was even more ghastly, her lips bluer, her eyes more watery. She wore a faded cotton gown and a slouching bonnet. When she walked, one could see that she was deformed, almost a hunchback. She trod softly, so as not to waken him, and went through into the room beyond. There she found by the half-extinguished fire an iron saucepan filled with cold boiled potatoes, which she put upon a broken chair with a pint-cup of ale. Placing the old candlestick beside this dainty repast, she untied her bonnet, which hung limp and wet over her face, and prepared to eat her supper. It was the first food that had touched her lips since morning. There was enough of it, however: there is not always. She was hungry,—one could see that easily enough,—and not drunk, as most of her companions would have been found at this hour. She did not drink, this woman,—her face told that, too,—nothing stronger than ale. Perhaps the weak, flaccid wretch had some stimulant in her pale life to keep her up,—some love or hope, it might be, or urgent need. When that stimulant was gone, she would take to whiskey. Man cannot live by work alone. While she was skinning the potatoes, and munching them, a noise behind her made her stop.

"Janey!" she called, lifting the candle and peering into the darkness. "Janey, are you there?"

A heap of ragged coats was heaved up, and the face of a young girl emerged, staring sleepily at the woman.

"Deborah," she said, at last, "I'm here the night."

"Yes, child. Hur's welcome," she said, quietly eating on.

The girl's face was haggard and sickly; her eyes were heavy with sleep and hunger: real Milesian eyes they were, dark, delicate blue, glooming out from black shadows with a pitiful fright.

"I was alone," she said, timidly.

"Where's the father?" asked Deborah, holding out a potato, which the girl greedily seized.

"He's beyant,—wid Haley,—in the stone house." (Did you ever hear the word *jail* from an Irish mouth?) "I came here. Hugh told me never to stay me-lone."

"Hugh?"

"Yes."

A vexed frown crossed her face. The girl saw it, and added quickly,—

"I have not seen Hugh the day, Deb. The old man says his watch lasts till the mornin'."

The woman sprang up, and hastily began to arrange some bread and flitch in a tin pail, and to pour her own measure of ale into a bottle. Tying on her bonnet, she blew out the candle.

"Lay ye down, Janey dear," she said, gently, covering her with the old rags. "Hur can eat the potatoes, if hur's hungry."

"Where are ye goin', Deb? The rain's sharp."

"To the mill, with Hugh's supper."

"Let him bide till th' morn. Sit ye down."

"No, no,"—sharply pushing her off. "The boy'll starve."

She hurried from the cellar, while the child wearily coiled herself up for sleep. The rain was falling heavily, as the woman, pail in hand, emerged from the mouth of the alley, and turned down the narrow street, that stretched out, long and black, miles before her. Here and there a flicker of gas lighted an uncertain space of muddy footwalk and gutter; the long rows of houses, except an occasional lager-bier shop, were closed; now and then she met a band of mill-hands skulking to or from their work.

Not many even of the inhabitants of a manufacturing town know the vast machinery of system by which the bodies of workmen are governed, that goes on unceasingly from year to year. The hands of each mill are divided into watches that relieve each other as regularly as the sentinels of an army. By night and day the work goes on, the unsleeping engines groan and shriek, the fiery pools of metal boil and surge. Only for a day in the week, in half-courtesy to public censure, the fires are partially veiled; but as soon as the clock strikes midnight, the great furnaces break forth with renewed fury, the clamor begins with fresh, breathless vigor, the engines sob and shriek like "gods in pain."

As Deborah hurried down through the heavy rain, the noise of these thousand engines sounded through the sleep and shadow of the city like far-off thunder. The mill to which she was going lay on the river, a mile below the city-limits. It was far, and she was weak, aching from standing twelve hours at the spools. Yet it was her almost nightly walk to take this man his supper, though at every square she sat down to rest, and she knew she should receive small word of thanks.

Perhaps, if she had possessed an artist's eye, the picturesque oddity of the scene might have made her step stagger less, and the path seem shorter; but to her the mills were only "summat deilish to look at by night."

The road leading to the mills had been quarried from the solid rock, which rose abrupt and bare on one side of the cinder-covered road, while the river, sluggish and black, crept past on the other. The mills for rolling iron are simply immense tent-like roofs, covering acres of ground, open on every side. Beneath these roofs Deborah looked in on a city of fires, that burned hot and fiercely in the night. Fire in every horrible form: pits of flame waving in the wind; liquid metal-flames writhing in tortuous streams through the sand; wide caldrons filled with boiling fire, over which bent ghastly wretches stirring the strange brewing; and through all, crowds of half-clad men, looking like revengeful ghosts in the red light, hurried, throwing masses of glittering fire. It was like a street in Hell. Even Deborah muttered, as she crept through, " 'T looks like t' Devil's place!" It did,—in more ways than one.

She found the man she was looking for, at last, heaping coal on a furnace. He had not time to eat his supper; so she went behind the furnace, and waited. Only a few men were with him, and they noticed her only by a "Hyur comes t' hunchback, Wolfe."

Deborah was stupid with sleep; her back pained her sharply; and her teeth chattered with cold, with the rain that soaked her clothes and dripped from her at every step. She stood, however, patiently holding the pail, and waiting.

"Hout, woman! ye look like a drowned cat. Come near to the fire,"—said one of the men, approaching to scrape away the ashes.

She shook her head. Wolfe had forgotten her. He turned, hearing the man, and came closer.

"I did no' think; gi' me my supper, woman."

She watched him eat with a painful eagerness. With a woman's quick instinct, she saw that he was not hungry,—was eating to please her. Her pale, watery eyes began to gather a strange light.

"Is't good, Hugh? T'ale was a bit sour, I feared."

"No, good enough." He hesitated a moment. "Ye're tired, poor lass! Bide here till I go. Lay down there on that heap of ash, and go to sleep."

He threw her an old coat for a pillow, and turned to his work. The heap was the refuse of the burnt iron, and

was not a hard bed; the half-smothered warmth, too,
penetrated her limbs, dulling their pain and cold shiver.

Miserable enough she looked, lying there on the ashes
like a limp, dirty rag,—yet not an unfitting figure to
crown the scene of hopeless discomfort and veiled crime:
more fitting, if one looked deeper into the heart of
things,—at her thwarted woman's form, her colorless
life, her waking stupor that smothered pain and hunger,—even more fit to be a type of her class. Deeper yet
if one could look, was there nothing worth reading in this
wet, faded thing, half-covered with ashes? no story of a
soul filled with groping passionate love, heroic un-
selfishness, fierce jealousy? of years of weary trying to
please the one human being whom she loved, to gain one
look of real heart-kindness from him? If anything like
this were hidden beneath the pale, bleared eyes, and
dull, washed-out-looking face, no one had ever taken the
trouble to read its faint signs: not the half-clothed
furnace-tender, Wolfe, certainly. Yet he was kind to her:
it was his nature to be kind, even to the very rats that
swarmed in the cellar; kind to her in just the same way.
She knew that. And it might be that very knowledge
had given to her face its apathy and vacancy more than
her low, torpid life. One sees that dead, vacant look steal
sometimes over the rarest, finest of women's faces,—in
the very midst, it may be, of their warmest summer's
day; and then one can guess at the secret of intolerable
solitude that lies hid beneath the delicate laces and brilliant smile. There was no warmth, no brilliancy, no summer for this woman; so the stupor and vacancy had time
to gnaw into her face perpetually. She was young, too,
though no one guessed it; so the gnawing was the fiercer.

She lay quiet in the dark corner, listening, through the
monotonous din and uncertain glare of the works, to the
dull plash of the rain in the far distance,—shrinking back
whenever the man Wolfe happened to look towards her.
She knew, in spite of all his kindness, that there was that
in her face and form which made him loathe the sight
of her. She felt by instinct, although she could not comprehend it, the finer nature of the man, which made him
among his fellow-workmen something unique, set apart.
She knew, that, down under all the vileness and coarse-

ness of his life, there was a groping passion for whatever
was beautiful and pure,—that his soul sickened with disgust at her deformity, even when his words were kindest.
Through this dull consciousness, which never left her,
came, like a sting, the recollection of the dark blue eyes
and lithe figure of the little Irish girl she had left in the
cellar. The recollection struck through even her stupid
intellect with a vivid glow of beauty and of grace. Little
Janey, timid, helpless, clinging to Hugh as her only
friend: that was the sharp thought, the bitter thought,
that drove into the glazed eyes a fierce light of pain.
You laugh at it? Are pain and jealousy less savage realities down here in this place I am taking you to than in
your own house or your own heart,—your heart, which
they clutch at sometimes? The note is the same, I fancy,
be the octave high or low.

If you could go into this mill where Deborah lay, and
drag out from the hearts of these men the terrible tragedy of their lives, taking it as a symptom of the disease
of their class, no ghost Horror would terrify you more.
A reality of soul-starvation, of living death, that meets
you every day under the besotted faces on the street,—
I can paint nothing of this, only give you the outside
outlines of a night, a crisis in the life of one man: whatever muddy depth of soul-history lies beneath you can
read according to the eyes God has given you.

Wolfe, while Deborah watched him as a spaniel its
master, bent over the furnace with his iron pole, unconscious of her scrutiny, only stopping to receive orders.
Physically, Nature had promised the man but little. He
had already lost the strength and instinct vigor of a man,
his muscles were thin, his nerves weak, his face (a meek,
woman's face) haggard, yellow with consumption. In the
mill he was known as one of the girl-men: "Molly
Wolfe" was his *sobriquet*. He was never seen in the
cockpit, did not own a terrier, drank but seldom; when
he did, desperately. He fought sometimes, but was always thrashed, pommelled to a jelly. The man was game
enough, when his blood was up: but he was no favorite
in the mill; he had the taint of school-learning on him,—
not to a dangerous extent, only a quarter or so in the

free-school in fact, but enough to ruin him as a good hand in a fight.

For other reasons, too, he was not popular. Not one of themselves, they felt that, though outwardly as filthy and ash-covered; silent, with foreign thoughts and longings breaking out through his quietness in innumerable curious ways: this one, for instance. In the neighboring furnace-buildings lay great heaps of the refuse from the ore after the pig-metal is run. *Korl* we call it here: a light, porous substance, of a delicate, waxen, flesh-colored tinge. Out of the blocks of this korl, Wolfe, in his off-hours from the furnace, had a habit of chipping and moulding figures,—hideous, fantastic enough, but sometimes strangely beautiful: even the mill-men saw that, while they jeered at him. It was a curious fancy in the man, almost a passion. The few hours for rest he spent hewing and hacking with his blunt knife, never speaking, until his watch came again,—working at one figure for months, and, when it was finished, breaking it to pieces perhaps, in a fit of disappointment. A morbid, gloomy man, untaught, unled, left to feed his soul in grossness and crime, and hard, grinding labor.

I want you to come down and look at this Wolfe, standing there among the lowest of his kind, and see him just as he is, that you may judge him justly when you hear the story of this night. I want you to look back, as he does every day, at his birth in vice, his starved infancy; to remember the heavy years he has groped through as boy and man,—the slow, heavy years of constant, hot work. So long ago he began, that he thinks sometimes he has worked there for ages. There is no hope that it will ever end. Think that God put into this man's soul a fierce thirst for beauty,—to know it, to create it; to *be*—something, he knows not what,—other than he is. There are moments when a passing cloud, the sun glinting on the purple thistles, a kindly smile, a child's face, will rouse him to a passion of pain,—when his nature starts up with a mad cry of rage against God, man, whoever it is that has forced this vile, slimy life upon him. With all this groping, this mad desire, a great blind intellect stumbling through wrong, a loving poet's heart, the man was by habit only a coarse, vulgar laborer, familiar with sights and words you would blush to name. Be just: when I tell you about this night, see him as he is. Be just,—not like man's law, which seizes on one isolated fact, but like God's judging angel, whose clear, sad eye saw all the countless cankering days of this man's life, all the countless nights, when, sick with starving, his soul fainted in him, before it judged him for this night, the saddest of all.

I called this night the crisis of his life. If it was, it stole on him unawares. These great turning-days of life cast no shadow before, slip by unconsciously. Only a trifle, a little turn of the rudder, and the ship goes to heaven or hell.

Wolfe, while Deborah watched him, dug into the furnace of melting iron with his pole, dully thinking only how many rails the lump would yield. It was late,— nearly Sunday morning; another hour, and the heavy work would be done,—only the furnaces to replenish and cover for the next day. The workmen were growing more noisy, shouting, as they had to do, to be heard over the deep clamor of the mills. Suddenly they grew less boisterous,—at the far end, entirely silent. Something unusual had happened. After a moment, the silence came nearer; the men stopped their jeers and drunken choruses. Deborah, stupidly lifting up her head, saw the cause of the quiet. A group of five or six men were slowly approaching, stopping to examine each furnace as they came. Visitors often came to see the mills after night: except by growing less noisy, the men took no notice of them. The furnace where Wolfe worked was near the bounds of the works; they halted there hot and tired: a walk over one of these great foundries is no trifling task. The woman, drawing out of sight, turned over to sleep. Wolfe, seeing them stop, suddenly roused from his indifferent stupor, and watched them keenly. He knew some of them: the overseer, Clarke,—a son of Kirby, one of the mill-owners,—and a Doctor May, one of the town-physicians. The other two were strangers. Wolfe came closer. He seized eagerly every chance that brought him into contact with this mysterious class that shone down on him perpetually with the glamour of another order of being. What made the difference between

them? That was the mystery of his life. He had a vague
notion that perhaps to-night he could find it out. One of
the strangers sat down on a pile of bricks, and beckoned
young Kirby to his side.

"This *is* hot, with a vengeance. A match, please?"—
lighting his cigar. "But the walk is worth the trouble. If
it were not that you must have heard it so often, Kirby,
I would tell you that your works look like Dante's
Inferno."

Kirby laughed.

"Yes. Yonder is Farinata himself in the burning
tomb,"—pointing to some figure in the shimmering
shadows.

"Judging from some of the faces of your men," said
the other, "they bid fair to try the reality of Dante's
vision, some day."

Young Kirby looked curiously around, as if seeing the
faces of his hands for the first time.

"They're bad enough, that's true. A desperate set, I
fancy. Eh, Clarke?"

The overseer did not hear him. He was talking of net
profits just then,—giving, in fact, a schedule of the an-
nual business of the firm to a sharp peering little Yan-
kee, who jotted down notes on a paper laid on the crown
of his hat: a reporter for one of the city-papers, getting
up a series of reviews of the leading manufactories. The
other gentlemen had accompanied them merely for
amusement. They were silent until the notes were finished, drying their feet at the furnaces, and sheltering
their faces from the intolerable heat. At last the overseer
concluded with—

"I believe that is a pretty fair estimate, Captain."

"Here, some of you men!" said Kirby, "bring up those
boards. We may as well sit down, gentlemen, until the
rain is over. It cannot last much longer at this rate."

"Pig-metal,"—mumbled the reporter,—"um!—coal
facilities,—um!—hands employed, twelve hundred,—bi-
tumen,—um!—all right, I believe, Mr. Clarke;—sinking-
fund,—what did you say was your sinking-fund?"

"Twelve hundred hands?" said the stranger, the young
man who had first spoken. "Do you control their
votes, Kirby?"

"Control? No." The young man smiled complacently. "But my father brought seven hundred votes to the polls for his candidate last November. No force-work, you understand,—only a speech or two, a hint to form themselves into a society, and a bit of red and blue bunting to make them a flag. The Invincible Roughs,—I believe that is their name. I forget the motto: 'Our country's hope,' I think."

There was a laugh. The young man talking to Kirby sat with an amused light in his cool gray eye, surveying critically the half-clothed figures of the puddlers, and the slow swing of their brawny muscles. He was a stranger in the city,—spending a couple of months in the borders of a Slave State, to study the institutions of the South,— a brother-in-law of Kirby's,—Mitchell. He was an amateur gymnast,—hence his anatomical eye; a patron, in a *blasé* way, of the prize-ring; a man who sucked the essence out of a science or philosophy in an indifferent, gentlemanly way; who took Kant, Novalis, Humboldt, for what they were worth in his own scales; accepting all, despising nothing, in heaven, earth, or hell, but one-idead men; with a temper yielding and brilliant as summer water, until his Self was touched, when it was ice, though brilliant still. Such men are not rare in the States.

As he knocked the ashes from his cigar, Wolfe caught with a quick pleasure the contour of the white hand, the blood-glow of a red ring he wore. His voice, too, and that of Kirby's, touched him like music,—low, even, with chording cadences. About this man Mitchell hung the impalpable atmosphere belonging to the thoroughbred gentleman. Wolfe, scraping away the ashes beside him, was conscious of it, did obeisance to it with his artist sense, unconscious that he did so.

The rain did not cease. Clarke and the reporter left the mills; the others, comfortably seated near the furnace, lingered, smoking and talking in a desultory way. Greek would not have been more unintelligible to the furnace-tenders, whose presence they soon forgot entirely. Kirby drew out a newspaper from his pocket and read aloud some article, which they discussed eagerly. At every sentence, Wolfe listened more and more like a dumb, hopeless animal, with a duller, more stolid look creeping over his face, glancing now and then at Mitchell, marking acutely every smallest sign of refinement, then back to himself, seeing as in a mirror his filthy body, his more stained soul.

Never! He had no words for such a thought, but he knew now, in all the sharpness of the bitter certainty, that between them there was a great gulf never to be passed. Never!

The bells of the mills rang for midnight. Sunday morning had dawned. Whatever hidden message lay in the tolling bells floated past these men unknown. Yet it was there. Veiled in the solemn music ushering the risen saviour was a key-note to solve the darkest secrets of a world gone wrong,—even this social riddle which the brain of the grimy puddler grappled with madly to-night.

The men began to withdraw the metal from the caldrons. The mills were deserted on Sundays, except by the hands who fed the fires, and those who had no lodgings and slept usually on the ash-heaps. The three strangers sat still during the next hour, watching the men cover the furnaces, laughing now and then at some jest of Kirby's.

"Do you know," said Mitchell, "I like this view of the works better than when the glare was fiercest? These heavy shadows and the amphitheatre of smothered fires are ghostly, unreal. One could fancy these red smouldering lights to be the half-shut eyes of wild beasts, and the spectral figures their victims in the den."

Kirby laughed. "You are fanciful. Come, let us get out of the den. The spectral figures, as you call them, are a little too real for me to fancy a close proximity in the darkness,—unarmed, too."

The others rose, buttoning their over-coats, and lighting cigars.

"Raining, still," said Doctor May, "and hard. Where did we leave the coach, Mitchell?"

"At the other side of the works.—Kirby, what's that?"

Mitchell started back, half-frightened, as, suddenly turning a corner, the white figure of a woman faced him in the darkness,—a woman, white, of giant proportions, crouching on the ground, her arms flung out in some wild gesture of warning.

"Stop! Make that fire burn there!" cried Kirby, stopping short.

The flame burst out, flashing the gaunt figure into bold relief.

Mitchell drew a long breath.

"I thought it was alive," he said, going up curiously. The others followed.

"Not marble, eh?" asked Kirby, touching it.

One of the lower overseers stopped.

"Korl, Sir."

"Who did it?"

"Can't say. Some of the hands; chipped it out in off-hours."

"Chipped to some purpose, I should say. What a flesh-tint the stuff has! Do you see, Mitchell?"

"I see."

He had stepped aside where the light fell boldest on the figure, looking at it in silence. There was not one line of beauty or grace in it: a nude woman's form, muscular, grown coarse with labor, the powerful limbs instinct with some one poignant longing. One idea: there it was in the tense, rigid muscles, the clutching hands, the wild, eager face, like that of a starving wolf's. Kirby and Doctor May walked around it, critical, curious. Mitchell stood aloof, silent. The figure touched him strangely.

"Not badly done," said Doctor May. "Where did the fellow learn that sweep of the muscles in the arm and hand? Look at them! They are groping,—do you see?—clutching: the peculiar action of a man dying of thirst."

"They have ample facilities for studying anatomy," sneered Kirby, glancing at the half-naked figures.

"Look," continued the Doctor, "at this bony wrist, and the strained sinews of the instep! A working-woman,—the very type of her class."

"God forbid!" muttered Mitchell.

"Why?" demanded May. "What does the fellow intend by the figure? I cannot catch the meaning."

"Ask him," said the other, dryly. "There he stands,"—pointing to Wolfe, who stood with a group of men, leaning on his ash-rake.

The Doctor beckoned him with the affable smile

which kind-hearted men put on, when talking with these people.

"Mr. Mitchell has picked you out as the man who did this,—I'm sure I don't know why. But what did you mean by it?"

"She be hungry."

Wolfe's eyes answered Mitchell, not the Doctor.

"Oh-h! But what a mistake you have made, my fine fellow! You have given no sign of starvation to the body. It is strong,—terribly strong. It has the mad, half-despairing gesture of drowning."

Wolfe stammered, glanced appealingly at Mitchell, who saw the soul of the thing, he knew. But the cool, probing eyes were turned on himself now,—mocking, cruel, relentless.

"Not hungry for meat," the furnace-tender said at last.

"What then? Whiskey?" jeered Kirby, with a coarse laugh.

Wolfe was silent a moment, thinking.

"I dunno," he said, with a bewildered look. "It mebbe. Summat to make her live, I think,—like you. Whiskey ull do it, in a way."

The young man laughed again. Mitchell flashed a look of disgust somewhere,—not at Wolfe.

"May," he broke out impatiently, "are you blind? Look at that woman's face! It asks questions of God, and says, 'I have a right to know.' Good God, how hungry it is!"

They looked a moment; then May turned to the mill-owner:—

"Have you many such hands as this? What are you going to do with them? Keep them at puddling iron?"

Kirby shrugged his shoulders. Mitchell's look had irritated him.

"*Ce n'est pas mon affaire.* I have no fancy for nursing infant geniuses. I suppose there are some stray gleams of mind and soul among these wretches. The Lord will take care of his own; or else they can work out their own salvation. I have heard you call our American system a ladder which any man can scale. Do you doubt it? Or perhaps you want to banish all social ladders, and put us all on a flat table-land,—eh, May?"

The Doctor looked vexed, puzzled. Some terrible problem lay hid in this woman's face, and troubled these men. Kirby waited for an answer, and, receiving none, went on, warming with his subject.

"I tell you, there's something wrong that no talk of 'Liberté' or 'Égalité' will do away. If I had the making of men, these men who do the lowest part of the world's work should be machines,—nothing more,—hands. It would be kindness. God help them! What are taste, reason, to creatures who must live such lives as that?" He pointed to Deborah, sleeping on the ash-heap. "So many nerves to sting them to pain. What if God had put your brain, with all its agony of touch, into your fingers, and bid you work and strike with that?"

"You think you could govern the world better?" laughed the Doctor.

"I do not think at all."

"That is true philosophy. Drift with the stream, because you cannot dive deep enough to find bottom, eh?"

"Exactly," rejoined Kirby. "I do not think. I wash my hands of all social problems,—slavery, caste, white or black. My duty to my operatives has a narrow limit,— the pay-hour on Saturday night. Outside of that, if they cut korl, or cut each other's throats, (the more popular amusement of the two,) I am not responsible."

The Doctor sighed,—a good honest sigh, from the depths of his stomach.

"God help us! Who is responsible?"

"Not I, I tell you," said Kirby, testily. "What has the man who pays them money to do with their souls' concerns, more than the grocer or butcher who takes it?"

"And yet," said Mitchell's cynical voice, "look at her! How hungry she is!"

Kirby tapped his boot with his cane. No one spoke. Only the dumb face of the rough image looking into their faces with the awful question, "What shall we do to be saved?" Only Wolfe's face, with its heavy weight of brain, its weak, uncertain mouth, its desperate eyes, out of which looked the soul of his class,—only Wolfe's face turned towards Kirby's. Mitchell laughed,—a cool, musical laugh.

"Money has spoken!" he said, seating himself lightly

on a stone with the air of an amused spectator at a play. "Are you answered?"—turning to Wolfe his clear, magnetic face.

Bright and deep and cold as Arctic air, the soul of the man lay tranquil beneath. He looked at the furnace-tender as he had looked at a rare mosaic in the morning; only the man was the more amusing study of the two.

"Are you answered? Why, May, look at him! *'De profundis clamavi.'* Or, to quote in English, 'Hungry and thirsty, his soul faints in him.' And so Money sends back its answer into the depths through you, Kirby! Very clear the answer, too!—I think I remember reading the same words somewhere:—washing your hands in Eau de Cologne, and saying, 'I am innocent of the blood of this man. See ye to it!' "

Kirby flushed angrily.

"You quote Scripture freely."

"Do I not quote correctly? I think I remember another line, which may amend my meaning: 'Inasmuch as ye did it unto one of the least of these, ye did it unto me.' Deist? Bless you, man, I was raised on the milk of the Word. Now, Doctor, the pocket of the world having uttered its voice, what has the heart to say? You are a philanthropist, in a small way,—*n'est ce pas?* Here, boy, this gentleman can show you how to cut korl better,—or your destiny. Go on, May!"

"I think a mocking devil possesses you to-night," rejoined the Doctor, seriously.

He went to Wolfe and put his hand kindly on his arm. Something of a vague idea possessed the Doctor's brain that much good was to be done here by a friendly word or two: a latent genius to be warmed into life by a waited-for sun-beam. Here it was: he had brought it. So he went on complacently:—

"Do you know, boy, you have it in you to be a great sculptor, a great man?—do you understand?" (talking down to the capacity of his hearer: it is a way people have with children, and men like Wolfe,)—"to live a better, stronger life than I, or Mr. Kirby here? A man may make himself anything he chooses. God has given you stronger powers than many men,—me, for instance."

May stopped, heated, glowing with his own magnanimity. And it was magnanimous. The puddler had drunk in every word, looking through the Doctor's flurry, and generous heat, and self-approval, into his will, with those slow, absorbing eyes of his.

"Make yourself what you will. It is your right."

"I know," quietly. "Will you help me?"

Mitchell laughed again. The Doctor turned now, in a passion,—

"You know, Mitchell, I have not the means. You know, if I had, it is in my heart to take this boy and educate him for"—

"The glory of God, and the glory of John May."

May did not speak for a moment; then, controlled, he said,—

"Why should one be raised, when myriads are left?—I have not the money, boy," to Wolfe, shortly.

"Money?" He said it over slowly, as one repeats the guessed answer to a riddle, doubtfully. "That is it? Money?"

"Yes, money,—that is it," said Mitchell, rising, and drawing his furred coat about him. "You've found the cure for all the world's diseases.—Come, May, find your good-humor, and come home. This damp wind chills my very bones. Come and preach your Saint-Simonian doctrines to-morrow to Kirby's hands. Let them have a clear idea of the rights of the soul, and I'll venture next week they'll strike for higher wages. That will be the end of it."

"Will you send the coach-driver to this side of the mills?" asked Kirby, turning to Wolfe.

He spoke kindly: it was his habit to do so. Deborah, seeing the puddler go, crept after him. The three men waited outside. Doctor May walked up and down, chafed. Suddenly he stopped.

"Go back, Mitchell! You say the pocket and the heart of the world speak without meaning to these people. What has its head to say? Taste, culture, refinement? Go!"

Mitchell was leaning against a brick wall. He turned his head indolently, and looked into the mills. There hung about the place a thick, unclean odor. The slightest motion of his hand marked that he perceived it, and his insufferable disgust. That was all. May said nothing, only quickened his angry tramp.

"Besides," added Mitchell, giving a corollary to his answer, "it would be of no use. I am not one of them."

"You do not mean"—said May, facing him.

"Yes, I mean just that. Reform is born of need, not pity. No vital movement of the people's has worked down, for good or evil; fermented, instead, carried up the heaving, cloggy mass. Think back through history, and you will know it. What will this lowest deep— thieves, Magdalens, negroes—do with the light filtered through ponderous Church creeds, Baconian theories, Goethe schemes? Some day, out of their bitter need will be thrown up their own light-bringer,—their Jean Paul, their Cromwell, their Messiah."

"Bah!" was the Doctor's inward criticism. However, in practice, he adopted the theory; for, when, night and morning, afterwards, he prayed that power might be given these degraded souls to rise, he glowed at heart, recognizing an accomplished duty.

Wolfe and the woman had stood in the shadow of the works as the coach drove off. The Doctor had held out his hand in a frank, generous way, telling him to "take care of himself, and to remember it was his right to rise." Mitchell had simply touched his hat, as to an equal, with a quiet look of thorough recognition. Kirby had thrown Deborah some money, which she found, and clutched eagerly enough. They were gone now, all of them. The man sat down on the cinder-road, looking up into the murky sky.

" 'T be late, Hugh. Wunnot hur come?"

He shook his head doggedly, and the woman crouched out of his sight against the wall. Do you remember rare moments when a sudden light flashed over yourself, your world, God? when you stood on a mountain-peak, seeing your life as it might have been, as it is? one quick instant, when custom lost its force and every-day usage? when your friend, wife, brother, stood in a new light? your soul was bared, and the grave,—a foretaste of the nakedness of the Judgment-Day? So it came before him, his life, that night. The slow tides of pain he had borne gathered themselves up and surged against his soul. His squalid daily life, the brutal coarseness eating into his brain, as the ashes into his skin: before, these things had been a dull aching into his consciousness; to-night, they were reality. He gripped the filthy red shirt that clung, stiff with soot, about him, and tore it savagely from his arm. The flesh beneath was muddy with grease and ashes,—and the heart beneath that! And the soul? God knows.

Then flashed before his vivid poetic sense the man who had left him,—the pure face, the delicate, sinewy limbs, in harmony with all he knew of beauty or truth. In his cloudy fancy he had pictured a Something like this. He had found it in this Mitchell, even when he idly scoffed at his pain: a Man all-knowing, all-seeing, crowned by Nature, reigning,—the keen glance of his eye falling like a sceptre on other men. And yet his instinct taught him that he too—He! He looked at himself with sudden loathing, sick, wrung his hands with a cry, and then was silent. With all the phantoms of his heated, ignorant fancy, Wolfe had not been vague in his ambitions. They were practical, slowly built up before him out of his knowledge of what he could do. Through years he had day by day made this hope a real thing to himself,—a clear, projected figure of himself, as he might become.

Able to speak, to know what was best, to raise these men and women working at his side up with him: sometimes he forgot this defined hope in the frantic anguish to escape,—only to escape,—out of the wet, the pain, the ashes, somewhere, anywhere,—only for one moment of free air on a hill-side, to lie down and let his sick soul throb itself out in the sunshine. But to-night he panted for life. The savage strength of his nature was roused; his cry was fierce to God for justice.

"Look at me!" he said to Deborah, with a low, bitter laugh, striking his puny chest savagely. "What am I worth, Deb? Is it my fault that I am no better? My fault? My fault?"

He stopped, stung with a sudden remorse, seeing her hunchback shape writhing with sobs. For Deborah was crying thankless tears, according to the fashion of women.

"God forgi' me, woman! Things go harder wi' you nor me. It's a worse share."

He got up and helped her to rise; and they went doggedly down the muddy street, side by side.

"It's all wrong," he muttered, slowly,—"all wrong! I dunnot understan'. But it'll end some day."

"Come home, Hugh!" she said, coaxingly; for he had stopped, looking around bewildered.

"Home,—and back to the mill!" He went on saying this over to himself, as if he would mutter down every pain in this dull despair.

She followed him through the fog, her blue lips chattering with cold. They reached the cellar at last. Old Wolfe had been drinking since she went out, and had crept nearer the door. The girl Janey slept heavily in the corner. He went up to her, touching softly the worn white arm with his fingers. Some bitterer thought stung him, as he stood there. He wiped the drops from his forehead, and went into the room beyond, livid, trembling. A hope, trifling, perhaps, but very dear, had died just then out of the poor puddler's life, as he looked at the sleeping, innocent girl,—some plan for the future, in which she had borne a part. He gave it up that moment, then and forever. Only a trifle, perhaps, to us: his face grew a shade paler,—that was all. But, somehow, the man's soul, as God and the angels looked down on it, never was the same afterwards.

Deborah followed him into the inner room. She carried a candle, which she placed on the floor, closing the door after her. She had seen the look on his face, as he turned away: her own grew deadly. Yet, as she came up to him her eyes glowed. He was seated on an old chest, quiet, holding his face in his hands.

"Hugh!" she said, softly.

He did not speak.

"Hugh, did hur hear what the man said,—him with the clear voice? Did hur hear? Money, money,—that it wud do all?"

He pushed her away,—gently, but he was worn out; her rasping tone fretted him.

"Hugh!"

The candle flared a pale yellow light over the cob-

webbed brick walls, and the woman standing there. He
looked at her. She was young, in deadly earnest; her
faded eyes, and wet, ragged figure caught from their
frantic eagerness a power akin to beauty.

"Hugh, it is true! Money ull do it! ·Oh, Hugh, boy,
listen till me! He said it true! It is money!"

"I know. Go back! I do not want you here."

"Hugh, it is t' last time. I'll never worrit hur again."

There were tears in her voice now, but she choked
them back.

"Hear till me only to-night! If one of t' witch people
wud come, them we heard of t' home, and gif hur all
hur wants, what then? Say, Hugh!"

"What do you mean?"

"I mean money."

Her whisper shrilled through his brain.

"If one of t' witch dwarfs wud come from t' lane
moors to-night, and gif hur money, to go out,—*out*, I
say,—out, lad, where t' sun shines, and t' heath grows,
and t' ladies walk in silken gownds, and God stays all t'
time,—where t' man lives that talked to us to-night,—
Hugh knows,—Hugh could walk there like a king!"

He thought the woman mad, tried to check her, but
she went on, fierce in her eager haste.

"If *I* were t' witch dwarf, if I had t' money, wud hur
thank me? Wud hur take me out o' this place wid hur and
Janey? I wud not come into the gran' house hur wud build,
to vex hur wid t' hunch,—only at night, when t' shadows
were dark, stand far off to see hur."

Mad? Yes! Are many of us mad in this way?

"Poor Deb! poor Deb!" he said, soothingly.

"It is here," she said, suddenly jerking into his hand
a small roll. "I took it! I did it! Me, me!—not hur! I shall
be hanged, I shall be burnt in hell, if anybody knows I
took it! Out of his pocket, as he leaned against t' bricks.
Hur knows?"

She thrust it into his hand, and then, her errand done,
began to gather chips together to make a fire, choking
down hysteric sobs.

"Has it come to this?"

That was all he said. The Welsh Wolfe blood was honest. The roll was a small green pocket-book containing

one or two gold pieces, and a check for an incredible amount, as it seemed to the poor puddler. He laid it down, hiding his face again in his hands.

"Hugh, don't be angry wud me! It's only poor Deb,— hur knows?"

He took the long skinny fingers kindly in his.

"Angry? God help me, no! Let me sleep. I am tired."

He threw himself heavily down on the wooden bench, stunned with pain and weariness. She brought some old rags to cover him.

It was late on Sunday evening before he awoke. I tell God's truth, when I say he had then no thought of keeping this money. Deborah had hid it in his pocket. He found it there. She watched him eagerly, as he took it out.

"I must gif it to him," he said, reading her face.

"Hur knows," she said with a bitter sigh of disappointment. "But it is hur right to keep it."

His right! The word struck him. Doctor May had used the same. He washed himself, and went out to find this man Mitchell. His right! Why did this chance word cling to him so obstinately? Do you hear the fierce devils whisper in his ear, as he went slowly down the darkening street?

The evening came on, slow and calm. He seated himself at the end of an alley leading into one of the larger streets. His brain was clear to-night, keen, intent, mastering. It would not start back, cowardly, from any hellish temptation, but meet it face to face. Therefore the great temptation of his life came to him veiled by no sophistry, but bold, defiant, owning its own vile name, trusting to one bold blow for victory.

He did not deceive himself. Theft! That was it. At first the word sickened him; then he grappled with it. Sitting there on a broken cart-wheel, the fading day, the noisy groups, the church-bells' tolling passed before him like a panorama, while the sharp struggle went on within. This money! He took it out, and looked at it. If he gave it back, what then? He was going to be cool about it.

People going by to church saw only a sickly mill-boy watching them quietly at the alley's mouth. They did not know that he was mad, or they would not have gone by so quietly: mad with hunger; stretching out his hands to the world, that had given so much to them, for leave to live the life God meant him to live. His soul within him was smothering to death; he wanted so much, thought so much, and *knew*—nothing. There was nothing of which he was certain, except the mill and things there. Of God and heaven he had heard so little, that they were to him what fairy-land is to a child: something real, but not here; very far off. His brain, greedy, dwarfed, full of thwarted energy and unused powers, questioned these men and women going by, coldly, bitterly, that night. Was it not his right to live as they,—a pure life, a good, true-hearted life, full of beauty and kind words? He only wanted to know how to use the strength within him. His heart warmed, as he thought of it. He suffered himself to think of it longer. If he took the money?

Then he saw himself as he might be, strong, helpful, kindly. The night crept on, as this one image slowly evolved itself from the crowd of other thoughts and stood triumphant. He looked at it. As he might be! What wonder, if it blinded him to delirium,—the madness that underlies all revolution, all progress, and all fall?

You laugh at the shallow temptation? You see the error underlying its argument so clearly,—that to him a true life was one of full development rather than self-restraint? that he was deaf to the higher tone in a cry of voluntary suffering for truth's sake than in the fullest flow of spontaneous harmony? I do not plead his cause. I only want to show you the mote in my brother's eye: then you can see clearly to take it out.

The money,—there it lay on his knee, a little blotted slip of paper, nothing in itself; used to raise him out of the pit; something straight from God's hand. A thief! Well, what was it to be a thief? He met the question at last, face to face, wiping the clammy drops of sweat from his forehead. God made this money—the fresh air, too— for his children's use. He never made the difference between poor and rich. The Something who looked down on him that moment through the cool gray sky had a kindly face, he knew,—loved his children alike. Oh, he knew that!

There were times when the soft floods of color in the

crimson and purple flames, or the clear depth of amber
in the water below the bridge, had somehow given him
a glimpse of another world than this,—of an infinite
depth of beauty and of quiet somewhere,—somewhere,—a depth of quiet and rest and love. Looking up
now, it became strangely real. The sun had sunk quite
below the hills, but his last rays struck upward, touching
the zenith. The fog had risen, and the town and river
were steeped in its thick, gray damp; but overhead, the
sun-touched smoke-clouds opened like a cleft ocean,—
shifting, rolling seas of crimson mist, waves of billowy
silver veined with blood-scarlet, inner depths unfathom-
able of glancing light. Wolfe's artist-eye grew drunk with
color. The gates of that other world! Fading, flashing
before him now! What, in that world of Beauty, Content,
and Right, were the petty laws, the mine and thine, of
mill-owners and mill-hands?

A consciousness of power stirred within him. He stood
up. A man,—he thought, stretching out his hands,—free
to work, to live, to love! Free! His right! He folded the
scrap of paper in his hand. As his nervous fingers took
it in, limp and blotted, so his soul took in the mean
temptation, lapped it in fancied rights, in dreams of improved existences, drifting and endless as the cloud-seas
of color. Clutching it, as if the tightness of his hold would
strengthen his sense of possession, he went aimlessly
down the street. It was his watch at the mill. He need
not go, need never go again, thank God!—shaking off
the thought with unspeakable loathing.

Shall I go over the history of the hours of that night?
how the man wandered from one to another of his old
haunts, with a half-consciousness of bidding them farewell,—lanes and alleys and back-yards where the mill-
hands lodged,—noting, with a new eagerness, the filth
and drunkenness, the pig-pens, the ash-heaps covered
with potato-skins, the bloated, pimpled women at the
doors,—with a new disgust, a new sense of sudden triumph, and, under all, a new, vague dread, unknown before, smothered down, kept under, but still there? It left
him but once during the night, when, for the second time
in his life, he entered a church. It was a sombre Gothic
pile, where the stained light lost itself in far-retreating

arches; built to meet the requirements and sympathies
of a far other class than Wolfe's. Yet it touched, moved
him uncontrollably. The distances, the shadows, the still,
marble figures, the mass of silent kneeling worshippers,
the mysterious music, thrilled, lifted his soul with a wonderful pain. Wolfe forgot himself, forgot the new life he
was going to live, the mean terror gnawing underneath.
The voice of the speaker strengthened the charm; it was
clear, feeling, full, strong. An old man, who had lived
much, suffered much; whose brain was keenly alive,
dominant; whose heart was summer-warm with charity.
He taught it to-night. He held up Humanity in its grand
total; showed the great world-cancer to his people. Who
could show it better? He was a Christian reformer; he
had studied the age thoroughly; his outlook at man had
been free, world-wide, over all time. His faith stood sublime upon the Rock of Ages; his fiery zeal guided vast
schemes by which the gospel was to be preached to all
nations. How did he preach it to-night? In burning, light-
laden words he painted the incarnate Life, Love, the
universal Man: words that became reality in the lives of
these people,—that lived again in beautiful words and
actions, trifling, but heroic. Sin, as he defined it, was a
real foe to them; their trials, temptations, were his. His
words passed far over the furnace-tender's grasp, toned
to suit another class of culture; they sounded in his ears
a very pleasant song in an unknown tongue. He meant
to cure this world-cancer with a steady eye that had
never glared with hunger, and a hand that neither poverty nor strychnine-whiskey had taught to shake. In this
morbid, distorted heart of the Welsh puddler he had
failed.

Wolfe rose at last, and turned from the church down
the street. He looked up; the night had come on foggy,
damp; the golden mists had vanished, and the sky lay
dull and ash-colored. He wandered again aimlessly down
the street, idly wondering what had become of the cloud-
sea of crimson and scarlet. The trial-day of this man's
life was over, and he had lost the victory. What followed
was mere drifting circumstance,—a quicker walking over
the path,—that was all. Do you want to hear the end of
it? You wish me to make a tragic story out of it? Why,

in the police-reports of the morning paper you can find a dozen such tragedies: hints of shipwrecks unlike any that ever befell on the high seas; hints that here a power was lost to heaven,—that there a soul went down where no tide can ebb or flow. Commonplace enough the hints are,—jocose sometimes, done up in rhyme.

Doctor May, a month after the night I have told you of, was reading to his wife at breakfast from this fourth column of the morning-paper: an unusual thing,—these police-reports not being, in general, choice reading for ladies; but it was only one item he read.

"Oh, my dear! You remember that man I told you of, that we saw at Kirby's mill?—that was arrested for robbing Mitchell? Here he is; just listen:—'Circuit Court. Judge Day. Hugh Wolfe, operative in Kirby & John's Loudon Mills. Charge, grand larceny. Sentence, nineteen years hard labor in penitentiary.'—Scoundrel! Serves him right! After all our kindness that night! Picking Mitchell's pocket at the very time!"

His wife said something about the ingratitude of that kind of people, and then they began to talk of something else.

Nineteen years! How easy that was to read! What a simple word for Judge Day to utter! Nineteen years! Half a lifetime!

Hugh Wolfe sat on the window-ledge of his cell, looking out. His ankles were ironed. Not usual in such cases; but he had made two desperate efforts to escape. "Well," as Haley, the jailer, said, "small blame to him! Nineteen years' imprisonment was not a pleasant thing to look forward to." Haley was very good-natured about it, though Wolfe had fought him savagely.

"When he was first caught," the jailer said afterwards, in telling the story, "before the trial, the fellow was cut down at once,—laid there on that pallet like a dead man, with his hands over his eyes. Never saw a man so cut down in my life. Time of the trial, too, came the queerest dodge of any customer I ever had. Would choose no lawyer. Judge gave him one, of course. Gibson it was. He tried to prove the fellow crazy; but it wouldn't go. Thing was plain as day-light: money found on him. 'Twas a hard sentence,—all the law allows; but it was for 'xample's sake. These mill-hands are gettin' onbearable. When the sentence was read, he just looked up, and said the money was his by rights, and that all the world had gone wrong. That night, after the trial, a gentleman came to see him here, name of Mitchell,—him as he stole from. Talked to him for an hour. Thought he came for curiosity, like. After he was gone, thought Wolfe was remarkable quiet, and went into his cell. Found him very low; bed all bloody. Doctor said he had been bleeding at the lungs. He was as weak as a cat; yet, if ye'll b'lieve me, he tried to get a-past me and get out. I just carried him like a baby, and threw him on the pallet. Three days after, he tried it again: that time reached the wall. Lord help you! he fought like a tiger,—giv' some terrible blows. Fightin' for life, you see; for he can't live long, shut up in the stone crib down yonder. Got a death-cough now. 'T took two of us to bring him down that day; so I just put the irons on his feet. There he sits, in there. Goin' to-morrow, with a batch more of 'em. That woman, hunchback, tried with him,—you remember?— she's only got three years. 'Complice. But *she's* a woman, you know. He's been quiet ever since I put on irons: giv' up, I suppose. Looks white, sick-lookin'. It acts different on 'em, bein' sentenced. Most of 'em gets reckless, devilish-like. Some prays awful, and sings them vile songs of the mills, all in a breath. That woman, now, she's desper't'. Been beggin' to see Hugh, as she calls him, for three days. I'm a-goin' to let her in. She don't go with him. Here she is in this next cell. I'm a-goin' now to let her in."

He let her in. Wolfe did not see her. She crept into a corner of the cell, and stood watching him. He was scratching the iron bars of the window with a piece of tin which he had picked up, with an idle, uncertain, vacant stare, just as a child or idiot would do.

"Tryin' to get out, old boy?" laughed Haley. "Them irons will need a crow-bar beside your tin, before you can open 'em."

Wolfe laughed, too, in a senseless way.

"I think I'll get out," he said.

"I believe his brain's touched," said Haley, when he came out.

The puddler scraped away with the tin for half an
hour. Still Deborah did not speak. At last she ventured
nearer, and touched his arm.

"Blood?" she said, looking at some spots on his coat
with a shudder.

He looked up at her. "Why, Deb!" he said, smiling,—
such a bright, boyish smile, that it went to poor Deborah's heart directly, and she sobbed and cried out loud.

"Oh, Hugh, lad! Hugh! dunnot look at me, when it
wur my fault! To think I brought hur to it! And I loved
hur so! Oh, lad, I dud!"

The confession, even in this wretch, came with the
woman's blush through the sharp cry.

He did not seem to hear her,—scraping away diligently at the bars with the bit of tin.

Was he going mad? She peered closely into his face.
Something she saw there made her draw suddenly
back,—something which Haley had not seen, that lay
beneath the pinched, vacant look it had caught since the
trial, or the curious gray shadow that rested on it. That
gray shadow,—yes, she knew what that meant. She had
often seen it creeping over women's faces for months,
who died at last of slow hunger or consumption. That
meant death, distant, lingering: but this—Whatever it
was the woman saw, or thought she saw, used as she
was to crime and misery, seemed to make her sick with
a new horror. Forgetting her fear of him, she caught his
shoulders, and looked keenly, steadily, into his eyes.

"Hugh!" she cried, in a desperate whisper,—"oh, boy,
not that! for God's sake, not *that!*"

The vacant laugh went off his face, and he answered
her in a muttered word or two that drove her away. Yet
the words were kindly enough. Sitting there on his pallet,
she cried silently a hopeless sort of tears, but did not
speak again. The man looked up furtively at her now
and then. Whatever his own trouble was, her distress
vexed him with a momentary sting.

It was market-day. The narrow window of the jail
looked down directly on the carts and wagons drawn up
in a long line, where they had unloaded. He could see,
too, and hear distinctly the clink of money as it changed
hands, the busy crowd of whites and blacks shoving,

pushing one another, and the chaffering and swearing at the stalls. Somehow, the sound, more than anything else had done, wakened him up,—made the whole real to him. He was done with the world and the business of it. He let the tin fall, and looked out, pressing his face close to the rusty bars. How they crowded and pushed! And he,—he should never walk that pavement again! There came Neff Sanders, one of the feeders at the mill, with a basket on his arm. Sure enough, Neff was married the other week. He whistled, hoping he would look up; but he did not. He wondered if Neff remembered he was there,—if any of the boys thought of him up there, and thought that he never was to go down that old cinder-road again. Never again! He had not quite understood it before; but now he did. Not for days or years, but never!—that was it.

How clear the light fell on that stall in front of the market! and how like a picture it was, the dark-green heaps of corn, and the crimson beets, and golden melons! There was another with game: how the light flickered on that pheasant's breast, with the purplish blood dripping over the brown feathers! He could see the red shining of the drops, it was so near. In one minute he could be down there. It was just a step. So easy, as it seemed, so natural to go! Yet it could never be—not in all the thousands of years to come—that he should put his foot on that street again! He thought of himself with a sorrowful pity, as of some one else. There was a dog down in the market, walking after his master with such a stately, grave look!—only a dog, yet he could go backwards and forwards just as he pleased: he had good luck! Why, the very vilest cur, yelping there in the gutter, had not lived his life, had been free to act out whatever thought God had put into his brain; while he—No, he would not think of that! He tried to put the thought away, and to listen to a dispute between a countryman and a woman about some meat; but it would come back. He, what had he done to bear this?

Then came the sudden picture of what might have been, and now. He knew what it was to be in the penitentiary,—how it went with men there. He knew how in these long years he should slowly die, but not until soul

and body had become corrupt and rotten,—how, when
he came out, if he lived to come, even the lowest of the
mill-hands would jeer him,—how his hands would be
weak, and his brain senseless and stupid. He believed he
was almost that now. He put his hand to his head, with
a puzzled, weary look. It ached, his head, with thinking.
He tried to quiet himself. It was only right, perhaps; he
had done wrong. But was there right or wrong for such
as he? What was right? And who had ever taught him?
He thrust the whole matter away. A dark, cold quiet
crept through his brain. It was all wrong; but let it be!
It was nothing to him more than the others. Let it be!

The door grated, as Haley opened it.

"Come, my woman! Must lock up for t' night. Come,
stir yerself!"

She went up and took Hugh's hand.

"Good-night, Deb," he said, carelessly.

She had not hoped he would say more; but the tired
pain on her mouth just then was bitterer than death. She
took his passive hand and kissed it.

"Hur'll never see Deb again!" she ventured, her lips
growing colder and more bloodless.

What did she say that for? Did he not know it? Yet
he would not be impatient with poor old Deb. She had
trouble of her own, as well as he.

"No, never again," he said, trying to be cheerful.

She stood just a moment, looking at him. Do you
laugh at her, standing there, with her hunchback, her
rags, her bleared, withered face, and the great despised
love tugging at her heart?

"Come, you!" called Haley, impatiently.

She did not move.

"Hugh!" she whispered.

It was to be her last word. What was it?

"Hugh, boy, not *THAT!*"

He did not answer. She wrung her hands, trying to be
silent, looking in his face in an agony of entreaty. He
smiled again, kindly.

"It is best, Deb. I cannot bear to be hurted any more."

"Hur knows," she said, humbly.

"Tell my father good-bye; and—and kiss little Janey."

She nodded, saying nothing, looked in his face again, and went out of the door. As she went, she staggered.

"Drinkin' to-day?" broke out Haley, pushing her before him. "Where the Devil did you get it? Here, in with ye!" and he shoved her into her cell, next to Wolfe's, and shut the door.

Along the wall of her cell there was a crack low down by the floor, through which she could see the light from Wolfe's. She had discovered it days before. She hurried in now, and, kneeling down by it, listened, hoping to hear some sound. Nothing but the rasping of the tin on the bars. He was at his old amusement again. Something in the noise jarred on her ear, for she shivered as she heard it. Hugh rasped away at the bars. A dull old bit of tin, not fit to cut korl with.

He looked out of the window again. People were leaving the market now. A tall mulatto girl, following her mistress, her basket on her head, crossed the street just below, and looked up. She was laughing; but, when she caught sight of the haggard face peering out through the bars, suddenly grew grave, and hurried by. A free, firm step, a clear-cut olive face, with a scarlet turban tied on one side, dark, shining eyes, and on the head the basket poised, filled with fruit and flowers, under which the scarlet turban and bright eyes looked out half-shadowed. The picture caught his eye. It was good to see a face like that. He would try to-morrow, and cut one like it. *To-morrow!* He threw down the tin, trembling, and covered his face with his hands. When he looked up again, the daylight was gone.

Deborah, crouching near by on the other side of the wall, heard no noise. He sat on the side of the low pallet, thinking. Whatever was the mystery which the woman had seen on his face, it came out now slowly, in the dark there, and became fixed,—a something never seen on his face before. The evening was darkening fast. The market had been over for an hour; the rumbling of the carts over the pavement grew more infrequent: he listened to each, as it passed, because he thought it was to be for the last time. For the same reason, it was, I suppose, that he strained his eyes to catch a glimpse of each passer-by, wondering who they were, what kind of homes they were

going to, if they had children,—listening eagerly to every
chance word in the street, as if—(God be merciful to
the man! what strange fancy was this?)—as if he never
should hear human voices again.

It was quite dark at last. The street was a lonely one.
The last passenger, he thought, was gone. No,—there
was a quick step: Joe Hill, lighting the lamps. Joe was a
good old chap; never passed a fellow without some joke
or other. He remembered once seeing the place where
he lived with his wife. "Granny Hill" the boys called
her. Bedridden she was; but so kind as Joe was to her!
kept the room so clean!—and the old woman, when he
was there, was laughing at "some of t' lad's foolishness."
The step was far down the street; but he could see him
place the ladder, run up, and light the gas. A longing
seized him to be spoken to once more.

"Joe!" he called, out of the grating. "Good-bye, Joe!"

The old man stopped a moment, listening uncertainly;
then hurried on. The prisoner thrust his hand out of the
window, and called again, louder; but Joe was too far
down the street. It was a little thing; but it hurt him,—
this disappointment.

"Good-bye, Joe!" he called, sorrowfully enough.

"Be quiet!" said one of the jailers, passing the door,
striking on it with his club.

Oh, that was the last, was it?

There was an inexpressible bitterness on his face, as
he lay down on the bed, taking the bit of tin, which he
had rasped to a tolerable degree of sharpness, in his
hand,—to play with, it may be. He bared his arms, looking intently at their corded veins and sinews. Deborah,
listening in the next cell, heard a slight clicking sound,
often repeated. She shut her lips tightly, that she might
not scream, the cold drops of sweat broke over her, in
her dumb agony.

"Hur knows best," she muttered at last, fiercely
clutching the boards where she lay.

If she could have seen Wolfe, there was nothing about
him to frighten her. He lay quite still, his arms outstretched, looking at the pearly stream of moonlight
coming into the window. I think in that one hour that
came then he lived back over all the years that had gone

before. I think that all the low, vile life, all his wrongs, all his starved hopes, came then, and stung him with a farewell poison that made him sick unto death. He made neither moan nor cry, only turned his worn face now and then to the pure light, that seemed so far off, as one that said, "How long, O Lord? how long?"

The hour was over at last. The moon, passing over her nightly path, slowly came nearer, and threw the light across his bed on his feet. He watched it steadily, as it crept up, inch by inch, slowly. It seemed to him to carry with it a great silence. He had been so hot and tired there always in the mills! The years had been so fierce and cruel! There was coming now quiet and coolness and sleep. His tense limbs relaxed, and settled in a calm languor. The blood ran fainter and slow from his heart. He did not think now with a savage anger of what might be and was not; he was conscious only of deep stillness creeping over him. At first he saw a sea of faces: the mill-men,—women he had known, drunken and bloated,—Janeys timid and pitiful,—poor old Debs: then they floated together like a mist, and faded away, leaving only the clear, pearly moonlight.

Whether, as the pure light crept up the stretched-out figure, it brought with it calm and peace, who shall say? His dumb soul was alone with God in judgment. A Voice may have spoken for it from far-off Calvary, "Father, forgive them, for they know not what they do!" Who dare say? Fainter and fainter the heart rose and fell, slower and slower the moon floated from behind a cloud, until, when at last its full tide of white splendor swept over the cell, it seemed to wrap and fold into a deeper stillness the dead figure that never should move again. Silence deeper than the Night! Nothing that moved, save the black nauseous stream of blood dripping slowly from the pallet to the floor!

There was outcry and crowd enough in the cell the next day. The coroner and his jury, the local editors, Kirby himself, and boys with their hands thrust knowingly into their pockets and heads on one side, jammed into the corners. Coming and going all day. Only one woman. She came late, and outstayed them all. A Quaker, or Friend, as they call themselves. I think this woman was known by that name in heaven. A homely body, coarsely dressed in gray and white. Deborah (for Haley had let her in) took notice of her. She watched them all—sitting on the end of the pallet, holding his head in her arms—with the ferocity of a watch-dog, if any of them touched the body. There was no meekness, or sorrow, in her face; the stuff out of which murderers are made, instead. All the time Haley and the woman were laying straight the limbs and cleaning the cell, Deborah sat still, keenly watching the Quaker's face. Of all the crowd there that day, this woman alone had not spoken to her,—only once or twice had put some cordial to her lips. After they all were gone, the woman, in the same still, gentle way, brought a vase of wood-leaves and berries, and placed it by the pallet, then opened the narrow window. The fresh air blew in, and swept the woody fragrance over the dead face. Deborah looked up with a quick wonder.

"Did hur know my boy wud like it? Did hur know Hugh?"

"I know Hugh now."

The white fingers passed in a slow, pitiful way over the dead, worn face. There was a heavy shadow in the quiet eyes.

"Did hur know where they'll bury Hugh?" said Deborah in a shrill tone, catching her arm.

This had been the question hanging on her lips all day.

"In t' town-yard? Under t' mud and ash? T' lad'll smother, woman! He wur born on t' lane moor, where t' air is frick and strong. Take hur out, for God's sake, take hur out where t' air blows!"

The Quaker hesitated, but only for a moment. She put her strong arm around Deborah and led her to the window.

"Thee sees the hills, friend, over the river? Thee sees how the light lies warm there, and the winds of God blow all the day? I live there,—where the blue smoke is, by the trees. Look at me." She turned Deborah's face to her own, clear and earnest. "Thee will believe me? I will take Hugh and bury him there to-morrow."

Deborah did not doubt her. As the evening wore on, she leaned against the iron bars, looking at the hills that rose far off, through the thick sodden clouds, like a bright, unattainable calm. As she looked, a shadow of their solemn repose fell on her face: its fierce discontent faded into a pitiful, humble quiet. Slow, solemn tears gathered in her eyes: the poor weak eyes turned so hopelessly to the place where Hugh was to rest, the grave heights looking higher and brighter and more solemn than ever before. The Quaker watched her keenly. She came to her at last, and touched her arm.

"When thee comes back," she said, in a low, sorrowful tone, like one who speaks from a strong heart deeply moved with remorse or pity, "thee shall begin thy life again,—there on the hills. I came too late; but not for thee,—by God's help, it may be."

Not too late. Three years after, the Quaker began her work. I end my story here. At evening-time it was light. There is no need to tire you with the long years of sunshine, and fresh air, and slow, patient Christ-love, needed to make healthy and hopeful this impure body and soul. There is a homely pine house, on one of these hills, whose windows overlook broad, wooded slopes and clover-crimsoned meadows,—niched into the very place where the light is warmest, the air freest. It is the Friends' meeting-house. Once a week they sit there, in their grave, earnest way, waiting for the Spirit of Love to speak, opening their simple hearts to receive His words. There is a woman, old, deformed, who takes a humble place among them: waiting like them: in her gray dress, her worn face, pure and meek, turned now and then to the sky. A woman much loved by these silent, restful people; more silent than they, more humble, more loving. Waiting: with her eyes turned to hills higher and purer than these on which she lives,—dim and far off now, but to be reached some day. There may be in her heart some latent hope to meet there the love denied her here,—that she shall find him whom she lost, and that then she will not be all-unworthy. Who blames her? Something is lost in the passage of every soul from one eternity to the other,—something pure and beautiful, which might have been and was not: a hope, a talent, a love, over which the soul mourns, like Esau deprived of his birthright. What blame to the meek Quaker, if she took her lost hope to make the hills of heaven more fair?

Nothing remains to tell that the poor Welsh puddler once lived, but this figure of the mill-woman cut in korl. I have it here in a corner of my library. I keep it hid behind a curtain,—it is such a rough, ungainly thing. Yet there are about it touches, grand sweeps of outline, that show a master's hand. Sometimes,—to-night, for instance,—the curtain is accidentally drawn back, and I see a bare arm stretched out imploringly in the darkness, and an eager, wolfish face watching mine: a wan, woful face, through which the spirit of the dead korl-cutter looks out, with its thwarted life, its mighty hunger, its unfinished work. Its pale, vague lips seem to tremble with a terrible question. "Is this the End?" they say,— "nothing beyond?—no more?" Why, you tell me you have seen that look in the eyes of dumb brutes,—horses dying under the lash. I know.

The deep of the night is passing while I write. The gas-light wakens from the shadows here and there the objects which lie scattered through the room: only faintly, though; for they belong to the open sunlight. As I glance at them, they each recall some task or pleasure of the coming day. A half-moulded child's head; Aphrodite; a bough of forest-leaves; music; work; homely fragments, in which lie the secrets of all eternal truth and beauty. Prophetic all! Only this dumb, woful face seems to belong to and end with the night. I turn to look at it. Has the power of its desperate need commanded the darkness away? While the room is yet steeped in heavy shadow, a cool, gray light suddenly touches its head like a blessing hand, and its groping arm points through the broken cloud to the far East, where, in the flickering, nebulous crimson, God has set the promise of the Dawn.

—1861

STEPHEN CRANE
(1871–1900)

The fourteenth child of a Methodist minister, the Reverend Dr. Jonathan Townley Crane, and a Methodist revivalist, journalist, and speaker, Mary Peck Crane, Stephen Crane was born in New Jersey. After the death of her husband, when Stephen was nine years old, Mary Crane relocated her family to Asbury Park, a fashionable summer resort town on the New Jersey shore. There, Mrs. Crane and Stephen collected news about the activities of the affluent summer vacationers for items and essays they could easily publish, since one of Stephen's older brothers headed a *New York Tribune* agency for summer news stories. Crane spent two years at Claverack Military School, followed by a semester at Lafayette College in Easton, Pennsylvania. In 1891, during one semester at Syracuse University, he completed a first draft of "Maggie: A Girl of the Streets." Using the pseudonym Johnston Smith, Crane published "Maggie" in 1893 at his own expense. Rejecting the intense religious background of his parents, Crane depicted a godless universe that was indifferent to the lives and suffering of human beings. A revised version of "Maggie" that named Crane as the author was published in New York in 1896. An early Naturalist writer, he described his philosophy of using fiction "to show that environment is a tremendous thing in the world and frequently shapes lives." During his short career, Crane wrote *The Red Badge of Courage* (1895), a classic American war novel, *George's Mother* (1896), *The Open Boat and Other Tales of Adventure* (1898), *The Monster and Other Stories* (1899), *Great Battles of the World* (1901), and *Last Words* (1902).

Maggie: A Girl of the Streets

CHAPTER I

A very little boy stood upon a heap of gravel for the honor of Rum Alley. He was throwing stones at howling urchins from Devil's Row who were circling madly about the heap and pelting him.

His infantile countenance was livid with the fury of battle. His small body was writhing in the delivery of oaths.

"Run, Jimmie, run! Dey'll git yehs!" screamed a retreating Rum Alley child.

"Naw," responded Jimmie with a valiant roar, "dese micks can't make me run."

Howls of renewed wrath went up from Devil's Row throats. Tattered gamins on the right made a furious assault on the gravel heap. On their small, convulsed faces shone the grins of true assassins. As they charged, they threw stones and cursed in shrill chorus.

The little champion of Rum Alley stumbled precipitately down the other side. His coat had been torn to shreds in a scuffle, and his hat was gone. He had bruises on twenty parts of his body, and blood was dripping from a cut in his head. His wan features looked like those of a tiny, insane demon.

On the ground, children from Devil's Row closed in on their antagonist. He crooked his left arm defensively about his head and fought with madness. The little boys ran to and fro, dodging, hurling stones and swearing in barbaric trebles.

From a window of an apartment house that uprose from amid squat, ignorant stables, there leaned a curious woman. Some laborers, unloading a scow at a dock at the river, paused for a moment and regarded the fight. The engineer of a passive tugboat hung lazily over a railing and watched. Over on the Island, a worm of yellow convicts came from the shadow of a grey ominous building and crawled slowly along the river's bank.

A stone had smashed in Jimmie's mouth. Blood was bubbling over his chin and down upon his ragged shirt. Tears made furrows on his dirt-stained cheeks. His thin legs had begun to tremble and turn weak, causing his small body to reel. His roaring curses of the first part of the fight had changed to a blasphemous chatter.

In the yells of the whirling mob of Devil's Row children there were notes of joy like songs of triumphant savagery. The little boys seemed to leer gloatingly at the blood upon the other child's face.

Down the avenue came boastfully sauntering a lad of sixteen years, although the chronic sneer of an ideal manhood already sat upon his lips. His hat was tipped over his eye with an air of challenge. Between his teeth, a cigar stump was tilted at the angle of defiance. He walked with a certain swing of the shoulders which appalled the timid. He glanced over into the vacant lot in which the little raving boys from Devil's Row seethed about the shrieking and tearful child from Rum Alley.

"Gee!" he murmured with interest. "A scrap. Gee!"

He strode over to the cursing circle, swinging his shoulders in a manner which denoted that he held victory in his fists. He approached at the back of one of the most deeply engaged of the Devil's Row children.

"Ah, what d' hell," he said, and smote the deeply-engaged one on the back of the head. The little boy fell to the ground and gave a tremendous howl. He scrambled to his feet, and perceiving, evidently, the size of his assailant, ran quickly off, shouting alarms. The entire Devil's Row party followed him. They came to a stand a short distance away and yelled taunting oaths at the boy with the chronic sneer. The latter, momentarily, paid no attention to them.

"What d' hell, Jimmie?" he asked of the small champion.

Jimmie wiped his blood-wet features with his sleeve.

"Well, it was dis way, Pete, see! I was goin' t' lick dat Riley kid and dey all pitched on me."

Some Rum Alley children now came forward. The party stood for a moment exchanging vainglorious remarks with Devil's Row. A few stones were thrown at long distances, and words of challenge passed between small warriors. Then the Rum Alley contingent turned slowly in the direction of their home street. They began to give, each to each, distorted versions of the fight. Causes of retreat in particular cases were magnified. Blows dealt in the fight were enlarged to catapultian power, and stones thrown were alleged to have hurtled with infinite accuracy. Valor grew strong again, and the little boys began to brag with great spirit.

"Ah, we blokies kin lick d' hull damn Row," said a child, swaggering.

Little Jimmie was striving to stanch the flow of blood from his cut lips. Scowling, he turned upon the speaker.

"Ah, where d' hell was yehs when I was doin' all d' fightin'?" he demanded. "Youse kids makes me tired."

"Ah, go ahn," replied the other argumentatively.

Jimmie replied with heavy contempt. "Ah, youse can't fight, Blue Billie! I kin lick yeh wid one han'."

"Ah, go ahn," replied Billie again.

"Ah," said Jimmie threateningly.

"Ah," said the other in the same tone.

They struck at each other, clinched, and rolled over on the cobble stones.

"Smash 'im, Jimmie, kick d' damn guts out of 'im," yelled Pete, the lad with the chronic sneer, in tones of delight.

The small combatants pounded and kicked, scratched and tore. They began to weep and their curses struggled in their throats with sobs. The other little boys clasped their hands and wriggled their legs in excitement. They formed a bobbing circle about the pair.

A tiny spectator was suddenly agitated.

"Cheese it, Jimmie, cheese it! Here comes yer fader," he yelled.

The circle of little boys instantly parted. They drew away and waited in ecstatic awe for that which was about to happen. The two little boys fighting in the modes of four thousand years ago, did not hear the warning.

Up the avenue there plodded slowly a man with sullen eyes. He was carrying a dinner-pail and smoking an apple-wood pipe.

As he neared the spot where the little boys strove, he regarded them listlessly. But suddenly he roared an oath and advanced upon the rolling fighters.

"Here, you Jim, git up, now, while I belt yer life out, yeh damned disorderly brat."

He began to kick into the chaotic mass on the ground. The boy Billie felt a heavy boot strike his head. He made a furious effort and disentangled himself from Jimmie. He tottered away, damning.

Jimmie arose painfully from the ground and confronting his father, began to curse him. His parent kicked him. "Come home, now," he cried, "an' stop yer jawin', er I'll lam the everlasting head off yehs."

They departed. The man paced placidly along with the applewood emblem of serenity between his teeth. The boy followed a dozen feet in the rear. He swore luridly, for he felt that it was degradation for one who aimed to be some vague kind of a soldier, or a man of blood with a sort of sublime license, to be taken home by a father.

<h3 style="text-align:center">CHAPTER II</h3>

Eventually they entered into a dark region where, from a careening building, a dozen gruesome doorways gave up loads of babies to the street and the gutter. A wind of early autumn raised yellow dust from cobbles and swirled it against an hundred windows. Long streamers of garments fluttered from fire-escapes. In all unhandy places there were buckets, brooms, rags and bottles. In the street infants played or fought with other infants or sat stupidly in the way of vehicles. Formidable women, with uncombed hair and disordered dress, gossiped while leaning on railings, or screamed in frantic quarrels. Withered persons, in curious postures of submission to something, sat smoking pipes in obscure corners. A thousand odors of cooking food came forth to the street. The building quivered and creaked from the weight of humanity stamping about in its bowels.

A small ragged girl dragged a red, bawling infant along the crowded ways. He was hanging back, baby-like, bracing his wrinkled, bare legs.

The little girl cried out: "Ah, Tommie, come ahn. Dere's Jimmie and fader. Don't be a-pullin' me back."

She jerked the baby's arm impatiently. He fell on his face, roaring. With a second jerk she pulled him to his feet, and they went on. With the obstinacy of his order, he protested against being dragged in a chosen direction. He made heroic endeavors to keep on his legs, denounced his sister and consumed a bit of orange peeling which he chewed between the times of his infantile orations.

As the sullen-eyed man, followed by the blood-covered

boy, drew near, the little girl burst into reproachful cries. "Ah, Jimmie, youse bin fightin' agin."

The urchin swelled disdainfully.

"Ah, what d'hell, Mag. See?"

The little girl upbraided him. "Youse allus fightin', Jimmie, an' yeh knows it puts mudder out when yehs come home half dead, an' it's like we'll all get a poundin'."

She began to weep. The babe threw back his head and roared at his prospects.

"Ah, what d' hell!" cried Jimmie. "Shut up er I'll smack yer mout'. See?"

As his sister continued her lamentations, he suddenly struck her. The little girl reeled and, recovering herself, burst into tears and quaveringly cursed him. As she slowly retreated her brother advanced dealing her cuffs. The father heard and turned about.

"Stop that, Jim, d'yeh hear? Leave yer sister alone on the street. It's like I can never beat any sense into yer damned wooden head."

The urchin raised his voice in defiance to his parent and continued his attacks. The babe bawled tremendously, protesting with great violence. During his sister's hasty manœuvres, he was dragged by the arm.

Finally the procession plunged into one of the gruesome doorways. They crawled up dark stairways and along cold, gloomy halls. At last the father pushed open a door and they entered a lighted room in which a large woman was rampant.

She stopped in a career from a seething stove to a pan-covered table. As the father and children filed in she peered at them.

"Eh, what? Been fightin' agin, by Gawd!" She threw herself upon Jimmie. The urchin tried to dart behind the others and in the scuffle the babe, Tommie, was knocked down. He protested with his usual vehemence, because they had bruised his tender shins against a table leg.

The mother's massive shoulders heaved with anger. Grasping the urchin by the neck and shoulder she shook him until he rattled. She dragged him to an unholy sink, and, soaking a rag in water, began to scrub his lacerated face with it. Jimmie screamed in pain and tried to twist his shoulders out of the clasp of the huge arms.

The babe sat on the floor watching the scene, his face in contortions like that of a woman at a tragedy. The father, with a newly-ladened pipe in his mouth, sat in a backless chair near the stove. Jimmie's cries annoyed him. He turned about and bellowed at his wife:

"Let the damned kid alone for a minute, will yeh, Mary? Yer allus poundin' 'im. When I come nights I can't git no rest 'cause yer allus poundin' a kid. Let up, d'yeh hear? Don't be allus poundin' a kid."

The woman's operations on the urchin instantly increased in violence. At last she tossed him to a corner where he limply lay weeping.

The wife put her immense hands on her hips, and with a chieftain-like stride approached her husband.

"Ho," she said, with a great grunt of contempt. "An' what in the devil are you stickin' your nose for?"

The babe crawled under the table and, turning, peered out cautiously. The ragged girl retreated and the urchin in the corner drew his legs carefully beneath him.

The man puffed his pipe calmly and put his great muddied boots on the back part of the stove.

"Go t' hell," he said tranquilly.

The woman screamed and shook her fists before her husband's eyes. The rough yellow of her face and neck flared suddenly crimson. She began to howl.

He puffed imperturbably at his pipe for a time, but finally arose and went to look out at the window into the darkening chaos of back yards.

"You've been drinkin', Mary," he said. "You'd better let up on the bot', ol' woman, or you'll git done."

"You're a liar. I ain't had a drop," she roared in reply. They had a lurid altercation, in which they damned each other's souls with frequence.

The babe was staring out from under the table, his small face working in his excitement. The ragged girl went stealthily over to the corner where the urchin lay.

"Are yehs hurted much, Jimmie?" she whispered timidly.

"Not a damn bit! See?" growled the little boy.

"Will I wash d' blood?"

"Naw!"

"Will I——"

"When I catch dat Riley kid I'll break 'is face! Dat's right! See?"

He turned his face to the wall as if resolved to grimly bide his time.

In the quarrel between husband and wife, the woman was victor. The man seized his hat and rushed from the room, apparently determined upon a vengeful drunk. She followed to the door and thundered at him as he made his way down stairs.

She returned and stirred up the room until her children were bobbing about like bubbles.

"Git outa d' way," she persistently bawled, waving feet with their dishevelled shoes near the heads of her children. She shrouded herself, puffing and snorting, in a cloud of steam at the stove, and eventually extracted a frying-pan full of potatoes that hissed.

She flourished it. "Come t' yer suppers, now," she cried with sudden exasperation. "Hurry up, now, er I'll help yeh!"

The children scrambled hastily. With prodigious clatter they arranged themselves at table. The babe sat with his feet dangling high from a precarious infant chair and gorged his small stomach. Jimmie forced, with feverish rapidity, the grease-enveloped pieces between his wounded lips. Maggie, with side glances of fear of interruption, ate like a small pursued tigress.

The mother sat blinking at them. She delivered reproaches, swallowed potatoes and drank from a yellow-brown bottle. After a time her mood changed and she wept as she carried little Tommie into another room and laid him to sleep, with his fists doubled, in an old quilt of faded red and green grandeur. Then she came and moaned by the stove. She rocked to and fro upon a chair, shedding tears and crooning miserably to the two children about their "poor mother" and "yer fader, damn 'is soul."

The little girl plodded between the table and the chair with a dish-pan on it. She tottered on her small legs beneath burdens of dishes.

Jimmie sat nursing his various wounds. He cast furtive glances at his mother. His practised eye perceived her gradually emerge from a muddled mist of sentiment until her brain burned in drunken heat. He sat breathless.

Maggie broke a plate.

The mother started to her feet as if propelled.

"Good Gawd," she howled. Her glittering eyes fastened on her child with sudden hatred. The fervent red of her face turned almost to purple. The little boy ran to the halls, shrieking like a monk in an earthquake.

He floundered about in darkness until he found the stairs. He stumbled, panic-stricken, to the next floor. An old woman opened a door. A light behind her threw a flare on the urchin's face.

"Eh, Gawd, child, what is it dis time? Is yer fader beatin' yer mudder, or yer mudder beatin' yer fader?"

CHAPTER III

Jimmie and the old woman listened long in the hall. Above the muffled roar of conversation, the dismal wailings of babies at night, the thumping of feet in unseen corridors and rooms, and the sound of varied hoarse shoutings in the street and the rattling of wheels over cobbles, they heard the screams of the child and the roars of the mother die away to a feeble moaning and a subdued bass muttering.

The old woman was a gnarled and leathery personage who could don, at will, an expression of great virtue. She possessed a small music box capable of one tune, and a collection of "God bless yehs" pitched in assorted keys of fervency. Each day she took a position upon the stones of Fifth Avenue, where she crooked her legs under her and crouched immovable and hideous, like an idol. She received daily a small sum in pennies. It was contributed, for the most part, by persons who did not make their homes in that vicinity.

Once, when a lady had dropped her purse on the sidewalk, the gnarled woman had grabbed it and smuggled it with great dexterity beneath her cloak. When she was arrested she had cursed the lady into a partial swoon, and with her aged limbs, twisted from rheumatism, had almost kicked the stomach out of a huge policeman whose conduct upon that occasion she referred to when she said, "The police, damn 'em!"

"Eh, Jimmie, it's cursed shame," she said. "Go, now,

like a dear an' buy me a can, an' if yer mudder raises 'ell all night yehs can sleep here."

Jimmie took a tendered tin-pail and seven pennies and departed. He passed into the side door of a saloon and went to the bar. Straining up on his toes he raised the pail and pennies as high as his arms would let him. He saw two hands thrust down to take them. Directly the same hands let down the filled pail and he left.

In front of the gruesome doorway he met a lurching figure. It was his father, swaying about on uncertain legs.

"Give me d' can. See?" said the man.

"Ah, come off! I got dis can fer dat ol' woman an' it 'ud be dirt t' swipe it. See?" cried Jimmie.

The father wrenched the pail from the urchin. He grasped it in both hands and lifted it to his mouth. He glued his lips to the under edge and tilted his head. His throat swelled until it seemed to grow near his chin. There was a tremendous gulping movement and the beer was gone.

The man caught his breath and laughed. He hit his son on the head with the empty pail. As it rolled clanging into the street, Jimmie began to scream and kicked repeatedly at his father's shins.

"Look at d' dirt what yeh done me," he yelled. "D' ol' woman 'ill be raisin' hell."

He retreated to the middle of the street, but the man did not pursue. He staggered toward the door.

"I'll club hell outa yeh when I ketch yeh," he shouted, and disappeared.

During the evening he had been standing against a bar drinking whiskies and declaring to all comers, confidentially: "My home reg'lar livin' hell! Damndes' place! Reg'lar hell! Why do I come an' drin' whisk' here thish way? 'Cause home reg'lar livin' hell!"

Jimmie waited a long time in the street and then crept warily up through the building. He passed with great caution the door of the gnarled woman, and finally stopped outside his home and listened.

He could hear his mother moving heavily about among the furniture of the room. She was chanting in a mournful voice, occasionally interjecting bursts of volcanic wrath at the father, who, Jimmie judged, had sunk down on the floor or in a corner.

"Why d' blazes don' chere try t' keep Jim from fightin'? I'll break yer jaw," she suddenly bellowed.

The man mumbled with drunken indifference. "Ah, wha' d' hell. W'a's odds? Wha' makes kick?"

"Because he tears 'is clothes, yeh damn fool," cried the woman in supreme wrath.

The husband seemed to become aroused. "Go t' hell," he thundered fiercely in reply. There was a crash against the door and something broke into clattering fragments. Jimmie partially suppressed a yell and darted down the stairway. Below he paused and listened. He heard howls and curses, groans and shrieks—a confused chorus as if a battle were raging. With it all there was the crash of splintering furniture. The eyes of the urchin glared in his fear that one of them would discover him.

Curious faces appeared in doorways, and whispered comments passed to and fro. "Ol' Johnson's raisin' hell agin."

Jimmie stood until the noises ceased and the other inhabitants of the tenement had all yawned and shut their doors. Then he crawled up stairs with the caution of an invader of a panther den. Sounds of labored breathing came through the broken door-panels. He pushed the door open and entered, quaking.

A glow from the fire threw red hues over the bare floor, the cracked and soiled plastering, and the overturned and broken furniture.

In the middle of the floor lay his mother asleep. In one corner of the room his father's limp body hung across the seat of a chair.

The urchin stole forward. He began to shiver in dread of awakening his parents. His mother's great chest was heaving painfully. Jimmie paused and looked down at her. Her face was inflamed and swollen from drinking. Her yellow brows shaded eye-lids that had grown blue. Her tangled hair tossed in waves over her forehead. Her mouth was set in the same lines of vindictive hatred that it had, perhaps, borne during the fight. Her bare, red arms were thrown out above her head in an attitude of exhaustion, something, mayhap, like that of a sated villain.

The urchin bended over his mother. He was fearful lest she should open her eyes, and the dread within him was so strong, that he could not forbear to stare, but hung as if fascinated over the woman's grim face.

Suddenly her eyes opened. The urchin found himself looking straight into an expression, which, it would seem, had the power to change his blood to salt. He howled piercingly and fell backward.

The woman floundered for a moment, tossed her arms about her head as if in combat, and again began to snore.

Jimmie crawled back into the shadows and waited. A noise in the next room had followed his cry at the discovery that his mother was awake. He grovelled in the gloom, his eyes riveted upon the intervening door.

He heard it creak, and then the sound of a small voice came to him. "Jimmie! Jimmie! Are yehs dere?" it whispered. The urchin started. The thin, white face of his sister looked at him from the doorway of the other room. She crept to him across the floor.

The father had not moved, but lay in the same death-like sleep. The mother writhed in uneasy slumber, her chest wheezing as if she were in the agonies of strangulation. Out at the window a florid moon was peering over dark roofs, and in the distance the waters of a river glimmered pallidly.

The small frame of the ragged girl was quivering. Her features were haggard from weeping, and her eyes gleamed with fear. She grasped the urchin's arm in her little trembling hands and they huddled in a corner. The eyes of both were drawn, by some force, to stare at the woman's face, for they thought she need only to awake and all the fiends would come from below.

They crouched until the ghost-mists of dawn appeared at the window, drawing close to the panes, and looking in at the prostrate, heaving body of the mother.

CHAPTER IV

The babe, Tommie, died. He went away in an insignificant coffin, his small waxen hand clutching a flower that the girl, Maggie, had stolen from an Italian.

She and Jimmie lived.

The inexperienced fibres of the boy's eyes were hardened at an early age. He became a young man of leather. He lived some red years without laboring. During that time his sneer became chronic. He studied human nature in the gutter, and found it no worse than he thought he had reason to believe it. He never conceived a respect for the world, because he had begun with no idols that it had smashed.

He clad his soul in armor by means of happening hilariously in at a mission church where a man composed his sermons of "you's." Once a philosopher asked this man why he did not say "we" instead of "you." The man replied, "What?"

While they got warm at the stove, he told his hearers just where he calculated they stood with the Lord. Many of the sinners were impatient over the pictured depths of their degradation. They were waiting for soup-tickets.

A reader of words of wind-demons might have been able to see the portions of a dialogue pass to and fro between the exhorter and his hearers.

"You are damned," said the preacher. And the reader of sounds might have seen the reply go forth from the ragged people: "Where's our soup?"

Jimmie and a companion sat in a rear seat and commented upon the things that didn't concern them, with all the freedom of English tourists. When they grew thirsty and went out their minds confused the speaker with Christ.

Momentarily, Jimmie was sullen with thoughts of a hopeless altitude where grew fruit. His companion said that if he should ever meet God he would ask for a million dollars and a bottle of beer.

Jimmie's occupation for a long time was to stand on street-corners and watch the world go by, dreaming blood-red dreams at the passing of pretty women. He menaced mankind at the intersections of streets.

On the corners he was in life and of life. The world was going on and he was there to perceive it.

He maintained a belligerent attitude toward all well-dressed men. To him fine raiment was allied to weakness, and all good coats covered faint hearts. He and his order were kings, to a certain extent, over the men of untarnished clothes, because these latter dreaded, perhaps, to be either killed or laughed at.

Above all things he despised obvious Christians and ciphers with the chrysanthemums of aristocracy in their button-holes. He considered himself above both of these classes. He was afraid of nothing.

When he had a dollar in his pocket his satisfaction with existence was the greatest thing in the world. So, eventually, he felt obliged to work. His father died and his mother's years were divided up into periods of thirty days.

He became a truck driver. There was given to him the charge of a pains-taking pair of horses and a large rattling truck. He invaded the turmoil and tumble of the down-town streets and learned to breathe maledictory defiance at the police who occasionally used to climb up, drag him from his perch and punch him.

In the lower part of the city he daily involved himself in hideous tangles. If he and his team chanced to be in the rear he preserved a demeanor of serenity, crossing his legs and bursting forth into yells when foot passengers took dangerous dives beneath the noses of his champing horses. He smoked his pipe calmly for he knew that his pay was marching on.

If his charge was in the front and if it became the key-truck of chaos, he entered terrifically into the quarrel that was raging to and fro among the drivers on their high seats, and sometimes roared oaths and violently got himself arrested.

After a time his sneer grew so that it turned its glare upon all things. He became so sharp that he believed in nothing. To him the police were always actuated by malignant impulses and the rest of the world was composed, for the most part, of despicable creatures who were all trying to take advantage of him and with whom, in defense, he was obliged to quarrel on all possible occasions. He himself occupied a down-trodden position which had a private but distinct element of grandeur in its isolation.

The greatest cases of aggravated idiocy were, to his mind, rampant upon the front platforms of all of the street cars. At first his tongue strove with these beings, but he eventually became superior. In him grew a majestic contempt for those strings of street cars that followed him like intent bugs.

He fell into the habit, when starting on a long journey, of fixing his eye on a high and distant object, commanding his horses to start and then going into a trance of observation. Multitudes of drivers might howl in his rear, and passengers might load him with opprobrium, but he would not awaken until some blue policeman turned red and began to frenziedly seize bridles and beat the soft noses of the responsible horses.

When he paused to contemplate the attitude of the police toward himself and his fellows, he believed that they were the only men in the city who had no rights. When driving about, he felt that he was held liable by the police for anything that might occur in the streets, and that he was the common prey of all energetic officials. In revenge, he resolved never to move out of the way of anything, until formidable circumstances, or a much larger man than himself forced him to it.

Foot passengers were mere pestering flies with an insane disregard for their legs and his convenience. He could not comprehend their desire to cross the streets. Their madness smote him with eternal amazement. He was continually storming at them from his throne. He sat aloft and denounced their frantic leaps, plunges, dives and straddles.

When they would thrust at, or parry, the noses of his champing horses, making them swing their heads and move their feet, and thus disturbing a stolid dreamy repose, he swore at the men as fools, for he himself could perceive that Providence had caused it clearly to be written, that he and his team had the unalienable right to stand in the proper path of the sun chariot, and if they so minded, obstruct its mission or take a wheel off.

And if the god-driver had had a desire to step down, put up his flame-colored fists and manfully dispute the right of way, he would have probably been immediately opposed by a scowling mortal with two sets of hard knuckles.

It is possible, perhaps, that this young man would have derided, in an axle-wide alley, the approach of a flying ferry boat. Yet he achieved a respect for a fire engine. As one charged toward his truck, he would drive fearfully upon a sidewalk, threatening untold people with annihilation. When an engine struck a mass of blocked trucks, splitting it into fragments, as a blow annihilates a cake of ice, Jimmie's team could usually be observed high and safe, with whole wheels, on the sidewalk. The fearful coming of the engine could break up the most intricate muddle of heavy vehicles at which the police had been swearing for the half of an hour.

A fire engine was enshrined in his heart as an appalling thing that he loved with a distant dog-like devotion. It had been known to overturn a street car. Those leaping horses, striking sparks from the cobbles in their forward lunge, were creatures to be ineffably admired. The clang of the gong pierced his breast like a noise of remembered war.

When Jimmie was a little boy, he began to be arrested. Before he reached a great age, he had a fair record.

He developed too great a tendency to climb down from his truck and fight with other drivers. He had been in quite a number of miscellaneous fights, and in some general barroom rows that had become known to the police. Once he had been arrested for assaulting a Chinaman. Two women in different parts of the city, and entirely unknown to each other, caused him considerable annoyance by breaking forth, simultaneously, at fateful intervals, into wailings about marriage and support and infants.

Nevertheless, he had, on a certain star-lit evening, said wonderingly and quite reverently: "D' moon looks like hell, don't it?"

CHAPTER V

The girl, Maggie, blossomed in a mud puddle. She grew to be a most rare and wonderful production of a tenement district, a pretty girl.

None of the dirt of Rum Alley seemed to be in her veins. The philosophers up stairs, down stairs and on the same floor, puzzled over it.

When a child, playing and fighting with gamins in the

street, dirt disguised her. Attired in tatters and grime, she went unseen.

There came a time, however, when the young men of the vicinity, said: "Dat Johnson goil is a puty good looker." About this period her brother remarked to her: "Mag, I'll tell yeh dis! See? Yeh've edder got t' go t' hell er go t' work!" Whereupon she went to work, having the feminine aversion of going to hell.

By a chance, she got a position in an establishment where they made collars and cuffs. She received a stool and a machine in a room where sat twenty girls of various shades of yellow discontent. She perched on the stool and treadled at her machine all day, turning out collars with a name which might have been noted for its irrelevancy to anything connected with collars. At night she returned home to her mother.

Jimmie grew large enough to take the vague position of head of the family. As incumbent of that office, he stumbled up stairs late at night, as his father had done before him. He reeled about the room, swearing at his relations, or went to sleep on the floor.

The mother had gradually arisen to such a degree of fame that she could bandy words with her acquaintances among the police-justices. Court-officials called her by her first name. When she appeared they pursued a course which had been theirs for months. They invariably grinned and cried out: "Hello, Mary, you here again?" Her grey head wagged in many courts. She always besieged the bench with voluble excuses, explanations, apologies and prayers. Her flaming face and rolling eyes were a familiar sight on the Island. She measured time by means of sprees, and was eternally swollen and dishevelled.

One day the young man, Pete, who as a lad had smitten the Devil's Row urchin in the back of the head and put to flight the antagonists of his friend, Jimmie, strutted upon the scene. He met Jimmie one day on the street, promised to take him to a boxing match in Williamsburg, and called for him in the evening.

Maggie observed Pete.

He sat on a table in the Johnson home and dangled his checked legs with an enticing nonchalance. His hair was curled down over his forehead in an oiled bang. His pugged nose seemed to revolt from contact with a bristling moustache of short, wire-like hairs. His blue double-breasted coat, edged with black braid, was buttoned close to a red puff tie, and his patent-leather shoes looked like weapons.

His mannerisms stamped him as a man who had a correct sense of his personal superiority. There was valor and contempt for circumstances in the glance of his eye. He waved his hands like a man of the world, who dismisses religion and philosophy, and says "Rats!" He had certainly seen everything and with each curl of his lip, he declared that it amounted to nothing. Maggie thought he must be a very "elegant" bartender.

He was telling tales to Jimmie.

Maggie watched him furtively, with half-closed eyes, lit with a vague interest.

"Hully gee! Dey makes me tired," he said. "Mos' e'ry day some farmer comes in an' tries t' run d' shop. See? But dey gits t'rowed right out! I jolt dem right out in d' street before dey knows where dey is! See?"

"Sure," said Jimmie.

"Dere was a mug come in d' place d' odder day wid an idear he wus goin' t' own d' place! Hully gee, he wus goin' t' own d' place! I see he had a still on an' I didn' wanna giv 'im no stuff, so I says: 'Git d' hell outa here an' don' make no trouble,' I says like dat! See? 'Git d' hell outa here an' don' make no trouble'; like dat. 'Git d' hell outa here,' I says. See?"

Jimmie nodded understandingly. Over his features played an eager desire to state the amount of his valor in a similar crisis, but the narrator proceeded.

"Well, d' blokie he says: 'T' hell wid it! I ain' lookin' for no scrap,' he says—see? 'But,' he says, 'I'm 'spectable cit'zen an' I wanna drink an' purtydamnsoon, too.' See? 'D' hell,' I says. Like dat! 'D' hell,' I says. See? 'Don' make no trouble,' I says. Like dat. 'Don' make no trouble.' See? Den d' mug he squared off an' said he was fine as silk wid his dukes—see? An' he wanned a drink damnquick. Dat's what he said. See?"

"Sure," repeated Jimmie.

Pete continued. "Say, I jes' jumped d' bar an' d' way

I plunked dat blokie was outa sight. See? Dat's right! In d' jaw! See? Hully gee, he t'rowed a spittoon t'ru d' front windee. Say, I t'aut I'd drop dead. But d' boss, he comes in after an' he says, 'Pete, yehs done jes' right! Yeh've gota keep order an' it's all right.' See? 'It's all right,' he says. Dat's what he said."

The two held a technical discussion.

"Dat bloke was a dandy," said Pete, in conclusion, "but he hadn' oughta made no trouble. Dat's what I says t' dem: 'Don' come in here an' make no trouble,' I says, like dat. 'Don' make no trouble.' See?"

As Jimmie and his friend exchanged tales descriptive of their prowess, Maggie leaned back in the shadow. Her eyes dwelt wonderingly and rather wistfully upon Pete's face. The broken furniture, grimy walls, and general disorder and dirt of her home of a sudden appeared before her and began to take a potential aspect. Pete's aristocratic person looked as if it might soil. She looked keenly at him, occasionally, wondering if he was feeling contempt. But Pete seemed to be enveloped in reminiscence.

"Hully gee," said he, "dose mugs can't phase me. Dey knows I kin wipe up d' street wid any t'ree of dem."

When he said, "Ah, what d' hell!" his voice was burdened with disdain for the inevitable and contempt for anything that fate might compel him to endure.

Maggie perceived that here was the ideal man. Her dim thoughts were often searching for far away lands where, as God says, the little hills sing together in the morning. Under the trees of her dream-gardens there had always walked a lover.

CHAPTER VI

Pete took note of Maggie.

"Say, Mag, I'm stuck on yer shape. It's outa sight," he said, parenthetically, with an affable grin.

As he became aware that she was listening closely, he grew still more eloquent in his descriptions of various happenings in his career. It appeared that he was invincible in fights.

"Why," he said, referring to a man with whom he

had had a misunderstanding, "dat mug scrapped like a damned dago. Dat's right. He was dead easy. See? He t'aut he was a scrapper! But he foun' out diff'ent! Hully gee."

He walked to and fro in the small room, which seemed then to grow even smaller and unfit to hold his dignity, the attribute of a supreme warrior. That swing of the shoulders which had frozen the timid when he was but a lad had increased with his growth and education at the ratio of ten to one. It, combined with the sneer upon his mouth, told mankind that there was nothing in space which could appall him. Maggie marvelled at him and surrounded him with greatness. She vaguely tried to calculate the altitude of the pinnacle from which he must have looked down upon her.

"I met a chump d' odder day way up in d' city," he said. "I was goin' t' see a frien' of mine. When I was a-crossin' d' street d' chump runned plump inteh me, an' den he turns aroun' an' says, 'Yer insolen' ruffin,' he says, like dat. 'Oh, gee,' I says, 'oh, gee, go t' hell an' git off d' eart'!' I says, like dat. See? 'Go t' hell an' git off d' eart',' like dat. Den d' blokie he got wild. He says I was a contempt'ble scoun'el, er somethin' like dat, an' he says I was doom' t' everlastin' pe'dition, er somethin' like dat. 'Gee,' I says, 'gee! D' hell I am,' I says. 'D' hell I am,' like dat. An' den I slugged 'im. See?"

With Jimmie in his company, Pete departed in a sort of a blaze of glory from the Johnson home. Maggie, leaning from the window, watched him as he walked down the street.

Here was a formidable man who disdained the strength of a world full of fists. Here was one who had contempt for brass-clothed power; one whose knuckles could defiantly ring against the granite of law. He was a knight.

The two men went from under the glimmering street-lamp and passed into shadows.

Turning, Maggie contemplated the dark, dust-stained walls, and the scant and crude furniture of her home. A clock, in a splintered and battered oblong box of varnished wood, she suddenly regarded as an abomination. She noted that it ticked raspingly. The almost vanished flowers in the carpet-pattern, she conceived to be newly hideous. Some faint attempts which she had made with blue ribbon, to freshen the appearance of a dingy curtain, she now saw to be piteous.

She wondered what Pete dined on.

She reflected upon the collar and cuff factory. It began to appear to her mind as a dreary place of endless grinding. Pete's elegant occupation brought him, no doubt, into contact with people who had money and manners. It was probable that he had a large acquaintance of pretty girls. He must have great sums of money to spend.

To her the earth was composed of hardships and insults. She felt instant admiration for a man who openly defied it. She thought that if the grim angel of death should clutch his heart, Pete would shrug his shoulders and say, "Oh, ev'ryt'ing goes."

She anticipated that he would come again shortly. She spent some of her week's pay in the purchase of flowered cretonne for a lambrequin. She made it with infinite care and hung it to the slightly-careening mantel, over the stove, in the kitchen. She studied it with painful anxiety from different points in the room. She wanted it to look well on Sunday night when, perhaps, Jimmie's friend would come. On Sunday night, however, Pete did not appear.

Afterward the girl looked at it with a sense of humiliation. She was now convinced that Pete was superior to admiration for lambrequins.

A few evenings later Pete entered with fascinating innovations in his apparel. As she had seen him twice and he wore a different suit each time, Maggie had a dim impression that his wardrobe was prodigious.

"Say, Mag," he said, "put on yer bes' duds Friday night an' I'll take yehs t' d' show. See?"

He spent a few moments in flourishing his clothes and then vanished, without having glanced at the lambrequin.

Over the eternal collars and cuffs in the factory Maggie spent the most of three days in making imaginary sketches of Pete and his daily environment. She imagined some half dozen women in love with him and thought he must lean dangerously toward an indefinite one, whom she pictured as endowed with great charms of person, but with an altogether contemptible disposition.

She thought he must live in a blare of pleasure. He had friends, and people who were afraid of him.

She saw the golden glitter of the place where Pete was to take her. It would be an entertainment of many hues and many melodies where she was afraid she might appear small and mouse-colored.

Her mother drank whiskey all Friday morning. With lurid face and tossing hair she cursed and destroyed furniture all Friday afternoon. When Maggie came home at half-past six her mother lay asleep amidst the wreck of chairs and a table. Fragments of various household utensils were scattered about the floor. She had vented some phase of drunken fury upon the lambrequin. It lay in a bedraggled heap in the corner.

"Hah," she snorted, sitting up suddenly, "where d' hell yeh been? Why d' hell don' yeh come home earlier? Been loafin' 'round d' streets. Yer gettin' t' be a reg'lar devil."

When Pete arrived Maggie, in a worn black dress, was waiting for him in the midst of a floor strewn with wreckage. The curtain at the window had been pulled by a heavy hand and hung by one tack, dangling to and fro in the draft through the cracks at the sash. The knots of blue ribbons appeared like violated flowers. The fire in the stove had gone out. The displaced lids and open doors showed heaps of sullen grey ashes. The remnants of a meal, ghastly, lay in a corner. Maggie's mother, stretched on the floor, blasphemed and gave her daughter a bad name.

CHAPTER VII

An orchestra of yellow silk women and bald-headed men on an elevated stage near the centre of a great green-hued hall, played a popular waltz. The place was crowded with people grouped about little tables. A battalion of waiters slid among the throng, carrying trays of beer glasses and making change from the inexhaustible vaults of their trousers pockets. Little boys, in the costumes of French chefs, paraded up and down the irregular aisles vending fancy cakes. There was a low rumble of conversation and a subdued clinking of glasses.

Clouds of tobacco smoke rolled and wavered high in air about the dull gilt of the chandeliers.

The vast crowd had an air throughout of having just quitted labor. Men with calloused hands and attired in garments that showed the wear of an endless drudging for a living, smoked their pipes contentedly and spent five, ten, or perhaps fifteen cents for beer. There was a mere sprinkling of men who smoked cigars purchased elsewhere. The great body of the crowd was composed of people who showed that all day they strove with their hands. Quiet Germans, with maybe their wives and two or three children, sat listening to the music, with the expressions of happy cows. An occasional party of sailors from a war-ship, their faces pictures of sturdy health, spent the earlier hours of the evening at the small round tables. Very infrequent tipsy men, swollen with the value of their opinions, engaged their companions in earnest and confidential conversation. In the balcony, and here and there below, shone the impassive faces of women. The nationalities of the Bowery beamed upon the stage from all directions.

Pete aggressively walked up a side aisle and took seats with Maggie at a table beneath the balcony.

"Two beehs!"

Leaning back he regarded with eyes of superiority the scene before them. This attitude affected Maggie strongly. A man who could regard such a sight with indifference must be accustomed to very great things.

It was obvious that Pete had visited this place many times before, and was very familiar with it. A knowledge of this fact made Maggie feel little and new.

He was extremely gracious and attentive. He displayed the consideration of a cultured gentleman who knew what was due.

"Say, what d' hell? Bring d' lady a big glass! What d' hell use is dat pony?"

"Don't be fresh, now," said the waiter, with some warmth, as he departed.

"Ah, git off d' eart'," said Pete, after the other's retreating form.

Maggie perceived that Pete brought forth all his elegance and all his knowledge of high-class customs for her benefit. Her heart warmed as she reflected upon his condescension.

The orchestra of yellow silk women and bald-headed men gave vent to a few bars of anticipatory music and a girl, in a pink dress with short skirts, galloped upon the stage. She smiled upon the throng as if in acknowledgment of a warm welcome, and began to walk to and fro, making profuse gesticulations and singing, in brazen soprano tones, a song, the words of which were inaudible. When she broke into the swift rattling measures of a chorus some half-tipsy men near the stage joined in the rollicking refrain and glasses were pounded rhythmically upon the tables. People leaned forward to watch her and to try to catch the words of the song. When she vanished there were long rollings of applause.

Obedient to more anticipatory bars, she reappeared amidst the half-suppressed cheering of the tipsy men. The orchestra plunged into dance music and the laces of the dancer fluttered and flew in the glare of gas jets. She divulged the fact that she was attired in some half dozen skirts. It was patent that any one of them would have proved adequate for the purpose for which skirts are intended. An occasional man bent forward, intent upon the pink stockings. Maggie wondered at the splendor of the costume and lost herself in calculations of the cost of the silks and laces.

The dancer's smile of enthusiasm was turned for ten minutes upon the faces of her audience. In the finale she fell into some of those grotesque attitudes which were at the time popular among the dancers in the theatres up-town, giving to the Bowery public the diversions of the aristocratic theatre-going public, at reduced rates.

"Say, Pete," said Maggie, leaning forward, "dis is great."

"Sure," said Pete, with proper complacence.

A ventriloquist followed the dancer. He held two fantastic dolls on his knees. He made them sing mournful ditties and say funny things about geography and Ireland.

"Do dose little men talk?" asked Maggie.

"Naw," said Pete, "it's some damn fake. See?"

Two girls, set down on the bills as sisters, came forth

and sang a duet which is heard occasionally at concerts given under church auspices. They supplemented it with a dance which of course can never be seen at concerts given under church auspices.

After they had retired, a woman of debatable age sang a negro melody. The chorus necessitated some grotesque waddlings supposed to be an imitation of a plantation darkey, under the influence, probably, of music and the moon. The audience was just enthusiastic enough over it to have her return and sing a sorrowful lay, whose lines told of a mother's love, and a sweetheart who waited and a young man who was lost at sea under harrowing circumstances. From the faces of a score or so in the crowd, the self-contained look faded. Many heads were bent forward with eagerness and sympathy. As the last distressing sentiment of the piece was brought forth, it was greeted by the kind of applause which rings as sincere.

As a final effort, the singer rendered some verses which described a vision of Britain annihilated by America, and Ireland bursting her bonds. A carefully prepared climax was reached in the last line of the last verse, when the singer threw out her arms and cried, "The star-spangled banner." Instantly a great cheer swelled from the throats of this assemblage of the masses, most of them of foreign birth. There was a heavy rumble of booted feet thumping the floor. Eyes gleamed with sudden fire, and calloused hands waved frantically in the air.

After a few moments' rest, the orchestra played noisily, and a small fat man burst out upon the stage. He began to roar a song and stamp back and forth before the foot-lights, wildly waving a silk hat and throwing leers broadcast. He made his face into fantastic grimaces until he looked like a devil on a Japanese kite. The crowd laughed gleefully. His short, fat legs were never still a moment. He shouted and roared and bobbed his shock of red wig until the audience broke out in excited applause.

Pete did not pay much attention to the progress of events upon the stage. He was drinking beer and watching Maggie.

Her cheeks were blushing with excitement and her eyes were glistening. She drew deep breaths of pleasure. No thoughts of the atmosphere of the collar and cuff factory came to her.

With the final crash of the orchestra they jostled their way to the sidewalk in the crowd. Pete took Maggie's arm and pushed a way for her, offering to fight with a man or two. They reached Maggie's home at a late hour and stood for a moment in front of the gruesome doorway.

"Say, Mag," said Pete, "give us a kiss for takin' yeh t' d' show, will yer?"

Maggie laughed, as if startled, and drew away from him.

"Naw, Pete," she said, "dat wasn't in it."

"Ah, what d' hell?" urged Pete.

The girl retreated nervously.

"Ah, what d' hell?" repeated he.

Maggie darted into the hall, and up the stairs. She turned and smiled at him, then disappeared.

Pete walked slowly down the street. He had something of an astonished expression upon his features. He paused under a lamp-post and breathed a low breath of surprise.

"Gawd," he said, "I wonner if I've been played fer a duffer."

CHAPTER VIII

As thoughts of Pete came to Maggie's mind, she began to have an intense dislike for all of her dresses.

"What d'hell ails yeh? What makes yeh be allus fixin' and fussin'? Good Gawd," her mother would frequently roar at her.

She began to note, with more interest, the well-dressed women she met on the avenues. She envied elegance and soft palms. She craved those adornments of person which she saw every day on the street, conceiving them to be allies of vast importance to women.

Studying faces, she thought many of the women and girls she chanced to meet, smiled with serenity as though forever cherished and watched over by those they loved.

The air in the collar and cuff establishment strangled her. She knew she was gradually and surely shriveling in the hot, stuffy room. The begrimed windows rattled incessantly from the passing of elevated trains. The place was filled with a whirl of noises and odors.

She became lost in thought as she looked at some of the grizzled women in the room, mere mechanical contrivances sewing seams and grinding out, with heads bended over their work, tales of imagined or real girlhood happiness, or of past drunks, or the baby at home, and unpaid wages. She wondered how long her youth would endure. She began to see the bloom upon her cheeks as something of value.

She imagined herself, in an exasperating future, as a scrawny woman with an eternal grievance. She thought Pete to be a very fastidious person concerning the appearance of women.

She felt that she should love to see somebody entangle their fingers in the oily beard of the fat foreigner who owned the establishment. He was a detestable creature. He wore white socks with low shoes. He sat all day delivering orations, in the depths of a cushioned chair. His pocketbook deprived them of the power of retort.

"What een hell do you sink I pie fife dolla a week for? Play? No, py tamn!"

Maggie was anxious for a friend to whom she could talk about Pete. She would have liked to discuss his admirable mannerisms with a reliable mutual friend. At home, she found her mother often drunk and always raving. It seemed that the world had treated this woman very badly, and she took a deep revenge upon such portions of it as came within her reach. She broke furniture as if she were at last getting her rights. She swelled with virtuous indignation as she carried the lighter articles of household use, one by one, under the shadows of the three gilt balls, where Hebrews chained them with chains of interest.

Jimmie came when he was obliged to by circumstances over which he had no control. His well-trained legs brought him staggering home and put him to bed some nights when he would rather have gone elsewhere.

Swaggering Pete loomed like a golden sun to Maggie.

He took her to a dime museum where rows of meek freaks astonished her. She contemplated their deformities with awe and thought them a sort of chosen tribe.

Pete, racking his brains for amusement, discovered the Central Park Menagerie and the Museum of Arts. Sunday afternoons would sometimes find them at these places. Pete did not appear to be particularly interested in what he saw. He stood around looking heavy, while Maggie giggled in glee.

Once at the Menagerie he went into a trance of admiration before the spectacle of a very small monkey threatening to thrash a cageful because one of them had pulled his tail and he had not wheeled about quickly enough to discover who did it. Ever after Pete knew that monkey by sight and winked at him, trying to induce him to fight with other and larger monkeys.

At the Museum, Maggie said, "Dis is outa sight."

"Oh hell," said Pete, "wait till next summer an' I'll take yehs to a picnic."

While the girl wandered in the vaulted rooms, Pete occupied himself in returning stony stare for stony stare, the appalling scrutiny of the watch-dogs of the treasures. Occasionally he would remark in loud tones: "Dat jay has got glass eyes," and sentences of the sort. When he tired of this amusement he would go to the mummies and moralize over them.

Usually he submitted with silent dignity to all that he had to go through, but, at times, he was goaded into comment.

"What d' hell," he demanded once. "Look at all dese little jugs! Hundred jugs in a row! Ten rows in a case an' 'bout a t'ousand cases! What d' blazes use is dem?"

In the evenings of week days he often took her to see plays in which the dazzling heroine was rescued from the palatial home of her treacherous guardian by the hero with the beautiful sentiments. The latter spent most of his time out at soak in pale-green snow storms, busy with a nickel-plated revolver, rescuing aged strangers from villains.

Maggie lost herself in sympathy with the wanderers swooning in snow storms beneath happy-hued church windows, while a choir within sang "Joy to the World."

To Maggie and the rest of the audience this was transcendental realism. Joy always within, and they, like the actor, inevitably without. Viewing it, they hugged themselves in ecstatic pity of their imagined or real condition.

The girl thought the arrogance and granite-heartedness of the magnate of the play was very accurately drawn. She echoed the maledictions that the occupants of the gallery showered on this individual when his lines compelled him to expose his extreme selfishness.

Shady persons in the audience revolted from the pictured villainy of the drama. With untiring zeal they hissed vice and applauded virtue. Unmistakably bad men evinced an apparently sincere admiration for virtue. The loud gallery was overwhelmingly with the unfortunate and the oppressed. They encouraged the struggling hero with cries, and jeered the villain, hooting and calling attention to his whiskers. When anybody died in the pale-green snow storms, the gallery mourned. They sought out the painted misery and hugged it as akin.

In the hero's erratic march from poverty in the first act, to wealth and triumph in the final one, in which he forgives all the enemies that he has left, he was assisted by the gallery, which applauded his generous and noble sentiments and confounded the speeches of his opponents by making irrelevant but very sharp remarks. Those actors who were cursed with the parts of villains were confronted at every turn by the gallery. If one of them rendered lines containing the most subtle distinctions between right and wrong, the gallery was immediately aware that the actor meant wickedness, and denounced him accordingly.

The last act was a triumph for the hero, poor and of the masses, the representative of the audience, over the villain and the rich man, his pockets stuffed with bonds, his heart packed with tyrannical purposes, imperturbable amid suffering.

Maggie always departed with raised spirits from these melodramas. She rejoiced at the way in which the poor and virtuous eventually overcame the wealthy and wicked. The theatre made her think. She wondered if the culture and refinement she had seen imitated, perhaps grotesquely, by the heroine on the stage, could be acquired by a girl who lived in a tenement house and worked in a shirt factory.

CHAPTER IX

A group of urchins were intent upon the side door of a saloon. Expectancy gleamed from their eyes. They were twisting their fingers in excitement.

"Here she comes," yelled one of them suddenly.

The group of urchins burst instantly asunder and its individual fragments were spread in a wide, respectable half-circle about the point of interest. The saloon door opened with a crash, and the figure of a woman appeared upon the threshold. Her grey hair fell in knotted masses about her shoulders. Her face was crimsoned and wet with perspiration. Her eyes had a rolling glare.

"Not a damn cent more of me money will yehs ever get—not a damn cent. I spent me money here fer t'ree years an' now yehs tells me yeh'll sell me no more stuff! T' hell wid yeh, Johnnie Murckre! 'Disturbance?' Disturbance be damned! T' hell wid yeh, Johnnie—"

The door received a kick of exasperation from within and the woman lurched heavily out on the sidewalk.

The gamins in the half-circle became violently agitated. They began to dance about and hoot and yell and jeer. Wide dirty grins spread over each face.

The woman made a furious dash at a particularly outrageous cluster of little boys. They laughed delightedly and scampered off a short distance, calling out over their shoulders to her. She stood tottering on the curb-stone and thundered at them.

"Yeh devil's kids," she howled, shaking her fists. The little boys whooped in glee. As she started up the street they fell in behind and marched uproariously. Occasionally she wheeled about and made charges on them. They ran nimbly out of reach and taunted her.

In the frame of a gruesome doorway she stood for a moment cursing them. Her hair straggled, giving her red features a look of insanity. Her great fists quivered as she shook them madly in the air.

The urchins made terrific noises until she turned and

disappeared. Then they filed off quietly in the way they had come.

The woman floundered about in the lower hall of the tenement house and finally stumbled up the stairs. On an upper hall a door was opened and a collection of heads peered curiously out, watching her. With a wrathful snort the woman confronted the door, but it was slammed hastily in her face and the key was turned.

She stood for a few minutes, delivering a frenzied challenge at the panels.

"Come out in d' hall, Mary Murphy, damn yeh, if yehs want a scrap. Come ahn, yeh overgrown terrier, come ahn."

She began to kick the door. She shrilly defied the universe to appear and do battle. Her cursing trebles brought heads from all doors save the one she threatened. Her eyes glared in every direction. The air was full of her tossing fists.

"Come ahn, d' hull damn gang of yehs, come ahn," she roared at the spectators. An oath or two, cat-calls, jeers and bits of facetious advice were given in reply. Missiles clattered about her feet.

"What d' hell's d' matter wid yeh?" said a voice in the gathered gloom, and Jimmie came forward. He carried a tin dinner-pail in his hand and under his arm a truckman's brown apron done in a bundle. "What d' hell's wrong?" he demanded.

"Come out, all of yehs, come out," his mother was howling. "Come ahn an' I'll stamp yer damn brains under me feet."

"Shet yer face, an' come home, yeh damned old fool," roared Jimmie at her. She strided up to him and twirled her fingers in his face. Her eyes were darting flames of unreasoning rage and her frame trembled with eagerness for a fight.

"T' hell wid yehs! An' who d' hell are yehs? I ain't givin' a snap of me fingers fer yehs," she bawled at him. She turned her huge back in tremendous disdain and climbed the stairs to the next floor.

Jimmie followed, cursing blackly. At the top of the flight he seized his mother's arm and started to drag her toward the door of their room.

"Come home, damn yeh," he gritted between his teeth.

"Take yer hands off me! Take yer hands off me!" shrieked his mother.

She raised her arm and whirled her great fist at her son's face. Jimmie dodged his head and the blow struck him in the back of the neck. "Damn yeh," he gritted again. He threw out his left hand and writhed his fingers about her middle arm. The mother and the son began to sway and struggle like gladiators.

"Whoop!" said the Rum Alley tenement house. The hall filled with interested spectators.

"Hi, ol' lady, dat was a dandy!"

"T'ree t' one on d' red!"

"Ah, quit yer damn scrappin'!"

The door of the Johnson home opened and Maggie looked out. Jimmie made a supreme cursing effort and hurled his mother into the room. He quickly followed and closed the door. The Rum Alley tenement swore disappointedly and retired.

The mother slowly gathered herself up from the floor. Her eyes glittered menacingly upon her children.

"Here, now," said Jimmie, "we've had enough of dis. Sit down, an' don' make no trouble."

He grasped her arm, and twisting it, forced her into a creaking chair.

"Keep yer hands off me," roared his mother again.

"Damn yer ol' hide," yelled Jimmie, madly. Maggie shrieked and ran into the other room. To her there came the sound of a storm of crashes and curses. There was a great final thump and Jimmie's voice cried: "Dere, damn yeh, stay still." Maggie opened the door now, and went warily out. "Oh, Jimmie!"

He was leaning against the wall and swearing. Blood stood upon bruises on his knotty fore-arms where they had scraped against the floor or the walls in the scuffle. The mother lay screeching on the floor, the tears running down her furrowed face.

Maggie, standing in the middle of the room, gazed about her. The usual upheaval of the tables and chairs had taken place. Crockery was strewn broadcast in fragments. The stove had been disturbed on its legs, and now leaned idiotically to one side. A pail had been upset and water spread in all directions.

The door opened and Pete appeared. He shrugged his shoulders. "Oh, Gawd," he observed.

He walked over to Maggie and whispered in her ear. "Ah, what d' hell, Mag? Come ahn and we'll have a hell of a time."

The mother in the corner upreared her head and shook her tangled locks.

"T' hell wid him and you," she said, glowering at her daughter in the gloom. Her eyes seemed to burn balefully. "Yeh've gone t' d' devil, Mag Johnson, yehs knows yehs have gone t' d' devil. Yer a disgrace t' yer people, damn yeh. An' now, git out an' go ahn wid dat doe-faced jude of yours. Go t' hell wid him, damn yeh, an' a good riddance. Go t' hell an' see how yeh likes it."

Maggie gazed long at her mother.

"Go t' hell now, an' see how yeh likes it. Git out. I won't have sech as yehs in me house! Git out, d'yeh hear! Damn yeh, git out!"

The girl began to tremble.

At this instant Pete came forward. "Oh, what d' hell, Mag, see," whispered he softly in her ear. "Dis all blows over. See? D' ol' woman 'ill be all right in d' mornin'. Come ahn out wid me! We'll have a hell of a time."

The woman on the floor cursed. Jimmie was intent upon his bruised fore-arms. The girl cast a glance about the room filled with a chaotic mass of debris, and at the writhing body of her mother.

"Go t' hell an' good riddance."

Maggie went.

CHAPTER X

Jimmie had an idea it wasn't common courtesy for a friend to come to one's home and ruin one's sister. But he was not sure how much Pete knew about the rules of politeness.

The following night he returned home from work at rather a late hour in the evening. In passing through the halls he came upon the gnarled and leathery old woman who possessed the music box. She was grinning in the

dim light that drifted through dust-stained panes. She
beckoned to him with a smudged forefinger.

"Ah, Jimmie, what do yehs t'ink I tumbled to, las'
night. It was d' funnies' t'ing I ever saw," she cried,
coming close to him and leering. She was trembling with
eagerness to tell her tale. "I was by me door las' night
when yer sister and her jude feller came in late, oh, very
late. An' she, the dear, she was a-cryin' as if her heart
would break, she was. It was d' funnies' t'ing I ever saw.
An' right out here by me door she asked him did he
love her, did he. An' she was a-cryin' as if her heart
would break, poor t'ing. An' him, I could see by d' way
what he said it dat she had been askin' orften, he says:
'Oh, hell, yes,' he says, says he, 'Oh, hell, yes.' "

Storm-clouds swept over Jimmie's face, but he turned
from the leathery old woman and plodded on up stairs.

"Oh, hell, yes," she called after him. She laughed a
laugh that was like a prophetic croak. " 'Oh, hell, yes,'
he says, says he, 'Oh, hell, yes.' "

There was no one in at home. The rooms showed that
attempts had been made at tidying them. Parts of the
wreckage of the day before had been repaired by an
unskilful hand. A chair or two and the table stood uncertainly upon legs. The floor had been newly swept. The
blue ribbons had been restored to the curtains, and the
lambrequin, with its immense sheaves of yellow wheat
and red roses of equal size, had been returned, in a worn
and sorry state, to its place at the mantel. Maggie's
jacket and hat were gone from the nail behind the door.

Jimmie walked to the window and began to look
through the blurred glass. It occurred to him to vaguely
wonder, for an instant, if some of the women of his
acquaintance had brothers.

Suddenly, however, he began to swear.

"But he was me frien'! I brought 'im here! Dat's d'
hell of it!"

He fumed about the room, his anger gradually rising
to the furious pitch.

"I'll kill d' jay! Dat's what I'll do! I'll kill d' jay!"

He clutched his hat and sprang toward the door. But it
opened and his mother's great form blocked the passage.

"What d' hell's d' matter wid yeh?" exclaimed she, coming into the rooms.

Jimmie gave vent to a sardonic curse and then laughed heavily.

"Well, Maggie's gone t' d' devil! Dat's what! See?"

"Eh?" said his mother.

"Maggie's gone t' d' devil! Are yehs deaf?" roared Jimmie, impatiently.

"D' hell she has," murmured the mother, astounded.

Jimmie grunted, and then began to stare out at the window. His mother sat down in a chair, but a moment later sprang erect and delivered a maddened whirl of oaths. Her son turned to look at her as she reeled and swayed in the middle of the room, her fierce face convulsed with passion, her blotched arms raised high in imprecation.

"May Gawd curse her forever," she shrieked. "May she eat nothin' but stones and d' dirt in d' street. May she sleep in d' gutter an' never see d' sun shine again. D' damn——"

"Here, now," said her son. "Take a drop on yerself, an' quit dat."

The mother raised lamenting eyes to the ceiling.

"She's d' devil's own chil', Jimmie," she whispered. "Ah, who would t'ink such a bad girl could grow up in our fambly, Jimmie, me son. Many d' hour I've spent in talk wid dat girl an' tol' her if she ever went on d' streets I'd see her damned. An' after all her bringin' up an' what I tol' her and talked wid her, she goes t' d' bad, like a duck t' water."

The tears rolled down her furrowed face. Her hands trembled.

"An' den when dat Sadie MacMallister next door to us was sent t' d' devil by dat feller what worked in d' soap-factory, didn't I tell our Mag dat if she——"

"Ah, dat's anudder story," interrupted the brother. "Of course, dat Sadie was nice an' all dat—but—see— it ain't dessame as if—well, Maggie was diff'ent—see— she was diff'ent."

He was trying to formulate a theory that he had always unconsciously held, that all sisters, excepting his own, could advisedly be ruined.

He suddenly broke out again. "I'll go t'ump hell out a d' mug what done her d' harm. I'll kill 'im! He t'inks he kin scrap, but when he gits me a-chasin' 'im he'll fin' out where he's wrong, d' damned duffer. I'll wipe up d' street wid 'im."

In a fury he plunged out of the doorway. As he vanished the mother raised her head and lifted both hands, entreating.

"May Gawd curse her forever," she cried.

In the darkness of the hallway Jimmie discerned a knot of women talking volubly. When he strode by they paid no attention to him.

"She allus was a bold thing," he heard one of them cry in an eager voice. "Dere wasn't a feller come t' d' house but she'd try t' mash 'im. My Annie says d' shameless t'ing tried t' ketch her feller, her own feller, what we useter know his fader."

"I could a' tol' yehs dis two years ago," said a woman, in a key of triumph. "Yessir, it was over two years ago dat I says t' my ol' man, I says, 'Dat Johnson girl ain't straight,' I says. 'Oh, hell,'' he says. 'Oh, hell.' 'Dat's all right,' I says, 'but I know what I knows,' I says, 'an' it 'ill come out later. You wait an' see,' I says, 'you see.' "

"Anybody what had eyes could see dat dere was somethin' wrong wid dat girl. I didn't like her actions."

On the street Jimmie met a friend. "What d' hell?" asked the latter.

Jimmie explained. "An' I'll t'ump 'im till he can't stand."

"Oh, what d' hell," said the friend. "What's d' use! Yeh'll git pulled in! Everybody 'ill be onto it! An' ten plunks! Gee!"

Jimmie was determined. "He t'inks he kin scrap, but he'll fin' out diff'ent."

"Gee!" remonstrated the friend. "What d' hell?"

CHAPTER XI

On a corner a glass-fronted building shed a yellow glare upon the pavements. The open mouth of a saloon called seductively to passengers to enter and annihilate sorrow or create rage.

The interior of the place was papered in olive and bronze tints of imitation leather. A shining bar of counterfeit massiveness extended down the side of the room. Behind it a great mahogany-imitation sideboard reached the ceiling. Upon its shelves rested pyramids of shimmering glasses that were never disturbed. Mirrors set in the face of the sideboard multiplied them. Lemons, oranges and paper napkins, arranged with mathematical precision, sat among the glasses. Many-hued decanters of liquor perched at regular intervals on the lower shelves. A nickel-plated cash register occupied a place in the exact centre of the general effect. The elementary senses of it all seemed to be opulence and geometrical accuracy.

Across from the bar a smaller counter held a collection of plates upon which swarmed frayed fragments of crackers, slices of boiled ham, dishevelled bits of cheese, and pickles swimming in vinegar. An odor of grasping, begrimed hands and munching mouths pervaded all.

Pete, in a white jacket, was behind the bar bending expectantly toward a quiet stranger. "A beeh," said the man. Pete drew a foam-topped glassful and set it dripping upon the bar.

At this moment the light bamboo doors at the entrance swung open and crashed against the wall. Jimmie and a companion entered. They swaggered unsteadily but belligerently toward the bar and looked at Pete with bleared and blinking eyes.

"Gin," said Jimmie.

"Gin," said the companion.

Pete slid a bottle and two glasses along the bar. He bended his head sideways as he assiduously polished away with a napkin at the gleaming wood. He wore a look of watchfulness.

Jimmie and his companion kept their eyes upon the bartender and conversed loudly in tones of contempt.

"He's a dindy masher, ain't he, by Gawd?" laughed Jimmie.

"Oh, hell, yes," said the companion, sneering. "He's great, he is. Git onto d' mug on d' blokie. Dat's enough to make a feller turn hand-springs in 'is sleep."

The quiet stranger moved himself and his glass a trifle

further away and maintained an attitude of oblivi-
ousness.

"Gee! ain't he hot stuff!"

"Git onto his shape! Great Gawd!"

"Hey," cried Jimmie, in tones of command. Pete came
along slowly, with a sullen dropping of the under lip.

"Well," he growled, "what's eatin' yehs?"

"Gin," said Jimmie.

"Gin," said the companion.

As Pete confronted them with the bottle and the
glasses, they laughed in his face. Jimmie's companion,
evidently overcome with merriment, pointed a grimy
forefinger in Pete's direction.

"Say, Jimmie," demanded he, "what d' hell is dat behind d' bar?"

"Damned if I knows," replied Jimmie. They laughed
loudly. Pete put down a bottle with a bang and turned
a formidable face toward them. He disclosed his teeth
and his shoulders heaved restlessly.

"You fellers can't guy me," he said. "Drink yer stuff
an' git out an' don' make no trouble."

Instantly the laughter faded from the faces of the two
men and expressions of offended dignity immediately
came.

"Who d' hell has said anyt'ing t' you," cried they in
the same breath.

The quiet stranger looked at the door calculatingly.

"Ah, come off," said Pete to the two men. "Don't
pick me up for no jay. Drink yer rum an' git out an'
don' make no trouble."

"Oh, d' hell," airily cried Jimmie.

"Oh, d' hell," airily repeated his companion.

"We goes when we git ready! See!" continued Jimmie.

"Well," said Pete in a threatening voice, "don' make
no trouble."

Jimmie suddenly leaned forward with his head on one
side. He snarled like a wild animal.

"Well, what if we does? See?" said he.

Hot blood flushed into Pete's face, and he shot a lurid
glance at Jimmie.

"Well, den we'll see who's d' bes' man, you or me,"
he said.

The quiet stranger moved modestly toward the door. Jimmie began to swell with valor.

"Don' pick me up fer no tenderfoot. When yeh tackles me yeh tackles one of d' bes' men in d' city. See? I'm a scrapper, I am. Ain't dat right, Billie?"

"Sure, Mike," responded his companion in tones of conviction.

"Oh, hell," said Pete, easily. "Go fall on yerself."

The two men again began to laugh.

"What d' hell is dat talkin'?" cried the companion.

"Damned if I knows," replied Jimmie with exaggerated contempt.

Pete made a furious gesture. "Git outa here now, an' don' make no trouble. See? Youse fellers er lookin' fer a scrap an' it's damn likely yeh'll fin' one if yeh keeps on shootin' off yer mout's. I know yehs! See? I kin lick better men dan yehs ever saw in yer lifes. Dat's right! See? Don' pick me up fer no stuff er yeh might be jolted out in d' street before yeh knows where yeh is. When I comes from behind dis bar, I t'rows yehs bote inteh d' street. See?"

"Oh, hell," cried the two men in chorus.

The glare of a panther came into Pete's eyes. "Dat's what I said! Unnerstan'?"

He came through a passage at the end of the bar and swelled down upon the two men. They stepped promptly forward and crowded close to him.

They bristled like three roosters. They moved their heads pugnaciously and kept their shoulders braced. The nervous muscles about each mouth twitched with a forced smile of mockery.

"Well, what d' hell yer goin' t' do?" gritted Jimmie.

Pete stepped warily back, waving his hands before him to keep the men from coming too near.

"Well, what d' hell yer goin' t' do?" repeated Jimmie's ally. They kept close to him, taunting and leering. They strove to make him attempt the initial blow.

"Keep back now! Don' crowd me," ominously said Pete.

Again they chorused in contempt. "Oh, hell!"

In a small, tossing group, the three men edged for positions like frigates contemplating battle.

"Well, why d' hell don' yeh try t' t'row us out?" cried Jimmie and his ally with copious sneers.

The bravery of bull-dogs sat upon the faces of the men. Their clenched fists moved like eager weapons.

The allied two jostled the bartender's elbows, glaring at him with feverish eyes and forcing him toward the wall.

Suddenly Pete swore furiously. The flash of action gleamed from his eyes. He threw back his arm and aimed a tremendous, lightning-like blow at Jimmie's face. His foot swung a step forward and the weight of his body was behind his fist. Jimmie ducked his head, Bowery-like, with the quickness of a cat. The fierce, answering blows of Jimmie and his ally crushed on Pete's bowed head.

The quiet stranger vanished.

The arms of the combatants whirled in the air like flails. The faces of the men, at first flushed to flame-colored anger, now began to fade to the pallor of warriors in the blood and heat of a battle. Their lips curled back and stretched tightly over the gums in ghoul-like grins. Through their white, gripped teeth struggled hoarse whisperings of oaths. Their eyes glittered with murderous fire.

Each head was huddled between its owner's shoulders, and arms were swinging with marvelous rapidity. Feet scraped to and fro with a loud scratching sound upon the sanded floor. Blows left crimson blotches upon pale skin. The curses of the first quarter minute of the fight died away. The breaths of the fighters came wheezingly from their lips and the three chests were straining and heaving. Pete at intervals gave vent to low, labored hisses, that sounded like a desire to kill. Jimmie's ally gibbered at times like a wounded maniac. Jimmie was silent, fighting with the face of a sacrificial priest. The rage of fear shone in all their eyes and their blood-colored fists whirled.

At a critical moment a blow from Pete's hand struck the ally and he crashed to the floor. He wriggled instantly to his feet and grasping the quiet stranger's beer glass from the bar, hurled it at Pete's head.

High on the wall it burst like a bomb, shivering fragments flying in all directions. Then missiles came to every man's hand. The place had heretofore appeared free of things to throw, but suddenly glasses and bottles went singing through the air. They were thrown point-blank at bobbing heads. The pyramid of shimmering glasses, that had never been disturbed, changed to cascades as heavy bottles were flung into them. Mirrors splintered to nothing.

The three frothing creatures on the floor buried themselves in a frenzy for blood. There followed in the wake of missiles and fists some unknown prayers, perhaps for death.

The quiet stranger had sprawled very pyrotechnically out on the sidewalk. A laugh ran up and down the avenue for the half of a block.

"Dey've t'rowed a bloke inteh d' street."

People heard the sound of breaking glass and shuffling feet within the saloon and came running. A small group, bending down to look under the bamboo doors, and watching the fall of glass and three pairs of violent legs, changed in a moment to a crowd.

A policeman came charging down the sidewalk and bounced through the doors into the saloon. The crowd bended and surged in absorbing anxiety to see.

Jimmie caught first sight of the on-coming interruption. On his feet he had the same regard for a policeman that, when on his truck, he had for a fire engine. He howled and ran for the side door.

The officer made a terrific advance, club in hand. One comprehensive sweep of the long night stick threw the ally to the floor and forced Pete to a corner. With his disengaged hand he made a furious effort at Jimmie's coat-tails. Then he regained his balance and paused.

"Well, well, you are a pair of pictures. What in hell have yeh been up to?"

Jimmie, with his face drenched in blood, escaped up a side street, pursued a short distance by some of the more law-loving, or excited individuals of the crowd.

Later, from a safe dark corner, he saw the policeman, the ally and the bartender emerge from the saloon. Pete locked the doors and then followed up the avenue in the rear of the crowd-encompassed policeman and his charge.

At first Jimmie, with his heart throbbing at battle heat, started to go desperately to the rescue of his friend, but he halted.

"Ah, what d' hell?" he demanded of himself.

CHAPTER XII

In a hall of irregular shape sat Pete and Maggie drinking beer. A submissive orchestra dictated to by a spectacled man with frowsy hair and in soiled evening dress, industriously followed the bobs of his head and the waves of his baton. A ballad singer, in a gown of flaming scarlet, sang in the inevitable voice of brass. When she vanished, men seated at the tables near the front applauded loudly, pounding the polished wood with their beer glasses. She returned attired in less gown, and sang again. She received another enthusiastic encore. She reappeared in still less gown and danced. The deafening rumble of glasses and clapping of hands that followed her exit indicated an overwhelming desire to have her come on for the fourth time, but the curiosity of the audience was not gratified.

Maggie was pale. From her eyes had been plucked all look of self-reliance. She leaned with a dependent air toward her companion. She was timid, as if fearing his anger or displeasure. She seemed to beseech tenderness of him.

Pete's air of distinguished valor had grown upon him until it threatened to reach stupendous dimensions. He was infinitely gracious to the girl. It was apparent to her that his condescension was a marvel.

He could appear to strut even while sitting still and he showed that he was a lion of lordly characteristics by the air with which he spat.

With Maggie gazing at him wonderingly, he took pride in commanding the waiters who were, however, indifferent or deaf.

"Hi, you, git a russle on yehs! What d' hell yehs lookin' at? Two more beehs, d'yeh hear?"

He leaned back and critically regarded the person of

a girl with a straw-colored wig who upon the stage was flinging her heels about in somewhat awkward imitation of a well-known danseuse.

At times Maggie told Pete long confidential tales of her former home life, dwelling upon the escapades of the other members of the family and the difficulties she had had to combat in order to obtain a degree of comfort. He responded in the accents of philanthropy. He pressed her arm with an air of reassuring proprietorship.

"Dey was damn jays," he said, denouncing the mother and brother.

The sound of the music which, through the efforts of the frowsy-headed leader, drifted to her ears in the smoke-filled atmosphere, made the girl dream. She thought of her former Rum Alley environment and turned to regard Pete's strong protecting fists. She thought of a collar and cuff manufactory and the eternal moan of the proprietor: "What een hale do you sink I pie fife dolla a week for? Play? No, py tamn!" She contemplated Pete's man-subduing eyes and noted that wealth and prosperity was indicated by his clothes. She imagined a future, rose-tinted, because of its distance from all that she had experienced before.

As to the present she perceived only vague reasons to be miserable. Her life was Pete's and she considered him worthy of the charge. She would be disturbed by no particular apprehensions, so long as Pete adored her as he now said he did. She did not feel like a bad woman. To her knowledge she had never seen any better.

At times men at other tables regarded the girl furtively. Pete, aware of it, nodded at her and grinned. He felt proud.

"Mag, yer a bloomin' good-looker," he remarked, studying her face through the haze. The men made Maggie fear, but she blushed at Pete's words as it became apparent to her that she was the apple of his eye.

Grey-headed men, wonderfully pathetic in their dissipation, stared at her through clouds. Smooth-cheeked boys, some of them with faces of stone and mouths of sin, not nearly so pathetic as the grey heads, tried to find the girl's eyes in the smoke wreaths. Maggie considered she was not what they thought her. She confined her glances to Pete and the stage.

The orchestra played negro melodies and a versatile drummer pounded, whacked, clattered and scratched on a dozen machines to make noise.

Those glances of the men, shot at Maggie from under half-closed lids, made her tremble. She thought them all to be worse men than Pete.

"Come, let's go," she said.

As they went out Maggie perceived two women seated at a table with some men. They were painted and their cheeks had lost their roundness. As she passed them the girl, with a shrinking movement, drew back her skirts.

CHAPTER XIII

Jimmie did not return home for a number of days after the fight with Pete in the saloon. When he did, he approached with extreme caution.

He found his mother raving. Maggie had not returned home. The parent continually wondered how her daughter could come to such a pass. She had never considered Maggie as a pearl dropped unstained into Rum Alley from Heaven, but she could not conceive how it was possible for her daughter to fall so low as to bring disgrace upon her family. She was terrific in denunciation of the girl's wickedness.

The fact that the neighbors talked of it, maddened her. When women came in, and in the course of their conversation casually asked, "Where's Maggie dese days?" the mother shook her fuzzy head at them and appalled them with curses. Cunning hints inviting confidence she rebuffed with violence.

"An' wid all d' bringin' up she had, how could she?" moaningly she asked of her son. "Wid all d' talkin' wid her I did an' d' t'ings I tol' her to remember? When a girl is bringed up d' way I bringed up Maggie, how kin she go t' d' devil?"

Jimmie was transfixed by these questions. He could not conceive how under the circumstances his mother's daughter and his sister could have been so wicked.

His mother took a drink from a bottle that sat on the table. She continued her lament.

"She had a bad heart, dat girl did, Jimmie. She was wicked t' d' heart an' we never knowed it."

Jimmie nodded, admitting the fact.

"We lived in d' same house wid her an' I brought her up an' we never knowed how bad she was."

Jimmie nodded again.

"Wid a home like dis an' a mudder like me, she went t' d' bad," cried the mother, raising her eyes.

One day Jimmie came home, sat down in a chair and began to wriggle about with a new and strange nervousness. At last he spoke shamefacedly.

"Well, look-a-here, dis t'ing queers us! See? We're queered! An' maybe it 'ud be better if I—well, I t'ink I kin look 'er up an'—maybe it 'ud be better if I fetched her home an'——"

The mother started from her chair and broke forth into a storm of passionate anger.

"What! Let 'er come an' sleep under d' same roof wid her mudder agin! Oh, yes, I will, won't I? Sure? Shame on yehs, Jimmie Johnson, fer sayin' such a t'ing t' yer own mudder—t' yer own mudder! Little did I t'ink when yehs was a babby playin' about me feet dat ye'd grow up t' say sech a t'ing t' yer mudder—yer own mudder. I never t'aut——"

Sobs choked her and interrupted her reproaches.

"Dere ain't nottin' t' raise sech hell about," said Jimmie. "I on'y says it 'ud be better if we keep dis t'ing dark, see? It queers us! See?"

His mother laughed a laugh that seemed to ring through the city and be echoed and re-echoed by countless other laughs. "Oh, yes, I will, won't I! Sure!"

"Well, yeh must take me for a damn fool," said Jimmie, indignant at his mother for mocking him. "I didn't say we'd make 'er inteh a little tin angel, ner nottin', but d' way it is now she can queer us! Don' che see?"

"Aye, she'll git tired of d' life atter a while an' den she'll wanna be a-comin' home, won' she, d' beast! I'll let 'er in den, won' I?"

"Well, I didn' mean none of dis prod'gal bus'ness anyway," explained Jimmie.

"It wa'n't no prod'gal dauter, yeh damn fool," said the mother. "It was prod'gal son, anyhow."

"I know dat," said Jimmie.

For a time they sat in silence. The mother's eyes gloated on the scene which her imagination called before her. Her lips were set in a vindictive smile.

"Aye, she'll cry, won' she, an' carry on, an' tell how Pete, or some odder feller, beats 'er an' she'll say she's sorry an' all dat an' she ain't happy, she ain't, and she wants to come home agin, she does."

With grim humor the mother imitated the possible wailing notes of the daughter's voice.

"Den I'll take 'er in, won't I? She kin cry 'er two eyes out on d' stones of d' street before I'll dirty d' place wid her. She abused an' ill-treated her own mudder—her own mudder what loved her an' she'll never git anodder chance dis side of hell."

Jimmie thought he had a great idea of women's frailty, but he could not understand why any of his kin should be victims.

"Damn her," he fervidly said.

Again he wondered vaguely if some of the women of his acquaintance had brothers. Nevertheless, his mind did not for an instant confuse himself with those brothers nor his sister with theirs. After the mother had, with great difficulty, suppressed the neighbors, she went among them and proclaimed her grief. "May Gawd forgive dat girl," was her continual cry. To attentive ears she recited the whole length and breadth of her woes.

"I bringed 'er up d' way a dauter oughta be bringed up, an' dis is how she served me! She went t' d' devil d' first chance she got! May Gawd forgive her."

When arrested for drunkenness she used the story of her daughter's downfall with telling effect upon the police-justices. Finally one of them said to her, peering down over his spectacles: "Mary, the records of this and other courts show that you are the mother of forty-two daughters who have been ruined. The case is unparalleled in the annals of this court, and this court thinks——"

The mother went through life shedding large tears of sorrow. Her red face was a picture of agony.

Of course Jimmie publicly damned his sister that he might appear on a higher social plane. But, arguing with himself, stumbling about in ways that he knew not, he, once, almost came to a conclusion that his sister would have been more firmly good had she better known why. However, he felt that he could not hold such a view. He threw it hastily aside.

CHAPTER XIV

In a hilarious hall there were twenty-eight tables and twenty-eight women and a crowd of smoking men. Valiant noise was made on a stage at the end of the hall by an orchestra composed of men who looked as if they had just happened in. Soiled waiters ran to and fro, swooping down like hawks on the unwary in the throng; clattering along the aisles with trays covered with glasses; stumbling over women's skirts and charging two prices for everything but beer, all with a swiftness that blurred the view of the coconut palms and dusty monstrosities painted upon the walls of the room. A "bouncer" with an immense load of business upon his hands, plunged about in the crowd, dragging bashful strangers to prominent chairs, ordering waiters here and there and quarreling furiously with men who wanted to sing with the orchestra.

The usual smoke cloud was present, but so dense that heads and arms seemed entangled in it. The rumble of conversation was replaced by a roar. Plenteous oaths heaved through the air. The room rang with the shrill voices of women bubbling over with drink-laughter. The chief element in the music of the orchestra was speed. The musicians played in intent fury. A woman was singing and smiling upon the stage, but no one took notice of her. The rate at which the piano, cornet and violins were going, seemed to impart wildness to the half-drunken crowd. Beer glasses were emptied at a gulp and conversation became a rapid chatter. The smoke eddied and swirled like a shadowy river hurrying toward some unseen falls. Pete and Maggie entered the hall and took chairs at a table near the door. The woman who was seated there made an attempt to occupy Pete's attention and, failing, went away.

Three weeks had passed since the girl had left home. The air of spaniel-like dependence had been magnified and showed its direct effect in the peculiar off-handedness and ease of Pete's ways toward her.

She followed Pete's eyes with hers, anticipating with smiles gracious looks from him.

A woman of brilliance and audacity, accompanied by a mere boy, came into the place and took seats near them.

At once Pete sprang to his feet, his face beaming with glad surprise.

"By Gawd, dere's Nellie," he cried.

He went over to the table and held out an eager hand to the woman.

"Why, hello, Pete, me boy, how are you," said she, giving him her fingers.

Maggie took instant note of the woman. She perceived that her black dress fitted her to perfection. Her linen collar and cuffs were spotless. Tan gloves were stretched over her well-shaped hands. A hat of a prevailing fashion perched jauntily upon her dark hair. She wore no jewelry and was painted with no apparent paint. She looked clear-eyed through the stares of the men.

"Sit down, and call your lady-friend over," she said to Pete. At his beckoning Maggie came and sat between Pete and the mere boy.

"I thought yeh were gone away fer good," began Pete, at once. "When did yeh git back? How did dat Buff'lo bus'ness turn out?"

The woman shrugged her shoulders. "Well, he didn't have as many stamps as he tried to make out, so I shook him, that's all."

"Well, I'm glad t' see yehs back in d' city," said Pete, with gallantry.

He and the woman entered into a long conversation, exchanging reminiscences of days together. Maggie sat still, unable to formulate an intelligent sentence as her addition to the conversation and painfully aware of it.

She saw Pete's eyes sparkle as he gazed upon the handsome stranger. He listened smilingly to all she said.

The woman was familiar with all his affairs, asked him about mutual friends, and knew the amount of his salary.

She paid no attention to Maggie, looking toward her once or twice and apparently seeing the wall beyond.

The mere boy was sulky. In the beginning he had welcomed the additions with acclamations.

"Let's all have a drink! What'll you take, Nell? And you, Miss What's-your-name. Have a drink, Mr.——, you, I mean."

He had shown a sprightly desire to do the talking for the company and tell all about his family. In a loud voice he declaimed on various topics. He assumed a patronizing air toward Pete. As Maggie was silent, he paid no attention to her. He made a great show of lavishing wealth upon the woman of brilliance and audacity.

"Do keep still, Freddie! You talk like a clock," said the woman to him. She turned away and devoted her attention to Pete.

"We'll have many a good time together again, eh?"

"Sure, Mike," said Pete, enthusiastic at once.

"Say," whispered she, leaning forward, "let's go over to Billie's and have a heluva time."

"Well, it's dis way! See?" said Pete. "I got dis lady frien' here."

"Oh, t' hell with her," argued the woman.

Pete appeared disturbed.

"All right," said she, nodding her head at him. "All right for you! We'll see the next time you ask me to go anywheres with you."

Pete squirmed.

"Say," he said, beseechingly, "come wid me a minit an' I'll tell yer why."

The woman waved her hand.

"Oh, that's all right, you needn't explain, you know. You wouldn't come merely because you wouldn't come, that's all."

To Pete's visible distress she turned to the mere boy, bringing him speedily out of a terrific rage. He had been debating whether it would be the part of a man to pick a quarrel with Pete, or would he be justified in striking him savagely with his beer glass without warning. But he recovered himself when the woman turned to renew her smilings. He beamed upon her with an expression that was somewhat tipsy and inexpressibly tender.

"Say, shake that Bowery jay," requested he, in a loud whisper.

"Freddie, you are so funny," she replied.

Pete reached forward and touched the woman on the arm.

"Come out a minit while I tells yeh why I can't go wid yer. Yer doin' me dirt, Nell! I never t'aut ye'd do me dirt, Nell. Come on, will yer?" He spoke in tones of injury.

"Why, I don't see why I should be interested in your explanations," said the woman, with a coldness that seemed to reduce Pete to a pulp.

His eyes pleaded with her. "Come out a minit while I tells yeh. On d' level, now."

The woman nodded slightly at Maggie and the mere boy, saying, " 'Scuse me."

The mere boy interrupted his loving smile and turned a shriveling glare upon Pete. His boyish countenance flushed and he spoke, in a whine, to the woman:

"Oh, I say, Nellie, this ain't a square deal, you know. You aren't goin' to leave me and go off with that duffer, are you? I should think—"

"Why, you dear boy, of course I'm not," cried the woman, affectionately. She bended over and whispered in his ear. He smiled again and settled in his chair as if resolved to wait patiently.

As the woman walked down between the rows of tables, Pete was at her shoulder talking earnestly, apparently in explanation. The woman waved her hands with studied airs of indifference. The doors swung behind them, leaving Maggie and the mere boy seated at the table.

Maggie was dazed. She could dimly perceive that something stupendous had happened. She wondered why Pete saw fit to remonstrate with the woman, pleading for forgiveness with his eyes. She thought she noted an air of submission about her leonine Pete. She was astounded.

The mere boy occupied himself with cock-tails and a

cigar. He was tranquilly silent for half an hour. Then he
bestirred himself and spoke.

"Well," he said sighing, "I knew this was the way it
would be. They got cold feet." There was another
stillness. The mere boy seemed to be musing.

"She was pulling m' leg. That's the whole amount of
it," he said, suddenly. "It's a bloomin' shame the way
that girl does. Why, I've spent over two dollars in drinks
to-night. And she goes off with that plug-ugly who looks
as if he had been hit in the face with a coin-die. I call
it rocky treatment for a fellah like me. Here, waiter,
bring me a cock-tail and make it damned strong."

Maggie made no reply. She was watching the doors.
"It's a mean piece of business," complained the mere
boy. He explained to her how amazing it was that anybody should treat him in such a manner. "But I'll get
square with her, you bet. She won't get far ahead of
yours truly, you know," he added, winking. "I'll tell her
plainly that it was bloomin' mean business. And she
won't come it over me with any of her 'now-Freddie-
dears.' She thinks my name is Freddie, you know, but
of course it ain't. I always tell these people some name
like that, because if they got onto your right name they
might use it sometime. Understand? Oh, they don't fool
me much."

Maggie was paying no attention, being intent upon the
doors. The mere boy relapsed into a period of gloom,
during which he exterminated a number of cock-tails
with a determined air, as if replying defiantly to fate.
He occasionally broke forth into sentences composed of
invectives joined together in a long chain.

The girl was still staring at the doors. After a time the
mere boy began to see cobwebs just in front of his nose.
He spurred himself into being agreeable and insisted
upon her having a charlotte-russe and a glass of beer.

"They's gone," he remarked, "they's gone." He
looked at her through the smoke wreaths. "Shay, lil' girl,
we mightish well make bes' of it. You ain't such bad-
lookin' girl, y'know. Not half bad. Can't come up to
Nell, though. No, can't do it! Well, I should shay not!
Nell fine-lookin' girl! F—i—n—ine. You look damn bad

longsider her, but by y'self ain't so bad. Have to do anyhow. Nell gone. On'y you left. Not half bad, though."

Maggie stood up.

"I'm going home," she said.

The mere boy started.

"Eh? What? Home," he cried, struck with amazement. "I beg pardon, did hear say home?"

"I'm going home," she repeated.

"Great Gawd, what hav'a struck?" demanded the mere boy of himself, stupefied.

In a semi-comatose state he conducted her on board an uptown car, ostentatiously paid her fare, leered kindly at her through the rear window and fell off the steps.

CHAPTER XV

A forlorn woman went along a lighted avenue. The street was filled with people desperately bound on missions. An endless crowd darted at the elevated station stairs and the horse cars were thronged with owners of bundles.

The pace of the forlorn woman was slow. She was apparently searching for some one. She loitered near the doors of saloons and watched men emerge from them. She furtively scanned the faces in the rushing stream of pedestrians. Hurrying men, bent on catching some boat or train, jostled her elbows, failing to notice her, their thoughts fixed on distant dinners.

The forlorn woman had a peculiar face. Her smile was no smile. But when in repose her features had a shadowy look that was like a sardonic grin, as if some one had sketched with cruel forefinger indelible lines about her mouth.

Jimmie came strolling up the avenue. The woman encountered him with an aggrieved air.

"Oh, Jimmie, I've been lookin' all over fer yehs——" she began.

Jimmie made an impatient gesture and quickened his pace.

"Ah, don't bodder me! Good Gawd!" he said, with the savageness of a man whose life is pestered.

The woman followed him along the sidewalk in somewhat the manner of a suppliant.

"But, Jimmie," she said, "yehs told me yeh'd——"

Jimmie turned upon her fiercely as if resolved to make
a last stand for comfort and peace.

"Say, fer Gawd's sake, Hattie, don' foller me from
one end of d' city t' d' odder. Let up, will yehs! Give
me a minute's res', can't yehs? Yehs makes me tired,
allus taggin' me. See? Ain' yehs got no sense? Do yehs
want people t' get onto me? Go chase yerself, fer
Gawd's sake."

The woman stepped closer and laid her fingers on his
arm. "But, look-a-here——"

Jimmie snarled. "Oh, go t' hell."

He darted into the front door of a convenient saloon
and a moment later came out into the shadows that surrounded the side door. On the brilliantly lighted avenue
he perceived the forlorn woman dodging about like a
scout. Jimmie laughed with an air of relief and went
away.

When he arrived home he found his mother clamoring. Maggie had returned. She stood shivering beneath
the torrent of her mother's wrath.

"Well, I'm damned," said Jimmie in greeting.

His mother, tottering about the room, pointed a quivering forefinger.

"Lookut her, Jimmie, lookut her. Dere's yer sister,
boy. Dere's yer sister. Lookut her! Lookut her!"

She screamed at Maggie with scoffing laughter.

The girl stood in the middle of the room. She edged
about as if unable to find a place on the floor to put
her feet.

"Ha, ha, ha," bellowed the mother. "Dere she stands!
Ain' she purty? Lookut her! Ain' she sweet, d' beast?
Lookut her! Ha, ha! lookut her!"

She lurched forward and put her red and seamed
hands upon her daughter's face. She bended down and
peered keenly up into the eyes of the girl.

"Oh, she's jes' dessame as she ever was, ain' she?
She's her mudder's putty darlin' yit, ain' she? Lookut
her, Jimmie! Come here, fer Gawd's sake, and lookut
her."

The loud, tremendous railing of the mother brought the denizens of the Rum Alley tenement to their doors. Women came in the hallways. Children scurried to and fro.

"What's up? Dat Johnson party on anudder tear?"

"Naw! Young Mag's come home!"

"D' hell yeh say?"

Through the open doors curious eyes stared in at Maggie. Children ventured into the room and ogled her, as if they formed the front row at a theatre. Women, without, bended toward each other and whispered, nodding their heads with airs of profound philosophy.

A baby, overcome with curiosity concerning this object at which all were looking, sidled forward and touched her dress, cautiously, as if investigating a red-hot stove. Its mother's voice rang out like a warning trumpet. She rushed forward and grabbed her child, casting a terrible look of indignation at the girl.

Maggie's mother paced to and fro, addressing the doorful of eyes, expounding like a glib showman. Her voice rang through the building.

"Dere she stands," she cried, wheeling suddenly and pointing with dramatic finger. "Dere she stands! Lookut her! Ain' she a dindy? An' she was so good as to come home t' her mudder, she was! Ain' she a beaut'? Ain' she a dindy? Fer Gawd's sake!"

The jeering cries ended in another burst of shrill laughter.

The girl seemed to awaken. "Jimmie——"

He drew hastily back from her.

"Well, now, yer a hell of a t'ing, ain' yeh?" he said, his lips curling in scorn. Radiant virtue sat upon his brow and his repelling hands expressed horror of contamination.

Maggie turned and went.

The crowd at the door fell back precipitately. A baby falling down in front of the door, wrenched a scream like that of a wounded animal from its mother. Another woman sprang forward and picked it up, with a chivalrous air, as if rescuing a human being from an on-coming express train.

As the girl passed down through the hall, she went

before open doors framing more eyes strangely micro-
scopic, and sending broad beams of inquisitive light into
the darkness of her path. On the second floor she met
the gnarled old woman who possessed the music box.

"So," she cried, " 'ere yehs are back again, are yehs?
An' dey've kicked yehs out? Well, come in an' stay wid
me t'-night. I ain' got no moral standin'."

From above came an unceasing babble of tongues,
over all of which rang the mother's derisive laughter.

CHAPTER XVI

Pete did not consider that he had ruined Maggie. If he
had thought that her soul could never smile again, he
would have believed the mother and brother, who were
pyrotechnic over the affair, to be responsible for it.

Besides, in his world, souls did not insist upon being
able to smile. "What d' hell?"

He felt a trifle entangled. It distressed him. Revela-
tions and scenes might bring upon him the wrath of the
owner of the saloon, who insisted upon respectability of
an advanced type.

"What d' hell do dey wanna raise such a smoke about
it fer?" demanded he of himself, disgusted with the attitude of the family. He saw no necessity that people
should lose their equilibrium merely because their sister
or their daughter had stayed away from home.

Searching about in his mind for possible reasons for
their conduct, he came upon the conclusion that Maggie's motives were correct, but that the two others
wished to snare him. He felt pursued.

The woman whom he had met in the hilarious hall
showed a disposition to ridicule him.

"A little pale thing with no spirit," she said. "Did you
note the expression of her eyes? There was something
in them about pumpkin pie and virtue. That is a peculiar
way the left corner of her mouth has of twitching, isn't
it? Dear, dear, Pete, what are you coming to?"

Pete asserted at once that he never was very much
interested in the girl. The woman interrupted him,
laughing.

"Oh, it's not of the slightest consequence to me, my

dear young man. You needn't draw maps for my benefit. Why should I be concerned about it?"

But Pete continued with his explanations. If he was laughed at for his tastes in women, he felt obliged to say that they were only temporary or indifferent ones.

The morning after Maggie had departed from home, Pete stood behind the bar. He was immaculate in white jacket and apron and his hair was plastered over his brow with infinite correctness. No customers were in the place. Pete was twisting his napkined fist slowly in a beer glass, softly whistling to himself and occasionally holding the object of his attention between his eyes and a few weak beams of sunlight that found their way over the thick screens and into the shaded room.

With lingering thoughts of the woman of brilliance and audacity, the bartender raised his head and stared through the varying cracks between the swaying bamboo doors. Suddenly the whistling pucker faded from his lips. He saw Maggie walking slowly past. He gave a great start, fearing for the previously-mentioned eminent respectability of the place.

He threw a swift, nervous glance about him, all at once feeling guilty. No one was in the room.

He went hastily over to the side door. Opening it and looking out, he perceived Maggie standing, as if undecided, on the corner. She was searching the place with her eyes.

As she turned her face toward him Pete beckoned to her hurriedly, intent upon returning with speed to a position behind the bar and to the atmosphere of respectability upon which the proprietor insisted.

Maggie came to him, the anxious look disappearing from her face and a smile wreathing her lips.

"Oh, Pete——" she began brightly.

The bartender made a violent gesture of impatience.

"Oh, my Gawd," cried he, vehemently. "What d' hell do yeh wanna hang aroun' here fer? Do yeh wanna git me inteh trouble?" he demanded with an air of injury.

Astonishment swept over the girl's features. "Why, Pete! yehs tol' me——"

Pete's glance expressed profound irritation. His coun-

tenance reddened with the anger of a man whose respectability is being threatened.

"Say, yehs makes me tired. See? What d' hell do yeh
wanna tag aroun' atter me fer? Yeh'll do me dirt wid d'
ol' man an' dey'll be hell t' pay! If he sees a woman
roun' here he'll go crazy an' I'll lose me job! See? Ain'
yehs got no sense? Don' be allus bodderin' me. See?
Yer brudder come in here an' raised hell an' d' ol' man
hada put up fer it! An' now I'm done! See? I'm done."

The girl's eyes stared into his face. "Pete, don't yeh
remem——"

"Oh, hell," interrupted Pete, anticipating.

The girl seemed to have a struggle with herself. She
was apparently bewildered and could not find speech.
Finally she asked in a low voice: "But where kin I go?"

The question exasperated Pete beyond the powers of
endurance. It was a direct attempt to give him some
responsibility in a matter that did not concern him. In
his indignation he volunteered information.

"Oh, go t' hell," cried he. He slammed the door furiously and returned, with an air of relief, to his
respectability.

Maggie went away.

She wandered aimlessly for several blocks. She
stopped once and asked aloud a question of herself:
"Who?"

A man who was passing near her shoulder, humor-
ously took the questioning word as intended for him.

"Eh? What? Who? Nobody! I didn't say anything,"
he laughingly said, and continued his way.

Soon the girl discovered that if she walked with such
apparent aimlessness, some men looked at her with calculating eyes. She quickened her step, frightened. As a
protection, she adopted a demeanor of intentness as if
going somewhere.

After a time she left rattling avenues and passed between rows of houses with sternness and stolidity
stamped upon their features. She hung her head for she
felt their eyes grimly upon her.

Suddenly she came upon a stout gentleman in a silk
hat and a chaste black coat, whose decorous row of but-
tons reached from his chin to his knees. The girl had

heard of the Grace of God and she decided to approach this man.

His beaming, chubby face was a picture of benevolence and kind-heartedness. His eyes shone good-will.

But as the girl timidly accosted him, he made a convulsive movement and saved his respectability by a vigorous side-step. He did not risk it to save a soul. For how was he to know that there was a soul before him that needed saving?

CHAPTER XVII

Upon a wet evening, several months after the last chapter, two interminable rows of cars, pulled by slipping horses, jangled along a prominent side street. A dozen cabs, with coat-enshrouded drivers, clattered to and fro. Electric lights, whirring softly, shed a blurred radiance. A flower dealer, his feet tapping impatiently, his nose and his wares glistening with rain-drops, stood behind an array of roses and chrysanthemums. Two or three theatres emptied a crowd upon the storm-swept pavements. Men pulled their hats over their eyebrows and raised their collars to their ears. Women shrugged impatient shoulders in their warm cloaks and stopped to arrange their skirts for a walk through the storm. People who had been constrained to comparative silence for two hours burst into a roar of conversation, their hearts still kindling from the glowings of the stage.

The pavements became tossing seas of umbrellas. Men stepped forth to hail cabs or cars, raising their fingers in varied forms of polite request or imperative demand. An endless procession wended toward elevated stations. An atmosphere of pleasure and prosperity seemed to hang over the throng, born, perhaps, of good clothes and of two hours in a place of forgetfulness.

In the mingled light and gloom of an adjacent park, a handful of wet wanderers, in attitudes of chronic dejection, was scattered among the benches.

A girl of the painted cohorts of the city went along the street. She threw changing glances at men who passed her, giving smiling invitations to those of rural or untaught pattern and usually seeming sedately uncon-

scious of the men with a metropolitan seal upon their
faces.

Crossing glittering avenues, she went into the throng
emerging from the places of forgetfulness. She hurried
forward through the crowd as if intent upon reaching a
distant home, bending forward in her handsome cloak,
daintily lifting her skirts and picking for her well-shod
feet the dryer spots upon the pavements.

The restless doors of saloons, clashing to and fro, disclosed animated rows of men before bars and hurrying
barkeepers.

A concert hall gave to the street faint sounds of swift,
machine-like music, as if a group of phantom musicians
were hastening.

A tall young man, smoking a cigarette with a sublime
air, strolled near the girl. He had on evening dress, a
moustache, a chrysanthemum, and a look of ennui, all
of which he kept carefully under his eye. Seeing the girl
walk on as if such a young man as he was not in existence, he looked back transfixed with interest. He stared
glassily for a moment, but gave a slight convulsive start
when he discerned that she was neither new, Parisian,
nor theatrical. He wheeled about hastily and turned his
stare into the air, like a sailor with a search-light.

A stout gentleman, with pompous and philanthropic
whiskers, went stolidly by, the broad of his back sneering
at the girl.

A belated man in business clothes, and in haste to
catch a car, bounced against her shoulder. "Hi, there,
Mary, I beg your pardon! Brace up, old girl." He
grasped her arm to steady her, and then was away running down the middle of the street.

The girl walked on out of the realm of restaurants and
saloons. She passed more glittering avenues and went
into darker blocks than those where the crowd travelled.

A young man in light overcoat and derby hat received
a glance shot keenly from the eyes of the girl. He
stopped and looked at her, thrusting his hands in his
pockets and making a mocking smile curl his lips.
"Come, now, old lady," he said, "you don't mean to tell
me that you sized me up for a farmer?"

A laboring man marched along with bundles under his

arms. To her remarks, he replied, "It's a fine evenin', ain't it?"

She smiled squarely into the face of a boy who was hurrying by with his hands buried in his overcoat pockets, his blond locks bobbing on his youthful temples, and a cheery smile of unconcern upon his lips. He turned his head and smiled back at her, waving his hands.

"Not this eve—some other eve!"

A drunken man, reeling in her pathway, began to roar at her. "I ain' ga no money, dammit," he shouted, in a dismal voice. He lurched on up the street wailing to himself, "Dammit, I ain' ga no money. Damn ba' luck. Ain' ga no more money."

The girl went into gloomy districts near the river, where the tall black factories shut in the street and only occasional broad beams of light fell across the pavements from saloons. In front of one of these places, whence came the sound of a violin vigorously scraped, the patter of feet on boards and the ring of loud laughter, there stood a man with blotched features.

Further on in the darkness she met a ragged being with shifting, blood-shot eyes and grimy hands.

She went into the blackness of the final block. The shutters of the tall buildings were closed like grim lips. The structures seemed to have eyes that looked over them, beyond them, at other things. Afar off the lights of the avenues glittered as if from an impossible distance. Street-car bells jingled with a sound of merriment.

At the feet of the tall buildings appeared the deathly black hue of the river. Some hidden factory sent up a yellow glare, that lit for a moment the waters lapping oilily against timbers. The varied sounds of life, made joyous by distance and seeming unapproachableness, came faintly and died away to a silence.

CHAPTER XVIII

In a partitioned-off section of a saloon sat a man with a half dozen women, gleefully laughing, hovering about him. The man had arrived at that stage of drunkenness where affection is felt for the universe.

"I'm good f'ler, girls," he said, convincingly. "I'm

damn good f'ler. An'body treats me right, I allus trea's zem right! See?"

The women nodded their heads approvingly. "To be sure," they cried in hearty chorus. "You're the kind of a man we like, Pete. You're outa sight! What yeh goin' to buy this time, dear?"

"An't'ing yehs wants, damn it," said the man in an abandonment of good-will. His countenance shone with the true spirit of benevolence. He was in the proper mood of missionaries. He would have fraternized with obscure Hottentots. And above all, he was overwhelmed in tenderness for his friends, who were all illustrious.

"An't'ing yehs wants, damn it," repeated he, waving his hands with beneficent recklessness. "I'm good f'ler, girls, an' if an'body treats me right I—here," called he through an open door to a waiter, "bring girls drinks, damn it. What 'ill yehs have, girls? An't'ing yehs wants, damn it!"

The waiter glanced in with the disgusted look of the man who serves intoxicants for the man who takes too much of them. He nodded his head shortly at the order from each individual, and went.

"Damn it," said the man, "w're havin' heluva time. I like you girls! Damn'd if I don't! Yer right sort! See?"

He spoke at length and with feeling, concerning the excellencies of his assembled friends.

"Don't try pull man's leg, but have a heluva time! Das right! Das way t' do! Now, if I sawght yehs tryin' work me fer drinks, wouldn' buy damn t'ing! But yer right sort, damn it! Yehs know how ter treat a f'ler, an' I stays by yehs 'til spen' las' cent! Das right! I'm good f'ler an' I knows when an'body treats me right!"

Between the times of the arrival and departure of the waiter, the man discoursed to the women on the tender regard he felt for all living things. He laid stress upon the purity of his motives in all dealings with men in the world and spoke of the fervor of his friendship for those who were amiable. Tears welled slowly from his eyes. His voice quavered when he spoke to his companions.

Once when the waiter was about to depart with an empty tray, the man drew a coin from his pocket and held it forth.

"Here," said he, quite magnificently, "here's quar'."

The waiter kept his hands on his tray.

"I don' want yer money," he said.

The other put forth the coin with tearful insistence.

"Here, damn it," cried he, "tak't! Yer damn goo' f'ler an' I wan' yehs tak't!"

"Come, come, now," said the waiter, with the sullen air of a man who is forced into giving advice. "Put yer mon in yer pocket! Yer loaded an' yehs on'y makes a damn fool of yerself."

As the latter passed out of the door the man turned pathetically to the women.

"He don' know I'm damn goo' f'ler," cried he, dismally.

"Never you mind, Pete, dear," said the woman of brilliance and audacity, laying her hand with great affection upon his arm. "Never you mind, old boy! We'll stay by you, dear!"

"Das ri'!" cried the man, his face lighting up at the soothing tones of the woman's voice. "Das ri', I'm damn goo' f'ler an' w'en anyone trea's me ri', I trea's zem ri'! Shee?"

"Sure!" cried the women. "And we're not goin' back on you, old man."

The man turned appealing eyes to the woman. He felt that if he could be convicted of a contemptible action he would die.

"Shay, Nell, damn it, I allus trea's yehs shquare, didn' I? I allus been goo' f'ler wi' yehs, ain't I, Nell?"

"Sure you have, Pete," assented the woman. She delivered an oration to her companions. "Yessir, that's a fact. Pete's a square fellah, he is. He never goes back on a friend. He's the right kind an' we stay by him, don't we, girls?"

"Sure," they exclaimed. Looking lovingly at him they raised their glasses and drank his health.

"Girlsh," said the man, beseechingly, "I allus trea's yehs ri', didn' I? I'm goo' f'ler, ain' I, girlsh?"

"Sure," again they chorused.

"Well," said he finally, "le's have nozzer drink, zen."

"That's right," hailed a woman, "that's right. Yer no

bloomin' jay! Yer spends yer money like a man. Dat's right."

The man pounded the table with his quivering fists.

"Yessir," he cried, with deep earnestness, as if someone disputed him. "I'm damn goo' f'ler, an' w'en anyone trea's me ri', I allus trea's—le's have nozzer drink."

He began to beat the wood with his glass.

"Shay!" howled he, growing suddenly impatient. As the waiter did not then come, the man swelled with wrath.

"Shay!" howled he again.

The waiter appeared at the door.

"Bringsh drinksh," said the man.

The waiter disappeared with the orders.

"Zat f'ler damn fool," cried the man. "He insul' me! I'm ge'man! Can' stan' be insul'! I'm goin' lickim when comes!"

"No, no!" cried the women, crowding about and trying to subdue him. "He's all right! He didn't mean anything! Let it go! He's a good fellah!"

"Din' he insul' me?" asked the man earnestly.

"No," said they. "Of course he didn't! He's all right!"

"Sure he didn' insul' me?" demanded the man, with deep anxiety in his voice.

"No, no! We know him! He's a good fellah. He didn't mean anything."

"Well, zen," said the man, resolutely, "I'm go' 'pol'gize!"

When the waiter came, the man struggled to the middle of the floor.

"Girlsh shed you insul' me! I shay damn lie! I 'pol'gize!"

"All right," said the waiter.

The man sat down. He felt a sleepy but strong desire to straighten things out and have a perfect understanding with everybody.

"Nell, I allus trea's yeh shquare, din' I? Yeh likes me, don' yehs, Nell? I'm goo' f'ler?"

"Sure!" said the woman.

"Yeh knows I'm stuck on yehs, don' yehs, Nell?"

"Sure," she repeated, carelessly.

Overwhelmed by a spasm of drunken adoration, he

drew two or three bills from his pocket, and with the trembling fingers of an offering priest, laid them on the table before the woman.

"Yehs knows, damn it, yehs kin have all I got, 'cause I'm stuck on yehs, Nell, damn't, I—I'm stuck on yehs, Nell—buy drinksh—damn't—we're havin' heluva time— w'en anyone trea's me ri'—I—damn't, Nell—we're havin' heluva—time."

Presently he went to sleep with his swollen face fallen forward on his chest.

The women drank and laughed, not heeding the slumbering man in the corner. Finally he lurched forward and fell groaning to the floor.

The women screamed in disgust and drew back their skirts.

"Come ahn," cried one, starting up angrily, "let's get out of here."

The woman of brilliance and audacity stayed behind, taking up the bills and stuffing them into a deep, irregularly-shaped pocket. A guttural snore from the recumbent man caused her to turn and look down at him.

She laughed. "What a damn fool," she said, and went.

The smoke from the lamps settled heavily down in the little compartment, obscuring the way out. The smell of oil, stifling in its intensity, pervaded the air. The wine from an overturned glass dripped softly down upon the blotches on the man's neck.

CHAPTER XIX

In a room a woman sat at a table eating like a fat monk in a picture.

A soiled, unshaven man pushed open the door and entered.

"Well," said he, "Mag's dead."

"What?" said the woman, her mouth filled with bread.

"Mag's dead," repeated the man.

"D' hell she is," said the woman. She continued her meal. When she finished her coffee she began to weep.

"I kin remember when her two feet was no bigger dan' yer t'umb, and she weared worsted boots," moaned she.

"Well, whata dat?" said the man.

"I kin remember when she weared worsted boots," she cried.

The neighbors began to gather in the hall, staring in at the weeping woman as if watching the contortions of a dying dog. A dozen women entered and lamented with her. Under their busy hands the rooms took on that appalling appearance of neatness and order with which death is greeted.

Suddenly the door opened and a woman in a black gown rushed in with outstretched arms. "Ah, poor Mary," she cried, and tenderly embraced the moaning one.

"Ah, what ter'ble affliction is dis," continued she. Her vocabulary was derived from mission churches. "Me poor Mary, how I feel fer yehs! Ah, what a ter'ble affliction is a disobed'ent chil'."

Her good, motherly face was wet with tears. She trembled in eagerness to express her sympathy. The mourner sat with bowed head, rocking her body heavily to and fro, and crying out in a high, strained voice that sounded like a dirge on some forlorn pipe.

"I kin remember when she weared worsted boots an' her two feets was no bigger dan yer t'umb an' she weared worsted boots, Miss Smith," she cried raising her streaming eyes.

"Ah, me poor Mary," sobbed the woman in black. With low, coddling cries, she sank on her knees by the mourner's chair, and put her arms about her. The other women began to groan in different keys.

"Yer poor misguided chil' is gone now, Mary, an' let us hope it's fer d' bes'. Yeh'll fergive her now, Mary, won't yehs, dear, all her disobed'ence? All her t'ankless behavior to her mudder an' all her badness? She's gone where her ter'ble sins will be judged."

The woman in black raised her face and paused. The inevitable sunlight came streaming in at the window and shed a ghastly cheerfulness upon the faded hues of the room. Two or three of the spectators were sniffling, and one was weeping loudly. The mourner arose and staggered into the other room. In a moment she emerged with a pair of faded baby shoes held in the hollow of her hand.

"I kin remember when she used to wear dem," cried she. The women burst anew into cries as if they had all been stabbed. The mourner turned to the soiled and unshaven man.

"Jimmie, boy, go git yer sister! Go git yer sister an' we'll put d' boots on her feets!"

"Dey won't fit her now, yeh damn fool," said the man.

"Go git yer sister, Jimmie," shrieked the woman, confronting him fiercely.

The man swore sullenly. He went over to a corner and slowly began to put on his coat. He took his hat and went out, with a dragging, reluctant step.

The woman in black came forward and again besought the mourner.

"Yeh'll fergive her, Mary! Yeh'll fergive yer bad, bad chil'! Her life was a curse an' her days were black an' yeh'll fergive yer bad girl? She's gone where her sins will be judged."

"She's gone where her sins will be judged," cried the other women, like a choir at a funeral.

"D' Lord gives and d' Lord takes away," said the woman in black, raising her eyes to the sunbeams.

"D' Lord gives and d' Lord takes away," responded the others.

"Yeh'll fergive her, Mary!" pleaded the woman in black. The mourner essayed to speak but her voice gave way. She shook her great shoulders frantically, in an agony of grief. The tears seemed to scald her face. Finally her voice came and arose in a scream of pain.

"Oh, yes, I'll fergive her! I'll fergive her!"

—1893

JACK LONDON
(1876–1916)

The illegitimate son of a father who was a traveling astrologer and spiritualist and a mother who performed as a medium, Jack London experienced poverty and deprivation from his earliest days. Beginning as an adolescent, he took jobs wherever he could find them, at various times working as an ice-wagon driver, pin-boy in a bowling alley, oyster pirate on a San Francisco ship, factory worker, and longshoreman. He traveled throughout the country riding in railroad boxcars as well as sailing to Japan as a crew member of a sealing ship. In 1897, he traveled to the Klondike in search of gold. In that year, he began to publish his stories. His first collection of stories, *The Son of the Wolf*, appeared in 1900. Although he never completed his freshman year at the University of California, London read widely and was particularly influenced by the works of Darwin, Marx, and Nietzsche. Among the fifty volumes of stories, novels, and essays he published during a highly successful writing career are the novels *The Call of the Wild* (1903), *The Sea-Wolf* (1904), *The Game* (1905), *White Fang* (1906), *Martin Eden* (1909), *Adventure* (1911), *The Mutiny of the Elsinore* (1914), and *The Star Rover* (1915). Some of his stories are collected in *Love of Life* (1906) and *When God Laughs and Other Stories* (1911).

The Apostate

Now I wake me up to work;
I pray the Lord I may not shirk.
If I should die before the night,
I pray the Lord my work's all right.
                              —Amen.

"IF you don't git up, Johnny, I won't give you a bite to eat!"

The threat had no effect on the boy. He clung stubbornly to sleep, fighting for its oblivion as the dreamer fights for his dream. The boy's hands loosely clenched themselves, and he made feeble, spasmodic blows at the air. These blows were intended for his mother, but she betrayed practiced familiarity in avoiding them as she shook him roughly by the shoulder.

"Lemme 'lone!"

It was a cry that began, muffled, in the deeps of sleep, that swiftly rushed upward, like a wail, into passionate belligerence, and that died away and sank down into an inarticulate whine. It was a bestial cry, as of a soul in torment, filled with infinite protest and pain.

But she did not mind. She was a sad-eyed, tired-faced woman, and she had grown used to this task, which she repeated every day of her life. She got a grip on the bedclothes and tried to strip them down; but the boy, ceasing his punching, clung to them desperately. In a huddle, at the foot of the bed, he still remained covered. Then she tried dragging the bedding to the floor. The boy opposed her. She braced herself. Hers was the superior weight, and the boy and bedding gave, the former instinctively following the latter in order to shelter against the chill of the room that bit into his body.

As he toppled on the edge of the bed it seemed that he must fall headfirst to the floor. But consciousness fluttered up in him. He righted himself and for a moment perilously balanced. Then he struck the floor on his feet. On the instant his mother seized him by the shoulders and shook him. Again his fists struck out, this time with more force and directness. At the same time his eyes opened. She released him. He was awake.

"All right," he mumbled.

She caught up the lamp and hurried out, leaving him in darkness.

"You'll be docked," she warned back to him.

He did not mind the darkness. When he had got into his clothes, he went out into the kitchen. His tread was very heavy for so thin and light a boy. His legs dragged with their own weight, which seemed unreasonable because they were such skinny legs. He drew a broken-bottomed chair to the table.

"Johnny!" his mother called sharply.

He arose as sharply from the chair and, without a word, went to the sink. It was a greasy, filthy sink. A smell came up from the outlet. He took no notice of it. That a sink should smell was to him part of the natural order, just as it was a part of the natural order that the soap should be grimy with dishwater and hard to lather. Nor did he try very hard to make it lather. Several splashes of the cold water from the running faucet completed the function. He did not wash his teeth. For that matter he had never seen a toothbrush, nor did he know that there existed beings in the world who were guilty of so great a foolishness as tooth washing.

"You might wash yourself wunst a day without bein' told," his mother complained.

She was holding a broken lid on the pot as she poured two cups of coffee. He made no remark, for this was a standing quarrel between them, and the one thing upon which his mother was hard as adamant. "Wunst" a day it was compulsory that he should wash his face. He dried himself on a greasy towel, damp and dirty and ragged, that left his face covered with shreds of lint.

"I wish we didn't live so far away," she said, as he sat down. "I try to do the best I can. You know that. But a dollar on the rent is such a savin', an' we've more room here. You know that."

He scarcely followed her. He had heard it all before, many times. The range of her thought was limited, and she was ever harking back to the hardship worked upon them by living so far from the mills.

"A dollar means more grub," he remarked sententiously. "I'd sooner do the walkin' an' git the grub."

He ate hurriedly, half chewing the bread and washing the unmasticated chunks down with coffee. The hot and muddy liquid went by the name of coffee. Johnny thought it was coffee—and excellent coffee. That was one of the few of life's illusions that remained to him. He had never drunk real coffee in his life.

In addition to the bread, there was a small piece of cold pork. His mother refilled his cup with coffee. As he was finishing the bread, he began to watch if more was forthcoming. She intercepted his questioning glance.

"Now, don't be hoggish, Johnny," was her comment.

"You've had your share. Your brothers an' sisters are smaller'n you."

He did not answer the rebuke. He was not much of a talker. Also, he ceased his hungry glancing for more. He was uncomplaining, with a patience that was as terrible as the school in which it had been learned. He finished his coffee, wiped his mouth on the back of his hand, and started to rise.

"Wait a second," she said hastily. "I guess the loaf kin stand you another slice—a thin un."

There was legerdemain in her actions. With all the seeming of cutting a slice from the loaf for him, she put loaf and slice back in the bread box and conveyed to him one of her own two slices. She believed she had deceived him, but he had noted her sleight of hand. Nevertheless, he took the bread shamelessly. He had a philosophy that his mother, what of her chronic sickliness, was not much of an eater anyway.

She saw that he was chewing the bread dry, and reached over and emptied her coffee cup into his.

"Don't set good somehow on my stomach this morning," she explained.

A distant whistle, prolonged and shrieking, brought both of them to their feet. She glanced at the tin alarm clock on the shelf. The hands stood at half-past five. The rest of the factory world was just arousing from sleep. She drew a shawl about her shoulders, and on her head put a dingy hat, shapeless and ancient.

"We've got to run," she said, turning the wick of the lamp and blowing down the chimney.

They groped their way out and down the stairs. It was clear and cold, and Johnny shivered at the first contact with the outside air. The stars had not yet begun to pale in the sky, and the city lay in blackness. Both Johnny and his mother shuffled their feet as they walked. There was no ambition in the leg muscles to swing the feet clear of the ground.

After fifteen silent minutes, his mother turned off to the right.

"Don't be late," was her final warning from out of the dark that was swallowing her up.

He made no response, steadily keeping on his way. In

the factory quarter, doors were opening everywhere, and he was soon one of a multitude that pressed onward through the dark. As he entered the factory gate the whistle blew again. He glanced at the east. Across a ragged sky line of housetops a pale light was beginning to creep. This much he saw of the day as he turned his back upon it and joined his work gang.

He took his place in one of many long rows of machines. Before him, above a bin filled with small bobbins, were large bobbins revolving rapidly. Upon these he wound the jute twine of the small bobbins. The work was simple. All that was required was celerity. The small bobbins were emptied so rapidly, and there were so many large bobbins that did the emptying, that there were no idle moments.

He worked mechanically. When a small bobbin ran out, he used his left hand for a brake, stopping the large bobbin and at the same time, with thumb and forefinger, catching the flying end of twine. Also, at the same time, with his right hand, he caught up the loose twine end of a small bobbin. These various acts with both hands were performed simultaneously and swiftly. Then there would come a flash of his hands as he looped the weaver's knot and released the bobbin. There was nothing difficult about weaver's knots. He once boasted he could tie them in his sleep. And for that matter, he sometimes did, toiling centuries long in a single night at tying an endless succession of weaver's knots.

Some of the boys shirked, wasting time and machinery by not replacing the small bobbins when they ran out. And there was an overseer to prevent this. He caught Johnny's neighbor at the trick, and boxed his ears.

"Look at Johnny there—why ain't you like him?" the overseer wrathfully demanded.

Johnny's bobbins were running full blast, but he did not thrill at the indirect praise. There had been a time . . . but that was long ago, very long ago. His apathetic face was expressionless as he listened to himself being held up as a shining example. He was the perfect worker. He knew that. He had been told so, often. It was a commonplace, and besides it didn't seem to mean anything to him any more. From the perfect worker he had evolved into the perfect machine. When his work went wrong, it was with him as with the machine, due to faulty material. It would have been as possible for a perfect nail die to cut imperfect nails as for him to make a mistake.

And small wonder. There had never been a time when he had not been in intimate relationship with machines. Machinery had almost been bred into him, and at any rate he had been brought up on it. Twelve years before, there had been a small flutter of excitement in the loom room of this very mill. Johnny's mother had fainted. They stretched her out on the floor in the midst of the shrieking machines. A couple of elderly women were called from their looms. The foreman assisted. And in a few minutes there was one more soul in the loom room than had entered by the doors. It was Johnny, born with the pounding, crashing roar of the looms in his ears, drawing with his first breath the warm, moist air that was thick with flying lint. He had coughed that first day in order to rid his lungs of the lint; and for the same reason he had coughed ever since.

The boy alongside of Johnny whimpered and sniffed. The boy's face was convulsed with hatred for the overseer who kept a threatening eye on him from a distance; but every bobbin was running full. The boy yelled terrible oaths into the whirling bobbins before him; but the sound did not carry half a dozen feet, the roaring of the room holding it in and containing it like a wall.

Of all this Johnny took no notice. He had a way of accepting things. Besides, things grow monotonous by repetition, and this particular happening he had witnessed many times. It seemed to him as useless to oppose the overseer as to defy the will of a machine. Machines were made to go in certain ways and to perform certain tasks. It was the same with the overseer.

But at eleven o'clock there was excitement in the room. In an apparently occult way the excitement instantly permeated everywhere. The one-legged boy who worked on the other side of Johnny bobbed swiftly across the floor to a bin truck that stood empty. Into this he dived out of sight, crutch and all. The superintendent of the mill was coming along, accompanied by a young man. He was well dressed and wore a starched shirt—a gentleman, in Johnny's classification of men, and also, "the Inspector."

He looked sharply at the boys as he passed along. Sometimes he stopped and asked questions. When he did so, he was compelled to shout at the top of his lungs, at which moments his face was ludicrously contorted with the strain of making himself heard. His quick eye noted the empty machine alongside of Johnny's, but he said nothing. Johnny also caught his eye, and he stopped abruptly. He caught Johnny by the arm to draw him back a step from the machine; but with an exclamation of surprise he released the arm.

"Pretty skinny," the superintendent laughed anxiously.

"Pipe stems," was the answer. "Look at those legs. The boy's got the rickets—incipient, but he's got them. If epilepsy doesn't get him in the end, it will be because tuberculosis gets him first."

Johnny listened, but did not understand. Furthermore he was not interested in future ills. There was an immediate and more serious ill that threatened him in the form of the inspector.

"Now, my boy, I want you to tell me the truth," the inspector said, or shouted, bending close to the boy's ear to make him hear. "How old are you?"

"Fourteen," Johnny lied, and he lied with the full force of his lungs. So loudly did he lie that it started him off in a dry, hacking cough that lifted the lint which had been settling in his lungs all morning.

"Looks sixteen at least," said the superintendent.

"Or sixty," snapped the inspector.

"He's always looked that way."

"How long?" asked the inspector, quickly.

"For years. Never gets a bit older."

"Or younger, I dare say. I suppose he's worked here all those years?"

"Off and on—but that was before the new law was passed," the superintendent hastened to add.

"Machine idle?" the inspector asked, pointing at the unoccupied machine beside Johnny's, in which the part-filled bobbins were flying like mad.

"Looks that way." The superintendent motioned the

overseer to him and shouted in his ear and pointed at the machine. "Machine's idle," he reported back to the inspector.

They passed on, and Johnny returned to his work, relieved in that the ill had been averted. But the one-legged boy was not so fortunate. The sharp-eyed inspector haled him out at arm's length from the bin truck. His lips were quivering, and his face had all the expression of one upon whom was fallen profound and irremediable disaster. The overseer looked astounded, as though for the first time he had laid eyes on the boy, while the superintendent's face expressed shock and displeasure.

"I know him," the inspector said. "He's twelve years old. I've had him discharged from three factories inside the year. This makes the fourth."

He turned to the one-legged boy. "You promised me, word and honor, that you'd go to school."

The one-legged boy burst into tears. "Please, Mr. Inspector, two babies died on us, and we're awful poor."

"What makes you cough that way?" the inspector demanded, as though charging him with crime.

And as in denial of guilt, the one-legged boy replied: "It ain't nothin'. I jes' caught a cold last week, Mr. Inspector, that's all."

In the end the one-legged boy went out of the room with the inspector, the latter accompanied by the anxious and protesting superintendent. After that monotony settled down again. The long morning and the longer afternoon wore away and the whistle blew for quitting time. Darkness had already fallen when Johnny passed out through the factory gate. In the interval the sun had made a golden ladder of the sky, flooded the world with its gracious warmth, and dropped down and disappeared in the west behind a ragged sky line of housetops.

Supper was the family meal of the day—the one meal at which Johnny encountered his younger brothers and sisters. It partook of the nature of an encounter, to him, for he was very old, while they were distressingly young. He had no patience with their excessive and amazing juvenility. He did not understand it. His own childhood was too far behind him. He was like an old and irritable man, annoyed by the turbulence of their young spirits

that was to him arrant silliness. He glowered silently
over his food, finding compensation in the thought that
they would soon have to go to work. That would take
the edge off of them and make them sedate and digni-
fied—like him. Thus it was, after the fashion of the
human, that Johnny made of himself a yardstick with
which to measure the universe.

During the meal, his mother explained in various ways
and with infinite repetition that she was trying to do the
best she could; so that it was with relief, the scant meal
ended, that Johnny shoved back his chair and arose. He
debated for a moment between bed and the front door,
and finally went out the latter. He did not go far. He sat
down on the stoop, his knees drawn up and his narrow
shoulders drooping forward, his elbows on his knees and
the palms of his hands supporting his chin.

As he sat there, he did no thinking. He was just resting. So far as his mind was concerned, it was asleep. His
brothers and sisters came out, and with other children
played noisily about him. An electric globe on the corner
lighted their frolics. He was peevish and irritable, that
they knew, but the spirit of adventure lured them into
teasing him. They joined hands before him, and, keeping
time with their bodies, chanted in his face weird and
uncomplimentary doggerel. At first he snarled curses at
them—curses he had learned from the lips of various
foremen. Finding this futile, and remembering his dignity, he relapsed into dogged silence.

His brother Will, next to him in age, having just
passed his tenth birthday, was the ringleader. Johnny did
not possess particularly kindly feelings toward him. His
life had early been embittered by continual giving over
and giving way to Will. He had a definite feeling that
Will was greatly in his debt and was ungrateful about it.
In his own playtime, far back in the dim past, he had
been robbed of a large part of that playtime by being
compelled to take care of Will. Will was a baby then,
and then, as now, their mother had spent her days in
the mills. To Johnny had fallen the part of little father
and little mother as well.

Will seemed to show the benefit of the giving over
and the giving way. He was well built, fairly rugged, as

tall as his elder brother and even heavier. It was as though the lifeblood of the one had been diverted into the other's veins. And in spirits it was the same. Johnny was jaded, worn out, without resilience, while his younger brother seemed bursting and spilling over with exuberance.

The mocking chant rose louder and louder. Will leaned closer as he danced, thrusting out his tongue. Johnny's left arm shot out and caught the other around the neck. At the same time he rapped his bony fist to the other's nose. It was a pathetically bony fist, but that it was sharp to hurt was evidenced by the squeal of pain it produced. The other children were uttering frightened cries, while Johnny's sister, Jennie, had dashed into the house.

He thrust Will from him, kicked him savagely on the shins, then reached for him and slammed him face downward in the dirt. Nor did he release him till the face had been rubbed into the dirt several times. Then the mother arrived, an anemic whirlwind of solicitude and maternal wrath.

"Why can't he leave me alone?" was Johnny's reply to her upbraiding. "Can't he see I'm tired?"

"I'm as big as you." Will raged in her arms, his face a mess of tears, dirt, and blood. "I'm as big as you now, an' I'm goin' to git bigger. Then I'll lick you—see if I don't."

"You ought to be to work, seein' how big you are," Johnny snarled. "That's what's the matter with you. You ought to be to work. An' it's up to your ma to put you to work."

"But he's too young," she protested. "He's only a little boy."

"I was younger'n him when I started to work."

Johnny's mouth was open, further to express the sense of unfairness that he felt, but the mouth closed with a snap. He turned gloomily on his heel and stalked into the house and to bed. The door of his room was open to let in warmth from the kitchen. As he undressed in the semidarkness he could hear his mother talking with a neighbor woman who had dropped in. His mother was crying, and her speech was punctuated with spiritless sniffles.

"I can't make out what's gittin' into Johnny," he could hear her say. "He didn't used to be this way. He was a patient little angel.

"An' he *is* a good boy," she hastened to defend. "He's worked faithful, an' he did go to work too young. But it wasn't my fault. I do the best I can, I'm sure."

Prolonged sniffling from the kitchen, and Johnny murmured to himself as his eyelids closed down, "You betcher life I've worked faithful."

The next morning he was torn bodily by his mother from the grip of sleep. Then came the meager breakfast, the tramp through the dark, and the pale glimpse of day across the house-tops as he turned his back on it and went in through the factory gate. It was another day, of all the days, and all the days were alike.

And yet there had been variety in his life—at the times he changed from one job to another, or was taken sick. When he was six, he was little mother and father to Will and the other children still younger. At seven he went into the mills—winding bobbins. When he was eight, he got work in another mill. His new job was marvelously easy. All he had to do was to sit down with a little stick in his hand and guide a stream of cloth that flowed past him. This stream of cloth came out of the maw of a machine, passed over a hot roller, and went on its way elsewhere. But he sat always in the one place, beyond the reach of daylight, a gas jet flaring over him, himself part of the mechanism.

He was very happy at that job, in spite of the moist heat, for he was still young and in possession of dreams and illusions. And wonderful dreams he dreamed as he watched the steaming cloth streaming endlessly by. But there was no exercise about the work, no call upon his mind, and he dreamed less and less, while his mind grew torpid and drowsy. Nevertheless, he earned two dollars a week, and two dollars represented the difference between acute starvation and chronic underfeeding.

But when he was nine, he lost his job. Measles was the cause of it. After he recovered, he got work in a glass factory. The pay was better, and the work demanded skill. It was piecework, and the more skillful he was, the bigger wages he earned. Here was incentive. And under this incentive he developed into a remarkable worker.

It was simple work, the tying of glass stoppers into small bottles. At his waist he carried a bundle of twine. He held the bottles between his knees so that he might work with both hands. Thus, in a sitting position and bending over his own knees, his narrow shoulders grew humped and his chest was contracted for ten hours each day. This was not good for the lungs, but he tied three hundred dozen bottles a day.

The superintendent was very proud of him, and brought visitors to look at him. In ten hours three hundred dozen bottles passed through his hands. This meant that he had attained machinelike perfection. All waste movements were eliminated. Every motion of his thin arms, every movement of a muscle in the thin fingers, was swift and accurate. He worked at high tension, and the result was that he grew nervous. At night his muscles twitched in his sleep, and in the daytime he could not relax and rest. He remained keyed up and his muscles continued to twitch. Also he grew sallow and his lint cough grew worse. Then pneumonia laid hold of the feeble lungs within the contracted chest, and he lost his job in the glassworks.

Now he had returned to the jute mills where he had first begun with winding bobbins. But promotion was waiting for him. He was a good worker. He would next go on the starcher, and later he would go into the loom room. There was nothing after that except increased efficiency.

The machinery ran faster than when he had first gone to work, and his mind ran slower. He no longer dreamed at all, though his earlier years had been full of dreaming. Once he had been in love. It was when he first began guiding the cloth over the hot roller, and it was with the daughter of the superintendent. She was much older than he, a young woman, and he had seen her at a distance only a paltry half-dozen times. But that made no difference. On the surface of the cloth stream that poured past him, he pictured radiant futures wherein he performed prodigies of toil, invented miraculous machines, won to the mastership of the mills, and in the end took her in his arms and kissed her soberly on the brow.

But that was all in the long ago, before he had grown too old and tired to love. Also, she had married and gone away, and his mind had gone to sleep. Yet it had been a wonderful experience, and he used often to look back upon it as other men and women look back upon the time they believed in fairies. He had never believed in fairies nor Santa Claus; but he had believed implicitly in the smiling future his imagination had wrought into the steaming cloth stream.

He had become a man very early in life. At seven, when he drew his first wages, began his adolescence. A certain feeling of independence crept up in him, and the relationship between him and his mother changed. Somehow, as an earner and breadwinner, doing his own work in the world, he was more like an equal with her. Manhood, full-blown manhood, had come when he was eleven, at which time he had gone to work on the night shift for six months. No child works on the night shift and remains a child.

There had been several great events in his life. One of these had been when his mother bought some California prunes. Two others had been the two times when she cooked custard. Those had been events. He remembered them kindly. And at that time his mother had told him of a blissful dish she would sometime make—"floating island," she had called it, "better than custard." For years he had looked forward to the day when he would sit down to the table with floating island before him, until at last he had relegated the idea of it to the limbo of unattainable ideals.

Once he found a silver quarter lying on the sidewalk. That, also, was a great event in his life, withal a tragic one. He knew his duty on the instant the silver flashed on his eyes, before even he had picked it up. At home, as usual, there was not enough to eat, and home he should have taken it as he did his wages every Saturday night. Right conduct in this case was obvious; but he never had any spending of his money, and he was suffering from candy hunger. He was ravenous for the sweets that only on red-letter days he had ever tasted in his life.

He did not attempt to deceive himself. He knew it was sin, and deliberately he sinned when he went on a fifteen-cent candy debauch. Ten cents he saved for a future orgy; but not being accustomed to the carrying of money, he lost the ten cents. This occurred at the time when he was suffering all the torments of conscience, and it was to him an act of divine retribution. He had a frightened sense of the closeness of an awful and wrathful God. God had seen, and God had been swift to punish, denying him even the full wages of sin.

In memory he always looked back upon that event as the one great criminal deed of his life, and at the recollection his conscience always awoke and gave him another twinge. It was the one skeleton in his closet. Also, being so made and circumstanced, he looked back upon the deed with regret. He was dissatisfied with the manner in which he had spent the quarter. He could have invested it better and, out of his later knowledge of the quickness of God, he would have beaten God out by spending the whole quarter at one fell swoop. In retrospect he spent the quarter a thousand times, and each time to better advantage.

There was one other memory of the past, dim and faded, but stamped into his soul everlasting by the savage feet of his father. It was more like a nightmare than a remembered vision of a concrete thing—more like the race memory of man that makes him fall in his sleep and that goes back to his arboreal ancestry.

This particular memory never came to Johnny in broad daylight when he was wide awake. It came at night, in bed, at the moment that his consciousness was sinking down and losing itself in sleep. It always aroused him to frightened wakefulness, and for the moment, in the first sickening start, it seemed to him that he lay crosswise on the foot of the bed. In the bed were the vague forms of his father and mother. He never saw what his father looked like. He had but one impression of his father, and that was that he had savage and pitiless feet.

His earlier memories lingered with him, but he had

no late memories. All days were alike. Yesterday or last year were the same as a thousand years—or a minute. Nothing ever happened. There were no events to mark the march of time. Time did not march. It stood always still. It was only the whirling machines that moved, and they moved nowhere—in spite of the fact that they moved faster.

When he was fourteen, he went to work on the starcher. It was a colossal event. Something had at last happened that could be remembered beyond a night's sleep or a week's payday. It marked an era. It was a machine Olympiad, a thing to date from. "When I went to work on the starcher," or, "after," or "before I went to work on the starcher," were sentences often on his lips.

He celebrated his sixteenth birthday by going into the loom room and taking a loom. Here was an incentive again, for it was piecework. And he excelled, because the clay of him had been molded by the mills into the perfect machine. At the end of three months he was running two looms, and, later, three and four.

At the end of his second year at the looms he was turning out more yards than any other weaver, and more than twice as much as some of the less skillful ones. And at home things began to prosper as he approached the full stature of his earning power. Not, however, that his increased earnings were in excess of need. The children were growing up. They ate more. And they were going to school, and schoolbooks cost money. And somehow, the faster he worked, the faster climbed the prices of things. Even the rent went up, though the house had fallen from bad to worse disrepair.

He had grown taller; but with his increased height he seemed leaner than ever. Also, he was more nervous. With the nervousness increased his peevishness and irritability. The children had learned by many bitter lessons to fight shy of him. His mother respected him for his earning power, but somehow her respect was tinctured with fear.

There was no joyousness in life for him. The procession of the days he never saw. The nights he slept away in twitching unconsciousness. The rest of the time he worked, and his consciousness was machine consciousness. Outside this his mind was a blank. He had no ideals, and but one illusion; namely, that he drank excellent coffee. He was a workbeast. He had no mental life whatever; yet deep down in the crypts of his mind, unknown to him, were being weighed and sifted every hour of his toil, every movement of his hands, every twitch of his muscles, and preparations were making for a future course of action that would amaze him and all his little world.

It was in the late spring that he came home from work one night aware of unusual tiredness. There was a keen expectancy in the air as he sat down to the table, but he did not notice. He went through the meal in moody silence, mechanically eating what was before him. The children um'd and ah'd and made smacking noises with their mouths. But he was deaf to them.

"D'ye know what you're eatin'?" his mother demanded at last, desperately.

He looked vacantly at the dish before him and vacantly at her.

"Floatin' island," she announced triumphantly.

"Oh," he said.

"Floating island," the children chorused loudly.

"Oh," he said. And after two or three mouthfuls, he added, "I guess I ain't hungry tonight."

He dropped the spoon, shoved back his chair, and arose wearily from the table.

"An' I guess I'll go to bed."

His feet dragged more heavily than usual as he crossed the kitchen floor. Undressing was a Titan's task, a monstrous futility, and he wept weakly as he crawled into bed, one shoe still on. He was aware of a rising, swelling something inside his head that made his brain thick and fuzzy. His lean fingers felt as big as his wrist, while in the ends of them was a remoteness of sensation vague and fuzzy like his brain. The small of his back ached intolerably. All his bones ached. He ached everywhere. And in his head began the shrieking, pounding, crashing, roaring of a million looms. All space was filled with flying shuttles. They darted in and out, intricately, amongst the stars. He worked a thousand looms himself, and ever they speeded up, faster and faster, and his brain unwound, faster and faster, and became the thread that fed the thousand flying shuttles.

He did not go to work next morning. He was too busy weaving colossally on the thousand looms that ran inside his head. His mother went to work, but first she sent for the doctor. It was a severe attack of the grippe, he said. Jennie served as nurse and carried out his instructions.

It was a very severe attack, and it was a week before Johnny dressed and tottered feebly across the floor. Another week, the doctor said, and he would be fit to return to work. The foreman of the loom room visited him on Sunday afternoon, the first day of his convalescence. The best weaver in the room, the foreman told his mother. His job would be held for him. He could come back to work a week from Monday.

"Why don't you thank 'im, Johnny?" his mother asked anxiously.

"He's ben that sick he ain't himself yet," she explained apologetically to the visitor.

Johnny sat hunched up and gazing steadfastly at the floor. He sat in the same position long after the foreman had gone. It was warm outdoors, and he sat on the stoop in the afternoon. Sometimes his lips moved. He seemed lost in endless calculations.

Next morning, after the day grew warm, he took his seat on the stoop. He had pencil and paper this time with which to continue his calculations, and he calculated painfully and amazingly.

"What comes after millions?" he asked at noon, when Will came home from school. "An' how d'ye work 'em?"

That afternoon finished his task. Each day, but without paper and pencil, he returned to the stoop. He was greatly absorbed in the one tree that grew across the street. He studied it for hours at a time, and was unusually interested when the wind swayed its branches and fluttered its leaves. Throughout the week he seemed lost in a great communion with himself. On Sunday, sitting on the stoop, he laughed aloud, several times, to the perturbation of his mother, who had not heard him laugh in years.

Next morning, in the early darkness, she came to his bed to rouse him. He had had his fill of sleep all week, and awoke easily. He made no struggle, nor did he attempt to hold on to the bedding when she stripped it from him. He lay quietly, and spoke quietly.

"It ain't no use, ma."

"You'll be late," she said, under the impression that he was still stupid with sleep.

"I'm awake, ma, an' I tell you it ain't no use. You might as well lemme alone. I ain't goin' to git up."

"But you'll lose your job!" she cried.

"I ain't goin' to git up," he repeated in a strange, passionless voice.

She did not go to work herself that morning. This was sickness beyond any sickness she had ever known. Fever and delirium she could understand; but this was insanity. She pulled the bedding up over him and sent Jennie for the doctor.

When that person arrived, Johnny was sleeping gently, and gently he awoke and allowed his pulse to be taken.

"Nothing the matter with him," the doctor reported. "Badly debilitated, that's all. Not much meat on his bones."

"He's always been that way," his mother volunteered.

"Now go 'way, ma, an' let me finish my snooze."

Johnny spoke sweetly and placidly, and sweetly and placidly he rolled over on his side and went to sleep.

At ten o'clock he awoke and dressed himself. He walked out into the kitchen, where he found his mother with a frightened expression on her face.

"I'm goin' away, ma," he announced, "an' I jes' want to say good-by."

She threw her apron over her head and sat down suddenly and wept. He waited patiently.

"I might a-known it," she was sobbing.

"Where?" she finally asked, removing the apron from her head and gazing up at him with a stricken face in which there was little curiosity.

"I don't know—anywhere."

As he spoke, the tree across the street appeared with

dazzling brightness on his inner vision. It seemed to lurk just under his eyelids, and he could see it whenever he wished.

"An' your job?" she quavered.

"I ain't never goin' to work again."

"My God, Johnny!" she wailed, "don't say that!"

What he had said was blasphemy to her. As a mother who hears her child deny God, was Johnny's mother shocked by his words.

"What's got into you, anyway?" she demanded, with a lame attempt at imperativeness.

"Figures," he answered. "Jes' figures. I've ben doin' a lot of figurin' this week, an' it's most surprisin'."

"I don't see what that's got to do with it," she sniffled.

Johnny smiled patiently, and his mother was aware of a distinct shock at the persistent absence of his peevishness and irritability.

"I'll show you," he said. "I'm plum' tired out. What makes me tired? Moves. I've ben movin' ever since I was born. I'm tired of movin', an' I ain't goin' to move any more. Remember when I worked in the glasshouse? I used to do three hundred dozen a day. Now I reckon I made about ten different moves to each bottle. That's thirty-six thousan' moves a day. Ten days, three hundred an' sixty thousan' moves a day. One month, one million an' eighty thousan' moves. Chuck out the eighty thousan'—" he spoke with the complacent beneficence of a philanthropist—"chuck out the eighty thousan', that leaves a million moves a month—twelve million moves a year.

"At the looms I'm movin' twic'st as much. That makes twenty-five million moves a year, an' it seems to me I've ben a movin' that way 'most a million years.

"Now this week I ain't moved at all. I ain't made one move in hours an' hours. I tell you it was swell, jes' settin' there, hours an' hours, an' doin' nothin'. I ain't never ben happy before. I never had any time. I've ben movin' all the time. That ain't no way to be happy. An' I ain't goin' to do it any more. I'm jes' goin' to set, an' set, an' rest, an' rest, and then rest some more."

"But what's goin' to come of Will an' the children?" she asked despairingly.

"That's it, 'Will an' the children,' " he repeated.

But there was no bitterness in his voice. He had long known his mother's ambition for the younger boy, but the thought of it no longer rankled. Nothing mattered any more. Not even that.

"I know, ma, what you've ben plannin' for Will—keepin' him in school to make a bookkeeper out of him. But it ain't no use, I've quit. He's got to go to work."

"An' after I have brung you up the way I have," she wept, starting to cover her head with the apron and changing her mind.

"You never brung me up," he answered with sad kindliness. "I brung myself up, ma, an' I brung up Will. He's bigger'n me, an' heavier, an' taller. When I was a kid, I reckon I didn't git enough to eat. When he come along an' was a kid, I was workin' an' earnin' grub for him too. But that's done with. Will can go to work, same as me, or he can go to hell, I don't care which. I'm tired. I'm goin' now. Ain't you goin' to say good-by?"

She made no reply. The apron had gone over her head again, and she was crying. He paused a moment in the doorway.

"I'm sure I done the best I knew how," she was sobbing.

He passed out of the house and down the street. A wan delight came into his face at the sight of the lone tree. "Jes' ain't goin' to do nothin'," he said to himself, half aloud, in a crooning tone. He glanced wistfully up at the sky, but the bright sun dazzled and blinded him.

It was a long walk he took, and he did not walk fast. It took him past the jute mill. The muffled roar of the loom room came to his ears, and he smiled. It was a gentle, placid smile. He hated no one, not even the pounding, shrieking machines. There was no bitterness in him, nothing but an inordinate hunger for rest.

The houses and factories thinned out and the open spaces increased as he approached the country. At last the city was behind him, and he was walking down a leafy lane beside the railroad track. He did not walk like a man. He did not look like a man. He was a travesty of the human. It was a twisted and stunted and nameless piece of life that shambled like a sickly ape, arms loose-hanging, stoop-shouldered, narrow-chested, grotesque and terrible.

He passed by a small railroad station and lay down in the grass under a tree. All afternoon he lay there. Sometimes he dozed, with muscles that twitched in his sleep. When awake, he lay without movement, watching the birds or looking up at the sky through the branches of the tree above him. Once or twice he laughed aloud, but without relevance to anything he had seen or felt.

After twilight had gone, in the first darkness of the night, a freight train rumbled into the station. When the engine was switching cars on to the sidetrack, Johnny crept along the side of the train. He pulled open the side door of an empty boxcar and awkwardly and laboriously climbed in. He closed the door. The engine whistled. Johnny was lying down, and in the darkness he smiled.

—1911

HAMLIN GARLAND
(1860–1940)

Born in a small Wisconsin village to which his father had moved the family from Maine, Hamlin Garland learned early about the brutalizing toil and poverty experienced by the unsuccessful seekers after "the American Dream." At the age of twenty-four, he left the Midwest for Boston where, essentially, he educated himself through extensive reading at the Boston Public Library. Ironically, the scenes which triggered his literary imagination and provided the material for his first tales were those of the harsh and dull farm life he encountered when he visited his family out West in 1887. His early stories were collected in *Main-Travelled Roads* (1891). This volume was expanded in 1910, when Garland included in the revised edition the stories of two other books: *Prairie Folk* (1893) and *Wayside Courtships* (1897). His most vital fiction reflects his desire for social and political reforms to help the struggling farm and working families he knew so well as a boy. Among his other works are *A Little Norsk* (1892), *Rose of Dutcher's Coolly* (1895), *Hesper* (1903), and the autobiographical narrative *A Son of the Middle Border* (1917).

Under the Lion's Paw

"Along this main-travelled road trailed an endless line of prairie schooners, coming into sight at the east, and passing out of sight over the swell to the west. We children used to wonder where they were going and why they went."

IT was the last of autumn and first day of winter coming together. All day long the plowmen on their prairie farms had moved to and fro on their wide level field through the falling snow, which melted as it fell, wetting them to the skin—all day, notwithstanding the frequent squalls of snow, the dripping, desolate clouds, and the muck of the furrows, black and tenacious as tar.

Under their dripping harness the horses swung to and fro silently, with that marvelous uncomplaining patience which marks the horse. All day the wild geese, honking wildly as they sprawled sidewise down the wind, seemed to be fleeing from an enemy behind, and with neck outthrust and wings extended, sailed down the wind, soon lost to sight.

Yet the plowman behind his plow, though the snow lay on his ragged greatcoat and the cold clinging mud rose on his heavy boots, fettering him like gyves, whistled in the very beard of the gale. As day passed, the snow, ceasing to melt, lay along the plowed land and lodged in the depth of the stubble, till on each slow round the last furrow stood out black and shining as jet between the plowed land and the gray stubble.

When night began to fall, and the geese, flying low, began to alight invisibly in the near cornfield, Stephen Council was still at work "finishing a land." He rode on his sulky-plow when going with the wind, but walked when facing it. Sitting bent and cold but cheery under his slouch hat, he talked encouragingly to his four-in-hand.

"Come round there, boys!—round agin! We got t' finish this land. Come in there, Dan! *Stiddy,* Kate!—stiddy! None o' y'r tantrums, Kittie. It's purty tuff, but gotta be did. *Tchk! tchk!* Step along, Pete! Don't let Kate git y'r single tree on the wheel. *Once* more!"

They seemed to know what he meant, and that this was the last round, for they worked with greater vigor than before.

"Once more, boys, an' sez I oats, an' a nice warm stall, an' sleep f'r all."

By the time the last furrow was turned on the land it was too dark to see the house, and the snow changing to rain again. The tired and hungry man could see the light from the kitchen shining through the leafless hedge, and lifting a great shout, he yelled, "Sup*per* f'r a half a dozen!"

It was nearly eight o'clock by the time he had finished his chores and started for supper. He was picking his way carefully through the mud when the tall form of a man loomed up before him with a premonitory cough.

"Waddy ye want?" was the rather startled question of the farmer.

"Well, ye see," began the stranger in a deprecating tone, "we'd like t' git in f'r the night. We've tried every house f'r the last two miles, but they hadn't any room f'r us. My wife's jest about sick, 'n' the children are cold and hungry—"

"Oh, y' want a stay all night, eh?"

"Yes, sir; it 'ud be a great accom—"

"Waal, I don't make it a practice t' turn anybuddy away hungry, not on sech nights as this. Drive right in. We ain't got much, but sech as it is—"

But the stranger had disappeared. And soon his steaming, weary team, with drooping heads and swinging single trees, moved past the well to the block beside the path. Council stood at the side of the "schooner" and helped the children out—two little half-sleeping children—and then a small woman with a babe in her arms.

"There ye go!" he shouted jovially to the children. "*Now* we're all right. Run right along to the house there, an' tell M'am Council you wants sumpthin' t' eat. Right this way, Mis'—keep right off t' the right there. I'll go an' git a lantern. Come," he said to the dazed and silent group at his side.

"Mother," he shouted as he neared the fragrant and warmly lighted kitchen, "here are some wayfarers an' folks who need sumpthin t' eat an' a place t'snooze." He ended by pushing them all in.

Mrs. Council, a large, jolly, rather coarse-looking woman, took the children in her arms. "Come right in, you little rabbits. 'Most asleep, hay? Now here's a drink o' milk f'r each o' ye. I'll have s'm tea in a minute. Take off y'r things and set up t' the fire."

While she set the children to drinking milk, Council got out his lantern and went out to the barn to help the stranger about his team, where his loud, hearty voice could be heard as it came and went between the haymow and the stalls.

The woman came to light as a small, timid, and discouraged-looking woman, but still pretty, in a thin and sorrowful way.

"Land sakes! An' you've travelled all the way from Clear Lake t'day in this mud! Waal! waal! No wonder you're all tired out. Don't wait f'r the men, Mis'—" She hesitated, waiting for the name.

"Haskins."

"Mis' Haskins, set right up to the table an' take a good swig o' tea, whilst I make y' s'm toast. It's green tea, an' it's good. I tell Council as I git older I don't seem t' enjoy Young Hyson n'r Gunpowder. I want the reel green tea, jest as it comes off'n the vines. Seems t' have more heart in it some way. Don't s'pose it has. Council says it's all in m' eye."

Going on in this easy way, she soon had the children filled with bread and milk and the woman thoroughly at home, eating some toast and sweet-melon pickles and sipping the tea.

"See the little rats!" she laughed at the children. "They're full as they can stick now, and they want to go to bed. Now don't git up, Mis' Haskins; set right where you are an' let me look after 'em. I know all about young ones, though I am all alone now. Jane went an' married last fall. But, as I tell Council, it's lucky we keep our health. Set right there, Mis' Haskins; I won't have you stir a finger."

It was an unmeasured pleasure to sit there in the warm, homely kitchen, the jovial chatter of the housewife driving out and holding at bay the growl of the impotent, cheated wind.

The little woman's eyes filled with tears which fell down upon the sleeping baby in her arms. The world was not so desolate and cold and hopeless, after all.

"Now I hope Council won't stop out there and talk politics all night. He's the greatest man to talk politics an' read the *Tribune*. How old is it?"

She broke off and peered down at the face of the babe.

"Two months 'n' five days," said the mother, with a mother's exactness.

"Ye don't say! I want t' know! The dear little pudzy-

wudzy!" she went on, stirring it up in the neighborhood
of the ribs with her fat forefinger.

"Pooty tough on 'oo to go gallivant'n' 'cross lots this
way."

"Yes, that's so; a man can't lift a mountain," said
Council, entering the door. "Sarah, this is Mr. Haskins
from Kansas. He's been eat up 'n' drove out by
grasshoppers."

"Glad t' see yeh! Pa, empty that washbasin 'n' give
him a chance t' wash."

Haskins was a tall man with a thin, gloomy face. His
hair was a reddish brown, like his coat, and seemed
equally faded by the wind and sun. And his sallow face,
though hard and set, was pathetic somehow. You would
have felt that he had suffered much by the line of his
mouth showing under his thin, yellow mustache.

"Hain't Ike got home yet, Sairy?"

"Hain't seen 'im."

"W-a-a-l, set right up, Mr. Haskins; wade right into
what we've got; 'tain't much, but we manage to live on
it—she gits fat on it," laughed Council, pointing his
thumb at his wife.

After supper, while the women put the children to
bed, Haskins and Council talked on, seated near the
huge cooking stove, the steam rising from their wet
clothing. In the Western fashion, Council told as much
of his own life as he drew from his guest. He asked but
few questions; but by and by the story of Haskins's struggles and defeat came out. The story was a terrible one,
but he told it quietly, seated with his elbows on his
knees, gazing most of the time at the hearth.

"I didn't like the looks of the country, anyhow," Haskins said, partly rising and glancing at his wife. "I was
ust t' northern Ingyannie, where we have lots a timber
'n' lots o' rain, 'n' I didn't like the looks o' that dry
prairie. What galled me the worst was goin' s' far away
acrosst so much fine land layin' all through here vacant."

"And the 'hoppers eat ye four years hand running,
did they?"

"Eat! They wiped us out. They chawed everything that
was green. They jest set around waitin' f'r us to die t'
eat us, too. My God! I ust t' dream of 'em sitt'n' 'round

on the bedpost, six feet long, workin' their jaws. They
eet the fork handles. They got worse 'n' worse till they
jest rolled on one another, piled up like snow in winter.
Well, it ain't no use; if I was t' talk all winter I couldn't
tell nawthin'. But all the while I couldn't help thinkin'
of all that land back here that nobuddy was usin', that
I ought a had 'stead o' bein' out there in that cussed
country."

"Waal, why didn't ye stop an' settle here?" asked Ike,
who had come in and was eating his supper.

"Fer the simple reason that you fellers wantid ten 'r
fifteen dollars an acre fer the bare land, and I hadn't no
money fer that kind o' thing."

"Yes, I do my own work," Mrs. Council was heard to
say in the pause which followed. "I'm a-gettin' purty
heavy t' be on m' laigs all day, but we can't afford t'
hire, so I keep rackin' around somehow, like a foun-
dered horse. S' lame—I tell Council he can't tell how
lame I am f'r I'm jest as lame in one laig as t'other."
And the good soul laughed at the joke on herself as she
took a handful of flour and dusted the biscuit board to
keep the dough from sticking.

"Well, I hain't *never* been very strong," said Mrs. Haskins. "Our folks was Canadians an' small-boned, and
then since my last child I hain't got up again fairly. I
don't like t' complain—Tim has about all he can bear
now—but they was days this week when I jest wanted
to lay right down an' die."

"Waal, now, I'll tell ye," said Council from his side of
the stove, silencing everybody with his good-natured
roar, "I'd go down and *see* Butler, *anyway,* if I was you.
I guess he'd let you have his place purty cheap; the
farm's all run down. He's ben anxious t' let t' some-
buddy next year. It 'ud be a good chance fer you. Anyhow, you go to bed and sleep like a babe. I've got some
plowin' t' do anyhow, an' we'll see if somethin' can't be
done about your case. Ike, you go out an' see if the
horses is all right, an' I'll show the folks t' bed."

When the tired husband and wife were lying under
the generous quilts of the spare bed, Haskins listened a
moment to the wind in the eaves, and then said with a
slow and solemn tone:

"There are people in this world who are good enough
t' be angels, an' only haff t' die to *be* angels."

II

Jim Butler was one of those men called in the West
"land poor." Early in the history of Rock River he had
come into the town and started in the grocery business
in a small way, occupying a small building in a mean
part of the town. At this period of his life he earned all
he got, and was up early and late, sorting beans, working
over butter, and carting his goods to and from the station. But a change came over him at the end of the
second year, when he sold a lot of land for four times
what he paid for it. From that time forward he believed
in land speculation as the surest way of getting rich.
Every cent he could save or spare from his trade he put
into land at forced sale, or mortgages on land, which
were "just as good as the wheat," he was accustomed
to say.

Farm after farm fell into his hands, until he was recognized as one of the leading landowners of the county.
His mortgages were scattered all over Cedar County,
and as they slowly but surely fell in he sought usually
to retain the former owner as tenant.

He was not ready to foreclose; indeed, he had the
name of being one of the "easiest" men in the town. He
let the debtor off again and again, extending the time
whenever possible.

"I don't want y'r land," he said. "All I'm after is the
int'rest on my money—that's all. Now if y' want 'o stay
on the farm, why, I'll give y' a good chance. I can't have
the land layin' vacant." And in many cases the owner
remained as tenant.

In the meantime he had sold his store; he couldn't
spend time in it; he was mainly occupied now with sitting
around town on rainy days, smoking and "gassin' with
the boys," or in riding to and from his farms. In fishing
time he fished a good deal. Doc Grimes, Ben Ashley,
and Cal Cheatham were his cronies on these fishing ex-
cursions or hunting trips in the time of chickens or par-

tridges. In winter they went to northern Wisconsin to shoot deer.

In spite of all these signs of easy life, Butler persisted in saying he "hadn't money enough to pay taxes on his land," and was careful to convey the impression that he was poor in spite of his twenty farms. At one time he was said to be worth fifty thousand dollars, but land had been a little slow of sale of late, so that he was not worth so much. A fine farm, known as the Higley place, had fallen into his hands in the usual way the previous year, and he had not been able to find a tenant for it. Poor Higley, after working himself nearly to death on it, in the attempt to lift the mortgage, had gone off to Dakota, leaving the farm and his curse to Butler.

This was the farm which Council advised Haskins to apply for; and the next day Council hitched up his team and drove down town to see Butler.

"You jest le' *me* do the talkin'," he said. "We'll find him wearin' out his pants on some salt barrel somew'er's; and if he thought you *wanted* a place, he'd sock it to you hot and heavy. You jest keep quiet; I'll fix 'im."

Butler was seated in Ben Ashley's store, telling "fish yarns," when Council sauntered in casually.

"Hello, But; lyin' agin, hay?"

"Hello, Steve! how goes it?"

"Oh, so-so. Too dang much rain these days. I thought it was goin' t' freeze f'r good last night. Tight squeak if I git m' plowin' done. How's farmin' with *you* these days?"

"Bad. Plowin' ain't half done."

"It 'ud be a religious idee f'r you t' go out an' take a hand y'rself."

"I don't haff to," said Butler with a wink.

"Got anybody on the Higley place?"

"No. Know of anybody?"

"Waal, no; not eggsackly. I've got a relation back t' Michigan who's b'en hot an' cold on the idee o' comin' West f'r some time. *Might* come if he could get a good layout. What do you talk on the farm?"

"Well, I d' know. I'll rent it on shares, or I'll rent it money rent."

"Waal, how much money, say?"

"Well, say ten per cent on the price—two-fifty."

"Waal, that ain't bad. Wait on 'im till 'e thrashes?"

Haskins listened eagerly to his important question, but Council was coolly eating a dried apple which he had speared out of a barrel with his knife. Butler studied him carefully.

"Well, knocks me out of twenty-five dollars interest."

"My relation 'll need all he's got t' git his crops in," said Council in the same indifferent way.

"Well, all right; *say* wait," concluded Butler.

"All right; this is the man. Haskins, this is Mr. Butler—no relation to Ben—the hardest working man in Cedar county."

On the way home Haskins said: "I ain't much better off. I'd like that farm; it's a good farm, but it's all run down, an' so'm I. I could make a good farm of it if I had half a show. But I can't stock it n'r seed it."

"Waal, now, don't you worry," roared Council in his ear. "We'll pull y' through somehow till next harvest. He's agreed t' hire it plowed, an' you can earn a hundred dollars ploughin', an' y' c'n git the seed o' me, an' pay me back when y' can."

Haskins was silent with emotion, but at last he said, "I ain't got nothin' t' live on."

"Now don't you worry 'bout that. You jest make your headquarters at ol' Steve Council's. Mother 'll take a pile o' comfort in havin' y'r wife an children 'round. Y' see Jane's married off lately, an' Ike's away a good 'eal, so we'll be darn glad t' have ye stop with us this winter. Nex' spring we'll see if y' can't git a start agin;" and he chirruped to the team, which sprang forward with the rumbling, clattering wagon.

"Say, looky here, Council, you can't do this. I never saw—" shouted Haskins in his neighbor's ear.

Council moved about uneasily in his seat and stopped his stammering gratitude by saying: "Hold on, now; don't make such a fuss over a little thing. When I see a man down, an' things all on top of 'm, I jest like t' kick em off an' help 'm up. That's the kind of religion I got, an' it's about the *only* kind."

They rode the rest of the way home in silence. And when the red light of the lamp shone out into the darkness of the cold and windy night, and he thought of this refuge for his children and wife, Haskins could have put his arm around the neck of his burly companion and squeezed him like a lover; but he contented himself with saying: "Steve Council, you'll git y'r pay f'r this some day."

"Don't want any pay. My religion ain't run on such business principles."

The wind was growing colder, and the ground was covered with a white frost, as they turned into the gate of the Council farm, and the children came rushing out, shouting "Papa's come!" They hardly looked like the same children who had sat at the table the night before. Their torpidity under the influence of sunshine and Mother Council had given way to a sort of spasmodic cheerfulness, as insects in winter revive when laid on the earth.

III

Haskins worked like a fiend, and his wife, like the heroic woman that she was, bore also uncomplainingly the most terrible burdens. They rose early and toiled without intermission till the darkness fell on the plain, then tumbled into bed, every bone and muscle aching with fatigue, to rise with the sun next morning to the same round of the same ferocity of labor.

The eldest boy, now nine years old, drove a team all through the spring, plowing and seeding, milked the cows, and did chores innumerable, in most ways taking the place of a man; an infinitely pathetic but common figure—this boy—on the American farm, where there is no law against child labor. To see him in his coarse clothing, his huge boots, and his ragged cap, as he staggered with a pail of water from the well, or trudged in the cold and cheerless dawn out into the frosty field behind his team, gave the city-bred visitor a sharp pang of sympathetic pain. Yet Haskins loved his boy, and would have saved him from this if he could, but he could not.

By June the first year the result of such Herculean toil began to show on the farm. The yard was cleaned up and sown to grass, the garden plowed and planted, and the house mended. Council had given them four of his cows.

"Take 'em an' run 'em on shares. I don't want a milk s' many. Ike's away s' much now, Sat'd'ys an' Sund'ys, I can't stand the bother anyhow."

Other men, seeing the confidence of Council in the newcomer, had sold him tools on time; and as he was really an able farmer, he soon had round him many evidences of his care and thrift. At the advice of Council he had taken the farm for three years, with the privilege of rerenting or buying at the end of the term.

"It's a good bargain, an' y' want 'o nail it," said Council. "If you have any kind ov a crop, you can pay y'r debts an' keep seed an' bread."

The new hope which now sprang up in the heart of Haskins and his wife grew great almost as a pain by the time the wide field of wheat began to wave and rustle and swirl in the winds of July. Day after day he would snatch a few moments after supper to go and look at it.

"Have ye seen the wheat t'day, Nettie?" he asked one night as he rose from supper.

"No, Tim, I ain't had time."

"Well, take time now. Le's go look at it."

She threw an old hat on her head—Tommy's hat—and looking almost pretty in her thin sad way, went out with her husband to the hedge.

"Ain't it grand, Nettie? Just look at it."

It was grand. Level, russet here and there, heavy-headed, wide as a lake, and full of multitudinous whispers and gleams of wealth, it stretched away before the gazers like the fabled field of the cloth of gold.

"Oh, I think—I *hope* we'll have a good crop, Tim; and oh, how good the people have been to us!"

"Yes; I don't know where we'd be t'day if it hadn't ben f'r Council and his wife."

"They're the best people in the world," said the little woman with a great sob of gratitude.

"We'll be in the field on Monday, sure," said Haskins, griping the rail on the fence as if already at the work of the harvest.

The harvest came, bounteous, glorious, but the winds

came and blew it into tangles, and the rain matted it here and there close to the ground, increasing the work of gathering it threefold.

Oh, how they toiled in those glorious days! Clothing dripping with sweat, arms aching, filled with briers, fingers raw and bleeding, backs broken with the weight of heavy bundles, Haskins and his man toiled on. Tommy drove the harvester while his father and a hired man bound on the machine. In this way they cut ten acres every day, and almost every night after supper, when the hand went to bed, Haskins returned to the field, shocking the bound grain in the light of the moon. Many a night he worked till his anxious wife came out to call him in to rest and lunch.

At the same time she cooked for the men, took care of the children, washed and ironed, milked the cows at night, made the butter, and sometimes fed the horses and watered them while her husband kept at the shocking. No slave in the Roman galleys could have toiled so frightfully and lived, for this man thought himself a free man, and that he was working for his wife and babes.

When he sank into his bed with a deep groan of relief, too tired to change his grimy, dripping clothing, he felt that he was getting nearer and nearer to a home of his own, and pushing the wolf of want a little farther from his door.

There is no despair so deep as the despair of a homeless man or woman. To roam the roads of the country or the streets of the city, to feel there is no rood of ground on which the feet can rest, to halt weary and hungry outside lighted windows and hear laughter and song within—these are the hungers and rebellions that drive men to crime and women to shame.

It was the memory of this homelessness, and the fear of its coming again, that spurred Timothy Haskins and Nettie, his wife, to such ferocious labor during that first year.

IV

" 'M, yes; 'm, yes; first-rate," said Butler as his eye took in the great garden, the pigpen, and the well-filled barnyard. "You're git'n' quite a stock around yer. Done well, eh?"

Haskins was showing Butler around the place. He had not seen it for a year, having spent the year in Washington and Boston with Ashley, his brother-in-law, who had been elected to Congress.

"Yes, I've laid out a good deal of money during the last three years. I've paid out three hundred dollars f'r fencin'."

"Um—h'm! I see, I see," said Butler while Haskins went on.

"The kitchen there cost two hundred; the barn ain't cost much in money, but I've put o lot o' time on it. I've dug a new well, and I—"

"Yes, yes. I see! You've done well. Stalk worth a thousand dollars," said Butler, picking his teeth with a straw.

"About that," said Haskins modestly. "We begin to feel 's if we wuz git'n' a home f'r ourselves; but we've worked hard. I tell ye we begin to feel it, Mr. Butler, and we're goin' t' begin t' ease up purty soon. We've been kind o' plannin' a trip back t' *her* folks after the fall plowin's done."

"*Eggs*-actly!" said Butler, who was evidently thinking of something else. "I suppose you've kine o' kalklated on stayin' here three years more?"

"Well, yes. Fact is, I think I c'n buy the farm this fall, if you'll give me a reasonable show."

"Um—m! What do you call a reasonable show?"

"Waal; say a quarter down and three years' time."

Butler looked at the huge stacks of wheat which filled the yard, over which the chickens were fluttering and crawling, catching grasshoppers, and out of which the crickets were singing innumerably. He smiled in a peculiar way as he said, "Oh, I won't be hard on yer. But what did you expect to pay f'r the place?"

"Why, about what you offered it for before, two thousand five hundred, or *possibly* the three thousand dollars," he added quickly as he saw the owner shake his head.

"This farm is worth five thousand and five hundred dollars," said Butler in a careless but decided voice.

"*What!*" almost shrieked the astounded Haskins.

"What's that? Five thousand? Why, that's double what you offered it for three years ago."

"Of course; and it's worth it. It was all run down then; now it's in good shape. You've laid out fifteen hundred dollars in improvements, according to your own story."

"But *you* had nothin' t' do about that. It's my work an' my money."

"You bet it was; but it's my land."

"But what's to pay me for all my—?"

"Ain't you had the use of 'em?" replied Butler, smiling calmly into his face.

Haskins was like a man struck on the head with a sandbag; he couldn't think; he stammered as he tried to say: "But—I never 'd git the use—You'd rob me. More'n that: you agreed—you promised that I could buy or rent at the end of three years at—"

"That's all right. But I didn't say I'd let you carry off the improvements, nor that I'd go on renting the farm at two-fifty. The land is doubled in value, it don't matter how; it don't enter into the question; an' now you can pay me five hundred dollars a year rent, or take it on your own terms at fifty-five hundred, or—git out."

He was turning away when Haskins, the sweat pouring from his face, fronted him, saying again:

"But *you've* done nothing to make it so. You hain't added a cent. I put it all there myself, expectin' to buy. I worked an' sweat to improve it. I was workin' f'r myself an' babes—"

"Well, why didn't you buy when I offered to sell? What y' kickin' about?"

"I'm kickin' about payin' you twice f'r my own things—my own fences, my own kitchen, my own garden."

Butler laughed. "You're too green t' eat, young feller. *Your* improvements! The law will sing another tune."

"But I trusted your word."

"Never trust anybody, my friend. Besides, I didn't promise not to do this thing. Why, man, don't look at me like that. Don't take me for a thief. It's the law. The reg'lar thing. Everybody does it."

"I don't care if they do. It's stealin' jest the same. You take three thousand dollars of my money. The work o'

my hands and my wife's." He broke down at this point.
He was not a strong man mentally. He could face hardship, ceaseless toil, but he could not face the cold and
sneering face of Butler.

"But I don't take it," said Butler coolly. "All you've
got to do is to go on jest as you've been a-doin', or give
me a thousand dollars down and a mortgage at ten per
cent on the rest."

Haskins sat down blindly on a bundle of oats nearby
and, with staring eyes and drooping head, went over the
situation. He was under the lion's paw. He felt a horrible
numbness in his heart and limbs. He was hid in a mist,
and there was no path out.

Butler walked about, looking at the huge stacks of
grain and pulling now and again a few handfuls out,
shelling the heads in his hands and blowing the chaff
away. He hummed a little tune as he did so. He had an
accommodating air of waiting.

Haskins was in the midst of the terrible toil of the last
year. He was walking again in the rain and the mud
behind his plow, he felt the dust and dirt of the thresh-
ing. The ferocious husking time, with its cutting wind
and biting, clinging snows, lay hard upon him. Then he
thought of his wife, how she had cheerfully cooked and
baked, without holiday and without rest.

"Well, what do you think of it?" inquired the cool,
mocking, insinuating voice of Butler.

"I think you're a thief and a liar!" shouted Haskins,
leaping up. "A black-hearted houn'!" Butler's smile
maddened him; with a sudden leap he caught a fork in
his hands and whirled it in the air. "You'll never rob
another man, damn ye!" he grated through his teeth, a
look of pitiless ferocity in his accusing eyes.

Butler shrank and quivered, expecting the blow; stood,
held hypnotized by the eyes of the man he had a moment before despised—a man transformed into an
avenging demon. But in the deadly hush between the
lift of the weapon and its fall there came a gush of faint,
childish laughter, and then across the range of his vision,
far away and dim, he saw the sun-bright head of his
baby girl as, with the pretty tottering run of a two-year-
old, she moved across the grass of the dooryard. His

hands relaxed; the fork fell to the ground; his head lowered.

"Make out y'r deed an' morgige, an' git off'n my land, an' don't ye never cross my line agin; if y' do, I'll kill ye."

Butler backed away from the man in wild haste and, climbing into his buggy with trembling limbs, drove off down the road, leaving Haskins seated dumbly on the sunny pile of sheaves, his head sunk into his hands.

—1889

FRANK NORRIS
(1870–1902)

Born in Chicago, Benjamin Franklin Norris was the son of an actress and an affluent businessman. Raised in Chicago and San Francisco, he briefly studied painting in Paris. Upon his return to America, he attended the University of California and, in 1894, spent a year at Harvard. There he studied under Professor Lewis E. Gates and worked on his first novel, *McTeague*, which was published in 1899. As a correspondent, Norris traveled to South Africa during the Boer War and to Cuba during the Spanish American War. A Naturalistic writer and chronicler of America's poor and working class, he wrote two novels that he hoped would educate people and influence their opinions about economic issues: *The Octopus* (1901), about wheat farmers, and *The Pit* (1903) about wheat brokers and investors. During a brief period as an editor at Doubleday, Page and Co., he was instrumental in getting that firm to accept and fulfill its contract to publish Theodore Dreiser's first novel, *Sister Carrie*. Among Norris's other works are *Moran of the Lady Letty* (1898), *Blix* (1899), *A Man's Woman* (1900), *The Responsibilities of the Novelist* (1903), *A Deal in Wheat and Other Stories* (1903), and *Vandover and the Brute*, a novel written in 1899 but unpublished until 1914 because the manuscript was lost in the San Francisco earthquake of 1906.

A Deal in Wheat

I The Bear—Wheat at Sixty-two

AS Sam Lewiston backed the horse into the shafts of his buckboard and began hitching the tugs to the whiffletree, his wife came out from the kitchen door of the house and drew near, and stood for some time at the horse's head, her arms folded and her apron rolled around them. For a long moment neither spoke. They had talked over the situation so long and so comprehensively the night before that there seemed to be nothing more to say.

The time was late in the summer, the place a ranch in southwestern Kansas, and Lewiston and his wife were two of a vast population of farmers, wheat growers, who at that moment were passing through a crisis—a crisis that at any moment might culminate in tragedy. Wheat was down to sixty-six.

At length Emma Lewiston spoke.

"Well," she hazarded, looking vaguely out across the ranch toward the horizon, leagues distant; "well, Sam, there's always that offer of brother Joe's. We can quit—and go to Chicago—if the worst comes."

"And give up!" exclaimed Lewiston, running the lines through the torets. "Leave the ranch! Give up! After all these years!"

His wife made no reply for the moment. Lewiston climbed into the buckboard and gathered up the lines. "Well, here goes for the last try, Emmie," he said. "Good-by, girl. Maybe things will look better in town today."

"Maybe," she said gravely. She kissed her husband good-by and stood for some time looking after the buckboard traveling toward the town in a moving pillar of dust.

"I don't know," she murmured at length; "I don't know just how we're going to make out."

When he reached town, Lewiston tied the horse to the iron railing in front of the Odd Fellows' Hall, the ground floor of which was occupied by the post-office, and went across the street and up the stairway of a building of brick and granite—quite the most pretentious structure of the town—and knocked at a door upon the first landing. The door was furnished with a pane of frosted glass, on which, in gold letters, was inscribed "Bridges & Co., Grain Dealers."

Bridges himself, a middle-aged man who wore a velvet skullcap and who was smoking a Pittsburg stogie, met the farmer at the counter and the two exchanged perfunctory greetings.

"Well," said Lewiston, tentatively, after a while.

"Well, Lewiston," said the other, "I can't take that wheat of yours at any better than sixty-two."

"Sixty-*two*."

"It's the Chicago price that does it, Lewiston. Truslow is bearing the stuff for all he's worth. It's Truslow and the bear clique that stick the knife into us. The price broke again this morning. We've just got a wire."

"Good heavens," murmured Lewiston, looking vaguely from side to side. "That—that ruins me. I *can't* carry my grain any longer—what with storage charges and—and—Bridges, I don't see just how I'm going to make out. Sixty-two cents a bushel! Why, man, what with this and with that it's cost me nearly a dollar a bushel to raise that wheat, and now Truslow—"

He turned away abruptly with a quick gesture of infinite discouragement.

He went down the stairs, and making his way to where his buckboard was hitched, got in, and, with eyes vacant, the reins slipping and sliding in his limp, half-open hands, drove slowly back to the ranch. His wife had seen him coming, and met him as he drew up before the barn.

"Well?" she demanded.

"Emmie," he said as he got out of the buckboard, laying his arm across her shoulder, "Emmie, I guess we'll take up with Joe's offer. We'll go to Chicago. We're cleaned out!"

II The Bull—Wheat at a Dollar-ten

. . .—*and said Party of the Second Part further covenants and agrees to merchandise such wheat in foreign ports, it being understood and agreed between the Party of the First Part and the Party of the Second Part that the wheat hereinbefore mentioned is released and sold to the Party of the Second Part for export purposes only, and not for consumption or distribution within the boundaries of the United States of America or of Canada.*

"Now, Mr. Gates, if you will sign for Mr. Truslow, I guess that'll be all," remarked Hornung when he had finished reading.

Hornung affixed his signature to the two documents

and passed them over to Gates, who signed for his principal client, Truslow—or, as he had been called ever since he had gone into the fight against Hornung's corner—the Great Bear. Hornung's secretary was called in and witnessed the signatures, and Gates thrust the contract into his Gladstone bag and stood up, smoothing his hat.

"You will deliver the warehouse receipts for the grain," began Gates.

"I'll send a messenger to Truslow's office before noon," interrupted Hornung. "You can pay by certified check through the Illinois Trust people."

When the other had taken himself off, Hornung sat for some moments gazing abstractedly toward his office windows, thinking over the whole matter. He had just agreed to release to Truslow, at the rate of one dollar and ten cents per bushel, one hundred thousand out of the two million and odd bushels of wheat that he, Hornung, controlled, or actually owned. And for the moment he was wondering if, after all, he had done wisely in not goring the Great Bear to actual financial death. He had made him pay one hundred thousand dollars. Truslow was good for this amount. Would it not have been better to have put a prohibitive figure on the grain and forced the Bear into bankruptcy? True, Hornung would then be without his enemy's money, but Truslow would have been eliminated from the situation, and that—so Hornung told himself—was always a consummation most devoutly, strenuously and diligently to be striven for. Truslow once dead was dead, but the Bear was never more dangerous than when desperate.

"But so long as he can't get *wheat*," muttered Hornung at the end of his reflections, "he can't hurt me. And he can't get it. That I *know*."

For Hornung controlled the situation. So far back as the February of that year an "unknown bull" had been making his presence felt on the floor of the Board of Trade. By the middle of March the commercial reports of the daily press had begun to speak of "the powerful bull clique"; a few weeks later that legendary condition of affairs implied and epitomized in the magic words "Dollar Wheat" had been attained, and by the first of

April, when the price had been boosted to one dollar and ten cents a bushel, Hornung had disclosed his hand, and in place of mere rumors, the definite and authoritative news that May wheat had been cornered in the Chicago Pit went flashing around the world from Liverpool to Odessa and from Duluth to Buenos Aires.

It was—as the veteran operators were persuaded—Truslow himself who had made Hornung's corner possible. The Great Bear had for once overreached himself, and believing himself all-powerful, had hammered the price just the fatal fraction too far down. Wheat had gone to sixty-two—for the time, and under the circumstances, an abnormal price. When the reaction came it was tremendous. Hornung saw his chance, seized it, and in a few months had turned the tables, had cornered the product, and virtually driven the bear clique out of the pit.

On the same day that the delivery of the hundred thousand bushels was made to Truslow, Hornung met his broker at his lunch club.

"Well," said the latter, "I see you let go that line of stuff to Truslow."

Hornung nodded; but the broker added:

"Remember, I was against it from the very beginning. I know we've cleared up over a hundred thou'. I would have fifty, times preferred to have lost twice that and *smashed Truslow dead*. Bet you what you like he makes us pay for it somehow."

"Huh!" grunted his principal. "How about insurance and warehouse charges, and carrying expenses on that lot? Guess we'd have had to pay those, too, if we'd held on."

But the other put up his chin, unwilling to be persuaded. "I won't sleep easy," he declared, "till Truslow is busted."

III The Pit

Just as Going mounted the steps on the edge of the pit the great gong struck, a roar of a hundred voices developed with the swiftness of successive explosions, the rush of a hundred men surging downward to the center of the pit filled the air with the stamp and grind of feet, a hundred hands in eager strenuous gestures tossed upward from out the brown of the crowd, the official reporter in his cage on the margin of the pit leaned far forward with straining ear to catch the opening bid, and another day of battle was begun.

Since the sale of the hundred thousand bushels of wheat to Truslow the "Hornung crowd" had steadily shouldered the price higher until on this particular morning it stood at one dollar and a half. That was Hornung's price. No one else had any grain to sell.

But not ten minutes after the opening Going was surprised out of all countenance to hear shouted from the other side of the pit these words:

"Sell May at one-fifty."

Going was for the moment touching elbows with Kimbark on one side and with Merriam on the other, all three belonging to the "Hornung crowd." Their answering challenge of "*Sold*" was as the voice of one man. They did not pause to reflect upon the strangeness of the circumstance. (That was for afterward.) Their response to the offer was as unconscious as reflex action and almost as rapid, and before the pit was well aware of what had happened the transaction of one thousand bushels was down upon Going's trading-card and fifteen hundred dollars had changed hands. But here was a marvel—the whole available supply of wheat cornered, Hornung master of the situation, invincible, unassailable; yet behold a man willing to sell, a Bear bold enough to raise his head.

"That was Kennedy, wasn't it, who made that offer?" asked Kimbark, as Going noted down the trade—"Kennedy, that new man?"

"Yes; who do you suppose he's selling for; who's willing to go short at this stage of the game?"

"Maybe he ain't short."

"Short! Great heavens, man; where'd he get the stuff?"

"Blamed if I know. We can account for every handful of May. Steady! Oh, there he goes again."

"Sell a thousand May at one-fifty," vociferated the bear-broker, throwing out his hand, one finger raised to indicate the number of "contracts" offered. This time it was evident that he was attacking the Hornung crowd deliberately, for, ignoring the jam of traders that swept toward him, he looked across the pit to where Going and Kimbark were shouting "*Sold! Sold!*" and nodded his head.

A second time Going made memoranda of the trade, and either the Hornung holdings were increased by two thousand bushels of May wheat or the Hornung bank account swelled by at least three thousand dollars of some unknown short's money.

Of late—so sure was the bull crowd of its position— no one even thought of glancing at the inspection sheet on the bulletin board. But now one of Going's messengers hurried up to him with the announcement that this sheet showed receipts at Chicago for that morning of twenty-five thousand bushels, and not credited to Hornung. Some one had got hold of a line of wheat overlooked by the "clique" and was dumping it upon them.

"Wire the chief," said Going over his shoulder to Merriam. This one struggled out of the crowd, and on a telegraph blank scribbled:

"Strong bear movement—New man—Kennedy—Selling in lots of five contracts—Chicago receipts twenty-five thousand."

The message was despatched, and in a few moments the answer came back, laconic, of military terseness.

"Support the market."

And Going obeyed, Merriam and Kimbark following, the new broker fairly throwing the wheat at them in thousand-bushel lots.

"Sell May at 'fifty; sell May; sell May." A moment's indecision, an instant's hesitation, the first faint suggestion of weakness, and the market would have broken under them. But for the better part of four hours they stood their ground, taking all that was offered, in constant communication with the Chief, and from time to time stimulated and steadied by his brief, unvarying command:

"Support the market."

At the close of the session they had bought in the twenty-five thousand bushels of May. Hornung's position was as stable as a rock, and the price closed even with the opening figure—one dollar and a half.

But the morning's work was the talk of all La Salle Street. Who was back of that raid? What was the meaning of this unexpected selling? For weeks the Pit trading had been merely nominal. Truslow, the Great Bear, from whom the most serious attack might have been expected, had gone to his country seat at Geneva Lake, in Wisconsin, declaring himself to be out of the market entirely. He went bass fishing every day.

IV The Belt Line

On a certain day toward the middle of the month, at a time when the mysterious Bear had unloaded some eighty thousand bushels upon Hornung, a conference was held in the library of Hornung's home. His broker attended it, and also a clean-faced, bright-eyed individual whose name of Cyrus Ryder might have been found upon the payroll of a rather well-known detective agency. For upward of half an hour after the conference began the detective spoke, the other two listening attentively, gravely.

"Then, last of all," concluded Ryder, "I made out I was a hobo, and began stealing rides on the Belt Line Railroad. Know the road? It just circles Chicago. Truslow owns it. Yes? Well, then I began to catch on. I noticed that cars of certain numbers—thirty-one naught thirty-four, thirty-two one ninety—well, the numbers don't matter, but anyhow, these cars were always switched on to the sidings by Mr. Truslow's main elevator D soon as they came in. The wheat was shunted in, and they were pulled out again. Well, I spotted one car and stole a ride on her. Say, look here, *that car went right around the city on the Belt, and came back to D again, and the same wheat in her all the time.* The grain was reinspected—it was raw, I tell you—and the warehouse receipts made out just as though the stuff had come in from Kansas or Iowa."

"The same wheat all the time!" interrupted Hornung.

"The same wheat—your wheat, that you sold to Truslow."

"Great snakes!" ejaculated Hornung's broker. "Truslow never took it abroad at all."

"Took it abroad! Say, he's just been running it around Chicago, like the supers in 'Shenandoah,' round an' round, so you'd think it was a new lot, an' selling it back to you again."

"No wonder we couldn't account for so much wheat."

"Bought it from us at one-ten, and made us buy it back—our own wheat—at one-fifty."

Hornung and his broker looked at each other in silence for a moment. Then all at once Hornung struck the arm of his chair with his fist and exploded in a roar of laughter. The broker stared for one bewildered moment, then followed his example.

"Sold! Sold!" shouted Hornung almost gleefully. "Upon my soul it's as good as a Gilbert and Sullivan show. And we—Oh, Lord! Billy, shake on it, and hats off to my distinguished friend, Truslow. He'll be President some day. Hey! What? Prosecute him? Not I."

"He's done us out of a neat hatful of dollars for all that," observed the broker, suddenly grave.

"Billy, it's worth the price."

"We've got to make it up somehow."

"Well, tell you what. We were going to boost the price to one seventy-five next week, and make that our settlement figure."

"Can't do it now. Can't afford it."

"No. Here; we'll let out a big link; we'll put wheat at two dollars, and let it go at that."

"Two it is, then," said the broker.

V The Bread Line

The street was very dark and absolutely deserted. It was a district on the "South Side," not far from the Chicago River, given up largely to wholesale stores, and after nightfall was empty of all life. The echoes slept but lightly hereabouts, and the slightest footfall, the faintest noise, woke them upon the instant and sent them clamoring up and down the length of the pavement between the iron-shuttered fronts. The only light visible came from the side door of a certain "Vienna" bakery, where at one o'clock in the morning loaves of bread were given away to any who should ask. Every evening about nine o'clock the outcasts began to gather about the side door. The stragglers came in rapidly, and the line—the "bread line," as it was called—began to form. By midnight it was usually some hundred yards in length, stretching almost the entire length of the block.

Toward ten in the evening, his coat collar turned up against the fine drizzle that pervaded the air, his hands in his pockets, his elbows gripping his sides, Sam Lewiston came up and silently took his place at the end of the line.

Unable to conduct his farm upon a paying basis at the time when Truslow, the "Great Bear," had sent the price of grain to sixty-two cents a bushel, Lewiston had turned over his entire property to his creditors, and, leaving Kansas for good, had abandoned farming, and had left his wife at her sister's boarding-house in Topeka with the understanding that she was to join him in Chicago so soon as he had found a steady job. Then he had come to Chicago and had turned workman. His brother Joe conducted a small hat factory on Archer Avenue, and for a time he found there a meagre employment. But difficulties had occurred, times were bad, the hat factory was involved in debts, the repealing of a certain import duty on manufactured felt overcrowded the home market with cheap Belgian and French products, and in the end his brother had resigned and gone to Milwaukee.

Thrown out of work, Lewiston drifted aimlessly about Chicago, from pillar to post, working a little, earning here a dollar, there a dime, but always sinking, till at last the ooze of the lowest bottom dragged at his feet and the rush of the great ebb went over him and engulfed him and shut him from the light, and a park bench became his home and the "bread line" his chief makeshift of subsistence.

He stood now in the infolding drizzle, sodden, stupefied with fatigue. Before and behind stretched the line. There was no talking. There was no sound. The street was empty. It was so still that the passing of a cablecar in the adjoining thoroughfare grated like prolonged rolling explosions, beginning and ending at immeasurable distances. The drizzle descended incessantly. After a long time midnight struck.

There was something ominous and gravely impressive in this interminable line of dark figures, close-pressed, soundless; a crowd, yet absolutely still; a close-packed, silent file, waiting, waiting in the vast deserted night-ridden street; waiting without a word, without a move-ment, there under the night and under the slow-moving mists of rain.

Few in the crowd were professional beggars. Most of them were workmen, long since out of work, forced into idleness by long-continued "hard times," by ill luck, by sickness. To them the "bread line" was a godsend. At least they could not starve. Between jobs here in the end was something to hold them up—a small platform, as it were, above the sweep of black water, where for a moment they might pause and take breath before the plunge.

The period of waiting on this night of rain seemed endless to those silent, hungry men; but at length there was a stir. The line moved. The side door opened. Ah, at last! They were going to hand out the bread.

But instead of the usual white-aproned undercook with his crowded hampers there now appeared in the doorway a new man—a young fellow who looked like a bookkeeper's assistant. He bore in his hand a placard, which he tacked to the outside of the door. Then he disappeared within the bakery, locking the door after him.

A shudder of poignant despair, an unformed, inarticu-late sense of calamity, seemed to run from end to end of the line. What had happened? Those in the rear, un-able to read the placard, surged forward, a sense of bit-ter disappointment clutching at their hearts.

The line broke up, disintegrated into a shapeless throng—a throng that crowded forward and collected in front of the shut door whereon the placard was affixed. Lewiston, with the others, pushed forward. On the plac-ard he read these words:

"Owing to the fact that the price of grain has been increased to two dollars a bushel, there will be no distribution of bread from this bakery until further notice."

Lewiston turned away, dumb, bewildered. Till morning he walked the streets, going on without purpose, without direction. But now at last his luck had turned. Overnight the wheel of his fortunes had creaked and swung upon its axis, and before noon he had found a job in the street-cleaning brigade. In the course of time he rose to be first shift-boss, then deputy inspector, then inspector, promoted to the dignity of driving a red wagon with rubber tires and drawing a salary instead of mere wages. The wife was sent for and a new start made.

But Lewiston never forgot. Dimly he began to see the significance of things. Caught once in the cogs and wheels of a great and terrible engine, he had seen—none better—its workings. Of all the men who had vainly stood in the "bread line" on that rainy night in early summer, he, perhaps, had been the only one who had struggled up to the surface again. How many others had gone down in the great ebb? Grim question; he dared not think how many.

He had seen the two ends of a great wheat operation—a battle between Bear and Bull. The stories (subsequently published in the city's press) of Truslow's counter move in selling Hornung his own wheat, supplied the unseen section. The farmer—he who raised the wheat—was ruined upon one hand; the working-man—he who consumed it—was ruined upon the other. But between the two, the great operators, who never saw the wheat they traded in, bought and sold the world's food, gambled in the nourishment of entire nations, practiced their tricks, chicanery and oblique shifty "deals," were reconciled in their differences, and went on through their appointed way, jovial, contented, enthroned, and unassailable.

—1903

MARY WILKINS FREEMAN
(1852–1930)

In 1877, at the age of twenty-five, Mary E. Wilkins accompanied her parents, who had suffered financial losses, in moving into the home of Thomas Pickman Tyler, where Mary's
mother, Eleanor, had accepted the job of housekeeper.
Mary, the only one of four Wilkins children to survive into
adulthood, had tried teaching for a year and had long been
attempting to sell her poems and stories. Not until 1881
(the year after her mother's death), did Freeman succeed
in selling any of her writing. Among almost forty volumes of
her work which were subsequently published are the novels
Jane Field (1893), *Pembroke* (1894), and *The Shoulders of
Atlas* (1908), as well as collections of her short stories: *A
Humble Romance and Other Stories* (1887), *A New England Nun and Other Stories* (1891), and *Six Trees* (1903).
When she married Dr. Charles Freeman in 1902, she left
New England to become a resident of Metuchen, New
Jersey.

Louisa

"I don't see what kind of ideas you've got in your
head for my part." Mrs. Britton looked sharply at
her daughter Louisa, but she got no response.

Louisa sat in one of the kitchen chairs close to the
door. She had dropped into it when she first entered.
Her hands were all brown and grimy with garden-mould;
it clung to the bottom of her old dress and her coarse
shoes.

Mrs. Britton, sitting opposite by the window, waited,
looking at her. Suddenly Louisa's silence seemed to
strike her mother's will with an electric shock; she recoiled, with an angry jerk of her head. "You don't know
nothin' about it. You'd like him well enough after you
was married to him," said she, as if in answer to an
argument.

Louisa's face looked fairly dull; her obstinacy seemed to cast a film over it. Her eyelids were cast down; she leaned her head back against the wall.

"Sit there like a stick if you want to!" cried her mother.

Louisa got up. As she stirred, a faint earthy odor diffused itself through the room. It was like a breath from a ploughed field.

Mrs. Britton's little sallow face contracted more forcibly. "I s'pose now you're goin' back to your potater patch," said she. "Plantin' potaters out there jest like a man, for all the neighbors to see. Pretty sight, I call it."

"If they don't like it, they needn't look," returned Louisa. She spoke quite evenly. Her young back was stiff with bending over the potatoes, but she straightened it rigorously. She pulled her old hat farther over her eyes.

There was a shuffling sound outside the door and a fumble at the latch. It opened, and an old man came in, scraping his feet heavily over the threshold. He carried an old basket.

"What you got in that basket, father?" asked Mrs. Britton.

The old man looked at her. His old face had the round outlines and naïve grin of a child.

"Father, what you got in that basket?"

Louisa peered apprehensively into the basket. "Where did you get those potatoes, grandfather?" said she.

"Digged 'em." The old man's grin deepened. He chuckled hoarsely.

"Well, I'll give up if he ain't been an' dug up all them potaters you've been plantin'!" said Mrs. Britton.

"Yes, he has," said Louisa. "Oh, grandfather, didn't you know I'd jest planted those potatoes?"

The old man fastened his bleared blue eyes on her face, and still grinned.

"Didn't you know better, grandfather?" she asked again.

But the old man only chuckled. He was so old that he had come back into the mystery of childhood. His motives were hidden and inscrutable; his amalgamation with the human race was so much weaker.

"Land sakes! don't waste no more time talkin' to him," said Mrs. Britton. "You can't make out whether he knows what he's doin' or not. I've give it up. Father, you jest set them pertaters down, an' you come over here an' set down in the rockin'-chair; you've done about 'nough work to-day."

The old man shook his head with slow mutiny.

"Come right over here."

Louisa pulled at the basket of potatoes. "Let me have 'em, grandfather," said she. "I've got to have 'em."

The old man resisted. His grin disappeared, and he set his mouth. Mrs. Britton got up, with a determined air, and went over to him. She was a sickly, frail-looking woman, but the voice came firm, with deep bass tones, from her little lean throat.

"Now, father," said she, "you jest give her that basket, an' you walk across the room, and you set down in that rockin'-chair."

The old man looked down into her little, pale, wedge-shaped face. His grasp on the basket weakened. Louisa pulled it away, and pushed past out of the door, and the old man followed his daughter sullenly across the room to the rocking-chair.

The Brittons did not have a large potato field; they had only an acre of land in all. Louisa had planted two thirds of her potatoes; now she had to plant them all over again. She had gone in the house for a drink of water; her mother had detained her, and in the mean-time the old man had undone her work. She began putting the cut potatoes back in the ground. She was careful and laborious about it. A strong wind, full of moisture, was blowing from the east. The smell of the sea was in it, although this was some miles inland. Louisa's brown calico skirt blew out in it like a sail. It beat her in the face when she raised her head.

"I've got to get these in to-day somehow," she muttered. "It'll rain to-morrow."

She worked as fast as she could, and the afternoon wore on. About five o'clock she happened to glance at the road—the potato field lay beside it—and she saw Jonathan Nye driving past with his gray horse and buggy. She turned her back to the road quickly, and listened until the rattle of the wheels died away. At six o'clock her mother looked out of the kitchen window and called her to supper.

"I'm comin' in a minute," Louisa shouted back. Then she worked faster than ever. At half-past six she went into the house, and the potatoes were all in the ground.

"Why didn't you come when I called you?" asked her mother.

"I had to get the potatoes in."

"I guess you wa'n't bound to get 'em all in to-night. It's kind of discouragin' when you work, an' get supper all ready, to have it stan' an hour, I call it. An' you've worked 'bout long enough for one day out in this damp wind, I should say."

Louisa washed her hands and face at the kitchen sink, and smoothed her hair at the little glass over it. She had wet her hair too, and made it look darker; it was quite a light brown. She brushed it in smooth straight lines back from her temples. Her whole face had a clear bright look from being exposed to the moist wind. She noticed it herself, and gave her head a little conscious turn.

When she sat down to the table her mother looked at her with admiration, which she veiled with disapproval.

"Jest look at your face," said she; "red as a beet. You'll be a pretty-lookin' sight before the summer's out, at this rate."

Louisa thought to herself that the light was not very strong, and the glass must have flattered her. She could not look as well as she had imagined. She spread some butter on her bread very sparsely. There was nothing for supper but some bread and butter and weak tea, though the old man had his dish of Indian-meal porridge. He could not eat much solid food. The porridge was covered with milk and molasses. He bent low over it, and ate large spoonfuls with loud noises. His daughter had tied a towel around his neck as she would have tied a pinafore on a child. She had also spread a towel over the tablecloth in front of him, and she watched him sharply lest he should spill his food.

"I wish I could have somethin' to eat that I could relish the way he does that porridge and molasses," said she. She had scarcely tasted anything. She sipped her weak tea laboriously.

Louisa looked across at her mother's meagre little figure in its neat old dress, at her poor small head bending over the tea-cup, showing the wide parting in the thin hair.

"Why don't you toast your bread, mother?" said she. "I'll toast it for you."

"No, I don't want it. I'd jest as soon have it this way as any. I don't want no bread, nohow. I want somethin' to relish—a herrin', or a little mite of cold meat, or somethin'. I s'pose I could eat as well as anybody if I had as much as some folks have. Mis' Mitchell was sayin' the other day that she didn't believe but what they had butcher's meat up to Mis' Nye's every day in the week. She said Jonathan he went to Wolfsborough and brought home great pieces in a market-basket every week. I guess they have everything."

Louisa was not eating much herself, but now she took another slice of bread with a resolute air. "I guess some folks would be thankful to get this," said she.

"Yes, I s'pose we'd ought to be thankful for enough to keep us alive, anybody takes so much comfort livin'," returned her mother, with a tragic bitterness that sat oddly upon her, as she was so small and feeble. Her face worked and strained under the stress of emotion; her eyes were full of tears; she sipped her tea fiercely.

"There's some sugar," said Louisa. "We might have had a little cake."

The old man caught the word. "Cake?" he mumbled, with pleased inquiry, looking up, and extending his grasping old hand.

"I guess we ain't got no sugar to waste in cake," returned Mrs. Britton. "Eat your porridge, father, an' stop teasin'. There ain't no cake."

After supper Louisa cleared away the dishes; then she put on her shawl and hat.

"Where you goin'?" asked her mother.

"Down to the store."

"What for?"

"The oil's out. There wasn't enough to fill the lamps this mornin'. I ain't had a chance to get it before."

It was nearly dark. The mist was so heavy it was almost rain. Louisa went swiftly down the road with the oil-
can. It was a half-mile to the store where the few staples
were kept that sufficed the simple folk in this little settlement. She was gone a half-hour. When she returned, she
had besides the oil-can a package under her arm. She
went into the kitchen and set them down. The old man
was asleep in the rocking-chair. She heard voices in the
adjoining room. She frowned, and stood still, listening.

"Louisa!" called her mother. Her voice was sweet, and
higher pitched than usual. She sounded the *i* in Louisa
long.

"What say?"

"Come in here after you've taken your things off."

Louisa knew that Jonathan Nye was in the sitting-
room. She flung off her hat and shawl. Her old dress
was damp, and had still some earth stains on it; her hair
was roughened by the wind, but she would not look
again in the glass; she went into the sitting room just as
she was.

"It's Mr. Nye, Louisa," said her mother, with effusion.

"Good-evenin', Mr. Nye," said Louisa.

Jonathan Nye half rose and extended his hand, but
she did not notice it. She sat down peremptorily in a
chair at the other side of the room. Jonathan had the
one rocking-chair; Mrs. Britton's frail little body was
poised anxiously on the hard rounded top of the carpet-
covered lounge. She looked at Louisa's dress and hair,
and her eyes were stony with disapproval, but her lips
still smirked, and she kept her voice sweet. She pointed
to a glass dish on the table.

"See what Mr. Nye has brought us over, Louisa,"
said she.

Louisa looked indifferently at the dish.

"It's honey," said her mother; "some of his own bees
made it. Don't you want to get a dish an' taste of it?
One of them little glass sauce dishes."

"No, I guess not," replied Louisa. "I never cared
much about honey. Grandfather'll like it."

The smile vanished momentarily from Mrs. Britton's
lips, but she recovered herself. She arose and went
across the room to the china closet. Her set of china

dishes was on the top shelves, the lower were filled with books and papers. "I've got somethin' to show you, Mr. Nye," said she.

This was scarcely more than a hamlet, but it was incorporated, and had its town books. She brought forth a pile of them, and laid them on the table beside Jonathan Nye. "There," said she, "I thought mebbe you'd like to look at these." She opened one and pointed to the school report. This mother could not display her daughter's accomplishments to attract a suitor, for she had none. Louisa did not own a piano or organ; she could not paint; but she had taught school acceptably for eight years—ever since she was sixteen—and in every one of the town books was testimonial to that effect, intermixed with glowing eulogy. Jonathan Nye looked soberly through the books; he was a slow reader. He was a few years older than Louisa, tall and clumsy, long-featured and long-necked. His face was a deep red with embarrassment, and it contrasted oddly with his stiff dignity of demeanor.

Mrs. Britton drew a chair close to him while he read. "You see, Louisa taught that school for eight year," said she; "an' she'd be teachin' it now if Mr. Mosely's daughter hadn't grown up an' wanted somethin' to do, an' he put her in. He was committee, you know. I dun' know as I'd ought to say so, an' I wouldn't want you to repeat it, but they do say Ida Mosely don't give very good satisfaction, an' I guess she won't have no reports like these in the town books unless her father writes 'em. See this one."

Jonathan Nye pondered over the fulsome testimony to Louisa's capability, general worth, and amiability, while she sat in sulky silence at the farther corner of the room. Once in a while her mother, after a furtive glance at Jonathan, engrossed in a town book, would look at her and gesticulate fiercely for her to come over, but she did not stir. Her eyes were dull and quiet, her mouth closely shut; she looked homely. Louisa was very pretty when pleased and animated, at other times she had a look like a closed flower. One could see no prettiness in her.

Jonathan Nye read all the school reports; then he

arose heavily. "They're real good," said he. He glanced
at Louisa and tried to smile; his blushes deepened.

"Now don't be in a hurry," said Mrs. Britton.

"I guess I'd better be goin'; mother's alone."

"She won't be afraid; it's jest on the edge of the
evenin'."

"I don't know as she will. But I guess I'd better be
goin'." He looked hesitatingly at Louisa.

She arose and stood with an indifferent air.

"You'd better set down again," said Mrs. Britton.

"No; I guess I'd better be goin'." Jonathan turned
towards Louisa. "Good-evenin'," said he.

"Good-evenin'."

Mrs. Britton followed him to the door. She looked
back and beckoned imperiously to Louisa, but she stood
still. "Now come again, do," Mrs. Britton said to the
departing caller. "Run in any time; we're real lonesome
evenin's. Father he sets an' sleeps in his chair, an' Louisa
an' me often wish somebody'd drop in; folks round here
ain't none too neighborly. Come in any time you happen
to feel like it, an' we'll both of us be glad to see you.
Tell your mother I'll send home that dish to-morrer, an'
we shall have a real feast off that beautiful honey."

When Mrs. Britton had fairly shut the outer door
upon Jonathan Nye, she came back into the sitting room
as if her anger had a propelling power like steam upon
her body.

"Now, Louisa Britton," said she, "you'd ought to be
ashamed of yourself—ashamed of yourself! You've
treated him like a—hog!"

"I couldn't help it."

"Couldn't help it! I guess you could treat anybody
decent if you tried. I never saw such actions! I guess you
needn't be afraid of him. I guess he ain't so set on you
that he means to ketch you up an' run off. There's other
girls in town full as good as you an' better-lookin'. Why
didn't you go an' put on your other dress? Comin' into
the room with that old thing on, an' your hair all in a
frowse! I guess he won't want to come again."

"I hope he won't," said Louisa, under her breath. She
was trembling all over.

"What say?"

"Nothin'."

"I shouldn't think you'd want to say anything, treatin' him that way, when he came over and brought all that beautiful honey! He was all dressed up, too. He had on a real nice coat—cloth jest as fine as it could be, an' it was kinder damp when he come in. Then he dressed all up to come over here this rainy night an' bring this honey." Mrs. Britton snatched the dish of honey and scudded into the kitchen with it. "Sayin' you didn't like honey after he took all that pains to bring it over!" said she. "I'd said I liked it if I'd lied up hill and down." She set the dish in the pantry. "What in creation smells so kinder strong an' smoky in here?" said she, sharply.

"I guess it's the herrin'. I got two or three down to the store."

"I'd like to know what you got herrin' for?"

"I thought maybe you'd relish 'em."

"I don't want no herrin's, now we've got this honey. But I don't know that you've got money to throw away." She shook the old man by the stove into partial wakefulness, and steered him into his little bedroom off the kitchen. She herself slept in one off the sitting-rooms; Louisa's room was up-stairs.

Louisa lighted her candle and went to bed, her mother's scolding voice pursuing her like a wrathful spirit. She cried when she was in bed in the dark, but she soon went to sleep. She was too healthfully tired with her outdoor work not to. All her young bones ached with the strain of manual labor as they had ached many a time this last year since she had lost her school.

The Brittons had been and were in sore straits. All they had in the world was this little house with the acre of land. Louisa's meagre school money had bought their food and clothing since her father died. Now it was almost starvation for them. Louisa was struggling to wrest a little sustenance from their stony acre of land, toiling like a European peasant woman, sacrificing her New England dignity. Lately she had herself split up a cord of wood which she had bought of a neighbor, paying for it in instalments with work for his wife.

"Think of a school-teacher goin' into Mis' Mitchell's house to help clean!" said her mother.

She, although she had been of poor, hard-working
people all her life, with the humblest surroundings, was
a born aristocrat, with that fiercest and most bigoted
aristocracy which sometimes arises from independent
poverty. She had the feeling of a queen for a princess
of the blood about her school-teacher daughter; her
working in a neighbor's kitchen was as galling and terrible to her. The projected marriage with Jonathan Nye
was like a royal alliance for the good of the state. Jonathan Nye was the only eligible young man in the place;
he was the largest land-owner; he had the best house.
There were only himself and his mother; after her death
the property would all be his. Mrs. Nye was an older
woman than Mrs. Britton, who forgot her own frailty in
calculating their chances of life.

"Mis' Nye is considerable over seventy," she said
often to herself; "an' then Jonathan will have it all."

She saw herself installed in that large white house as
reigning dowager. All the obstacle was Louisa's obstinacy, which her mother could not understand. She could
see no fault in Jonathan Nye. So far as absolute approval
went, she herself was in love with him. There was no
more sense, to her mind, in Louisa's refusing him than
there would have been in a princess refusing the fairy
prince and spoiling the story.

"I'd like to know what you've got against him," she
said often to Louisa.

"I ain't got anything against him."

"Why don't you treat him different, then, I want to
know?"

"I don't like him." Louisa said "like" shamefacedly,
for she meant love, and dared not say it.

"*Like!* Well, I don't know nothin' about such likin's
as some pretend to, an' I don't want to. If I see anybody
is good an' worthy, I like 'em, an' that's all there is
about it."

"I don't—believe that's the way you felt about—father," said Louisa, softly, her young face flushed red.

"Yes, it was. I had some common-sense about it."

And Mrs. Britton believed it. Many hard middle-aged
years lay between her and her own love-time, and nothing is so changed by distance as the realities of youth.

She believed herself to have been actuated by the same calm reason in marrying young John Britton, who had had fair prospects, which she thought should actuate her daughter in marrying Jonathan Nye.

Louisa got no sympathy from her, but she persisted in her refusal. She worked harder and harder. She did not spare herself in doors or out. As the summer wore on her face grew as sunburnt as a boy's, her hands were hard and brown. When she put on her white dress to go to meeting on a Sunday there was a white ring around her neck where the sun had not touched it. Above it her face and neck showed browner. Her sleeves were rather short, and there were also white rings above her brown wrists.

"You look as if you were turnin' Injun by inches," said her mother.

Louisa, when she sat in the meeting-house, tried slyly to pull her sleeves down to the brown on her wrists; she gave a little twitch to the ruffle around her neck. Then she glanced across, and Jonathan Nye was looking at her. She thrust her hands, in their short-wristed, loose cotton gloves, as far out of the sleeves as she could; her brown wrists showed conspicuously on her white lap. She had never heard of the princess who destroyed her beauty that she might not be forced to wed the man whom she did not love, but she had something of the same feeling, although she did not have it for the sake of any tangible lover. Louisa had never seen anybody whom she would have preferred to Jonathan Nye. There was no other marriageable young man in the place. She had only her dreams, which she had in common with other girls.

That Sunday evening before she went to meeting her mother took some old wide lace out of her bureau drawer. "There," said she, "I'm goin' to sew this in your neck an' sleeves before you put your dress on. It'll cover up a little; it's wider than the ruffle."

"I don't want it in," said Louisa.

"I'd like to know why not? You look a fright. I was ashamed of you this mornin'."

Louisa thrust her arms into the white dress sleeves peremptorily. Her mother did not speak to her all the

way to meeting. After meeting, Jonathan Nye walked
home with them, and Louisa kept on the other side of
her mother. He went into the house and stayed an hour.
Mrs. Britton entertained him, while Louisa sat silent.
When he had gone, she looked at her daughter as if she
could have used bodily force, but she said nothing. She
shot the bolt of the kitchen door noisily. Louisa lighted
her candle. The old man's loud breathing sounded from
his room; he had been put to bed for safety before they
went to meeting; through the open windows sounded
the loud murmur of the summer night, as if that, too,
slept heavily.

"Good-night, mother," said Louisa, as she went upstairs; but her mother did not answer.

The next day was very warm. This was an exception-
ally hot summer. Louisa went out early; her mother
would not ask her where she was going. She did not
come home until noon. Her face was burning; her wet
dress clung to her arms and shoulders.

"Where have you been?" asked her mother.

"Oh, I've been out in the field."

"What field?"

"Mr. Mitchell's."

"What have you been doin' out there?"

"Rakin' hay."

"Rakin' hay with the men?"

"There wasn't anybody but Mr. Mitchell and Johnny.
Don't, mother!"

Mrs. Britton had turned white. She sank into a chair.
"I can't stan' it nohow," she moaned. "All the daughter
I've got."

"Don't, mother! I ain't done any harm. What harm is
it? Why can't I rake hay as well as a man? Lots of
women do such things, if nobody round here does. He's
goin' to pay me right off, and we need the money. Don't,
mother!" Louisa got a tumbler of water. "Here, mother,
drink this."

Mrs. Britton pushed it away. Louisa stood looking
anxiously at her. Lately her mother had grown thinner
than ever; she looked scarcely bigger than a child. Presently she got up and went to the stove.

"Don't try to do anything, mother; let me finish getting dinner," pleaded Louisa. She tried to take the pan of biscuits out of her mother's hands, but she jerked it away.

The old man was sitting on the door-step, huddled up loosely in the sun, like an old dog.

"Come, father," Mrs. Britton called, in a dry voice, "dinner's ready—what there is of it!"

The old man shuffled in, smiling.

There was nothing for dinner but the hot biscuits and tea. The fare was daily becoming more meagre. All Louisa's little hoard of school money was gone, and her earnings were very uncertain and slender. Their chief dependence for food through the summer was their garden, but that had failed them in some respects.

One day the old man had come in radiant, with his shaking hands full of potato blossoms; his old eyes twinkled over them like a mischievous child's. Reproaches were useless; the little potato crop was sadly damaged. Lately, in spite of close watching, he had picked the squash blossoms, piling them in a yellow mass beside the kitchen door. Still, it was nearly time for the pease and beans and beets; they would keep them from starvation while they lasted.

But when they came, and Louisa could pick plenty of green food every morning, there was still a difficulty: Mrs. Britton's appetite and digestion were poor; she could not live upon a green-vegetable diet; and the old man missed his porridge, for the meal was all gone.

One morning in August he cried at the breakfast-table like a baby, because he wanted his porridge, and Mrs. Britton pushed away her own plate with a despairing gesture.

"There ain't no use," said she. "I can't eat no more garden-sauce nohow. I don't blame poor father a mite. You ain't got no feelin' at all."

"I don't know what I can do; I've worked as hard as I can," said Louisa, miserably.

"I know what you can do, and so do you."

"No, I don't, mother," returned Louisa, with alacrity. "He ain't been here for two weeks now, and I saw him with my own eyes yesterday carryin' a dish into the

Moselys', and I knew 'twas honey. I think he's after
Ida."

"Carryin' honey into the Moselys'? I don't believe it."

"He was; I saw him."

"Well, I don't care if he was. If you're a mind to act
decent now, you can bring him round again. He was
dead set on you, an' I don't believe he's changed round
to that Mosely girl as quick as this."

"You don't want me to ask him to come back here,
do you?"

"I want you to act decent. You can go to meetin'
tonight, if you're a mind to—I sha'n't go; I ain't got
strength 'nough—an' 'twouldn't hurt you none to hang
back a little after meetin', and kind of edge round his
way. 'Twouldn't take more'n a look."

"Mother!"

"Well, I don't care. 'Twouldn't hurt you none. It's the
way more'n one girl does, whether you believe it or not.
Men don't do all the courtin'—not by a long shot.
'Twon't hurt you none. You needn't look so scart."

Mrs. Britton's own face was a burning red. She looked
angrily away from her daughter's honest, indignant eyes.

"I wouldn't do such a thing as that for a man I liked,"
said Louisa; "and I certainly sh'an't for a man I don't
like."

"Then me an' your grandfather'll starve," said her
mother; "that's all there is about it. We can't neither of
us stan' it much longer."

"We could—"

"Could what?"

"Put a—little mortgage on the house."

Mrs. Britton faced her daughter. She trembled in
every inch of her weak frame. "Put a mortgage on this
house, an' by-an'-by not have a roof to cover us! Are
you crazy? I tell you what 'tis, Louisa Britton, we may
starve, your grandfather an' me, an' you can follow us
to the graveyard over there, but there's only one way
I'll ever put a mortgage on this house. If you have Jonathan Nye, I'll ask him to take a little one to tide us along
an' get your weddin' things."

"Mother, I'll tell you what I'm goin' to do."

"What?"

"I am goin' to ask Uncle Solomon."

"I guess when Solomon Mears does anythin' for us you'll know it. He never forgave your father about that wood lot, an' he's hated the whole of us ever since. When I went to his wife's funeral he never answered when I spoke to him. I guess if you go to him you'll take it out in goin'."

Louisa said nothing more. She began clearing away the breakfast dishes and setting the house to rights. Her mother was actually so weak that she could scarcely stand, and she recognized it. She had settled into the rocking-chair, and leaned her head back. Her face looked pale and sharp against the dark calico cover.

When the house was in order, Louisa stole up-stairs to her own chamber. She put on her clean old blue muslin and her hat, then she went slyly down and out the front way.

It was seven miles to her uncle Solomon Mears's, and she had made up her mind to walk them. She walked quite swiftly until the house windows were out of sight, then she slackened her pace a little. It was one of the fiercest dog-days. A damp heat settled heavily down upon the earth; the sun scalded.

At the foot of the hill Louisa passed a house where one of her girl acquaintances lived. She was going in the gate with a pan of early apples. "Hullo, Louisa," she called.

"Hullo, Vinnie."

"Where you goin'?"

"Oh, I'm goin' a little way."

"Ain't it awful hot? Say, Louisa, do you know Ida Mosely's cuttin' you out?"

"She's welcome."

The other girl, who was larger and stouter than Louisa, with a sallow, unhealthy face, looked at her curiously. "I don't see why you wouldn't have him," said she. "I should have thought you'd jumped at the chance."

"Should you if you didn't like him, I'd like to know?"

"I'd like him if he had such a nice house and as much money as Jonathan Nye," returned the other girl.

She offered Louisa some apples, and she went along

the road eating them. She herself had scarcely tasted food that day.

It was about nine o'clock; she had risen early. She calculated how many hours it would take her to walk the seven miles. She walked as fast as she could to hold out. The heat seemed to increase as the sun stood higher. She had walked about three miles when she heard wheels behind her. Presently a team stopped at her side.

"Good-mornin'," said an embarrassed voice.

She looked around. It was Jonathan Nye, with his gray horse and light wagon.

"Good-mornin'," said she.

"Goin' far?"

"A little ways."

"Won't you—ride?"

"No, thank you. I guess I'd rather walk."

Jonathan Nye nodded, made an inarticulate noise in his throat, and drove on. Louisa watched the wagon bowling lightly along. The dust flew back. She took out her handkerchief and wiped her dripping face.

It was about noon when she came in sight of her uncle Solomon Mears's house in Wolfsborough. It stood far back from the road, behind a green expanse of untrodden yard. The blinds on the great square front were all closed; it looked as if everybody were away. Louisa went around to the side door. It stood wide open. There was a thin blue cloud of tobacco smoke issuing from it. Solomon Mears sat there in the large old kitchen smoking his pipe. On the table near him was an empty bowl; he had just eaten his dinner of bread and milk. He got his own dinner, for he had lived alone since his wife died. He looked at Louisa. Evidently he did not recognize her.

"How do you do, Uncle Solomon?" said Louisa.

"Oh, it's John Britton's daughter! How d'ye do?"

He took his pipe out of his mouth long enough to speak, then replaced it. His eyes, sharp under their shaggy brows, were fixed on Louisa; his broad bristling face had a look of stolid rebuff like an ox; his stout figure, in his soiled farmer dress, surged over his chair. He sat full in the doorway. Louisa standing before him, the perspiration trickling over her burning face, set forth her case with a certain dignity. This old man was her mother's nearest relative. He had property and to spare. Should she survive him, it would be hers, unless willed away. She, with her unsophisticated sense of justice, had a feeling that he ought to help her.

The old man listened. When she stopped speaking he took the pipe out of his mouth slowly, and stared gloomily past her at his hay field, where the grass was now a green stubble.

"I ain't got no money I can spare jest now," said he. "I s'pose you know your father cheated me out of consider'ble once?"

"We don't care so much about money, if you have got something you could spare to—eat. We ain't got anything but garden-stuff."

Solomon Mears still frowned past her at the hay field. Presently he arose slowly and went across the kitchen. Louisa sat down on the door-step and waited. Her uncle was gone quite a while. She, too, stared over at the field, which seemed to undulate like a lake in the hot light.

"Here's some things you can take, if you want 'em," said her uncle, at her back.

She got up quickly. He pointed grimly to the kitchen table. He was a deacon, an orthodox believer; he recognized the claims of the poor, but he gave alms as a soldier might yield up his sword. Benevolence was the result of warfare with his own conscience.

On the table lay a ham, a bag of meal, one of flour, and a basket of eggs.

"I'm afraid I can't carry 'em all," said Louisa.

"Leave what you can't then." Solomon caught up his hat and went out. He muttered something about not spending any more time as he went.

Louisa stood looking at the packages. It was utterly impossible for her to carry them all at once. She heard her uncle shout to some oxen he was turning out of the barn. She took up the bag of meal and the basket of eggs and carried them out to the gate; then she returned, got the flour and ham, and went with them to a point beyond. Then she returned for the meal and eggs, and carried them past the others. In that way she traversed the seven miles home. The heat increased. She had eaten

nothing since morning but the apples that her friend had
given her. Her head was swimming, but she kept on.
Her resolution was as immovable under the power of
the sun as a rock. Once in a while she rested for a moment under a tree, but she soon arose and went on. It
was like a pilgrimage, and the Mecca at the end of the
burning, desert-like road was her own maiden independence.

It was after eight o'clock when she reached home. Her
mother stood in the doorway watching for her, straining
her eyes in the dusk.

"For goodness sake, Louisa Britton! where have you
been?" she began; but Louisa laid the meal and eggs
down on the step.

"I've got to go back a little ways," she panted.

When she returned with the flour and ham, she could
hardly get into the house. She laid them on the kitchen
table, where her mother had put the other parcels, and
sank into a chair.

"Is this the way you've brought all these things
home?" asked her mother.

Louisa nodded.

"All the way from Uncle Solomon's?"

"Yes."

Her mother went to her and took her hat off. "It's a
mercy if you ain't got a sunstroke," said she, with a
sharp tenderness. "I've got somethin' to tell you. What
do you s'pose has happened? Mr. Mosely has been here,
an' he wants you to take the school again when it opens
next week. He says Ida ain't very well, but I guess that
ain't it. They think she's goin' to get somebody. Mis'
Mitchell says so. She's been in. She says he's carryin'
things over there the whole time, but she don't b'lieve
there's anything settled yet. She says they feel so sure
of it they're goin' to have Ida give the school up. I told
her I thought Ida would make him a good wife, an' she
was easier suited than some girls. What do you s'pose
Mis' Mitchell says? She says old Mis' Nye told her that
there was one thing about it: if Jonathan had you, he
wa'n't goin' to have me an' father hitched on to him;
he'd look out for that. I told Mis' Mitchell that I guess
there wa'n't none of us willin' to hitch, you nor anybody

else. I hope she'll tell Mis' Nye. Now I'm a-goin' to turn you out a tumbler of milk—Mis' Mitchell she brought over a whole pitcherful; says she's got more'n they can use—they ain't got no pig now—an' then you go an' lay down on the sittin'-room lounge, an' cool off: an' I'll stir up some porridge for supper, an' boil some eggs. Father'll be tickled to death. Go right in there. I'm dreadful afraid you'll be sick. I never heard of anybody doin' such a thing as you have."

Louisa drank the milk and crept into the sitting-room. It was warm and close there, so she opened the front door and sat down on the step. The twilight was deep, but there was a clear yellow glow in the west. One great star had come out in the midst of it. A dewy coolness was spreading over everything. The air was full of bird calls and children's voices. Now and then there was a shout of laughter. Louisa leaned her head against the door-post.

The house was quite near the road. Some one passed—a man carrying a basket. Louisa glanced at him, and recognized Jonathan Nye by his gait. He kept on down the road toward the Moselys', and Louisa turned again from him to her sweet, mysterious, girlish dreams.

—1891

THEODORE DREISER
(1871–1945)

Son of a stern German Catholic father and an affectionate Mennonite mother, Dreiser, who was born in Terre Haute, Indiana, recalled among his earliest impressions his overwhelming pity at the sight of the holes in his mother's badly worn shoes. Himself a "have-not," he felt the enormous temptations of American materialist society, having, as a young man, withheld money from his employer in order to buy the overcoat he desperately wanted. Dreiser's advanced education consisted of a single year at the University of Indiana, which was financed by Mildred Fielding, a high school teacher who believed he had great potential. Essentially, he developed as a writer through studying on his own such theorists as Huxley, Tyndall, and Spencer, and through practical experience as a reporter for newspapers in St. Louis, Chicago, Pittsburgh, and New York. His first novel, *Sister Carrie* (1900), received virtually no distribution since the publisher, Doubleday, Page and Co., after signing a contract with Dreiser, developed reservations about the novel's morality. Among the novels subsequently published were *Jennie Gerhardt* (1911), *The Financier* (1912), *The Titan* (1914), *An American Tragedy* (1925), which was filmed in 1951 as *A Place in the Sun*, and *The Bulwark* (1946).

The Second Choice

Shirley Dear:

You don't want the letters. There are only six of them, anyhow, and think, they're all I have of you to cheer me on my travels. What good would they be to you—little bits of notes telling me you're sure to meet me—but me—think of me! If I send them to you, you'll tear them up, whereas if you leave them with me I can dab them with musk and ambergis and keep them in a little silver box, always beside me.

Ah, Shirley dear, you really don't know how sweet I
think you are, how dear! There isn't a thing we have
ever done together that isn't as clear in my mind as this
great big skyscraper over the way here in Pittsburgh,
and far more pleasing. In fact, my thoughts of you are
the most precious and delicious things I have, Shirley.

But I'm too young to marry now. You know that,
Shirley, don't you? I haven't placed myself in any way
yet, and I'm so restless that I don't know whether I
ever will, really. Only yesterday, old Roxbaum—that's
my new employer here—came to me and wanted to
know if I would like an assistant overseership on one
of his coffee plantations in Java, said there would not
be much money in it for a year or two, a bare living,
but later there would be more—and I jumped at it.
Just the thought of Java and going there did that, although I knew I could make more staying right here.
Can't you see how it is with me, Shirl? I'm too restless
and too young. I couldn't take care of you right, and
you wouldn't like me after a while if I didn't.

But ah, Shirley sweet, I think the dearest things of
you! There isn't an hour, it seems, but some little bit
of you comes back—a dear, sweet, bit—the night we
sat on the grass in Tregore Park and counted the stars
through the trees; that first evening at Sparrows Point
when we missed the last train and had to walk to
Langley. Remember the tree-toads, Shirl? And then
that warm April Sunday in Atholby woods! Ah, Shirl,
you don't want the six notes! Let me keep them. But
think of me, will you, sweet, wherever you go and
whatever you do? I'll always think of you, and wish
that you had met a better, saner man than me, and
that I really could have married you and been all you
wanted me to be. By-by, sweet. I may start for Java
within the month. If so, and you would want them,
I'll send you some cards from there if they have any.

> Your worthless
> ARTHUR

She sat and turned the letter in her hand, dumb with
despair. It was the very last letter she would ever get
from him. Of that she was certain. He was gone now,

once and for all. She had written him only once, not
making an open plea but asking him to return her letters,
and then there had come this tender but evasive reply,
saying nothing of a possible return but desiring to keep
her letters for old times' sake—the happy hours they
had spent together.

The happy hours! Oh, yes, yes, yes—the happy hours!

In her memory now, as she sat here in her home after
the day's work, meditating on all that had been in the
few short months since he had come and gone, was a
world of color and light—a color and light so transfigur-
ing as to seem celestial, but now, alas, wholly dissipated.
It had contained so much of all she had desired—love,
romance, amusement, laughter. He had been so gay and
thoughtless, or headstrong, so youthfully romantic, and
with such a love of play and change and to be saying
and doing anything and everything. Arthur could dance
in a gay way, whistle, sing after a fashion, play. He could
play cards and do tricks, and he had such a superior air,
so genial and brisk, with a kind of innate courtesy in it
and yet an intolerance for slowness and stodginess or
anything dull or dingy, such as characterized—but here
her thoughts fled from him. She refused to think of any
one but Arthur.

Sitting in her little bedroom now, off the parlor on
the ground floor in her home in Bethune Street, and
looking out over the Kessels' yard, and beyond that—
there being no fences in Bethune Street—over the
"yards" or lawns of the Pollards, Bakers, Cryders, and
others, she thought of how dull it must all have seemed
to him, with his fine imaginative mind and experiences,
his love of change and gaiety, his atmosphere of something better than she had ever known. How little she
had been fitted, perhaps, by beauty or temperament to
overcome this—the something—dullness in her work or
her home, which possibly had driven him away. For, although many had admired her to date, and she was
young and pretty in her simple way and constantly receiving suggestions that her beauty was disturbing to
some, still, he had not cared for her—he had gone.

And now, as she meditated, it seemed that this scene,
and all that it stood for—her parents, her work, her daily

shuttling to and fro between the drug company for which she worked and this street and house—was typical of her life and what she was destined to endure always. Some girls were so much more fortunate. They had fine clothes, fine homes, a world of pleasure and opportunity in which to move. They did not have to scrimp and save and work to pay their own way. And yet she had always been compelled to do it, but had never complained until now—or until he came, and after. Bethune Street, with its commonplace front yards and houses nearly all alike, and this house, so like the others, room for room and porch for porch, and her parents, too, really like all the others, had seemed good enough, quite satisfactory, indeed, until then. But now, now!

Here, in their kitchen, was her mother, a thin, pale, but kindly woman, peeling potatoes and washing lettuce, and putting a bit of steak or a chop or a piece of liver in a frying pan day after day, morning and evening, month after month, year after year. And next door was Mrs. Kessel doing the same thing. And next door Mrs. Cryder. And next door Mrs. Pollard. But, until now, she had not thought it so bad. But now—now—oh! And on all the porches or lawns all along this street were the husbands and fathers, mostly middle-aged or old men like her father, reading their papers or cutting the grass before dinner, or smoking and meditating afterward. Her father was out in front now, a stooped, forebearing, meditative soul, who had rarely anything to say—leaving it all to his wife, her mother, but who was fond of her in his dull, quiet way. He was a pattern-maker by trade, and had come into possession of this small, ordinary home via years of toil and saving, her mother helping him. They had no particular religion, as he often said, thinking reasonably human conduct a sufficient passport to heaven, but they had gone occasionally to the Methodist Church over in Nicholas Street, and she had once joined it. But of late she had not gone, weaned away by the other commonplace pleasures of her world.

And then in the midst of it, the dull drift of things, as she now saw them to be, he had come—Arthur Bristow—young, energetic, good-looking, ambitious, dreamful, and instanter, and with her never knowing quite how, the whole thing had been changed. He had appeared so swiftly—out of nothing, as it were.

Previous to him had been Barton Williams, stout, phlegmatic, good-natured, well-meaning, who was, or had been before Arthur came, asking her to marry him, and whom she allowed to half assume that she would. She had liked him in a feeble, albeit, as she thought, tender way, thinking him the kind, according to the logic of her neighborhood, who would make her a good husband, and, until Arthur appeared on the scene, had really intended to marry him. It was not really a love-match, as she saw now, but she thought it was, which was much the same thing, perhaps. But, as she now recalled, when Arthur came, how the scales fell from her eyes! In a trice, as it were, nearly, there was a new heaven and a new earth. Arthur had arrived, and with him a sense of something different.

Mabel Gove had asked her to come over to her house in Westleigh, the adjoining suburb, for Thanksgiving eve and day, and without a thought of anything, and because Barton was busy handling a part of the work in the despatcher's office of the Great Eastern and could not see her, she had gone. And then, to her surprise and strange, almost ineffable delight, the moment she had seen him, he was there—Arthur, with his slim, straight figure and dark hair and eyes and clean-cut features, as clean and attractive as those of a coin. And as he had looked at her and smiled and narrated humorous bits of things that had happened to him, something had come over her—a spell—and after dinner they had all gone round to Edith Barringer's to dance, and there as she had danced with him, somehow, without any seeming boldness on his part, he had taken possession of her, as it were, drawn her close, and told her she had beautiful eyes and hair and such a delicately rounded chin, and that he thought she danced gracefully and was sweet. She had nearly fainted with delight.

"Do you like me?" he had asked in one place in the dance, and, in spite of herself, she had looked up into his eyes, and from that moment she was almost mad over him, could think of nothing else but his hair and eyes and his smile and graceful figure.

Mabel Gove had seen it all, in spite of her determination that no one should, and on their going to bed later, back at Mabel's home, she had whispered:

"Ah, Shirley, I saw. You like Arthur, don't you?"

"I think he's very nice," Shirley recalled replying, for Mabel knew of her affair with Barton and liked him, "but I'm not crazy over him." And for this bit of treason she had sighed in her dreams nearly all night.

And the next day, true to a request and a promise made by him, Arthur had called again at Mabel's to take her and Mabel to a "movie" which was not so far away, and from there they had gone to an ice-cream parlor, and during it all, when Mabel was not looking, he had squeezed her arm and hand and kissed her neck, and she had held her breath, and her heart had seemed to stop.

"And now you're going to let me come out to your place to see you, aren't you?" he had whispered.

And she had replied, "Wednesday evening," and then written the address on a little piece of paper and given it to him.

But now it was all gone, gone!

This house, which now looked so dreary—how romantic it had seemed that first night *he* called—the front room with its commonplace furniture, and later in the spring, the veranda, with its vines just sprouting, and the moon in May. Oh, the moon in May, and June and July, when he was here! How she had lied to Barton to make evenings for Arthur, and occasionally to Arthur to keep him from contact with Barton. She had not even mentioned Barton to Arthur because—because—well, because Arthur was so much better, and somehow (she admitted it to herself now) she had not been sure that Arthur would care for her long, if at all, and then—well, and then, to be quite frank, Barton might be good enough. She did not exactly hate him because she had found Arthur—not at all. She still liked him in a way—he was so kind and faithful, so very dull and straightforward and thoughtful of her, which Arthur was certainly not. Before Arthur had appeared, as she well remembered, Barton had seemed to be plenty good enough—in fact, all that she desired in a pleasant, companionable way, calling for her, taking her places, bringing her flowers and candy, which Arthur rarely did, and for that, if nothing more, she could not help continuing to like him and to feel sorry for him, and besides, as she had admitted to herself before, if Arthur left her—. . . Weren't his parents better off than hers—and hadn't he a good position for such a man as he—one hundred and fifty dollars a month and the certainty of more later on? A little while before meeting Arthur, she had thought this very good, enough for two to live on at least, and she had thought some of trying it at some time or other—but now—now—

And that first night he had called—how well she remembered it—how it had transfigured the parlor next this in which she was now, filling it with something it had never had before, and the porch outside, too, for that matter, with its gaunt, leafless vine, and this street, too, even—dull, commonplace Bethune Street. There had been a flurry of snow during the afternoon while she was working at the store, and the ground was white with it. All the neighboring homes seemed to look sweeter and happier and more inviting than ever they had as she came past them, with their lights peeping from under curtains and drawn shades. She had hurried into hers and lighted the big red-shaded parlor lamp, her one artistic treasure, as she thought, and put it near the piano, between it and the window, and arranged the chairs, and then bustled to the task of making herself as pleasing as she might. For him she had gotten out her one best filmy house dress and done up her hair in the fashion she thought most becoming—and that he had not seen before—and powdered her cheeks and nose and darkened her eyelashes, as some of the girls at the store did, and put on her new gray satin slippers, and then, being so arrayed, waited nervously, unable to eat anything or to think of anything but him.

And at last, just when she had begun to think he might not be coming, he had appeared with that arch smile and a "Hello! It's here you live, is it? I was wondering. George, but you're twice as sweet as I thought you were, aren't you?" And then, in the little entryway, behind the closed door, he had held her and kissed her on the mouth a dozen times while she pretended to push

against his coat and struggle and say that her parents
might hear.

And, oh, the room afterward, with him in it in the red
glow of the lamp, and with his pale handsome face made
handsomer thereby, as she thought! He had made her
sit near him and had held her hands and told her about
his work and his dreams—all that he expected to do
in the future—and then she had found herself wishing
intensely to share just such a life—his life—anything that
he might wish to do; only, she kept wondering, with a
slight pain, whether he would want her to—he was so
young, dreamful, ambitious, much younger and more
dreamful than herself, although, in reality, he was several
years older.

And then followed that glorious period from Decem-
ber to this late September, in which everything which
was worth happening in love had happened. Oh, those
wondrous days the following spring, when, with the first
burst of buds and leaves, he had taken her one Sunday
to Atholby, where all the great woods were, and they
had hunted spring beauties in the grass, and sat on a
slope and looked at the river below and watched some
boys fixing up a sailboat and setting forth in it quite
as she wished she and Arthur might be doing—going
somewhere together—far, far away from all commonplace things and life! And then he had slipped his arm
about her and kissed her cheek and neck, and tweaked
her ear and smoothed her hair—and oh, there on the
grass, with the spring flowers about her and a canopy of
small green leaves above, the perfection of love had
come—love so wonderful that the mere thought of it
made her eyes brim now! And then had been days, Saturday afternoons and Sundays, at Atholby and Sparrows
Point, where the great beach was, and in lovely Tregore
Park, a mile or two from her home, where they could
go of an evening and sit in or near the pavilion and have
ice-cream and dance or watch the dancers. Oh, the stars,
the winds, the summer breath of those days! Ah, me!
Ah, me!

Naturally, her parents had wondered from the first
about her and Arthur, and her and Barton, since Barton
had already assumed a proprietary interest in her and

she had seemed to like him. But then she was an only child and a pet, and used to presuming on that, and they could not think of saying anything to her. After all, she was young and pretty and was entitled to change her mind; only, only—she had had to indulge in a career of lying and subterfuge in connection with Barton, since Arthur was headstrong and wanted every evening that he chose—to call for her at the store and keep her downtown to dinner and a show.

Arthur had never been like Barton, shy, phlegmatic, obedient, waiting long and patiently for each little favor, but, instead, masterful and eager, rifling her of kisses and caresses and every delight of love, and teasing and playing with her as a cat would a mouse. She could never resist him. He demanded of her her time and her affection without let or hindrance. He was not exactly selfish or cruel, as some might have been, but gay and unthinking at times, unconsciously so, and yet loving and tender at others—nearly always so. But always he would talk of things in the future as if they really did not include her—and this troubled her greatly—of places he might go, things he might do, which, somehow, he seemed to think or assume that she could not or would not do with him. He was always going to Australia sometime, he thought, in a business way, or to South Africa, or possibly to India. He never seemed to have any fixed clear future for himself in mind.

A dreadful sense of helplessness and of impending disaster came over her at these times, of being involved in some predicament over which she had no control, and which would lead her on to some sad end. Arthur, although plainly in love, as she thought, and apparently delighted with her, might not always love her. She began, timidly at first (and always, for that matter), to ask him pretty, seeking questions about himself and her, whether their future was certain to be together, whether he really wanted her—loved her—whether he might not want to marry some one else or just her, and whether she wouldn't look nice in a pearl satin wedding-dress with a long creamy veil and satin slippers and a bouquet of bridalwreath. She had been so slowly but surely saving to that end, even before he came, in connection with

Barton; only, after *he* came, all thought of the import of it had been transferred to him. But now, also, she was beginning to ask herself sadly, "Would it ever be?" He was so airy, so inconsequential, so ready to say: "Yes, yes," and "Sure, sure! that's right! Yes, indeedy; you bet! Say, kiddie, but you'll look sweet!" but, somehow, it had always seemed as if this whole thing were a glorious interlude and that it could not last. Arthur was too gay and ethereal and too little settled in his own mind. His ideas of travel and living in different cities, finally winding up in New York or San Francisco, but never with her exactly until she asked him, were too ominous, although he always reassured her gaily: "Of course! Of course!" But somehow she could never believe it really, and it made her intensely sad at times, horribly gloomy. So often she wanted to cry, and she could scarcely tell why.

And then, because of her affection for him, she had finally quarreled with Barton, or nearly that, if one could say that one ever really quarreled with him. It had been because of a certain Thursday evening a few weeks before about which she had disappointed him. In a fit of generosity, knowing that Arthur was coming Wednesday, and because Barton had stopped in at the store to see her, she had told him that he might come, having regretted it afterwards, so enamored was she of Arthur. And then when Wednesday came, Arthur had changed his mind, telling her he would come Friday instead, but on Thursday evening he had stopped in at the store and asked her to go to Sparrows Point, with the result that she had no time to notify Barton. He had gone to the house and sat with her parents until ten-thirty, and then, a few days later, although she had written him offering an excuse, had called at the store to complain slightly.

"Do you think you did just right, Shirley? You might have sent word, mightn't you? Who was it—the new fellow you won't tell me about?"

Shirley flared on the instant.

"Supposing it was? What's it to you? I don't belong to you yet, do I? I told you there wasn't any one, and I wish you'd let me alone about that. I couldn't help it last Thursday—that's all—and I don't want you to be fussing with me—that's all. If you don't want to, you needn't come any more, anyhow."

"Don't say that, Shirley," pleaded Barton. "You don't mean that, I won't bother you, though, if you don't want me any more."

And because Shirley sulked, not knowing what else to do, he had gone and she had not seen him since.

And then sometime later when she had thus broken with Barton, avoiding the railway station where he worked, Arthur had failed to come at his appointed time, sending no word until the next day, when a note came to the store saying that he had been out of town for his firm over Sunday and had not been able to notify her, but that he would call Tuesday. It was an awful blow. At the time, Shirley had a vision of what was to follow. It seemed for the moment as if the whole world had suddenly been reduced to ashes, that there was nothing but black charred cinders anywhere—she felt that about all life. Yet, it all came to her clearly then that this was but the beginning of just such days and just such excuses, and that soon, soon, he would come no more. He was beginning to be tired of her and soon he would not even make excuses. She felt it, and it froze and terrified her.

And then, soon after, the indifference which she feared did follow—almost created by her own thoughts, as it were. First, it was a meeting he had to attend somewhere one Wednesday night when he was to have come for her. Then he was going out of town again, over Sunday. Then he was going away for a whole week—it was absolutely unavoidable, he said, his commercial duties were increasing—and once he had casually remarked that nothing could stand in the way where she was concerned—never! She did not think of reproaching him with this; she was too proud. If he was going, he must go. She would not be willing to say to herself that she had ever attempted to hold any man. But, just the same, she was agonized by the thought. When he was with her, he seemed tender enough; only, at times, his eyes wandered and he seemed slightly bored. Other girls, particularly pretty ones, seemed to interest him as much as she did.

And the agony of the long days when he did not come any more for a week or two at a time! The waiting, the brooding, the wondering, at the store and here in her home—in the former place making mistakes at times because she could not get her mind off him and being reminded of them, and here at her own home at nights, being so absent-minded that her parents remarked on it. She felt sure that her parents must be noticing that Arthur was not coming any more, or as much as he had— for she pretended to be going out with him, going to Mabel Gove's instead—and that Barton had deserted her too, he having been driven off by her indifference, never to come any more, perhaps, unless she sought him out.

And then it was that the thought of saving her own face by taking up with Barton once more occurred to her, of using him and his affections and faithfulness and dullness, if you will, to cover up her own dilemma. Only, this ruse was not to be tried until she had written Arthur this one letter—a pretext merely to see if there was a single ray of hope, a letter to be written in a gentle-enough way and asking for the return of the few notes she had written him. She had not seen him now in nearly a month, and the last time she had, he had said he might soon be compelled to leave her awhile—to go to Pittsburgh to work. And it was his reply to this that she now held in her hand—from Pittsburgh! It was frightful! The future without him!

But Barton would never know really what had transpired, if she went back to him. In spite of all her delicious hours with Arthur, she could call him back, she felt sure. She had never really entirely dropped him, and he knew it. He had bored her dreadfully on occasion, arriving on off days when Arthur was not about, with flowers or candy, or both, and sitting on the porch steps and talking of the railroad business and of the whereabouts and doings of some of their old friends. It was shameful, she had thought at times, to see a man so patient, so hopeful, so good-natured as Barton, deceived in this way, and by her, who was so miserable over another. Her parents must see and know, she had thought at these times, but still, what else was she to do?

"I'm a bad girl," she kept telling herself. "I'm all wrong. What right have I to offer Barton what is left?" But still, somehow, she realized that Barton, if she chose to favor him, would only be too grateful for even the leavings of others where she was concerned, and that even yet, if she but deigned to crook a finger, she could have him. He was so simple, so good-natured, so stolid and matter of fact, so different to Arthur whom (she could not help smiling at the thought of it) she was loving now about as Barton loved her—slavishly, hopelessly.

And then, as the days passed and Arthur did not write any more—just this one brief note—she at first grieved horribly, and then in a fit of numb despair attempted, bravely enough from one point of view, to adjust herself to the new situation. Why should she despair? Why die of agony where there were plenty who would still sigh for her—Barton among others? She was young, pretty, very—many told her so. She could, if she chose, achieve a vivacity which she did not feel. Why should she brook this unkindness without a thought of retaliation? Why shouldn't she enter upon a gay and heartless career, indulging in a dozen flirtations at once—dancing and killing all thoughts of Arthur in a round of frivolities? There were many who beckoned to her. She stood at her counter in the drug store on many a day and brooded over this, but at the thought of which one to begin with, she faltered. After her late love, all were so tame, for the present anyhow.

And then—and then—always there was Barton, the humble or faithful, to whom she had been so unkind and whom she had used and whom she still really liked. So often self-reproaching thoughts in connection with him crept over her. He must have known, must have seen how badly she was using him all this while, and yet he had not failed to come and come, until she had actually quarreled with him, and any one would have seen that it was literally hopeless. She could not help remembering, especially now in her pain, that he adored her. He was not calling on her now at all—by her indifference she had finally driven him away—but a word, a word—she waited for days, weeks, hoping against hope, and then—

The office of Barton's superior in the Great Eastern terminal had always made him an easy object for her blandishments, coming and going, as she frequently did, via this very station. He was in the office of the assistant train-despatcher on the ground floor, where passing to and from the local, which, at times, was quicker than a street-car, she could easily see him by peering in; only, she had carefully avoided him for nearly a year. If she chose now, and would call for a message blank at the adjacent telegraph-window which was a part of his room, and raised her voice as she often had in the past, he could scarcely fail to hear, if he did not see her. And if he did, he would rise and come over—of that she was sure, for he never could resist her. It had been a wile of hers in the old days to do this or to make her presence felt by idling outside. After a month of brooding, she felt that she must act—her position as a deserted girl was too much. She could not stand it any longer really—the eyes of her mother, for one.

It was six-fifteen one evening when, coming out of the store in which she worked, she turned her step disconsolately homeward. Her heart was heavy, her face rather pale and drawn. She had stopped in the store's retiring-room before coming out to add to her charms as much as possible by a little powder and rouge and to smooth her hair. It would not take much to reallure her former sweetheart, she felt sure—and yet it might not be so easy after all. Suppose he had found another? But she could not believe that. It had scarcely been long enough since he had last attempted to see her, and he was really so very, very fond of her and so faithful. He was too slow and certain in his choosing—he had been so with her. Still, who knows? With this thought, she went forward in the evening, feeling for the first time the shame and pain that comes of deception, the agony of having to relinquish an ideal and the feeling of despair that comes to those who find themselves in the position of suppliants, stooping to something which in better days and better fortune they would not know. Arthur was the cause of this.

When she reached the station, the crowd that usually filled it at this hour was swarming. There were so many pairs like Arthur and herself laughing and hurrying away or so she felt. First glancing in the small mirror of a weighing scale to see if she were still of her former charm, she stopped thoughtfully at a little flower stand which stood outside, and for a few pennies purchased a tiny bunch of violets. She then went inside and stood near the window, peering first furtively to see if he were present. He was. Bent over his work, a green shade over his eyes, she could see his solid genial figure at a table. Stepping back a moment to ponder, she finally went forward and, in a clear voice asked.

"May I have a blank, please?"

The infatuation of the discarded Barton was such that it brought him instantly to his feet. In his stodgy, stocky way he rose, his eyes glowing with a friendly hope, his mouth wreathed in smiles, and came over. At the sight of her, pale, but pretty—paler and prettier, really, than he had ever seen her—he thrilled dumbly.

"How are you, Shirley?" he asked sweetly, as he drew near, his eyes searching her face hopefully. He had not seen her for so long that he was intensely hungry, and her paler beauty appealed to him more than ever. Why wouldn't she have him? he was asking himself. Why wouldn't his persistent love yet win her? Perhaps it might. "I haven't seen you in a month of Sundays, it seems. How are the folks?"

"They're all right, Bart," she smiled archly, "and so am I. How have you been? It has been a long time since I've seen you. I've been wondering how you were. Have you been all right? I was just going to send a message."

As he had approached, Shirley had pretended at first not to see him, a moment later to affect surprise, although she was really suppressing a heavy sigh. The sight of him, after Arthur, was not reassuring. Could she really interest herself in him any more? Could she?

"Sure, sure," he replied genially; "I'm always all right. You couldn't kill me, you know. Not going away, are you, Shirl?" he queried interestedly.

"No: I'm just telegraphing to Mabel. She promised to meet me to-morrow, and I want to be sure she will."

"You don't come past here as often as you did, Shirley," he complained tenderly. "At least, I don't seem to see you so often," he added with a smile. "It isn't anything I have done, is it?" he queried, and then, when she protested quickly, added: "What's the trouble, Shirl? Haven't been sick, have you?"

She affected all her old gaiety and ease, feeling as though she would like to cry.

"Oh, no," she returned; "I've been all right. I've been going through the other door, I suppose, or coming in and going out on the Langdon Avenue car." (This was true, because she had been wanting to avoid him.) "I've been in such a hurry, most nights, and I haven't had time to stop, Bart. You know how late the store keeps us at times."

He remembered, too, that in the old days she had made time to stop or meet him occasionally.

"Yes, I know," he said tactfully. "But you haven't been to any of our old card-parties either of late, have you? At least, I haven't seen you. I've gone to two or three, thinking you might be there."

That was another thing Arthur had done—broken up her interest in these old store and neighborhood parties and a banjo-and-mandolin club to which she had once belonged. They had all seemed so pleasing and amusing in the old days, but now. . . . In those days Bart had been her usual companion when his work permitted.

"No," she replied evasively, but with a forced air of pleasant remembrance; "I have often thought of how much fun we had at those, though. It was a shame to drop them. You haven't seen Harry Stull or Trina Trask recently, have you?" she inquired, more to be saying something than for any interest she felt.

He shook his head negatively, then added:

"Yes, I did, too; here in the waiting-room a few nights ago. They were coming down-town to a theater, I suppose."

His face fell slightly as he recalled how it had been their custom to do this, and what their one quarrel had been about. Shirley noticed it. She felt the least bit sorry for him, but much more for herself, coming back so disconsolately to all this.

"Well, you're looking as pretty as ever, Shirley," he continued, noting that she had not written the telegram and that there was something wistful in her glance. "Prettier, I think," and she smiled sadly. Every word that she tolerated from him was as so much gold to him, so much of dead ashes to her. "You wouldn't like to come down some evening this week and see 'The Mouse-Trap,' would you? We haven't been to a theater together in I don't know when." His eyes sought hers in a hopeful, doglike way.

So—she could have him again—that was the pity of it! To have what she really did not want, did not care for! At the least nod now he would come, and this very devotion made it all but worthless, and so sad. She ought to marry him now for certain, if she began in this way, and could in a month's time if she chose, but oh, oh— could she? For the moment she decided that she could not, would not. If he had only repulsed her—told her to go—ignored her—but no; it was her fate to be loved by him in this moving, pleading way, and hers not to love him as she wished to love—to be loved. Plainly, he needed some one like her, whereas, she, she—She turned a little sick, a sense of the sacrilege of gaiety at this time creeping into her voice, and exclaimed:

"No, no!" Then seeing his face change, a heavy sadness come over it, "Not this week, anyhow, I mean" ("Not so soon," she had almost said). "I have several engagements this week and I'm not feeling well. But"— seeing his face change, and the thought of her own state returning—"you might come out to the house some evening instead, and then we can go some other time."

His face brightened intensely. It was wonderful how he longed to be with her, how the least favor from her comforted and lifted him up. She could see also now, however, how little it meant to her, how little it could ever mean, even if to him it was heaven. The old relationship would have to be resumed in toto, once and for all, but did she want it that way now that she was feeling so miserable about this other affair? As she meditated, these various moods racing to and fro in her mind, Barton seemed to notice, and now it occurred to him that perhaps he had not pursued her enough—was too easily put off. She probably did like him yet. This evening, her present visit, seemed to prove it.

"Sure, sure!" he agreed. "I'd like that. I'll come out Sunday, if you say. We can go any time to the play. I'm sorry, Shirley, if you're not feeling well. I've thought of you a lot these days. I'll come out Wednesday, if you don't mind."

She smiled a wan smile. It was all so much easier than she had expected—her triumph—and so ashenlike in consequence, a flavor of dead-sea fruit and defeat about it all, that it was pathetic. How could she, after Arthur? How could he, really?

"Make it Sunday," she pleaded, naming the farthest day off, and then hurried out.

Her faithful lover gazed after her, while she suffered an intense nausea. To think—to think—it should all be coming to this! She had not used her telegraph-blank, and now had forgotten all about it. It was not the simple trickery that discouraged her, but her own future which could find no better outlet than this, could not rise above it apparently, or that she had no heart to make it rise above it. Why couldn't she interest herself in some one different to Barton? Why did she have to return to him? Why not wait and meet some other—ignore him as before? But no, no; nothing mattered now—no one—it might as well be Barton as any one, and she would at least make him happy and at the same time solve her own problem. She went out into the train-shed and climbed into her train. Slowly, after the usual pushing and jostling of a crowd, it drew out toward Latonia, that suburban region in which her home lay. As she rode, she thought.

"What have I just done? What am I doing?" she kept asking herself as the clacking wheels on the rails fell into a rhythmic dance and the houses of the brown, dry, endless city fled past in a maze. "Severing myself decisively from the past—the happy past—for supposing, once I am married, Arthur should return and want me again—suppose! Suppose!"

Below at one place, under a shed, were some market-gardeners disposing of the last remnants of their day's wares—a sickly, dull life, she thought. Here was Rutgers Avenue, with its line of red street-cars, many wagons and tracks and counterstreams of automobiles—how often had she passed it morning and evening in a shuttle-like way, and how often would, unless she got married! And here, now, was the river flowing smoothly between its banks lined with coal-pockets and wharves—away, away to the huge deep sea which she and Arthur had enjoyed so much. Oh, to be in a small boat and drift out, out into the endless, restless, pathless deep! Some-how the sight of this water, to-night and every night, brought back those evenings in the open with Arthur at Sparrows Point, the long line of dancers in Eckert's Pa-vilion, the woods at Atholby, the park, with the dancers in the pavilion—she choked back a sob. Once Arthur had come this way with her on just such an evening as this, pressing her hand and saying how wonderful she was. Oh, Arthur! Arthur! And now Barton was to take his old place again—forever, no doubt. She could not trifle with her life longer in this foolish way, or his. What was the use? But think of it!

Yes, it must be—forever now, she told herself. She must marry. Time would be slipping by and she would become too old. It was her only future—marriage. It was the only future she had ever contemplated really, a home, children, the love of some man whom she could love as she loved Arthur. Ah, what a happy home that would have been for her! But now, now—

But there must be no turning back now, either. There was no other way. If Arthur ever came back—but fear not, he wouldn't! She had risked so much and lost—lost him. Her little venture into true love had been such a failure. Before Arthur had come all had been well enough. Barton, stout and simple and frank and direct, had in some way—how, she could scarcely realize now—offered sufficient of a future. But now, now! He had enough money, she knew, to build a cottage for the two of them. He had told her so. He would do his best al-ways to make her happy, she was sure of that. They could live in about the state her parents were living in—or a little better, not much—and would never want. No

doubt there would be children, because he craved
them—several of them—and that would take up her
time, long years of it—the sad, gray years! But then Arthur, whose children she would have thrilled to bear,
would be no more, a mere memory—think of that!—and
Barton, the dull, the commonplace, would have achieved
his finest dream—and why?

Because love was a failure for her—that was why—
and in her life there would be no more true love. She
would never love any one again as she had Arthur. It
could not be, she was sure of it. He was too fascinating,
too wonderful. Always, always, wherever she might be,
whoever she might marry, he would be coming back,
intruding between her and any possible love, receiving
any possible kiss. It would be Arthur she would be loving or kissing. She dabbed at her eyes with a tiny handkerchief, turned her face close to the window and stared
out, and then as the environs of Latonia came into view,
wondered (so deep is romance): What if Arthur should
come back at some time—or now! Supposing he should
be here at the station now, accidentally or on purpose,
to welcome her, to soothe her weary heart. He had met
her here before. How she would fly to him, lay her head
on his shoulder, forget forever that Barton ever was, that
they had ever separated for an hour. Oh, Arthur!
Arthur!

But no, no; here was Latonia—here the viaduct over
her train, the long business street and the cars marked
"Center" and "Langdon Avenue" running back into the
great city. A few blocks away in treeshaded Bethune
Street, duller and plainer than ever, was her parents'
cottage and the routine of that old life which was now,
she felt, more fully fastened upon her than ever before—
the lawn-mowers, the lawns, the front porches all alike.
Now would come the going to and fro of Barton to business as her father and she now went to business, her
keeping house, cooking, washing, ironing, sewing for
Barton as her mother now did these things for her father
and herself. And she would not be in love really, as she
wanted to be. Oh, dreadful! She could never escape it
really, now that she could endure it less, scarcely for

another hour. And yet she must, must, for the sake of—
for the sake of—she closed her eyes and dreamed.

She walked up the street under the trees, past the
houses and lawns all alike to her own, and found her
father on their veranda reading the evening paper. She
sighed at the sight.

"Back, daughter?" he called pleasantly.

"Yes."

"Your mother is wondering if you would like steak or
liver for dinner. Better tell her."

"Oh, it doesn't matter."

She hurried into her bedroom, threw down her hat
and gloves, and herself on the bed to rest silently, and
groaned in her soul. To think that it had all come to
this!—Never to see him any more!—To see only Barton,
and marry him and live in such a street, have four or
five children, forget all her youthful companionships—
and all to save her face before her parents, and her future. Why must it be? Should it be, really? She choked
and stifled. After a little time her mother, hearing her
come in, came to the door—thin, practical, affectionate, conventional.

"What's wrong, honey? Aren't you feeling well to-
night? Have you a headache? Let me feel."

Her thin cool fingers crept over her temples and hair.
She suggested something to eat or a headache powder
right away.

"I'm all right, mother. I'm just not feeling well now.
Don't bother. I'll get up soon. Please don't."

"Would you rather have liver or steak to-night, dear?"

"Oh, anything—nothing—please don't bother—steak
will do—anything"—if only she could get rid of her and
be at rest.

Her mother looked at her and shook her head sympa-
thetically, then retreated quietly, saying no more. Lying
so, she thought and thought—grinding, destroying
thoughts about the beauty of the past, the darkness of
the future—until able to endure them no longer she got
up and, looking distractedly out of the window into the
yard and the house next door, stared at her future
fixedly. What should she do? What should she really do?
There was Mrs. Kessel in her kitchen getting her dinner

as usual, just as her own mother was now, and Mr. Kessel out on the front porch in his shirt-sleeves reading the evening paper. Beyond was Mr. Pollard in his yard, cutting the grass. All along Bethune Street were such houses and such people—simple, commonplace souls all—clerks, managers, fairly successful craftsmen, like her father and Barton, excellent in their way but not like Arthur the beloved, the lost—and here was she, perforce, or by decision of necessity, soon to be one of them, in some such street as this no doubt, forever and—. For the moment it choked and stifled her.

She decided that she would not. No, no, no! There must be some other way—many ways. She did not have to do this unless she really wished to—would not—only—. Then going to the mirror she looked at her face and smoothed her hair.

"But what's the use?" she asked herself wearily and resignedly after a time. "Why should I cry? Why shouldn't I marry Barton? I don't amount to anything, anyhow. Arthur wouldn't have me. I wanted him, and I am compelled to take some one else—or no one—what difference does it really make who? My dreams are too high, that's all. I wanted Arthur, and he wouldn't have me. I don't want Barton, and he crawls at my feet. I'm a failure, that's what's the matter with me."

And then, turning up her sleeves and removing a fichu which stood out too prominently from her breast, she went into the kitchen and looking about for an apron, observed:

"Can't I help? Where's the tablecloth?" and finding it among napkins and silverware in a drawer in the adjoining room, proceeded to set the table.

—1918

FRANCINE PROSE
(B. 1947)

Born in Brooklyn, New York, Francine Prose was educated at Brooklyn Friends, a Quaker elementary and high school; Radcliffe College, where she received a B.A.; and at Harvard University, where she received an M.A. She has taught creative writing at the University of Arizona and at Warren Wilson College in Swannanoa, North Carolina. Her stories have appeared in *The New Yorker*, *Antaeus*, *Atlantic*, *Commentary*, *Ploughshares*, and the *Pushcart Prize Volume XI*. She was awarded the Jewish Book Council Award in 1973 and the MMLE Award from *Mademoiselle* in 1975. Among her works are the novels *Judah the Pious* (1973), *The Glorious Ones* (1974), *Marie Laveau* (1977), *Animal Magnetism* (1978), *Household Saints* (1981), *Hungry Hearts* (1983), *Bigfoot Dreams* (1986), *Primitive People* (1992), *Hunters and Gatherers* (1995), and *Guided Tours of Hell: Novellas* (1998). Her stories are collected in *Women and Children First* (1988) and *The Peaceable Kingdom* (1993).

Everyone Had a Lobster

EVERYONE had a lobster. This was a serious problem. Roy, the SoHo contractor who'd served as a kind of treasurer for the lobster dinner, took Valerie aside and said he was sorry it wasn't pasta or bouillabaisse, something stretchable. Valerie should have telephoned in advance, they would have bought a lobster for her. Valerie thought: Shut up. Her friend Suzanne—Roy's girlfriend, in fact—had specifically told her not to arrive till after dinner; she said Valerie should start being discreet about having lived in the summer house for six weeks without having paid any rent.

The others, a lawyer, two therapists, a cameraman, a painter, a contractor, and so forth—were splitting the rent of this mini-Versailles with its enormous restaurant kitchen, its *Citizen Kane* fireplace, its French doors fac-

ing on Block Island Sound. But no one seemed to mind
that Valerie didn't contribute. They found her entertaining. They were all around thirty and felt that they used
to know more people like her. They said she was right
out there, right on the edge, by which they meant she
had no income and was a bit manic, lean, a fearless
swimmer, she had a terrific tan. Besides, they only saw
her on weekends. They worked weeks and came out
Friday nights, everyone but Suzanne, who was on vacation from teaching high school and had sublet her place
in the city. Weekdays, the house had felt empty, so Suzanne had tracked down Valerie at her parents'. Valerie
came for a visit and stayed.

Valerie liked the house, the shore. And Suzanne was
her oldest friend. But by August some things about her
life here felt like a job, a receptionist's job, not the chilly
receptionists of the rich, but of those borderline businesses that hire you to be constantly cheery and up.
Once Valerie had had such a job, at a carpet whole-
saler's. Her boyfriend then often had speed, and she
would do just a little before going to work. She wouldn't
take speed now—it was so hard to get and terrible on
your teeth—but she'd found an African bark called kavakava you could buy at the health food store and chew
and get a noticeable buzz.

She needed it to stay up, especially after a day like
this, a whole boiling summer Saturday driving the Long
Island Expressway after Suzanne suggested she clear out
for the day, keep a low profile for once. Valerie had
planned to go to the city; the museums would be air-
conditioned and empty. But she didn't expect so much
traffic in that direction, stalled, overheated cars, thirty
miles of steam pouring out from under hoods, and her
chewing kavakava, so that finally she pulled off the road
and followed signs to a state park where she was the
only white person on the beach.

At first this was a little disconcerting: She gave the
groups of Puerto Rican guys a wide berth, but no one
seemed even to notice her, or pay any attention. It was
as if she wasn't just white, but transparent. The point
was, everyone was busy with their own good times. She
stayed there all day, and later stopped at a Chinese res-

taurant where she ordered a dish of day-glo orange sweet and sour pork she would have been embarrassed to eat in front of anyone she knew.

She was positive that the people at the summer house would be long finished with dinner, but she walked in to find the table elegantly set, each individual lobster leaking cloudy water onto its individual plate. At least twenty people were seated around the table and at least five or six of them called to Valerie—"Eat! There's steamers and corn!" Valerie said she'd eaten, relishing the memory of her sweet and sour pork. They would be horrified, or else mistake her pleasure in it for some interest in edible kitsch. They were all very serious about food, they planned elaborate menus, all shopped and cooked like some semipro catering crew. Suzanne and Valerie had always liked cooking and eating, but last week Suzanne told Valerie she was going to strangle the next person who said "radicchio."

As Valerie caught Suzanne's eye, it occurred to her that everyone was saying, "Eat! There's steamers and corn!" but no one was saying a word about lobster despite the humongous red ones sitting right there on their plates. Suzanne put her hands over her lobster, as if to protect it from Valerie, and Valerie knew she wasn't mad about her showing up too early.

Valerie was always telling Suzanne she was too paranoid about the other people in the house. Suzanne's problem was that she made the least money of anyone—though not little enough to seem brave, like Valerie—and that her boyfriend Roy made the most. Roy wore the three-piece suits, the ponytail and potbelly of a rich California dope lawyer. He was bisexual, he liked to talk about his leather-bar night life. Especially when someone new—someone innocent and shockable—was around, Roy could get pretty graphic. He said he didn't worry about AIDS, every six months he went to Rumania and had his blood changed. Sometimes he would say this right in front of Suzanne, and Valerie would thank God that she wasn't leading Suzanne's life.

Not that Valerie felt she was leading her own life, exactly. Lately she had the sense she was stuck in some prelife, some in-between life, waiting for her serious life to start. For now, all that mattered was keeping interested. Lobsters were very low on her interest list, but she had to focus on them for a while before she could make herself look at Nasir, who was way at the top of the list. Nasir waited till she looked at him, then cracked the claw off his lobster, held it out to her, and at the same time motioned toward the seat next to his.

At that table, that art director's gourmet dream of perfect red lobsters on perfect sea-green glass plates, Nasir's ripping into that lobster seemed really kind of primitive and nasty. But Nasir could get away with it because he was so beautiful and graceful, and was basically a nice guy. Also, Valerie noticed, he held the lobster body so the juice dripped on the plate.

Everyone got quiet and waited to see what Valerie would do. For weeks she and Nasir had circled each other; it gave the atmosphere an erotic charge and was part of what people found entertaining. Valerie would have liked to sit next to Nasir. She was so drawn to him it scared her. One problem was Nasir's girlfriend, Iris, sitting across from him. But that wasn't it, exactly. No one liked Iris, and Nasir cheated on her constantly; last winter he and Suzanne were involved for about two weeks.

Nasir was Pakistani, British-educated, with a terrible and romantic history of loved ones disappeared into Zia's jails. Unlike everyone else in the house, all of whom were their professions, Nasir shot commercials for a living but was actually something else—a Marxist who dreamed of making political documentaries. So he too was more like the people these people used to know, and maybe that was part of the kinship Valerie felt with him. Also, they shared a similar manic edge. He was the only one she could have taken to the state park, the only one who would have seen what she saw in that Cantonese restaurant extravaganza of red and gold.

The last commercial Nasir shot was for a manufacturer of remote control lamps. Last weekend, Nasir brought twenty lamps out to the house and put them around the living room, and they all took turns standing in the center of the pitch black room making twenty lights dance on and off with the remote control wand. Nasir was always surprising them, turning out to know card tricks, to play stride piano and an amazing game of soccer. He had very large brown eyes, and the power of his attention was such that now, as Valerie laughed and shrugged off his lobster offer, she was so adrenalinized and trembly she had to sit right down next to Suzanne.

Suzanne said, "You chicken." She was all for Valerie having a romance with Nasir—partly, Valerie suspected, because then the responsibility for Valerie's continued presence would no longer be just Suzanne's. Last week, when they were alone in the house, Suzanne told Valerie that she and Nasir would be good together, they both had great bone structure. It was something a fifteen-year-old would say, but Valerie couldn't help asking, "Really?" or being embarrassed by how happy it made her.

Based on her own little fling with Nasir, Suzanne has warned Valerie not to expect too much, so Valerie could hardly tell her that what held her back, what kept her from even taking a lobster claw she might have liked, was that she expected the *world,* she had a sense that what happened with her and Nasir could be serious. She could imagine a life with Nasir, or anyway, time enough to find out who he was.

Dutifully, Suzanne asked if Valerie wanted a bite of her lobster, and Valerie said no, she didn't want to spoil her high, and showed Suzanne her little plastic bag of kavakava. Suzanne made a face. Up and down the table, they were talking about food. Roy was going on about lobsters, information he'd picked up from the man at the fish store, many incredibly boring facts about water temperature and seasons. Then Nasir said that when he first came to this country, he'd worked briefly at a restaurant with a fresh water tank in which there was one lobster no one would touch, a forty-eight-pounder named Captain Hank.

Someone asked Nasir where he'd been today, and he said, "I ran away with Valerie." Valerie was so shocked she laughed idiotically and said, "No, he didn't!" And where was Valerie? Valerie described the beach she'd been to as if she'd headed there on purpose, and when Roy asked how it was, she said, "Oh great, just like Carnival in Rio! You would have loved it, Roy!" Then she asked how their day at the beach had been, and after a funny silence, everyone said fine.

Valerie said, "What are you guys not telling me?" Suzanne whispered, "Hey, be quiet, okay?" But before anyone could answer, Valerie stood up—the kavakava was making her thirsty and unable to sit still. There was only wine and beer on the table; it would have been okay pharmacologically, but mixing alcohol and the root left a bad taste in her mouth. As she filled a glass at the kitchen sink, she heard someone behind her.

Nasir came close and said, "Wait till you see what's on today's tape. I'm gone a few hours and all hell breaks loose."

One custom of the house was that they videotaped the whole day—breakfast, grocery shopping, the beach— and watched it after dinner on TV. The only event left undocumented was dinner, which they were too busy eating to shoot. Mostly Nasir did the taping, the equipment was his, but he had shown everyone how to use it, and in his absence, Iris generally took over.

"Don't tell me—an orgy," said Valerie. Nasir just laughed, as did Valerie, thrilled by their apparent agreement that an orgy without the two of them seemed truly beneath contempt. "Then what?" she said. "A murder?"

"Believe me," said Nasir, "a murder would look healthy. Fun. Compared to what they've got taped, a murder would look like nursery school."

"Wow," said Valerie. But Nasir wouldn't say more. He said he hadn't seen it, only heard, and now it was hard for Valerie to insist, with ten people carrying in dirty lobster plates while ten more came in debating the best way to unmold crème caramel.

After dessert and the coffee, which took forever because the cappuccino machine could only make four cups at a time, they settled around the living room in front of the TV and turned off all the lights. Nearly everyone sat near the small screen, except for Valerie, who was chewing kavakava and pacing, and Nasir, standing and leaning against the back wall, his face lit and shadowed dramatically by the flickering TV.

The first shot was of people loading the van to go to the beach, and when the camera slipped and the picture swooped down, someone watching said, "Terrific, Iris."

The camera was riding shotgun. Gary, the lawyer, drove. When Valerie had first come to the house, Gary was clearly interested, but seemed like someone so used to women refusing him that she never even had to say no. Now he played to the video camera, giving his impression of a tour bus guide running down the sights. Gary shouldn't have tried, he was stiff at it, and faltered. Iris's camera caught every wrinkle of strain. Iris was a therapist, she used video in counseling, and somehow everyone she photographed looked as if they were toughing it out at some family crisis session. When Nasir did the taping, people looked more handsome and relaxed.

At the beach, Iris caught lots of unfortunate close-ups: squinty eyes, hairy backs, even some arm-skin flapping as shirts were pulled up over heads. Valerie thought: Trust Iris to show them the suddenly unmistakable signs of age. The camera made it obvious that Roy wouldn't take off his Hawaiian shirt, the audio blurred the drone of his voice as he sat on the sand holding court like some obese Polynesian king. Keeping its distance, the camera turned on a handful of people walking gingerly into the surf. Then Gary—not on the tape but in the room—said, "Oh, here's where I almost drowned."

"Here's *what*?" said Valerie, kneeling down at the back of the crowd around the TV.

"Almost drowned," Gary said, but just then the camera was occupied with a start-up soccer practice. Nasir had introduced the game to the house; they played often. Without him, the guys kicking the nerf ball around all looked a little adrift. Then a woman's voice—on the tape but off camera—said, "Hey, look out there!" and the lens turned toward the horizon where now in the water you could see a human form, moving oddly.

Another off-camera voice asked who that was, and someone else said, "I think it's Gary." A couple of seconds went by, then somebody asked, "You think he's in some kind of trouble?" Another pause, then somebody else said, "No." The camera turned back to the soccer players standing there lamely, like couples between dances, watching the ocean till someone said, "Are you sure he's all right?" Focus on Suzanne looking out at the water, then shrugging and saying, "I think he's okay," then going off to check something in the food hamper; the camera followed her the whole way, which took about a minute.

"Hey," said a voice on the audio track, "look at that!" The screen went black. Someone in the room said, "Jesus, Iris, this is where you blew it?" "Sand on the heads," Iris said. "I had to switch it on and off a few times."

When the image returned, the lens was scanning the water till it found that same form moving in place and two others speeding toward it. And now the camera zoomed in on two guys grabbing Gary and dragging him in toward the shore. This took a long time, too; finally everyone was wrapping towels around a gagging, shaking Gary.

Gary, in the room, said, "Thank God for the Coast Guard."

"You almost died," said Valerie. "Gary almost died, you guys."

"All right, Valerie," said Roy. "We can't *all* be world-class swimmers."

"You sons of bitches," Gary said. Then he laughed.

Valerie said, "I can't believe this."

Someone close beside her said, "You'd better believe it." It was Nasir. Valerie grabbed his shoulder and pulled herself toward him and began to whisper in his ear, but it wasn't sexual, really, it was like talking into a disembodied ear, the only one that would listen to her as she went on whispering, a hot, slightly sandy whisper. The kavakava had begun to bum her mouth. She asked what was wrong with these people, how could Gary sit there and joke with these assholes who had almost let him drown, who were too selfish and lazy to even find out if he had been drowning, and maybe for a little while, at dinner, knew they'd done something wrong, but seeing it on video had freed them, had let them pretend it was just something else on TV.

Nasir didn't answer. Instead he very gently placed his hand on the back of Valerie's neck. Valerie felt slightly queasy with lust, felt literally slightly sick. The warmth of his hand drew everything to the back of her neck, but everything was confused—sex, anger, exhaustion, fear, the kavakava which suddenly tasted awful. She said, "Christ. I need air."

She went out onto the lawn which sloped down to the Sound. It was a clear night and in the distance she could make out the lights of Block Island. After a while she heard people outside, near the door, getting the mountain of wood needed to make a fire in that cavernous fireplace.

When they'd gone in, and smoke was coming from the chimney, she went to the woodpile and got the smallest pieces and began to stack them near the far end of the lawn. She made many trips, adding on branches which had fallen during a rainstorm last week and still lay around on the grass. When she had enough for a sizable bonfire, she sneaked back into the house. Everyone was watching the fireplace, or reruns of SCTV. She ducked into the kitchen and got newspapers and a bottle of brandy.

The fire flared up so fast she jumped back. It went up in two stages, first it rose to two feet, then to about fifteen feet and stayed there, burning. Valerie stood with her back to the house, as near to the fire as she could. The fire didn't seem hot enough; she kept hugging herself and shivering. She imagined people up at the house, looking out the windows, laughing, maybe even applauding Valerie's latest crazy stunt. Then they would go back to the TV, or the bigger, nearer fire of their own.

Valerie really did feel crazed as she began to pace, slinking back and forth by the fire, like something out of *Cat People*. She gazed into the flames, putting herself in a kind of a trance which it took her some time to snap out of when Nasir came up beside her. "Great fire," he said.

"Thanks," said Valerie.

Then he said, "Give them a break, okay? They're scared too. Are you one hundred percent certain that you would have jumped in and saved him?"

Valerie was ninety-nine percent certain that she would at least have made sure someone did. But Nasir's words made her stop and think about the group in the house, about the terrible power of politeness, the desire that things remain civilized and well-mannered, the awful paralysis of the grateful guest. She looked back at the house and thought: No one lives there, no one has stakes there. They're all one another's guests.

It made her treasure Nasir even more, for quieting that part of her which was usually so harsh and quick to condemn. She thought: With Nasir, she would be a better person. She looked up into his face. They began to kiss, sweetly at first, then harder. After a while Nasir tipped his head back and as Valerie kissed his neck, he said, in a husky voice, "What about Suzanne?"

"What about Suzanne?" said Valerie.

"You two are friends, right?" he said. "Good friends. You can get her to come out here . . . the three of us . . ."

Valerie said, "No way."

Nasir laughed and hugged her. "All right," he said. "It doesn't matter." He kissed her a couple more times. But really, it mattered a lot, it beamed like a laser straight to the part of her brain that governed desire. It cut that part right out. All Valerie could see was herself and Suzanne and Nasir, like some sleazy cameraman might see them, pale blond Suzanne, dark Valerie, Nasir darker still. It amazed her that what you'd hoped was the start of your life could turn out to be a scene in someone else's porno movie.

Nasir said, "Okay, later maybe," and straightened his clothes and walked back up to the house. Valerie just stood there. After a while she caught a whiff of smoke from the fire which reminded her of autumn, and she thought how often in fall she had driven along the edge of the forest, beside all the color, and imagined it would be even brighter inside, inside the woods and that beauty. So she would park and walk into the forest, but it was worse there, the light was wrong, you couldn't see far enough, it had been brighter from the road. Now she stared at the fire, at the changing shapes, and thought how the very worst moments of waiting for life to begin are better—much better—than knowing it already has.

—1988

CHARLOTTE PERKINS GILMAN

(1860–1935)

Divorced from her first husband, Charles Stetson, at the age of thirty, Charlotte Perkins Gilman moved to California, where she supported herself by lecturing on the status of women and on socialism, teaching school, running a boarding house, editing newspapers, and writing. Among her works on social and feminist issues are *Women and Economics* (1898), *Concerning Children* (1900), *Human Work* (1904), and *The Man-made World; or Our Androcentric Culture* (1911). Among her novels are *The Crux* (1911) and *What Diantha Did* (1912), as well as three feminist, Utopian works—*Moving the Mountain* (1911), *Herland* (1915), and *With Her in Ourland* (1916). *The Living of Charlotte Perkins Gilman*, her autobiography, was published in 1935. Terminally and painfully ill with cancer, she chose to end her life.

Mrs. Beazley's Deeds

MRS. William Beazley was crouching on the floor of her living room over the store in a most peculiar attitude. It was what a doctor would call the "knee-chest position"; and the woman's pale, dragged out appearance quite justified the idea.

She was as one scrubbing a floor and then laying her cheek to it, a rather undignified little pile of bones, albeit discreetly covered with stringy calico.

A hard voice from below suddenly called "Maria!" and when she jumped nervously, and hurried downstairs in answer, the cause of the position became apparent— she had been listening at a stove-pipe hole.

In the store sat Mr. Beazley, quite comfortable in his back-tilted chair, enjoying a leisurely pipe and as leisurely conversation with another smoking, back-tilting man, beside the empty stove.

"This lady wants some cotton elastic," said he; "you know where those dewdabs are better'n I do."

A customer, also in stringy calico, stood at the counter. Mrs. Beazley waited on her with the swift precision of long practice, and much friendliness besides, going with her to the wagon afterward, and standing there to chat, her thin little hand on the wheel as if to delay it.

"Maria!" called Mr. Beazley.

"Oh, good land!" said Mrs. Janeway, gathering up the reins.

"Well—good-bye, Mrs. Janeway—do come around when you can; I can't seem to get down to Rockwell."

"Maria!" She hurried in. "Ain't supper ready yet?" inquired Mr. Beazley.

"It'll be ready at six, same as it always is," she replied wearily, turning again to the door. But her friend had driven off and she went slowly upstairs.

Luella was there. Luella was only fourteen, but a big, courageous-looking girl, and prematurely wise from many maternal confidences. "Now you sit down and rest," she said. "I'll set the table and call Willie and everything. Baby's asleep all right."

Willie, shrilly summoned from the window, left his water wheel reluctantly and came in dripping and muddy.

"Never mind, mother," said Luella. "I'll fix him up in no time; supper's all ready."

"I can't eat a thing," said Mrs. Beazley, "I'm so worried!" She vibrated nervously in the wooden rocker by the small front window. Her thin hands gripped the arms; her mouth quivered—a soft little mouth that seemed to miss the smiles naturally belonging to it.

"It's another of them deeds!" she was saying over and over in her mind. "He'll do it. He's no right to do it, but he will; he always does. He don't care what I want— nor the children."

When the supper was over, Willie went to bed, and Luella minding the store and the baby, Mr. Beazley tipped back his chair and took to his toothpick. "I've got another deed for you to sign, Mrs. Beazley," said he. "Justice Fielden said he'd be along tonight some time, and we can fix it before him—save takin' it to town."

"What's it about?" she demanded. "I've signed away enough already. What you sellin' now?"

Mr. Beazley eyed her contemptuously. The protest that had no power of resistance won scant consideration from a man like him.

"It's a confounded foolish law," said he, meditatively. "What do women know about business, anyway! You just tell him you're perfectly willin' and under no compulsion and sign the paper—that's all you have to do!"

"You might as well tell me what you're doin'—I have to read the deed anyhow."

"Much you'll make out of readin' the deed," said he, with some dry amusement, "and Justice Fielden lookin' on and waitin' for you!"

"You're going to sell the Rockford lot—I know it!" said she. "How can you do it, William! The very last piece of what father left me!—and it's mine—you can't sell it—I won't sign!"

Mr. Beazley minded her outcry no more than he minded the squawking of a to-be beheaded hen.

"Seems to me you know a lot," he observed, eyeing her with shrewd scrutiny. Then without a word he rose to his lank height, went out to the woodshed and hunted about, returning with an old piece of tin. This he took upstairs with him, and a sound of hammering told Mrs. Beazley that one source of information was closed to her completely.

"You'd better not take that up, Mrs. Beazley," said he, returning. "It makes it drafty round your feet up there. I always wondered at them intuitions of yours—guess they wasn't so remarkable after all.

"Now before Mr. Fielden comes, seein' as you are so far on to this business, we may as well talk it out. I suppose you'll admit that you're a woman—and that you don't know anything about business, and that it's a man's place to take care of his family to the best of his ability."

"You just go ahead and say what you want to—you needn't wait for any admits from me! What I know is my father left me a lot o' land—left it to me—to take care of me and the children, and you've sold it all—in spite of me—but this one lot."

"We've sold it, Mrs. Beazley; you've signed the deeds."

"Yes, I know I have—you made me."

"Now, Mrs. Beazley! Haven't you always told Justice Fielden that you were under no compulsion?"

"O yes—I told him so—what's the use of fightin' over everything! But that house in Rockford is mine—where I was brought up—and I want to keep it for the children. If you'd only live there, William, I'd take boarders and be glad to—to keep the old home! and you could sell that water power—or lease it—"

Mr. Beazley's face darkened. "You're talking nonsense, Mrs. Beazley—and too much of it. 'Women are words and men are deeds' is a good sayin'. But what's more to the purpose is Bible sayin'—this fool law is a mere formality—you know the real law—'Wives submit yourselves to your husbands!'"

He lit his pipe and rose to go outside, adding, "Oh, by the way, here 'tis Friday night, and I clean forgot to tell you—there's a boarder comin' tomorrow."

"A boarder—for who?"

"For you, I guess—you'll see more of her than I shall, seein' as it's a woman."

"William Beazley! Have you gone and taken a boarder without even askin' me?" The little woman's hands shook with excitement. Her voice rose in a plaintive crescendo, with a helpless break at the end.

"Saves a lot of trouble, you see; now you'll have no time to worry over it; and yet you've got a day to put her room in order."

"Her room! What room? We've got no room for ourselves over this store. William—I won't have it! I can't—I haven't the strength!"

"Oh, nonsense, Mrs. Beazley! You've got nothin' to do but keep house for a small family—and tend the store now and then when I'm busy. As to room, give her Luella's, of course. She can sleep on the couch, and Willie can sleep in the attic. Why, Morris Whiting's wife has six boarders—down at Ordway's there's eight."

"Yes—and they are near dead, both of them women! It's little they get from their boarders! Just trouble and work and the insultin' manners of those city people—

and their husbands pocketing all the money. And now you expect me—in four rooms—to turn my children out of doors to take one—and a woman at that; more trouble'n three men! I won't, I tell you!"

Luella came in at this point and put a sympathetic arm around her. "Bert Fielden was in just now," she told her father. "He says his father had to go to the city, and won't be back for some time—left word for you about it."

"Oh, well," said Mr. Beazley philosophically, "a few days more or less won't make much difference, I guess. That bein' the case you better help your mother wash up and then go to bed, both of you," and he took himself off to lounge on the steps of the store, smoking serenely.

Next day at supper time the boarder came. Mr. Beazley met her at the station and brought her and her modest trunk back with him. He took occasion on the journey to inform the lady that one reason for his making the arrangement was that he thought his wife needed company—intelligent company of her own sex.

"She's nervous and notional and kinder dreads it, now it's all arranged," he said; "but I know she'll like you first rate."

He himself was most favorably impressed, for the woman was fairly young, undeniably good looking, and had a sensible, prompt friendliness that was most attractive.

The drive was quite a long one and slower than mere length accounted for, owing to the nature of rural roads in mountain districts; and Mr. Beazley found himself talking more freely than was his habit with strangers, and pointing out the attractive features of the place with fluency.

Miss Lawrence was observant, interested, appreciative.

"There ought to be good water power in that river," she suggested; "what a fine place for a mill. Why, there was a mill, wasn't there?"

"Yes," said he. "That place belonged to my wife's father. Her father had a mill there in the old times when we had tanneries and saw mills all along in this country. They've cut out most of the hemlock now."

"That's a pleasant looking house on it, too. Do you live there?"

"No—we live quite a piece beyond—up at Shade City. This is Rockwell we're going through. It's a growin' place—if the railroad ever gets in here as they talk about."

Mr. Beazley looked wise. He knew a good deal more about that railroad than was worth while mentioning to a woman. Meanwhile he speculated inwardly on his companion's probable standing and profession.

"She's Miss, all right, and no chicken," he said to himself, "but looks young enough, too. Can't have much money or she'd not be boardin' with us, up there. Schoolma'am, I guess."

"Find school teachin' pretty wearin'?" he hazarded.

"School teaching? Oh, there are harder professions than that," she replied lightly. "Do I look so tired?

"I have a friend in the girls' high school who gets very much exhausted by summer time," she pursued. "When I am tired I prefer the sea; but this year I wanted a perfectly quiet place—and I believe I've found one. Oh, how pretty it is!" she cried as they rounded a steep hill shoulder and skirted the river to their destination. Shade City was well named, in part at least, for it stood in a crack of the mountains and saw neither sunrise nor sunset.

The southern sun warmed it at midday, and the north wind cooled it well; there was hardly room for the river and the road; and the "City" consisted of five or six houses, a blacksmith shop and "the store," strung along the narrow banks.

But the little pass had its strategic value for a country trader, lying between wide mountain valleys and concentrating all their local traffic.

"Maria!" called Mr. Beazley. "Here's Miss Lawrence. I'll take her trunk up right now. Luella! Show Miss Lawrence where her room is! You can't miss it, Miss Lawrence—we haven't got so many."

Mrs. Beazley's welcome left much to be desired; Luella wore an air of subdued hostility, and Willie, caught by his father in unobserved derision, was cuffed and warned to behave or he'd be sorry.

But Miss Lawrence took no notice. She came down to supper simply dressed, fresh and cheerful. She talked gaily, approved the food, soon won Luella's interest, and captured Willie by a small mechanical puzzle she brought out of her pocket. Her hostess remained cold, however, and stood out for some days against the constant friendliness of her undesired guest.

"I'll take care of my own room," said Miss Lawrence. "I like to, and then I've so little to do here—and you have so much. What would I prefer to eat? Whatever you have—it's a change I'm after, you know—not just what I get at home."

After a little while Mrs. Beazley owned to a friend and customer that her boarder was "no more trouble than a man, and a sight more agreeable."

"What does she do all the time?" asked the visitor. "You've got no piazza."

"She ain't the piazza kind," answered Mrs. Beazley. "She's doing what they call nature study. She tramps off with an opera glass and a book—Willie likes to go with her, and she's tellin' him a lot about birds and plants and stones and things. She gets mushrooms, too—and cooks them herself—and eats them. Says they are better than meat and cheaper. I don't like to touch them myself, but it does save money."

In about a week Mrs. Beazley hauled down her flag and capitulated. In two she grew friendly—in three, confidential, and when she heard through Luella and Bert Fielden that his father would soon be back now—her burden of trouble overflowed—the over-hanging loss of her last bit of property.

"It's not only because it's our old place and I love it," she said; "and it's not only because it would be so much better for the children—though that's enough—but it would be better business to live there—and I can't make him see it!"

"He thinks he sees way beyond it, doesn't he?"

"Of course—but you know how men are! Oh, no, you don't; you're not married. He's all for buyin' and sellin' and makin' money, and I think half the time he loses and won't let me know."

"The store seems to be popular, doesn't it?"

"Not so much as it would be if he'd attend to it. But he won't stock up as he ought to—and he takes everything he can scrape and puts it into land—and then sells that and gets more. And he swaps horses, and buys up stuff at 'vandoos' and sells it again—he's always speculatin'. And he won't let me send Luella to school—nor Willie half the time—and now—but I've no business talkin' to you like this, Miss Lawrence!"

"If it's any relief to your mind, Mrs. Beazley, I wish you would. It is barely possible that I may be of some use. My father is in the real estate business and knows a good deal about these mountain lands."

"Well, it's no great story—I'm not complainin' of Mr. Beazley, understand—only about this property. It does seem as if it was mine—and I do hate to sign deeds—but he will sell it off!"

"Why do you let him, if you feel sure he is wrong!"

"Let him!—Oh, well you ain't married! Let him! Miss Lawrence, you don't know men!"

"But still, Mrs. Beazley, if you want to keep your property——"

"Oh, Miss Lawrence, you don't understand—here am I and here's the children, and none of us can get away, and if I don't do as he says I must, he takes it out of us—that's all. You can't do nothin' with a man like that—and him with the Bible on his side!"

Miss Lawrence meditated for some moments.

"Have you ever thought of leaving him?" she ventured.

"Oh, yes, I've thought of it; my sister's always wantin' me to. But I don't believe in divorce—and if I did, this is New York state and I couldn't get it."

"It's pretty hard on the children, isn't it?"

"That's what I can't get reconciled to. I've had five children, Miss Lawrence. My oldest boy went off when he was only twelve, he couldn't stand his father—he used to punish him so—seems as if he did it to make me give in. So he never had proper schoolin' and can't earn much—he's fifteen now—I don't hear from him very often, and he never was very strong." Mrs. Beazley's eyes filled. "He hates the city, too, and he'd come back to me any day—if it wasn't for his father."

"You had five, you say?"

"Yes—there was a baby between Willie and this one—but it died. We're so far from a doctor, and he wouldn't hitch up—said it was all my nonsense till it was too late: And this baby's delicate—just the way he was!" The tears ran down now, but the faded little woman wiped them off resignedly and went on.

"It's worse now for Luella. Luella's at an age when she oughtn't to be tendin' store the whole time—she ought to be at a good school. There's too many young fellows hangin' around here already. Luella's large for her age, and pretty. I was good lookin' when I was Luella's age, Miss Lawrence, and I got married not much later—girls don't know nothin'!"

Miss Lawrence studied her unhappy little face with attention.

"How old should you think I was, Mrs. Beazley?"

Mrs. Beazley, struggling between politeness and keen observation, guessed twenty-seven.

"Ten years short," she answered cheerfully. "I was thirty-seven this very month."

"What!" cried the worn woman in calico. "You're older'n I am! I'm only thirty-two!"

"Yes, I'm a lot older, you see, and I'm going to presume on my age now, and on some business experience, and commit the unpardonable sin of interfering between man and wife—in the interest of the children. It seems to me, Mrs. Beazley, that you owe it them to make a stand.

"Think now—before it is too late. If you kept possession of this property in Rockwell, and had control of your share of what has been sold heretofore—could you live on it?"

"Why, I guess so. There's the house, my sister's in it now—she takes boarders and pays us rent—she thinks I get the money. We could make something that way."

"How much land is there?"

"There's six acres in all. There's the house lot right there in town, and the strip next to it down to the falls—we own the falls—both sides."

"Isn't that rather valuable? You could lease the water power, I should think."

"There was some talk of a 'lectric company takin' it—but it fell through. He wouldn't sell to them—said he'd sell nothin' to Sam Hunt—just because he was an old friend of mine. Sam keeps a good store down to Rockwell, and he was in that company—got it up, I think. Mr. Beazley was always jealous of Sam—and 'twan't me at all he wanted—'twas my sister."

"But, Mrs. Beazley, think. If you and your sister could keep house together you could make a home for the children, and your boy would come back to you. If you leased or sold the falls you could afford to send Luella away to school. Willie could go to school in town—the baby would do better down there where there is more sunlight, I'm sure—why do you not make a stand for the children's sake?"

Mrs. Beazley looked at her with a faint glimmer of hope. "If I only could," she said.

"Has Mr. Beazley any property of his own?" pursued Miss Lawrence.

"Property! He's got debts. Old ones and new ones. He was in debt when I married him—and he's made more."

"But the proceeds of these sales you tell me of?"

"Oh, he has some trick about that. He banks it in my name or something—so his creditors can't get it. He always gets ahead of everybody."

"M-m-m," said Miss Lawrence.

Mr. Beazley had a long ride before him the next day; he was to drive to Princeville for supplies.

An early breakfast was prepared and consumed, with much fault finding on his part—and he started off by six o'clock in a bad temper, unrestrained by the presence of Miss Lawrence, who had not come down.

"Whoa! Hold up!" he cried, stopping the horses with a spiteful yank as they had just settled into the collar.

"Maria!"

"Well—what you forgotten?"

"Forgot nothin'! I've remembered something; see that you're on hand tonight—don't go gallivantin' down to Rockwell or anywhere just because I'm off. Justice Fielden's comin' up and we've got to settle that business I told you about. See't you're here! Gid ap!"

The big wagon lumbered off across the bridge, around the corner, into the hidden wood road.

* * *

When Mr. Beazley returned the late dusk had fallen thickly in the narrow pass. He was angry at being late, for he had counted much on having this legal formality in his own house—where he could keep a sterner hand on his wife.

He was tired, too, and in a cruel temper, as the sweating horses showed.

"Willie!" he shouted. "Here you, Willie! Come and take the horses!" No hurrying, frightened child appeared.

"Maria!" he yelled. "Maria! Where's that young one! Luella! Maria!"

He clambered down, swearing under his breath; and rushed to the closed front door. It was locked.

"What in Halifax!" he muttered, shaking and banging vainly. Then he tried the side door—the back door—the woodshed—all were locked and the windows shut tight with sticks over them. His face darkened with anger.

"They've gone off—the whole of them—and I told her she'd got to be here tonight. Gone to Rockwell, of course, leavin' the store, too. We'll have a nice time when she comes back! That young one needs a lickin'."

He attended to the horses after a while, leaving the loaded wagon in the barn, and then broke a pane of glass in a kitchen window and let himself in.

A damp, clean, soapy smell greeted him. He struck matches and looked for a lamp. There was none. The room was absolutely empty. So were the closet, pantry and cellar. So were the four rooms upstairs and the attic. So was the store.

"Halifax!" said Mr. Beazley. He was thoroughly mystified now, and his rage died in bewilderment.

A knocking at the door called him.

It was not Justice Fielden, however, but Sam Hunt.

"I heard you brought up a load of goods today," said he easily; "and I thought you might like to sell 'em. I bought out the rest of the stuff this morning, and the store, and the good-will o' the business—and this lot isn't much by itself."

Mr. Beazley looked at him with a blackening countenance.

"You bought out this store, did you? I'd like to know who you bought it of!"

"Why, the owner, of course! Mrs. Beazley; paid cash on the nail, too. I've bought it, lock, stock and barrel— cows, horses, hens and cats. You don't own the wagon, even. As to your clothes—they're in that trunk yonder. However, keep your stuff—you'll need some capital," with this generous parting shot Mr. Hunt drove off.

Mr. Beazley retired to the barn. He had no wish to consult his neighbors for further knowledge.

Mrs. Beazley had gone to her sister, no doubt.

And she had dared to take this advantage of him—of the fact that the property stood in her name—Sam Hunt had put her up to it. He'd have the law on them—it was a conspiracy.

Then he went to sleep on the hay, muttering vengeance for the morrow.

The strange atmosphere awoke him early, and he breakfasted on some crackers from his wagon.

Then he grimly set forth on foot for the village, refusing offered lifts from the loads of grinning men who passed him. He presented himself at the door of his wife's house in the village at an early hour. Her sister opened it.

"Well," she said, holding the doorknob in her hand, "what do you want at this time in the morning?"

"I want my family," said he. "I'll have you know a man has some rights in his family at any rate."

"There's no family of yours in this house, William Beazley," said she grimly. "No, I'm not a liar—never had that reputation. You can come in and search the house if you please—after the boarders are up."

"Where is my wife?" he demanded.

"I don't know, thank goodness, and I don't think you'll find her very soon either," she added to herself, as he turned and marched off without further words.

In the course of the morning he presented himself at Justice Fielden's office.

"Gone off, has she?" inquired the Judge genially. "Or just gone visiting, I guess. Forgot to leave word."

"It's not only that, I want to know my rights in this

case, Judge. I've been to the bank—and she's drawn every cent. Every cent of my property."

"Wasn't it her property, Mr. Beazley?"

"Some of it was, and some of it wasn't. All I've made since we was married was in there, too. I've speculated quite a bit, you know, buying and selling—there was considerable money."

"How on earth could she get your money out of the bank?" asked Mr. Fielden.

"Why, it was in her name, of course; matter of business, you understand."

"Why, yes; I understand, I guess. Well, I don't see exactly what you can do about it, Mr. Beazley. You, technically gave her the property, you see, and she's taken it—that's all there is to it."

"She's sold out the store!" broke in Mr. Beazley, "all the stock, the fixtures—she couldn't do that, could she?"

"Appears as if she had, don't it? It was rather over-bearin' I do think, and you can bring suit for compensation for your services—you tended the store, of course?"

"If I knew where she was—" said Mr. Beazley slowly, with a grinding motion of his fingers. "But she's clean gone—and the children, too."

"If she remains away that constitutes desertion, of course," said the Judge briskly, "and your remedy is clear. You can get a separation—in due time. If you cared to live in another state long enough you could get a divorce—not in New York though. Being in New York, and not knowing where your wife is, I don't just see what you can do about it. Do you care to employ detectives?"

"No," said Mr. Beazley, "not yet."

Suddenly he started up.

"There's Miss Lawrence," said he. "She'll know something," and he darted out after her.

She came into the little office, calm, smiling, daintily arrayed.

"Do you know where my wife is, Miss Lawrence?" he demanded.

"Yes," she replied pleasantly.

"Well—where is she?"

"That I am not at liberty to tell you, Mr. Beazley. But

any communication you may wish to make to her you
can make through me. And I can attend to any immediate business. She has given me power of attorney."

Justice Fielden's small eyes were twinkling.

"You never knew you had a counsel learned in the
law at your place, did you? Miss Lawrence is the best
woman lawyer in New York, Mr. Beazley—just going
kinder incog, for a vacation."

"Are you at the bottom of all this deviltry?" said the
angry man, turning upon her fiercely.

"If you mean that Mrs. Beazley is acting under my
advice, yes. I found that she had larger business interests
than she supposed, and that they were not being well
managed. I happened to be informed as to real estate
values in this locality, and was able to help her. We
needed a good deal of ready money to take advantage
of our opportunity, and Mr. Hunt was willing to help us
out on the stock."

He set his teeth and looked at her with growing fury,
to which she paid no attention whatever.

"I advised Mrs. Beazley to take the children and go
away for a complete change and rest, and to leave me
to settle this matter. I was of the opinion that you and
I could make business arrangements more amicably
perhaps."

"What do you mean by business arrangements?" he
asked.

"We are prepared to make you this offer: If you will
sign the deed of separation I have here, agreeing to
waive all rights in the children and live out of the state,
we will give you five thousand dollars. In case you reap-
pear in the state you will be liable for debts, and for—
you remember that little matter of the wood lot deal?"

"That's a fair offer, I think," said Justice Fielden. "I
always told you that wood lot matter would get you into
trouble if your wife got on to it—and cared to push it.
I think you'd better take up with this proposition."

"What's she going to do—a woman alone? What are
the children going to do? A man can't give up his family
this way."

"You need not be at all concerned about that," she
answered. "Mrs. Beazley's plans are open and above-

board. She is going to enlarge her house and keep boarders. Her sister is to marry Mr. Hunt, as you doubtless know. The children are to be properly educated. There is nothing you need fear for your family."

"And how about me? I—if I could just talk to her?"

"That is exactly what I advised my client to avoid. She has gone to a quiet, pleasant place for this summer. She needs a long rest, and you and I can settle this little matter without any feeling, you see."

"What with summers in quiet places, and enlarging the house, you seem to have found a good deal more in that property than I did," said he with a sneer.

"That is not improbable," she replied sweetly. "Here is the agreement; take the offer or leave it."

"And if I don't take it? Then what'll you do?"

"Nothing. You may continue to live here if you insist—and pay your debts by your own exertions. You can get employment, no doubt, of your friends and neighbors."

Mr. Beazley looked out of the window. Quite a number of his friends and neighbors were gathered together around Hunt's store, and as each new arrival was told the story, they slapped their thighs and roared with laughter.

Judge Fielden, smiling dryly, threw up the sash.

"Clean as a whistle!" he heard Sturgis Black's strident voice. "Not as much as a cat to kick! Nobody to holler at! No young ones to lick! Nothin' whatsomever to eat! You should a heard him bangin' on the door!"

"And him a luggin' in that boarder just to spite her," crowed old Sam Wiley—"that was the last straw, I guess."

"Well, he was always an enterprisin' man," said Horace Johnson. "Better at specilatin' with his wife's property than workin' with his hands. Guess he'll have to hunt a job now, though."

"He ain't likely to git one in a hurry—not in this county—unless Sam Hunt'll take him in." Wiley yelled again at this.

"Have you got that deed drawn up?" said Mr. Beazley harshly—"I'll sign."

—1916

J. F. POWERS
(B. 1917)

In 1943, *Accent* published "Lions, Harts, Leaping Does," a short story which Powers had written while working in a Chicago bookstore. Selected for the volume *O. Henry Prize Stories* the following year, the story brought its author national recognition. Prior to this success, Powers, who went to work in the middle of the Depression, was employed as a department store clerk, door-to-door insurance salesman, and chauffeur. A graduate of Quincy College Academy, he has taught courses in writing at St. John's University in Collegeville, Minnesota, Marquette University, the University of Michigan, and Smith College. He has received Guggenheim and Rockefeller-*Kenyon Review* fellowships, and was awarded the National Book Award for his first novel, *Morte d'Urban*, in 1963. *Prince of Darkness and Other Stories* (1947), *The Presence of Grace* (1956), and *Look How the Fish Live* (1975) are collections of his stories.

Blue Island

ON the day the Daviccis moved into their house, Ethel was visited by a Welcome Wagon hostess bearing small gifts from local merchants, but after that by nobody for three weeks, only Ralph's relatives and door-to-door salesmen. And then Mrs. Hancock came smiling. They sat on the matching green chairs which glinted with threads of what appeared to be gold. In the picture window, the overstimulated plants grew wild in pots.

Mrs. Hancock had guessed right about Ethel and Ralph, that they were newlyweds. "Am I right in thinking you're of Swedish descent, Mrs. Davicky? You, I mean?"

Ethel smiled, as if taking a compliment, and said nothing.

"I only ask because so many people in the neighborhood are. I'm not, myself," said Mrs. Hancock. She was unnaturally pink, with tinted blue hair. Her own sharp-looking teeth were transparent at the tips. "But you're so fair."

"My maiden name was Taylor," Ethel said. It was, and it wasn't—it was the name she'd got at the orphanage. Wanting a cigarette, she pushed the silver box on the coffee table toward Mrs. Hancock.

Mrs. Hancock used one of her purple claws to pry up the first cigarette from the top layer. "A good old American name like mine."

She was making too much of it, Ethel thought, and wondered about Mrs. Hancock's maiden name.

"Is your husband in business, Mrs. Davicky?"

"Yes, he is." Ethel put the lighter—a simple column of silver, the mate to the box—to Mrs. Hancock's cigarette and then to her own.

"Not here in Blue Island?"

"No." From here on, it could be difficult. Ralph was afraid that people in the neighborhood would disapprove of his business. "In Minneapolis." The Mohawk Inn, where Ethel had worked as a waitress, was first-class—thick steaks, dark lights, an electric organ—but Ralph's other places, for which his brothers were listed as the owners, were cut-rate bars on or near Washington Avenue. "He's a distributor," Ethel said, heading her off. "Non-alcoholic beverages mostly." It was true. Ralph had taken over his family's wholesale wine business, never much in Minneapolis, and got it to pay by converting to soft drinks.

Mrs. Hancock was noticing the two paintings which, because of their size and the lowness of the ceiling, hung two feet from the floor, but she didn't comment on them. "Lovely, lovely," she said, referring to the driftwood lamp in the picture window. A faraway noise came from her stomach. She raised her voice. "But you've been lonely, haven't you? I could see it when I came in. It's this neighborhood."

"It's very nice," said Ethel quickly. Maybe Mrs. Hancock was at war with the neighbors, looking for an ally.

"I suppose you know Mrs. Nilgren," said Mrs. Hancock, nodding to the left.

"No, but I've seen her. Once she waved."

"She's nice. Tied down with children, though." Mrs. Hancock nodded to the right. "How about old Mrs. Mann?"

"I don't think anybody's there now."

"The Manns are away! California. So you don't know anybody yet?"

"No."

"I'm surprised you haven't met some of them at the Cashway."

"I never go there," Ethel said. "Ralph—that's my husband—he wants me to trade at the home-owned stores."

"Oh?" Mrs. Hancock's stomach cut loose again. "I didn't know people still felt that way." Mrs. Hancock looked down the street, in the direction of the little corner store. "Do they do much business?"

"No," said Ethel. The old couple who ran it were suspicious of her, she thought, for buying so much from them. The worst of it was that Ralph had told her to open a charge account, and she hadn't, and she never knew when he'd stop there and try to use it. There was a sign up in the store that said: In God We Trust—All Others Pay Cash.

"I'll bet that's it," Mrs. Hancock was saying. "I'm afraid people are pretty clannish around here—and the Wagners have so many friends. They live one-two-three-five houses down." Mrs. Hancock had been counting the houses across the street. "Mr. Wagner's the manager of the Cashway."

Ethel was holding her breath.

"I'm afraid so," said Mrs. Hancock.

Ethel sighed. It was Ralph's fault. She'd always wanted to trade at the Cashway.

Mrs. Hancock threw back her head, inhaling, and her eyelids like a doll's, came down. "I'm afraid it's your move, Mrs. Davicky."

Ethel didn't feel that it was her move at all and must have shown it.

Mrs. Hancock sounded impatient. "Invite 'em in. Have 'em in for a morning coffee."

"I couldn't do that," Ethel said. "I've never been to a coffee." She'd only read about coffees in the women's magazines to which Ralph had subscribed for her. "I wouldn't know what to do."

"Nothing to it. Rolls, coffee, and come as you are. Of course nobody really does, not really." Mrs. Hancock's stomach began again. "Oh, shut up," she said to it. "I've just come from one too many." Mrs. Hancock made a face, showing Ethel a brown mohair tongue. She laughed at Ethel. "Cheer up. It wasn't in this neighborhood."

Ethel felt better. "I'll certainly think about it," she said.

Mrs. Hancock rose, smiling, and went over to the telephone. "You'll do it right now," she said, as though being an older woman entitled her to talk that way to Ethel. "They're probably dying to get inside this lovely house."

After a moment, Ethel, who was already on her feet, having thought that Mrs. Hancock was leaving, went over and sat down to telephone. In the wall mirror she saw how she must appear to Mrs. Hancock. When the doorbell had rung, she'd been in too much of a hurry to see who it was to do anything about her lips and hair. "Will they know who I am?"

"Of course." Mrs. Hancock squatted on the white leather hassock with the phone book. "And you don't have to say I'm coming. Oh, I'll come. I'll be more than happy to. You don't need me, though. All you need is confidence."

And Mrs. Hancock was right. Ethel called eight neighbors, and six could come on Wednesday morning, which Mrs. Hancock had thought would be the best time for her. Two of the six even sounded anxious to meet Ethel, and, surprisingly, Mrs. Wagner was one of these.

"You did it all yourself," said Mrs. Hancock.

"With your help," said Ethel, feeling indebted to Mrs. Hancock, intimately so. It was as if they'd cleaned the house together.

They were saying good-by on the front stoop when Ralph rolled into the driveway. Ordinarily at noon he parked just outside the garage, but that day he drove in—without acknowledging them in any way. "Mr. Daveechee," Ethel commented. For Mrs. Hancock, after listening to Ethel pronounce her name for all the neighbors, was still saying "Davicky."

Mrs. Hancock stayed long enough to get the idea that Ralph wasn't going to show himself. She went down the front walk saying, " 'Bye now."

While Mrs. Hancock was getting into her car, which seemed a little old for the neighborhood, Ralph came out of the garage.

Mrs. Hancock waved and nodded—which, Ethel guessed, was for Ralph's benefit, the best Mrs. Hancock could do to introduce herself at the distance. She drove off. Too late, Ralph's hand moved up to wave. He stared after Mrs. Hancock's moving car with a look that just didn't belong to him, Ethel thought, a look that she hadn't seen on his face until they moved out to Blue Island.

During lunch, Ethel tried to reproduce her conversation with Mrs. Hancock, but she couldn't tell Ralph enough. He wanted to know the neighbors' names, and she could recall the names of only three. Mrs. Wagner, one of them, was very popular in the neighborhood, and her husband . . .

"You go to the Cashway then. Some of 'em sounded all right, huh?"

"Ralph, they all sounded all right, real friendly. The man next door sells insurance. Mr. Nilgren."

Ethel remembered that one of the husbands was a lawyer and told Ralph that. He left the table. A few minutes later Ethel heard him driving away.

It had been a mistake to mention the lawyer to Ralph. It had made him think of the shooting they'd had at the Bow Wow, one of the joints. There had been a mix-up, and Ralph's home address had appeared in the back pages of one of the papers when the shooting was no longer news. Ethel doubted that the neighbors had seen the little item. Ralph might be right about the lawyer, though, who would probably have to keep up with everything like that.

Ralph wouldn't have worried so much about such a little thing in the old days. He was different now. It was hard to get him to smile. Ethel could remember how he

would damn the Swedes for slapping higher and higher
taxes on liquor and tobacco, but now, when she pointed
out a letter some joker had written to the paper suggesting a tax on coffee, or when she showed him the
picture of the wife of the Minnesota senator—the fearless one—christening an ore boat with a bottle of milk,
which certainly should've given Ralph a laugh, he was
silent.

It just made Ethel sick to see him at the windows,
watching Mr. Nilgren, a sandy-haired, dim-looking man
who wore plaid shirts and a red cap in the yard. Mr.
Nilgren would be raking out his hedge, or wiring up the
skinny little trees, or washing his car if it was Sunday
morning, and there Ralph would be, behind a drape.
One warm day Ethel had seen Mr. Nilgren in the yard
with a golf club, and had said, "He should get some of
those little balls that don't go anywhere." It had been
painful to see Ralph then. She could almost *hear* him
thinking. He would get some of those balls and give
them to Mr. Nilgren as a present. No, it would look
funny if he did. Then he got that sick look that seemed
to come from wanting to do a favor for someone who
might not let him do it.

A couple of days later Ethel learned that Ralph had
gone to an indoor driving range to take golf lessons. He
came home happy, with a club he was supposed to swing
in his spare time. He'd made a friend, too, another beginner. They were going to have the same schedule and
be measured for clubs. During his second lesson, however, he quit. Ethel wasn't surprised, for Ralph, though
strong, was awkward. She was better than he was with
a hammer and nails, and he mutilated the heads of
screws. When he went back the second time, it must
have been too much for him, finding out he wasn't any
better, after carrying the club around the house for three
days. Ethel asked about the other beginner, and at first
Ralph acted as though she'd made him up, and then he
hotly rejected the word "friend," which she'd used. Finally he said, "If you ask me, that bastard's played
before!"

That was just like him. At the coffee, Ethel planned
to ask the women to come over soon with their hus-

bands, but she was afraid some of the husbands wouldn't
take to Ralph. Probably he could buy insurance from
Mr. Nilgren. He would want to do something for the
ones who weren't selling anything, though—if there were
any like that—and they might misunderstand Ralph. He
was used to buying the drinks. He should relax and take
the neighbors as they came. Or move.

She didn't know why they were there anyway. It was
funny. After they were married, before they left on their
honeymoon, Ralph had driven her out to Blue Island
and walked her through the house. That was all there
was to it. Sometimes she wondered if he'd won the
house at cards. She didn't know why they were there
when they could just as well be living at Minnetonka or
White Bear, where they could keep a launch like the
one they'd hired in Florida—and where the houses were
far apart and neighbors wouldn't matter so much. What
were they waiting for? Some of the things they owned,
she knew, were for later. They didn't need sterling for
eighteen in Blue Island. And the two big pictures were
definitely for later. She didn't know what Ralph liked
about his picture, which was of an Indian who looked
all in sitting on a horse that looked all in, but he had
gone to the trouble of ordering it from a regular art
store. Hers was more cheerful, the palace of the Doge
of Venice, Italy. Ralph hadn't wanted her to have it at
first. He was really down on anything foreign. (There
were never any Italian dishes on the menu at the Mohawk.) But she believed he liked her for wanting that
picture, for having a weakness for things Italian, for
him—and even for his father and mother, whom he was
always sorry to see and hadn't invited to the house.
When they came anyway, with his brothers, their wives
and children (and wine, which Ralph wouldn't touch),
Ralph was in and out, upstairs and down, never long in
the same room with them, never encouraging them to
stay when they started to leave. They called him "Rock"
or "Rocky," but Ralph didn't always answer to that. To
one of the little boys who had followed him down into
the basement, Ethel had heard him growl, "The name's
Ralph"—that to a nine-year-old. His family must have
noticed the change in Ralph, but they were wrong if

they blamed her, just because she was a little young for
him, a blonde, and not a Catholic—not that Ralph went
to church. In fact, she thought Ralph would be better
off with his family for his friends, instead of counting so
much on the neighbors. She liked Ralph's family and
enjoyed having them in the house.

And if Ralph's family hadn't come around, the neighbors might even think they weren't properly married,
that they had a love nest going there. Ethel didn't blame
the neighbors for being suspicious of her and Ralph. Mr.
Nilgren in his shirt and cap that did nothing for him, he
belonged there, but not Ralph, so dark, with his dark
blue suits, pearl-gray hats, white jacquard shirts—and
with her, with her looks and platinum hair. She tried to
dress down, to look like an older woman, when she went
out. The biggest thing in their favor, but it wasn't noticeable yet, was the fact that she was pregnant.

Sometimes she thought Ralph must be worrying about
the baby—as she was—about the kind of life a little kid
would have in a neighborhood where his father and
mother didn't know anybody. There were two pre-school
children at the Nilgrens'. Would they play with the Davicci kid? Ethel didn't ever want to see that sick look
of Ralph's on a child of hers.

That afternoon two men in white overalls arrived from
Minneapolis in a white truck and washed the windows
inside and out, including the basement and garage.
Ralph had sent them. Ethel sat in the dining room and
polished silver to the music of *Carmen* on records. She
played whole operas when Ralph wasn't home.

In bed that night Ralph made her run through the
neighbors again. Seven for sure, counting Mrs. Hancock.
"Is that all?" Ethel said she was going to call the neighbor who hadn't been home. "When?" When she got the
number from Mrs. Hancock. "When's that?" When Mrs.
Hancock phoned, if she phoned . . . And that was where
Ralph believed Ethel had really fallen down. She didn't
have Mrs. Hancock's number—or address—and there
wasn't a Hancock listed for Blue Island in the phone
book. "How about next door?" Mrs. Nilgren was still
coming. "The other side?" The Manns were still away,

in California, and Ralph knew it. "They might come
back. Ever think of that? You don't wanna leave them
out." *Them,* he'd said, showing Ethel what was expected
of her. He wanted those husbands. Ethel promised to
watch for the return of the Manns. "They could come
home in the night." Ethel reminded Ralph that a person
in her condition needed a lot of sleep, and Ralph left
her alone then.

Before Ralph was up the next morning, Ethel started
to clean the house. Ralph was afraid the house cleaning
wouldn't be done right (*he* spoke of her condition) and
wanted to get another crew of professionals out from
Minneapolis. Ethel said it wouldn't look good. She said
the neighbors expected them to do their own house
cleaning—*and window washing.* Ralph shut up.

When he came home for lunch, Ethel was able to say
that Mrs. Hancock had called and that the neighbor who
hadn't been home could come to the coffee. Ethel had
talked to her, and she had sounded very friendly. "That's
three of 'em, huh?" Ethel was tired of that one, but told
him they'd *all* sounded friendly to her. "Mrs. Hancock
okay?" Mrs. Hancock was okay. More than happy to be
coming. Ralph asked if Ethel had got Mrs. Hancock's
phone number and address. No. "Why not?" Mrs. Hancock would be there in the morning. That was why—
and Ralph should get a hold on himself.

In the afternoon, after he was gone, Ethel put on one
of her new conservative dresses and took the bus to
Minneapolis to buy some Swedish pastry. She wanted
something better than she could buy in Blue Island. In
the window of the store where they'd bought Ralph's
Indian, there were some little miniatures, lovely New
England snow scenes. She hesitated to go in when she
saw the sissy clerk was on duty again. He had made
Ralph sore, asking how he'd like to have the Indian
framed in birch bark. The Mohawk was plastered with
birch bark, and Ralph thought the sissy recognized him
and was trying to be funny. "This is going into my
home!" Ralph had said, and ordered the gold frame
costing six times as much as the Indian. However, he'd
taken the sissy's advice about having a light put on it.
Ethel hesitated, but she went in. In his way, the sissy

was very nice, and Ethel went home with five little Old
English prints. When she'd asked about the pictures in
the window, the New England ones, calling them "landscapes," he'd said "snowscapes" and looked disgusted,
as if they weren't what she should want.

When she got home, she hung the prints over the sofa
where there was a blank space, and they looked fine in
their shiny black frames. She didn't say anything to
Ralph, hoping he'd notice them, but he didn't until after
supper. "Hey, what *is* this?" he said. He bounced off
the sofa, confronting her.

"Ralph, they're cute!"

"Not in my home!"

"Ralph, they're humorous!" The clerk had called
them that. Ralph called them drunks and whores. He
had Ethel feeling ashamed of herself. It was hard to
believe that she could have felt they were just fat and
funny and just what their living room needed, as the
clerk had said. Ralph took them down. "Man or woman
sell 'em to you?" Ethel, seeing what he had in mind,
knew she couldn't tell him where she'd got them. She
lied. "I was in Dayton's . . ."

"A woman—all right, then *you* can take 'em back!"

She was scared. Something like that was enough to
make Ralph regret *marrying* her—and to remind her
again that she couldn't have made him. If there had been
a showdown between them, he would've learned about
her first pregnancy. It would've been easy for a lawyer
to find out about that. She'd listened to an old doctor
who'd told her to go ahead and have it, that she'd love
her little baby, who hadn't lived, but there would be a
record anyway. She wasn't sorry about going to a regular
hospital to have it, though it made it harder for her now,
having that record. She'd done what she could for the
baby. She hated to think of the whole thing, but when
she did, as she did that evening, she knew she'd done
her best.

It might have been a bad evening for her, with Ralph
brooding on her faults, if a boy hadn't come to the door
selling chances on a raffle. Ralph bought all the boy had,
over five dollars' worth, and asked where he lived in the
neighborhood. "I live in Minneapolis."

"Huh? Whatcha doin' way out here then?" The boy said it was easier to sell chances out there. Ethel, who had been doing the dishes, returned to the sink before Ralph could see her. He went back to his *Reader's Digest,* and she slipped off to bed, early, hoping his mind would be occupied with the boy if she kept out of sight.

He came to bed after the ten o'clock news. "You awake?" Ethel, awake, but afraid he wanted to talk neighbors, moaned remotely. "If anybody comes to the door sellin' anything, make sure it's somebody local."

In the morning, Ralph checked over the silver and china laid out in the dining room and worried over the pastry. "Fresh?" Fresh! She'd put it in the deep freeze right away and it hadn't even thawed out yet. "Is that *all*?" That was all, and it was more than enough. She certainly didn't need a whole quart of whipping cream. "Want me to call up for something to go with this?" No. "Turkey or a ham? I maybe got time to go myself if I go right now." He carried on like that until ten o'clock, when she got rid of him, saying, "You wouldn't want to be the only man, Ralph."

Then she was on her own, wishing Mrs. Hancock would come early and see her through the first minutes.

But Mrs. Wagner was the first to arrive. After that, the neighbors seemed to ring the bell at regular intervals. Ethel met them at the door, hung their coats in the hall closet, returning each time to Mrs. Wagner in the kitchen. They were all very nice, but Mrs. Wagner was the nicest.

"Now let's just let everything be," she said after they'd arranged the food in the dining room. "Let's go in and meet your friends."

They found the neighbors standing before the two pictures. Ethel snapped on the spotlights. She heard little cries of pleasure all around.

"Heirlooms!"

"Is Mr. Davitchy a collector?"

"Just likes good things, huh?"

"I just love this lamp."

"I just *stare* at it when I go by."

"So do I."

Ethel, looking at her driftwood lamp, her plants, and beyond, stood in a haze of pleasure. Earlier, when she was giving her attention to Mrs. Nilgren (who was telling about the trouble "Carl" had with his trees), Ethel had seen Ralph's car cruise by, she thought, and now again, but this time there was no doubt of it. She recognized the rather old one parked in front as Mrs. Hancock's, but where was Mrs. Hancock?

"Hello, everybody!"

Mrs. Hancock had let herself in, and was hanging up her coat.

Ethel disappeared into the kitchen. She carried the coffee-pot, which had been on *low,* into the dining room, where they were supposed to come and help themselves. She stood by the pot, nervous, ready to pour, hoping that someone would look in and see that she was ready, but no one did.

She went to see what they were doing. They were still sitting down, listening to Mrs. Hancock. She'd had trouble with her car. That was why she was late. She saw Ethel. "I can see you want to get started," she said, rising. "So do I."

Ethel returned to the dining room and stood by the coffee-pot.

Mrs. Hancock came first. "Starved," she said. She carried off her coffee, roll, and two of the little Swedish cookies, and Ethel heard her in the living room rallying the others.

They came then, quietly, and Ethel poured. When all had been served, she started another pot of coffee, and took her cup and a cookie—she wasn't hungry—into the living room.

Mrs. Hancock, sitting on the hassock, had a bottle in her hand. On the rug around her were some brushes and one copper pan. "Ladies," she was saying, "now here's something new." Noticing Ethel, Mrs. Hancock picked up the pan. "How'd you like to have this for your kitchen? Here."

Ethel crossed the room. She carried the pan back to where she'd been standing.

"This is no ordinary polish," continued Mrs. Hancock, shaking the bottle vigorously. "This is what is known as liquefied ointment. It possesses rare medicinal properties. It renews wood. It gives you a base for polishing—something to shine that simply wasn't there before. There's nothing like it on the market—not in the polish field. It's a Shipshape product, and you all know what that means." Mrs. Hancock opened the bottle and dabbed at the air. "Note the handy applicator." Snatching a cloth from her lap, she rubbed the leg of the coffee table—"remove all foreign matter first"—and dabbed at the leg with the applicator. "This does for wood what liniment does for horses. It relaxes the grain, injects new life, *soothes* the wood. Well, how do you like it?" she called over to Ethel.

Ethel glanced down at the pan, forgotten in her hand.

"Pass it around," said Mrs. Hancock.

Ethel offered the pan to Mrs. Nilgren, who was nearest.

"I've seen it, thanks."

Ethel moved to the next neighbor.

"I've seen it."

Ethel moved on. "Mrs. Wagner, have you?"

"Many times"—with a smile.

Ethel looked back where she'd been standing before she started out with the pan—and went the other way, finally stepping into the hallway. There she saw a canvas duffel bag on the side of which was embossed a pennant flying the word SHIPSHAPE. And hearing Mrs. Hancock—"And this is new, girls. Can you all see from where you're sitting?"—Ethel began to move again. She kept right on going.

Upstairs, in the bedroom, lying down, she noticed the pan in her hand. She shook it off. It hit the headboard of the bed, denting the traditional mahogany, and came to rest in the satin furrow between Ralph's pillow and hers. Oh, God! In a minute, she'd have to get up and go down to them and do *something*—but then she heard the coat hangers banging back empty in the closet downstairs, and the front door opening and, finally, closing. There was a moment of perfect silence in the house before her sudden sob, then another moment before she heard someone coming, climbing the carpeted stairs.

Ethel foolishly thought it would be Mrs. Wagner, but of course it was Mrs. Hancock, after her pan.

She tiptoed into the room, adjusted the venetian blind, and seated herself lightly on the edge of the bed. "Don't think I don't know how you feel," she said. "Not that it shows yet. I wasn't *sure,* dear." She looked into Ethel's eyes, frightening her.

As though only changing positions, Ethel moved the hand that Mrs. Hancock was after.

"My ointment would fix that, restore the surface," said Mrs. Hancock, her finger searching the little wound in the headboard. She began to explain, gently—like someone with a terrible temper warming up: "When we first started having these little Shipshape parties, they didn't tell each other. They do now, oh, yes, or they would if I'd let them. I'm on to them. They're just in it for the mops now. You get one, you know, for having the party in your home. It's collapsible, ideal for the small home or travel. But the truth is you let me down! Why, when you left the room the way you did, you didn't give them any choice. Why, I don't think there's one of that crowd—with the exception of May Wagner—that isn't using one of my free mops! Why, they just walked out on me!"

Ethel, closing her eyes, saw Mrs. Hancock alone, on the hassock, with her products all around her.

"It's a lot of pan for the money," Mrs. Hancock was saying now. She reached over Ethel's body for it. "You'll love your little pan," she said, fondling it.

Ethel's eyes were resisting Mrs. Hancock, but her right hand betrayed her.

"Here?" Mrs. Hancock opened a drawer, took out a purse, and handed it over, saying, "Only $12.95."

Ethel found a five and a ten.

"You *do* want the ointment, don't you? The pan and the large bottle come to a little more than this, but it's not enough to worry about."

Mrs. Hancock got up, apparently to leave.

Ethel thought of something. "You do live in Blue Island, don't you?" Ralph would be sure to ask about that—if she had to tell him. And she would!

"Not any more, thank God."

Ethel nodded. She wasn't surprised.

Mrs. Hancock, at the door, peeked out—reminding Ethel of a bored visitor looking for a nurse who would tell her it was time to leave the patient. "You'll find your ointment and mop downstairs," she said. "I just know everything's going to be all right." Then she smiled and left.

When, toward noon, Ethel heard Ralph come into the driveway, she got out of bed, straightened the spread, and concealed the pan in the closet. She went to the window and gazed down upon the crown of his pearl-gray hat. He was carrying a big club of roses.

—1956

KATE BRAVERMAN

(B. 1950)

Born in Philadelphia and raised in Los Angeles, Kate Braverman received a B.A. from the University of California at Berkeley. She was a founding member of the Los Angeles Women's Building and the Venice Poetry Workshop. The California landscape is often of thematic significance in her writing, and one reviewer has asserted that "the Braverman voice has become one of L.A.'s most compelling." Her poetry, stories, and essays have appeared in numerous magazines, such as *American Short Fiction*, the *American Voice*, *Antaeus*, *Kenyon Review*, the *Paris Review*, *Quarterly West*, and *Story*. She has published three novels: *Lithium for Medea* (1979), *Palm Latitudes* (1988), and *Wonders of the West* (1993). *Squandering the Blue* (1990) and *Small Craft Warnings* (1998) are collections of her stories. Her poems are collected in *Milk Run* (1977), *Lullaby for Sinners* (1980), *Hurricane Warnings* (1987), and *Postcard from August* (1990).

Over the Hill

SHE lives on the side of a mountain above Sunset Boulevard in Beverly Hills. The hill rises in the backyard where Frank has built a gazebo. Small square slabs of stone, like the indented plaques on graves in the cemeteries of Los Angeles, form a path to the gazebo. The stones lead past the wooden fence dense with bougainvillea, past the herb garden with its basil and sage, past the circular cluster of rosebushes and the patch planted with annuals, then the stalks of canna and gladiolas and bird of paradise. And the orchids, of course, surrounding one side of the swimming pool.

Jessica sits in the gazebo in the late afternoon. The school bus has brought her children home. Maria is cooking dinner. Jessica waits for sunset as if it were a punctuation that should mean something. At such moments, the city is astonishing with detail. She can see to the south past the Baldwin Hills and the airport and farther, to some ghastly urban infestation one passes only by car when driving to Newport Beach or La Jolla. A place called City of Commerce or City of Industry or some incorporated slum that advertises legal gambling.

From her white wood-slat bench in the gazebo, Jessica can watch the sunset and then the lights of the city asserting themselves, and later, the constant wash of silver and red and green in the sky which are a sort of avant-grade choreography of planes and helicopters. The lights are tiered, they rise from the land and fall from the sky, as if in mute celebration.

"Think of the wildlife Ryan and Ashley have," Frank says. "That's an advantage."

Jessica considers this acre of hill with its iris and roses and borders of bougainvillea, its orange and lemon trees, its hedges of red-and-yellow hibiscus, its bird of paradise and yellow and red and magenta orchids. The gardener made Ashley an old-fashioned swing with rope and a wooden seat. It hangs from the avocado tree and sails out over the hill, over the square indented stones leading to the white wood gazebo. The graves in the cemetery where her father is buried are like these stones. It seems that the dead do not have markers that rise anymore. In this region, they have outlawed idolatry, even in its remote forms. It is near the millennium. We know nothing here will change. We are not waiting for our dead to rise. Even the cemeteries lie in isolated areas, at the end of freeways one has never before heard of. You leave your dead there and never return. You are not afraid of being haunted. The dead could not find you if they wanted to.

But what of the wildlife Frank always mentions? Jessica sits in the gazebo and thinks of the deer, coyotes, squirrels, raccoons, and rabbits that inhabit this acre of hill. Her son, Ryan, is nine. The gardener built a house for him in a tree, a kind of fort with nailed-together pine boards and old curtains in a permanently open window. Ryan has a BB gun and a slingshot. He shoots at anything that moves across the backyard, even cats and dogs belonging to the neighbors. Is his boyhood being enriched by the wildlife?

"Think of the color," Frank says.

She sits in the gazebo and considers the color. The sky is Kauai blue even in August. In the hills where she lives, in these Beverly Hills, the contours remain vivid and assured. These skies are not tainted by smog and the human residues that slope upward from cities. It might be a region in an elemental state of grace. Or a region where pollution has been completely banished, where there has been some complex accommodation. And the greens seem mysteriously illuminated, as if their essences had been somehow defined and freed.

"It's the green of money," Frank says. He is serious.

And the greens contain a kind of crispness, a moist clarity. This is a green you cannot intrude on. It is an absolute assertion. This is the climate that only money can buy. There is no vegetation too exotic or difficult. Here the Japanese and Mexican gardeners arrive at sunrise with bulbs from Australia, China, India, Madagascar, Kauai, and Peru. There should be lilies in the pools, she thinks, and peacocks and jaguars in the tall night grass. Or perhaps they already have this, closer to Sunset Boulevard, in the gated villas she drives past. Or perhaps near the top of Mulholland, where the Persians build their fortresses.

"You have no idea what things cost," Frank points out.

He gives her a computer printout that his accountant has devised. Lists of numbers for services, car insurance, health insurance, homeowners' insurance, gas and water and electricity, food, liquor, chauffeur, car payments, house repairs, school tuition, psychiatrist, swimming pool maintenance, tennis lessons, violin lessons, restaurants, airline and theater tickets, hairdresser, clothing, pediatrician, dentist, orthodontist. There are more numbers, three full pages of them, but Jessica has seen enough.

These numbers are not real, she knows this. Frank's accountant can make numbers appear or disappear. He's not a bookkeeper, Frank likes to say, he's a magician. Now you see it, now you don't. Her husband's accountant creates pages of numbers to substantiate Frank's transitory versions of reality. This is the way Frank's cities are peopled. These are the bridges, the aqueducts and clouds. These are the rituals where one bows to carved stones. These are the slow syllables released into darkness. These are the litanies, the way to bury and raise the dead. These are the creation myths and the cycles of destruction.

"You'll have to economize," Frank tells her. Then he says he won't pay for Westford Academy anymore, or Ashley's violin lessons or Ryan's karate classes. Her children will have to attend public schools. Frank's accountant will make the stocks and bonds disappear. He will make Frank's assets confused and ambiguous. Frank is an attorney. He knows how to go to court, what a judge and jury will find credible. Frank specializes in these matters, these unique parameters. And she will have to rent an apartment in an inferior part of the city where her neighbors will speak languages she does not want to know.

Sometimes Frank takes her to these apartments. They hire real-estate agents for this, usually women who look unhappy. These real-estate agents open the doors of apartments for them. They inspect these town houses and condominiums. They open closets and cabinets. They pull blinds and look where the view should be, but there is none. There is only an alley, a parking lot, or the terrace of the apartment across the courtyard. Always there is a carport with graffiti. And on the terrace, old boxes of diapers and shopping carts upended, a mattress with springs showing, parts of a bicycle, a container for plants, objects that are deprived of context and gutted. Why are these stained things on display? The real-estate agents, who seem to be women just awoken from terrible dreams, women with a fresh sense of small atrocities, offer nothing by way of explanation.

Sometimes Jessica and Frank take the keys. Then they go to these apartments and town houses and condominiums by themselves. They stand on brown carpet that smells somehow of insect repellent and sand, marginal educations and savage divorces, and some anonymous misery that might be random or cyclic or some unearthly confluence of both. They walk across the tiny rooms.

She would take only the children's beds and one sofa. There isn't space for more. She begins to feel feverish, breathless and trembling all at once. She thinks this is what malaria must be. We have a kind of emotional malaria now, all of us, poised near the millennium.

"Lie down," Frank says.

She stares at him. They are alone in the town house with the new brown carpet that already looks faded and dull, as if indicative of the sort of dreams one would have here, something inconsequential, intrinsically small, flawed, incapable of transcending itself. She is still staring at Frank, wondering if he realizes she is sick. Is this why he wants her to lie down? And where can she do this, these miniature rooms are empty.

"On the floor," Frank says. "Now."

She lies down on the floor. The ceiling seems to be composed of an immensity of tiny rocks like the surface of the moon. She thinks of the boulevard below, with its decades of balconies where women with their received secrets and tainted memories stand by windows in rain. Or sleep at last with a sense of the moon and the jungle and some ineluctable other. She closes her eyes.

"No. On your hands and knees," Frank says. He sounds annoyed. He has taken off his jacket. He is unbuttoning his shirt.

Later, in the bath, Jessica notices her elbows have been scraped. They are raw. The skin on her knees is red. She knows this injury is called a rug burn. This is not the first time this has happened.

"I don't think you could live in a place like that," Frank says at dinner. "Or could you?"

"No," she quickly agrees. "Of course not."

The maid, Maria, cleans the plates from the table. Ashley is playing a video game upstairs with her best friend, Tiffany. Ryan is spending the night with a friend on a yacht at the Marina. Frank has lit the fire in the den. She can smell wood burning. Frank tells Maria that they will have their brandy by the fire. She hears these instructions occurring across a confused and agitated distance that is inaccessible. She feels as if she is somehow under anesthesia.

Jessica sits on the brick ledge in front of the fireplace. Her body is a series of burns. There is the heat of the fire on her face, the burn of her scraped elbows and knees, and now the cognac in her chest and how she can feel the liquid in her legs and arms.

Outside, in the courtyard between the study windows and the side garden of roses and yellow canna, she can hear the rain fall. Soon it will be time to prepare for the holidays. There will be the shopping, of course, the baking, the wrapping, the decorating of the house and tree and grounds. There will be the matter of the menus, the wreaths, the Christmas linens and china. She will get a noble pine this year. And perhaps along the iron-slatted perimeter of gate she will have the gardener hang silver lights. Last year they were the only house with red-and-green lights. Everyone else on the street used just silver. We are becoming streamlined and closer to the stars, she thinks.

"Can you imagine Christmas in that apartment?" Frank asks. His voice contains wonder and contempt in equal measure.

She glances at Maria. They look into each other's eyes, startled. Maria leaves a silver tray on the mahogany coffee table in front of the sofa where Frank is sitting. There are grapes and strawberries in a crystal bowl. There is a plate with four types of white cheese. There is a larger glass plate with chocolates and raspberry cookies.

"Without a fireplace? Or a dining room?" Frank continues. He is arranging a plate with cheese and fruit and cookies. He hands this to her.

The apartments that Frank takes her to only have living rooms. The dining room has disappeared like the markers on graves. We give our dead indented slabs. We know they are not coming out of the ground. And we don't need dining rooms. We eat standing up in the kitchen or on a sofa in front of the television. A dining room implies a world where a family gathers and shares food. There are no families anymore, only women with children. Is that what one learns from the architecture? Is this how rooms speak?

But yes, she can imagine Christmas in the town house

with the brown carpet the color of all the subtle crimes of trapped people. It would rain. She would hang a wreath on the living-room door. She would hold Ashley's hand. She would leave the piano behind. These rooms cannot accommodate pianos. This is a world without musical instruments. In this region, people walk with radios on their heads. But she could still play Mozart on the stereo. Or perhaps she will not be able to afford a record player. But she would have a radio. She is certain of this. Ashley has a dozen radios. Ashley has underwater radios and radios inside stuffed raccoons and bears. She is almost positive Frank will allow the children to take their possessions.

They would have to leave behind the toys that wouldn't fit into a small apartment. She would be getting a two-bedroom apartment. Frank has explained this to her. Ashley and Ryan will have the bedrooms. She will sleep in the living room on a bed that opens from the sofa. And there won't be room for Ashley's dollhouses, for Ryan's electric trains, for Ashley's simulated kitchen with three-foot-high mock appliances, and the easel, the synthesizers, the twin stuffed polar bears with eyes that glow in the dark.

There are moments when she thinks she could divest herself of these things effortlessly, as if they had never been, all the opulent and sophisticated clutter. She could become smaller, less encumbered, a size appropriate to her new surroundings. She could become deceptive, like her circumstances. No one would know what she was thinking.

"You couldn't survive in that apartment. Just you and the children," Frank reminds her.

He is going to recite the separate elements that accumulate and by their density become the illusion of a fact. They are an empty weight. And he is going to tell her exactly what she cannot survive. There is the miniature ugliness, the cheap rugs with their aggrieved and ruined scent and all they imply, the windows with their squalid antiviews of terraces lined with offensive debris where exiled women memorize the textures of premature burial. There are the carports with the names of gangs written in spray paint, there is pavement and no gardens.

And her children in public schools where they are the minority and larger children who speak Spanish and Korean and Vietnamese would waylay them in these scars of southern California alleys. And she would have to wake at seven, even when she has had insomnia and not slept at all, that night or the night before. She will have to rise at seven and make their breakfasts and put their lunches into brown paper bags and drive them to the imposing and dangerous public school. Then she would return to the apartment and clean it, sweep and do the laundry, iron and shop, make the beds, fold her blankets into the hall closet, and transform her bed back into a sofa. She would be required to carry wash to and from a shared laundry facility where coins were necessary.

Jessica wonders how women do this and the other labor of stove and floor, of bathroom, toilet, and tile. How do they master the intricacies of so many surfaces? How is it possible to provide such services and also do conventional work, go to offices, remain the appropriate hours? What happens when your children are sick?

When Jessica reaches this particular juncture, when she imagines the feverish Ashley in an unadorned room in a stucco building ripped by the noise from radios and cars and words shouted in alien languages, Jessica reaches for a glass. She finishes the cognac. Frank pours her another.

"Think of summer there," Frank says. He is looking into her face, as if there was something he expected to find on the surface of her skin. "In the Valley? Without a pool? When it's eighty-five here it's a hundred and five there."

It was curious how the outlying areas were assaulted by the elements, how the act of a few miles of geography could produce such dramatic results. The Valley lay between them like the Mojave desert, vast and intractable.

It occurs to her that leaving Frank would be the psychological equivalent of crossing Donner Pass. If she could survive the leaving, the metaphorical mountains, the hardship of winter, the disease and death and cannibalism, if she could find the faith and intelligence to outwit this, she would be delivered. She would come to inhabit another region entirely. At such moments, she

envisions the San Fernando Valley as it once was, with
its unmolested acres of orange groves and grapefruit
trees where blue jays dived blind into hot nectar. Men
came there during the war and never left. They recognized there was no border to this valley, no rules to
this astonished terrain, with its citrus orchards, its vistas
without obstacles. Here the dead could be deposited at
the end of an off-ramp.

"I won't pay for Dr. Rivers," Frank tells her. "You
can't expect me to."

She has been seeing Dr. Rivers three days a week for
two and a half years. Dr. Rivers wants her to leave
Frank. He wants her to take an apartment in the Valley.

"Where in the Valley?" she asks.

"I don't know the Valley," Dr. Rivers says. He seems
pleased with himself. "I've never been there."

"You've never been there?" she repeats, stunned.
Until Frank began taking her to inspect condominiums,
she had rarely been to the Valley. Or over the hill.
That's how the real-estate agents describe it. Over the
hill.

"I'm from western Ohio," Dr. Rivers says.

"But you've lived here for years," she recognizes. His
attitude feeds her fear. She realizes that she hates him.

"I live on the Westside. My practice is on the Westside. My patients live on the Westside." Dr. Rivers
smiles. It is simple for him, where and how people live.

"When I move out, Frank won't pay for my treatment," she tells Dr. Rivers later that week.

"I think he'll pay," Dr. Rivers says. He is looking out
the window. The window faces the Hollywood Hills. On
the other side of the hills is the Valley.

Jessica stares at her psychiatrist. He is absolutely
wrong.

"What if Frank refuses?" she continues. "I won't be
able to afford coming here."

"Then you can't afford it," Dr. Rivers says. He has
picked up a pen. He taps it on the surface of the desk,
as if playing an invisible drum.

When she walks into the wind after the session, when
she looks at the cold gray slate of autumn sky, it seems
possible that she could divest herself of Dr. Rivers ef-

fortlessly. She could leave him behind with the piano, the toy dollhouses, the miniature kitchen set with plastic stove and refrigerator, the Ping Pong table, the indoor volleyball equipment, and all that takes up space and gives her nothing.

Now rain is falling. Soon it will be the holidays. She will buy a noble pine as she does every year. She will make Aunt Glenda's St. Louis brownies. She will buy her presents at Neiman-Marcus. Frank's secretary will provide her with a list of names and addresses and a budget. Later, Frank will ask her where she wants to go for her birthday. Her birthday is in January. He will recite the names of cities and resorts, Paris and London, Palm Springs and Hawaii. And she will say Kauai, as she does every year. We have swallows inside us, Jessica thinks suddenly. Our ideas are like walled missions. We return to them again and again, even when they feed us poison.

"Did I hurt you today?" Frank asks. "In the apartment?" He seems somehow hopeful.

Now, because she wants to deny and wound him, she shakes her head no.

"Let me see," Frank says. He is walking toward the fireplace where she sits on the brick ledge with her many concealed flames. He is reaching across the invisible Mojave Desert that stretches between them, wherever they are. He is touching her elbow with his lips.

"I have new movies," Frank whispers against her burned skin.

Jessica saw the bag in a corner of the den, the flagrantly yellow plastic bag from the video rental shop. Frank thinks she should enjoy these pornographic movies. He believes she would enjoy them if she simply let herself. He thinks she deliberately refuses to allow these images to bring her pleasure. He does not understand there is no arrangement of her personality which would allow her to find a sustaining impulse in these reels. These movies seem to have been shot in apartments similar to the ones she has been touring. She can almost smell the anonymous ruined brown carpeting. Beyond the curtained windows, Jessica thinks, are streets where we are always cold and know small atrocities by lamplight. Here the sea is remembered and the proportions of the heart are washed by thoughts of ancient places and orchids the color of silence. In these apartments young women are taken with force. There are lurid combinations. Women with burns on their elbows and knees.

"I saw Monty," Frank is telling her, his voice soft. "He came by the office."

Monty is Frank's drug connection. What Frank is really saying is that he has cocaine and pornographic movies. He thinks this is somehow an inducement for her. Frank is a divorce lawyer, after all. They have been married sixteen years. Frank thinks he knows the parameters of acceptable marital behavior. It's his specialty. He thinks this is how people live.

She closes her eyes. The rain is falling harder now. The windowpanes radiate a chill. It is probably only a drizzle in the Valley, she thinks, or a light mist. She imagines this mist falling across the wide boulevards with their relentless rows of condominiums and their alleys of carports brutalized by graffiti, by trash, by stolen and abandoned shopping carts. The Valley is a vast plain stretching indefinitely to the feet of the barren and hallucinatory mountains. In this Valley lie the living graves of women at the millennium. It is a grid of town-house condominiums where women live alone or alone with children. Women who had nervous breakdowns but can no longer afford treatment. Children who leave behind their dollhouses and violin lessons to come to apartments where they do not speak the languages of their neighbors. They watch television in the long afternoons until their mothers return from work. When the children are sick, special arrangements are made. When she solves this equation, when she can understand what they do with the sick children, then she will be able to leave. Perhaps she could ask someone. The woman who does her manicure, perhaps. Or the clerk at the cleaners. Or even her maid. Maybe Maria knows.

She imagines that she is standing on a balcony of an apartment where she lives alone with her children. It is a moment when she knows there is only earth and silence and a trembling in crowds in all the ruined latitudes. And how we wake to sudden clarities and men with knives and mesas and years. How we know that we are simply bodies with hands, words, and blood in nights of impossible gatherings beneath jacaranda trees.

"Your knees?" Frank is repeating. "Are they scraped, too?" He is finished with her arms. He is standing. He is balanced like a baseball catcher in front of the fireplace. He is lifting her robe and studying her knees. He is bringing his face to her legs.

Now there is the rain falling. Now there are her clandestine flames. And how one day she is going to leave. She is certain. She will simply walk out in the morning, as if she were going to the gym or the florist or a medical appointment. She will drive over Mulholland instead, down into the enormous concrete mouth of the Valley. One day she will go over the hill. She will take her children and nothing else and this divestiture will free her. It will be like crossing Donner Pass. It will be the end of isolation and spiritual starvation. It will be what happens after a woman has been alone with prophecies of cancer and water and madness and savage inhabitations in the primitive country. It will be like returning in the last light, in the same transparencies where we long for boats and splendor. It will be like discovering that time and space are indeed a continuum. It will be like arriving in another century. It will be like finding God.

—1990

KATE CHOPIN
(1851–1904)

In 1879, Kate Chopin, her husband, Oscar, and five sons moved from New Orleans to Cloutierville, a small town in Louisiana where she gave birth to the last of her children, her daughter Lelia. Occupied with family concerns, she had never written a single word for publication, and her literary career, which was to begin when she was thirty-eight years old, was still a decade away. After the death of Oscar, she returned to her native St. Louis, and several years later, in 1889, two of her stories and a poem appeared. The following year, her first novel, *At Fault*, was published, and within a short period of time she had established herself as a short story writer of national reputation. Most of her stories were collected in two volumes, *Bayou Folk* (1894) and *A Night in Acadie* (1897). Amid a storm of abuse from literary critics, her masterpiece, the novel *The Awakening*, was published in 1899.

A Pair of Silk Stockings

LITTLE Mrs. Sommers one day found herself the unexpected possessor of fifteen dollars. It seemed to her a very large amount of money, and the way in which it stuffed and bulged her worn old *porte-monnaie* gave her a feeling of importance such as she had not enjoyed for years.

The question of investment was one that occupied her greatly. For a day or two she walked about apparently in a dreamy state, but really absorbed in speculation and calculation. She did not wish to act hastily, to do anything she might afterward regret. But it was during the still hours of the night when she lay awake revolving plans in her mind that she seemed to see her way clearly toward a proper and judicious use of the money.

A dollar or two should be added to the price usually paid for Janie's shoes, which would insure their lasting an appreciable time longer than they usually did. She would buy so and so many yards of percale for new shirt waists for the boys and Janie and Mag. She had intended to make the old ones do by skilful patching. Mag should have another gown. She had seen some beautiful patterns, veritable bargains in the shop windows. And still there would be left enough for new stockings—two pairs apiece—and what darning that would save for a while! She would get caps for the boys and sailor-hats for the girls. The vision of her little brood looking fresh and dainty and new for once in their lives excited her and made her restless and wakeful with anticipation.

The neighbors sometimes talked of certain "better days" that little Mrs. Sommers had known before she had ever thought of being Mrs. Sommers. She herself indulged in no such morbid retrospection. She had no time—no second of time to devote to the past. The needs of the present absorbed her every faculty. A vision of the future like some dim, gaunt monster sometimes appalled her, but luckily to-morrow never comes.

Mrs. Sommers was one who knew the value of bargains; who could stand for hours making her way inch by inch toward the desired object that was selling below cost. She could elbow her way if need be; she had learned to clutch a piece of goods and hold it and stick to it with persistence and determination till her turn came to be served, no matter when it came.

But that day she was a little faint and tired. She had swallowed a light luncheon—no! when she came to think of it, between getting the children fed and the place righted, and preparing herself for the shopping bout, she had actually forgotten to eat any luncheon at all!

She sat herself upon a revolving stool before a counter that was comparatively deserted, trying to gather strength and courage to charge through an eager multitude that was besieging breast-works of shirting and figured lawn. An all-gone limp feeling had come over her and she rested her hand aimlessly upon the counter. She wore no gloves. By degrees she grew aware that her hand had encountered something very soothing, very pleasant to touch. She looked down to see that her hand lay upon a pile of silk stockings. A placard near by announced that they had been reduced in price from two dollars and fifty cents to one dollar and ninety-eight cents; and a young girl who stood behind the counter asked her if she wished to examine their line of silk hosiery. She smiled, just as if she had been asked to inspect a tiara of diamonds with the ultimate view of purchasing it. But she went on feeling the soft, sheeny luxurious things— with both hands now, holding them up to see them glisten, and to feel them glide serpent-like through her fingers.

Two hectic blotches came suddenly into her pale cheeks. She looked up at the girl.

"Do you think there are any eights-and-a-half among these?"

There were any number of eights-and-a-half. In fact, there were more of that size than any other. Here was a light-blue pair; there were some lavender, some all black and various shades of tan and gray. Mrs. Sommers selected a black pair and looked at them very long and closely. She pretended to be examining their texture, which the clerk assured her was excellent.

"A dollar and ninety-eight cents," she mused aloud. "Well, I'll take this pair." She handed the girl a five-dollar bill and waited for her change and for her parcel. What a very small parcel it was. It seemed lost in the depths of her shabby old shopping-bag.

Mrs. Sommers after that did not move in the direction of the bargain counter. She took the elevator, which carried her to an upper floor into the region of the ladies' waiting-rooms. Here, in a retired corner, she exchanged her cotton stockings for the new silk ones which she had just bought. She was not going through any acute mental process or reasoning with herself, nor was she striving to explain to her satisfaction the motive of her action. She was not thinking at all. She seemed for the time to be taking a rest from that laborious and fatiguing function and to have abandoned herself to some mechanical impulse that directed her actions and freed her of responsibility.

How good was the touch of the raw silk to her flesh! She felt like lying back in the cushioned chair and reveling for a while in the luxury of it. She did for a little while. Then she replaced her shoes, rolled the cotton stockings together and thrust them into her bag. After doing this she crossed straight over to the shoe department and took her seat to be fitted.

She was fastidious. The clerk could not make her out; he could not reconcile her shoes with her stockings, and she was not too easily pleased. She held back her skirts and turned her feet one way and her head another way as she glanced down at the polished, pointed-tipped boots. Her foot and ankle looked very pretty. She could not realize that they belonged to her and were a part of herself. She wanted an excellent and stylish fit, she told the young fellow who served her, and she did not mind the difference of a dollar or two more in the price so long as she got what she desired.

It was a long time since Mrs. Sommers had been fitted with gloves. On rare occasions when she had bought a pair they were always "bargains," so cheap that it would have been preposterous and unreasonable to have expected them to be fitted to the hand.

Now she rested her elbow on the cushion of the glove counter, and a pretty, pleasant young creature, delicate and deft of touch, drew a long-wristed "kid" over Mrs. Sommers' hand. She smoothed it down over the wrist and buttoned it neatly, and both lost themselves for a second or two in admiring contemplation of the little symmetrical gloved hand. But there were other places where money might be spent.

There were books and magazines piled up in the window of a stall a few paces down the street. Mrs. Sommers bought two high-priced magazines such as she had been accustomed to read in the days when she had been accustomed to other pleasant things. She carried them without wrapping. As well as she could she lifted her skirts at the crossings. Her stockings and boots and well-fitting gloves had worked marvels in her bearing—had given her a feeling of assurance, a sense of belonging to the well-dressed multitude.

She was very hungry. Another time she would have stilled the cravings for food until reaching her own home, where she would have brewed herself a cup of tea and taken a snack of anything that was available.

But the impulse that was guiding her would not suffer her to entertain any such thought.

There was a restaurant at the corner. She had never entered its doors; from the outside she had sometimes caught glimpses of spotless damask and shining crystal, and soft-stepping waiters serving people of fashion.

When she entered her appearance created no surprise, no consternation, as she had half feared it might. She seated herself at a small table alone, and an attentive waiter at once approached to take her order. She did not want a profusion: she craved a nice and tasty bite—a half dozen blue-points, a plump chop with cress, a something sweet—a crème-frappée, for instance; a glass of Rhine wine, and after all a small cup of black coffee.

While waiting to be served she removed her gloves very leisurely and laid them beside her. Then she picked up a magazine and glanced through it, cutting the pages with a blunt edge of her knife. It was all very agreeable. The damask was even more spotless than it had seemed through the window, and the crystal more sparkling. There were quiet ladies and gentlemen, who did not notice her, lunching at the small tables like her own. A soft, pleasing strain of music could be heard, and a gentle breeze was blowing through the window. She tasted a bite, and she read a word or two, and she sipped the amber wine and wiggled her toes in the silk stockings. The price of it made no difference. She counted the money out to the waiter and left an extra coin on his tray, whereupon he bowed before her as before a princess of royal blood.

There was still money in her purse, and her next temptation presented itself in the shape of a matinée poster.

It was a little later when she entered the theatre, the play had begun and the house seemed to her to be packed. But there were vacant seats here and there, and into one of them she was ushered, between brilliantly dressed women who had gone there to kill time and eat candy and display their gaudy attire. There were many others who were there solely for the play and acting. It is safe to say there was no one present who bore quite the attitude which Mrs. Sommers did to her surroundings. She gathered in the whole—stage and players and people in one wide impression, and absorbed it and enjoyed it. She laughed at the comedy and wept—she and the gaudy woman next to her wept over the tragedy. And they talked a little together over it. And the gaudy woman wiped her eyes and sniffled on a tiny square of filmy, perfumed lace and passed little Mrs. Sommers her box of candy.

The play was over, the music ceased, the crowd filed out. It was like a dream ended. People scattered in all directions. Mrs. Sommers went to the corner and waited for the cable car.

A man with keen eyes, who sat opposite to her, seemed to like the study of her small, pale face. It puzzled him to decipher what he saw there. In truth, he saw nothing—unless he were wizard enough to detect a poignant wish, a powerful longing that the cable car would never stop anywhere, but go on and on with her forever.

—1897

KATHERINE ANNE PORTER
(1890–1980)

Born in Indian Creek, Texas, Katherine Anne Porter supported herself as a ghost writer, newspaper reporter, and magazine writer. In 1930, a collection titled *Flowering Judas and Other Stories* appeared, but only five years later, after the addition of four other tales, did it achieve its final form. In 1931 she received a Guggenheim Fellowship, making possible her trips to Mexico and Germany. Best known as a writer of short stories, she received both a National Book Award and a Pulitzer Prize in 1966 for her work in this genre. Among the collections of her stories are *Pale Horse, Pale Rider* (1939), *The Leaning Tower and Other Stories* (1944), and *Collected Stories* (1965). *The Days Before* (1952), a collection of essays and book reviews, was revised and enlarged to be republished as *The Collected Essays and Occasional Writings of Katherine Anne Porter* in 1965, while *The Never-Ending Wrong* (1977) is a brief memoir of her protest during the Sacco-Vanzetti case. Her only novel, *Ship of Fools* (1962), was made into a film in 1965.

He

LIFE was very hard for the Whipples. It was hard to feed all the hungry mouths, it was hard to keep the children in flannels during the winter, short as it was: "God knows what would become of us if we lived north," they would say: keeping them decently clean was hard. "It looks like our luck won't never let up on us," said Mr. Whipple, but Mrs. Whipple was all for taking what was sent and calling it good, anyhow when the neighbors were in earshot. "Don't ever let a soul hear us complain," she kept saying to her husband. She couldn't stand to be pitied. "No, not if it comes to it that we have to live in a wagon and pick cotton around

the country," she said, "nobody's going to get a chance
to look down on us."

Mrs. Whipple loved her second son, the simple-
minded one, better than she loved the other two children
put together. She was forever saying so, and when she
talked with certain of her neighbors, she would even
throw in her husband and her mother for good measure.

"You needn't keep on saying it around," said Mr.
Whipple, "you'll make people think nobody else has any
feelings about Him but you."

"It's natural for a mother," Mrs. Whipple would remind him. "You know yourself it's more natural for a
mother to be that way. People don't expect so much of
fathers, some way."

This didn't keep the neighbors from talking plainly
among themselves. "A Lord's pure mercy if He should
die," they said. "It's the sins of the fathers," they agreed
among themselves. "There's bad blood and bad doings
somewhere, you can bet on that." This behind the Whipples' backs. To their faces everybody said, "He's not so
bad off. He'll be all right yet. Look how He grows!"

Mrs. Whipple hated to talk about it, she tried to keep
her mind off it, but every time anybody set foot in the
house, the subject always came up, and she had to talk
about Him first, before she could get on to anything else.
It seemed to ease her mind. "I wouldn't have anything
happen to Him for all the world, but it just looks like I
can't keep Him out of mischief. He's so strong and active, He's always into everything; He was like that since
He could walk. It's actually funny sometimes, the way
He can do anything; it's laughable to see Him up to His
tricks. Emly has more accidents; I'm forever tying up
her bruises, and Adna can't fall a foot without cracking
a bone. But He can do anything and not get a scratch.
The preacher said such a nice thing once when he was
here. He said, and I'll remember it to my dying day,
'The innocent walk with God—that's why He don't get
hurt.' " Whenever Mrs. Whipple repeated these words,
she always felt a warm pool spread in her breast, and
the tears would fill her eyes, and then she could talk
about something else.

He did grow and He never got hurt. A plank blew off

the chicken house and struck Him on the head and He never seemed to know it. He had learned a few words, and after this He forgot them. He didn't whine for food as the other children did, but waited until it was given Him; He ate squatting in the corner, smacking and mumbling. Rolls of fat covered Him like an overcoat, and He could carry twice as much wood and water as Adna. Emly had a cold in the head most of the time—"she takes that after me," said Mrs. Whipple—so in bad weather they gave her the extra blanket off His cot. He never seemed to mind the cold.

Just the same, Mrs. Whipple's life was a torment for fear something might happen to Him. He climbed the peach trees much better than Adna and went skittering along the branches like a monkey, just a regular monkey. "Oh, Mrs. Whipple, you hadn't ought to let Him do that. He'll lose His balance sometime. He can't rightly know what He's doing."

Mrs. Whipple almost screamed out at the neighbor. "He *does* know what He's doing! He's as able as any other child! Come down out of there, you!" When He finally reached the ground she could hardly keep her hands off Him for acting like that before people, a grin all over His face and her worried sick about Him all the time.

"It's the neighbors," said Mrs. Whipple to her husband. "Oh, I do mortally wish they would keep out of our business. I can't afford to let Him do anything for fear they'll come nosing around about it. Look at the bees, now. Adna can't handle them, they sting him up so; I haven't got time to do everything, and now I don't dare let Him. But if He gets a sting He don't really mind."

"It's just because He ain't got sense enough to be scared of anything," said Mr. Whipple.

"You ought to be ashamed of yourself," said Mrs. Whipple, "talking that way about your own child. Who's to take up for Him if we don't, I'd like to know? He sees a lot that goes on, He listens to things all the time. And anything I tell Him to do He does it. Don't never let anybody hear you say such things. They'd think you favored the other children over Him."

"Well, now I don't, and you know it, and what's the use of getting all worked up about it? You always think the worst of everything. Just let Him alone, He'll get along somehow. He gets plenty to eat and wear, don't He?" Mr. Whipple suddenly felt tired out. "Anyhow, it can't be helped now."

Mrs. Whipple felt tired too, she complained in a tired voice. "What's done can't never be undone, I know that as good as anybody; but He's my child, and I'm not going to have people say anything. I get sick of people coming around saying things all the time."

In the early fall Mrs. Whipple got a letter from her brother saying he and his wife and two children were coming over for a little visit next Sunday week. "Put the big pot in the little one," he wrote at the end. Mrs. Whipple read this part out loud twice, she was so pleased. Her brother was a great one for saying funny things. "We'll just show him that's no joke," she said, "we'll just butcher one of the sucking pigs."

"It's a waste and I don't hold with waste the way we are now," said Mr. Whipple. "That pig'll be worth money by Christmas."

"It's a shame and a pity we can't have a decent meal's vittles once in a while when my own family comes to see us," said Mrs. Whipple. "I'd hate for his wife to go back and say there wasn't a thing in the house to eat. My God, it's better than buying up a great chance of meat in town. There's where you'd spend the money!"

"All right, do it yourself then," said Mr. Whipple. "Christamighty, no wonder we can't get ahead!"

The question was how to get the little pig away from his ma, a great fighter, worse than a Jersey cow. Adna wouldn't try it: "That sow'd rip my insides out all over the pen." "All right, old fraidy," said Mrs. Whipple, "*He's* not scared. Watch *Him* do it." And she laughed as though it was all a good joke and gave Him a little push towards the pen. He sneaked up and snatched the pig right away from the teat and galloped back and was over the fence with the sow raging at His heels. The little black squirming thing was screeching like a baby in a tantrum, stiffening its back and stretching its mouth to the ears. Mrs. Whipple took the pig with her face stiff and sliced its throat with one stroke. When He saw the blood. He gave a great jolting breath and ran away. "But He'll forget and eat plenty, just the same," thought Mrs. Whipple. Whenever she was thinking, her lips moved making words. "He'd eat it all if I didn't stop Him. He'd eat up every mouthful from the other two if I'd let Him."

She felt badly about it. He was ten years old now and a third again as large as Adna, who was going on fourteen. "It's a shame, a shame," she kept saying under her breath, "and Adna with so much brains!"

She kept on feeling badly about all sorts of things. In the first place it was the man's work to butcher; the sight of the pig scraped pink and naked made her sick. He was too fat and soft and pitiful-looking. It was simply a shame the way things had to happen. By the time she had finished it up, she almost wished her brother would stay at home.

Early Sunday morning Mrs. Whipple dropped everything to get Him all cleaned up. In an hour He was dirty again, with crawling under fences after a possum, and straddling along the rafters of the barn looking for eggs in the hayloft. "My Lord, look at you now after all my trying! And here's Adna and Emly staying so quiet. I get tired trying to keep you decent. Get off that shirt and put on another, people will say I don't half dress you!" And she boxed Him on the ears, hard. He blinked and blinked and rubbed His head, and His face hurt Mrs. Whipple's feelings. Her knees began to tremble, she had to sit down while she buttoned His shirt. "I'm just all gone before the day starts."

The brother came with his plump healthy wife and two great roaring hungry boys. They had a grand dinner, with the pig roasted to a crackling in the middle of the table, full of dressing, a pickled peach in his mouth and plenty of gravy for the sweet potatoes.

"This looks like prosperity all right," said the brother; "you're going to have to roll me home like I was a barrel when I'm done."

Everybody laughed out loud; it was fine to hear them laughing all at once around the table. Mrs. Whipple felt warm and good about it. "Oh, we've got six more of these; I say it's as little as we can do when you come to see us so seldom."

He wouldn't come into the dining room, and Mrs. Whipple passed it off very well. "He's timider than my other two," she said, "He'll just have to get used to you. There isn't everybody He'll make up with, you know how it is with some children, even cousins." Nobody said anything out of the way.

"Just like my Alfy here," said the brother's wife. "I sometimes got to lick him to make him shake hands with his own grandmammy."

So that was over, and Mrs. Whipple loaded up a big plate for Him first, before everybody. "I always say He ain't to be slighted, no matter who else goes without," she said, and carried it to Him herself.

"He can chin Himself on the top of the door," said Emly, helping along.

"That's fine, He's getting along fine," said the brother.

They went away after supper. Mrs. Whipple rounded up the dishes, and sent the children to bed and sat down and unlaced her shoes. "You see?" she said to Mr. Whipple. "That's the way my whole family is. Nice and considerate about everything. No out-of-the-way remarks—they *have* got refinement. I get awfully sick of people's remarks. Wasn't that pig good?"

Mr. Whipple said, "Yes, we're out three hundred pounds of pork, that's all. It's easy to be polite when you come to eat. Who knows what they had in their minds all along?"

"Yes, that's like you," said Mrs. Whipple. "I don't expect anything else from you. You'll be telling me next that my own brother will be saying around that we made Him eat in the kitchen! Oh, my God!" She rocked her head in her hands, a hard pain started in the very middle of her forehead. "Now it's all spoiled, and everything was so nice and easy. All right, you don't like them and you never did—all right, they'll not come here again soon, never you mind! But they *can't* say He wasn't dressed every lick as good as Adna—oh, honest, sometimes I wish I was dead!"

"I wish you'd let up," said Mr. Whipple. "It's bad enough as it is."

*   *   *

It was a hard winter. It seemed to Mrs. Whipple that they hadn't ever known anything but hard times, and now to cap it all a winter like this. The crops were about half of what they had a right to expect; after the cotton was in it didn't do much more than cover the grocery bill. They swapped off one of the plow horses, and got cheated, for the new one died of the heaves. Mrs. Whipple kept thinking all the time it was terrible to have a man you couldn't depend on not to get cheated. They cut down on everything, but Mrs. Whipple kept saying there are things you can't cut down on, and they cost money. It took a lot of warm clothes for Adna and Emly, who walked four miles to school during the three-months session. "He sets around the fire a lot, He won't need so much," said Mr. Whipple. "That's so," said Mrs. Whipple, "and when He does the outdoor chores He can wear your tarpaullion coat. I can't do no better, that's all."

In February He was taken sick, and lay curled up under His blanket looking very blue in the face and acting as if He would choke. Mr. and Mrs. Whipple did everything they could for Him for two days, and then they were scared and sent for the doctor. The doctor told them they must keep Him warm and give Him plenty of milk and eggs. "He isn't as stout as He looks, I'm afraid," said the doctor. "You've got to watch them when they're like that. You must put more cover onto Him, too."

"I just took off His big blanket to wash," said Mrs. Whipple, ashamed. "I can't stand dirt."

"Well, you'd better put it back on the minute it's dry," said the doctor, "or He'll have pneumonia."

Mr. and Mrs. Whipple took a blanket off their own bed and put His cot in by the fire. "They can't say we didn't do everything for Him," she said, "even to sleeping cold ourselves on His account."

When the winter broke He seemed to be well again, but He walked as if His feet hurt Him. He was able to run a cotton planter during the season.

"I got it all fixed up with Jim Ferguson about breeding

the cow next time," said Mr. Whipple. "I'll pasture the bull this summer and give Jim some fodder in the fall. That's better than paying out money when you haven't got it."

"I hope you didn't say such a thing before Jim Ferguson," said Mrs. Whipple. "You oughtn't to let him know we're so down as all that."

"Godamighty, that ain't saying we're down. A man is got to look ahead sometimes. He can lead the bull over today. I need Adna on the place."

At first Mrs. Whipple felt easy in her mind about sending Him for the bull. Adna was too jumpy and couldn't be trusted. You've got to be steady around animals. After He was gone she started thinking, and after a while she could hardly bear it any longer. She stood in the lane and watched for Him. It was nearly three miles to go and a hot day, but He oughtn't to be so long about it. She shaded her eyes and stared until colored bubbles floated in her eyeballs. It was just like everything else in life, she must always worry and never know a moment's peace about anything. After a long time she saw Him turn into the side lane, limping. He came on very slowly, leading the big hulk of an animal by a ring in the nose, twirling a little stick in His hand, never looking back or sideways, but coming on like a sleepwalker with His eyes half shut.

Mrs. Whipple was scared sick of bulls; she had heard awful stories about how they followed on quietly enough, and then suddenly pitched on with a bellow and pawed and gored a body to pieces. Any second now that black monster would come down on Him, my God, He'd never have sense enough to run.

She mustn't make a sound nor a move; she mustn't get the bull started. The bull heaved his head aside and horned the air at a fly. Her voice burst out of her in a shriek, and she screamed at Him to come on, for God's sake. He didn't seem to hear her clamor, but kept on twirling His switch and limping on, and the bull lumbered along behind him as gently as a calf. Mrs. Whipple stopped calling and ran towards the house, praying under her breath: "Lord, don't let anything happen to

Him. Lord, you *know* people will say we oughtn't to have sent Him. You *know* they'll say we didn't take care of Him. Oh, get Him home, safe home, safe home, and I'll look out for Him better! Amen."

She watched from the window while He led the beast in, and tied him up in the barn. It was no use trying to keep up, Mrs. Whipple couldn't bear another thing. She sat down and rocked and cried with her apron over her head.

From year to year the Whipples were growing poorer and poorer. The place just seemed to run down of itself, no matter how hard they worked. "We're losing our hold," said Mrs. Whipple. "Why can't we do like other people and watch for our best chances? They'll be calling us poor white trash next."

"When I get to be sixteen I'm going to leave," said Adna. "I'm going to get a job in Powell's grocery store. There's money in that. No more farm for me."

"I'm going to be a schoolteacher," said Emly. "But I've got to finish the eighth grade, anyhow. Then I can live in town. I don't see any chances here."

"Emly takes after my family," said Mrs. Whipple. "Ambitious every last one of them, and they don't take second place for anybody."

When fall came Emly got a chance to wait on table in the railroad eating-house in the town near by, and it seemed such a shame not to take it when the wages were good and she could get her food too, that Mrs. Whipple decided to let her take it, and not bother with school until the next session. "You've got plenty of time," she said. "You're young and smart as a whip."

With Adna gone too, Mr. Whipple tried to run the farm with just Him to help. He seemed to get along fine, doing His work and part of Adna's without noticing it. They did well enough until Christmas time, when one morning He slipped on the ice coming up from the barn. Instead of getting up He thrashed round and round, and when Mr. Whipple got to Him, He was having some sort of fit.

They brought Him inside and tried to make Him sit up, but He blubbered and rolled, so they put Him to bed and Mr. Whipple rode to town for the doctor. All the way there and back he worried about where the money was to come from: it sure did look like he had about all the troubles he could carry.

From then on He stayed in bed. His legs swelled up double their size, and the fits kept coming back. After four months, the doctor said, "It's no use, I think you'd better put Him in the County Home for treatment right away. I'll see about it for you. He'll have good care there and be off your hands."

"We don't begrudge Him any care, and I won't let Him out of my sight," said Mrs. Whipple. "I won't have it said I sent my sick child off among strangers."

"I know how you feel," said the doctor. "You can't tell me anything about that, Mrs. Whipple. I've got a boy of my own. But you'd better listen to me. I can't do anything more for Him, that's the truth."

Mr. and Mrs. Whipple talked it over a long time that night after they went to bed. "It's just charity," said Mrs. Whipple, "that's what we've come to, charity! I certainly never looked for this."

"We pay taxes to help support the place just like everybody else," said Mr. Whipple, "and I don't call that taking charity. I think it would be fine to have Him where He'd get the best of everything . . . and besides, I can't keep up with these doctor bills any longer."

"Maybe that's why the doctor wants us to send Him—he's scared he won't get his money," said Mrs. Whipple.

"Don't talk like that," said Mr. Whipple, feeling pretty sick, "or we won't be able to send Him."

"Oh, but we won't keep Him there long," said Mrs. Whipple. "Soon's He's better, we'll bring Him right back home."

"The doctor has told you and told you time and again He can't ever get better, and you might as well stop talking," said Mr. Whipple.

"Doctors don't know everything," said Mrs. Whipple, feeling almost happy. "But anyhow, in the summer Emly can come home for a vacation, and Adna can get down for Sundays: we'll all work together and get on our feet again, and the children will feel they've got a place to come to."

All at once she saw it full summer again, with the

garden going fine, and new white roller shades up all over the house, and Adna and Emly home, so full of life, all of them happy together. Oh, it could happen, things would ease up on them.

They didn't talk before Him much, but they never knew just how much He understood. Finally the doctor set the day and a neighbor who owned a double-seated carryall offered to drive them over. The hospital would have sent an ambulance, but Mrs. Whipple couldn't stand to see Him going away looking so sick as all that. They wrapped Him in blankets, and the neighbor and Mr. Whipple lifted Him into the back seat of the carryall beside Mrs. Whipple, who had on her black shirt waist. She couldn't stand to go looking like charity.

"You'll be all right, I guess I'll stay behind," said Mr. Whipple. "It don't look like everybody ought to leave the place at once."

"Besides, it ain't as if He was going to stay forever," said Mrs. Whipple to the neighbor. "This is only for a little while."

They started away, Mrs. Whipple holding to the edges of the blankets to keep Him from sagging sideways. He sat there blinking and blinking. He worked His hands out and began rubbing His nose with His knuckles, and then with the end of the blanket. Mrs. Whipple couldn't believe what she saw; He was scrubbing away big tears that rolled out of the corners of His eyes. He sniveled and made a gulping noise. Mrs. Whipple kept saying, "Oh, honey, you don't feel so bad, do you? You don't feel so bad, do you?" for He seemed to be accusing her of something. Maybe He remembered that time she boxed His ears, maybe He had been scared that day with the bull, maybe He had slept cold and couldn't tell her about it; maybe He knew they were sending Him away for good and all because they were too poor to keep Him. Whatever it was, Mrs. Whipple couldn't bear to think of it. She began to cry, frightfully, and wrapped her arms tight around Him. His head rolled on her shoulder: she had loved Him as much as she possibly could, there were Adna and Emly who had to be thought of too, there was nothing she could do to make up to Him for His life. Oh, what a mortal pity He was ever born.

They came in sight of the hospital, with the neighbor driving very fast, not daring to look behind him.

—1930

• TILLIE OLSEN

(B. 1913)

Born in Nebraska, Tillie Olsen came of age during the Great Depression. She left high school in order to get a job and has commented that "public libraries were my college." Committed to social and political activism, she worked to help organize meatpacking workers in Omaha and Kansas City and participated in the general strike of 1934 in San Francisco. In 1943, she married Jack Olsen, who shared her commitment to the labor movement. Only when the youngest of the couple's four children was old enough to attend school was Olsen able to return to the writing she had begun to publish in the 1930s. "Tell Me a Riddle," the title story of a volume of four of her tales, won the O. Henry Award for best American short story in 1961. Olsen edited Rebecca Harding Davis's *Life in the Iron Mills* (1972) and published a novel *Yonnondio: From the Thirties* (1974). The title refers to her rediscovering the manuscript of this novel almost forty years after the demands of family and work caused her to set it aside for lack of time. In 1978, she published *Silences*, a feminist nonfiction work. She has taught at Amherst College, Stanford University, M.I.T., and the University of Massachusetts at Boston and is the recipient of fellowships from the Guggenheim Foundation and the National Endowment for the Humanities.

I Stand Here Ironing

I STAND here ironing, and what you asked me moves tormented back and forth with the iron.

"I wish you would manage the time to come in and talk with me about your daughter. I'm sure you can help me understand her. She's a youngster who needs help and whom I'm deeply interested in helping."

"Who needs help." Even if I came, what good would it do? You think because I am her mother I have a key, or that in some way you could use me as a key? She has lived for nineteen years. There is all that life that has happened outside of me, beyond me.

And when is there time to remember, to sift, to weigh, to estimate, to total? I will start and there will be an interruption and I will have to gather it all together again. Or I will become engulfed with all I did or did not do, with what should have been and what cannot be helped.

She was a beautiful baby. The first and only one of our five that was beautiful at birth. You do not guess how new and uneasy her tenancy in her now-loveliness. You did not know her all those years she was thought homely, or see her poring over her baby pictures, making me tell her over and over how beautiful she had been—and would be, I would tell her—and was now, to the seeing eye. But the seeing eyes were few or nonexistent. Including mine.

I nursed her. They feel that's important nowadays. I nursed all the children, but with her, with all the fierce rigidity of first motherhood, I did like the books then said. Though her cries battered me to trembling and my breasts ached with swollenness, I waited till the clock decreed.

Why do I put that first? I do not even know if it matters, or if it explains anything.

She was a beautiful baby. She blew shining bubbles of sound. She loved motion, loved light, loved color and music and textures. She would lie on the floor in her blue overalls patting the surface so hard in ecstasy her hands and feet would blur. She was a miracle to me, but when she was eight months old I had to leave her day-times with the woman downstairs to whom she was no miracle at all, for I worked or looked for work and for Emily's father, who "could no longer endure" (he wrote in his good-bye note) "sharing want with us."

I was nineteen. It was the pre-relief, pre-WPA world of the depression. I would start running as soon as I got off the streetcar, running up the stairs, the place smelling sour, and awake or asleep to startle awake, when she saw me she would break into a clogged weeping that could not be comforted, a weeping I can hear yet.

After a while I found a job hashing at night so I could

be with her days, and it was better. But it came to where I had to bring her to his family and leave her.

It took a long time to raise the money for her fare back. Then she got chicken pox and I had to wait longer. When she finally came, I hardly knew her, walking quick and nervous like her father, looking like her father, thin, and dressed in a shoddy red that yellowed her skin and glared at the pockmarks. All the baby loveliness gone.

She was two. Old enough for nursery school they said, and I did not know then what I know now—the fatigue of the long day, and the lacerations of group life in nurseries that are only parking places for children.

Except that it would have made no difference if I had known. It was the only place there was. It was the only way we could be together, the only way I could hold a job.

And even without knowing, I knew. I knew the teacher that was evil because all these years it has curdled into my memory, the little boy hunched in the corner, her rasp, "why aren't you outside, because Alvin hits you? that's no reason, go out, scaredy." I knew Emily hated it even if she did not clutch and implore "don't go Mommy" like the other children, mornings.

She always had a reason why we should stay home. Momma, you look sick, Momma. I feel sick. Momma, the teachers aren't there today, they're sick. Momma, we can't go, there was a fire there last night. Momma, it's a holiday today, no school, they told me.

But never a direct protest, never rebellion. I think of our others in their three-, four-year-oldness—the explosions, the tempers, the denunciations, the demands—and I feel suddenly ill. I put the iron down. What in me demanded that goodness in her? And what was the cost, the cost to her of such goodness?

The old man living in the back once said in his gentle way: "You should smile at Emily more when you look at her." What *was* in my face when I looked at her? I loved her. There were all the acts of love.

It was only with the others I remembered what he said, and it was the face of joy, and not of care or tightness or worry I turned to them—too late for Emily. She does not smile easily, let alone almost always as her brothers and sisters do. Her face is closed and sombre, but when she wants, how fluid. You must have seen it in her pantomimes, you spoke of her rare gift for comedy on the stage that rouses a laughter out of the audience so dear they applaud and applaud and do not want to let her go.

Where does it come from, that comedy? There was none of it in her when she came back to me that second time, after I had had to send her away again. She had a new daddy now to learn to love, and I think perhaps it was a better time.

Except when we left her alone nights, telling ourselves she was old enough.

"Can't you go some other time, Mommy, like tomorrow?" she would ask. "Will it be just a little while you'll be gone? Do you promise?"

The time we came back, the front door open, the clock on the floor in the hall. She rigid awake. "It wasn't just a little while. I didn't cry. Three times I called you, just three times, and then I ran downstairs to open the door so you could come faster. The clock talked loud. I threw it away, it scared me what it talked."

She said the clock talked loud again that night I went to the hospital to have Susan. She was delirious with the fever that comes before red measles, but she was fully conscious all the week I was gone and the week after we were home when she could not come near the new baby or me.

She did not get well. She stayed skeleton thin, not wanting to eat, and night after night she had nightmares. She would call for me, and I would rouse from exhaustion to sleepily call back: "You're all right, darling, go to sleep, it's just a dream," and if she still called, in a sterner voice, "now go to sleep, Emily, there's nothing to hurt you." Twice, only twice, when I had to get up for Susan anyhow, I went in to sit with her.

Now when it is too late (as if she would let me hold and comfort her like I do the others) I get up and go to her at once at her moan or restless stirring. "Are you awake, Emily? Can I get you something?" And the answer is always the same: "No, I'm all right, go back to sleep, Mother."

They persuaded me at the clinic to send her away to a convalescent home in the country where "she can have the kind of food and care you can't manage for her, and you'll be free to concentrate on the new baby." They still send children to that place. I see pictures on the society page of sleek young women planning affairs to raise money for it, or dancing at the affairs, or decorating Easter eggs or filling Christmas stockings for the children.

They never have a picture of the children so I do not know if the girls still wear those gigantic red bows and the ravaged looks on the every other Sunday when parents can come to visit "unless otherwise notified"—as we were notified the first six weeks.

Oh it is a handsome place, green lawns and tall trees and fluted flower beds. High up on the balconies of each cottage the children stand, the girls in their red bows and white dresses, the boys in white suits and giant red ties. The parents stand below shrieking up to be heard and the children shriek down to be heard, and between them the invisible wall "Not To Be Contaminated by Parental Germs or Physical Affection."

There was a tiny girl who always stood hand in hand with Emily. Her parents never came. One visit she was gone. "They moved her to Rose College," Emily shouted in explanation. "They don't like you to love anybody here."

She wrote once a week, the labored writing of a seven-year-old. "I am fine. How is the baby. If I write my leter nicly I will have a star. Love." There never was a star. We wrote every other day, letters she could never hold or keep but only hear read—once. "We simply do not have room for children to keep any personal possessions," they patiently explained when we pieced one Sunday's shrieking together to plead how much it would mean to Emily, who loved so to keep things, to be allowed to keep her letters and cards.

Each visit she looked frailer. "She isn't eating," they told us.

(They had runny eggs for breakfast or mush with lumps, Emily said later, I'd hold it in in my mouth and not swallow. Nothing ever tasted good, just when they had chicken.)

It took us eight months to get her released home, and only the fact that she gained back so little of her seven lost pounds convinced the social worker.

I used to try to hold and love her after she came back, but her body would stay stiff, and after a while she'd push away. She ate little. Food sickened her, and I think much of life too. Oh she had physical lightness and brightness, twinkling by on skates, bouncing like a ball up and down up and down over the jump rope, skimming over the hill; but these were momentary.

She fretted about her appearance, thin and dark and foreign-looking at a time when every little girl was supposed to look or thought she should look a chubby blonde replica of Shirley Temple. The doorbell sometimes rang for her, but no one seemed to come and play in the house or be a best friend. Maybe because we moved so much.

There was a boy she loved painfully through two school semesters. Months later she told me how she had taken pennies from my purse to buy him candy. "Licorice was his favorite and I brought him some every day, but he still liked Jennifer better'n me. Why, Mommy?" The kind of question for which there is no answer.

School was a worry to her. She was not glib or quick in a world where glibness and quickness were easily confused with ability to learn. To her overworked and exasperated teachers she was an overconscientious "slow learner" who kept trying to catch up and was absent entirely too often.

I let her be absent, though sometimes the illness was imaginary. How different from my now-strictness about attendance with the others. I wasn't working. We had a new baby, I was home anyhow. Sometimes, after Susan grew old enough, I would keep her home from school, too, to have them all together.

Mostly Emily had asthma, and her breathing, harsh and labored, would fill the house with a curiously tranquil sound. I would bring the two old dresser mirrors and her boxes of collections to her bed. She would select beads and single earrings, bottle tops and shells, dried flowers and pebbles, old postcards and scraps, all sorts of oddments; then she and Susan would play Kingdom, setting up landscapes and furniture, peopling them with action.

Those were the only times of peaceful companionship between her and Susan. I have edged away from it, that poisonous feeling between them, that terrible balancing of hurts and needs I had to do between the two, and did so badly, those earlier years.

Oh there are conflicts between the others too, each one human, needing, demanding, hurting, taking—but only between Emily and Susan, no, Emily toward Susan that corroding resentment. It seems so obvious on the surface, yet it is not obvious. Susan, the second child, Susan, golden- and curly-haired and chubby, quick and articulate and assured, everything in appearance and manner Emily was not; Susan, not able to resist Emily's precious things, losing or sometimes clumsily breaking them; Susan telling jokes and riddles to company for applause while Emily sat silent (to say to me later: that was *my* riddle, Mother, I told it to Susan); Susan, who for all the five years' difference in age was just a year behind Emily in developing physically.

I am glad for that slow physical development that widened the difference between her and her contemporaries, though she suffered over it. She was too vulnerable for that terrible world of youthful competition, of preening and parading, of constant measuring of yourself against every other, of envy, "If I had that copper hair," "If I had that skin. . . ." She tormented herself enough about not looking like the others, there was enough of the unsureness, the having to be conscious of words before you speak, the constant caring—what are they thinking of me? without having it all magnified by the merciless physical drives.

Ronnie is calling. He is wet and I change him. It is rare there is such a cry now. That time of motherhood is almost behind me when the ear is not one's own but must always be racked and listening for the child cry, the child call. We sit for a while and I hold him, looking out over the city spread in charcoal with its soft aisles of light. "*Shoogily*," he breathes and curls closer. I carry him back to bed, asleep. *Shoogily.* A funny word, a family word, inherited from Emily, invented by her to say: *comfort.*

In this and other ways she leaves her seal, I say aloud. And startle at my saying it. What do I mean? What did I start to gather together, to try and make coherent? I was at the terrible, growing years. War years. I do not remember them well. I was working, there were four smaller ones now, there was not time for her. She had to help be a mother, and housekeeper, and shopper. She had to set her seal. Mornings of crisis and near hysteria trying to get lunches packed, hair combed, coats and shoes found, everyone to school or Child Care on time, the baby ready for transportation. And always the paper scribbled on by a smaller one, the book looked at by Susan then mislaid, the homework not done. Running out to that huge school where she was one, she was lost, she was a drop; suffering over the unpreparedness, stammering and unsure in her classes.

There was so little time left at night after the kids were bedded down. She would struggle over books, always eating (it was in those years she developed her enormous appetite that is legendary in our family) and I would be ironing, or preparing food for the next day, or writing V-mail to Bill, or tending the baby. Sometimes, to make me laugh, or out of her despair, she would imitate happenings or types at school.

I think I said once: "Why don't you do something like this in the school amateur show?" One morning she phoned me at work, hardly understandable through the weeping: "Mother, I did it. I won, I won; they gave me first prize; they clapped and clapped and wouldn't let me go."

Now suddenly she was Somebody, and as imprisoned in her difference as she had been in anonymity.

She began to be asked to perform at other high schools, even in colleges, then at city and statewide affairs. The first one we went to, I only recognized her that first moment when thin, shy, she almost drowned herself into the curtains. Then: Was this Emily? The control, the command, the convulsing and deadly clowning, the spell, then the roaring, stamping audience, unwilling to let this rare and precious laughter out of their lives.

Afterwards: You ought to do something about her with a gift like that—but without money or knowing how, what does one do? We have left it all to her, and the gift has as often eddied inside, clogged and clotted, as been used and growing.

She is coming. She runs up the stairs two at a time with her light graceful step, and I know she is happy tonight. Whatever it was that occasioned your call did not happen today.

"Aren't you ever going to finish the ironing, Mother? Whistler painted his mother in a rocker. I'd have to paint mine standing over an ironing board." This is one of her communicative nights and she tells me everything and nothing as she fixes herself a plate of food out of the icebox.

She is so lovely. Why did you want me to come in at all? Why were you concerned? She will find her way.

She starts up the stairs to bed. "Don't get me up with the rest in the morning." "But I thought you were having midterms." "Oh, those," she comes back in, kisses me, and says quite lightly, "in a couple of years when we'll all be atom-dead they won't matter a bit."

She has said it before. She *believes* it. But because I have been dredging the past, and all that compounds a human being is so heavy and meaningful in me, I cannot endure it tonight.

I will never total it all. I will never come in to say: She was a child seldom smiled at. Her father left me before she was a year old. I had to work her first six years when there was work, or I sent her home and to his relatives. There were years she had care she hated. She was dark and thin and foreign-looking in a world where the prestige went to blondeness and curly hair and dimples, she was slow where glibness was prized. She was a child of anxious, not proud, love. We were poor and could not afford for her the soil of easy growth. I was a young mother, I was a distracted mother. There were the other children pushing up, demanding. Her younger sister seemed all that she was not. There were years she did not want me to touch her. She kept too much in herself, her life was such she had to keep too much in herself. My wisdom came too late. She has much to her and probably nothing will come of it. She is a child of her age, of depression, of war, of fear.

Let her be. So all that is in her will not bloom—but in how many does it? There is still enough left to live by. Only help her to know—help make it so there is cause for her to know—that she is more than this dress on the ironing board, helpless before the iron.

—1961

ALICE WALKER
(B. 1944)

Born in Eatonton, Georgia (a community where many African-Americans were struggling tenant-farmers), Alice Walker was educated at Spelman College and Sarah Lawrence College. She has served as a voter registration worker in Georgia, a Head Start program worker in Mississippi, and an employee at New York City's Welfare Department. She has been a writer in residence or visiting professor at Jackson State College, Tougaloo College, Wellesley College, the University of Massachusetts at Boston, the University of California at Berkeley, and Brandeis University. She is a recipient of an award from The American Academy and Institute of Arts and Letters (1974), a National Book Critics Circle Award nomination (1982), an American Book Award (1983), the Pulitzer Prize (1983), a D.H.L. from the University of Massachusetts (1983), an O. Henry Award (1986), a Langston Hughes Award—New York City College (1989), a Freedom to Write Award, PEN West (1990), and a Literary Ambassador Award from the University of Oklahoma Center for Poets and Writers (1998). Among her works are the poetry collections *Revolutionary Petunias and Other Poems* (1973), *Goodnight, Willie Lee, I'll See You in the Morning* (1979), *Horses Make a Landscape More Beautiful* (1984), and *Her Blue Body Everything We Know: Earthling Poems, 1965–1990 Complete* (1991). Among her novels are *The Third Life of Grange Copeland* (1970); *Meridian* (1976); *The Color Purple* (1982), which won the Pulitzer Prize and American Book Award in 1983 and was made into a highly successful film in 1985; *The Temple of My Familiar* (1989); and *Possessing the Secret of Joy* (1992). Among her nonfiction works are *In Search of Our Mothers' Gardens: Womanist Prose* (1983), *Living by the Word: Selected Writings, 1973–1987* (1988), and *Anything We Love Can Be Saved: A Writer's Activism* (1997). Her stories are collected in *In Love and Trouble: Stories of Black Women* (1973) and *You Can't Keep a Good Woman Down* (1981).

Everyday Use

for your grandmama

I will wait for her in the yard that Maggie and I made so clean and wavy yesterday afternoon. A yard like this is more comfortable than most people know. It is not just a yard. It is like an extended living room. When the hard clay is swept clean as a floor and the fine sand around the edges lined with tiny, irregular grooves, anyone can come and sit and look up into the elm tree and wait for the breezes that never come inside the house.

Maggie will be nervous until after her sister goes: she will stand hopelessly in corners, homely and ashamed of the burn scars down her arms and legs, eying her sister with a mixture of envy and awe. She thinks her sister has held life always in the palm of one hand, that "no" is a word the world never learned to say to her.

You've no doubt seen those TV shows where the child who has "made it" is confronted, as a surprise, by her own mother and father, tottering in weakly from back-stage. (A pleasant surprise, of course: What would they do if parent and child came on the show only to curse out and insult each other?) On TV mother and child embrace and smile into each other's faces. Sometimes the mother and father weep, the child wraps them in her arms and leans across the table to tell how she would not have made it without their help. I have seen these programs.

Sometimes I dream a dream in which Dee and I are suddenly brought together on a TV program of this sort. Out of a dark and soft-seated limousine I am ushered into a bright room filled with many people. There I meet a smiling, gray, sporty man like Johnny Carson who shakes my hand and tells me what a fine girl I have. Then we are on the stage and Dee is embracing me with tears in her eyes. She pins on my dress a large orchid, even though she has told me once that she thinks orchids are tacky flowers.

In real life I am a large, big-boned woman with rough, man-working hands. In the winter I wear flannel night-gowns to bed and overalls during the day. I can kill and clean a hog as mercilessly as a man. My fat keeps me hot in zero weather. I can work outside all day, breaking ice to get water for washing; I can eat pork liver cooked over the open fire minutes after it comes steaming from the hog. One winter I knocked a bull calf straight in the brain between the eyes with a sledge hammer and had the meat hung up to chill before nightfall. But of course all this does not show on television. I am the way my daughter would want me to be: a hundred pounds lighter, my skin like an uncooked barley pancake. My hair glistens in the hot bright lights. Johnny Carson has much to do to keep up with my quick and witty tongue.

But that is a mistake. I know even before I wake up. Who ever knew a Johnson with a quick tongue? Who can even imagine me looking a strange white man in the eye? It seems to me I have talked to them always with one foot raised in flight, with my head turned in which-ever way is farthest from them. Dee, though. She would always look anyone in the eye. Hesitation was no part of her nature.

"How do I look, Mama?" Maggie says, showing just enough of her thin body enveloped in pink skirt and red blouse for me to know she's there, almost hidden by the door.

"Come out into the yard," I say.

Have you ever seen a lame animal, perhaps a dog run over by some careless person rich enough to own a car, sidle up to someone who is ignorant enough to be kind to him? That is the way my Maggie walks. She has been like this, chin on chest, eyes on ground, feet in shuffle, ever since the fire that burned the other house to the ground.

Dee is lighter than Maggie, with nicer hair and a fuller figure. She's a woman now, though sometimes I forget. How long ago was it that the other house burned? Ten, twelve years? Sometimes I can still hear the flames and feel Maggie's arms sticking to me, her hair smoking and her dress falling off her in little black papery flakes. Her eyes seemed stretched open, blazed open by the flames reflected in them. And Dee. I see her standing off under the sweet gum tree she used to dig gum out of; a look of concentration on her face as she watched the last dingy gray board of the house fall in toward the red-hot brick chimney. Why don't you do a dance around the ashes? I'd wanted to ask her. She had hated the house that much.

I used to think she hated Maggie, too. But that was before we raised the money, the church and me, to send her to Augusta to school. She used to read to us without pity; forcing words, lies, other folks' habits, whole lives upon us two, sitting trapped and ignorant underneath her voice. She washed us in a river of make-believe, burned us with a lot of knowledge we didn't necessarily need to know. Pressed us to her with the serious way she read, to shove us away at just the moment, like dimwits, we seemed about to understand.

Dee wanted nice things. A yellow organdy dress to wear to her graduation from high school; black pumps to match a green suit she'd made from an old suit somebody gave me. She was determined to stare down any disaster in her efforts. Her eyelids would not flicker for minutes at a time. Often I fought off the temptation to shake her. At sixteen she had a style of her own: and knew what style was.

I never had an education myself. After second grade the school was closed down. Don't ask my why: in 1927 colored asked fewer questions than they do now. Sometimes Maggie reads to me. She stumbles along good-naturedly but can't see well. She knows she is not bright. Like good looks and money, quickness passed her by. She will marry John Thomas (who has mossy teeth in an earnest face) and then I'll be free to sit here and I guess just sing church songs to myself. Although I never was a good singer. Never could carry a tune. I was always better at a man's job. I used to love to milk till I was hooked in the side in '49. Cows are soothing and slow and don't bother you, unless you try to milk them the wrong way.

I have deliberately turned my back on the house. It

is three rooms, just like the one that burned, except the roof is tin; they don't make shingle roofs any more. There are no real windows, just some holes cut in the sides, like the portholes in a ship, but not round and not square, with rawhide holding the shutters up on the outside. This house is in a pasture, too, like the other one. No doubt when Dee sees it she will want to tear it down. She wrote me once that no matter where we "choose" to live, she will manage to come see us. But she will never bring her friends. Maggie and I thought about this and Maggie asked me, "Mama, when did Dee ever *have* any friends?"

She had a few. Furtive boys in pink shirts hanging about on washday after school. Nervous girls who never laughed. Impressed with her they worshiped the well-turned phrase, the cute shape, the scalding humor that erupted like bubbles in lye. She read to them.

When she was courting Jimmy T she didn't have much time to pay to us, but turned all her faultfinding power on him. He *flew* to marry a cheap city girl from a family of ignorant flashy people. She hardly had time to recompose herself.

When she comes I will meet—but there they are!

Maggie attempts to make a dash for the house, in her shuffling way, but I stay her with my hand. "Come back here," I say. And she stops and tries to dig a well in the sand with her toe.

It is hard to see them clearly through the strong sun. But even the first glimpse of leg out of the car tells me it is Dee. Her feet were always neat-looking, as if God himself had shaped them with a certain style. From the other side of the car comes a short, stocky man. Hair is all over his head a foot long and hanging from his chin like a kinky mule tail. I hear Maggie suck in her breath. "Uhnnnh," is what it sounds like. Like when you see the wriggling end of a snake just in front of your foot on the road. "Uhnnnh."

Dee next. A dress down to the ground, in this hot weather. A dress so loud it hurts my eyes. There are yellows and oranges enough to throw back the light of the sun. I feel my whole face warming from the heat waves it throws out. Earrings gold, too, and hanging down to her shoulders. Bracelets dangling and making noises when she moves her arm up to shake the folds of the dress out of her armpits. The dress is loose and flows, and as she walks closer, I like it. I hear Maggie go "Uhnnnh" again. It is her sister's hair. It stands straight up like the wool on a sheep. It is black as night and around the edges are two long pigtails that rope about like small lizards disappearing behind her ears.

"Wa-su-zo-Tean-o!" she says, coming on in that gliding way the dress makes her move. The short stocky fellow with the hair to his navel is all grinning and he follows up with "Asalamalakim, my mother and sister!" He moves to hug Maggie but she falls back, right up against the back of my chair. I feel her trembling there and when I look up I see the perspiration falling off her chin.

"Don't get up," says Dee. Since I am stout it takes something of a push. You can see me trying to move a second or two before I make it. She turns, showing white heels through her sandals, and goes back to the car. Out she peeks next with a Polaroid. She stoops down quickly and lines up picture after picture of me sitting there in front of the house with Maggie cowering behind me. She never takes a shot without making sure the house is included. When a cow comes nibbling around the edge of the yard she snaps it and me and Maggie *and* the house. Then she puts the Polaroid in the back seat of the car, and comes up and kisses me on the forehead.

Meanwhile Asalamalakim is going through motions with Maggie's hand. Maggie's hand is as limp as a fish, and probably as cold, despite the sweat, and she keeps trying to pull it back. It looks like Asalamalakim wants to shake hands but wants to do it fancy. Or maybe he don't know how people shake hands. Anyhow, he soon gives up on Maggie.

"Well," I say. "Dee."

"No, Mama," she says. "Not 'Dee,' Wangero Leewanika Kemanjo!"

"What happened to 'Dee'?" I wanted to know.

"She's dead," Wangero said. "I couldn't bear it any longer, being named after the people who oppress me."

"You know as well as me you was named after your aunt Dicie," I said. Dicie is my sister. She named Dee. We called her "Big Dee" after Dee was born.

"But who was *she* named after?" asked Wangero.

"I guess after Grandma Dee," I said.

"And who was she named after?" asked Wangero.

"Her mother," I said, and saw Wangero was getting tired. "That's about as far back as I can trace it," I said. Though, in fact, I probably could have carried it back beyond the Civil War through the branches.

"Well," said Asalamalakim, "there you are."

"Uhnnnh," I heard Maggie say.

"There I was not," I said, "before 'Dicie' cropped up in our family, so why should I try to trace it that far back?"

He just stood there grinning, looking down on me like somebody inspecting a Model A car. Every once in a while he and Wangero sent eye signals over my head.

"How do you pronounce this name?" I asked.

"You don't have to call me by it if you don't want to," said Wangero.

"Why shouldn't I?" I asked. "If that's what you want us to call you, we'll call you."

"I know it might sound awkward at first," said Wangero.

"I'll get used to it," I said. "Ream it out again."

Well, soon we got the name out of the way. Asalamalakim had a name twice as long and three times as hard. After I tripped over it two or three times he told me to just call him Hakim-a-barber. I wanted to ask him was he a barber, but I didn't really think he was, so I didn't ask.

"You must belong to those beef-cattle peoples down the road," I said. They said "Asalamalakim" when they met you, too, but they didn't shake hands. Always too busy: feeding the cattle, fixing the fences, putting up salt-lick shelters, throwing down hay. When the white folks poisoned some of the herd the men stayed up all night with rifles in their hands. I walked a mile and a half just to see the sight.

Hakim-a-barber said, "I accept some of their doctrines, but farming and raising cattle is not my style."

(They didn't tell me, and I didn't ask, whether Wangero (Dee) had really gone and married him.)

We sat down to eat and right away he said he didn't eat collards and pork was unclean. Wangero, though, went on through the chitlins and corn bread, the greens and everything else. She talked a blue streak over the sweet potatoes. Everything delighted her. Even the fact that we still used the benches her daddy made for the table when we couldn't afford to buy chairs.

"Oh, Mama!" she cried. Then turned to Hakim-a-barber. "I never knew how lovely these benches are. You can feel the rump prints," she said, running her hands underneath her and along the bench. Then she gave a sigh and her hand closed over Grandma Dee's butter dish. "That's it!" she said. "I knew there was something I wanted to ask you if I could have." She jumped up from the table and went over in the corner where the churn stood, the milk in it clabber by now. She looked at the churn and looked at it.

"This churn top is what I need," she said. "Didn't Uncle Buddy whittle it out of a tree you all used to have?"

"Yes," I said.

"Uh huh," she said happily. "And I want the dasher, too."

"Uncle Buddy whittle that, too?" asked the barber.

Dee (Wangero) looked up at me.

"Aunt Dee's first husband whittled the dash," said Maggie so low you almost couldn't hear her. "His name was Henry, but they called him Stash."

"Maggie's brain is like an elephant's," Wangero said, laughing. "I can use the churn top as a centerpiece for the alcove table," she said, sliding a plate over the churn, "and I'll think of something artistic to do with the dasher."

When she finished wrapping the dasher the handle stuck out. I took it for a moment in my hands. You didn't even have to look close to see where hands pushing the dasher up and down to make butter had left a kind of sink in the wood. In fact, there were a lot of small sinks; you could see where thumbs and fingers had sunk into the wood. It was beautiful light yellow wood,

from a tree that grew in the yard where Big Dee and
Stash had lived.

After dinner Dee (Wangero) went to the trunk at the
foot of my bed and started rifling through it. Maggie
hung back in the kitchen over the dishpan. Out came
Wangero with two quilts. They had been pieced by
Grandma Dee and then Big Dee and me had hung them
on the quilt frames on the front porch and quilted them.
One was in the Lone Star pattern. The other was Walk
Around the Mountain. In both of them were scraps of
dresses Grandma Dee had worn fifty and more years
ago. Bits and pieces of Grandpa Jarrell's Paisley shirts.
And one teeny faded blue piece, about the size of a
penny matchbox, that was from Great Grandpa Ezra's
uniform that he wore in the Civil War.

"Mama," Wangero said sweet as a bird. "Can I have
these old quilts?"

I heard something fall in the kitchen, and a minute
later the kitchen door slammed.

"Why don't you take one or two of the others?" I
asked. "These old things was just done by me and Big
Dee from some tops your grandma pieced before she
died."

"No," said Wangero. "I don't want those. They are
stitched around the borders by machine."

"That'll make them last better," I said.

"That's not the point," said Wangero. "These are all
pieces of dresses Grandma used to wear. She did all this
stitching by hand. Imagine!" She held the quilts securely
in her arms, stroking them.

"Some of the pieces, like those lavender ones, come
from old clothes her mother handed down to her," I
said, moving up to touch the quilts. Dee (Wangero)
moved back just enough so that I couldn't reach the
quilts. They already belonged to her.

"Imagine!" she breathed again, clutching them closely
to her bosom.

"The truth is," I said, "I promised to give them quilts
to Maggie, for when she marries John Thomas."

She gasped like a bee had stung her.

"Maggie can't appreciate these quilts!" she said.

"She'd probably be backward enough to put them to everyday use."

"I reckon she would," I said. "God knows I been saving 'em for long enough with nobody using 'em. I hope she will!" I didn't want to bring up how I had offered Dee (Wangero) a quilt when she went away to college. Then she had told me they were old-fashioned, out of style.

"But they're *priceless*!" she was saying now, furiously; for she has a temper. "Maggie would put them on the bed and in five years they'd be in rags. Less than that!"

"She can always make some more," I said. "Maggie knows how to quilt."

Dee (Wangero) looked at me with hatred. "You just will not understand. The point is these quilts, *these* quilts!"

"Well," I said, stumped. "What would *you* do with them?"

"Hang them," she said. As if that was the only thing you *could* do with quilts.

Maggie by now was standing in the door. I could almost hear the sound her feet made as they scraped over each other.

"She can have them, Mama," she said, like somebody used to never winning anything, or having anything reserved for her. "I can 'member Grandma Dee without the quilts."

I looked at her hard. She had filled her bottom lip with checkerberry snuff and it gave her face a kind of dopey, hangdog look. It was Grandma Dee and Big Dee who taught her how to quilt herself. She stood there with her scarred hands hidden in the folds of her skirt. She looked at her sister with something like fear but she wasn't mad at her. This was Maggie's portion. This was the way she knew God to work.

When I looked at her like that something hit me in the top of my head and ran down to the soles of my feet. Just like when I'm in church and the spirit of God touches me and I get happy and shout. I did something I never had done before: hugged Maggie to me, then dragged her on into the room, snatched the quilts out of Miss Wangero's hands and dumped them into Maggie's lap. Maggie just sat there on my bed with her mouth open.

"Take one or two of the others," I said to Dee.

But she turned without a word and went out to Hakim-a-barber.

"You just don't understand," she said, as Maggie and I came out to the car.

"What don't I understand?" I wanted to know.

"Your heritage," she said. And then she turned to Maggie, kissed her, and said, "You ought to try to make something of yourself, too, Maggie. It's really a new day for us. But from the way you and Mama still live you'd never know it."

She put on some sunglasses that hid everything above the tip of her nose and her chin.

Maggie smiled; maybe at the sunglasses. But a real smile, not scared. After we watched the car dust settle I asked Maggie to bring me a dip of snuff. And then the two of us sat there just enjoying, until it was time to go in the house and go to bed.

—1973

GLORIA NAYLOR
(B. 1950)

After serving as a missionary for the Jehovah's Witnesses from 1968 through 1975, Gloria Naylor, a native New Yorker, earned a B.A. at Brooklyn College. While a student, she began writing the seven interconnected stories that form *The Women of Brewster Place* (1982), a collection that won an American Book Award for First Fiction and was made into a television miniseries starring and produced by Oprah Winfrey. Naylor earned an M.A. in Afro-American Studies at Yale University and has taught creative writing and American literature at George Washington University, New York University, Boston University, and Cornell. A recipient of grants from the Guggenheim Foundation and the National Endowment for the Arts, she has published *Linden Hills* (1985), *Mama Day* (1988), *Bailey's Café* (1992), and *The Men of Brewster Place* (1998). *Bailey's Café* was adapted for the stage and premiered at the Hartford Stage Company in 1994.

Kiswana Browne

FROM the window of her sixth-floor studio apartment, Kiswana could see over the wall at the end of the street to the busy avenue that lay just north of Brewster Place. The late-afternoon shoppers looked like brightly clad marionettes as they moved between the congested traffic, clutching their packages against their bodies to guard them from sudden bursts of the cold autumn wind. A portly mailman had abandoned his cart and was bumping into indignant window-shoppers as he puffed behind the cap that the wind had snatched from his head. Kiswana leaned over to see if he was going to be successful, but the edge of the building cut him off from her view.

A pigeon swept across her window, and she marveled at its liquid movements in the air waves. She placed her dreams on the back of the bird and fantasized that it would glide forever in transparent silver circles until it ascended to the center of the universe and was swallowed up. But the wind died down, and she watched with a sigh as the bird beat its wings in awkward, frantic movements to land on the corroded top of a fire escape on the opposite building. This brought her back to earth.

Humph, it's probably sitting over there crapping on those folks' fire escape, she thought. Now, that's a safety hazard. . . . And her mind was busy again, creating flames and smoke and frustrated tenants whose escape was being hindered because they were slipping and sliding in pigeon shit. She watched their cussing, haphazard descent on the fire escapes until they had all reached the bottom. They were milling around, oblivious to their burning apartments, angrily planning to march on the mayor's office about the pigeons. She materialized placards and banners for them, and they had just reached the corner, boldly sidestepping fire hoses and broken glass, when they all vanished.

A tall copper-skinned woman had met this phantom parade at the corner, and they had dissolved in front of her long, confident strides. She plowed through the remains of their faded mists, unconscious of the lingering wisps of their presence on her leather bag and black fur-trimmed coat. It took a few seconds for this transfer from one realm to another to reach Kiswana, but then suddenly she recognized the woman.

"Oh, God, it's Mama!" She looked down guiltily at the forgotten newspaper in her lap and hurriedly circled random job advertisements.

By this time Mrs. Browne had reached the front of Kiswana's building and was checking the house number against a piece of paper in her hand. Before she went into the building she stood at the bottom of the stoop and carefully inspected the condition of the street and the adjoining property. Kiswana watched this meticulous inventory with growing annoyance but she involunarily followed her mother's slowly rotating head, forcing herself to see her new neighborhood through the older woman's eyes. The brightness of the unclouded sky seemed to join forces with her mother as it high-lighted every broken stoop railing and missing brick. The afternoon sun glittered and cascaded across even the tiniest fragments of broken bottle, and at that very moment the wind chose to rise up again, sending unswept grime flying into the air, as a stray tin can left by careless garbage collectors went rolling noisily down the center of the street.

Kiswana noticed with relief that at least Ben wasn't sitting in his usual place on the old garbage can pushed against the far wall. He was just a harmless old wino, but Kiswana knew her mother only needed one wino or one teenager with a reefer within a twenty-block radius to decide that her daughter was living in a building seething with dope factories and hang-outs for derelicts. If she had seen Ben, nothing would have made her believe that practically every apartment contained a family, a Bible, and a dream that one day enough could be scraped from those meager Friday night paychecks to make Brewster Place a distant memory.

As she watched her mother's head disappear into the building, Kiswana gave silent thanks that the elevator was broken. That would give her at least five minutes' grace to straighten up the apartment. She rushed to the sofa bed and hastily closed it without smoothing the rumpled sheets and blanket or removing her nightgown. She felt that somehow the tangled bedcovers would give away the fact that she had not slept alone last night. She silently apologized to Abshu's memory as she heartlessly crushed his spirit between the steel springs of the couch. Lord, that man was sweet. Her toes curled involuntarily at the passing thought of his full lips moving slowly over her instep. Abshu was a foot man, and he always started his lovemaking from the bottom up. For that reason Kiswana changed the color of the polish on her toenails every week. During the course of their relationship she had gone from shades of red to brown and was now into the purples. I'm gonna have to start mixing them soon, she thought aloud as she turned from the couch and raced into the bathroom to remove any traces of Abshu from there. She took up his shaving cream and razor and threw them into the bottom drawer of her dresser beside her diaphragm. Mama wouldn't dare pry into my drawers right in front of me, she thought as she slammed the drawer shut. Well, at least not the *bottom* drawer. She may come up with some sham excuse for opening the top drawer, but never the bottom one.

When she heard the first two short raps on the door, her eyes took a final flight over the small apartment, desperately seeking out any slight misdemeanor that might have to be defended. Well, there was nothing she could do about the crack in the wall over that table. She had been after the landlord to fix it for two months now. And there had been no time to sweep the rug, and everyone knew that off-gray always looked dirtier than it really was. And it was just too damn bad about the kitchen. How was she expected to be out job-hunting every day and still have time to keep a kitchen that looked like her mother's, who didn't even work and still had someone come in twice a month for general cleaning. And besides . . .

Her imaginary argument was abruptly interrupted by a second series of knocks, accompanied by a penetrating, "Melanie, Melanie, are you there?"

Kiswana strode toward the door. She's starting before she even gets in here. She knows that's not my name anymore.

She swung the door open to face her slightly flushed mother. "Oh, hi, Mama. You know, I thought I heard a knock, but I figured it was for the people next door, since no one hardly ever calls me Melanie." Score one for me, she thought.

"Well, it's awfully strange you can forget a name you answered to for twenty-three years," Mrs. Browne said, as she moved past Kiswana into the apartment. "My, that was a long climb. How long has your elevator been out? Honey, how do you manage with your laundry and groceries up all those steps? But I guess you're young, and it wouldn't bother you as much as it does me." This long string of questions told Kiswana that her mother had no intentions of beginning her visit with another argument about her new African name.

"You know I would have called before I came, but you don't have a phone yet. I didn't want you to feel that I was snooping. As a matter of fact, I didn't expect to find you home at all. I thought you'd be out looking for a job." Mrs. Browne had mentally covered the entire apartment while she was talking and taking off her coat.

"Well, I got up late this morning. I thought I'd buy the afternoon paper and start early tomorrow."

"That sounds like a good idea." Her mother moved toward the window and picked up the discarded paper and glanced over the hurriedly circled ads. "Since when do you have experience as a fork-lift operator?"

Kiswana caught her breath and silently cursed herself for her stupidity. "Oh, my hand slipped—I meant to circle file clerk." She quickly took the paper before her mother could see that she had also marked cutlery salesman and chauffeur.

"You're sure you weren't sitting here moping and daydreaming again?" Amber specks of laughter flashed in the corner of Mrs. Browne's eyes.

Kiswana threw her shoulders back and unsuccessfully tried to disguise her embarrassment with indignation.

"Oh, God, Mama! I haven't done that in years—it's for kids. When are you going to realize that I'm a woman now?" She sought desperately for some womanly thing to do and settled for throwing herself on the couch and crossing her legs in what she hoped looked like a nonchalant arc.

"Please, have a seat," she said, attempting the same tones and gestures she'd seen Bette Davis use on the late movies.

Mrs. Browne, lowering her eyes to hide her amusement, accepted the invitation and sat at the window, also crossing her legs. Kiswana saw immediately how it should have been done. Her celluloid poise clashed loudly against her mother's quiet dignity, and she quickly uncrossed her legs. Mrs. Browne turned her head toward the window and pretended not to notice.

"At least you have a halfway decent view from here. I was wondering what lay beyond that dreadful wall—it's the boulevard. Honey, did you know that you can see the trees in Linden Hills from here?"

Kiswana knew that very well, because there were many lonely days that she would sit in her gray apartment and stare at those trees and think of home, but she would rather have choked than admit that to her mother.

"Oh, really, I never noticed. So how is Daddy and things at home?"

"Just fine. We're thinking of redoing one of the extra bedrooms since you children have moved out, but Wilson insists that he can manage all that work alone. I told him that he doesn't really have the proper time or energy for all that. As it is, when he gets home from the office, he's so tired he can hardly move. But you know you can't tell your father anything. Whenever he starts complaining about how stubborn you are, I tell him the child came by it honestly. Oh, and your brother was by yesterday," she added, as if it had just occurred to her.

So that's it, thought Kiswana. That's why she's here.

Kiswana's brother, Wilson, had been to visit her two days ago, and she had borrowed twenty dollars from him to get her winter coat out of layaway. That son-of-a-bitch probably ran straight to Mama—and after he swore he wouldn't say anything. I should have known, he was always a snotty-nosed sneak, she thought.

"Was he?" she said aloud. "He came by to see me, too, earlier this week. And I borrowed some money from him because my unemployment checks hadn't cleared in the bank, but now they have and everything's just fine." There, I'll beat you to that one.

"Oh, I didn't know that," Mrs. Browne lied. "He never mentioned you. He had just heard that Beverly was expecting again, and he rushed over to tell us."

Damn. Kiswana could have strangled herself.

"So she's knocked up again, huh?" she said irritably.

Her mother started. "Why do you always have to be so crude?"

"Personally, I don't see how she can sleep with Willie. He's such a dishrag."

Kiswana still resented the stance her brother had taken in college. When everyone at school was discovering their blackness and protesting on campus, Wilson never took part; he had even refused to wear an

Afro. This had outraged Kiswana because, unlike her, he was dark-skinned and had the type of hair that was thick and kinky enough for a good "Fro." Kiswana had still insisted on cutting her own hair, but it was so thin and fine-textured, it refused to thicken even after she washed it. So she had to brush it up and spray it with lacquer to keep it from lying flat. She never forgave Wilson for telling her that she didn't look African, she looked like an electrocuted chicken.

"Now that's some way to talk. I don't know why you have an attitude against your brother. He never gave me a restless night's sleep, and now he's settled with a family and a good job."

"He's an assistant to an assistant junior partner in a law firm. What's the big deal about that?"

"The job has a future, Melanie. And at least he finished school and went on for his law degree."

"In other words, not like me, huh?"

"Don't put words into my mouth, young lady. I'm perfectly capable of saying what I mean."

Amen, thought Kiswana.

"And I don't know why you've been trying to start up with me from the moment I walked in. I didn't come here to fight with you. This is your first place away from home, and I just wanted to see how you were living and if you're doing all right. And I must say, you've fixed this apartment up very nicely."

"Really, Mama?" She found herself softening in the light of her mother's approval.

"Well, considering what you had to work with." This time she scanned the apartment openly.

"Look, I know it's not Linden Hills, but a lot can be done with it. As soon as they come and paint, I'm going to hang my Ashanti print over the couch. And I thought a big Boston Fern would go well in that corner, what do you think?"

"That would be fine, baby. You always had a good eye for balance."

Kiswana was beginning to relax. There was little she did that attracted her mother's approval. It was like a rare bird, and she had to tread carefully around it lest it fly away.

"Are you going to leave that statue out like that?"

"Why, what's wrong with it? Would it look better somewhere else?"

There was a small wooden reproduction of a Yoruba goddess with large protruding breasts on the coffee table.

"Well," Mrs. Browne was beginning to blush, "it's just that it's a bit suggestive, don't you think? Since you live alone now, and I know you'll be having male friends stop by, you wouldn't want to be giving them any ideas. I mean, uh, you know, there's no point in putting yourself in any unpleasant situations because they may get the wrong impressions and uh, you know, I mean, well . . ." Mrs. Browne stammered on miserably.

Kiswana loved it when her mother tried to talk about sex. It was the only time she was at a loss for words.

"Don't worry, Mama." Kiswana smiled. "That wouldn't bother the type of men I date. Now maybe if it had big feet . . ." And she got hysterical, thinking of Abshu.

Her mother looked at her sharply. "What sort of gibberish is that about feet? I'm being serious, Melanie."

"I'm sorry, Mama." She sobered up. "I'll put it away in the closet," she said, knowing that she wouldn't.

"Good," Mrs. Browne said, knowing that she wouldn't either. "I guess you think I'm too picky, but we worry about you over here. And you refuse to put in a phone so we can call and see about you."

"I haven't refused, Mama. They want seventy-five dollars for a deposit, and I can't swing that right now."

"Melanie, I can give you the money."

"I don't want you to be giving me money—I've told you that before. Please, let me make it by myself."

"Well, let me lend it to you, then."

"No!"

"Oh, so you can borrow money from your brother, but not from me."

Kiswana turned her head from the hurt in her mother's eyes. "Mama, when I borrow from Willie, he makes me pay him back. You never let me pay you back," she said into her hands.

"I don't care. I still think it's downright selfish of you

to be sitting over here with no phone, and sometimes we don't hear from you in two weeks—anything could happen—especially living among these people."

Kiswana snapped her head up. "What do you mean, *these people.* They're my people and yours, too, Mama— we're all black. But maybe you've forgotten that over in Linden Hills."

"That's not what I'm talking about, and you know it. These streets—this building—it's so shabby and run-down. Honey, you don't have to live like this."

"Well, this is how poor people live."

"Melanie, you're not poor."

"No, Mama, *you're* not poor. And what you have and I have are two totally different things. I don't have a husband in real estate with a five-figure income and a home in Linden Hills—*you* do. What I have is a weekly unemployment check and an overdrawn checking account at United Federal. So this studio on Brewster is all I can afford."

"Well, you could afford a lot better," Mrs. Browne snapped, "if you hadn't dropped out of college and had to resort to these dead-end clerical jobs."

"Uh-huh, I knew you'd get around to that before long." Kiswana could feel the rings of anger begin to tighten around her lower backbone, and they sent her forward onto the couch. "You'll never understand, will you? Those bourgie schools were counterrevolutionary. My place was in the streets with my people, fighting for equality and a better community."

"Counterrevolutionary!" Mrs. Browne was raising her voice. "Where's your revolution now, Melanie? Where are all those black revolutionaries who were shouting and demonstrating and kicking up a lot of dust with you on that campus? Huh? They're sitting in wood-paneled offices with their degrees in mahogany frames, and they won't even drive their cars past this street because the city doesn't fix potholes in this part of town."

"Mama," she said, shaking her head slowly in disbelief, "how can you—a black woman—sit there and tell me that what we fought for during the Movement wasn't important just because some people sold out?"

"Melanie, I'm not saying it wasn't important. It was

damned important to stand up and say that you were proud of what you were and to get the vote and other social opportunities for every person in this country who had it due. But you kids thought you were going to turn the world upside down, and it just wasn't so. When all the smoke had cleared, you found yourself with a fistful of new federal laws and a country still full of obstacles for black people to fight their way over—just because they're black. There was no revolution, Melanie, and there will be no revolution."

"So what am I supposed to do, huh? Just throw up my hands and not care about what happens to my people? I'm not supposed to keep fighting to make things better?"

"Of course, you can. But you're going to have to fight within the system, because it and these so-called 'bourgie' schools are going to be here for a long time. And that means that you get smart like a lot of your old friends and get an important job where you can have some influence. You don't have to sell out, as you say, and work for some corporation, but you could become an assemblywoman or a civil liberties lawyer or open a freedom school in this very neighborhood. That way you could really help the community. But what help are you going to be to these people on Brewster while you're living hand-to-mouth on file-clerk jobs waiting for a revolution? You're wasting your talents, child."

"Well, I don't think they're being wasted. At least I'm here in day-to-day contact with the problems of my people. What good would I be after four or five years of a lot of white brainwashing in some phony, prestige institution, huh? I'd be like you and Daddy and those other educated blacks sitting over there in Linden Hills with a terminal case of middle-class amnesia."

"You don't have to live in a slum to be concerned about social conditions, Melanie. Your father and I have been charter members of the NAACP for the last twenty-five years."

"Oh, God!" Kiswana threw her head back in exaggerated disgust. "That's being concerned? That middle-of-the-road, Uncle Tom dumping ground for black Republicans!"

"You can sneer all you want, young lady, but that

organization has been working for black people since the turn of the century, and it's still working for them. Where are all those radical groups of yours that were going to put a Cadillac in every garage and Dick Gregory in the White House? I'll tell you where."

I knew you would, Kiswana thought angrily.

"They burned themselves out because they wanted too much too fast. Their goals weren't grounded in reality. And that's always been your problem."

"What do you mean, my problem? I know exactly what I'm about."

"No, you don't. You constantly live in a fantasy world—always going to extremes—turning butterflies into eagles, and life isn't about that. It's accepting what is and working from that. Lord, I remember how worried you had me, putting all that lacquered hair spray on your head. I thought you were going to get lung cancer—trying to be what you're not."

Kiswana jumped up from the couch. "Oh, God, I can't take this anymore. Trying to be something I'm not—trying to be something I'm not, Mama! Trying to be proud of my heritage and the fact that I was of African descent. If that's being what I'm not, then I say fine. But I'd rather be dead than be like you—a white man's nigger who's ashamed of being black!"

Kiswana saw streaks of gold and ebony light follow her mother's flying body out of the chair. She was swung around by the shoulders and made to face the deadly stillness in the angry woman's eyes. She was too stunned to cry out from the pain of the long fingernails that dug into her shoulders, and she was brought so close to her mother's face that she saw her reflection, distorted and wavering, in the tears that stood in the older woman's eyes. And she listened in that stillness to a story she had heard from a child.

"My grandmother," Mrs. Browne began slowly in a whisper, "was a full-bloodied Iroquois, and my grandfather a free black from a long line of journeymen who had lived in Connecticut since the establishment of the colonies. And my father was a Bajan who came to this country as a cabin boy on a merchant mariner."

"I know all that," Kiswana said, trying to keep her lips from trembling.

"Then, know this." And the nails dug deeper into her flesh. "I am alive because of the blood of proud people who never scraped or begged or apologized for what they were. They lived asking only one thing of this world—to be allowed to be. And I learned through the blood of these people that black isn't beautiful and it isn't ugly—black is! It's not kinky hair and it's not straight hair—it just is.

"It broke my heart when you changed your name. I gave you my grandmother's name, a woman who bore nine children and educated them all, who held off six white men with a shotgun when they tried to drag one of her sons to jail for 'not knowing his place.' Yet you needed to reach into an African dictionary to find a name to make you proud.

"When I brought my babies home from the hospital, my ebony son and my golden daughter, I swore before whatever gods would listen—those of my mother's people or those of my father's people—that I would use everything I had and could ever get to see that my children were prepared to meet this world on its own terms, so that no one could sell them short and make them ashamed of what they were or how they looked—whatever they were or however they looked. And Melanie, that's not being white or red or black—that's being a mother."

Kiswana followed her reflection in the two single tears that moved down her mother's cheeks until it blended with them into the woman's copper skin. There was nothing and then so much that she wanted to say, but her throat kept closing up every time she tried to speak. She kept her head down and her eyes closed, and thought, Oh, God, just let me die. How can I face her now?

Mrs. Browne lifted Kiswana's chin gently. "And the one lesson I wanted you to learn is not to be afraid to face anyone, not even a crafty old lady like me who can outtalk you." And she smiled and winked.

"Oh, Mama, I . . ." and she hugged the woman tightly.

"Yeah, baby." Mrs. Browne patted her back. "I know."

She kissed Kiswana on the forehead and cleared her throat. "Well, now, I better be moving on. It's getting late, there's dinner to be made, and I have to get off my feet—these new shoes are killing me."

Kiswana looked down at the beige leather pumps. "Those are really classy. They're English, aren't they?"

"Yes, but, Lord, do they cut me right across the instep." She removed the shoe and sat on the couch to massage her foot.

Bright red nail polish glared at Kiswana through the stockings. "Since when do you polish your toenails?" she gasped. "You never did that before."

"Well . . ." Mrs. Browne shrugged her shoulders, "your father sort of talked me into it, and, uh, you know, he likes it and all, so I thought, uh, you know, why not, so . . ." And she gave Kiswana an embarrassed smile.

I'll be damned, the young woman thought, feeling her whole face tingle. Daddy's into feet! And she looked at the blushing woman on her couch and suddenly realized that her mother had trod through the same universe that she herself was now traveling. Kiswana was breaking no new trails and would eventually end up just two feet away on that couch. She stared at the woman she had been and was to become.

"But I'll never be a Republican," she caught herself saying aloud.

"What are you mumbling about, Melanie?" Mrs. Browne slipped on her shoe and got up from the couch.

She went to get her mother's coat. "Nothing, Mama. It's really nice of you to come by. You should do it more often."

"Well, since it's not Sunday, I guess you're allowed at least one lie."

They both laughed.

After Kiswana had closed the door and turned around, she spotted an envelope sticking between the cushions of her couch. She went over and opened it up; there was seventy-five dollars in it.

"Oh, Mama, darn it!" She rushed to the window and started to call to the woman, who had just emerged from the building, but she suddenly changed her mind and sat down in the chair with a long sigh that caught in the upward draft of the autumn wind and disappeared over the top of the building.

—1980